CRYSTAL AWAKENING

CRYSTAL AWAKENING

SHATTERED LEGACY ✦ BOOK ONE

ANDREW ROWE
AND
KAYLEIGH NICOL

Podium

Podium

Foreword

This book represents a wonderful milestone to me—the first book in the Arcane Ascension universe by another author. I'm delighted and thrilled that Kayleigh has ascended to the challenge of writing this book. I certainly didn't make it easy for her. I'd like to thank her, as well as her husband, for being patient with my obsessive world building and magic system notes and corrections. Thank you to Jess Richards for suggesting this team-up and helping facilitate it. I'd also like to thank all of our many beta readers, my agent and his assistant, and our team at Podium Audio for making this all possible.

Readers, I hope you love this story and many more in the years to come.

—Andrew Rowe

A Word before We Begin . . .

Some of you are probably thinking: Wait a minute—is this an Andrew Rowe book or a Kayleigh Nicol book? And the answer is: both!

Andrew Rowe has graciously invited me into his expanded universe to write a series set in his world of Kaldwyn. To truly appreciate this book, a background of Andrew's Arcane Ascension series is recommended but not necessarily required. A synopsis of the magic system as well as the setting has been included at the beginning of this book, and we've added a helpful appendix at the end. I hope these additions will help answer any questions you might have in regard to the setting, magic system, and characters.

For those of you familiar with Andrew Rowe's work, you may find my style of writing to be quite different. Rather than attempt to mimic Andrew's style (as we all know his feelings on mimics), I have incorporated similar elements from Andrew's other works while using my words to tell a story in his world. For consistency, I have chosen to emulate Andrew's use of brackets and italics to distinguish between telepathic communication and personal thoughts. For example, a person's thoughts *will appear in italics, like this.* A telepathic message [will be braced by square brackets, like this]. A character who communicates only through telepathic speech will use angle brackets <to make it immediately obvious that they are the one speaking>. Any other forms of speech, such as sign language, will be denoted in quotations and indicated in the narrative.

Just as in Andrew's other works, I use the singular "they/them" for agender and nonbinary characters, as well as characters whose gender has not yet been determined by the narrator. For example: "The cloaked and hooded person shook their head."

I am deeply honored to have been invited into Andrew Rowe's expanded universe, and I am excited to share the Shattered Legacy series with all of you!

~Kayleigh Nicol

Crystal Awakening

MAGIC INTRODUCTION

Hey Sal,

If you're reading this, you must have made your way to one of the spires. I wasn't sure where you'd go when you arrived on the continent, so I sent copies to the Soaring Wings in each major nation. I hope that you've found your way here quickly enough for this to be useful. I figured the old man wouldn't bother telling you anything about the local magic before he sent you, so a quick primer might be useful.

You've probably sorted out some of this on your own, but I'm going to start with some basics, just to make sure.

You aren't going to find many dominion sorcerers around here. Instead, the local magic comes in the form of attunements—mystical marks granted to people who take "Judgments," a personal test inside any one of these gigantic towers they call the "Soaring Spires." The spires are extremely important to the locals, both for these Judgments and for people who attempt to climb to the top. The people who try to ascend through them are called "climbers," and they're seeking the top to have a meeting with the local goddess, Selys, who they believe grants wishes to anyone who reaches there. Oh, the spires are filled with monsters and treasure, too. You'd like them. Some people make careers out of just going in and looting the treasure—they're called "delvers." The spires constantly change, similar to Xixian Vaults, including having new monsters and traps on a regular basis. Don't ask me how that works.

Anyway, back to magic.

Each spire offers different attunements, and each attunement has different powers. As someone uses an attunement, it gets more powerful, granting new abilities. When this happens, the mark itself changes in design, and it also generates a different-colored aura that represents the attunement's current level.

If you're thinking this sounds similar to dominion marks from back on Mythralis, you're not wrong. It's the same underlying concept, but these are more sophisticated than most of the dominion marks I've seen, since they're designed to replace conventional sorcery entirely. As for why you don't see other sorts of sorcery here . . . well, that's complicated, and I won't get into it here. Sorry. I can talk to you about it when I see you in person, maybe?

Anyway, attunements.

As I said, there are a bunch of varieties. They have profession-style names and give thematic powers tied to that profession, like "Summoner" and "Elementalist." You'd probably like the "Soulblade" one, or maybe "Swordmaster"— but I'd advise you against taking any Judgments right away. I don't know if attunements would work on you properly. The natives here don't seem to have quite the same underlying biology that Mythralians do. You may need to do some research on compatibility before you try to get yourself a mark. Sorry.

Attunement levels are a big deal here, both culturally and in terms of the power they provide. A quick list:

Quartz (Colorless Aura)—The first level. Gives you access to two base mana types, which we'd call prime dominions back at home, and one composite mana type. The composite isn't always usable directly—sometimes it just powers functions of the attunement mark itself. You also get an attunement-specific ability. Summoners can make contracts with monsters, for example, which is neat. Enchanters get the ability to imbue mana directly into runes, which is super complicated and extremely important to how Kaldwyn's technology differs from ours.

Carnelian (Red Aura)—At this level, people get a shroud, which is basically a permanent defensive aura that works against both physical and magical attacks. Instead, it provides a layer of resistance, almost like trying to push through an opposing magnetic field. This makes it more effective against ranged attacks, since melee fighters can usually push through the field, but something like an arrow might lose enough force that it doesn't deal any damage. This shroud is a critical feature to attunements in general, and it gets stronger with each subsequent level.

Sunstone (Orange Aura)—At Sunstone, people gain the ability to manipulate their own shroud, suppressing and reshaping it. This is extremely useful for hiding power or using the shroud in creative ways, like blocking attacks by compressing it into a single region rapidly, or infusing the shroud with mana of a specific type. This is also the highest level most people ever reach. There's a concept called the "Sunstone wall" where it gets progressively harder to increase the power of an attunement when you reach this point. It has to do with the reliance of attunements on gathering ambient mana and most locations not having enough mana to support growth, but that's a bit too technical to worry about much here.

Citrine (Yellow Aura)—This is where you start to see people who are truly powerful. This offers access to a new base mana type, and talented people of this level also can learn to wield the composite mana types of that type and the others they have access to, greatly increasing their power and flexibility. Most veteran fighters tend to end up around this level, if they survive that long.

Emerald (Green Aura)—The highest known level. This grants the ability to actively manipulate ambient mana, basically allowing you to use the mana in your region to your advantage. This can help you starve enemies of mana or just use it to power your own spells and abilities. I haven't met a lot of Emeralds—there are supposedly only a dozen or so in each nation, although I think that's an understatement—but the ones I have met are extremely impressive. Think of them as being in the same power range as the various dominion lords back home, although there's a fair bit of variation in both. You'd struggle against one, assuming you're still the same strength as when we last met.

Sapphire (Blue Aura)—There are stories of a level above Emerald, but I've never seen a human with one. Some monsters have a blue aura, though. I think this might be exclusive to the strongest monsters in the spires—creatures called "god beasts" and their descendants.

Aside from the level of an attunement, the location on the body it falls is also important. A quick overview of those:

Hand Mark—A mark on the hand allows for easier direction of mana into long-ranged attacks. Point at someone, boom. Your traditional blasty sorcerers tend to have one of these, or . . .

Lung Mark—This mark assists with putting mana into the air when you speak, then using that mana for casting wide-area spells. Great for gigantic explosions. This is your classic area-of-effect caster mark.

Heart Mark—This mark allows you to charge up a bunch of mana inside the body, then release it all at once for a powerful effect. Generates slow, but extremely powerful bursts.

Leg Mark—This style of mark helps distribute spells directly through touch. With this, you can empower your own weapons, cast spells on allies you're touching, or just blast an enemy you're punching. Probably the closest to your own style, Sal.

Mind Mark—A mind mark is designed for casting internal beneficial spells—things like casting a healing spell on yourself or something to increase your own abilities. Something like your Body of Stone technique would be similar to what people with a mind mark specialize in.

Note that mark locations don't mean that's the only way someone can use magic—it just assists them with doing that style of magic to make it easier. Veterans generally learn to use other ways to cast spells eventually, but it takes time and practice. You should expect most Citrines to be able to cast spells in at least two or three different ways.

I hope this all helps make things a little easier for you when you arrive. I wish I could tell you where I'm going to be, but I don't know yet. The problem with my back has been getting worse, and I'm going to need to find a local solution soon. The spires might help, and I'm planning to check through those . . . but I don't know how far I'll get before I run out of time.

I miss you, I hope you're well, and I can't wait to see you again.

*,*

Wrynn

CHAPTER 1

SAGE

Seer (hand mark), Citrine

Sage bounced on the balls of his feet, willing the line to move faster, though objectively he knew it was his own fault for arriving so late, just as he knew there was nothing he could have done differently that morning. He kept running his hands over his pockets and belt pouches, muttering softly to himself under his breath as he checked off his list of supplies.

"Cane, return bell, shield sigil." He touched the dueling cane hooked through his belt, and the smallest pouch tied near it, then touched the enchanted metal brooch fastened to his protective tunic. "Rations, potions, and water." He tugged the strap to his satchel, shifting its weight as a way of confirming its contents. "Cloak." He caught the fabric between his fingers, giving it a light tug. "Glasses." A light tap against the frame, confirming their presence on his face.

A final check, one he didn't murmur aloud, cupped a medium-sized pouch hanging from his belt, this one positioned farther back so it wouldn't be upset by a hasty draw or mistaken for something important during a time of crisis. His fingers found the rounded shape of the enchanted object, soothed that it was there as he expected it to be, but irritated that it was the reason he was running so late. He'd arrived at the Enchanter's shop on time—a little early, in fact—but the Enchanter herself had arrived late. It was a thoroughly aggravating reminder that even a Seer could fail to plan for every possible scenario.

"Next!" A harried and gruff-looking woman waved Sage forward. She stood behind a counter beneath the awning marked for the Soaring Wings that administered access to the Tortoise Spire of Dalenos. The spire loomed just beyond the edge of the awning, massive and coal-black, wide enough to make the bright and sunny day seem shadowed and gloomy. Sage still remembered when standing in the spire's shadow made him feel wary and anxious; now he only felt that way for making his companions wait on his arrival. "Climber identification and team name?"

"Sage, ah, I mean, Seiji Hayden. I'm with the Guiding Star team."

He rocked from foot to foot as the woman made a loud humming sound, scanning a page in the massive book before her. The Soaring Wings not only protected the Soaring Spires of the goddess Selys, but they also protected civilians from attacks originating from the Soaring Spires. Luckily, attacks were rare, so for the most part, they acted as administrators, confirming identities of climbers as well as keeping records of Judgments. This climb had been registered with the Soaring Wings a week ago, when Lani and Nieve recruited the final two climbers they needed for a full team. Why was it taking so long for the administrator to find the team's registration? The others should have all checked in by now.

"Hm, nope. No team by that name listed here." She gave Sage a pedantic look. "Do you have the right date and time, Mr. Hayden?"

"What? No, I'm sure it's—" Sage cut himself off with a groan. "I'm sorry, I forgot it's a legacy team name. Can you look up Guiding Star Legacy?"

The imperious woman gave Sage a level stare as she flipped a page in her book. She set a finger to the page, dragging it down slowly as she scanned the list of teams scheduled to climb. It was a foolish mistake on Sage's part, but he usually checked in with at least one other team member, if not all of them, so it was usually someone else who checked him in. Yet another mistake of timing to add to this morning's tally.

"Hm." The woman tapped the page, frowning darkly. "You know, you can't just keep guessing team names until you get one right. The team gets charged for every gate teleport our Wayfarers perform."

"I know, it was my mistake. But that really is my team," Sage insisted, trying to sound patient rather than whiny. "I'm sorry, I'm a bit anxious because I'm running late this morning. The team is registered under Nieve Yukihara, it's her family's legacy."

Sage didn't need to divine the future in order to interpret the malicious glint in the administrator's eye: he was about to be even later than expected.

"Let's just double-check and make sure you really are Seiji Hayden, a member of the Guiding Star Legacy team," the woman said, tapping something in her notes and holding her pen to the page as if marking her place. "Can you show me your attunement mark?"

Sage sighed and held out his right hand, showing her the Seer attunement mark, stark as a tattoo against his pale skin. The question was more invasive than it seemed, and Sage could only be thankful he had a hand mark. He would have been embarrassed to show a heart or leg mark, especially with the line of other climbers just behind him, waiting to reach the Soaring Wings' Wayfarers, stationed to send climbers to their desired spire gates.

The woman grunted as if dissatisfied but made a check in her book. "Current level?"

"Citrine." He was both proud and a little abashed to say so out loud. It was the second-highest recognized level, so hard to reach that people often referred to it as "breaching the Sunstone wall." He'd only recently reached Citrine, but the few people he had told so far all seemed impressed.

"Hmph." The administrator, it seemed, was not. "What floor is your team currently starting at?"

"Ah, last time we started at seventeen and got up to eighteen." Sage hedged, unsure what notes the administrator's book held. "We're starting on the nineteenth floor today for the first time. We have a key."

"I see that," she said with an air of aloof calm, the type of air that said "I can do this all day." "You mentioned your team leader, Miss Yukihara. What's her attunement and level?"

As frustrated as he was, Sage knew he didn't have a choice but to give in to the administrator's demands. His team had taken two full months off between climbs, a gap that hadn't been necessary since floors eight and nine, which was the last time they'd needed to recruit a new climber. While Sage mostly climbed for the challenge and the profit, his oldest friend Nieve made no secret of the fact that she wanted to reach the top of the spire and make a request of the goddess. As reaching the top of a spire could often take the course of a lifetime, breaks as long as this one tended to make Nieve restless and irritated; if this climb got delayed because of Sage's tardiness, he had no illusions that Nieve would drag him to the nearest dueling ground and demand satisfaction. In order to avoid a few bruises, Sage ducked his head and silently invoked a spell in order to speed up his check-in process.

Divine Future.

The vision played out rapidly, like a memory crystal viewed at the fastest setting. The woman was planning to ask Sage about each of his teammates in turn, drawing out the interaction as a petty power play over Sage's apparent impatience. He let his breath out slowly, keeping his tone as calm and even as possible while he answered all her future questions.

"Nieve has a Champion attunement. She leveled up to Citrine on the last climb, same as I did. Emiko is our Cloudcaller, still Sunstone level. Lani is an Acolyte, she's been Citrine for a while, I believe she's a midrange Citrine, if your records show that. Our Soulblade is—"

The woman grunted but didn't quite get a word out before Sage shook his head, reminding himself that Ren and Wyle had both retired after the last climb.

"Wait, I'm sorry, we have new climbers on our roster this time." Sage checked his pocket for a folded piece of paper. He pulled it open, squinting at Nieve's messy writing. "We have a new Wayfarer, by the name of Aldis Somers. He's, ah, Sunstone. And the other one is Hane." No last name was listed, but Nieve had written a note after their name so Sage wouldn't address them incorrectly when they met. "They're a Citrine-level Wavewalker."

"They? A follower of Wydd?" the administrator asked in a bored tone.

"I haven't met them, so I don't really know." Sage tried not to fidget and give away his impatience. "Look, I'm very sorry for forgetting to say that this is a legacy team. I'm running late and that's my problem, not yours. We found a key to a nineteenth-floor gateway on our last climb, which is higher than any of us have ever been before. I'm sure my teammates are all just as excited to get started as I am."

Excited and probably impatient. Sage expected at least one tongue-lashing by the time he arrived. *If* he ever arrived.

The woman sighed, adding a roll of her eyes for a grander effect. "Fine, fine, go on through. Take the line into consideration next time so you don't keep your team waiting."

"Yes, thank you, yes." Sage rushed through the gate, gritting his teeth as he banged his knee against the latch. "I'll remember for next time. Thanks again!"

Hopefully next time isn't delayed by a sleepy Enchanter, Sage thought, checking the pouch tied just behind his left hip once again. It was still there, of course. It might be enchanted, but it wasn't going to vanish just because he took his mind off it for a moment. He'd wanted to give it to Lani at the beginning of the climb, but that was out now. She wouldn't thank him if she realized it was the reason he was late.

"Hi!" Sage put a cheery smile on his face for the Soaring Wings Wayfarer, putting the administrator out of his mind. "I need to get to the southern gate on the nineteenth floor, please."

"No problem!" the Wayfarer chirped, giving Sage the kind of smile most people could only conjure in the first hour of their shift. "Have a great climb!"

"Thanks, you too!" Sage cringed as he realized his mistake—he'd expected the Wayfarer to say "Have a nice day," making his response awkward at best. Luckily, the teleportation spell had already taken effect, thankfully ending the interaction rather abruptly.

Sage's relief was short-lived. He might have avoided further awkwardness with the Wayfarer, but that only meant he now had to face his team after arriving late.

"Look who finally decided to show up." That drawl was unmistakably Nieve, her hand hooked over the hilt of her custom-made and custom-enchanted katana. "Would have been nice if you'd told me yesterday that you were going to be late."

"I'm sorry, everyone." Sage ducked his head, abashed, holding back a quip about conserving his mana for the climb. "I didn't mean to keep you waiting."

"Do you have everything this time?" Lani asked archly, her arms folded over her chest. She was roughly the same height as Sage, but she had an imperious way of seeming to glare down at him. "If you forgot your canteen this time—"

"I have it!" Sage reached back to swing his satchel forward of his cloak, pointing to the canteen lashed to the side. "I have everything this time, I promise."

"Stop picking on him, you guys!" Emiko jumped forward, looping an arm around Sage's waist and leaning in for a quick hug. "It gave us some time to get to know our new teammates! Sage, come meet Hane and—"

"Aldis! Aldis Somers." A portly fair-skinned man bounded forward, clasping Sage's hand so suddenly that he very nearly pulled it away out of surprise. The new Wayfarer was taller than Sage by perhaps an inch, with close-cropped brown hair and twinkling blue eyes. He wore a dueling cane on his belt, similar to Sage's, and wore plain but sturdy-looking quilted armor, typical of most climbers. "How unexpected to be climbing the Dalenos spire with a fellow Valian! After reading the team roster, I thought everyone else was going to be Dalen!" He paused in the middle of pumping Sage's hand, seemingly aware of the faux pas he'd just made. "Er, not that I have any problem with Dalen climbers. It's just nice to see a face from home!"

"I'm, ah, not Valian." Sage tried to break the grip on his hand without seeming rude. "Sorry for any confusion over my name. Everyone calls me Sage."

Aldis chuckled heartily, nudging Sage with his elbow as he moved to stand by Sage's side. "That's really appropriate considering you're the Seer! Nice to meet you, Sage."

"Ah, yes. Thank you." Sage shifted sideways, a little put off by Aldis's overly friendly greeting. He told himself it was because his team hadn't had to recruit new climbers in years, so he just wasn't used to meeting new people. Aldis seemed well-meaning, if a little eager. "Nice to meet you, too."

"He's really nice," Emiko said in a stage whisper, grinning up at Aldis. She took Sage by the hand and tugged him across the balcony outside the spire gateway. "Come meet our new Ren!"

Nieve made a noise deep in her throat that Sage recognized as dubious. Lani shot her a look that he interpreted as "be nice." Sage had no idea of the newcomer's talent, but he knew how difficult it would be to fill the hole Ren's retirement left in their team. And as the other frontline fighter, Nieve would be the one working most closely with the so-called new Ren.

The newcomer, a slender youth a few inches shorter than Sage lounged back against the railing encircling the balcony. They wore black clothing, faded to gray in patches around the knees and elbows, showing its use. Dark hair was cut to chin length, longer in the front than the back. Their arms were crossed over their chest, but they lifted a hand in greeting.

"Hane," they said by way of introduction. "Wavewalker."

"Welcome," Sage said, offering a smile even though the stranger offered nothing by way of expression. "Sorry I'm late. I promise it doesn't happen often."

Hane shrugged, saying nothing in return.

"Hane's a professional contract climber," Lani put in, standing next to the gate, one hand tapping her belt purse lightly. Sage had learned to gauge her mood by how loudly she made the coins jingle. Right now, the sound was low and muffled, placing her mood at "feigned patience." "They're only with us for this one climb."

Sage cringed. "I didn't realize that. Sorry, Hane. I hope you won't judge the rest of the team based on my tardiness."

"It's fine," Hane said in a tone that lacked emotional indicators. "If everyone's here, can we get started?"

"Ah, yes. Right. Sorry." Resh it all, Sage could just not stop apologizing today, and the climb hadn't even started yet! His stomach churned unpleasantly as he turned to face Lani and Nieve, both flanking the gate to the nineteenth floor. "Should I have a look?"

"You mean do your job?" Nieve asked with a taunting smirk. Sage knew her well enough to understand that she wasn't in a bad mood—not yet, anyway—but she'd pick on him regardless for being late. "Why do you think we keep bringing you along? We don't enjoy your company that much."

"Rude, Nieve!" Emiko protested, hooking her arm through Sage's defensively. The way she huffed into her chest and held her head stubbornly high made her look as threatening as a songbird. "I'm sure Sage has a very good reason for being late and you haven't even asked what it is yet!"

"It's nothing!" Sage said quickly, eyes darting away from Lani. "Nothing at all. Just slept in today. Totally my fault and I accept responsibility for it."

Nieve's grin was wolfish and bright against her dark skin. "Yeah, you will." She thumped Sage on the shoulder with the back of her knuckles, not really a punch, but not gentle either. Sage scowled at her and jostled her with his shoulder, intentionally wedging himself between her and Lani.

Nieve and Emiko were as good as sisters: Sage had taken all his climbing classes with both of them, had even taken his Judgment on the same day as the both of them. There wasn't a single embarrassing story they didn't know about each other, no life event that wasn't at least partially shared among the three of them, no biting remarks withheld, nor did they hide their relief when they all came out of a challenge together and unharmed. The three of them had started this climbing team under Nieve's parents' legacy, mostly for the discount it offered when registering as a climbing team. The team itself had gone through some changes since those early days, but the three of them remained, stalwart and unflappable, and probably would until one of them retired, or died while climbing.

So it was a particularly cruel joke of fate that had both Nieve and Sage vying for the affections of the same woman.

Lani glowered at the two of them, the jingling of coins growing louder. "Let's get a move on, Sage, we don't want to sit out here any longer than we already have. Nieve, you've got the key ready?"

"Right here." Nieve smirked as she held up a gray iron key, the reward they'd earned at the end of their last climb—the one that nearly killed them all. Even though they had all survived, two of their former team members had decided to hang up their climbing gear for good. Not that Sage had been too surprised: he expected to hear word of an engagement soon.

Sage hid a scowl as he tapped the side of his glasses: he was the one who had actually grabbed that key before ringing out of the last climb, yet Nieve was the one who looked victorious as she tapped it against her palm. He hated to think that she'd been cozying up to Lani while he'd been anxiously waiting for the Enchanter to open up shop that morning. He wouldn't score any points with Lani by giving her the gift now; if she knew it was the reason he'd been late, she'd eschew it on principle. Sage would have to pick his moment and give it to her later, hoping that when she made the connection, she would find it amusing rather than annoying.

Channeling a touch of mental mana into his glasses, Sage activated the Divination runes etched into the frame as he sized up the gateway through the lenses. Images flashed by too quickly for him to identify as more than a blur, sounds crashing one on top of the other in a cacophonous roar. He kept his eyes wide and unblinking, focusing on the gateway beyond the flashing images. The visions weren't as important to process as they were to simply be seen and known: knowledge was power, especially in the eyes of a Seer.

The images continued to flicker one after the other as Sage held his attunement-marked hand out toward the spire's gateway. "Divine Future." He said it aloud to let his team know he was focusing, though he'd done this enough times by now that most of them knew not to interrupt him. But better to be safe than sorry with new climbers in the mix.

In general, Seeing the future through a spire door or gateway didn't work. Once inside a spire room, Sage's attunement could be used to view the future, or rather possible futures, depending on how his actions changed the outcome of each foreseen reality. But early on in his climbing career—probably around floor six or seven—Sage's enchanted glasses had turned up in a treasure chest after a particularly grueling challenge. They were specifically designed to work in the Tortoise Spire and must have spent a long time within it in order to possess the wealth of information they held for each floor, room, and challenge. But they could only show what had happened in the past. While assessing a particular door or gateway with the divination glasses, Sage's attunement could interpret the data into a vision of what awaited them on the other side.

The images on Sage's glasses continued to flicker even as his vision went blank, wiped clean like a slate. In his mind's eye, a new set of images took shape behind the rise of a velvet curtain, revealing bits and pieces of what was to come. A fortress surrounded by high walls with storm clouds rapidly approaching. Lightning flashed behind the fort three times; Sage was careful to keep count. A two-headed monster with the second head constantly shapeshifting into something new while the first head remained human, a glowing sword clasped in its hand. A deep, dark lake with something shadowy twisting within its depths. A hand holding out a key that flickered with golden light. And finally, the quickest flicker of reflected light off a surface Sage couldn't make out, along with the toll of a bell. That was new. He'd never Seen anything quite like that last part before.

"It looks like a scenario room," Sage told the team, watching the vision as it played out in his head. "We're defending a fortress. We'll move on if we can survive a siege for three days. The invading army is a mix of human soldiers, some attuned, and a lot of monsters of varying types. There's also something about a lake with some treasure, maybe a monster battle? And . . . a trading sequence. Completing the trading sequence gets us an extra key for later on."

"Any specific warnings?" Lani asked, direct as usual. "Traps? Traitors? Death?"

"Wait a minute!" Aldis protested, pushing forward in front of Nieve and Emiko. "You can See through a gateway? That's not supposed to be possible! Why isn't that a skill listed on your team roster?"

Still leaning back against the railing, Hane tipped their head to the side. "Are you hiding your attunement level? Are you actually an Emerald Seer?"

"No!" Sage flushed. He'd gotten so used to his glasses that he forgot how unique they were, especially in combination with his attunement. "It's these glasses. I got them as a treasure a few years ago. It's almost like a memory crystal that's recorded a lot of different rooms within the spire, and when I focus my Sight through the lenses, it shows me the upcoming challenge. It's not all that special."

"It sounds special," Aldis assured him. "Did you have an Enchanter take a look at those? If there's no patent for them yet, you could be wearing a fortune on your face."

"Ah, that's . . ."

"We're getting off topic," Lani said sternly. "Sage? Anything else we need to know?"

"Right, sorry." He concentrated on Lani's earlier question. "No traps, at least not right inside the doorway. As for our allies at the fortress, I'll need to meet them before I can be sure." Sage double-tapped the side of his glasses, deactivating the Divination runes. He turned, putting his back to the gateway in order to study each of his team members. Even with an attunement designed to show the future, there was no guaranteed spell that could accurately predict a team member's death. Everyone who climbed a spire courted death closely; it was a risk climbers accepted the moment they crossed the threshold. The best Sage could do was use a passive warning spell he called Divine Imminent Threat that would hopefully give him a few seconds' warning to try to avert disaster. He cast the spell silently over each of his teammates, hoping, as always, that it wouldn't be necessary.

"Nothing I can See from here, Lani," Sage said, gaze lingering on her just a touch longer than on anyone else. He felt a familiar touch of heat in his cheeks as he looked away. Her hair looked nice today, all in braids that were twisted into an elegant knot on the top of her head. By the end of every climb, everyone looked so ragged and battered that sometimes he forgot how elegant she could be. Although if Wyle were here, she would have already started taking bets on how long Lani's intricate braided knot would last after the climb began. She used to take bets on Emiko's two hair buns, too, but in all the years he'd climbed with her, Sage had never seen Emiko's hair out of place. It had taken him far longer than it should have to realize she was using enchanted clasps in her hair to keep it from falling out, but he'd never said a thing to anyone—save from placing the occasional winning bet.

"Good. Thanks, Sage. Final checks, everyone." Lani dropped her hands to her belt, touching the sheathed dirk on the right, the pouch marked with a first-aid symbol tucked right behind it, the hilt of her cutlass on the left, her coin purse, then finally the tiny pouch containing her return bell. With her gloves folded through her belt, Sage couldn't miss the fact that she'd lost another fingertip. This time it was her left ring finger. He flushed as he noticed, gaze darting away as he made his own final equipment check. He knew it would only start a fight if he said anything, so as much as he hated it, he stayed silent. Fighting wouldn't change Lani's mind and all it would do was sour the run. He wished she'd accept a loan from a friend sometimes, rather than surrendering her hand to the mercies of the collection agency. Even if it didn't affect him in any direct way, he hated to see her lose another knuckle. Too many more and it would start to impact her ability to climb.

But he'd seen loan offers play out more than once, and they never ended well. Even eternally stingy Nieve had offered to lend Lani cash when she needed it, and Lani had viciously rebuked the offer. After that, neither he nor Nieve had brought it up again. It was almost a challenge now, as if the first one of them to bring it up would lose. Sage shot a subtle glance sideways over at Nieve as he checked his dueling cane once more, trying to see if she'd noticed. By the tight pinch of her lips and her determined stare at the ground, Sage guessed she had.

"Everyone set their anchors, right?" Lani asked as the shuffling tapered off. "Hane, Aldis, did you set your anchors near the team flag?"

Hane nodded, still standing at the edge of the group gathered around the spire gateway.

"I planted mine at the Soaring Wings check-in station," Aldis said, making a vague motion with his hand. "I can always teleport to you after we ring out." He chuckled in a way that suggested he was covering up nerves. "Unless you suspect we'll be out of mana by the end of all this."

"It's hard to say," Lani admitted, ruthlessly honest. By the grim expression on her face, Sage knew she was thinking back to the end of their last climb. "We nearly lost people on our last climb and we were all drained by the time we were able to ring out. This is a new floor for us and the current plan is to at least make it up to the twentieth floor or higher."

"Or find another gate key." Nieve tossed the gray gate key up so that it flipped once before she caught it again. "Our last climb lasted ten days and we managed to get through two floors. I expect this one will take longer."

"If you come early next time, I'll show you where our flag is," Emiko offered, smiling brightly at Aldis. "If you want to climb with us again."

"Ah, thank you." Aldis's face was shiny with sweat already. Sage didn't think it was that hot on the balcony outside the gate. "I'll take you up on that offer for next time."

"We'll see about next time." Lani's tone was cool. Direct. "Your experience isn't what I'd like it to be. For your sake, I hope your travel mana specialization and your doorway theory make up for your level. If not, we'll look for a new Wayfarer next time."

Aldis's cheeks flared red, as if embarrassed, and he muttered something Sage couldn't quite make out. Not that Sage blamed him for that response: Lani often gave the impression of being cold or uncaring, but that was far from the truth. She was reserved, sure, but her levelheaded leadership had saved the team more than once, and as a healer, she was unparalleled for her level. If it weren't for her one heretical habit, the temple would probably have hired her to climb with a government-sponsored team, earning a salary in addition to any treasures recovered. When Sage thought about it that way, he was almost thankful that Lani's missing fingertips gave her away. But that was selfish thinking and he knew it.

"Okay, so after we get the lay of the land, we'll divvy up the tasks and get to work," Lani ordered. Sage grunted as Nieve grabbed his shoulder and dragged him backward so she could get to the gateway. He made a face at her as she shouldered past him, only looking back to bare her teeth in a feral grin. "Sage, once we get the basic rundown, take another look, okay?"

"Yes, Lani," Sage replied promptly.

"Yes, Lani," Nieve repeated mockingly. The grit and grind of the key was loud enough that only Sage heard her. He pretended that he hadn't, anyway. The gray stone slab of a door rippled outward from the lock, but not in the same way that water rippled. The movement was more like a shiver through scales, or the ruffled quills of a bird. It always made Sage think of goose bumps. The last ripple ended and the gray stone door faded, the key vanishing along with it. The space beyond was an inky black, not so much a doorway as a portal that would take them to their first challenge of the climb. Nieve swept back from the doorway, deliberately standing in front of Sage as she swept her arm out graciously. "After you, fearless leader."

Sage couldn't help but feel a tiny pinprick of jealousy when Lani gave her little purse-lipped smile, the one that said she was amused but not *that* amused. He reached back and checked the pouch tied to his belt again, feeling the object through the sturdy canvas. The timing was still bad, he knew that, but he wanted so badly to show Nieve up just then. She wasn't even all that interested in Lani! At least, not the same way he was.

"All right, let's go." Rather than step through the portal, Lani reached out and cupped her hand over one of Emiko's hair buns, shaking Emiko's head back and forth as the shorter woman squealed a protest. One brief smile, and then Lani stepped through the portal and vanished. Nieve was a little rougher, tugging on Emiko's hair bun until Emiko huffed and crossed her arms, appearing put out. Nieve grinned, then jumped through the portal after Lani. Sage was about to repeat the gesture but stopped at the mystified looks from both Hane and Aldis.

"Ah, sorry." Sage cupped his hand over one of Emiko's hair buns and shook lightly. "It's a preclimb ritual. We've done this since we started climbing."

"Yes, you have to!" Emiko declared, all signs of irritation vanished from her face. "It's bad luck if you don't."

"I thought preclimb rituals involved prayers and incense," Aldis said, looking taken aback. "You don't offer a prayer to the spire's visage? Or invoke the god beast? What is the significance of pulling on a teammate's hair?"

Sage exchanged a look with Emiko, her shoulders lifting in a shrug.

"It's just what we've always done," Sage replied simply. "Our Visage Katashi is busy enough without all the climber teams praying to him. As for Genbu, we're taught he prefers action to prayers."

"I lit some incense at the temple and prayed for a safe climb yesterday," Emiko added on. "Is praying before a climb something Valian teams do before a climb?"

"I'm not sure about Valian teams," Aldis huffed. "But most of the preclimb rituals I've seen at this spire usually at least mention Katashi or Genbu."

"From what I've seen, praying doesn't make much of a difference." The soft, clear voice made Sage jump, clasping a hand to his heart. How had he forgotten that Hane was still on the balcony with them? The Wavewalker turned to Emiko, a hand outstretched but stopping short of actually touching her. "May I?"

"Yep!" Emiko dipped her head, though it wasn't necessary as Hane stood about a head taller than she did. They placed a finger in the center of her hair bun, wiggled it once, then stepped through the portal.

"Rather unorthodox for a healer to go through first, isn't it?" Aldis asked, eyeing the dark portal beyond the gate with no small amount of trepidation. Emiko sidled up beside him and nudged him with her elbow, smiling as she pointed up at her hair buns. "Oh, fine, if you insist." He gave the nearest hair bun a tiny twist. "Will that do?"

"Yep!" Emiko reached up and squeezed both her hair buns before looping her arms through Sage's and Aldis's. "Let's go! One, two, three, jump!"

Sage jumped when Emiko did, holding his breath out of habit. The darkness swallowed him completely.

The climb had begun.

CHAPTER 2

ALDIS

Wayfarer—Travel Specialization (hand mark), Sunstone

Aldis staggered as solid ground formed under his feet. Jumping through the portal hadn't been the greatest idea, in his opinion, but the Cloud-caller hadn't given him much choice in the matter. Aldis freed his arm from hers, straightened his tunic, and looked around to get his bearings.

The six of them stood on a wide, flat walkway atop a long stretch of wall surrounding what appeared to be a military base. The wall was an impressive height, high enough that Aldis chose to stare out over the distance beyond the fort, rather than peer down at the neat and orderly buildings kept safe behind the fort walls. Without checking a compass, he wasn't entirely sure which direction he was facing, but he could see that the fortress was nestled in something of a valley, making it a choke point for whatever lay beyond. A low cloud of dust hovered on the horizon, thick near the ground and more nebulous above. An approaching army, perhaps? The ground ahead of the fortress had been cleared of trees and scrub about a mile out, most likely to improve visibility. Unfortunately, it had the added benefit of making a nice, clear path for an army to march straight through.

Are those reinforcements? Aldis wondered hopefully. If they weren't, they would be in trouble. The fortress seemed small—much too small to muster a force against the one coming toward them. What had Sage said? That they only needed to last here for three days? Maybe it was a simple matter of shoring up defenses and weathering the storm.

The wooden walkway shuddered beneath heavy, urgent footsteps, bringing Aldis's focus back to the walkway on the wall. A man dressed in an old-fashioned army uniform bearing the sash of a commander approached the six of them rapidly, stopping far enough back to bow formally.

"You must be the reinforcements I sent for," the man said brusquely. "Well met. You've arrived just in time." He looked out over the wall, countenance darkening beneath a close-trimmed black beard. "They'll be on us by sunset, and that's just the vanguard. I expect we'll see them camped out there tomorrow if they don't overrun us tonight."

"What can you tell us about the enemy army?" the Acolyte asked, a little too directly in Aldis's opinion. Shouldn't she have started with a "Thanks for meeting us here," or something like that?

"Hey." Aldis nudged Sage, whispering as the commander answered Lani's question. "Shouldn't you be the one taking point? You're the Seer, so that means you're the one who makes the plan, right?"

Sage shook his head and leaned away, craning forward to hear what the fortress commander was saying. "I just listen and look ahead. Lani makes the plans."

Aldis huffed, rocking back on his heels. The whole team dynamic felt odd to him. Having never had a team of his own, Aldis bounced around as a Wayfarer for hire, sometimes climbing with a group two or three times until the group either disbanded or ended his contract in order to hire someone else. There had been a lot of chatter in the contract-climber circles when the Guiding Star Legacy team posted two openings—even better was the fact that their former teammates had retired, rather than dying on a climb. The posting had requested a Citrine-level Wayfarer, but he'd leveraged his specialization in travel magic, setting himself apart from other Wayfarers even though he was only Sunstone level. Lucky for him, the specialization was easy to prove, as the attunement mark on his hand had changed from the standard Wayfarer attunement mark once he'd earned his specialization.

But his hypothesis for altering spire doorways probably hadn't hurt, either.

Goddess, did he hope that actually worked. If it didn't, he'd probably be looking for a new climber team all over again.

Of the team, Aldis had only met Lani and Nieve prior to today. They'd met at a popular tavern for climbers, where Lani, and to a lesser extent, Nieve, had drilled him on his experience, hypothetical challenges, and spell knowledge. Despite his specialty for casting complex travel magic, he knew he was lacking in actual climbing experience, which was why he'd shared his idea about spire portals and how they might be altered to shorten a climb. Lani had tried to brush him off there, but Nieve had been intrigued. He might have made it sound more like he was certain it would work rather than an untested hypothesis in order to secure his position on the team, which was probably the only reason they'd selected him rather than a Citrine-level Wayfarer, but even if his idea didn't pan out, he was hopeful he could at least break through the Sunstone wall and finally reach Citrine this climb. Even if the Guiding Star Legacy team wouldn't take him back, a Citrine attunement could open up other doors.

Lani stood with her back to Aldis, her posture ramrod straight, her hair perfectly coiled atop her head. She had a stern air about her; he'd noticed that during their meeting at the tavern. She didn't smile often, and she had a habit of resting her hands on her hips, giving her an imperious countenance. She looked fit but not so fit that she lost her curves. High cheekbones and sun-bronzed skin gave her an almost exotic look, despite the black hair and dark eyes common in Dalenos. By all accounts, she was an exceptional Acolyte, but Aldis silently wondered about her bedside manner as a healer.

Sage, the Seer, stood to Lani's left, one step behind her, nodding as the fortress commander laid out the situation. His gear looked fairly standard, well maintained but not at all flashy. His cloak looked reversible, and if it was anything like Aldis's, one side would be imbued with a weak warming spell, while the other side would have a cooling spell. The only notable item Sage wore—besides those marvelous glasses, of course—was a dueling cane double the standard length, making it almost as long as a sword. Perhaps it had one or two more functions than a normal cane; Aldis had seen that before. Sage himself was a puzzle Aldis couldn't quite crack. In all the teams he'd joined so far, if the team's Seer wasn't the leader, then they were at least a co-leader. But Sage hadn't been involved in the interview process, nor did he seem interested in addressing the fortress commander. He seemed content just to listen and let Lani ask all the questions. That was strange, wasn't it? Almost as strange as the Seer using a Valian variant of his name while still claiming to be Dalen. White skin, hazel eyes, and sandy hair gave him a distinctly Valian appearance. Having grown up in Valia, Aldis found it comforting to be climbing with someone who reminded him of home.

Nieve, the Champion and nominally the team's leader, didn't appear to be paying the fortress commander any attention at all. She was leaning against a merlon along the wall, a wide grin on her face as she looked down on the approaching army. The Guiding Star Legacy team was registered under her name, but she seemed uninterested in leading it. At least, she had seemed that way during Aldis's interview up until he mentioned his doorway hypothesis. At that point, she'd had no problem pulling rank over Lani—a fact Aldis had filed away for later. She looked like she might be from Caelford, or at least had a Caelish parent. She was tall, taller than Aldis by almost a head. Her skin was a rich brown, but her hair wasn't thick or curly in the way of some Caelish people. She wore it long and loose, save for a bright red headband tied around her forehead, covering her attunement mark. The only weapons that Aldis could see were on her belt: a small war hammer with a sharp spike opposite the blunt end, and a simple katana with an elongated hilt, similar to that of an odachi. Why would anyone need that much of a grip for a simple katana? Perhaps it was a strange piece of treasure she'd found while climbing. The rest of her gear had a patchwork quality to it, too, so the katana didn't seem entirely out of place. The rest of her teammates wore quality gear that had seen some use, but Nieve's gear looked older, almost as if it had been inherited, or bought secondhand.

To the complete contrary, the little Cloudcaller was wearing some of the most expensive gear Aldis had ever seen. Instead of the usual quilted tunic and thick leggings, she wore a stylish kimono patterned with clouds cut to about the length of a standard tunic with storm-blue leggings underneath. Her boots were only ankle high and stamped with little sparkling gems. He didn't see any weapons on her, but she wore a strange enchanted device on her belt as well as a bandolier of various mana crystals across her chest. Aldis used the spell Detect Aura to see the enchantments on her gear and flinched. The strange-looking box on her hip flared with light, only visible to him while the spell was active. Her clothing, her boots, and even something hidden in her hair were enchanted, the magical aura glittering in a way that indicated intricate spellwork and careful layering to avoid interference with other spells. Her hair was black as midnight, twisted up into two tight buns on the top of her head, her eyes an amber brown that always seemed to be lit with a smile. Her skin was pale, almost white, giving Aldis the uneasy feeling that she was probably a Dalen noble. Ostensibly she was the same age as everyone else on the team, but she gave the impression of being younger. Not just by her height but by the way she hummed lightly to herself, rocking on her heels as she shaped a little cloud between her hands, blowing puffs of air at it to make it look like a bunny.

The only person on the team that Aldis kind of knew was Hane, but only in a passing "Oh, that's *that* Wavewalker" kind of way. Not that Hane stood out at all. In fact, Aldis never would have noticed them if they weren't constantly being pointed out by other climbers. They had a slight build with typical Dalenos features: black hair, dark eyes, olive skin. They didn't wear expensive clothes or enchanted jewelry or even custom weaponry that Aldis could see. There was nothing about them that stood out, except their whispered reputation. The rumor among contract climbers was that Hane was secretly an Emerald-level Wavewalker who never climbed with the same team twice. Aldis had secretly inspected Hane's shroud a few times in the past using the spell Detect Aura, but each time he did, it only appeared as a yellowish-gold color, indicating a Citrine level. Not that that meant much:

shrouds could be suppressed, after all. Secretly, Aldis hoped the rumors were true: he'd never seen an Emerald's shroud before.

Hane lounged back against the rampart, arms folded loosely, giving the impression of listening to the commander while also taking stock of the scenario as a whole. Aldis looked around again, noticing things he hadn't given proper attention to before, like the distant shimmer of a lake, half hidden by the curve of a tree-studded hillside, and the sharp-edged barren slopes of the hills behind the fortress, dotted with caves that all appeared to be joined by steel tracks. Mine carts on rails, possibly? If the fortress protected mines full of precious metals, Aldis could surmise why the attacking army was here.

"Thank you for explaining the situation so frankly, Commander," Lani was saying, a finality in her tone that caught Aldis's ear. "It seems my team has their work cut out for them. Please allow us a brief conference, and then we'll get right to work."

"I'll let the barracks officer know to expect you. A squire will show you to your rooms once you are ready." The commander took a step back, bowed, then turned and marched away. Lani's bow in response was slightly belated, but at least she made the attempt at courtesy.

"Okay." Lani clapped her hands as she turned to face the rest of the team. "Who wants to do what, and what do you need?"

Aldis startled: Were they separating this quickly? Right inside the spire gate? Weren't they supposed to stick together and work as a team? Or was this how it worked on the higher floors? Most importantly: What did they expect *him* to do?

"I'm gonna round up the troops and run them through some drills," Nieve volunteered. "Looks like we have a few hours before that army gets here, which gives me a little time to whip the soldiers here into shape, then let them cool off before the attack."

"Are you leading troops out?" Lani asked.

"Probably." The Champion shrugged carelessly. "A good offense is the best defense and all that. Unless Sage says differently."

"I didn't See anything worth worrying about on my second look," Sage put in. "I'm going to start the trading sequence for now. When the attack is a little more imminent, I can look again."

"If it's all right, I'd like to be teleported to the lake." Hane nodded to the sliver of lake barely visible in the distance. "I'd like to take care of the lake monster problem early on in the scenario and be back by the time things start to get rough here."

Start to get rough? Aldis wondered. *Don't you see the army bearing down on us right now?*

Lani frowned. "On your own? That's a little risky, don't you think? If you can wait until after the first attack, we can split the team so that half of us stay here at the fort, and the other half go deal with the lake monster."

Hane rolled a shoulder in something approximating a shrug. "You don't need me here for the opening attack. If the monster isn't something I can handle on my own, I'll report back. Unless you're concerned about me making off with the treasure."

"No, of course not, your reputation is impeccable. It's a matter of safety, not trust," Lani insisted.

"I'll be fine," Hane said mildly. Their gaze drifted and Aldis suddenly found all eyes on him. "You can send me that far, can't you?"

"Er, that is . . ." Aldis hedged, nervous for reasons he couldn't fully identify. "The distance is no trouble, but with all the tree cover, I can't see a safe place to set you."

"Just drop me over the lake," Hane instructed. "I'll be fine from there."

"Er . . ." Aldis looked around for confirmation from Sage, Nieve, and finally Lani before getting a terse nod from the Acolyte. "Okay. Ready?"

Hane dipped their chin. Silently, Aldis reached for his travel sorcery and looked out over the lake in the distance. He picked a high spot over the center of the lake, then held his attunement-marked hand out toward Hane. As the Wavewalker vanished, the rest of the team turned to look out over the lake, as if expecting to see Hane reappear over the distance.

"Keep in touch with them," Lani ordered, freeing the gloves that had been folded over her belt. "What else was there?"

"Ooh, ooh!" The little Cloudcaller bobbed on her toes, hand in the air as if volunteering for something exciting. "I still have a lot of transference mana crystals from the last climb! I can help reinforce the inner curtain wall."

"Thanks, Emi, that'll be helpful." A flash of one of the Acolyte's rare smiles. As she pulled her gloves on, Aldis noticed something that made his stomach drop. "It sounds like the leadership here is a bit of a mess. I'm going to work with the commander to—"

"Whoa!" Aldis couldn't help the outburst. One missing fingertip might just be a climbing mishap, but three missing fingertips? Two pinkies and a ring finger? That wasn't accidental. As all eyes once again turned toward him, Aldis forced a weak chuckle. "It's just— Well, you look like you've had a run-in with some Haven Securities collection agents."

Lani's expression barely changed, but something like a shiver moved through the rest of the group. Sage and Nieve each actually took a step back, while Emiko bit her lower lip and dropped her gaze, weight shifting from side to side as if uncomfortable.

"You mean this?" Lani asked, holding up her right hand, the tip of her pinky missing. "Or this?" Her left was missing the tip of her ring finger and two joints from her pinky.

"Ouch." Aldis grimaced sympathetically. "I'm sorry, pardon the terrible joke. I'm sure it was just a really unlucky bite from a monster. Or two."

"Why?" Lani asked, her eyes narrowing into sharp points. "Because losing them to a monster is better than having them quickly and cleanly removed by a collections agent?"

"Oh, I didn't mean to imply you were a gambler!" Aldis laughed in the hopes that the others would join in and diffuse some of the tension. "No, that would be against the goddess's teachings, and heretical, and—"

"I *am* a gambler," Lani said, tone flat as she set her hands on her hips, missing fingertips in full view. "Is that a problem?"

"It looks like it has been," Aldis observed, gesturing to her hands. "But it doesn't have to be. The temple has all sorts of clinics and support available to help—"

A long, thin whine emerged from Emiko's throat, her brows tightly furrowed, and she looked between Aldis and Lani, concern evident in her wide, bright eyes. Nieve reached out and pulled Emiko to the side, putting an arm around her shoulders as if comforting her. Aldis watched, confused. These were Lani's friends and teammates. If they knew about her gambling problem, why not chime in and agree? Surely they weren't all gambling addicts.

Aldis furtively checked everyone else's hands, cool relief washing over him as he failed to find any other missing fingertips.

"I'm just saying you can get help for your problem," Aldis said as gently as possible.

Nieve hissed, her face scrunched up as if preparing for a blow. Sage turned away, pretending to take an interest in a broken lantern set into a crenel.

"It's *not* a problem," Lani snapped, storming forward so quickly that Aldis backed up several steps. "Sometimes, I win big. Sometimes, I lose big. That's part of the fun. And if I can't pay my debts in time, it's me who loses part of a finger. Not you, and not anyone else. Care to explain how any of that is a problem?"

Aldis sputtered, glancing around for support from Lani's so-called friends. Sage was cleaning the lenses of his glasses with fastidious focus. Nieve was staring up into the sky, her arm still wrapped around Emiko, who pressed in close to her friend's side.

"I'm just trying to help," Aldis finally managed, feeling wrong-footed and cornered. "There's no need to get upset about it."

"I don't need your help, and the fact that you think I do, without even bothering to get to know me, is extremely offensive." Though Lani had to be an inch or two shorter than he was, she seemed to loom over him as she set her hands on her hips. "I wouldn't presume to ask you what you spend your cut of the treasure on, so why is it any of your business what I do with my cut?"

"I can't see what you're so upset about!" Aldis burst out, looking around once again for support. "Why would any sane person choose to play a game where losing might mean the loss of a body part?"

"Why climb the spires, then?" Nieve asked, finally speaking up. "As many people die inside these spires as those who find life-changing amounts of treasure. It's a gamble, isn't it?"

Aldis's face felt flame-hot. "That's . . . that's entirely—"

"You don't always die in the spires," Emiko said without looking up. For once she sounded sullen and somber, her eyes downcast. "One of our earliest climbing friends lost half her leg in a climb, and that was where her attunement was."

"Climbing *is* a gamble," Sage added, piling on. "But we accept the risks when we step through the gateway. It's the same for Lani: she knows the risks and she pays the price when she loses."

"So you can either accept that, or we can find a new climber to take your place," Nieve said firmly. "Choose quickly, because we've been standing around out here for far too long already."

"But— It's not— I didn't—" Aldis fought to find the right words. "I never said I didn't want to continue. We're already here, we might as well get on with it."

"Fine," Lani said sharply, pulling her gloves on with small, sharp tugs. "We do need to be getting on with it. I'll be with the fortress commander, fixing the command structure here." Her eyes glinted like twin daggers as they darted up to meet Aldis's. "What are you going to be doing?"

"Ah . . ." He didn't know. Most of the time, he simply followed along behind the group, casting teleportation and communication spells when needed. It didn't help that he hadn't really been paying attention when the commander had outlined the situation. "I'll just—" He looked around, hopeful for a suggestion. His eyes landed on his fellow Valian. "I'll stick with Sage. In case he needs my help with the trading sequence."

Lani rolled her eyes, hands settling on her hips again. With her gloves on, it was impossible to tell that she'd ever lost even a single fingertip. "Fine. Just stay out of everyone's way. Meet in front of the north gate before the attack."

That last comment must have been aimed at everyone by the shuffling and murmurs of agreement. Emiko chanted something quickly and softly under her breath right before a nebulous cloud formed around her, lifting her off her feet and carrying her over the curtain wall and down into the fortress. Nieve and Sage exchanged a look that seemed to communicate something, though Aldis couldn't tell exactly what it was. Nieve walked away alongside Lani, leaving Sage with a sour look on his face. He finished polishing the lenses of his glasses and set them on his nose again before leaning in to study the nearby lantern again.

"Right." Aldis forced a smile, pushing through the awkward silence. "So, ah . . . What, exactly, did your last Wayfarer do in these sorts of situations?"

"Wyle usually stuck close to Lani, so she could communicate with everyone when plans changed," Sage explained. A songbird landed on the lantern's rusty carry-hook to trill a short tune, but Sage waved it away almost impatiently. "It's probably for the best if you stay with me. I'm usually the one who Sees plans changing, anyway."

"Oh, thank the goddess!" Sage seemed like a good sort. Even if he did let Lani and Nieve run the show. "Doesn't it make you uncomfortable? Climbing with someone who forsakes the teachings?"

Sage took a moment to answer. There must have been something intensely interesting about that lantern, because Sage picked it up carefully, holding it at both the top and bottom. The metal and glass rattled ominously; surely the lantern had to be broken beyond repair. "It doesn't bother me. Nieve and Emi are more religious than I am and they're fine with it. And I guess if the goddess really hated gambling so much, she wouldn't allow casinos to exist. I feel like it's a personal choice, and just as Lani says, it doesn't affect anyone but her."

"Yes, but . . ." Aldis hedged. "Isn't it still wrong? For instance, if you murdered someone and got away with it, murder is still wrong. How is gambling—"

Sage straightened up, turning to give Aldis an exasperated look. "If you want to debate morals and religious teachings, you ought to be in a temple, not a spire. Lani is a close friend of all of us and you're not going to win this argument. So you can either choose to accept it, or we can call the group together right now and stop our climb. Which is it going to be?"

Aldis held his hands palm up defensively, surprised by the almost hostile tone. "I'm not trying to pick a fight, I just—"

Sage turned away abruptly, cradling the creaking and cracking lantern against his chest. "I'll find Lani and let her know you need to quit. We'll just have to call Hane back and—"

"No, wait!" Aldis grabbed Sage's shoulder to stop him. "I don't want to quit! I want to climb. With your team."

"With our whole team," Sage stressed, holding Aldis's eyes intently.

"Yes. Your whole team," Aldis said, shoulders slumping. "I was just startled, that's all. The other climbers who interviewed for this spot all said your team is one of the best for its rank. I want to be here."

"Part of the reason we're among the best is because we function well as a team," Sage said, freeing his shoulder from Aldis's grasp and walking toward the stairs down to the inner fortress. He watched his step carefully as he continued. "Nieve and Emi and I all took our Judgments on the same day and we've been together ever since. Lani and Ren—he was our Soulblade—were only in the class ahead of ours. Wyle joined maybe a year after that and we've been solid as a team since then. I think we're all a little nervous with the change in our team's dynamic."

"You all seem quite close," Aldis admitted, following Sage closely. "But how did you manage to get into the actual Judgment classes? I thought foreigners all had to pass a series of tests in order to take Judgments in the Tortoise Spire."

"I'm not— Ugh." Sage stopped on the stairs and looked back. "Look, my parents came from Valia, but they moved to Dalenos before I was born. I may look like one, but I'm not a foreigner. I've never even been to Valia. Dalenos is my home."

Something clicked in Aldis's head. "Oh! So that's why your name is Seiji, isn't it? To, ah, blend in, as it were?"

"Yeah." Sage rolled his eyes. "Something like that, anyway. It didn't work as intended." Sage sighed and continued down the stairs. "What about you? You speak the language very well, but if you took the foreigner versions of the Judgment tests, then you can't have been here long."

"My parents were merchants. I used to travel with them between Valia and Dalenos all the time. A while back, they settled in Dalenos permanently and gave up their trade. They mostly work as local translators now." They had changed their last name, too, but that was supposed to be a secret, so Aldis didn't share it. "That was maybe four or five years ago, which means I've officially lived in Dalenos longer than I lived in Valia, what with all the back and forth over the years." Anxious about being caught in a lie, Aldis quickly changed the subject. "Why are you carrying around that broken lantern? Do we need it for some reason?"

Sage sighed. "How experienced are you with trading sequences within scenarios?"

"Not at all," Aldis admitted cheerfully. "I've heard people talk about them, but I never understood the point."

"The point is usually an extra treasure by the end of the scenario," Sage explained, eyes scanning the fort now that they were on the ground level.

The open area in front of the fort's gate was full of soldiers in various states of dress, with almost no one wearing a full uniform. Nieve stood in front of them, ordering them to fall into ranks. "It's almost always a key, which is helpful to have at the beginning of a climb."

"Ah." Aldis nodded agreeably. "I can see how that would be advantageous. Do you use your Sight to tell you where it goes?"

"I try not to. There are usually clues, but in a pinch, I'll use my Sight." Sage set off following the fortress wall, avoiding the assembly of soldiers. "Once, I got the sequence wrong—I think I missed a clue, or a fork in the sequence—and ended up with the exact same item I'd started with." Sage chuckled ruefully. "I wanted to start over and try to figure out where I messed up, but Lani was already mad at me, so we just moved on. I get it right most of the time, though."

Aldis managed to hold back a comment about Lani always seeming angry. He liked Sage, but the man could be defensive of his friends. Or maybe it was just Lani he was defensive of. "So how do you know where to take the lantern? Was there a clue on it?"

"I think so. Sometimes it's hard to tell." Sage flagged down a passing squire and asked where, of all things, the postmaster was located. The squire answered, pointed, then scurried away. "I think I know where to take this one. Follow me."

As with most spire scenarios that Aldis had been in before, this one paid meticulous attention to detail, from the number of barracks necessary to house all the not-real soldiers, to the cobwebs in the eaves of the storehouses. Even the smell from the privy trench seemed real enough as Aldis and Sage passed by it. The fort was contained within four walls, each stalwartly facing a cardinal direction and joined at the corner by four watchtowers. It looked very neat at the outset, but Aldis couldn't help but notice small things that unsettled him. For instance, all the storehouses they passed either were empty or had a just-looted quality about them: boxes stacked haphazardly, some open, some tipped over, and some with boxes stacked disorderly in the walkways between buildings rather than safely tucked away behind a locked door. Weapon racks were stationed along the walls so soldiers could grab them quickly if the fort came under attack, but most of the metal appeared rusted, with the wooden hafts looking mildewed and rotten. And he couldn't forget the sight of the soldiers congregated in front of Nieve in the central courtyard, most of them looking like they had been tossed out of bed, some still hungover. What sort of army was this, to be so unprepared with an enemy force barreling toward their gates?

Aldis would have asked Sage if he had any idea what battle this scenario was meant to represent, but then the scent of fresh-baked bread caught his nose, quashing his questions in favor of his appetite. They were passing the mess hall, a long, low building built in the dead center of the fortress, the scents of baking bread and roasting meat strong through the open windows. Aldis wanted to detour, but Sage refused to stop and Aldis didn't want to be left on his own. Scenarios weren't always what they seemed: even in a protected setting like this, there could be assassins, traps, or hidden monsters.

Across from the mess hall was the command center, built with two levels of offices and meeting rooms and crowned with the tallest building inside the fort walls: the bell tower. In Aldis's experience, army bells were used to signal anything from mealtimes to imminent attacks, which was the prime reason for its central location within the fortress. That wasn't what made him nervous, however. It was the fact that Sage was circling around behind the command center and ascending the bell tower stairs.

"Are you really sure the bell ringer needs a broken lantern?" Aldis asked, wary of the staircase. "I think a working one would be more fitting to negoti-ate the stairs at night."

"Hm?" Sage paused on the third step. "Oh, no, we're not going all the way to the top. And anyway, the rope for the bell is here." Sage pointed to a thick rope looped around a metal anchor attached to the wall. "I think the stairs only go up that high for maintenance. We're just going up to meet the postmaster."

"Ah." Aldis looked for a way to teleport up, rather than take the stairs, but he wasn't entirely sure which landing Sage needed. And it seemed bad form to let Sage go on his own, so he mustered and started up behind Sage. "What clue led you to the postmaster?"

"I'll tell you if I'm right," Sage called back. "The clue could have been mis-leading. Or, you know, not a clue at all and just a coincidence."

Aldis was beginning to understand why most groups skipped trading sequences in scenarios, despite the chance at an extra key. By the time Sage arrived at the first door leading into the bell tower, Aldis was sweating. He mopped his face with a handkerchief as Sage rapped lightly on the door before pushing it open. There was a dark cloth drape just past the doorway that Sage lifted aside so Aldis could pass through.

He immediately wished he hadn't: a sharp, acrid odor assaulted his nose, bringing tears to his eyes. The tower was narrow and, from this angle, extremely tall, being built entirely around an iron ladder that disappeared into a loft far above. The small space carried a ringing echo, which was dem-onstrated by what seemed to be hundreds of birds, all trilling, singing, coo-ing, or cawing, which made the space intolerable enough, but worse still: just about every surface Aldis could see—the ladder, the ledges to the outside, the floor, all of it—was coated in thick white bird droppings.

Sage made a noise of disgust, proving that Seers can't See everything. He reached into a pocket and pulled out a handkerchief, using it to open a second door in the wall adjacent to the stairs. Aldis hurried to follow him, trying to cover both ears and hold his nose at the same time, thinking anything had to be better than this.

The door opened to the roof of the command center, which made it better than the cacophonous aviary that was the bell tower, but only because it wasn't enclosed by walls. Birds sat along the waist-high walls around the roof, most of them pigeons by the look of them. There were almost as many droppings out here as inside the tower, but at least the open air mitigated the stench. The only surface that wasn't lined with birds was a long table covered in rolled and folded papers, with a single gray-haired man rustling through the papers, tossing them seemingly haphazardly into unmarked baskets.

"If you've a message to send, just leave it!" the postmaster groused, not deigning to look up from the stack of letters he was currently sorting. "If you're looking for a letter, I'll have it down in receiving as soon as it's sorted. Which would go a lot faster without interruptions, by the way!"

"Sorry to bother you," Sage said, his tone cordially polite. "I'm with the reinforcements that just arrived and I'm familiarizing myself with the fortress. It's a pleasure to make your acquaintance."

It certainly is not, Aldis thought to himself, scraping the sole of his boot on a wooden plank. He didn't like the looks of all those birds, silently judging him with their black, beady eyes. There were small crates and cages lining one wall of the roof, but instead of housing birds, they stored sacks of birdseed, millet, and straw. It seemed the postmaster had given up on caging the birds and was instead protecting his supplies from being assaulted by the winged pests. The "post office" seemed an utter wreck, from the sorting system on the table to the broken buckets and barrels the birds perched on. This certainly wasn't a job he envied.

"Oh. Well, in that case, welcome." The postmaster finally looked up from sorting scrolls into baskets, a look of pleasant surprise in his rheumy eyes. "The new people don't usually come by to— Oh my! What is that you have?"

"This?" Sage asked, holding up the broken lantern. "It's just a bit of trash. I was going to toss it in the midden."

"You don't need that?" The postmaster set down his stack of mail and plucked a pair of tiny glasses off the end of his nose. "Those mirrors would make perfect enrichment for my birds! Is it possible I could have it?"

Sage hummed thoughtfully, as if thinking it over. As he did, the postmaster looked around and grabbed what appeared to be the first random object within reach.

"Here! You can have this." Sage was presented with a brass-wire birdcage, the pretty type that usually hung from a stand and housed a canary. "It's not big enough for my birds and I don't have a use for it. Will you take it in exchange for the mirrors?"

"Sure, that seems fair." Sage smiled agreeably as he passed over the broken lantern for the old-fashioned birdcage. "Thank you. I look forward to seeing you around the fort."

"Likewise, likewise!" The postmaster was already puttering away, examining the lantern as if determining the best way to take it apart. Sage turned away, but before he could grasp the door handle to the bell tower, Aldis set a hand on his shoulder to stop him. Nothing was worth going back through that disgusting room and down all those stairs. Instead, Aldis teleported them both to the ground just outside the command center.

"If I'd known we were going to the roof, I could have taken us there in the first place," Aldis griped, searching his pockets for a sweet-smelling sachet. He dabbed it against his neck, then held it under his nose. "How did you know to go to the post office?"

"There was a bird on the lantern right as we passed through the gateway," Sage explained, scraping his boots on the packed earth. "Even after it flew away, another one landed in the same spot later. It was half a guess, but I'm glad it panned out."

"Let's hope the next part of this sequence is somewhere cleaner. Like a dungeon." Aldis pressed the sachet between his hands for a burst of perfumed air, then tucked it away. "I meant to ask earlier, but how does all of this lead to a key or a treasure? Because it looks like you just traded one piece of garbage for another piece of garbage."

Sage actually laughed at that. "Yeah, a lot of trades start off that way. Maybe that's why a lot of groups skip this part of scenarios. Here, let's bring this into the light and take a better look at it."

The towering fortress walls kept about a third of the fort in shadow at any given time of the day, and Aldis and Sage happened to be standing in the thick of it. A short walk took them back to the central courtyard, where Nieve was attempting to run the army's troops through a series of basic drills, but even Aldis could see that it wasn't going well. Soldiers kept running into one another or turning the wrong way when throwing a practice punch and hitting the person next to them. It made him skeptical that this fort was even meant to survive the oncoming attack.

In the light of the open courtyard, Sage held up the brass-wire birdcage, turning it this way and that as he muttered softly to himself. As interested as Aldis was in seeing the trading sequence through, something else caught and hooked his attention.

"It's a little broken, but the metal is good," Sage murmured, tapping the brass bars. "Missing the cage door, so not for a pet. The smith? No, it has to be good for more than scrap metal . . ."

"Sage?" Aldis clasped his shoulder and pointed. "What is your Cloudcaller doing?"

"Emi? Oh." Sage looked up, squinting through his glasses. The girl with the twin hair buns was floating close to the wall on her little vapor-cloud. That wasn't all that strange: Aldis could cast a levitation spell, too. What was strange was that she appeared to be moving her arms like a conductor, singing a cheerful little tune as shaped stone blocks dragged themselves out of a jumbled pile and drifted up to her, as if buoyed by some invisible force. She'd tap the stone and send it off toward the wall, where it would fit itself tightly against the other stones in neat, orderly rows. As they watched, she fiddled with something on her belt without ever missing a note of her song. "She's reinforcing the wall, like she said she would."

"Yes, but how?" Aldis asked, unable to stop staring at the strange orchestra. He couldn't quite make out Emiko's words over the distance, just the singsong quality of her spell-chant. "Is that a stone-calling spell? Cloudcallers don't have access to stone mana. Wind magic, then? But she'd have to be a high Emerald for that level of precision. Does she have a second attunement, or a crystal mark or something like that?"

"No, no, that's all her mana diffuser." Sage's explanation wasn't an explanation at all, and Aldis let him know it with a deadpan stare. "The enchanted device on her belt? You must have seen it. It draws mana out of crystals, and Emi channels that mana into her spells. We collected a lot of transference mana crystals on our last climb and Emi didn't use them all up." He made a derisive noise in the back of his throat as he resumed studying the birdcage. "Stupid Nieve, wanting to wake up *all* the mechanical golems."

"Wait, wait, I still don't understand." Aldis pointed to Emiko. "You're saying that there's an enchanted device that lets anyone just use any type of mana in any sort of spell? How have I not heard of this? My family used to ship enchanted items to Dalenos all the time!"

"It's a prototype," Sage replied. "You'll have to ask Emi about it if you want to know more, but it's not widely available yet. I think it only works with lung marks, or something like that. She only got it because the Enchanter was asking her family for an investment so they could keep making improvements to it."

"Ah." That made more sense than it didn't. Aldis had known many inventive Enchanters in Valia, all trying to create the next "essential" in climbing gear, but supplies were expensive and the enchanting process could take years. "So she comes from a rich family, then?"

Sage snorted. "You could say that. She's a Ryotsu."

Aldis spun around from watching Emiko so quickly he staggered before catching his balance. "Ryotsu? As in *Archduke Ryotsu*? You mean, that little girl is royalty?"

"She's short, but she's twenty-two." Sage frowned. "I hardly think it's fair to call her—"

"Yes, sorry, of course." Aldis waved off the objection. "But you're telling me that she's a *princess*?"

"No!" Sage laughed again. "She's not in the direct line of inheritance, otherwise I don't think she'd be allowed to climb with a team like ours. She's from a branch family, she's just the only climber with the right type of attunement to use the mana diffuser. Look, don't treat her any different just because I told you. She hates it when people get all formal around her."

"Yes, but . . . a Ryotsu." Aldis shook his head, turning to watch Emiko once more. How had he missed seeing that on the team roster? "What does someone like that need to climb the spires for?"

"What does anyone climb the spires for?" Sage asked with a nonchalant shrug. He touched his glasses, turning his attention to the cage again before stopping himself and looking up at Aldis again. "Unless there's something you're climbing for?"

"Ah, no." Aldis faked a grin, feeling a line of sweat run down the center of his back. "Just treasure, money, and fame: the usual."

CHAPTER 3

NIEVE

Champion (mind mark), Citrine

Nieve paced the top of the battlements over the fortress's gate, one hand resting on her sword hilt as she watched the attacking army draw closer and closer. The earlier training session had been draining and she'd released the soldiers sooner than intended; they were only making more mistakes than progress, anyway. In a few days, she could have them whipped into shape, but for now, prowling the ramparts and watching her enemy draw nearer soothed her aggravation.

A little, anyway.

She hated these scenarios with set times, knowing that even if she could eradicate the entire army in the space of an hour (unlikely, but Nieve could dream) the scenario would still last for three whole days. Not only that, but there seemed to be a spite factor in rooms where climbers accomplished their goals too quickly, so even if she could eradicate the army, they would probably find themselves under attack by a facsimile of a god beast, or something equally unfair. No, the safest thing to do was let the scenario play out little by little, no matter how irritating Nieve found that to be.

"Wearing down the stones?" Lani called as she came up the nearest set of stairs. "Don't tell Emi: she's already a little hoarse from reinforcing the walls."

"I'll make it up to her," Nieve replied, chuckling. "Whenever we get to the monster-killing portion of this climb, she can have my cut of the mana crystals."

"How generous," Lani retorted drily. "Did one of the squires come take your bags?"

"Yeah, a while ago. I didn't see where they took them, though."

"We have our own barracks. I'll show you later," Lani promised. "I was thinking standard watch rotation through the night."

"You know that's fine with me," Nieve replied, rolling her shoulders in a shrug. Normally she loved a little one-on-one time with Lani, but not when she was already frustrated over incompetence and gearing up for a fight. And it was funnier when she could annoy Sage, anyway. "Did you talk to the newbies about night watches yet?"

"Not yet." Lani made a face. "I don't know if I trust Aldis to take it seriously, and I don't even know if Hane plans on returning tonight or not."

Both turned and looked out at the hazy lake in the distance. Trees and low hills obscured the shores, but Nieve could just see a puddle of blue on the horizon.

"Should I send someone to check on them?" Lani asked, arms folded over her chest, a single finger tapping on her elbow. "Emi's resting her voice right now, there's no reason she couldn't pop through a portal and back again."

Nieve shrugged. "They seemed pretty confident. And their climber feats were pretty astounding. Hane didn't come off as arrogant to me, so I think they'd really come back and ask for help if they needed it."

"You're right. I know you're right." Lani massaged her forehead, looking tense. "I'm just nervous with new climbers on the roster. It's not even that I don't have faith in the new recruits, it's just . . . different."

"It does feel really strange without Ren and Wyle," Nieve admitted, glancing out over the valley again. "But it feels good to be back inside the spire again. I can't remember the last time we took two months off between climbs before. I was getting antsy."

"I could tell," Lani chuckled. "You were taking on so many duels and side gigs I was half afraid you were going to be the next Haven Securities goon paying me a late-night visit."

Nieve couldn't help the tiny flick of her eyes down at Lani's gloved hands. Lani's gambling habit didn't bother her—not really—but she didn't think it was something to joke about, either. "You know I'd never do that to you."

"I know, Nieve. I know." Lani's sigh was belied by the hard set of her mouth: a thin line beneath her eyes that seemed to stare straight through the distant horizon.

"You know I'd help you if you asked, right?" Nieve asked, as gently as she could. Even with her friends, Lani could get snappish. To lighten any unintended sting, she added: "It doesn't have to be a loan; I could just take care of those Haven goons for you."

Nieve cracked her knuckles suggestively, hoping to win a smile from the taciturn gambler, but Lani didn't offer even the slightest hint of amusement. She remained implacably focused as she studied the terrain and the approaching army below.

"I'll have Sage do a final check right before the battle," Lani said, as if she hadn't heard Nieve's offer. "I've changed a few of the officer positions here, but platoon management will be up to you for now. You've been granted the title of field captain, so everyone going out onto the battlefield should listen to you. I'll probably have Emi and Aldis sit back on defense, but Sage and I will be out there with you."

"You can hang back on defense, too, you know," Nieve pointed out, though she knew this time would be no different than any other time she suggested their healer take a supporting role. "With a Wayfarer, there's no reason why you need to be on the battlefield yourself."

"I'll get rusty if I stay out of the fight." Lani set her hand over the hilt of her cutlass, a lack of humor in her grin. "And I like being close enough to heal whoever I can. I imagine we get some sort of bonus for keeping as many of the defending soldiers alive as possible."

"Well, there is that," Nieve allowed. She clicked her tongue and set her foot against the wall. "Is there any way to speed this up? I'm getting bored of waiting."

Lani inclined her head toward the stairs. "Come down and meet a few of the officers. That'll help pass the time."

"Fine," Nieve grumbled, following Lani down the stairs. She took note of the newly reinforced walls, thicker now with more layers of stone, though Emi's hasty construction had left a layer of stone dust on everything nearby. Nieve had felt the wall vibrating subtly beneath her feet as Emi modified it, but it was different seeing all those neat rows of stone fitted tightly against each other, perfectly sized against the walls. Emi really put that little mana-crystal gadget to work for herself. Nieve didn't put too much stock into enchanted items beyond the basic protective ones; she had her sword and that was all she really needed.

". . . still don't understand how someone trades a silk embroidered hand fan for a leather collar!" Aldis and Sage passed in front of them, Aldis talking animatedly while Sage smiled and waved in acknowledgment. "I haven't even seen any dogs here. Who is going to want a leather collar?"

"Don't ask questions you don't want the answers to," Sage said wisely, slowing to a stop. "Are there any updates?"

"We were coming to ask you that," Lani replied. Nieve didn't miss the slightly bitter expression on her face when she looked at Aldis. "I've made all the changes to the army that I can prior to the attack; can you peek and see if it's going to be enough?"

Sage touched the side of his glasses, eyes staring sightlessly for a moment, and then he blinked and shook his head as if to clear it. "I don't See anything worth worrying about for now. It's just a probing attack to gauge our defenses, really. All humans, only one supporting attuned officer."

Lani shot a look over at Nieve, who made a face back at her.

"You want me to go easy on them, don't you?" Nieve asked.

"It doesn't hurt," Lani replied. "You know as well as I do that challenges scale. If we come out too strong, the spire will just increase the challenge."

Nieve groaned and rolled her eyes. "I know that you're right, I just hate it. You're turning what could be a ten-minute quick fix into something long and drawn out. People make more mistakes the longer a battle goes on, you know."

"That's why we'll have Sage right there with us," Lani said, shooting him a quick smile. "Right?"

"Right." He grinned back, but Nieve caught the flare of pink in his cheeks. He always lit up whenever Lani smiled at him. Sometimes Nieve wished he'd hurry up and confess his feelings to Lani. Nieve didn't expect that Lani reciprocated such feelings; the gambler had a lone-wolf quality about her and didn't seem ready to settle down the way Ren and Wyle had. But even lone wolves had needs, didn't they? Nieve respected Sage enough to try to keep her feelings—or rather, her hands—to herself, but if he was never going to say anything to Lani, was it really so bad if she did?

I'm just irritated because I want a good fight, Nieve told herself, touching the locket hidden beneath her dueling vest. It was really too bad that she was going to have to hold back in this first fight. The most important thing was keeping her friends and teammates safe, but resh it felt good to let loose and tear through an enemy army. If climbing the spire was something she could do on her own, she wouldn't be waiting around for an assault, she'd already be leading an attack force against them.

It was probably a good thing Nieve had a team, or else she would have accidentally killed herself in a challenge a long time ago.

"It's not going to be long now," Sage commented. "Should we start mustering for the attack?"

"Might as well," Lani said with a shrug. "If Emiko isn't too drained, maybe she can do something about the unfortunate weapon situation. Wyle, can you—sorry, Aldis, can you call Emi in?"

Nieve ground her teeth together, impatient for the fight to begin and hating the fact that she couldn't see anything from down here. How close was the enemy army now? Would the single attuned officer be at the front of the charge, or would she have to go looking for them? What kind of attunement was it? Sage had said it was a supporting attunement, so maybe something like an Illusionist or a Sentinel. Either could be tricky, but nothing Nieve couldn't handle.

"Do you want a window?" Sage asked kindly.

"Yes," Nieve said, stopping in her tracks. She hadn't realized she'd started pacing. "Please."

Sage handed something over to Aldis, making the Wayfarer blink in surprise. "Take this to the chief hostler and trade it for a book in really old binding. You'll be on defense, so you have a little time."

Aldis huffed indignantly but took the small leather object. "At least this one makes sense. A hostler can use this as a leather strap for a piece of harness or something. I have no idea what the cook was using it for."

Aldis vanished abruptly, leaving the three old friends behind. Lani cocked her head to the side.

"Do you think he meant that, or was he trying to sound more innocent than he is?"

"I don't know that he's ever had a thought he didn't immediately verbalize," Sage grumbled, waving his hand in a small circle. "He's not a bad guy, just . . . chatty. Remember, Nieve, this is just a window. Don't try to punch anyone through it."

"Oh, I'm gonna punch someone," Nieve threatened teasingly. She punched Sage lightly on the shoulder. He grinned and returned the gesture.

A vision of the battlefield hovered in midair, about the size of the circle Sage had swung his hand through. It wasn't as clear as it could be, but it served well enough to abate some of Nieve's impatience. Wyle used to make viewing portals, which could be used to drop surprise attacks down on their enemies and one time—one time!—Nieve had forgotten she was looking through one of Sage's windows rather than one of Wyle's portals and tried to drop a spell through it. Her teammates never failed to remind her of that particular embarrassment.

"Their ranks are disorderly," Nieve reported after watching through the window a bit. "Armor and weapons all look like they've seen hard use. I wouldn't be surprised if this first wave is just untrained peasants and prisoners."

"That makes them an almost even match for the sorry state these troops are in," Lani muttered. "Where are Emi and—"

Aldis reappeared in their midst, holding out a thick book with crumbling binding. "Here it is. Although I can't see how anyone else has a use for a book on old-style harnesses and bridles other than the hostler who gave it to me."

Sage's ears burned pink the moment his hand touched the book. Nieve snatched it out of his hand and flipped it open to a random page. She guffawed loudly and turned the book just enough to show Lani. Lani smirked, her eyes crinkling at the corners.

"I'm sure trading it won't be a problem," Nieve said, snapping it closed before handing it back to Sage. Sage looked a little embarrassed as he tucked the book away in a satchel. Aldis just looked confused. "But maybe don't trade it right away. Might be fun to flip through on watch tonight."

"Watch?" Aldis asked, because apparently that was a more pressing issue than trading the book. "Surely we've been given rooms inside the barracks. Why would we need to set a watch?"

"Because scenarios can throw surprises at you at any time, and as long as someone is awake to warn us, we can respond to changes faster." Lani's tone was dry as she answered the question. Clearly, she wasn't yet over her awkward exchange with Aldis earlier. "Where is Emi? Did you call her when I asked?"

Aldis put his hands up defensively, but his expression was anything but. "I did call her and she's on her way. And if you questioned your last Wayfarer like this, then I'm not surprised that they quit."

"Okay." Nieve stepped in front of Lani, blocking whatever verbal or physical assault the Acolyte might have launched. "Look, there's Emi now. You know how she gets after casting for a long time. She probably went to put her head down. Have we checked in with Hane recently?"

"I contacted them right after I checked in with the Cloudcaller," Aldis replied a little sharply. "They said they are fine, they're just taking their time scouting the lake. They don't need any assistance from us at this time."

"Thank you, Aldis," Sage said in his peacekeeping voice. With a gesture to the magical window he'd created earlier, he added: "The enemy forces are marshaling. We need to get our troops squared up."

"Finally," Nieve sighed, feeling genuine relief. She cracked the knuckles on both fists, grinning madly. "It's been too long since I've been in a good fight! I'm going to enjoy this."

Lani and Sage laughed as Emi trotted up to the group. She looked a little tired but still ready for the next part of the scenario. She smiled and waved cheerily but didn't speak aloud. More than likely her voice was hoarse from all her casting earlier reinforcing the walls.

"I'll get the commander to organize two units. That should be enough, shouldn't it?" Lani peered at the magical window, trying to make a quick head count of the enemy soldiers. "I don't want to bring out too many because apparently Nieve is just going to eat this first wave alive."

Nieve cackled. "You know it."

Lani shook her head, but she was smiling. "Emi, Aldis, you're on the rampart. Call out anything strange or unexpected, but you shouldn't need to attack unless we call for it. Sage and I will be down with Nieve on the battlefield. And while you're up there—" Lani had started turning away but now turned back to face Aldis. "Make sure to keep an ear out in case we need a quick teleport back to the fort."

"You mean, do my— Oof." Aldis covered his ribs, where Sage had just elbowed him. Lani glowered darkly at the both of them before turning and striding away, lifting a hand to beckon the fort's commander.

Emi waved a hand, catching Nieve's attention. Though she probably could have said it, she used her hands to sign the words: "Do you want cover for the battlefield?"

"I hope not," Nieve said, looking through Sage's window again. "I want to see what I'm doing for my first battle in two months."

"Like you haven't been dueling in competitions for the past two months," Sage pointed out. To Aldis, he added: "I'd hold off on the backtalk for a little while. Just until you get to know the team better. Lani's just doing her job, too."

"I don't understand the point of an Acolyte being a team leader," Aldis grouched, though he kept his voice low. Lani was speaking to the fortress commander, but she wasn't that far away. "And the rest of you seem so easygoing."

"We've just known each other a real long time," Emi signed. "Don't worry, you'll get there. You're one of us now."

"I'm sorry, what was that, now?" Aldis asked, looking to Sage. "I never picked up the trick of reading signs."

"She just said we've known each other a long time and that you'll get used to it," Sage explained. He left off the second part, which Nieve silently approved of, though Emi made a face at him. Aldis was a teammate, sure, but he wasn't "one of them" just yet. Emi had always been quick to trust and fast to make friends. Nieve preferred to survive a few battles alongside someone before extending the "one of us" courtesy. That was really how you got to know a person, after all.

By Sage's carefully neutral expression, he seemed to feel the same way, though Nieve wasn't entirely certain what metric he used to test a person's mettle. Emi had always been the most accepting out of the three of them, but Nieve wondered if Sage was having the same reservations about Aldis as she was having. Melding as a team was important, and so far, Aldis didn't seem the type to meld naturally.

Come to that, neither did Hane. Who insisted on taking a solo mission to fight what was most definitely a lake monster?

Wish I'd thought of it, Nieve thought grudgingly. *I like fighting lake monsters.*

Emi gasped and pointed at Sage's window, drawing their attention to the enemy advancing toward the fortress. She took Aldis's hand and tugged while pointing up at the ramparts.

"I— What?" Aldis looked flustered. "Oh, you want me to take you—"

They vanished as Aldis was speaking; the last of Aldis's sentence finished out of earshot. Nieve looked to Sage, cocking an eyebrow.

"He's not a bad guy," Sage said without conviction. He swept his hand through his window spell, dissipating it. Most of the enemy forces had marched beyond it by now, anyway. "Shouldn't we get moving? I assume you're leading the charge."

"Of course." Nieve grinned. "Make sure you stay out of my way. Duels are nothing like war games, and I want to let loose."

"Just don't go all out on this first fight," Sage reminded her, unnecessarily. "We're here for a while and this is only the first fight in the first room."

"Yeah, yeah." Nieve rolled her eyes. She slid her sword from its sheath and leaned it back against her shoulder, watching as Lani and the fortress commander ordered the soldiers to form ranks. "I don't tell you how to See, you don't tell me how to fight. That's how this works, Sage."

"Actually, part of my job is telling you how to fight," Sage pointed out, one hand hooked around the dueling cane on his hip. "For instance, if we were going up against monsters, or an army of attuned—"

Nieve spun on her heel and looped her free arm around the back of Sage's neck, bending him low and cradling his head against her side. He struggled but couldn't free himself. "I'm sorry, what were you saying, Seer? Do I even need to point out that you didn't See that coming?"

"Real mature, Nieve!" Sage wasn't weak by any means, but Nieve had the leverage to keep him pinned in the headlock, no matter how he tried to pull free. "You know I wasn't looking. C'mon, let go! Or else I'll tell Aldis you're up for a good, long religious discussion through the first and second watches tonight."

"You wouldn't."

"I can already See it happening," Sage declared. "Him mocking you for thinking the top of the spire is a literal rather than figurative destination, and how acceptance of shortcomings is itself a feat of—"

Sage made a noise like "hrk" as Nieve released him, bumping him forward with her hip to make him stumble. "You are the absolute worst, you know that?"

"Better that than a brute," Sage retorted, though the tone was still playful. Nieve *was* a bit of a brute; she didn't consider that a flaw. Just as she didn't consider Sage being a know-it-all as a flaw. It took all sorts to make it this high inside a spire, especially at their current ranks as freshly minted Citrines.

"Why do you two always start acting like children right before a fight?" Lani asked, striding up to them. "We're about to open the gates. Are you both ready?"

"Yes, Lani," they intoned together to the tune of "Yes, Mom." Nieve flipped her grip on her hilt, tightened the knot of her headband, then strode toward the head of the army, where the commander waited to give the signal to open the gates.

"We have two platoons marching out to follow your orders with two more on standby," the commander informed her crisply. "Ready to go on your mark."

"Good." Nieve cut a look over at Sage. His gaze went distant before he nodded at her. All good to head out, then. "Have the soldiers follow me out, but hold ranks until my man gives the signal to attack." She pointed to Sage, who raised a hand, acknowledging the troops. They'd done this more than enough times to know each other's strategies without discussing them, but if Nieve was being honest, she missed Ren charging into battle alongside her. Hane was meant to fill that role, but they were off fighting a lake monster (which Nieve was *not* jealous of). It wasn't that Nieve couldn't fight on her own, or that Sage and Lani weren't enough, but . . . it felt a little bit like she was leaving her back open without someone who could keep up with her on the battlefield. Not that she could say she'd feel better with an unknown element like Hane at her back, but it would have been a good trial run. Maybe she should have insisted harder that Hane stick around, at least until they pushed through to the core of the scenario.

Too late for that now, Nieve told herself, squaring her shoulders as the gates creaked open. *Maybe I'll have time between fights to go out to the lake, help them kill a monster or two, then bring them back to finish up this siege.*

That sounded like a plan.

Nieve began striding forward before the gates were fully open, advancing on the "army" ahead of her. The soldiers looked just as motley in person as they had seemed through Sage's window earlier. Nieve would have felt badly about what was about to happen if they weren't all simulacra, or summoned creatures, or illusions, or whatever they were. She'd long since stopped questioning how the spire did what it did; all she needed to do was win.

Hold back, hold back, hold back. Nieve repeated the refrain over and over so she wouldn't forget once the battle began. *Gotta make it good, but not too good. Don't want to summon a god beast by being too awesome.*

Before receiving her attunement, Nieve had prayed for something that lent itself well to combat. She had always been a talented fighter, like her parents and her grandmother, and while she would have accepted whichever attunement the goddess felt fit to bless her with, she'd longed for something powerful, something she could use to bolster her strength. And she'd gotten it—only not in the way she'd expected. While thrilled to receive a Champion attunement, initially she'd been disappointed at the placement of her attunement. Hand and heart marks were easier for casting spells over a distance, and leg marks worked best at close range and weapon enhancement. The best thing about having a mind mark was the ability to silently reinforce her body, making it stronger, faster, more resistant to physical and mental attacks. But learning how to project ice spells outside her body as other Champions did had taken a frustrating amount of practice. It came naturally to her now, though she still lacked refinement when casting spells. She wasn't resourceful like Emi or precise like Lani. But overall, she couldn't complain about her Champion attunement's location, even if it did mean having a mark like a tattoo in the middle of her forehead. At least she didn't have to bare her chest every time she was required to show her attunement mark.

I guess using Frost Form would be overkill, Nieve considered, though she felt a little naked entering a fight without it. Frost Form made her skin as hard to cut as solid ice, while also protecting her mind from mental attacks. It probably wasn't necessary for this fight, especially as her shroud would protect her from any physical attacks by the enemy soldiers. She could reevaluate her strategy when she found the attuned officer within the army.

Rather than cast Frost Form, her go-to battle spell, Nieve cast Enhance Strength instead, more for intimidation than anything else. The feeling of enhancement mana doubling the strength of her muscles felt like drawing her first full breath after being submerged under water. Goddess, but it had been too long since her last real fight. Holding back was going to be a struggle.

Hopefully the attuned officer would put up a good fight.

She knew she was grinning as she strode forward all on her own, the sword held out at her side as familiar as her own arm. She was eager, but she didn't rush, as if knowing the fight was imminent calmed her. She didn't look back, trusting that Sage and Lani would know when to give the signal for the defending army to charge. Besides, looking back exposed her back to the enemy, and she didn't want to risk that, no matter how weak these guys looked. She hadn't climbed this high just to start taking poor risks now. She looked for the attuned officer that Sage had mentioned but didn't see anyone who stood out to her among the front ranks of the weary and poorly attired enemy soldiers. Hopefully they would make themselves known after Nieve cut down enough of their soldiers.

As soon as Nieve could make out the eyes of her enemies, she leaned into the wind and raced forward, her enhancement-strengthened legs carrying her fast enough to appear as a blur to anyone without perception mana. She blew right past the first rank, the second rank, the third. Startled cries sounded all around her, with more people scrambling away from than toward her. When she judged herself to have reached just about the center of their ranks, she skidded to a stop and raised her sword above her head.

"Surrender?" She made sure to shout it as a question rather than her own declaration. It had been Sage's idea to offer the option of surrender in these scenarios, and though Nieve hated to solve anything without resorting to violence, both Emiko and Lani had agreed and Nieve acquiesced to the group majority. Thankfully, no one had ever taken her up on her quite generous offer.

And today seemed to be no different.

"Never!" a soldier shouted, rallying their nearby comrades and shaking a spear at Nieve. She grinned as they squared their shoulders and leveled their weapons.

"Don't forget that I offered." Nieve took a deep breath, clasping the elongated hilt of her sword in both hands and lowering the tip until it just touched the ground. She visualized the spell in her mind first, then felt it shift within her, moving to the center of her chest, then out through her arms. Her breath misted the air as she commanded: "Freeze."

Ice grew along the blade of her katana, frosting it at first, then thickening, spreading, until the slim metal blade was entirely encased in a new shape: longer than Nieve was tall with a wide, double-edged blade in the style of a zanbatou. The ice made it a good deal heavier, but with the enhancement mana running through her body, it was no trouble at all to handle. Nieve grinned as she leaned the ice blade back on her shoulder, looking around at the reactions of the nearby enemy soldiers.

Because the sword wasn't the only thing she'd frozen.

In a radius of about fifty feet spreading outward from where she stood, ice covered the battlefield, encasing the ankles of enemy soldiers, bringing them to a stumbling or sliding stop. There were shouts of surprise and cries of pain as many fell, while others attempted to chip away at the ice with their weapons or struggled and stamped at the imprisoning ice. Nieve took advantage of the chaos to glance back at her teammates, ensuring that no one had gotten past her to them.

Sage was just drawing his dueling cane, shouting something she couldn't hear, but the two platoons of defending soldiers surged forward, racing for the entrapped army, weapons drawn. She couldn't see Lani, but then Lani usually hung back, prioritizing care for the injured over fighting. Raising her gaze, Nieve could see Aldis and Emi watching from the ramparts. She saluted them once with her sword, then swept it down in a wide arc.

Satisfied that everyone was safe—or as safe as anyone ever was inside a spire—Nieve centered herself in a prepared stance, sweeping her blade low and angled. She grinned as the first enemy soldier freed himself from the ice and charged toward her, screaming as he brought his sword down in a slash. Nieve met his charge with her braced ice zanbatou, turning it aside easily, then reversing her stroke as if her sword weighed no more than a feather. The blade was no less sharp for the ice that encased it, severing the soldier's arm and head from his body. As blood bounced on the ice, Nieve looked up grinning, seeing the expressions of her opponents change from rage to fear to dread.

Finally! Time to get started.

LANI

Acolyte (hand mark), Citrine

Nieve looks like a monster when she gets going, Lani thought idly, picking her way over the trampled earth between the gate and the clashing armies. Not that her maniacal energy didn't serve a good purpose: the defending army at the fortress was no well-trained military unit. Lani's impression was that these were poor commoners or farmers starved off their lands, lured by the promise of pay, food, and a roof over their heads. Maybe they'd been taught how to hold a sword or a spear, but they were by no means soldiers.

Which raised the question: what battle was this scenario based on? These mine-filled hills could be anywhere near the Vanreach mountains, and the uniforms looked like something out of a history tome, so it certainly wasn't something in recent history. She hadn't heard a name she'd recognized, neither person nor city, making her wonder if this was an entirely fictional scenario, or maybe just one of the lesser-known skirmishes in an unimportant country backwater. Sage might know if she asked him. He was far from bookish, but he had a good memory for things Lani forgot about as soon as she completed her attunement classes. Besides, knowing the exact place and time was secondary to finessing the scenario and getting all the little details just right, which was what Lani actually excelled at, anyway.

Nieve's war cry rose over the tumult of the battlefield, making Lani look up in time to see a vibrant arc of blood soar above the battlefield before splashing to the icy ground.

Well, we all have different approaches to problem solving, Lani thought, with half a smile on her face.

A fallen soldier sat at the edge of Nieve's ice field clutching his ankle and moaning. Lani pointed and sent a regeneration spell his way as she passed. Anyone following in Nieve's wake risked a slip-and-fall injury thanks to the sheet of ice she had laid down to trap her opponents' feet, so Lani took the time to move slowly and carefully, cleaning up the mess Nieve had created. Not that she was at all resentful; they all had their specialties.

Speaking of which: Lani had just crouched to heal someone injured by an actual weapon when a blast of mana blew past her shoulder, knocking aside an enemy soldier who had apparently been pretending to be dead. Lani didn't even look up from her healing spell.

"I could have handled that," she said, loud enough to be heard without looking away from her patient.

"I know, I Saw," Sage called back. "Just trying to be efficient, that's all."

Lani huffed a laugh and brushed her hands off on her leggings as she stood up. "All right, soldier, up and at 'em, just watch your step on the ice."

"Even though I'm injured?" the soldier asked piteously. At Lani's glare, he started to rise, then stopped, moaning piteously. "My arm! It's broken!"

"What?" Lani scoffed. "Your arm is not broken, I just healed you."

"It is! Look!" The soldier pointed frantically. "That's bone! Bone sticking out of my arm!"

There was something on the soldier's sleeve, but it couldn't possibly be bone: Lani's diagnostic spell would have told her of any broken bones. She caught at the thin shard of . . . whatever that was, and tugged. The shard came away neatly, having been stuck to the soldier's uniform by frozen blood. The soldier looked sheepish as Lani held it up in front of him.

"You're fine," she informed him, in no uncertain terms. "Get back out there."

"Yes, Captain." The soldier trudged back onto the battlefield, halfheartedly drawing his sword.

"Wyle would give him terrible odds on surviving the fight," Sage commented darkly.

"Hm?" There was something strange about the supposed "bone" she'd plucked off the soldier's sleeve. She could have sworn she heard it make a sound when she touched it, something like a hum, but it was silent now. At first, she'd thought it a broken piece of metal, from either a weapon or a building material, but upon inspection, it looked more like glass, or crystal. The ends were needle-sharp and it measured the length of her palm to the tip of her longest finger. Light glinted off a sheared-off edge, a prismatic rainbow catching and holding her eye.

"Lani?" Sage nudged her in the side with his elbow. "Er, that soldier just took a pretty bad cut. I think she might need a healer."

"Which one?" Distracted by the injury, Lani tucked the mysterious shard away in a belt purse. It was probably nothing, but she couldn't discount the possibility that it might be a piece of treasure. She'd study it later, when she had the time.

The soldier Sage pointed out was down on one knee with her arms wrapped around her midsection. Lani helped her stretch out flat, then set to healing her with Sage standing sentinel over both of them. The soldier would survive, but once she was healed enough to stand, Lani sent her back to the fort to recover from blood loss. It was no good sending a dizzy soldier back to the front lines.

Lani tamped the blood off her gloves, then accepted a hand up from Sage. Ice crackled under their feet as they looked out toward where the fighting was hardest. "Did you want to go help Nieve?"

Sage didn't answer right away. Instead, he lifted his dueling cane, took careful aim at nothing Lani could see, then fired a burst of mana. A hurled javelin reached the apex of its arc, only to be blasted aside by Sage's shot. "I'm keeping an eye out for strays. Nieve's doing fine on her own, don't you think?"

"Probably a little too well," Lani agreed. "I'm all for a challenging scenario, but I'd like a little time to get used to our new teammates before we leap without looking."

"Nieve's just blowing off steam," Sage said with a shrug. "You know how she gets between climbs."

An animalistic war cry roared from the center of the battlefield. Lani cringed as several wet-sounding thumps hit the ice hard enough to make it shiver.

Sage flinched. "Maybe she could hold back just a little bit."

Bemused, Lani crossed her arms and sighed. "Let's try to mitigate it where we can. Does this fortress have a jail? I didn't have much of a chance to look around."

"Yes, it does, but we'll want to reinforce it before we lock anyone away down there." Sage looked thoughtful for a moment. "In fact, I think the jail guard is the next stop on my trading sequence."

"That's good. I'll ask Emi to fix up the cells before we lock up anyone. You can check to make sure it's secure when you get there." Lani hooked her hand over the hilt of her cutlass and tested the ice beneath her boots. The surface layer was melting, making it slick and dangerous. "Hold the last line of defense, will you?"

Sage lifted his dueling cane and fired another blast of mana just past her shoulder, knocking down a thrown hand axe. "Can do."

Lani smirked fondly. "Show-off."

The edges of Nieve's ice field were brittle, so at first Lani's steps broke through to the earth below, giving her reasonably solid footing. Farther in, where the ice lay thicker, she used a spell she called Sharpen Vision, a perception spell that helped her pick out the surest footing and avoid slick spots. As she passed wounded and whimpering soldiers, she held her attunement-marked hand out toward them, directing regeneration spells at the ones wearing the uniform of the fortress. She couldn't mend bone or reattach a severed limb, but a regeneration spell would fix surface injuries and soothe pulled muscles and tendons. Not everyone bothered to heal the spire's constructs since they were more like simulacra than "real" people, but it tugged at Lani's conscience to simply ignore them. If it came down to healing a simulacrum or one of her teammates, the choice was obvious, but without the burden of choice, Lani would heal everyone she feasibly could. Later on, she would probably end up healing the enemy soldiers they took captive—if Nieve left any of them alive.

Lani knew better than to get too close to Nieve as she fought with the unbridled fury of a mountain oni, but since that was where most of the injured were, she stayed right on the fringe of the fighting. Finding a gut-cut ally soldier, Lani drew her cutlass and used it as an anchor so she could kneel down without slipping at the soldier's side. She used a diagnostic spell to probe the injury before setting to work sealing up all the internal organs properly and purifying the beginnings of infection. Once, an injury like this would have taken all her concentration, but she'd done this enough times to remain alert against attack. For the moment, it seemed most of the enemy soldiers were either running away or otherwise occupied. The nearby grunts and clashes of weapons seemed to indicate that Nieve was currently engaged with a worthy opponent, or, more likely, opponents.

Just as she was finishing up her healing spell on the injured soldier, a hollow thud sounded from nearby, sending something skidding across the ice toward Lani. She stoutly refused to look at it but batted it away with her sword as she stood and drew it from the ice. The freshly healed soldier made the mistake of looking at whatever it was and promptly threw up. Lani fixed Nieve with a dark glare.

"What?" Nieve shouted, whirling her ice zanbatou before leaning it back against her shoulder. Her face was streaked with blood, but it looked more like splash-back rather than an injury. "That one actually had an attunement. A foreign one, I think. What's that one that makes shrouds harder to cut through?"

"Ask Sage," Lani called back, helping the sick-looking soldier to their feet before sending them back to the fort with a point. "I distinctly recall asking that you keep your severed body parts to yourself."

"Hey, you're the one who came all the way out here," Nieve replied with a shrug. "It's not my fault you're in the splash zone."

Lani faked a gag. Scenes like this were nothing new, but they weren't her favorite thing, either. "Did you even think of trying to take that officer alive? We could have questioned them."

"That shroud thing was causing a lot of trouble," Nieve insisted. "I mean, I was fine, but our soldiers were getting kinda demoralized. I made the call."

Lani sighed; it was probably the right call under the circumstances, but it made her miss Ren's level head even more. "Does any of that blood belong to you?"

"Blood?" Nieve grabbed the tail end of her red headband and dabbed it against her face. She glanced at it before tossing it over her shoulder. "I don't see any blood."

Lani rolled her eyes. She shouldn't have bothered asking. If Nieve was hurt, she'd ask for healing. If she was still joking around, it meant she was fine.

"What happened to going easy on them?" Lani asked pointedly. "I can't imagine this"—she gestured to the circle of carnage that formed a loose ring around where Nieve stood—"could be defined as 'going easy.'"

"I'm letting them run away, aren't I?" Nieve jerked her chin, indicating the soldiers running past, most having dropped their weapons to run faster. It seemed the death of their officer had broken their morale. That, or maybe it was the pile of severed limbs at Nieve's feet. Either way, it certainly did look as if the enemy army was breaking and running. "I could have shaped the ice spell like a sickle and sent it out at shoulder height. A few broken ankles are better than decapitating half the army, right?"

"Moderately," Lani said drily. "You know I can't heal broken ankles, and we have to get all the injured back to the fort somehow."

"That's what the Wayfarer's for, isn't it?"

Lani made a face. "I don't know if he's got the stomach for . . . this."

"Eh." Nieve shrugged. "If he faints, I'll carry him." Nieve took a deep breath, giving Lani just enough warning to brace herself against the following bellow: "Form up ranks! Defend! Let anyone without a weapon surrender or run!"

The ice under Lani's feet cracked and sang with the sound of dropped steel. The few enemies still fighting cast their weapons down and ran, leaving the injured ones behind to fend for themselves. When one of the fort's soldiers fired an arrow at a retreating enemy, a wall of ice shot up from the ground, catching the arrow midflight. The archer looked stunned for a moment, then withered under Nieve's harsh glare. The archer slunk back into the defensive ranks, obviously trying to lose themselves among the other soldiers.

"There. I cleared the field for you," Nieve said, turning a grin back on Lani. "If I held back any more than that, I would have had to leave my sword back inside the fort."

"Ugh, don't do that." Lani swiped the length of her blade with a cloth, then sheathed it. "I've seen the wreckage left behind when you punch someone while wearing ice gauntlets."

Nieve threw her head back and roared a laugh. Lani turned back toward the fort and raised her hand to the sky. Aldis and Emi were little more than silhouettes against the rampart, but a moment later, she heard Aldis's mental voice inside her head.

[Did you need me to teleport you?] Aldis asked.

[No. Thanks. Could you ask Emi if she would head down to the fort's jail and reinforce the cells there? We're going to be sending prisoners there once they're healed enough to walk,] Lani requested. She waited a minute, watching the silhouettes at the top of the gate confer.

[Emiko says that's fine and wants to know if you'd like a healing rain before she goes,] Aldis returned.

[Yes, a healing rain would be very welcome right now,] Lani confirmed. It would help melt some of Nieve's ice as well as take the burden of healing off Lani just a little. As Lani knelt to help the next-closest soldier moaning in pain, clouds began to form overhead, and by the time she straightened up, a misty rain was falling.

"Is that Emi's work?" Nieve asked, pointing up at the clouds.

"Yes, she's helping out with healing." More precisely, Emi's spell was more of a regeneration rain than a healing rain, but that was longer to say, so Emi had always just called it a healing rain whenever she mixed life mana into her rain spell. "Are you sure you don't need anything healed? Any bad cuts or possible poisoning?"

"Nah. My shoulder is a little sore, but that's it." Nieve rolled her shoulder once as she sheathed her sword—now a slim, single-edged katana once again. A sheath of ice formed over her shoulder like a pauldron, perfectly fitted against her body. "Nothing a little ice won't fix."

"Everyone's a show-off," Lani muttered. "Head back and stand guard over the medic area. Make sure the enemy fighters don't cause any trouble once they're healed. The fort jail won't be ready to receive them all just yet, but I imagine no one will try to start anything with you standing around intimidatingly."

"Ha, looming! That's where I shine." Nieve's grin looked ominous against her blood-covered face. "See you when you get back."

They clasped each other's forearm firmly, a sort of informal salute, and then Nieve set her feet and glided back to the fort with ice-skating-like movements. Emi's rain had wet the ice, making normal movement difficult, so gliding was the easiest way to move. Lani, however, braced herself and slammed her heel through the ice layer, cracking the ice enough to give herself some steady footing. Once she was certain she wasn't going to slip and fall, she scanned the overcast battlefield, looking for anyone who needed more than a simple regeneration spell. Sage skated up, using his sword-length dueling cane like a pole to keep himself balanced.

"Red dot system?" he inquired.

Lani nodded. "Red dots for enemies, blue dots for teleportation. Signal Aldis to let him know the plan."

Sage nodded, then skated away. It was a system they had worked out for taking prisoners: Sage had access to light mana and could cast a small glowing orb of light over a person's head, of any color he chose. A blue light indicated someone who could not walk back to the fort themself. A red dot indicated an enemy soldier, who would receive healing and care prior to being escorted to the jail.

Lani picked her steps across the icy field carefully, stopping occasionally to heal those who needed it most, whether friend or foe. She couldn't mend severed limbs or bones, but internal injuries, infections, and poisonings were simple enough with a little effort. Luckily, it seemed that no one had been using poison-dipped weapons, or else Emi's healing rain would have done more damage than good to them. Lani could also fix concussions and other brain injuries, but as that took a little more strength than a minor healing, she saved those spells for the fort's fighters, rather than spending them on the enemy. Kindness on a battlefield only went so far.

Emi's healing rain gradually melted Nieve's field of ice, turning it all into ankle-deep mud, which, in Lani's opinion, was not much better. Still, she slogged through the mud until either everyone was limping their way toward the fort, or the ones unable to walk had been teleported inside. She thought longingly of her extra-thick socks tucked away in the satchel she'd left back at the barracks. Was there anything worse than wet socks?

"Need a hand?" Sage asked, standing at the fortress entrance. He looked a little tired, the skin around his eyes tight and pinched. He'd need to take some downtime soon, but Lani still needed him to push through a little while longer.

"No, I'm fine," Lani insisted. The ground here was dry and firm, but mud was caked on the bottoms of her boots, making every step feel rounded and uneven. She clasped Sage's shoulder for balance as she scraped the sole of each boot against the packed-earth road. "What's the count? Can we hold all the prisoners?"

"Emi hasn't come back from the jail yet, but Aldis took a look with her before he popped up here." Sage looked a little peaked, with red flags coloring his cheeks. He must have worked harder during the fight than Lani had noticed. "He said there's plenty of space, but the prison guard complained about having to feed all of them."

"We'll just let them all cool their heels in jail overnight, and then tomorrow we'll see if some of them will flip and fight for our side," Lani recommended. "They were only fodder for the other side, there's no reason they can't be fodder for us, too."

"That sounds a little harsh," Sage commented. "Maybe we can offer them other ways to help out, too, instead of just feeding them back to the army we're asking them to betray."

"Sometimes I think you're too softhearted for this," Lani said, tousling Sage's hair before passing him to walk through the fort gates. "But it's a good idea. Give me a bit to check out how we're supplied and I'll figure something out. Maybe we can work out a deal that for anyone with valuable information on our enemy, they can choose a fort task, like construction or privy duty. Can you look ahead and figure out when the next wave is coming?"

"Yeah, just a minute." Sage took a drink from his canteen, then sat down in the shade of the fort's inner wall, closing his eyes. He only Saw like that when he was tired. Lani made a note to send him to get some rest afterward.

Wish I had a moment to change my socks, she thought wistfully as the fort commander approached her.

"A bold first skirmish!" the commander said, congratulating her. "So few casualties and using only two platoons! It seems almost too good to be true. Perhaps we should march on the enemy camp now with all our forces and eliminate the threat at its source."

"That can't be a good sign," Lani grumbled, more to herself than anything. To the commander, she explained: "This was just a probing attack, meant to assess our strengths and weaknesses. We shouldn't expect every wave of soldiers to be so poorly trained. I expect the next attack will be quite different. Get those gates closed and secured, and put archers on all the walls as lookouts. I'll confer with my people and let you know how we should proceed."

"Yes, Captain!" Lani wasn't sure if a fort commander should be saluting a captain, but she went with it. Her socks and boots still squishing, she made her way over to the hastily erected infirmary tent.

One line of cots hosted the fort's injured, steadily being churned out of their places as medics decided they were "healed enough" by the regeneration spells, and the other line of cots overflowed with young people marked by

Sage's red-light spell, all hunkered away from Nieve, who strode up and down before them with one hand on her sword.

"Stop terrorizing the villagers, you oni," Lani said, poking Nieve in the side. "Isn't it enough you dismembered many of them?"

"I did offer to let them surrender," Nieve replied with a careless shrug.

Lani rolled her eyes. She turned and addressed the injured. "I want you all to know that you will not be harmed. Once you are well enough, you will be dismissed to the dungeon." The jail was probably nothing like a dungeon, but the imagery was the important thing. "Tomorrow, you will be given a choice. I pray to the goddess that you make the right one."

Most of the enemy combatants ducked their heads and looked away, scared as bunnies. Maybe Sage's idea to let them work for the fort was better than giving them weapons and shoving them right back onto the battle-field. She shook her head ruefully. Thinking so piteously was likely to get her killed here. This was still a floor-nineteen challenge: she couldn't let her guard down.

Lani requested that Aldis create a portal from the infirmary to the jail after confirming with Emi that the cells had been reinforced. She looked longingly toward the barracks where her personal effects had been stored, wondering if she had time to change her socks and let her boots dry out, but Sage was just picking his head up from his hands and blinking the light out of his eyes. Lani didn't like the look on his face: in all likelihood, the next chal-lenge of this scenario wasn't going to be an easy one.

"What is it?" Lani asked, offering a hand down to Sage.

He frowned as he let her pull him to his feet. "Full team meeting."

Lani grimaced. "That bad? Is it Hane?"

Sage shook his head and adjusted his glasses. "I was focusing on the fort. I didn't See Hane at all."

"I'll have to ask Aldis if he's heard anything," Lani reminded herself. She ran a hand back over her head, checking to make sure her hair was still twisted in its bun: long habit from Wyle's old bets. She let a breath out, look-ing around for their teammates. "Wait here, I'll ask Aldis to call everyone in."

Emi popped through Aldis's portal returning from the jail, and Nieve left two officers in charge of watching over the injured enemies, shuffling them through the portal to the jail once they were healed enough. Sage was rub-bing his temple with a pained expression as Lani assembled the team around him.

"I'm going to have to lie down for a little while after this," Sage explained. "And what I have isn't all that clear, but we need to start developing a strategy now."

"All right," Lani agreed. "And you're sure we shouldn't call Hane in from the lake?"

"Everything seemed quiet when I checked in earlier," Aldis reported. "They didn't seem terribly busy; probably wouldn't be the worst thing to call them in."

"No, I didn't see them helping us and I worry that bringing them in now will change what I Saw," Sage said. "It's going to be a proper siege this time: keep the gates closed, no troops on the ground, though we'll want troops ready to go in case the gates are breached."

Lani tensed at that. Was there a real possibility of the gates breaking? This early in the scenario?

"We'll want archers and guards on the walls, mostly clustered near the front, but best to be prepared on all sides in case they go around."

"They?" Nieve asked. "Does the enemy have enough forces to surround the fort? In that case, why not just go around?"

"No, they don't have that many troops. Yet." Lani didn't like the sound of that. "There's going to be a battering ram and a fully armed and armored ground force that we need to keep out at all costs. Nieve can reinforce the gates with an ice wall and Emi can finish shoring up the walls before they get here. What we really have to worry about are the . . ." Sage hesitated, grimacing. "The flying pigs."

"The . . ." Lani blinked. "Excuse me, the what?"

"I know, I know, it's not clear." Sage rubbed his forehead. "That's the best I have for you. Something is going to be flying, smaller than a horse, bigger than a dog, and in my vision, they look like pigs. Arrows won't work and we do not want these things falling inside the fort."

Lani exchanged a look with Nieve. Sage was always on point with his visions, but sometimes they didn't make complete sense until the challenge actually started.

"Fine. We'll prepare for—I can't believe I'm saying this—flying pigs." Lani resisted the urge to shake her head. "How long do we have before this attack begins?"

"One hour after nightfall," Sage reported with a weak smile.

"Of course." Lani pinched the bridge of her nose. "Okay, Sage, go take a nap, we'll need you rested and—"

"Wait, sorry, I forgot that part." Sage squeezed his eyes closed and rubbed the back of his neck. "I'm not participating in the wall defense later. I'll be doing something else."

Lani waited for more, but it seemed that was all Sage was planning on saying. "Is that something you'll tell us about later?"

"Yes," Sage agreed. "I will tell you all later."

Another code, meaning Sage was afraid to say it out loud for fear of changing a future outcome. Lani hated an unknown variable, but she trusted Sage.

"All right." Lani clapped her palms together. "No Hane and no Sage. Emi, how will you be doing after you finish all the walls?"

"I can push through." Emi used her hands to sign the words. "If wind magic is all I need to blow away the, um, flying pigs, then I'll be fine." She looked like she was barely withholding laughter. Not that Lani could blame her.

"Why don't you go get started on the walls now?" Lani suggested. "The sooner you get finished, the sooner you can rest."

"I can start, but my belt is running low on transference crystals," Emi signed.

"I'll grab the reserve crystals from the supplies." Nieve lifted a hand, sounding disappointed as she volunteered. "I doubt I'll be of much use if the assault is mostly aerial, anyway."

"Wash up, too," Lani ordered. "You are absolutely terrifying with all the dried blood on your face."

"Yes, Lani," Nieve said with a vicious eye roll.

"Aldis, you must have some wind spells, right?" Lani asked, ignoring Nieve's sass.

"Er, yes, I do." Aldis looked nervous. "I can also open portals to send the, ah, flying pigs back the way they came from. Or elsewhere, if that's preferable."

"Either way works." Lani shifted, flinching at the wet squelch in her boots. "Rest up if you can. Everyone but Sage, reconvene here at nightfall. I'll alert the commander and have ground troops on standby. Sage, make sure to call out if anything changes. And everyone, stay alert. Remember, we've been surprised before."

The group broke apart after utterances of general agreement. Nieve slung an arm over Emi's shoulders, only to get shoved away with a squealed protest of "Gross!" Aldis looked nervous for a second, as if afraid to separate from the group, then started to follow Sage, who stopped him by thrusting the book of "bridles and harnesses" into his hands, telling him who to trade it with and what for. Aldis vanished in a blink. Lani stared longingly off toward the barracks, then shook her head and went in search of the fort commander.

Strategy was more important than fresh socks right now.

CHAPTER 5

HANE

Wavewalker (leg mark), Citrine

The lake was so peacefully serene that Hane took care not to leave ripples as they walked along its surface. They were keeping close to the shore, certain that the blue-black center of the lake was where the monster—along with the treasure—lay hidden. The lake itself wasn't all that big—not when compared to Lake Selden in Dalenos. It didn't hide nearly as much as Lake Selden did, either, though it did have a few secrets that Sage hadn't predicted. Perhaps they had been hidden from his Sight, or maybe he simply hadn't been looking for them. Few could "see" as clearly beneath watery depths as Wavewalkers could.

A loud chatter from the shoreline made Hane cock their head and listen. A bird having an argument with a squirrel. Such an odd thing for a spire scenario to include. Who came up with such illusions? Why bother including it? Hane guessed that few people bothered coming out of their way to visit the lake in this scenario, as it took time and resources away from the main objective, which was defending the fortress. It made sense to include a hidden treasure, guarded by a monster of some sort, because climbers certainly thrived on such challenges. But why the added dressings of birds and squirrels and fish and sunning lizards on the shore? Who was that for?

Maybe one day I'll ask the goddess directly, Hane thought with no real conviction. Hane doubted any climber had ever come face to face with the goddess Selys, and even if they did, there were far more important questions to ask.

A disturbance in the surface tension of the lake. Hane crouched on the balls of their feet, laying a hand so gently atop the water that it didn't disturb the surface. They had already determined that the monster was a lake serpent, a bit smaller and less powerful than a typical water serpent. It slept curled around a small hoard of treasure, the lateral lines of its body on alert for any water disturbance that indicated anything large enough to eat. If Hane sensed a disturbance in the lake's surface, it wouldn't be long before the serpent did, too. The serpent might not sense Hane's movement, but if it peeked its head up for a snack, it would most certainly see them. Depending on what the disturbance was, Hane could use it as a diversion and strike at the serpent while it was intent on its meal. It would be easy enough to do, but only if the disturbance was something the serpent could eat. If, say, a tree had fallen into the lake, the serpent wouldn't be distracted, only angry. And that was a poor combination, in Hane's experience. Better to identify the source of the disturbance quickly, before the serpent woke up.

It was most likely a monster splashing around in the shallows that had disturbed the lake: there were plenty of them moving around just beyond the treeline, but by dropping onto the lake itself, Hane had avoided meeting any of them. Most likely, something had come to the water's edge to drink, or to wash. Hane didn't mind letting the serpent snap up something small, like a wild boar, or something dangerous, like a troll. But sacrificing anything with humanlike intelligence, like ogres or goblins, gave Hane conflicted feelings. They were spire constructs, and thus not "real," but Hane had spent enough time in the Tortoise Spire to know that these beings had enough sentience to consider themselves real. Which made their goals and motivations every bit as intentional and "real" as Hane's. Who were they to judge a being's sense of self? It wasn't as if Hane had much of an existence, anyway.

As Hane attempted to discern whether the disturbance to the lake was worth checking out, they sensed an uncoiling deep within the lake's depths. The serpent. It was waking up.

The serpent would know the difference between a fallen tree and a potential meal, wouldn't it? Hane wondered, straightening from their crouch. They lifted a hand to shade their eyes, seeking the origin of the disturbance. The serpent was moving sluggishly for now, the surface of the lake seemingly motionless, belying the hidden danger. Hane had to decide quickly: hide, and wait for an opportunity to attack, or determine what, exactly, had disturbed the lake in the first place.

If experience had taught Hane anything, it was that the spires seemed to have a sick sense of humor: if they didn't check the source of the disturbance, they would likely end up regretting it.

Hane cushioned the portion of their shroud beneath their feet with a layer of water mana, then propelled themself forward over the water in a long, smooth glide using a controlled burst of transference mana. The most straightforward mana type for creating motion or aiding movement was transference mana, which Hane used in most of their spells to one extent or another. While some combat-attuned used enhancement mana to protect themselves against heavy blows and attacks, Hane used transference mana to avoid attacks entirely by dodging, darting, leaping, or running. And transference mana had other uses, besides.

With a leg mark, Hane's spells always worked best through direct contact, so as they slid along the surface of the lake, they kept at least part of their attention on their Sense Water spell. It was like "seeing" beneath the surface and more like sensing displacement or voids within deeps, then interpreting those blank spaces into a more meaningful context. Rough, jagged objects were often rocks. Anything of a rectangular shape was often a treasure chest. Long, sinewy, and wound tight around itself? That was a serpent. It was easy with objects that were stationary. Less so with things that moved, like whatever was disturbing the lake's surface and disturbing the serpent's rest. Hane could determine the direction of the disturbance but not the source.

Hane's spell kept "watch" over the serpent as they scanned the shore for the cause of the disturbance. The size of the serpent wasn't all that troubling; lake serpents weren't as dangerous as their cousin-species: sea serpents and water serpents. Judging by the size of this serpent, Hane didn't think they'd have much trouble dealing with it alone. In fact, more people around would likely just bring more monsters crashing in on them, making this a bigger mess than it had to be.

Speaking of which . . .

Hane sighed internally, finally catching sight of the source of the water disturbance.

A humanoid child.

Of course it was a humanoid child. No challenge this high up in a spire could ever be that straightforward, could it?

Can I just leave them there? Hane wondered. *If I divert the serpent's attention, will it still try to attack the child?*

Hane sensed a "rumbling" coming from the depths of the lake. If they had to guess, they'd say the serpent was stretching. It hadn't set off in any particular direction yet, still hovering over the hoard in the center of the lake.

I could use the diversion, Hane thought. *I could warn the child to run and let the serpent chase them, then get the serpent from behind while it's distracted.*

But even as they considered it, they knew it was too great a risk. Even if the child managed to avoid the serpent—however unlikely that was—they risked running directly into another monster hidden within the forest. No, the only thing to do was remove the child from danger and hope the lake serpent never saw either of them. Once the child was safe, Hane could come back for the serpent.

"Better make it count," Hane whispered, reaching back to remove a single tonfa from the harness on their back. Like most spire gear, Hane's tonfa were both enchanted to function similar to dueling canes, allowing them to blast either transference or water mana from the distal end. For close combat, they were constructed to be sturdy enough to deliver skull-crushing blows at need, or defend against blades or bludgeoning weapons, making the tonfa fairly versatile. Hane left the tonfa's pair holstered, keeping their other arm free.

Pointing the end of the tonfa out behind them, Hane charged their shroud with a thin layer of water mana once more, then fired a blast of transference mana out behind them. The blast sent them shooting forward along the surface of the water, directly at the child splashing playfully in the shallows. The child froze at the sight of Hane's approach, looking puzzled but not frightened. Hane felt the rapid displacement of the water beneath the surface just as they got an arm around the child's waist and heaved them up onto a shoulder. Hane sent a surge of transference mana through their legs and feet to push off the water's surface, leaping away just as the serpent's head burst through the surface of the lake, spraying water outward from the center of the lake like an explosion.

Hane landed lightly in the crux of a tree, cupping one hand over the child's mouth as the child had begun to shriek at some point—either when Hane scooped them up or when the serpent reared its head; Hane wasn't sure exactly why the child was shrieking, but they definitely needed to stop. Thin branches and leaves whipped back in Hane's face, displaced by the serpent's violent hiss, giving Hane only the barest of glimpses of the monster. The scales were an opalescent white, with a blue-green fin along its spine like webbed ridging, cresting the highest at the top of the serpent's head. It was immense, but Hane had already known its size based on the water it displaced within the lake, so that wasn't much of a surprise, except maybe to the child who had suddenly gone wide-eyed and silent. It was clearly a lake serpent, which meant it wasn't about to start flying—or at least Hane hoped it wasn't. And while most monsters of the serpent class had excellent senses of smell, lake serpents were more given to sensing water and air displacement, sacrificing smell almost entirely. So if they held very, very still, there was a chance the serpent wouldn't find them.

Just in case, Hane cast a dispersal spell through their shroud, combining transference and water mana to spread out the water droplets on both themself and the child evenly, giving them a sort of camouflage against the serpent's sight.

The waves rolling out of the center of the lake gradually stilled, though the serpent still turned its head this way and that, clearly searching for whatever had disturbed its waters. Hane held perfectly still, one hand still pressed tight to the child's mouth. For their part, the child seemed to have fallen still, grasping the base context of the situation. After what seemed like long, breathless minutes, the serpent hissed again, then plunged back into the depths of the lake, long sinewy body looping on itself until finally ending with a splash of a fan tail.

Hane exhaled slowly, waiting an extra beat before stepping out of the tree they'd landed in. They set the child down gently and crouched down to eye level. From a distance, the child had appeared human, but now that Hane took the time to really look the child over, they noted the slit pupils in amber-colored eyes and a fluffy red tail curled partially between their legs.

"Kitsune?" Hane asked, voice low in case there were monsters nearby.

The child nodded once, gazing up at Hane with something like hope mixed with distrust. Though they fell into the broad category of "monster," kitsune were generally more reasonable than most, though they could be tricksters at times. This one seemed fairly young, having only one visible tail.

"You got a place to go?" Hane asked the young kitsune.

The child nodded, sniffling softly, eyes darting away.

"You know how to get there?"

Another sullen nod.

"Can you get there on your own?"

A sharply inhaled breath and shaking of the head.

Hane covered their face with their palm. "Great. An escort quest. Just what I needed."

The child reached out and took Hane's hand, looking up with big watery eyes.

"Yeah, I know the drill." Hane sighed, rising from their crouch to look around. "Point me in the direction and stay as quiet as possible. I'll get you out of here."

Into the monster-infested woods, exactly where Hane didn't want to be. If they stepped lightly, they might be able to avoid the worst of all the possible encounters. And on the bright side, there was probably a reward waiting for the child's safe return. At the very least, Hane didn't expect a family of kitsune to be hostile toward them after escorting their child home.

But then it would be another long trek back to the lake again to fight a serpent who was now angry for having missed a meal and possibly alerted to an adventurer in the area.

Hane sighed heavily.

Next time, Hane thought, *I'll ask the Seer to look specifically for escort quests.*

CHAPTER 6

ℰMIKO

Cloudcaller (lung mark), Sunstone

miko yawned and leaned heavily against Nieve's side. Nieve wrapped an arm around her and patted her shoulder. It would have been nice to catch a break after using so much magic already in this scenario, but there wasn't time. It had taken the rest of the evening to reinforce the walls, and after a single rushed meal, Lani had called the team together to talk through their plan.

"Everyone here?" Lani asked. "Emi, Nieve, Aldis? Have we checked in with Hane recently?"

"They were busy," Aldis said, yawning widely. "Didn't seem like they needed anything."

"Were they in combat with the lake monster?" Lani pressed.

"It didn't seem like it, but they didn't want to talk." Emiko had to squint to see Aldis shrug: Lani had ordered that all the torches and lights remain unlit, so the enemy would be surprised by their counterattack. "They had all their survival supplies with them, so I imagine they're fine for tonight. Probably doing better than we are, come to that."

"If they're bored, you can always port them back here, can't you?" Lani asked.

"Yes, but that's not the impression they gave me." A brief, intense staring contest between Aldis and Lani made Emiko shuffle anxiously. "I'll ask if they want a portal back the next time I talk to them."

"Fine." Lani let out a breath. "Okay, Emi, I'm sorry to have to ask so much of you today, but you're our primary defense on this one. I need a fog layer on the ground to slow down the enemy troops, a light spell above the fort to aid the archers, and then wind spells to push back the, uh . . ." She grimaced. "Flying pigs. Or whatever they actually are."

"I can do it," Emiko confirmed, speaking aloud because it was hard to read hand signs in the dark. "But I'll have to rest my voice tomorrow."

"Hopefully we can all catch a little rest tomorrow," Lani said, her hand cupped over the rounded swell of her coin purse. "Aldis, you're on the wall with wind and teleport spells; Nieve, you're on the ground, in case we need to send you out to hack apart a battering ram."

"Why can't I just pop outside the walls after Emi's laid down the fog?" Nieve asked. "A Sense Water spell should help me see through the fog and take out the battering ram carriers before they get anywhere near the gate."

"Nieve, you're the reason the challenge escalated so quickly," Lani replied almost wearily. "If you had taken it easy earlier, we might have had a chance to rest between assault waves. As it is, you can spend your downtime training with the reserve troops. The sooner we give them the means to fight back on their own, the quicker we can leave the fighting to them and give ourselves some much-needed breaks."

"I have a question." Aldis's tone made Emiko brace herself for another argument like the one just outside the gateway. "Was this outpost originally outfitted with any attuned? If so, then where are said attuned?"

"The commander says the only attuned here are healers, and not very well-trained ones at that. Consider it part of the challenge."

Aldis huffed in irritation but didn't say anything out loud. Emiko understood the sentiment: fellow attuned in the fort would have taken some of the burden of victory off them, but supposedly for this scenario, their climbing team had been called in as a team of specialists to aid in the defense of the fortress, meaning they were the only attuned available to help. It wasn't all that strange as a scenario, but it was inconvenient. Too bad that didn't mean they wouldn't be up against any attuned in the attacking army.

"All right, Emi, fog first if you don't mind," Lani said, giving her a nod. "I'll have Aldis contact you when we're ready for the light."

"Gotcha!" Emiko said, clasping her hands in front of her chest. She drew a deep breath, filling her lungs with air as well as mana. On the exhale, she breathed out power. "Make me light as air/Lift me up to soar above/Goddess, grant me wings."

Her riding cloud formed around and beneath her, gently taking her up above her friends' heads, then just high enough to see over the wall surrounding the fortress. It was too dark to see the enemy forces moving, but here and there she caught flickers of shielded torchlight. For now, the enemy was still approaching the main gate of the fortress, but soon they would encircle the entire fort, so her spell had to be ring-shaped. She held a picture of the fort within her mind as she closed her eyes and began to chant.

"Mist rise and fog grow/Blot out ground and walls and sky/Hide us from our foes."

Emiko opened her eyes slowly, still holding the image of the fort surrounded by dense fog in her mind's eye. The imagery was even more important than the words when shaping a spell, but Emiko's background in poetry helped her put just the right amount of mana into her spells. It wasn't just the words, but the breath, the force, and the delivery that gave life to what she envisioned through the lung-marked attunement. Her most-used spells, like levitation and rain, were standards that she had memorized long before beginning her career as a climber, but she also had a knack for creating spells on the spot, which came in handy when using different mana types through her mana diffuser.

Thick, gray fog seemed to bloom straight out of the walls of the fort, billowing outward in silent menace. Just as she had willed it, it stayed relatively low, perhaps only ten feet off the ground. It looked as uniform as a blanket at first, but slowly swirls and dips appeared, giving proof to the movement below.

[Emiko.] Aldis's telepathic voice was different from Wyle's. Where hers had been a clarion call, Aldis's began with something like the sound of a teacup being set upon a saucer, then a soft voice as if he were speaking right beside her. She would grow used to it, but for now the connection felt weaker than Wyle's, like she had to strain to hear it. [The archers on the walls have all been warned. We're ready for your light spell.]

[Just a moment,] Emiko sent back. She never had any trouble using spells meant for a Cloudcaller. She could shape air and water all day long without breaking a sweat. But the ability to create clouds and rain wasn't all that helpful for a climber team, not in most challenges, anyway. Emiko's mana diffuser allowed her to use any base mana type and weave it into her spells so long as she had the correct mana crystal to power it. But doing so left a burn in her throat, like the feeling after drinking far too much citrus. If she pushed further than that, she could lose her voice, making her all but useless to her teammates. After this, she really needed a day to rest her voice. Sleep and a big meal or two wouldn't go amiss, either.

Emiko ran her hand along her bandolier, holstered with mana crystals of all types. While most teams sold the mana crystals recovered on climbs, Team Guiding Star Legacy collected them as a valued resource—the Class Three mana crystals, anyway, as that was the only size the diffuser could effectively utilize. The diffuser couldn't use compound mana crystals, like lightning or poison crystals, but those were harder to find and sold at better rates anyway. Her bandolier carried the types of mana crystals she used most, such as life crystals for healing spells, fire crystals to create lightning, and umbral mana to fuse into her fog spells for darkness. It took her a moment to find a crystal of light mana along her belt—she didn't normally stock too many of them, since Sage had access to light mana—and formed the words to a spell in her mind before speaking them aloud.

"First light, pure and strong/Gold and bright, rise up the dawn/Hark! Here comes the sun."

A Cloudcaller's natural spell affinity was for rain, which made it easiest for her to weave mana like light or life through a cloud-based spell. With the light mana crystal inserted into the diffuser, Emiko envisioned clouds filled with the sun's first light of the day, rich and golden and brilliant enough to give light to the fortress without blinding anyone on the ramparts. The golden cloud bloomed like a flower, hovering directly above the center of the fort, unmoved by wind. Emiko smiled as she massaged her throat. She wasn't done yet, but the rest of her spells should be much smaller by comparison: targeted air spells were easy compared to infusing clouds with external mana.

Emiko exhaled, using her breath to lower her cloud to just over the ramparts, where Lani stood looking out over the sea of fog.

"Nice work, Emi." Lani grinned up at her for the space of a moment: high praise from the Acolyte. "Are you still good to work a few wind spells?"

Emiko beamed and nodded, conserving her voice for the next spell.

"Good." Lani gazed down at the swirling fog, fingers drumming against her belt purse. "I guess we'll find out soon if any of our enemies are attuned if they try to blow the fog away. You should probably position yourself on the east wall, as Aldis is on the . . ."

Lani trailed off, frowning down at the mist. Emiko followed her gaze, leaning over the side of her little cloud to peer down the length of the wall. Parts of the fog were glowing, flickering in mysterious constellations far below the fortress walls. It made sense that the enemy would uncover their torches and lanterns now that they were close, but these lights were brighter than that, and stranger still: they weren't moving.

"What are they doing?" Lani murmured. "Fire magic? No, it looks too steady for that. Light magic, maybe? But why cast light spells when they could just blow the fog away? Unless the light is a weapon somehow?"

Emiko gasped and pointed as an odd shape rose through the mist, breaking through slowly enough that the mist seemed to swell and burst around it. It looked like a very small hot-air balloon carrying a . . . pickle barrel? A sideways pickle barrel, with small clockwork wings attached to the wooden staves? The tiny wings weren't quite flapping in unison, yet they were still managing to propel the barrel forward toward the fortress in little fits and starts. It was such an odd-looking thing that for a moment, it seemed Emiko, Lani, and even all the archers along the wall were transfixed by the sight of it.

"Oh, oh!" Emiko forgot about saving her voice as she realized what she was looking at. "There's a tied bag inside the barrel! The tied end looks a little like a snout! These are—"

"Sage's flying pigs!" Lani realized. "Archers, take care not to—"

Emiko heard the twang of a bow before Lani finished speaking. She drew a deep breath, but she knew it was going to be too late to finish the chant in time. The arrow struck the straining bag inside the barrel and popped it. A noxious purple cloud burst out, leaving streaks like inky tendrils against Emi's golden light.

"Wind who bows to none/I call upon our contract/Heed my every whim!" Emiko shouted the words rapidly, putting as much force behind the spell as she could. She thrust her hand out, pointing at the purple cloud. "Away!"

Wind roared past her, following her point and blowing the purple cloud away from the fort, but by then more poison-gas barrels were already breaking through the layer of fog.

"Don't shoot the barrels!" Lani shouted. "Aldis, spread the word!"

Even with the order echoing inside her head, as it likely did in every mind within the fort, a few arrows still took flight, bursting the gas balloons cradled within the pickle barrels.

"Away! Away! Away!" Emi shouted, pointing at each one in turn. Her spell gave her control of the winds for a limited amount of time, usually based on the amount of power she put behind the spell. Winds whipped past her, shooting toward the streaks of purple gas, tearing them apart into nothing before they could reach the fort.

"Do we know what the gas is?" a nearby archer on the wall asked.

"No," Lani replied grimly. "And I'd rather not find out. It's probably safe to assume it's some sort of poison. Try to blow the balloons away whole, without bursting them."

Pushing the balloons away was easy, but despite their best efforts, sometimes the sack holding the gas still exploded. Perhaps the wooden planks that made up the barrels were lined with nails or wooden splinters, just to guarantee the air sack would burst. Emiko shouted harder, faster winds at the plumes of erupted gas but more targeted, gentle winds at the barrels floating lazily along. At first, the pickle-barrel balloons only came at them from the gate side of the fortress, but gradually they were spreading out along the wall, growing more diffuse but coming from a wider radius.

They're spreading out beneath the fog, Emiko realized, watching the pattern of balloons erupting through the fog. *If they encircle the fort, Aldis and I might miss a few of these ugly pig balloons.*

Worse still was the sudden crack of wood on wood that sent shivers running up from the gate to the ramparts. Lani clutched the wall, rocked off her feet by the sudden impact. She snarled a curse, then turned and shouted down to the inside of the fort. "Shield the gate!"

After sending two balloons crashing into each other, then blowing away the purple gas, Emiko spared a glance down. She could just barely make out Nieve's figure by the tails of her red headband whipping out behind her. Stationed inside the fort near the gate, Nieve had been running night drills on rotating platoons, having the soldiers gather weapons and torches, then form up ranks all without running into each other in the near-dark. Now, Nieve cut off her current drill to spin around and face the massive fortress gateway. Emiko couldn't make out a clear shout or gesture, but suddenly twin ice walls burst upward from the ground, shielding the fort's gate from within and without. The second impact of a battering ram sounded like a crackle of lightning, but it didn't shake the wall near so much as the first time.

That'll hold them, Emiko thought, turning back to her work. She leaned to the side, urging her cloud to carry her to the eastern side of the fort, where more and more "flying pigs" were floating up. Her own fog layer was working against them by hiding the spots where these balloons might launch from, making the archers all but useless, especially as the balloons bumped their way up along the walls directly. Emiko really didn't want to find out what that noxious purple gas might do if anyone breathed it in.

One balloon was just cresting the wall in front of two scared-looking archers when Emiko blew it straight back down toward the ground. It erupted along the way, but she blasted it hard enough to break the gas apart before it could seep through the walls—if it could, in fact, seep into the fort. Maybe it could, or maybe Emiko's reinforced walls would stop it; she just didn't want to take the chance that the gas might permeate the walls, so she kept blowing it down, down until her winds actually pierced the fog layer, puffing the mist outward for the briefest of moments before it began to knit itself together again. But not before Emiko caught sight of a small group of enemy soldiers preparing to let another balloon-barrel fly. Two of them held torches as three others worked on securing an empty balloon to the sideways barrel. One of them made a gesture almost like cupping fire off the closest torch and waving it at the balloon before the balloon inflated, straining to lift free. One person held the barrel steady as two others worked clockwork gear-shafts to wind up the wings on either side of the barrel, but that was all she saw before the fog closed over them. She waited until the balloon rose up through the fog before directing her wind spell at it, punching it right back down on the group that had sent it off. She was too far away to hear any coughing or cries of pain, but gradually the torchlight beneath the fog winked out.

The torches! Emiko realized with a gasp. *They're using attuned to pull hot air off the torches into the balloons so they float! That means wherever the torches are, there's a whole group of fighters sending up the flying pigs!*

Emiko looked around frantically for Lani; she hadn't realized she'd flown so far past the ramparts in order to shoot down the poison-gas balloons. She wheeled her cloud back around, shooting for the rampart above the gate. Lani looked mildly alarmed as Emiko halted in front of her, signing frantically.

The trouble with shaping her wind spell to "heed her every whim" was that it turned certain words into commands, which meant if she didn't speak carefully, she might accidentally give a command she didn't mean to give. Canceling the command spell would mean having to cast it all over again, which would slow her response in case of an emergency, so rather than speak aloud, Emiko used hand signs to explain what she observed.

"The torches are where they launch the flying pigs from!" Emiko signed rapidly. "Have the archers shoot the glowing fog!"

"That's brilliant, Emi!" Lani peered over the edge of the rampart, looking down. "How did I not see that pattern?"

"Torches keep moving," Emiko signed. "And the little wings move the balloons before they break the fog layer. Not your fault."

"Of course." Lani shook her head. She twisted around, looking for Aldis, but he'd moved farther away along the wall, moving with the current wave of flying pigs. "I'll go tell Aldis to spread the word. Keep it up just a little longer, Emi!"

"Away!" Emiko cried, pointing at a nearby barrel. Air mana swept past her in a pointed attack, sending the balloon reeling away from the rampart. She gave Lani a quick nod, then shot forward on her cloud, shooting down more barrels with blasts of wind. Wind spells rarely taxed her, but her throat was raw already from using all that transference mana to build up the walls. A coughing fit nearly made her miss a balloon just cresting the ramparts. She managed to blow it back, but not before scared archers fled from in front of it.

Gradually, the archers on the wall began shooting volleys into the glowing dots within the mist. It wasn't as satisfying as Emiko had hoped it would be— no big explosions, no real indication that any arrows had landed, but far fewer balloons were rising from the fog, giving Emiko a bit of a break in calling the wind. The light spell on her dawn-cloud was waning, too, barely a soft glow compared to the golden radiance it had been when she first cast it. Hopefully this battle wouldn't last much longer, or else she'd need to refresh her light spell, which would interrupt her command of the winds. She wasn't sure how well Aldis was holding up, but she was beginning to break into coughing fits every time she directed the wind at a new target. In order to save her voice and her mana, Emiko tried blowing away multiple balloon-barrels with single commands but with limited success. Often when the balloons careened into each other, the sacks would burst, and Emiko would have to blow away the poison cloud left behind.

The fight had been going on for perhaps two hours when Emiko was forced to release her levitation spell and land on the ramparts opposite where Aldis stood. The ramparts shuddered on sporadic occasion, meaning the battering ram hadn't quite given up yet. The only other sound aside from her calls for the wind were the twang of bowstrings. A lull in the flying pigs made Emiko panic, wondering if she had somehow missed one. She spun in a circle, looking for any floating barrels, only to have her head keep spinning after her feet had stopped moving. She could hear the roar of her heartbeat in her ears and tasted blood on the back of her tongue. She could push through—she had to, because she couldn't be useless this time—but for how much longer? Each breath felt heavy, laborious, like it would be easiest to simply stop breathing for just a little while. Maybe she'd overdone it by going right from reinforcing the walls to shooting down the poison-gas balloons. Maybe she should have asked Lani to come up with a different solution.

A shadow rose in front of her, dark against the dim glow of her dawn-cloud. Emiko gasped and pointed, but only a copper-flavored cough emerged from her gasping throat. Her knees went weak beneath her and the world spun dizzily, but before she could fall, someone had their arm around her waist and levered her arm over their shoulders, lifting her up.

"Don't worry, Emi. I've got you."

"Sage?" Emiko felt her wind spell swirl and break right before a violent coughing knocked her knees out beneath her, nearly dragging Sage down to the walkway with her. He grunted and readjusted his grip around her waist, helping her find her feet.

"It's okay, you don't need to talk," he assured her. "It's almost over, don't push yourself so much."

She took in a breath that burned, of half a mind to reply, then slowly let it go. Sage was taking slow, careful steps, but it was still hard to draw enough breath to walk. The world kept almost falling away every time she took a step, so she closed her eyes and leaned against Sage's side, letting him half carry her.

"You shouldn't push yourself this hard," Sage told her, his soft voice soothing in her ears. "You can tell us when we're asking too much of you, you know. We could have found a different strategy."

I want to help all of you, Emiko thought but didn't attempt to verbalize. She couldn't sign, either, not with one arm looped behind Sage's neck for support. *I let you all down last climb. You and Nieve, you fought with everything you had, but when Ren went down, I panicked. I couldn't chant, I couldn't help, I was worse than useless to you: I became one more person to protect. And I wasn't even hurt!*

Even after two months and Ren's total recovery, Emiko still couldn't forgive herself for her reaction to Ren's near-fatal injury that ended their last climb. And in protecting Emiko and Lani, who was focused entirely on healing Ren, Nieve had nearly died as well. And Emiko hadn't even been able to conjure a healing rain spell. She'd never felt so helpless in her life. Worst of all was learning that afterward, when they recovered, both Nieve and Sage had broken through the Sunstone wall and achieved Citrine status. If Emiko had been able to keep her head and continue her spellcasting, she probably would have reached Citrine as well. Now she felt hopelessly behind and worried that one day, her fellow teammates—the friends she had been climbing with since the beginning—might ask her to leave the group entirely. And after that disastrous last climb, she couldn't even blame them.

Truth be told, Emiko already feared that that day was coming. She had been ever since Lani had suggested that they fill Ren's and Wyle's positions with Citrine-level climbers. It had been a relief to learn that Aldis was still only Sunstone as well.

"I know Nieve and Lani keep pushing us to ascend," Sage continued, unaware of Emiko's secret fears and doubts. "But we can always just spend a little time clearing rooms and floors just to collect treasure and improve our abilities. If you need more time to grow your mana pool, we can wait for you. It's no use climbing if we don't do it together."

Emiko sniffled and tried not to cry. How did Sage always know what to say? Even before he'd earned his Seer attunement, he'd always been the one to encourage, to lift others up. Well, maybe not Nieve, but that was because Nieve tended to punch anyone who got too sentimental.

As she began to feel steadier on her feet, Emiko leaned less against Sage and instead walked alongside him, holding on to his arm so she didn't weave or sway. She wanted to ask Sage if this had been his secret mission all along—catching her before she burned herself out of mana—but before she could try to whisper the question, the looming shape of a balloon-barrel rose menacingly over the side of the rampart. She drew a breath, readying the spell in her mind, but Sage was already raising a hand toward the balloon, scarcely deigning to look at it as some unseen spell sent it spinning away.

What was that? Sage didn't have air mana, or really any attack spells at all. Had he simply wafted it away somehow? She squeezed his hand and gave him a questioning look.

"Oh, I just shaped some death mana at it to repel it," he explained, looking a little sheepish. "The gas inside uses death mana as part of the poison. I tried learning a few death spells when we were on break, but they're really hard to practice safely."

Oh, that was right: Sage's tertiary mana was death mana. It would have come in after his attunement reached Citrine, which would have happened while he was recovering from their last climb. The same thing would have happened to Nieve, too, but Emiko couldn't remember what a Champion's tertiary mana type was. Mental or perception, or something like that. She wondered if Nieve had thought to study and train during the break, too, or if she had spent all her time in duels and challenges, like normal.

A Cloudcaller's tertiary mana type was perception, but Emiko's hadn't developed yet; it wouldn't until she reached Citrine. Maybe if she had kept her wits about her when Ren went down last time . . . During the break, she'd gone to visit Ren to make sure he was recovering well. Wyle had been right by his side, cheerful as usual until she caught a minute alone with Emiko. It turned out that the two of them, Emiko and Wyle, were the only ones who hadn't reached Citrine after that last, fateful climb: unsurprising, since they had both been too shocked to continue fighting once Ren dropped. Though at least in Wyle's case, it was nearly excusable: she and Ren were lovers. Emiko had just been that scared to see one of her friends so badly injured that she wasn't certain he was going to survive.

If I can't save my friends, what's the point in climbing? Emiko wondered, putting her head down as she trudged alongside Sage. *Maybe I should have retired when Ren and Wyle did. Maybe I should have listened to my family and become a poet. I don't want to quit, but I don't want to be a burden, either.*

Dark thoughts always crowded in when Emiko felt particularly useless. Sage had told the group he wouldn't be available to help out tonight, yet here he was, carrying Emiko because she was too weak to walk. Too weak to even speak. The very definition of a burden.

"Sage, is that— Emi!" Emiko blinked dark thoughts away in time to see Lani running toward them. She dropped to her knees in front of Emiko, eyes wide with concern. "Did you overdo it again? Emi, I asked you to tell me if you needed help!"

Emiko would have shaken her head, but Lani's cool hands were pressed against the sides of her neck. Icy magic trickled through her skin, numbing her throat and soothing away the rawness like a balm. Breathing slowly became easier and the world stopped tilting around her.

"Are you okay now?" Sage asked, his arm still wrapped around her, holding her upright.

Emiko nodded, centering her weight and leaning away from Sage. He let her go but stayed ready to catch her as she wobbled. She smiled weakly, then sat down against the wall, tucking her legs in tightly beneath her.

"Did you already finish what you were working on?" Lani asked Sage as Emiko settled in against the wall.

"Yeah." Sage ran a hand back through his hair before crossing his arms. Then uncrossing them. He started to put his hands in his pockets, then stopped and hooked his thumbs through his belt instead. Emiko smiled: Sage always acted nervous whenever he spoke to Lani. It was actually kind of adorable. "We had a traitor inside the walls, that's all. I had to catch her red-handed trying to free the prisoners we took. She drugged the prison guard, so I had to stay until he woke up. She's tied up inside the commander's office now, waiting for a court-martial or something, I guess."

"Good catch," Lani said with a nod. "You could have had Nieve check it out. She's been prowling around the courtyard this whole time, waiting for something to do."

"The battering ram was a wild card." Sage shook his head. "I wanted her to be near the gate in case anything went wrong. Has it all been pretty straightforward?"

"Everything except for your flying pigs," Lani scoffed. "You couldn't have mentioned they were poisonous flying pigs?"

Sage held his hands up helplessly. "My Divination glasses can only piece together fragments of rooms and scenarios that have happened before. We're entering territory that few climbers ever reach, so they're not showing me as much as they did on the lower floors. Without them, my visions are a little hazier, but at least you had some warning, right?"

"I suppose," Lani muttered doubtfully. She leaned over the edge of the wall for a quick look down. "The fog's clearing and Emi's light spell is almost out. The archers are shooting those poison-gas balloons faster than they can get them airborne now. They've got cover over the battering ram, but they haven't put a dent in Nieve's ice wall yet. And yet, they're still not retreating." Lani tapped a hand against her belt purse, the coins inside jingling softly. "Any thoughts on how to make them break?"

"Sure," Sage said, rolling his shoulders in a shrug. "Send Nieve out to harry the ones on the battering ram. If that doesn't break them, nothing will."

Lani grinned wickedly. "Ooh, I like it." She turned away to signal to Aldis farther along the wall. Lani missed Sage's glowing smile, but Emiko didn't.

The duck of his head, the lift of his ears, the shy way he hunched his shoulders. Yeah, her old friend had it bad. Too bad her other old friend had the exact same interest in the exact same person. Intragroup romances had the most potential to ruin a climbing team—after death and dismemberment, of course—so it was something Emiko kept an eye on. Ren and Wyle had managed to pull it off, but only because they'd been meant for each other since day one. So far, Lani hadn't shown any interest in either Sage or Nieve, nor even seemed to notice their flirtations, so Emiko thought that as long as no one confessed, there wouldn't be a problem.

She didn't know how she would handle it if her group of friends split over something so small.

Lani must have gotten in contact with Aldis, who teleported Nieve outside the gate, because Emiko heard a familiar, feral battle roar echoing up the wall of ice that defended the gate. Steel rang against steel, but only briefly, heralding the beginning of the end. Lani crouched down in front of Emiko to meet her eyes.

"Are you still hurting?" Lani asked kindly. "Can I heal anything else?"

Emiko shook her head. She folded her hands together and placed them beside her head, feigning sleep for a moment.

"I'll ask Aldis to send you down to the barracks, all right?" Lani asked.

Emiko nodded.

"Sage, do you need to turn in, too?" Lani asked, straightening.

"No, I rested earlier." He shuffled nervously. "I can stay out here a little while longer."

He's hoping Lani will stay, too, Emiko thought, watching the shift of his eyes. *He's trying to be alone with her.* Fearing a confession of love, Emiko leaned forward and caught Lani's sleeve, giving her a pleading look.

Aren't you tired, too? Emiko asked with her eyes. *You've been working nonstop since we walked through the gateway. Don't you think you've earned a break?*

Lani gave her a blank look back for a moment, then blinked. Then yawned. She squeezed Emiko's hand before helping her up and pulling her flush against her side to support Emiko's weight. Emiko leaned into her heavily, intentionally letting her eyelids droop, as if she couldn't remain standing for one more minute.

"Can you See anything happening between now and the dawn?" Lani asked Sage, ever diligent.

Sage stared out over the deeply shadowed battlefield, his eyes unfocused. "No. I don't See anything until midday tomorrow."

"Good." Lani yawned. "Nieve said she had first watch tonight, but wake me up if she gets hurt out there. I'll ask Aldis to send Emi and me down to the barracks. You've got command, but you can wake me for the second watch if you need to."

"Ah . . ." Sage looked disappointed, but only for a moment. "Okay. I'll try to get Aldis to take the second shift, to let you sleep. Good night, you guys."

"Good night, Sage."

Emiko waved wearily, looping her arm around Lani's waist to hold on through Aldis's teleport. It wasn't that she didn't want her friend to be happy.

She just wanted to keep the team dynamic as it was for at least a little while longer.

CHAPTER 7

SAGE

Seer (hand mark), Citrine

Beautiful!" Aldis declared, holding a hand-carved Crowns piece up to the sun. "The detail is exquisite! You traded a dagger for this entire set? These pieces look to be hand-carved by a master!"

"A decorative dagger," Sage explained. "Silver blade, gold-wrapped hilt, glass jewel in the pommel. Not at all practical."

"Even so, this set is just gorgeous!" Aldis set the piece he'd been looking at back in its velveted slot, then drew out the next piece. "Where did you get the dagger?"

"I traded the music box for it. You remember, you got the music box from—"

"From the prison guard, yes." Aldis couldn't seem to stop himself from touching every single Crowns piece in turn. Not that Sage could blame him: the set was beautiful. Not only were the pieces hand-carved, but the box itself was stylized with carvings. Even the latch that held the box closed looked to be a custom design: something conical with a pointed tip, like a sideways silo. Sage thought that might be a clue to the next step in the trading sequence, but there was no grain storage in or near the fortress, so perhaps he was wrong on that count. Maybe it was something in the carvings on the box? He wanted to take a closer look, but Aldis seemed reluctant to let go of the set.

Sage had been working on the trading sequence for most of the morning, while Emiko and Nieve were still resting and Lani was stuck in conferences with the fort's leadership. Now that the midday attack was almost on them, Sage and Aldis were killing time atop the ramparts over the fort's gate, waiting for the others to arrive. It was more soothing to admire the Crowns set than it was to watch the approach of the hulking pitch-and-timber-constructed war machines looming ever closer to the fortress walls.

"Couldn't you just keep this as a spire treasure?" Aldis asked, admiring another piece. "What's the incentive to trade it away?"

"I've never tried keeping anything from a trading sequence," Sage replied, squinting at a carved panel along one side of the box. It looked like a sequence of practice targets, but none were pierced by arrows. "There's probably no penalty for keeping it, but I'd rather have an extra door key. A Crowns set isn't going to help us in future challenges, and this is only the first room."

"You're right, of course." Aldis sighed heavily as he closed the box, fitting the latch in place with something almost akin to reverence. "Seems a shame, though. A set like this could sell for quite a bit. Not as much as something enchanted, but it's still quite a novelty."

"Do you play Crowns?" Sage asked, examining the relief carved into the top of the box. It was a pitched battle, meant to represent the pieces locked in combat, but Sage scoured the details for a hint of where the box might need to go. Sage used to play Crowns before his Judgment, but he hadn't found anyone to play against since he'd become a Seer. It would be nice to have a partner to play against between climbs if Aldis were to become a permanent member of the team. If not, seeing him between climbs would probably be awkward.

Aldis chuckled. "Do I play? You're looking at the runner-up champion in a Valian tournament just three years back. I still say I got robbed on that final exchange. If that piece exchange had happened just one turn sooner . . . Bah." He shook his head, clearly still upset over whatever had happened.

"Why three years ago?" Sage asked. "Dalenos has tournaments, too. Have you tried entering any, or could you not afford the entry fee?"

"No, it's . . ." Aldis shifted his weight from foot to foot, eyes suspiciously averted. "Personal. What are we trading this for? Something worthy, I hope."

"I'm not sure," Sage admitted, filing away a note about Aldis's sudden reluctance to talk about something. Not that he was curious, it just seemed like a decent tactic to get him to stop talking sometimes. "When I tried using my Sight, the paths diverged. Not so much as a fork, but more like a trident. I can tell one path brings us back to the broken lantern, but the other two were too jumbled to make out."

Aldis looked disgusted. "How does a genuine work of art like this turn into that broken lantern we had at the start of all of this?"

"Technically, it would be a different broken lantern we can use to start the sequence over again, but . . ." Sage exhaled slowly, turning the box over to check the other side. There was an odd smudge over the carving of the rifleman. Sage scrubbed at it mindlessly. "I'll mull it over for a bit and if I can't figure it out by tonight, I'll use a more direct Sight spell. Usually, the path that's harder to accomplish yields the better results."

"Sage. Aldis," Lani called from the stairs, lifting a hand in greeting as they turned toward her. Nieve and Emiko were right behind her, followed by another twenty or so soldiers, whom Nieve directed to wait by the stairs while the team conferred. Lani gave Aldis a critical glare. "Would have been nice to be teleported up, but now that we're all here: Sage, can you take a peek, please?"

Sage missed Aldis's retort as he blinked and cast his Divine Future spell. Not much had changed from his earlier vision of the battle to come, but it was clearer now: he Saw himself and Nieve leading teams of soldiers through portals in order to destroy the enemy's war machines before they could begin firing on the fortress; he Saw pillars of smoke and the fiery burst of explosions. He could hear screams as well as the clash of metal, the groan of heavy wood and the slow drip-drip of something wet. He tried to envision his targets in more detail, but instead a vision of the Crowns set superseded the vision, blocking out the siege weapon in the background. Was he meant to trade it with someone on the battlefield? How would he know who? He filed that information away, resolving to take the box along with him, even though it seemed a strange thing to do. When he switched his focus over to Nieve, he only Saw her silhouette, as if a brilliant light beamed behind her. He Saw Lani, covered in grime and blood as she healed arrow-shot soldiers on the ramparts, Saw Aldis sweating as he opened portal after portal, a bloodstain coloring the shoulder of his tunic, and, hazier, he Saw Emi surrounded by fiercely whipping winds, her hands cupped together as if in prayer. And more clearly than the rest of his companions, Sage Saw Hane standing near the center of a blue-black lake, body tightly coiled as they gripped a tonfa in each hand.

Strange, Sage thought. *That must be a much closer eventuality than everyone else's.*

He let his breath out as the visions subsided, organizing the visions into useful information to share with the team.

"Nothing vastly different from my peek this morning," Sage reported. "The foot soldiers will have battering rams, siege ladders, and raiding platforms, all of which will spread out to encircle the walls. Nieve, keep an eye out for any attuned on the battlefield, I think you're meant to fight them."

"Yes!" Nieve pumped a fist in the air. "Don't tell me anything else, I want my victory to be a surprise."

Sage rolled his eyes. "Emiko, try to preserve your voice and your mana as much as possible, we'll need you for a big cast near the end."

"Can you See when I'll need to be ready?" Emiko signed, face quizzical.

Sage shook his head. "I think you'll know it when you see it. And Aldis." Sage paused to gently remove the Crowns case from Aldis's hands. "Watch out for arrows."

"Shouldn't be many who can shoot as high as the walls. Not accurately, anyway," Aldis groused, seemingly more upset by the loss of the Crowns set. "Do you really need to take that with you? Or will you settle a dispute on the battlefield by playing a game against someone?"

"I don't want to miss an opportunity to trade it," Sage replied, tucking the set safely inside his satchel. "The most challenging trade gets the best reward, and what's more challenging than trading with an enemy?"

Aldis muttered something and crossed his arms over his chest. Sage felt he understood the sentiment: the Crowns board was almost nice enough to keep, and playing a game would be a nice way to relax between battles. It just wasn't worth the end cost.

"Good. Keep us informed if you See anything else." Lani hooked her bare hands through her belt, missing fingertips in clear view. "Aldis, have you checked in with Hane today?"

"Yes, they said they were busy." Aldis still appeared to be sulking over the loss of the Crowns set.

Lani waited a beat, clearly expecting more. "Busy doing what? Were they safe? Were they injured? Were they able to sleep safely through the night?"

"As far as I know, they got better sleep than I did," Aldis grumbled. "They said something about a kitsune village. Nonhostile. They don't need any support from us. That's all I know."

"Next time, I want a better report than 'They're busy,'" Lani demanded in clipped tones. She took a breath, smoothed her expression, then addressed all of them together. "All right, so with no changes from this morning, Nieve will place an ice shield over the fort's gate at the start of battle; then, Aldis, your job will be creating portals for the siege teams. Nieve, I assume that crew you brought up are the soldiers you picked to sabotage the siege weapons?"

"Yep!" Nieve grinned, hooking her hands through her sword belt. "Just some standouts from the battle yesterday. And a few irregulars."

By her grin, Sage had an idea of what to expect: specialists in demolition and, more than likely, explosions. Good for bringing down siege weapons but usually tough on team support.

By Lani's uneasy expression, she understood, too. "Okay, let's get them split into two teams so you and Sage can brief them on what to expect. Sage—" Lani hedged, looking uncertain. "This would normally be Ren's job. Are you sure you're meant to lead one of the strike teams?"

"I'm certain, Lani," Sage confirmed, checking the gear on his belt. His hand brushed the pouch near the back of his belt, reminding him that he still had the enchanted object he meant to give to Lani, but the timing never seemed right. He skipped over the pouch, making sure his satchel was secured behind him and wouldn't impede his ability to fight. "I worked with Nieve on my combat skills over the break, and I know I'm no Ren, but this is a guerrilla team, not the vanguard. Trust me, I'll be fine."

Truth to tell, Sage had hoped to earn a combat attunement during his Judgment all those years ago. He'd worked alongside Nieve in training his body to be ready for one: sparring, running, lifting weights, all of that. Even then, he'd acknowledged that Nieve was better than he was—she just had a talent for force and violence that Sage flinched from. It wasn't that his Seer attunement was a poor fit for his abilities, it just wasn't something that easily translated into a physical combat role, so he'd adjusted his training accordingly. He'd kept up most of the physical training, though. No one survived a spire without being able to defend oneself.

Lani's mouth twisted to the side before she shot a look over at Nieve. Though Lani had been on Sage's team almost since the beginning, Nieve had known him since childhood and had the best grasp of his combat abilities. So even though he felt a twinge resentful over being questioned, Sage understood that Lani's concern came from a place of caring.

Nieve shrugged lazily. "He's not bad, when he's not inside his head. If he says he can do it, let him do it."

"It's not as strange as putting an Acolyte on the front lines," Aldis muttered. When everyone turned to glare at him, he shrugged defensively. "What? That's not just my opinion. If your healer's not safe, no one's safe."

"You forgot the part about not irritating the healer," Lani informed him sharply. "Or more to the point: don't."

Aldis rolled his eyes. "At this point, I'm convinced that you find everything irritating. Look, I'll be connected to everyone anyway, what with all the portals back and forth. If Sage calls out a warning, I can transmit it right away."

"I guess that will have to do." Lani still looked uncertain. "Are you sure, Sage? We have options; you don't need to force yourself into this."

That was actually mildly insulting, but Sage couldn't really blame her. After all, he'd rarely stepped up into the forefront of a fight before, preferring to provide cover from behind. "It's fine, Lani. I'm not even all that nervous. I can actually beat Nieve in a duel one out of three times."

"Yeah, because you cheat," Nieve growled. "Stupid Sight. I'd destroy you in a fair fight."

"What's a fair fight?" Sage challenged. "Care to place a wager on who destroys the most siege weapons?"

"Yea— Wait." Nieve's expression went from elated to wary within the space of a blink. "Do you already know who wins? Because it's cheating if you already know."

Sage shrugged in a way that he hoped looked mysterious and superior. He didn't actually know the outcome of the wager—or if there would even be a wager; he just liked ruffling Nieve's feathers.

"Fine!" Nieve spat. "I don't care what you Saw, I'm still going to beat you!"

"That's the spirit." Lani rolled her eyes. "Okay, so Aldis is running communication and portals; Nieve and Sage are taking the demolition teams behind enemy lines to destroy the siege weapons; Emi, you're in reserve until the endgame; and I'll stay back to heal or call out changes to the plan. Everyone got that?"

"Yes!" Sage chorused his affirmative along with everyone else's, using a smile to cover his nerves. He set his hand over his dueling cane, trying not to fidget. He'd been in battle before—it was unavoidable, really, when climbing the Tortoise Spire. But he'd never volunteered to lead before: it had always been Nieve the Champion and Ren the Soulblade charging headfirst into battle, while the others hung back and picked off strays. Being the tip of the spear for once felt . . . odd.

"C'mon, let me introduce you to your team," Nieve called, waving Sage over. "They should at least know your face before you take them into the dragon's throat."

Nieve's chosen soldiers all had the same wild, battle-crazed look in their eyes that Sage was used to seeing on Nieve. She separated the group into two teams, running through brief introductions before sending Sage and his crew to the left of the gate while she held a conference with hers to the right. Likely, she was telling them about her wager of destroying more siege weapons than Sage's crew. Although, since they hadn't really bet anything, Sage wasn't sure how that would be at all motivating for the soldiers.

Most of his crew were seasoned veterans with wild-eyed excitement for combat, but there was also a mechanical engineer as well as a demolitions expert. Sage hammered out a brief plan, giving both of the technical experts time to dismantle the siege weapons while the others held off the enemy. The plan was to have Aldis drop them in via portal just behind the siege weapon and bank on the enemy facing toward the fort. The trick would be in keeping the soldiers close enough to guard the trebuchet or catapult without giving chase into the ranks upon ranks of soldiers who were even now besieging the fort.

"Sage!" Lani hollered. "Get ready! Nieve's team is dropping in!"

Sage spun, standing up a little too eagerly as he looked out toward the siege weapons. He hadn't even noticed them creeping close enough to hit the walls. A flash of light and magic to the right of the gate was Aldis opening a portal. With a mighty roar, Nieve charged through the portal, her team shouting and surging through behind her. What criteria had she used to pick which war machine she was attacking? Or was she letting Aldis choose her targets for her?

Sage closed his eyes and drew a deep breath. This was exactly what Nieve meant about him getting inside his own head. Just because Nieve was attacking at random didn't mean he had to do the same. Silently, he tapped the side of his glasses, imbuing the left lens with a passive spell he called Foresight. It would show him what was about to happen a few seconds before it happened, allowing him to react accordingly. To pick his first target, he used Divine Future, focusing on a trebuchet straight out from the gate of the fortress. The portal opened to the rear of the war machine, disgorging Sage and his team, but something must have been wrong with the trebuchet, because the technicians were all clustered around behind it, shouting at each other over the ratchet and clank of tools. Someone looked up and shouted, pointing at Sage's advancing team. Sage turned his focus to a different war machine, searching for a softer target. The next one he picked happened to have an extra-vigilant guard keeping watch right where the portal would open, so he skipped that one as well. The third pitch-and-timber construction he selected with his Sight showed the guards and technicians facing the fortress, completely unaware of the portal opening up behind them. It seemed as good a place as any to begin, so Sage marked it as his first target.

"Gather up!" Sage called, his voice weaker than he meant for it to be. He cleared his throat as his crew of ten gathered around. To Aldis, he shouted: "The trebuchet three ticks to the east! There!"

Aldis followed his point, squinting over the distance. He nodded once and a portal opened in front of Sage, like a doorway splitting reality. Behind him lay the rest of the wall, but before him were the fresh-cut logs making up a trebuchet. Just as he'd Seen, the majority of enemy soldiers were facing away from them as Sage waved his crew through the portal. That didn't last long as one of his team planted their greatsword through the chest of one of the trebuchet's technicians.

Sage burst through the portal just as the other technicians and guards surrounding the trebuchet turned to face them, the portal winking shut the second their last crew member was through. Sage felt a thread of connection in the back of his mind linking him to Aldis. He could request a portal back at any moment, or, at a note of true panic and peril, the Wayfarer should be able to teleport him back alone if faster transport was necessary. Or at least, that was how it worked with Wyle. Sage found himself wishing they'd discussed this part of the plan a little more.

But it was too late now: Sage was deep behind enemy lines, with only ten soldiers under his command and no way out until he asked for it.

Might as well get the job done.

Sage's two technicians were already working on tearing the trebuchet apart, with the mechanical engineer dismantling the axle from beneath and the demolitions expert scaling the sides up to the pivot. Luck was on their side so far, as it seemed there weren't any archers nearby, but one daring soldier decided to throw his sword at the demolitions expert. It wouldn't have killed her, but Sage caught the flash of an image from his Foresight spell—of the hilt of the thrown sword hitting the demolitions expert hard enough to knock her off the wooden beams—so he shot a blast of gray mana at the sword, knocking it away from her. He blasted the weaponless soldier next, just in case he had any more inventive ideas.

Sage spun around, looking for someone else to fight, but it seemed the element of surprise had worked almost a little too well: the guards and technicians either were already down or they had run away. Of course, running away could only lead to reinforcements heading their way soon, so Sage stayed wary.

"Stick close to the target, don't get lured off!" Sage shouted when one of the warriors in the point position looked like they might run off in search of a fight. "The second this thing falls is the moment we port back to—"

A shiver ran up through the wooden frame of the trebuchet, one wheel popping off the end of an axle as it tilted to the side. Sage's panic split down the middle as the demo expert nearly fell off the pivot point and he lost sight of the engineer beneath the hulking construction.

"A little warning next time!" the demolition expert shouted down, regaining her balance. "You almost blew out my candle!"

"Yeah, I'll remember that the next time I almost get crushed!" the engineer shouted, crawling out from beneath the tilted axle. Sage offered a hand down to him, helping him up. "The axle already had an internal crack running through it. I didn't expect it to split so easily."

"I'm glad you weren't hurt," Sage told the simulacra, or magical construct, or whatever the engineer actually was. "Is that enough to keep them from using it, or—"

A ringing thud cut him off as the young woman swung down from the arm, landing on the tilted base.

"I've got a slow fuse on the rotation joint," she said, pointing above her head. "That's gonna blow out in about seventeen seconds."

"Isn't that—" Sage cut himself off. Of course it was dangerous, all of this was dangerous. He cleared away the thought with a shake of his head. "All right, form a perimeter to defend, but not too close! Don't get caught in the—"

Demolitions leapt off the base, slamming into Sage's chest and knocking him flat. It didn't hurt too much, his Foresight giving him just enough warning to turn and catch her as she dove. A second later he understood what had happened: a small explosion triggered on the pivot, sending the arm crashing down. The demo soldier had knocked him clear out of the way.

Would have been nicer if she'd just told him to move, but hey. At least everyone was safe.

"Aldis," Sage wheezed, pushing himself up to sitting. "Portal. Now."

Two of his soldiers seized Sage's arms and pulled him to his feet just as a doorway-sized portal opened in front of him. Sage staggered through with his crew, one hand over his chest at the point of impact where the demo expert had hit him. She was still grinning like mad as she hopped unhurriedly through the portal. It narrowed and shut behind her, leaving the wreckage of the trebuchet behind them.

"Are you okay?" Lani rushed toward him, working her hand under his. "Did you get—" She blew out a frustrated breath as she backed away and crossed her arms. "You're not even bruised. Don't act like the walking wounded when you're not even injured, Sage, you had me worried!"

"Just winded," Sage admitted, wincing as he straightened up. "I'm fine. Give me a moment to catch my breath."

"Nieve and her crew are already on their second," Lani advised, looking out toward wherever Aldis had sent them. She shifted her gaze back, lifted an elegant eyebrow. "You should try and catch up."

Sage felt his heart pound at the realization that no one else from their team stood close enough to overhear them: for the first instant since beginning this climb, he was alone with Lani! His hand itched to reach inside the small belt purse hanging at his right hip, but he shook his head to clear it. This was most certainly *not* the time for that.

"Let's go, Captain!" The demolitions girl slapped Sage's shoulder. "I've got a whole bag of tricks I haven't tried yet!"

"Yeah, I bet," Sage replied, more than a little nervous. He gave Lani one more smile before scanning the battlefield for his next target. Lifting his voice, he called: "All right, Aldis, take us to . . ." A touch of Divine Future to look ahead. "That one."

"Got you." The portal opened and Sage's crew dove through.

Unlike the last trebuchet, this one already had the arm pinned down and the payload loaded in the slingshot. Sage blasted the mound of boulders in the sling with gray mana, scattering them outward. A technician leapt away from the pile and lunged at him, wielding something that looked like a pry bar. It wasn't nearly as heavy as Nieve's sword could become, though, so Sage parried it and tripped the technician by hooking her ankle. He placed the end of his dueling cane against the back of the technician's neck, not too hard, but enough to be a threat.

"Surrender or run," Sage offered, hoping she'd take the deal.

Instead, she hissed a curse and tried to fling a handful of dirt up at him.

Sage gritted his teeth and channeled his death mana through the dueling cane. His death spells were still weak—too weak to be used over any sort of distance—but with his cane pressed directly against her spine, the contact was enough to cause just enough damage to render her helpless. Mottled gray skin grew out from the tip of the cane, spreading like a bruise. The nerves there would be temporarily paralyzed, leaving her gasping and twitching. She'd probably recover: Sage's death magic was still new and fairly weak, but she wouldn't enjoy the next half hour or so.

"I did offer to let you run," Sage said weakly, feeling his gut churn sickly. He tried telling himself that this was better than Nieve dismembering people, but it still affected him more than he'd thought it would.

While Sage mulled over his crisis of conscience, his glasses flared red with a splash of blood. No, wait—that was just his Foresight spell activating on his left lens. Sage got his dueling cane up in time to fire a blast of gray mana at one of his teammates, barely getting them out of the way of a swing from a double-bladed axe. A brutish warrior taller than Nieve and twice as thick swung the axe up easily, letting the haft fall back against his shoulder as he fixed his gaze on Sage. Sage waved his teammates back as the large warrior advanced on him. He tried keeping one eye on the future while keeping the other in his present as he lined up a shot with his cane—just enough to knock the warrior back—but his hand trembled, his doubt betraying him. He had Aldis's name half formed in his mind when—

Crunch!

The counterweight for the slingshot landed in the center of the trebuchet's frame, making it seem as if the warrior vanished. As the wooden beams creaked and fell apart, it became grossly apparent that the warrior had not, in fact, managed to pull a disappearing act.

The demo expert slid down the arm of the trebuchet, smirking. "You're welcome."

"Tha—" Foresight moved him before he was conscious of doing anything, but right before a bullet took the demo expert through the chest, Sage swung his cane around, catching her across the middle and toppling her over backward off the beam. The boom of the bullet muffled the sound of her rough landing, but at least she could recover from a fall. Sage completed his spin, dueling cane dropping low to point at a technician on their knees, hands shaking as they fumbled drawing the hammer on their gun.

Light! Sage tapped the rune that allowed him to channel light mana through his dueling cane, blinding the technician so that they cried out and covered their eyes with their free arm, but the hand holding the gun was still trembling and outstretched.

Don't see too many guns in scenarios, the rational side of Sage's brain told him coldly. The rest of him felt frozen with panic. His Divine Future spell hadn't warned him of a gun on the battlefield, and he didn't have the right types of mana to defend himself or his teammates against bullets. Panic tasted like bile on the back of his tongue, and then inspiration struck, as divine as it seemed unlikely. Trembling slightly, Sage waited until the gun wielder's vision cleared, then slowly and carefully set his dueling cane down on the ground.

"Hey," he called in a voice that shook.

The youth blinked at him in shock, seemingly having no context for an enemy striking up a conversation in the middle of a battlefield. At least that made two of them.

"You don't really want to be here, do you?" Sage took in the youth's skinny arms, the malnourished look on their face, the violent tremors that made the barrel of the gun shift unexpectedly from target to target. This wasn't a trained soldier, this was a youngster who had been chosen for a particular skill. Sage could only hope and pray that he was right about that as he reached back for the satchel on his belt.

"You—don't!" the technician shouted, clearly terrified, gun shaking too much to make a clean shot. But even the panicked got lucky sometimes. "K-keep your hands where I c-c-can see them!"

"You don't have to do this," Sage said with a calm he didn't feel. "You don't want to hurt us, and we don't want to hurt you, either. I have something for you, okay? It's not a weapon, it's—it's a gift. Okay?"

"What are you doing?" the scared technician demanded through chattering teeth. "D-don't move or—"

"Look." Sage tugged at his belt until the satchel sat over his hip. He flipped it open to show the youth there was nothing dangerous inside. "No tricks, just an offer so you can put that gun down. It's a chance for something different. Something better. That's what you were trying to accomplish all along, wasn't it?"

He didn't really know what he was saying, he just knew that the tone of voice was having a soothing effect on the gun-wielder, and that behind terror, he saw intrigue. The youth wanted an excuse not to kill them; they wanted a reason to run away.

Sage pulled out the Crowns board with the hand-carved pieces, holding it out the long way to extend it toward the youth. The youth rocked back on their heels, eyes darting to the set, then back up again, gun trembling in their grip.

"I never wanted this," the youth said, a near-hysterical pitch to their voice. Tears gathered at the corners of their eyes. "My mother pushed me to it! She wanted me to be a commander like she was!"

"But that's not you, is it?" Sage asked, voice still low. "You know there's another way. A way to live a life you can be proud of. So why don't you put that down so you can take this? Take this and go."

Sage could feel the incredulous stares of his comrades as he waited, holding the Crowns set out to the scared youth. Everything wavered in the balance of those lost, watery eyes and that violently shaking gun. After a long, breathless minute, the technician tossed the gun down, seized the Crowns board in both hands, then turned tail and ran.

"Don't chase!" Sage ordered. His knees gave out as relief crashed over him like a wave, but he managed to make it look like he was picking up his dueling cane. At least, he hoped he did. "Is demolitions okay?"

"Got 'er, boss!" someone shouted. "Looks dazed, but she's fine. Goethem's got a cut through his leg, though."

"Good. I mean, not about Goethem." Sage hadn't foreseen the injury, but perhaps that was because trading the Crowns box had taken priority over a nonfatal injury. He'd have to consider that another time; such a mistake would be inexcusable if it involved Lani or Emi or any of his climbing teammates. As the soldiers helped up Goethem and the demolitions expert, Sage inched toward the gun and picked it up by the butt distastefully. He didn't know much about guns—they weren't common in Dalenos—but this one had a rounded chamber that appeared to be full of bullets, so he placed it gingerly inside his satchel. The casing from the single fired shot looked distractingly familiar, the color almost a dead ringer for the latch on the Crowns set.

[Aldis. I need a port for my crew. Please let Lani know we're coming in with two injured.]

[Got it.]

This time, the portal didn't open up over the fort's gate but somewhere else along the ramparts. Sage walked through last, making sure the demo expert and the injured warrior were carried through before him. The demolition expert was still grinning, but her eyes looked a little absent. Sage cringed inwardly at that; it was possible he'd given her a concussion by knocking her off the arm of the trebuchet. Once the portal to the battlefield was safely closed, Sage helped his injured teammates sit down against the low wall and offered them each a drink of water. Demolitions refused, laughing in a dazed manner, but the swordsman gulped at the water like it was a healing potion.

Lani was crouched nearby, in the lee of the wall, as she healed a near-fatal arrow wound. Not wanting to disturb her just yet, Sage checked his demolitions expert by using a light spell focused on the tip of his finger to observe the dilation on her pupils. By her uneven blink and the jerky nod of her head, as if she were trying to fall asleep, he confirmed his diagnosis of a concussion. He wet a handkerchief from his canteen and patted her face gently to keep her awake. As he did, he couldn't help but watch Lani at work.

Her twisted bun made up of braids was slowly coming undone, a few ends hanging down like the tails of a whip. A distinct, bloody handprint marred her upper arm, like someone had grabbed hold of her there. There was a streak of soot or something smudged across her cheekbone, but nowhere near as much blood and grime as Sage had seen in his vision earlier. Which meant this battle was far from being over. He'd known it would be a long one, but after two short forays behind enemy lines, he was ready to call it quits. Maybe if they dropped Nieve into the center of the army to soften it up, then sent Emiko's tornado ripping through it, they could end it early.

But then, that only opened them up to harder challenges moving forward, and none of them wanted that.

Lani looked up, wiping her hands on a bloody cloth, looking past Sage to his injured charges. "Let me see." Lani pushed Sage's hands away from the young woman's face. She placed her index fingers lightly on the explosion expert's temples, staring at her hard. "Have you had anything to drink? You look pale."

At first, Sage thought she was talking to the demo expert, then realized the question had been addressed to him. "I'm fine. I was just worried."

"She's fine. Don't worry." Lani glanced back quickly. "Drink your water. Take some deep breaths. Need me to take over for you in the field?"

"No." Sage reached for the canteen hooked to his satchel, then snatched his hand away abruptly as he remembered the gun. "I'm just getting into the groove of it. It'll be better now that I'm not scanning for a trade anymore."

"You made a trade?" Lani frowned. "With an enemy combatant?"

"Yeah." Sage made two attempts to open his satchel, then took the whole thing off and set it down next to Lani. "Can you hold on to that? I really don't want to take it with me and risk losing it, you know?"

Lani remained still, with her hands set over the demolition expert's head for a little while longer, then sat back, stretching her neck from side to side before flipping open the satchel. Her eyes widened briefly before she folded it closed again. "That's a first, isn't it?"

"Right?" Sage chuckled nervously. "I mean, I know some climbers use them, but . . . Hey, kid, how are you feeling?"

"Good." Demolitions sat up and shook her head a little more violently than necessary. When she stopped, she was grinning. "When do I get to blow up more stuff?"

Sage chuckled as he offered her his hand, helping her to her feet. Lani shifted sideways, waving a hand over the swordsman's injured leg before casting a spell that began to knit the muscle and skin back together.

"No broken bone," she pronounced as she worked. "But he should stay back for a little bit and drink a little water. Take one of the reserve soldiers on the wall near Aldis. When he's rested, he should be good to go back out. Nieve's replaced two of her fighters already."

Resh, but Nieve worked fast! How many war machines had she destroyed while he'd been sweet-talking a trade out of an enemy? Sage sighed and silently cast a Divine Future spell, picking out the next few targets for his team while he waited for Lani to finish. He missed her reach for a hand up until she knocked the back of her hand against his. Blushing deeply, Sage helped Lani up to her feet. She groaned and dug her fists into the small of her back.

"I can't ask Aldis to teleport the injured down to the field tent while he's casting portal spells for you and Nieve," Lani explained, frowning as she brushed the tails of her braids off her neck. "It's just a lot more work for me to go running up and down the ramparts, looking for injured soldiers."

"I'm sure they all appreciate it, Lani," Sage offered, hand twitching as he considered whether now could be the right time.

"Hey, hey, what are we waiting for?" The demolitions expert had an impish grin on her face as she toyed with a specialized long-wicked candle, a flame flickering at the distal end. "Let's go blow up more things!"

Sage gave up the idea with a hard sigh; his team was waiting for him, and every minute he delayed was a minute that allowed Nieve to pull further ahead.

"Drink some water first," Lani said firmly, detaching Sage's canteen from his satchel as she scooped it up from the walkway. Sage drank obediently as she fastened the satchel onto her belt. "And then go catch up to Nieve. I think she's at her fourth war machine already."

"Damn," Sage swore lightly, hooking his canteen through a belt loop. "That's okay, I've got a few good ones lined up. Just watch, I'll catch up."

Lani looked bemused, half a smile on her face. "Okay. Just be safe."

"Will do!" Sage lifted a hand in farewell, trotting along the wall ahead of his team. First, he needed a new soldier to replace the one that needed a rest.

Next, he needed to tell Aldis which trebuchets were his, so Nieve didn't get any further ahead. Nieve would call it cheating, but Sage called it winning.

CHAPTER 8

ALDIS

Wayfarer—Travel Specialization (hand mark), Sunstone

[Need a port back, no injured!] Nieve's mental voice felt like a shout directly inside Aldis's skull. Had it been like this with this team's last Wayfarer? How had they wrangled this mess of climbers? Were they simply more skilled, or did they rely on the same animal instincts as these hooligans?

Aldis opened a portal nearby, not so close that he would get run over by the exiting warriors, but close enough that he could count the soldiers as they leapt through, then snap the portal shut before anything else could pass. He would have preferred to teleport someone onto a battlefield location, as that eliminated the chance for an arrow or a thrown spear to skip through, but for moving groups of people safely and accurately, a portal spell was simply more practical.

"That's eight for us!" Nieve crowed, punching one of her teammates on the shoulder, who turned and punched her right back with enthusiasm. "Might pause for a minute and take a break. I'm starving!" She plopped down with her back against the rampart, drinking heartily from her canteen. After surfacing with a gasp, she asked: "How many has Sage's group got?"

Aldis hedged, keeping his eyes on the battlefield over the ramparts. The siege ladders were consistently getting torn down before the walls could be breached, but there seemed to be no end to them. "You should head down to the mess tent for some lunch. Don't want your team getting sloppy because of empty stomachs."

"Why? Is that where Sage is?" Nieve asked with a laugh. She adjusted her headband, tightening the knot at the back of her head. She smelled like sweat and steel and smoke, which made sense as most of the war machines her team destroyed went up in flames. Pillars of thick, black smoke dotted the horizon, making it seem later in the day than it actually was. Aldis wished it were later; then it would be over sooner. In theory, anyway.

"No, he and his crew are still on the field." Aldis tried distracting her attention from the original question without taking his attention off the fight. He had to keep an "ear" open to hear Sage if he called for a portal. "I know you said no injured, but perhaps you should have your people checked? I worry that some of them may have inhaled some smoke."

"Anyone need to get looked at?" Nieve asked, her shout down the line making Aldis twitch. "Anyone coughing? No? Nah, we're fine." Nieve stretched her arms over her head, groaning loudly before pulling her sword arm over her chest and holding it. Aldis could only guess that lopping off heads left and right put a great deal of strain on one's shoulder. "Did you forget the count? Sage isn't still on his third war machine, is he? If he is, maybe you should send me in to help."

Apparently, Nieve was not to be deterred. Aldis sighed and finally admitted the current count. "His team has felled eleven weapons. They're on their twelfth now."

"What?!" Nieve scrambled to her feet, throwing herself halfway over a merlon and shading her eyes to look out over the battlefield. She counted something in a low whisper, stopping at number eight. "But all those burning ones are mine! How can he be at twelve when there's nothing on fire?"

"I think he's using his Sight to pick his targets." It was a guess, but it seemed a fair one. Sage had been requesting very specific sites for portals, often jumping from one to the next without returning to the fort unless someone on his crew was injured. Nieve came back after every skirmish to report her count (as if Aldis couldn't see the burning wreckage left behind) and let Aldis choose her targets for her. It was clever on Sage's part, if that was what he was doing, though Aldis didn't quite understand why a Seer felt the need to compete with a Champion in the first place. "And they aren't burning their targets. I think they're just breaking them beyond repair."

"But burning is the best way to ensure they can't be used again!" Nieve protested. "There isn't going to be anything left but charcoal."

"Does the wood take a while to catch?" Aldis asked quizzically. It was the only logical reason Nieve and her crew took so long to down each weapon: holding defensive positions until the fire was too far along to be stopped. "That's probably how they're moving faster, then. If they're destroying the wheels or the throwing arm, it's just as ruined. The pieces can maybe be used for kindling, or maybe a new construction from scratch, but it's not as if we're going to give them the time to build entirely new siege weapons."

"That's so technical, though!" Nieve protested. "Starting a fire is faster. And guaranteed to work! How does he even know if he's breaking them beyond repair?"

"I don't know," Aldis admitted. "It could be that his Sight is helping him, but I think it's more that soldier with the dangerous-looking tool belt. If someone who looked like that actually got up one of those siege ladders, I'd teleport myself out to the lake. Whatever monster Hane's fighting over there would be better than a smirking demolitionist."

"Nothing explodes cleanly after it gets a little wet. Or cold. Or both," Nieve said carelessly. She curled her fingers over the far side of the merlon and leaned back, stretching long, like a cat. When she straightened, she sighed and tossed the long tails of her headband over her shoulder. "Up and at 'em, soldiers! We've gotta close the gap with stupid Sage and his crew. Let's go!"

The groans and protests of Nieve's people were cut off by a calm and collected voice within Aldis's head: [Aldis, can I get a port to the second-eastmost catapult? It will be a short trip, and then I'll need a port back to base.]

[Right away.] Aldis never minded hearing Sage's mental voice. Maybe it was because mental mana was the primary mana source to his attunement, or maybe he was just more considerate than Nieve and Lani, but there was something soothing about his voice, like a bit of mint in a glass of lemonade. [I'll keep an ear out for you.]

In an unfamiliar place, like a scenario inside a spire, it helped for Aldis to be able to see where he was sending people. There were many factors that influenced how far a Wayfarer could send someone, but nothing was more important than familiarity. In a city he knew like the back of his hand, such as Tenkai, Aldis could teleport a person halfway across the city as gently and easily as moving a piece on a Crowns board. Whereas here, over terrain Aldis had not personally surveyed, on a battlefield where positioning was paramount, Aldis maintained intense focus on both the entry and exit portals, doing his best to set them so no one would lose their footing upon stepping through, and hopefully where the enemy was least expecting a strike team to appear. The element of surprise had been in his favor at the beginning of the battle, not now with so many war machines burning or disabled; it was getting harder to pick a safe place for each new portal. Though his eyes were beginning to ache from squinting over long distances, Aldis maintained watch over the portals until Sage's entire crew was through, then hastily snapped the portals shut.

With the urgency over, Aldis blinked and looked around, jumping back when he found Nieve standing shoulder to shoulder with him, her arms folded as she leaned slowly and steadily against him.

"Are you finished?" Nieve asked pointedly. "My team needs a portal, too."

"I was prioritizing the team out on the—"

"I know, I know! That's why I didn't shake you or anything." Nieve grinned. "I'm impatient, that's all. You'll get used to it. Now let's go!"

Aldis blew out a breath in frustration, then picked a siege weapon at random. He opened a portal on the rampart, which Nieve practically dove through headfirst, her crew following her recklessly close. Despite their earlier protests, they seemed eager to return to the fight.

"How did their last Wayfarer keep up with this lot?" Aldis muttered to himself, dabbing sweat off his face with his sleeve. A voice from behind nearly made him jump over the rampart.

"If you think Nieve is bad, Wyle was worse." Aldis placed a hand over his chest and spun around, finding Emiko hovering on a little cloud behind him. She stepped off her cloud and sat in a crenellation on the far side of the walkway, swinging her legs back against the stonework. "She's louder and way more reckless, just in, like, a behind-the-ranks sort of way."

"I can't even begin to fathom what that means," Aldis informed her drily before turning to look out over the battlefield once again. "Aren't you supposed to be saving your voice? Or are you okay to talk?"

"I can talk a little." Emiko spoke softly, but her tone was still pleasant and breezy. "No one expects you to be Wyle, by the way. Not really. It's just difficult adjusting to new team members. It takes time, like Nieve said."

"How did this Wyle deal with all the yelling?" Aldis pointed to his head, meaning the loud shouts inside his skull. "Isn't that distracting?"

Emiko giggled, swinging her legs like a child. "Wyle was the loudest of anyone. She said it was to make sure we heard her over whatever we were doing, but she was just loud in general. She liked to sing, too. She didn't have a lung placement like me, but she'd sing her spells anyway. With her heart attunement, she'd dance and wave her arms around when placing portals or casting teleports. We used to laugh about it when she made a particularly weird motion."

"Did she ever get mad about getting laughed at?" Aldis asked.

"No, I think that was why she did it. To make us laugh." Emiko cupped her chin in her hands, resting her elbows on her knees. "And if you think Lani is serious, then you wouldn't have liked Ren. Wyle made it her mission in life to make him laugh at least once per climb."

"And? How did that work out for her?"

"Well, they retired from climbing together, so pretty good, I guess." Emiko kicked her heels off the wall. "It's a little sad for us, but I'm happy for them."

She looked wistful, and maybe a little sad. Remembering what Sage had said about her family, Aldis couldn't stop himself from asking: "Did you consider retiring? When your friends quit?"

"Oh, no, of course not." She beamed brightly. "I met Ren and Wyle through climbing, but Sage and Nieve and I took our Judgments together. I want to climb as long as they keep climbing."

"Ah." Seemed strange, especially as she had no real need for anything, being related to the archduke as she was. Maybe it was a need to prove herself? Aldis would have thought she'd accomplished that already, especially as a Cloudcaller reaching the nineteenth floor of the Tortoise Spire. Wasn't that good enough, for someone who had no need of a fortune?

I would have quit, Aldis thought, swiping his sleeve over his face. *If I had a name and money, you wouldn't catch me risking my life in here.*

But saying that out loud would only invite questions into his background, and he couldn't have that. Not while his parents had risked so much to keep themselves safe. Risking his life for himself was one thing; risking exposing his parents was another.

Most Wayfarers could make good lives for themselves, especially if they were willing to leave Dalenos, which had a higher-than-average concentration of Wayfarers. Nobles all over Kaldwyn liked to hire Wayfarers for quick and safe transportation or communication, and such jobs often offered housing in addition to a generous salary. But Aldis's false name wouldn't hold up to the intense background checks such nobles often ran, which greatly limited his options for a comfortable lifestyle.

No matter. He'd lived the good life before; he'd have it again. And this climb was where he would finally get the chance to prove himself.

As long as they made it through this scenario alive.

[Aldis, port back to the wall with injured.]

[Opening portal.] Aldis searched for Lani first, locating her on the wall before taking care to set the portal where Sage and his crew wouldn't step on any of the injured soldiers she was healing. He didn't quite understand the concept of healing the spire's constructs—they weren't real, after all—but perhaps that was a factor this particular challenge took under consideration. Maybe one of the factors of success depended on how many of these soldiers they kept alive in the end; who could say? Maybe that was even the secret to this team's success: treating the constructs as if they were real. Anything was possible within a spire.

"You know, Wyle couldn't use portals the way you do," Emiko commented, swinging her heels so they bounced off the stones of the low wall. "She could only cast about four portals of that size, and then she'd be finished. She used to say that the spell for portals gave her double vision a lot of the time."

"There is a double-vision effect sometimes," Aldis agreed. "The spell creates a door in two different locations, both of which you have to pay close attention to in order to set the portal correctly." With no small amount of pride, Aldis held up his hand, showing Emiko his attunement mark. "I may only be a Sunstone Wayfarer, but my travel specialization is fairly unique. One might say I've mastered the casting of portals."

"Oooh!" Emiko leaned forward from her perch. "Wow, Wyle never had anything like that. How'd you get it?"

"Study. Practice. Dedication." He said it airily, in an "if I can do it, anyone can do it" sort of way, but really, it had taken an intense amount of hard work and repetition to earn his travel specialization. After earning his attunement, Aldis had had trouble finding teams willing to climb with him (he'd assumed it was the fact that he was Valian), so he buried himself in books, learning the theory behind teleportation, communication, and portals. "I frequently volunteer my services at the temple in Tenkai, assisting Katashi's priests on their missions. I found a mentor there who helped teach me a few tricks to casting portals until it came as easily as a teleport spell."

What he didn't say was that he volunteered at the temple only when he couldn't find enough work as a corner teleporter. In Tenkai, it was common practice for Wayfarers to earn a little extra money by offering teleportation around the city. Unfortunately, some corner teleporters could be territorial about their locations, and Aldis had found himself chased off by higher-level Wayfarers more often than not. The temple never turned away a helping hand, but it didn't offer much in the way of payment, either. The work did grant him access to the temple's grand library, though, and practicing portals often enough to earn a specialization mark had definitely made it worthwhile. Since his attunement mark had changed to indicate his skill, he hadn't had nearly as much trouble finding a climbing group to join.

But Aldis didn't want to get into all of that. Especially not in front of a noble.

He cast around for a quick change of subject, his eyes falling on Sage talking to Lani on a distant rampart. They were too far away to be heard over the sounds of battle, but even over the distance, he couldn't miss Sage's bashful demeanor as he spoke to the Acolyte.

"So are those two . . . together?" Aldis asked, mildly curious. "It would explain why he was so defensive of her yesterday."

"Hm? Oh, Sage and Lani?" Emiko shook her head. "No, not together. Lani's really against teammates dating. Ren and Wyle kept their relationship a secret"—she held her hands up in a motion that implied it wasn't secret at all—"so Lani wouldn't find out. I think she knew, but she pretended she didn't. It can get really messy when climbers get romantically entangled."

"Finally, something I agree with her on," Aldis muttered, scanning the battlefield again. Smoke was just beginning to rise off the siege weapon Nieve's crew had gone to destroy. She probably wouldn't ask for a portal for another few minutes as the fire caught. He leaned over the battlements, glancing down at the gate below, still blocked by an impenetrable ice wall. The crews with battering rams were bypassing the gate entirely and hammering at the walls instead. Aldis may have had his doubts in the beginning about having the Cloudcaller reinforce the walls, but he wasn't complaining now. "When climbers on the same team start dating each other, they make poor decisions in regard to protecting each other, and if one of them dies, it makes it harder for the other to keep doing their job."

"I think that's true of all close climbing groups, regardless of whether they're romantically involved or not." There was something sour in Emiko's voice, a note Aldis wasn't used to hearing in her tone. He frowned and looked back at her. "I know I can't just go on chanting when something happens to one of my friends. How can anyone focus when someone they love is in danger?"

"Maybe that's a reason not to get too attached to climbing partners," Aldis suggested, turning back to the battle raging against the fortress walls. With one hand extended down toward one of the battering ram crews, Aldis estimated the circumference of the steel-capped log they were using. Just as the crew slammed the ram forward, Aldis opened a tiny portal in front of it with the corresponding portal opening at the base of a siege ladder, just about to be sent up. The battering ram caved in the base of the ladder, sending it toppling down sideways and crashing on a good number of enemy soldiers. "Not that the free-for-all method is much better, where the fewer team members who come out means more treasure for the ones that do. There should be some level of trust, but I think it gets sticky when your teammates are your friends."

"Does that mean you don't want to climb with us again?" Emiko asked, sounding hurt.

"No, no, I didn't mean that." Aldis shook his head firmly. The girl was rich, with one of the best-connected families in Dalenos: the last thing he wanted to do was offend her. "I'm only saying that personal relationships inside a climbing group can lead to—"

Something slammed into Aldis's shoulder hard enough to cut him off. At first he was just confused. The pain of the arrow in his shoulder reached him later, when his mind caught up to it. Even then, he was still more confused than anything else: How had an arrow hit him straight on when all the archers were on the ground?

"Wind who bows to none/I call upon our contract/Heed my every whim!" Emiko pushed off her seat on the wall, power thrumming in the air around her. She thrust her hand out, as if shoving the air before her. "There!"

Aldis followed the motion, watching as a nexus of wind whirled around her before gusting forward and slamming into—a floating platform of archers? No, that wasn't right. The platform was on a rolling base, as high as the wall around the fort, wide enough to carry ten soldiers—although all ten of them were tumbling through a freefall now, thanks to Emiko's wind spell. But how had that platform gotten so close?

"Illusion magic!" Emiko leaned over the edge of the wall, pointing down. "Look! There's more coming."

Aldis stared down bewildered, his hand pressed to the shaft of the arrow. His shroud and dueling tunic had taken most of the impact out of the hit, which meant the arrowhead wasn't buried beneath his skin, but every movement made the razor-sharp tip cut a little more into the meat of his shoulder. He could teleport it out cleanly, but then the open wound would bleed. Where was Lani? Did he have time to teleport to her for a quick healing before Nieve called for a portal? Or should he just teleport the arrow out now and risk the blood loss?

"See there?" Emiko grabbed Aldis's sleeve and pointed almost straight down, ignoring his gasp of pain. "See those empty lanes between the platoons? They're moving the invisible raiding platforms down those paths!"

Emiko gasped a breath and repeated her earlier chant, throwing a hand out toward nothing once again, but then Aldis heard screams come from the pocket of empty air and suddenly there were bodies falling from a great height. He still held his hand over the arrow in his shoulder, staring in disbelief. Invisible raiding platforms? How was that fair?

Emiko slapped her palm against a merlon, commanding Aldis's focus, but he only blinked and stared when she began making hand signs. With a frustrated sigh, she released a breath that sent out swirling currents of air around her.

"Tell Lani and the others!" Emiko demanded, taking a step back from the wall. She held her hands in front of her chest, palms facing each other but not quite touching. "And bring Nieve's crew back. They shouldn't be down there for this."

Emiko took a deep breath, her shoulders rising as she ducked her chin. Aldis lost the chant against the roar of wind along the wall. He felt the first clear twinge of pain from the arrow when he tried moving his left arm and abruptly stopped.

[Invisible raiding platforms moving through the ground troops to assault the wall.] Aldis sent the same message to Lani, Sage, and Nieve. He didn't want to distract Emiko while she was chanting. [Look for the empty swaths between ground units. Cloudcaller is chanting . . . something. Recalling Nieve and the assault unit.]

Even after receiving the affirmative from Nieve, it took Aldis a moment to remember where she was on the battlefield. There were so many smoking black plumes along the horizon that it was hard to find the most recent one. He ended up using his mental connection to Nieve in order to find her location, setting the portal to bring her and her team back to the ramparts.

"I don't think they can salvage that one now, anyway," Nieve said as she strode through the portal. "Even if Emi douses the fire with a rainstorm."

"I don't know if that's a rainstorm," Aldis replied, glancing up at the sky, suddenly blue-black with churning clouds. "It looks a little more ominous than a storm."

"Oh." Nieve's dark complexion went just a little pale. "Where's Lani? Does she know—"

"Know what? I'm here." Lani trotted up to them, Sage just behind her. "Oh, Aldis, you're—let me get that."

"Lani, Emi's still chanting," Nieve called as Aldis teleported the arrow out of his shoulder. He tossed it over the side of the wall, petulantly hoping it found a target down there by mere chance.

"So that's—" Lani turned away from Aldis as if to spare a glance, then halted. Aldis gritted his teeth against the pain in his shoulder. It sure would be nice to get healed, but as long as he didn't try moving his left arm, it wasn't so bad. Lani's eyes widened at whatever Emiko was chanting. "Sage?"

"It's going to be fine," Sage counseled. "But we've got to give her time. We should spread out along the walls and watch for those raiding parties on the platforms."

"Right." Lani nodded, swallowing visibly. "So that's—" She flicked a hand toward Aldis. "—That. Try not to move too much while that stitches up."

Aldis scowled. Not a healing spell, then, but a quick-and-dirty regeneration. It would get the job done, but over time rather than all at once. The pain lingered as the wound began stitching itself closed.

"Nieve, you'll stay right here and protect Emi," Lani ordered. "Sage, head to the east wall, I'll take the west. Aldis, are you good to get to the north-facing wall?"

"I'd feel better with a proper healing spell," Aldis countered. "If I'm running around fighting off raiders, a regeneration spell could wear out before the injury is fully healed."

Lani's eyes narrowed briefly before she smoothed away the expression of annoyance. She held her attunement-marked hand out toward him, her palm glowing with a pale green light.

"It's a scratch. It'll heal up faster than you realize," Lani determined, her hand dropping to her side. "I need to conserve my mana for life-threatening emergencies. Sage, didn't you say Nieve would be fighting an attuned opponent?"

"More than likely," Sage put in, most unhelpful in Aldis's opinion. "It wasn't too clear, but if Nieve is staying to protect Emi, then it's likely—"

"Less talking, more defending!" Nieve shouted, an ice wall bursting up from the rampart to catch a volley of arrows. "Lani, the left! Raiders!"

Lani cursed, one hand slapping a belt pouch that jingled. "On my way!" She turned and bolted.

"Sorry, Aldis." At least Sage sounded like he meant it. The Seer was hurrying away in the opposite direction from Lani but stopped to shout over his shoulder. "Keep an eye out for stray winds! Emi doesn't always have control of this spell!"

Well, that was an important bit of information, Aldis thought crossly. Then, worried, he wondered whether that had been a prediction or just a bit of friendly advice. He considered asking Sage via a communication spell, but the last thing he wanted to be was a distraction, especially to someone else with as much a mental attunement as his own. Distractions could be deadly in the middle of a fight.

Winds whipped around him, tugging not just at his clothes and hair but at Aldis's belt pouches and the dueling cane hooked on his belt. A look up gave him a sense of vertigo: the sky above the fort—or rather, centered over Emiko, specifically—churned and swirled in a nexus of black and gray clouds. As he watched, the vortex shifted, smooth as a shadow, to hover over the thickest concentration of enemy forces still marching toward the fortress. Pitch-dark clouds whirled, spun, and *stretched*, craning down from the sky like a single probing finger. The moment the cloud funnel touched down, dust erupted like the spray of a wave, and as it moved, it left destruction in its wake.

"She'll move it closer to the fort when she's got more control of it." Nieve's voice was tight. Aldis noted that for once she looked dead serious, which struck a discordant note of panic in his chest. "You should get to the far side of the fort and help with the defenses there. Keep an ear out and I'll try to let you know when it's coming."

"Yes, well." Aldis pulled his hand away from his shoulder, grimacing as his hand stuck to the dried blood. There was no fresh bleeding, though, and the pain felt slightly dulled. No doubt it was still healing, but at least he'd taken the arrow in his left shoulder and he was right-hand dominant. "I suppose that is the prudent course of action. Unless it would be better to send her somewhere safe within the fort?"

Aldis pointed to Emiko, eyes only half open as she chanted under her breath. Nieve shook her head. "Better to keep her here than move her and risk an attuned opponent sneaking into the fortress to get her. I'll keep her safe, don't worry."

Aldis didn't doubt that Nieve could keep Emiko safe; she was certainly more suited to the job than he was. It was just that in the short time that he'd come to know her, he'd come to feel the need to protect Emiko. Perhaps it was her innocent-seeming nature, or the "little sister" feeling she brought out in him. More likely it was because she was unerringly friendly and welcoming where some of her teammates came off as either distant or cold. He whispered a short prayer to the goddess for Emiko's safety, then hastily teleported himself to the far side of the fort, to the center of the walkway facing north.

The black wind funnel wasn't as easy to see from this side of the fort, especially for anyone down on the ground, although there were a good number of battering rams trying their luck along the walls. The archers here took careful shots aimed directly down, but after seeing how few arrows remained in the barrels here, Aldis called for a halt. The same wide paths between the ground troops were visible here as they were in front of the fort, which meant those invisible towers were on their way, if not here already.

"Wind Detection." Aldis turned his palm out, casting a spell that should allow him to feel the movement of air nearby. Hopefully not all of those paths leading through the enemy army up to the walls of the fort had rolling towers moving along them, but at least some of them had to. There: in at least two separate "lanes," Aldis could sense not just a large amount of displaced air but also the rapid breathing of soldiers preparing to charge. He couldn't create a portal large enough to move the whole tower, nor did he have the type of spell that could remove the invisibility spell from the towers. But he might be able to stop the towers before they made it all the way to the fort.

Using his Detect Wind spell, Aldis approximated where the closest tower was in its approach and set a portal like a trench in the road just ahead of it. An average Wayfarer might have considered the placement of the attached exit portal to be trivial, but Aldis placed it just over one of the battering rams, so that when the rolling tower hit the portal-trench, its front wheels landed heavily along the top of the battering ram, ripping it out of the grip of the soldiers hammering away with it. The tower itself hit the trench hard enough that several soldiers were flung off the top of it. It didn't topple forward the way Aldis hoped it would, but it did turn visible. Once the soldiers who remained on the platform could be seen, Aldis gave the orders to the archers to shoot.

An arrow skipped out of nowhere, catching Aldis by enough surprise that he teleported out of its path, his heart pummeling itself against his ribs like a trapped hummingbird. Belatedly, he realized he could have simply put a portal in the path of the arrow and sent it back to where it came from, but it was too late now. All he could do was use his Detect Wind spell to locate the next invisible tower, although this time it was harder. Because of the first tower hitting his portal-trench, this tower was no longer rolling toward the fort, but instead the archers atop it were firing at targets along the ramparts.

"Can't say I blame them," Aldis muttered, casting a cone of wind ahead of himself to send further arrows off-target. "All right, then. Time to prove I do know how to use a dueling cane."

He took the dueling cane off his belt but kept it pointed down at the walkway. As he pinpointed the central location where the arrows were coming from, he opened a portal directly beneath his dueling cane, with the corresponding portal exiting just in front of the archers, though slightly below where they'd be aiming to shoot—he didn't need any of them noticing the portal and trying to shoot through it. With minimal movement, Aldis sent a flurry of blasts of gray mana through his dueling cane, shifting the exit portal ever so slightly, using his Detect Wind spell to ensure that he'd cleared the top of the platform completely before closing the portal and hooking the cane back on his belt.

"And of course, no one saw that," Aldis muttered, taking the brief respite to check his injured shoulder. It still felt sore, but upon examination, it seemed the skin had healed over. The injury wasn't as bad as it could have been, but he still felt Lani had been a little callous in using only a regeneration spell. Would she have done the same if someone else had taken an arrow in the shoulder?

Maybe if the team didn't invite him back for a second climb, he'd write a complaint about the Acolyte so future applicants would know what they were getting into. Was it unprofessional to point out that she was also a gambler? He certainly would have liked to know that prior to joining. Come to that, how had he missed seeing her fingertips during the interview? Had she been wearing gloves? Aldis couldn't remember.

Aldis's introspection was cut short by the screams and cries ranging along the rampart. He lifted his head, looking out toward the west with everyone else.

Emiko's black wind funnel curved around the corner of the fort, eerie in the way it followed a set path, rather than veering off into wanton destruction. The whipping winds roared louder than the crash of battle, picking up war machines as if they were toys and tossing them down haphazardly, leaving a trail of ruin in their path. As Aldis watched, the black winds crunched through a mobile platform tower he hadn't even noticed, turning it visible just before it exploded into kindling, tossing the soldiers up like a juggler's act before they vanished inside the core of the whirlwind.

Aldis gaped, then grumbled, "Show-off."

NIEVE

Champion (mind mark), Citrine

Nieve paced the length of the gate along the rampart, impatiently tapping her sword against her shoulder. She'd shaped a half dome of ice over Emiko to protect her from arrows as she concentrated on her black wind funnel. Nieve had seen her lose control of this spell before. It wasn't one that dissipated on its own, didn't break up and fracture and float away, no. When this spell went badly, it spun out of control, recognizing neither friend nor foe as it ripped apart the scenario. If she squinted really hard at the funnel, Nieve could make out lifeless forms tossed along the winds like no more than leaves caught in a breeze. Soldiers fled before it, but the winds were strong even from a distance, and anyone slow to move out of its way was quickly caught in the vortex.

But Nieve wasn't watching the funnel. No, that was Emi's job. Nieve's job was to watch Emi.

Because any hero worth their salt would want to target the person maintaining the spell of abject terror and destruction.

And Nieve hadn't forgotten that there was at least one attuned on the enemy's side who had turned the raiding platforms invisible.

An Illusionist? Nieve wondered. *Seems too obvious. Perhaps a foreign attunement is more likely. Like a Mesmer, or an Enchanter. Or maybe the invisibility on the platforms was the result of some sort of device? But would that really extend to the people on the platforms?*

Nieve shook her head to clear it. Speculation was not her strong suit. She was a more "deal with the problems as they come" type of fighter. Figuring out strategies ahead of time was more Sage's and Lani's thing. Nieve's way was a little messier, but it got the job done.

She could only wait and hope that there was actually an enemy combatant on their way to come kill Emi right now, because all the useful little contraptions—the invisible raiding platforms, the flying pigs, and even the siege weapons were all beginning to make her think all the enemy's attuned were the bookish types, the ones that made her feel like a bully for beating them up. She wanted a *real* fight, against someone she could challenge herself against and feel good about beating. And after all those quick strikes against ill-prepared siege weapon defenders, she longed for a proper opponent.

Nieve checked the wall to either side of the gate and, finding it clear, turned to check on her friends. She couldn't see Aldis on the far side of the fort, but that was where Emi's black wind funnel was currently ripping apart the enemy's ranks, so he was probably safe for now. The raiders who had breached Lani's rampart had spilled desperately off the platforms before the funnel tore them to splinters, and many of the soldiers there were still fighting, Lani included. Sage appeared to be successfully defending against the raiding platforms on his wall, but she wouldn't give him too much credit for that; it had to be easy when his Sight nullified the utility of a good invisibility spell.

Nieve heard an ominous creaking noise, like wood clacking against wood. She froze midstep, tilted her head, and listened. It was faint, almost hidden by the roar of the winds, the cries of the soldiers, and the ring of steel on steel, but it was there. An approaching invisible platform, perhaps? Nieve turned her sword, encasing the blade in fanglike icicles, then swept it in a wide arc, parallel with the wall. The icicles broke off, flung from the blade in a curved line, numerous enough that had anything been in their way, they would have struck and shattered. Instead, they flew unerringly straight, falling only to gravity rather than meeting an invisible force.

Nieve took a step back, putting her back against Emi's protective dome. She heard something like the crack of wood against stone, and perhaps the creak of rope stretched taut. Based on what she had seen so far, this army definitely had more than its share of mechanical surprises up its sleeve, so Nieve couldn't begin to guess what this new noise might signify. What she could assume was that if there was a hidden device nearby, it would need a human element in order to be a threat.

I hate using this spell, Nieve thought, her upper lip curling on instinct. *This is Sage's thing, not mine.*

She drew a breath and focused inwardly on her attunement mark, located in the center of her forehead. She didn't close her eyes—she wouldn't blind herself to an ambush—but she did let her vision go fuzzy. Mental mana was her least favorite mana, as well as her weakest as it had only become available since the last climb, but Sage had taught her a few spells during the break between climbs. The easiest spell would be Detect Aura, which would allow her to see magic and shrouds, or sometimes spells and enchanted items, but anything cloaked in invisibility would be protected from such a basic spell and Nieve didn't have the experience necessary to tweak the spell the way Sage probably could. So instead, she used a different spell.

Detect Mind.

If someone was approaching, either on an invisible platform or otherwise, the spell should be able to detect their presence. In theory.

Nieve's unfocused vision slid along the rampart, coming into sharp focus at a place where the rampart met the observatory tower. She glanced around again, making sure she wasn't leaving Emi vulnerable, then silently stalked over to the corner where her spell thought it found something. The sounds of wood groaning and rope straining grew louder as she approached, though she still saw nothing. She braced a hip against the wall and carefully peered over, looking for whatever her Detect Mind spell had found.

Most elemental types of mana had a color when viewed by a simple Detect Aura spell: red for fire spells, blue for water spells. Even the more abstract mana types had casting colors, like Nieve's enhancement spells, which she'd always seen as white. But mental mana was different. Rather than manifesting as a color, it looked like peering through poorly made glass: clear but wavy, bubbly. Nieve only noticed it because she knew what she was looking for, but even then, she nearly missed it: a warped space of empty air right up against the wall, very nearly to the top. Nieve shrugged her sword off her shoulder, blinking away her Detect Mind spell and preparing to shape ice along the blade of her sword.

Searing light burst from the point Nieve was focused on, making her cry out and block the light with her free hand. With tears of pain rolling down her cheeks, Nieve forced herself into a defensive stance as she blinked away the light scars on her vision. She conjured ice along her sword, making the blade wide and flat, holding it across her body like a shield. She heard the clack of hard-soled shoes landing on the wall and forced her eyes open, searching for her opponent.

"Clever of you to find me, but not soon enough." The voice was lilting and teasing, carrying the bite of a smirk. Nieve could just barely make out a form in front of her, short and lithe, no visible weapons. Yet. "Your spellcaster is being troublesome. Get out of my way, or die."

"That's my line," Nieve snarled. She whipped her sword out straight from her shoulder, shifting the ice to elongate the blade into a longsword. It should have reached her opponent, cutting them in half, but the light seemed to bend around them, Nieve's blade passing by without a scratch. She swore as she corrected her strike: her opponent had scaled the wall while invisible. She should have anticipated what it meant to fight against someone who could cast illusory spells.

"Oooh, so close!" The still-blurry person burst into movement, somersaulting over Nieve's sloppy second swing and ducking beneath her guard. Nieve's vision cleared just enough to catch the silvery glint of metal claws extending from leather wrist wraps on her opponent's arms. She swore out loud as she activated her Frost Form spell, reinforcing her body to be as hard and unyielding as ice. She felt the metal claws rake against her leather tunic, digging deep but skating off her hardened skin. As Nieve reversed her strike to bring the butt of her sword down on her opponent's head, the hooded person flipped backward and out of the way, landing in a half crouch with their claws out in front of them.

"That tickled," Nieve taunted, annoyed that her opponent had gotten close enough to cut her protective vest. "Come a little closer and I'll show you how it's done."

"Ha! Tempting." Now that Nieve could see more clearly, she saw that her opponent was scarcely taller than Emiko, loose clothing strapped tight against her skin by flat leather bands around her upper arms, wrists, thighs and ankles. Her shoulders and midriff were bare, showing off hard muscles in a way that Nieve appreciated. She wore a headscarf that left only her eyes visible, twinkling like dark stars. "But I'm the one showing off here."

She turned her wrist sharply, metal claws catching the light. But instead of a simple flash or glint, the light burst outward, hitting Nieve's still-watering eyes. Her eyes snapped shut against her will, the sound of running steps along the rampart her only clue that the woman was attacking again. She stepped out wide, bracing herself for impact. Between her protective shroud and her body reinforced by Frost Form, there wasn't much that could really hurt her—at least, not without a stronger attunement or access to elemental magic that countered ice. If she couldn't see her opponent, she'd invite her to attack her first. All she needed was to get one hand on her opponent and the fight would be over.

A heavy weight against her sword, like someone had grabbed it with both hands. Nieve attempted to swing it back, but suddenly it was much lighter than it had been, making her stagger off-balance. Forcing her eyes open, she saw that her ice blade was gone, leaving behind only the single-edged katana.

"What—" Was it an illusion? Could an illusion make her blade lighter in her hands? Only a fire spell should have been able to evaporate her sword like that, and a powerful one at that, yet she hadn't felt any heat.

More importantly: the claw-wielding fighter wasn't in front of Nieve anymore. She had ducked Nieve's blade and was running to the ice dome covering Emi.

Close! Nieve shaped the dome almost without thinking, snapping it shut protectively around Emiko. She'd left the dome partially open in order to keep an eye on Emi, as well as to keep her from getting too cold within it. It closed like a clamshell just before the would-be assassin could dive through the opening claws first. Metal screeched over the smooth ice, leaving thin tracks but unable to break through. The sound set Nieve's teeth on edge, the little hairs on her arms and neck standing on end.

"Ah, quick thinking!" The woman's eyes crinkled at the corners. "But not quite enough."

She set her hand against the dome, blue magic flickering around her fingertips. The ice dome shimmered wetly, light glinting off its polished surface.

"A water spell?" Nieve redoubled her ice spell, freezing the water that was trickling free from beneath the enemy fighter's hand. The Illusionist attunement was a common one from the Tortoise Spire, so Nieve had a passing familiarity with it, but she'd never heard of an Illusionist having access to water mana before. Unless her opponent had two attunements? Or was the melting ice just an illusion as well? No, she had definitely manipulated Nieve's ice sword somehow; there had to be more than simple illusions at play here.

Someone else might have taken the time to try to puzzle it out, but Nieve simply charged, swinging her katana down on the woman's outstretched arm. The woman whipped her arm away at the last second, lifting her metal claws to her eye level and rotating her wrist, sending spears of light lancing at Nieve's eyes. Nieve squinted through her eyelashes, driving the attacker back and away from Emi's dome.

"How long can she stay in there?" the woman taunted, dodging Nieve's slashes with small, twisting movements. "Is there air? Is she cold? If she opens her eyes to darkness, will she be scared and call that death-wind to save herself?"

"Emi is strong, she'll be fine," Nieve replied, shaping ice along her sword again. "If you need someone to worry about, you should put yourself at the top of the list."

"Dangerous! I like it." The woman winked. Damn, but that was kinda cute. "What's your name, Tails?"

Tails? Oh, right, her headband. She liked to leave the ends long so she could adjust it easily, but the red stood out vibrantly against her hair, so it wasn't the first time she'd heard the nickname. "Nieve. But you can call me your doom, on account of our very limited acquaintance."

"That's nice. Good banter is important." She nodded sagely. "I'm Ana. But you can call me—"

Light sparked off every reflective surface, not just Ana's claws, but off Emi's dome and Nieve's own sword, too, driving lances of burning light deep into Nieve's eyes. She squeezed them shut and, relying on her Frost Form to protect her from a sudden attack, she broadened her stance to block Ana's path to Emi's protective dome.

"The light-bringer. Much catchier than 'your doom,' wouldn't you say?"

Nieve turned her head, eyes leaking tears as she slashed blindly with her sword. Ana was moving, based on the footsteps Nieve could hear, but she couldn't see a goddess-cursed thing. She felt an attack strike at her midsection, catching at her tunic again. She swung for the space in front of her but caught only empty air. Ana was quick. Athletic, too. And if Nieve couldn't see her to land a hit, how was she going to fight?

Maybe if I knew her second attunement, Nieve thought, keeping her back to Emi's dome. *Something with water mana, but that's half the attunements from Tortoise Spire. She melted my sword, but the ice dome slowed her down. She's fast, so maybe something with transference mana, like a Wavewalker?*

Wait. Nieve was assuming Ana's use of light mana was from an Illusionist attunement, but what if that assumption was wrong? If Ana was an Illusionist, why hadn't she used any illusions yet? Nieve hated dueling Illusionists: they were always casting weird spells to make it look like they had eight arms, or body doubles, or creating hazard traps in the terrain. So far, Ana had only turned herself invisible and used tricks of the light. Did that mean . . .

Nieve concentrated, casting a spell she'd barely practiced using this way, but it seemed her only option at this point. If she couldn't use her eyes, she'd have to use something else. It wouldn't work if Ana was an Illusionist, but just maybe that last quip had been a bit of a hint.

In casting Detect Mind, Nieve felt her hold on Frost Form falter. As she struggled to keep her protective spell active, Detect Mind weakened to the point that she could no longer make out the warped-space bubble that marked Ana's mind. It felt as if the two spells repelled each other, or that focusing on one weakened the other. Perhaps this was something Nieve could overcome with training, especially as her mental mana was still relatively new, but for now, she needed to find a way to fight without relying on her eyes, and for that, Detect Mind was the more relevant spell. Trusting in her shroud to protect her from those vicious claws, Nieve released Frost Form and put her faith in Detect Mind.

She waited until Ana darted in close for another attack, then spun her blade, catching those claws against the edge, shaping ice over them to trap them within her blade. Ana shouted out as Nieve completed her spin, sword crashing down against the wall, Ana's hands trapped by the claws encased in ice.

"How did— Ah." Ana's eyes flickered through surprise, then wariness. "The same way you found me earlier, right? Have you figured me out?"

"Illuminator, right?" Nieve peeked through her lashes, relaxing when she saw nothing reflective before her. She shifted so that even the ice-covered blade of her sword wasn't in her direct line of sight. "I haven't dueled anyone with that attunement yet. I guess I thought it was more like a healing attunement rather than an offensive one. But if you don't have perception mana, you can't trick a Detect Mind spell."

"You're smarter than you look." Ana's eyes glinted maliciously. "But if I don't have an offensive attunement, then why am I the one they sent up here?"

"Um . . ." Nieve stuttered over that. Ana was fast and no doubt those claws could be deadly, but she wasn't particularly strong. Had she been wrong? Or was Ana still hiding a second attunement? Or maybe Ana wasn't the only infiltrator?

Nieve snapped her head up, scanning with her Detect Mind spell, searching for any other invisible individuals.

"Close, but still a miss." Ana swung her leg up, bracing the sole of her boot against Nieve's leg, and kicked off her, ripping her claws free of the ice as she flipped backward, landing neatly on the centermost merlon over the gate. She faced out over the battlefield, putting her back toward Nieve, though she shot a wink over her shoulder. She held her arms out wide, metal claws glittering, and then slowly her entire body began to glow. Not just glow, but shine like the beacon of a lighthouse. Nieve squinted and turned her face away as a beam of pure light encased Ana entirely, shooting up through Emi's dark, churning clouds, even causing the ones directly overhead to break apart.

Shielding her eyes against Ana's sudden burst of radiance, Nieve cast a hurried glance around the fortress for her teammates. The ice dome around Emi was still closed and solid, but it looked slick, as if the brilliant rays of light were beginning to melt it. On one far rampart, she saw Lani still fighting viciously, her cutlass slicing one way, then reversing for a second chop. But as fierce as Lani looked, the soldiers around her looked overwhelmed and exhausted, some even sagging against the rampart wall, weapons heavy in their hands. A fresh wave of attackers was surging up a raiding platform, fists upraised toward the beacon that was Ana. A glance over at Sage's rampart showed a similar scene: two raiding platforms were anchored against the wall, attacking warriors pinching in from two sides as defenders raised their hands in surrender. Sage was still standing, but for how much longer? He had to be tired after leading all those forays behind enemy lines earlier. As she watched, Sage twisted to look back at her, touching his glasses as he eyed the column of light that engulfed Ana entirely.

Resh it, there's more to her attunement than just spears of light, Nieve realized, gritting her teeth against the burn of the light. *Somehow, she's demoralizing our troops while bolstering her own. She's the rallying cry.*

And I've gotta douse her.

Nieve exhaled slowly, firming her grip on her sword.

Time to show them that we have our own Champion.

Nieve spun around to face the Illuminator, yanking her headband down over her eyes. She couldn't see, but that didn't mean she couldn't fight. Light still poured in around the edges of her headband and through the lids of her eyes, but her Detect Mind spell was still active, showing the wavy distortion over Ana's location within the brilliant beam of light. Nieve swung her sword back behind her, reshaping the ice along it into a long thick pole, favoring range over accuracy, then swung for Ana's body.

Ana vaulted the pole, but she lost her concentration on her brilliant-beam-of-light spell. Nieve saw the window of warped space against the blood-colored backs of her eyes hesitate for a moment—doubtless confused over Nieve's self-imposed blindness—then saw it move laterally along the wall, presumably hopping from merlon to merlon. Nieve pivoted on her back foot and swung her pole-sword again, higher and at an angle this time so it would be harder to jump. She felt an impact along the shaft of her ice pole, saw the blurry space of air hovering over it, as if Ana had grabbed hold of it, allowing it to carry her over the walkway. Nieve released her spell, the ice rapidly turning into water, giving Ana nothing to hold on to.

Nieve wished she could have seen the look of surprise in Ana's eyes, as well as whatever heroic acrobatics kept her from falling over the edge of the wall. The scrape of metal on stone made her think Ana had used the claws to catch herself and to help her scramble over the rampart. If she was relieved from her near miss, she didn't show it; instead that warped-space blob dove headlong at Nieve and her very ordinary steel sword.

This spell is no good for close combat, Nieve realized, backing away. She couldn't tell if Ana's claws were extended in front of her for a charging attack or poised behind her for a stronger slice. She could only roughly judge where Ana's head was at any given moment, and even that was difficult as the light beyond her headband changed from bright to dark to bright again.

Resh it, I'm going to have to ask Sage to teach me a better spell for this, Nieve thought, bringing her sword up between herself and Ana as she retreated blindly. *He's always taking shots at stuff with his eyes closed. He'll probably make me do something stupid, like say "Please."*

Nieve managed to score a hit on Ana as she reversed the strike of her sword, slamming back with the hilt rather than bringing the blade around. Ana's shroud softened the blow, though, so it didn't knock her out cold, it only sent her staggering sideways. Nieve felt the pressure of Ana's claws rake across her midsection, but her shroud dulled the cut, the leather tunic snagging, but not sliced through. She changed her grip on her sword, driving it downward with both hands, but the blurry bubble of mind-space swung around in a circle and before Nieve could understand the motion, something crashed into her legs, sweeping her down to crash-land on her back. A spin-kick. Ana had taken her down with a spin-kick.

Unable to see where Ana was as she fell, Nieve shaped an ice wall, and based on a pretty loud grunt, she was pretty sure Ana slammed into it. Light flared beyond Nieve's blindfold and she felt the water in her ice wall melt away, pooling on the walkway, but it gave her enough time to get to her feet and change the shape of the ice along her sword, switching it to the broad blade of a zanbatou for use as a shield as well as a weapon.

It took a moment to find the wavy splotch in Nieve's vision, but just as she readied her sword to strike, the splotch moved in an unexpected direction, making it hard to strike. Ana must have jumped up onto the inner ledge of the rampart for that splotch to be so high up, and in the precious moments it took to locate her, Ana was already moving, that wavy bubble of space switching from high placement, then low, then high again in rapid order.

Flips? Nieve guessed. *She's doing flips along the—*

Stars broke out over Nieve's vision before she understood what had happened. Ana had used the momentum of her flips not only to disorient her but to slam her knee into Nieve's face, hard enough for her nose to crunch under the impact. She felt blood run down her face as pain radiated outward, bringing fresh tears to her eyes as she pivoted, still tracking that blurry spot in her mind's eye. Frost Form likely would have prevented that, or at least dulled the attack somewhat, but Detect Mind was still the more important spell for tracking Ana's movements. Nieve gritted her teeth against the pain, redoubling her efforts to focus on the moving target that represented Ana's mind.

Ana tried to follow up with a diving charge, but Nieve swept her aside this time, moving almost more on instinct than on what she could "see." She batted Ana away with the flat of her sword while her free hand pinched her nose, molding an ice cast over it. She hoped it wasn't too badly broken, or else Lani wouldn't be able to fix it, but it wouldn't be the first time she broke her nose during a climb, and probably not the last, either. It still hurt enough to make her see stars, though.

Brilliance flared ahead of Nieve, confusing her for a second before she realized Ana thought she was reaching up to remove her blindfold and had thought to catch her with a flash of light. Playing along, Nieve staggered backward, crying out as if in surprise but carefully keeping the sword between herself and Ana. She saw the blurry space of air racing after her, running along the rampart this time instead of the ledge. Nieve grinned wickedly as Ana stepped into the pool of water she had created when she'd melted Nieve's ice wall from earlier.

Freeze! Nieve commanded silently. The blurry splotch in her vision dropped into a headlong fall as Ana screamed, unable to catch herself. Nieve swung her sword, reshaping it as it whistled through the air, becoming narrower, sharper, bearing down on the small space of blurred air.

A screech of metal on ice, but Ana managed to divert the blade with her claws. A sudden surge of movement in front of her, and then Nieve felt Ana's shoulder connect with her midsection, hard enough to send her sliding back along the ice coating the walkway. Without missing a beat, Nieve yanked her war hammer off her belt, spinning the short haft in her hand, its heft and grip as familiar as that of her sword. She cast a spell as she slid back, shifting her weight to continue the slide, even picking up speed as she spun, putting her back to where she sensed Ana to be. A pillar of ice shot up in the center of the walkway, just to Nieve's left. With the icepick side of her hammer turned out, she pierced the pillar and used it as a pivot point to swing back around, gaining momentum on the ice.

The bubble of warped space that showed Ana's location ducked and weaved, trying to make it tough for Nieve to follow, but as quickly as Nieve was moving, Ana would have had to move fast, too. Nieve swung her sword out behind her, bending deep at the knees to compel her slide. She saw Ana duck just as low, likely preparing a claws-out charge. Just before they could collide, Nieve tucked her leg and rolled, continuing her slide on her back, driving her opposite foot up into where she estimated Ana's center of mass to be. The guttural grunt that followed told her she'd hit her target dead-on, Ana's weight crumpling around her kick. Nieve shook her off, tossing down both her hammer and her sword as she rolled to her feet, catching Ana by the collar as well as her belt. Taking a minute to orient herself, Nieve turned toward the battlefield, lifting Ana over her head.

"I hope you've got a way to survive this," Nieve said, grinning. "Because I'd sure enjoy a rematch on open ground."

"No, wait! Don't—" But Nieve had already tossed her over the side of the wall, a scream unspooling behind her as she fell.

Without chancing a look down, Nieve pulled her headband off her eyes and jumped up on the closest merlon, tossing her head back in a triumphant roar as she raised her fist holding the crimson headband as a sign of victory. Rallying cries came from the soldiers along the walls, hopefully renewing their vigor in the fight now that the Illuminator had been cast down.

After confirming that the ice dome over Emi remained unscathed, Nieve took a moment to catch her breath, tying her headband over her forehead attunement mark once again and tightening the knot behind her head. She hadn't had a fight that challenging in a while, which kept a grin on her face as she gathered her dropped weapons.

Keeping an eye out for any other invisible fighters, Nieve paced back to the ice dome, placing her hammer back in its loop on her belt. She reshaped the protective dome around Emi, opening up the front so Emi was no longer sealed inside. Finally, she checked the corner of the wall Ana had ascended and found a wood-and-rope pulley construction anchored by grappling hooks, which must have been made invisible using a trick of light mana. Nieve cut it down but saved the grappling hooks, looping them through her belt.

"Doing all right, Mi-mi?" Nieve asked, returning to the dome. Emi didn't respond, but her eyes moved rapidly beneath her lids, her cheeks flushed and pink. Nieve reached out, cupping Emi's cheek to check for warmth. Emi's skin was cool, but still soft, her breath warm enough to create puffs of steam as she exhaled. Nieve nodded and reshaped the ice again, smoothing the space directly in front of Emi into a seat. She sank down on it, hands grasping the hilt of her sword, point-down between her feet.

The fight might be winding down, but it wasn't over yet. Nieve held her vigilance in front of Emi's protective dome. Anyone coming for Emi would have to go through her first.

CHAPTER 10

LANI

Acolyte (hand mark), Citrine

Is that it?" Lani gasped, impatiently swiping braids over her shoulder as she looked from side to side. "Are there any others?"

"With the reinforcements from the north wall, we're just about clear!" a lieutenant reported.

"Good. Then we need to—" A clear tone sounded within Lani's mind. She held up a hand, halting her order as well as asking that the lieutenant wait a moment. If there was one thing she liked better about Aldis as the team's Wayfarer—just one thing—it was how he started mental communication. No matter how many times she'd asked, Wyle had always opened every communication with a shouted "Hey!" inside Lani's mind, disrupting her concentration every time. Aldis sent a noise like the toll of a bell, letting her know to expect his voice inside her mind.

[Sage requested that I connect everyone, save for Emiko,] Aldis explained a moment after the tone ended. [And Hane, obviously.]

Lani rolled her eyes. Obviously.

[It's just mop up from here,] came Sage's voice. [Nieve, wake up Emi gently, then take over Lani's side so she can head to the medical tent. Aldis, if you're clear, then I could use your help. There's another wave tonight, so use mana wisely.]

[Thanks, Sage. When you get a chance, find a quiet place and clear your head.] Lani cleaned the blade of her cutlass with the swipe of a cloth, then sheathed it, the click of the hilt feeling like a note of finality. She glanced up and down the rampart, making sure no one nearby was critically wounded before making her request. [Aldis, can I get a teleport down to the medical tent?]

[Sending you now.]

Lani closed her eyes as she felt the magic flow over her. She released a long, slow breath before opening her eyes again, the groans and whimpers of the injured informing her that she had arrived. The aftermath of a battle was usually the most strenuous part of a scenario for her. After a battle, Nieve would crow and cavort, drink and flirt before fatigue caught up to her, knocking her out cold. Ren had been a bit of the same, just on a smaller scale. If Emi didn't require any healing, she would drink a honeyed tea and sit near one of her teammates as she rested her voice. Sometimes she sat with Lani as she worked her way through the healer's tent; other times she'd curl up next to Sage and doze. Sage would often find a safe place slightly out of the way to meditate, already looking ahead to the next battle. Although, perhaps with him taking a larger part in today's battle, maybe he would take a page from Nieve's book and do a little bragging. Aldis would probably complain about something. That seemed to be his normal state whenever he wasn't actively offending people.

The medical tent was less a tent and more a canvas awning over thick, flat pads laid out in neat rows. Healers and trained medics moved among the injured, washing wounds, applying bandages, and offering draughts of potions. Lani took a moment to fix her hair into a serviceable bun at the back of her head, then made her way to the victims with the worst injuries. As per her instructions to the fort commander, the soldiers most in need of healing were all grouped together, making it easy for her to cast minor healing spells on all of them at once.

Before she got started, she held her hand out toward the injured and cast a silent spell she simply called Mortality. It was a hybrid of perception and life mana, allowing her to assess a person's worst injuries to see how much healing it would take to save them. The spell generally manifested as a dull red glow over an injury: the darker the red, the more mana required for healing. As cold as it sounded, she couldn't spend good mana on a life that was already lost. At least, not on spire constructs such as these.

By her spell's assessment, at least three of the soldiers were too far gone for her to save. Two were unconscious, either from pain or blood loss, and the third was gasping wetly. Lani knelt beside him, taking a potion out of a pouch.

"This will help," she said soothingly. "It will make the pain stop. Do you want it?"

Whether the soldier understood or not, Lani couldn't say. He met her eyes and nodded, opening his mouth so she could pour the liquid on his tongue. As she turned away to begin healing those who could be saved, she heard his gasps slowly die off, peace finally taking him.

Lani didn't waste time on prayers: too many others needed her help, or else they, too, would pass beyond her ability to save. She walked between the neat rows of padded cots, casting regeneration spells on those who couldn't be saved by simple stitches and bandages. She closed lacerations, eased head wounds, fixed internal organs, and knitted muscles and blood vessels back together again. Broken bones would have to heal on their own, but at least she could make sure any injuries to the body caused by jagged ends wouldn't cause anyone to bleed out. These were the moments when Lani toyed with the idea of getting a second Judgment with the hopes of getting an attunement that used stone mana in order to heal bone, but that mana type wasn't common to Dalenos Judgments and going anywhere else would be expensive. And she didn't want to make her team wait while she traveled somewhere to maybe get an attunement with the right mana type. Something like Emi's mana diffuser would be more practical, but those weren't available on the open market yet, and even if they were, she recalled the long hours of training Emi put into using hers, all the failed spells, the mistakes and the expense of the mana crystals lost to training. But what if she only needed a diffuser that could use stone mana crystals? That way, there would be a limit to the number of spells she'd have to learn, and mending bones was all she really intended to do with it. But even if such a device existed, Lani imagined it wouldn't be cheap, so she'd need a pretty big win to be able to afford one.

That's not impossible, Lani mused as she used a spell to help set a broken leg, holding it steady while a medic wrapped it in a splint. *My cold streak on Bandit's Run is bound to end soon. And that one Tiles wheel has been pretty reliable lately. After I see what my cut is from this run, maybe I can ask Sage about his parents' contacts in Valia . . .*

"Lani? Sorry, Lani?"

Lani blinked, surprised to hear her name spoken so softly, as if the speaker was worried about rousing her. Probably smart, though, considering she was holding four pieces of a leg bone together while the splint was being properly fitted. Sage was crouched on the other side of the patient's pallet, trying to catch her eyes. "Sorry, Sage. What is it?"

"I don't mean to interrupt," he said, smiling ruefully. "But we've got a few injuries that need to be seen to. Nothing dire, so no need to rush. I just wanted to see if you were almost finished here?"

"Yes, sorry." Lani shook her head. "I lost track of the time. I'll be right out."

"Thanks, Lani."

No one else inside the medical tent was in mortal danger anyway, and her teammates outranked the constructs of the spire. Lani finished helping with the leg she was setting, then used a clean cloth soaked in boiled water to wash her hands. If anyone on her team had been seriously injured, they would have come to her immediately, rather than waiting around politely. Still, she should have thought to check on them sooner. The battle had been nearly over already when she'd asked to be teleported down to the medical tent.

Long habit had Lani checking her gear as she exited the tent; careless climbers didn't make it very high in the spires. Her cutlass was sheathed on her hip, but she made a mental note to clean it more thoroughly a little later. She drummed her fingers against her coin purse, then smoothed a hand over her return bell's pouch, checking for its presence carefully to ensure that she hadn't lost it. It was the single most important piece of a climber's equipment, and the one Lani least wanted to lose. After that, she tapped the shield sigil on her vest, then the dirk on her hip. The dirk was enchanted with a light spell: if she unsheathed it, it would glow bright enough to light a small room, or illuminate a path in the dark. It didn't get much use with Sage's and Emiko's spells, but it was a comfort to have in case she was ever separated from the two of them. Behind the dirk was her emergency medical kit, then behind her belt was Sage's satchel, heavy with the weight of the traded gun. She had to give that back to him; trading sequences weren't puzzles that interested her, though she appreciated that Sage liked doing them. Having an extra key was always handy during a climb.

What was that? Lani brushed her hand over her pocket, feeling something like the vibration of a plucked string. She winced at a sharp edge pricking her hand as she drew it from her pocket.

Oh, yes, that strange shard she'd plucked from the injured soldier's sleeve. She'd forgotten about pocketing it; she'd been so tired the night before, she hadn't thought to examine it with the aura-detecting monocle she used to check treasure for enchantments. It didn't look like very much, so perhaps it was nothing, but as she held it pinched between her fingers, she could swear she felt it shivering. Was it reacting to something? Or was she merely tired and the shaking was coming from her? Either seemed likely, but neither was as important as healing her teammates. Perhaps Sage could take a look at it if he wasn't too taxed from the battle.

Lani's teammates waited just far enough away from the healing tent to be out of the way of the bustle of injured people being helped onto cots or healers rushing around for more water or clean bandages. Sage lifted a hand to wave her over. As she approached, she assessed each of her team members with a healer's eye, looking for grievous injuries or anything that might force her to end the climb early, such as broken bones. She didn't like the look of Nieve's nose, but then Nieve had insisted on continuing to climb with a broken nose before. Hopefully it wasn't all that bad. Emiko sat curled around herself, arms wrapped around herself as if cold. Aldis was gripping his right hand, his lower lip pinched between his teeth. She didn't see any blood, save for the arrow wound he'd taken earlier, so it was likely just mana strain. Sage looked roughed up and dirty, but he still smiled as she approached. She didn't miss him wincing at every loud noise, though. If he wasn't on the verge of a headache, he would be soon.

Lani set her hands on her hips and cocked an eyebrow. "Sorry about the wait, fellows. Who's first?"

Aldis, predictably, shuffled forward, then stopped, shooting a look over at Nieve. She was seated on a supply crate with her head tipped back as she pinched the bridge of her nose. Ghastly rivulets of wet and dried blood ran over her chin and down her neck to soak the collar of her shirt. For all that, though, she seemed in high spirits; perhaps she had found herself a worthy opponent within this scenario.

"Get the fearless warrior over there," Sage said, waving in Nieve's direction. "The sooner she gets healed, the sooner she can wash her face."

"If I must," Lani sighed, shaking her head at the mess. She stopped to hand Sage the shard of broken crystal on her way over to Nieve. "Can you take a look at that for me? I found it yesterday. It's probably nothing, but I'd hate to lose it if it turns out to be important."

"Thanks, Lani."

That was weird. Why was he thanking her for what was probably a useless task? No matter: healing Nieve was what mattered right now.

Nieve grinned at Lani's approach through bloody teeth, adding to the grim visage.

"Is it broken?" Lani asked, pressing close against the crate and Nieve's knee in order to reach Nieve's face.

"If it is, I'm still good to climb." Nieve took her hand away from the bridge of her nose, leaving behind a cast made of ice. She groped blindly through a pocket, bloody fingers marring what had previously been a clean handkerchief. "Just do it, Lani, I'm ready."

At least Nieve knew how to set her own nose, though at this point that was hardly worth marveling after. Lani's nose had been broken once on a climb, and the pain had nearly been enough to black her out before she could heal it. Maybe the enhancement mana played a role, or maybe Nieve was just a masochist, but Lani had seen her set her own nose in the middle of a fight and then charge back into the fray. Nothing seemed to slow Nieve down for long.

"It looks like it's mostly tissue damage, which is good," Lani said, using a spell to assess the injury. "I can pop the cartilage back into place, but it won't be fully healed. You might want to take a potion before you go to bed tonight. Ready?"

"Yeah, yeah, just—" Nieve grunted as Lani cast her minor healing spell, the tissue rearranging enough to pop the cartilage into its proper shape. Her expression was pained for only a moment before she pushed Lani's hand away and lifted the handkerchief to her nose. Lani knew well enough to turn away as Nieve blew her nose, though by the greenish expression on Aldis's face, he hadn't known what to expect. Sage stared determinedly down at the crystal shard, refusing to look up, though his grimace said he'd seen it before. Emi buried her head in her hands, leaning in against Sage's side as if for comfort.

Nieve sucked in a long breath through her nose, exhaling through her mouth. "Ah, so much better."

Lani withdrew her own handkerchief and wet it with a little conjured water. "Clean your face, you're scaring the kids."

Nieve rolled her eyes. "Yes, Lani."

"Okay, Emi, you're up." Lani crouched in front of Emiko, touching her hands to Emi's throat. There wasn't a lot to heal, as Emi had only used one prolonged wind spell, but she was still chilled from sitting in Nieve's protective ice dome, so Lani made sure to improve circulation to help her warm up faster. Lani stood up, grinding her fists into her lower back to stretch before turning to face the two men. "Who's next? Sage?"

Aldis started forward, then stopped, shooting a questioning look over at Sage. Sage shook his head, waving Aldis forward as he continued squinting at the crystal shard.

"Quite a bit of mana strain," Aldis reported, looking put out for some reason. "Casting so many portals over such a long time isn't easy, you know."

"Yes, I'm sure." Lani tried to keep her tone neutral as she soothed the swollen muscles in Aldis's wrist and arm. She knew enough Wayfarers to know that portal magic was a much more difficult spell than teleportation, but Aldis had continually bragged about his travel specialization in his climber interview, making it sound as if he could cast portals for days without feeling an inch of strain. She wasn't surprised to find he'd overstated himself a bit, but it was something she'd remember if Aldis requested a reference when searching for a new team to join.

But for now, keeping Aldis healthy enough to continue climbing was the priority, so Lani put aside her annoyance and checked him with a diagnostic spell, healing a few other aches and bruises as well as checking the arrow wound from earlier. Once the task was complete, she dropped his arm and stepped back.

"Okay, Sage, are you—"

"Lani, where did you get this?" Sage asked, holding up the crystal shard. "I've never seen anything like this before. Were there any other pieces to it? Was this something you traded for?"

Lani blinked, startled. "No, I just found it. It was stuck to a soldier's uniform when I healed them yesterday. They thought it was a broken bone."

"No, this is . . . This is something." Sage held the crystal at its points, rolling it between his fingers. "I don't know what it is, but it's important."

"Important how?" Lani asked, her hand tapping a belt purse thoughtfully. "Is it a treasure?"

Aldis crowded in close, holding a hand over the shard while Emi grabbed a handful of Sage's belt and levered herself to her feet, pressing close to his side to peer at it. Lani felt irritated that her aura monocle was back with her gear at the barracks, preventing her from seeing whatever Sage was seeing.

"Oh my!" Aldis murmured, eyebrows lifting almost to his hairline. "That's not a Sapphire enchantment, is it? I've never seen anything like that before."

"Not Sapphire, no. And I don't think it's an enchantment." Sage sounded unsure of himself, eyes narrow as he stared at the shard. "This might not even be a standard aura. I think these colors might indicate mana types, rather than the colors of a shroud."

"You're seeing more than one color?" Lani asked, trying to keep the irritation out of her voice. "What colors are they?"

"Sorry, Lani." Sage ducked his head sheepishly. "One's a bright blue, the other is like a bluish purple. That's the best way I can describe it. But there aren't any runes, and these edges make it look like it was broken off of something. Maybe it's a piece of something bigger? It just feels incomplete to me."

"Maybe it's a key to something," Aldis suggested, sounding eager. "Have you heard those rumors? Treasure chests that require oddly shaped keys found throughout the spire? Or secret pathways to avoid challenges?"

"Maybe." Sage didn't sound convinced. "What does your Sense Life spell say about it, Lani? It isn't alive, is it?"

Lani's mouth pinched; she was frustrated with herself for not thinking of that first. It didn't look like a living thing, but that didn't mean it wasn't. She held a hand out toward it and cast a Sense Life spell on the shard. The spell would bathe anything living with a greenish aura that only Lani would see. The shard didn't take on such an aura, but the spell did reveal something.

"No life aura," Lani explained, moving to her left, then her right in order to examine the shard from more angles. "But there's something I've never seen before. It's almost like a . . . shadow?" Lani shrugged, finding it hard to describe. "It has this nebulous, filmy aura about it, but I have no idea what that means."

"How odd." Sage had his scholar's face on, the one he wore most often during more cerebral challenges. "Let me try something: Detect Spirit."

"Ah, I don't know that one," Aldis commented, looking slightly smug for some reason. "I understand that spirit is quite difficult to work with. I didn't have the time to practice any of those spells while focusing on my specialization."

Lani kept herself from rolling her eyes. Barely.

"I don't use it often," Sage admitted, speaking slowly, his eyes scanning the shard as if he were reading something. "I don't have much practice with it, but . . . I do think I see something. Just like Lani says, it's filmy and not clearly defined, but it looks like . . . a spider's web? Or like little lines stretching out in all directions, but they fade after only a few inches." Sage blinked hard like his eyes had gone dry, then shook his head. "I think it's trying to be a part of a whole again. Whatever this shard came from, it's still connected to its missing parts somehow."

"Can we trace those lines to their source?" Lani asked, intrigued. A puzzle this big had to result in some epic-level treasure. Her pulse sped up just thinking about it. "Maybe we're meant to use it as a compass."

"Maybe. I don't know." Sage shrugged as he handed the crystal shard back to Lani. "The lines don't seem to lead anywhere for now. I think we need to activate it somehow, first. For now, Aldis and I can keep an eye out for anything else that shows this aura pattern. I think finding more of its pieces might be the key to unlocking its power."

A scavenger hunt for broken shards with mysterious auras? Lani was already theorizing how much such a treasure might be worth as she took the shard back. There were people who liked to buy spire oddities as collection pieces, and an aura as odd as the one Sage described could certainly be worth a line of credit at the casino. If they found the whole treasure, it might be enough to earn Lani a high-roller tag for at least a week. Was it worth going back to where she'd found the shard initially? Or was this a challenge meant to take up multiple rooms of their current floor? Lani resolved to keep her aura monocle close at hand from now on, so she could keep an eye out for the mysterious aura as well.

"Did you try predicting its future?" Aldis asked, gazing at the shard in a way that made Lani feel defensive. She tucked it in a pocket, glaring at him until he shifted his gaze.

"I did earlier, but I didn't see anything." Sage touched his forehead, a pinched and pained expression on his face. "I probably just need to rest for a bit. Or eat something. I think the last time I ate was breakfast."

"Yes, food!" Nieve cheered, kicking her heels against the supply crate she was perched on. She'd been so quiet, Lani had nearly forgotten she was there. "I'm starved! Let's head to the mess hall and grab a bite before the troops get all the good vittles."

"Just a minute." Lani set her fingers against Sage's temples, easing his growing headache. "We still need to check in with Hane, set the watch rotation, and check for any more upcoming surprises."

Aldis muttered something under his breath that sounded like "pointless." Lani glared at him and he mumbled that he was reaching out to Hane. Rather than distract him, she pursed her lips and finished healing Sage.

"Well, Sage?" she asked, taking a step back. "Anything to report? Or are we looking at a quiet night?"

"We're not that lucky," Sage said with a rueful shake of his head. "I took a look ahead while you were in the healing tent. We've got stealth climbers coming in periodically through the night, most of them attuned."

"Are they trying to sneak in and open the gates?" Lani asked. "Or are they coming after a target?"

"Targets," Sage said promptly. "They're coming after us."

Nieve groaned theatrically, rolling back on her supply crate so her arms and legs hung over at awkward angles as she kicked and thrashed. "I hate assassination runs! The good fights are always at the end and I can never stay awake that long!"

"Is it— Do you fight in rotations?" Aldis asked, turning to Lani. At her nod, he continued. "So why not take the final rotation?"

"Nieve's adrenaline only lasts so long before she crashes," Lani explained. "She'll be good for the first rotation, but by the second she'll be exhausted." Lani drummed her fingers on her hip, feeling the tip of the crystal shard in her pocket. "We used to have Ren take the final watch; he was always good for an early-morning fight."

"When Wyle wasn't keeping him up late," Emi signed. Lani chuckled along with Nieve and Sage.

"Hm . . . without Ren—or Hane, rather . . ." Lani hummed thoughtfully.

"I can do it," Sage offered, looking tired yet hopeful as he adjusted his glasses. "It's better that I sleep sooner rather than later anyway; I used a lot of spells today and I need time to recover."

"Yes, but . . ." Lani hesitated. It wasn't that she doubted Sage's skills, except . . . well, she kind of did. Dueling was a far cry from facing assassins in the dark, especially when he was already tired from spellcasting. "Maybe we need a different approach for the harder fights. Sage, team up with Aldis. If you can predict where the assassins are coming from, Aldis can port them back down to the ground again. Or just drop them, if that takes the same mana cost."

Aldis grumbled, starting to cross his arms but flinching as the motion reminded him of the soreness in his mana-burned hand and wrist. He opened and closed his hand, as if loosening some stiffness. "Watch shifts and night fights. Any chance of a nap tomorrow?"

Sage shrugged. "Looking that far ahead is useless right now. What happens tomorrow will be based on how well we handle the assassins."

"No matter what we do, the teams are uneven," Lani said, thinking out loud. "With Nieve on the first shift and Aldis and Sage on the last, someone is going to have to take two shifts."

"Nah," Nieve said, groaning as she pushed herself up to sitting. "The first wave is always the easiest, so just leave it to me. You and Emi can take the middle shift, and then you can kick those two out of bed for the last one." She jerked her chin at Sage and Aldis, who each gave her a grudging look. "I can use some of my guys from the demo teams earlier, too. We'll be fine."

There was no evidence to support Nieve's assertion, but it seemed a safe bet as long as the assassination run followed the typical pattern of beginning soft, then building up to stronger fighters near the end.

"Sage, what time will the attacks begin?"

"Just after nightfall." He hedged his answer. "The assassins will start climbing the walls at nightfall. It'll take longer for them to actually reach the top of the walls. And they can be knocked down if you can find them before they reach the top."

"Watch out for invisibility spells," Nieve added. "Hey, Sage!" He dodged as she chucked her bloodied handkerchief at him, earning a look of brotherly condescension from him. "Did you happen to see if any of the assassins are this hooded woman named Ana? I fought her over the gate earlier."

"I'm not looking that specifically, even if I were inclined to give you that information." Making a disgusted face, Sage prodded the ball of blood and snot with his dueling cane. A cone of brilliant light radiated from the end of it, bright enough that Lani couldn't look directly at it. When the light went away, the handkerchief was crumpled but looked clean of the mess Nieve had made of it. A cleansing spell made of light mana: that was a new one. Sage must have been studying hard since the last climb.

"Thanks, friend." Nieve grinned. "Toss that back to me?"

"No, I don't think I will." Sage scraped the end of his cane against the hard-packed earth, as if even the light spell wasn't enough to purify Nieve's handkerchief. "If I had fire mana, I would have burned it."

"Mean." Nieve kicked her heel against the supply crate. Nieve's smirk and sudden, intense eye contact made Lani shift her weight back on her heels. "Hey, wanna hit the baths after dinner? We have until nightfall, right? You scrub my back, I'll scrub yours."

Goddess, a bath did sound good, but what was up with that grin on Nieve's face? It looked almost sinister.

"I want a bath!" Emi spoke up, hand up in the air as if volunteering for something exciting. "I'll scrub your back, Nieve!"

Nieve looked half annoyed and half amused, but Sage, scowling lightly, spoke up before she could.

"Actually, Lani, I was hoping we might take a minute to consult about the . . . item I got from the trading sequence," Sage said, looking slightly flushed. "I wanted to look it over in case there was a clue on it. You still have it, right?"

Lani set her hand over the satchel on her belt, feeling the weight of the gun inside. "Yes, I have it. You can't See who needs it?"

Sage shook his head, one hand toying with a pouch tied to his belt. "I haven't tried looking yet, but it felt right when I gave it to you. I think you must have the better relationship with whoever needs it. I thought we might talk about it after dinner?"

"Is it not still the Crowns board?" Aldis asked, looking confused. "When did you find time for a trade?"

"It was an unexpected path," Sage admitted, with a shrug. "But I'm pretty sure this is what gets us the key."

"I don't know who would want it, but I can hang on to it for now." Lani said, setting her hand over the satchel hooked to her belt. "But I think we've all pushed it hard enough for today. Food, then bed. No unnecessary spells or revels tonight."

"But baths?" Emi asked with wide, hopeful eyes.

"Yes, baths," Lani agreed with a weary sigh. "Food first, though."

"And drinks!" Nieve crowed, jumping down from the supply crate. She stepped on her own handkerchief as she attempted to throw an arm over Sage's neck. He ducked her, walking backward to keep his distance. "Let's go! Want me to scrub your back for you later, Sage?"

"No. I don't even want to turn my back on you." Sage unhooked his dueling cane from his belt, using it to keep Nieve at a distance. "You should probably bathe before you eat anything. You smell almost as offensive as you look."

"C'mere, gimme a hug!"

"I *will* blast you."

Emiko shook her head indulgently, pinching the corner of Nieve's handkerchief as she lifted it. She waved cheerily before following after Nieve and

Sage, headed toward the mess hall. Lani was dismayed to find herself alone with Aldis.

The feeling, it seemed, was mutual.

"Hane's asleep," he reported, face grim as if he expected her to berate him. "I think they were in a fight earlier, around the same time we were. They're not hurt, but that's all I know."

Lani sighed, turning her face toward the lake, though she couldn't see it with the fort's walls in the way. "If it were anyone else, I'd want someone to go check on them and make sure everything's all right. I'm afraid they'd be insulted, though, given how strong they are." She wavered a moment, then considered Aldis. "Do you have the mana reserves for it? To pop over to the lake and check on Hane?"

"I'd rather eat and let my mana recover, if it's all the same," Aldis said with a shrug. "If they're fine, they're not going to thank me for checking up on them. If they're not fine, I don't want to meet the monster that got them."

Lani frowned at his cowardice but couldn't fault his logic. Hane was a frontline fighter and a top-notch one at that. They weren't the type of climber who forgot things like rations or volunteered for tasks that were above their level. And sending Aldis on his own seemed needlessly risky, especially as rest and recovery was the best thing for mana strain, despite her healing.

"Fine. I have to go talk to the commander anyway, I'll see if he can't spare an exploration team to head out to the lake and see if they can't find Hane. You should go eat and rest with the others. I'll be there shortly."

"Okay." Aldis shifted his weight, as if to go, but his eyes dropped to Lani's hips. No, not her hips. The satchel Sage had given her. "Excuse me, but I'm dying of curiosity. What did he trade that beautiful Crowns set for?"

Oh, right. Aldis had been following Sage's trading sequence almost from the beginning of the scenario. It made sense he'd want to know. Lani flipped open the satchel, showing him without taking it out.

"He didn't tell me what happened," Lani explained. "He just asked me to hold on to it so it wouldn't get lost while he was popping back and forth."

"Ah." Aldis reached out as if to touch the gun, then thought better of it, drawing his hand back to his chest. "I much preferred the Crowns set."

"I don't even know if this is loaded," Lani mused thoughtfully, tying the satchel closed again. "You know, firearms aren't a bad weapon for Wayfarers. Wyle didn't use one, but she thought about getting one. Some Wayfarers use them to great advantage."

"Yes, but they're also heavy, expensive, and you have to keep buying ammunition for them, or so I've come to understand," Aldis pointed out. "My dueling cane works fine. Although, if we happened to find one during our climb—one that's not part of a trading sequence—I might consider it."

"I hear they're hard to aim, too," Lani considered.

Aldis shrugged. "Not if you shoot through a portal."

"Cheater."

"House advantage."

Was that . . . was that a gambling joke? Lani was so taken aback, she couldn't even respond. Aldis looked uncomfortable, too, mumbling something about dinner before turning and skulking away. If it had been intentional, had it been meant as a barb? Or was he attempting to be friendly? To make up for first impressions? What was she supposed to think about that?

I miss Ren and Wyle, Lani thought unexpectedly. *Climbs were so much easier when I knew exactly what to expect from people.*

As much as she wanted to eat and bathe, Lani reported to the command center first, informing the fort commander of Sage's prediction of assassins during the night, as well as requesting a team of outriders to head to the lake and check on Hane. The commander listened politely, agreeing with her recommendations, and then, very tactfully, asked Lani if she and her teammates already knew where the baths were located. Lani couldn't even bring herself to feel affronted: she knew exactly how terrible she looked after battle, never mind the way she smelled.

So despite her hunger, Lani opted to bathe first. The grime from sweat and the smell of blood and death lingered on her skin like a morbid bouquet, dulling the edge of her hunger anyway. And bathing alone was so much more relaxing than bathing with her teammates. Even if Sage and Nieve weren't arguing like children, she'd still catch them sneaking glances at her missing fingertips, and that just wasn't something she felt up to dealing with tonight.

The fort had no bathhouses, only tubs of water that were freshened periodically, and thin wooden screens for privacy. The basins were big enough for maybe three people if no one minded getting a little cozy, but for now the tubs were empty. It seemed everyone else from today's battle had opted for food over cleanliness. Still, Lani took a moment to set privacy screens around her selected tub and grabbed a basket of bathing supplies, setting it on a stool within easy reach.

She didn't peel her gloves off until she had stripped nearly the rest of her clothing away, feeling the padded portions that hid her missing fingertips. She flexed her hands, noting the distant soreness of her left ring finger before slipping into the basin to wash.

She wasn't ashamed of her gambling habit—actually, for the most part she was quite proud of her winning streaks. And when she lost, well, that was part of the game and she took her losses graciously. No, what she couldn't stand was the pity in her friends' eyes when they saw she'd lost another toss she couldn't afford to pay in time. No, Sage, Nieve, and Emiko never said anything directly against her gambling—not anymore, at least—but that didn't stop the sympathetic looks and the unsolicited offers of financial assistance. Lani didn't want their help in paying her debts: she just wanted to be allowed to win or lose as fate decreed. That was it.

The water was cool enough that Lani bathed hurriedly, dunking her head beneath the water, then reaching over the rim of the tub for soap and scrub-stone. With her hair bound in tight braids, she didn't bother to wash it so much as rinse it, wringing it out once she was sure she'd gotten all the battle-field gore out of it. She scrubbed her skin hard enough to feel scraped raw by the time she finally felt clean. After that, it was simply a matter of picking dried blood out from under her fingernails.

At least I have fewer fingernails than most people, Lani told herself with no small amount of dark humor. Even so, she only finished one hand before she was shivering too much to continue. She sloshed out of the tub, wrapping a towel around herself and taking a seat on a nearby bench, where she continued cleaning her nails.

Something glittered in the small pile of her folded clothes. Lani squinted at it briefly before realizing it was the shard she'd had Sage examine. It must have fallen out of her pocket when she'd disrobed.

A blue and bluish-purple aura, Lani mused, grateful for the distraction from the cold. *No, Sage said it wasn't an aura. Mana types, maybe? What mana types would be blue and bluish-purple? I'll have to take a look at it through my monocle later.*

Water mana, maybe? Or air? Lani couldn't remember what mana type was associated with purple, never mind bluish-purple. It would help her to see the colors for herself. Maybe Sage had some notes about colors being associated with mana types. It would be easier to speculate if she knew what the colors meant.

Not all spire treasures were tangible rewards that could be sold for a profit, and often the more arduous a challenge or a task, the more detail-oriented, or time-consuming, or more insurmountable-seeming, the more likely the reward would be akin to a visage's favor. An additional attunement, perhaps, or boosted growth to an existing attunement. As enticing as that possibility was to most climbers, Lani would trade it for a trunk full of gold in a hummingbird's heartbeat.

Lani wouldn't roll the dice on Katashi's favor securing a fresh line of credit for her at the casino.

Lani needed a big win this time: after two months between climbs, she'd run through all her savings and exhausted every line of credit she could get her hands on. She could only hope to earn enough on this climb to tide over her gambling habit while she and Nieve interviewed new teammates again. Or she could just win big: she was due for a windfall any day now.

Her nails finally clean, Lani looped her braids up into a bun, then rushed to pull her clothes on. As she grabbed her leggings, the crystal shard rolled away into a small puddle left when she'd climbed out of the tub. After tugging her boots on over bare feet (she was *not* putting those gross socks back on), she stooped to pick the crystal shard up.

Then promptly dropped it in surprise.

The crystal . . . it was humming!

Lani stared dumbly down at it, half-concerned it might be dangerous, then startled at the sound of voices nearby. She moved aside a privacy screen as she recognized the voices of her teammates.

"Lani, you washed already? No fair!" Nieve called, her battered leather tunic already peeled off and set aside. "Come back and join us! Mi-mi's gonna heat up the water, but only for the ladies."

"Lani said no unnecessary spells!" Sage argued. "And using a whole fire mana crystal for only one bath is a waste, anyway. It could easily warm up two baths."

"Wait, before you undress—just wait." Lani pointed down at the crystal at her feet. "That shard from earlier. It's . . . I don't know, it's like it's humming or vibrating, or something."

A silent pause, then a sudden rush over to Lani's tub. Nieve nearly stepped on the shard in her haste. Emi crouched down and poked at it.

"Is it?" Emi asked, doubtfully. "I don't hear anything."

"The colors haven't changed," Sage observed, fingertips pressed against his glasses. "Maybe you struck it against something and you felt the vibrations."

"No, I—maybe." As cold and hungry as she was, Lani couldn't be certain Sage was wrong. "But this isn't the first time it's done this. I keep thinking it's . . . I don't know, reacting to something."

"It's not doing anything now," Emiko said, holding the shard up to the light. "I don't hear anything or feel anything. What do you think it was reacting to?"

"Maybe it was one of the mana types it's tied to!" Aldis said eagerly, looking around as if he expected to find a clue lying about in plain sight. "Were you casting any spells? Did it indicate a direction? Was the humming constant, or did it pulse like a rhythm or a wave?"

"I only picked it up from where it fell," Lani explained with a shrug. "I wasn't casting a spell and the vibrations didn't last long enough for me to tell if there was any rhythm to it."

"Try dropping it," Aldis suggested. "Maybe falling did something to it."

"But that wasn't—" Too late: Emi had already let the shard fall from her fingers. With the anticipation of a withheld breath, everyone watched and waited—so of course, nothing happened.

"Maybe I am tired," Lani admitted reluctantly. "I probably should have eaten before washing."

"We're all tired," Sage said sympathetically. "I can walk you back to the mess hall, if you want. Or the barracks, if you just want some rations before you go to bed."

"She doesn't want you walking her anywhere until you stop smelling like a dead octopus at low tide," Nieve taunted, scooping up a handful of water from the tub and splashing it at Sage. "And if she's that tired, she could just ask Aldis to—"

A shrill squeal from Emiko cut everyone off, Nieve and Lani reaching for swords that weren't on their belts at the moment. Emi had stooped to pick up the crystal again, but now, faintly but entirely unmistakably, the slim shard was humming. Drawing her hand back a few times, Emi bit her lower lip, then snatched up the crystal as if it were venomous. She held it at arm's length, goose bumps rippling up her arm.

"It's shivering!" Emi exclaimed, wide-eyed. "I can feel it. It feels like . . . like it's whispering."

"The colors still haven't changed," Sage said, Aldis nodding as if in confirmation. "Maybe somewhere nearby someone's using the right type of spell to activate it, but I thought we were the only attuned in the whole—"

"The water!" Lani gasped. "It fell into a puddle just now. And my hands were wet when I touched it at the medic tent!"

Nieve grabbed the shard from Emi's hand and plunged it into the tub, holding it submerged for long moments. Lani itched to reach in and take it from her, or at least touch it to feel what Nieve was feeling. The others crowded around the tub, staring intently at the shard.

"It's definitely vibrating," Nieve said, holding the shard in a fist. "Has it changed at all? Aura-wise?"

"You can use Detect Aura, too, Nieve," Sage reminded her drily. "But no, it hasn't."

"It seems a bit sharper, though, doesn't it?" Aldis asked. "The colors, I mean. The pattern seems more distinct somehow."

Lani held a hand over the water's surface, casting her Sense Life spell. The crystal still failed to register an aura of life, but the hazy shadow she had seen earlier almost seemed to flicker and surge with movement. Or maybe that was just an effect of the vibrations under the water?

"Sage, can you try Detect Spirit again?" Lani requested. "Just in case it's trying to point us toward a piece of itself?"

Sage touched his glasses, the skin around his eyes looking pinched and shadowed. Lani felt chagrined: she should have waited until after Sage had rested to ask him for another spell. As bad as she felt for pushing him, Lani still waited anxiously to hear the results of the spell.

"The spirit aura is still really thin," Sage said shaking his head. "I might just be tired, but I can't see any change. It's actually harder to see under the water. I can try again tomorrow, though."

"Do you think it has a connection to water mana?" Aldis mused, stroking his chin. "The blue color and the humming when wet seem to indicate some alignment with water. I wonder if searching the lake might yield any of its missing pieces?"

"Maybe the next time you check in with Hane, you can ask them to look for something like this," Lani suggested. "If there is a piece in the lake, it's likely it'll be part of the reward for defeating the lake monster."

"Or we could just go to the lake," Nieve suggested, drawing the shard from the tub, giving it a shake that sent water droplets flying. "Help Hane slay a water monster, then do a little searching. See if we can dig up another piece like this one."

"It might be a broader challenge than one contained in a single room," Sage pointed out. "Like a floor challenge rather than a room challenge."

"I thought the same thing earlier," Lani agreed, catching Nieve's hand and extracting the crystal shard. As she dried it off with a cloth, the humming abated. "We can ask Hane if they found anything like it at the lake, but based on how thin the spirit aura sounds, I think it more likely the pieces are farther away than the lake of this scenario."

"Well, at least we know it reacts to water," Nieve said, dropping down onto a bench. She began untying the laces of her boots, obviously still intending to wash up. "Maybe we can grab an empty jar from the mess hall and suspend it in water, like a compass. See if it points us anywhere special."

"That's not the worst idea," Sage admitted, looking pained to say so. "I don't think water is the mana type it's connected to. The blue is wrong, and it doesn't explain the purplish color. I can check my notes later, see if I have anything that equates colors to—"

Just then, Lani's stomach gurgled urgently, drawing stares from her teammates. With a rueful sigh, she dropped the shard into her pocket again.

"As exciting as this discovery is, I'm afraid I won't last much longer without eating something. And you all need to bathe." Lani smiled as she tugged one of Emiko's hair buns. "We'll pick this up later, okay? Maybe Hane will know something about it when they get back."

A muttered round of agreement, followed by the sounds of belts unbuckling and boots being kicked off. Sage scooped up a handful of water and dumped it down Nieve's back as she tugged off a boot, calling it payback for earlier. Lani slipped away before Nieve chucked Sage bodily into a tub. It was good to see her teammates relax after a long day, but all the same, she was grateful for having bathed earlier.

She was even more grateful for the lucky find that would hopefully line her pockets for her next trip to the casino.

Hours later, even after bathing and a heavy meal, Lani couldn't sleep. It wasn't the crystal shard keeping her awake, although she had begun to daydream about the treasures she hoped it might reveal. No, her sleep was troubled by the knowledge that Nieve was defending against an assassin attack all on her own, with only the spire constructs to watch her back. Nieve thought herself nigh indestructible, but Lani had put her back together one too many times to believe that anymore. Her conscience urged her to get up and simply remain awake through two watch shifts, but logic dictated she get what little rest she could while it was possible to do so.

Nieve would be fine; objectively, Lani knew that to be true. And she wasn't on her own, either; she had a platoon of armed and forewarned soldiers watching the walls alongside her. Forewarned was forearmed, and Nieve's battle prowess was respectable. Still, Lani hated that she was on watch alone.

And what of Hane? Asleep in the middle of the day, if Aldis was to be believed. Out in the wilds on their own, facing down a lake monster and whatever else lived down by the lake. Had they been injured? Did they still have their supplies? The unrest was almost bad enough for Lani to want to wake up Aldis and have him check on them, but that meant waking the irritable Wayfarer, and he had been the first to fall deeply asleep, snoring heavily almost as soon as his head hit the pillow. Waking him before his watch would start a fight Lani didn't want to deal with in the middle of the night. Still, it might be worthwhile to ask Aldis to check when she woke him for his shift later.

Exhausted but unable to find enough peace to sleep, Lani pulled the crystal shard out from beneath her pillow, holding it at the pointed ends to roll it between her fingers. She had finally gotten a chance to view it through her aura monocle, seeing the strange colors that Sage had attempted to describe. The blue was closer to turquoise and threaded through with swirls of indigo. Just the memory of it now was hypnotizing; even if the object proved worthless, Lani could still sell it to a collector for a moderate price. But she predicted it was far from useless.

Watching the dim light bounce through the crystal shard and create prismatic rainbows made Lani think of the spin of the Tiles wheel. She could almost hear the soft *tick-tick-tick* as the wheel spun, lulling her slowly to sleep. The crystal was just about as heavy as her eyelids when Sage thrashed violently in his bed, rolling out of it and fighting off the blanket as if it had attacked him.

"Something big!" he gasped, catching Lani's eyes in the near dark. "No, powerful! Something—it's coming!"

Lani was out of bed and pulling her boots on—they all slept in their gear during scenarios—before she started asking questions. "How sure are you? Is this just a nightmare, or a vision?"

"Hard to tell the difference," Sage admitted, still wild-eyed as he tried pulling his boots on the wrong feet. "Emi! Aldis! Up! Nieve might be in danger!"

Emi slid off the bunk over Lani's, scrubbing determinedly at her eyes and mumbling to herself. She conjured water cupped between her hands and splashed her face with it before lashing her mana diffuser around her waist. She got it upside down the first time and had to try again.

"I swear, if you people run attack drills in the middle of the night, I'm making a complaint against your team in the official registry!" Aldis grouched, the only one of them who had to pull on his dueling tunic over his shirt. "Overnight watches! Rotating assassin shifts! Midnight panics!"

"What did you think the nineteenth floor would be like?" Lani snapped, slipping the crystal shard into her pocket. Ever since the vibration discovery, she'd been loath to part with it. "The first floor wasn't exactly kittens and rainbows either, so suck it up!"

"There was that one room," Emi mused, looking almost drunk with sleep. She rolled to the floor in almost slow motion while attempting to pull on her boot. "Weren't there rainbows? They cut things, like knives."

Lani looped her braids into a knot at the back of her head, sparing just enough time to glare at Emiko's two perfect hair buns, then dashed to the door with Sage at her side. The other two could catch up.

The fort was eerily deserted, lit only by orange torchlight at posted guard stations. Lani scanned the walls, but she couldn't make out Nieve's silhouette against the night sky. She wasn't down already, was she? Lani couldn't imagine Nieve losing a fight without alerting the entire base to the battle first, but she'd heard of stranger things happening in the higher levels of the spire. She sprinted up the stairs to the ramparts, Sage close behind. Both were panting hard as they arrived at the top, but nothing could have prepared them for what awaited them.

Nieve stood with one foot braced against a crenellation, her arms folded over her knee. She looked mildly alarmed to see them at the top of the stairs, but other than that, she looked fine. Maybe bored. Emi and Aldis appeared opposite her a moment later, earning a second raised eyebrow. Nieve scratched her chin idly.

"Did Sage have a bad dream?" she asked, turning back toward Lani and Sage.

"Oh, for the love of the goddess!" Aldis threw his hands up in the air. "Really? All that for nothing?"

"No," Sage protested, his face going red as Lani turned toward him. "No, it— I'm sure! Something is coming." He swallowed hard and looked around. "How many assassin attacks have there been? What attunements did they have?"

"None." Nieve's face soured.

"All unattuned?" Sage sounded puzzled.

"None, as in: no attacks." Nieve stomped her boot down, an expression of deep annoyance written on her face. "There hasn't been a single attack. And I've been using that Detect Mind spell you taught me, so they're not getting by using invisibility. So where's the enemy, Sage?"

"I've been telling you that my glasses don't work the same on these levels, so my Sight is less reliable on this floor," Sage said defensively. "But still, I know I Saw this. The attacks and now . . . now something . . ."

Sage's hand cupped his forehead, almost as if he were in pain. Lani set a hand on his shoulder bracingly.

"We knew the possibility of it being a dream," she counseled, trying to sound calm though inwardly she was just as disappointed and upset as the others. Waking up in a panic was no way to approach a challenge. "Look, Nieve, I'm sorry you didn't get your fight, but why not trade out now for—"

"Look!" Emi was lying flat over a crenellation, pointing to something in the distance. "There, do you see?"

Lani rushed to the wall, Sage and Nieve taking up positions beside her. Aldis cast a scowl downward, then lifted his eyebrows in surprise.

"Aldis!" Lani ordered, but the Wayfarer was already in motion, casting his hand out and activating a teleportation spell. A breath later, Hane stood atop the wall along with them, looking moderately surprised to see them all.

"I didn't want to wake you by asking for a portal," Hane explained, mostly to Aldis. "Are you all awake tonight because we're not expecting an attack tomorrow?"

"No, there's—" Sage stopped himself, leaning over the wall to look down. "There was supposed to be an attack tonight."

Hane cocked their head to the side. "Were they attuned, decked out in wall climbing gear?"

"Er, probably?" Sage guessed.

Hane shrugged. "I ran into a group like that on my way here. I handled it."

Lani exchanged a look with Sage. They *handled* it?

"What kind of monster is in the lake?" Nieve asked eagerly. "Is it big? Can we take it? We might have a little time right now if you took care of the assassins."

Hane fell quiet a moment, then tugged on the strap of their satchel over their shoulder, pulling it forward. The bag appeared empty, but when Hane reached into it and turned it upside down, a spill of mana crystals, weapons, and even armor spilled out onto the walkway.

"Oooh!" Emi raced forward, burying her hands in the mana crystals, most likely looking for ones she could use in her mana diffuser. "So many water crystals! Oh, here's an enhancement crystal! Ah! And transference!"

Lani chuckled, elbowing Sage in the ribs. "I think I found your something powerful. Lucky for us, they're on our side."

"But, how . . ." Sage still looked perplexed, like he wasn't entirely certain what he was seeing was real.

"Next time," Hane said, quietly but seriously. "Please check for escort quests."

CHAPTER 11

ḢANE

Wavewalker (leg mark), Citrine

W e'll try to check in regularly, but until we know what we're facing, we won't know what timing between communiqués will look like," Lani said, addressing the team as she tugged at the edges of her gloves. "Let's follow the standard six-hour wait before assuming anything has gone terribly wrong. Aldis, you'll be able to send a message immediately in case we have to ring out for safety, right?"

"Goddess, don't let it come to that," Aldis prayed fervently, tearing his eyes away from Lani's hands in order to look skyward beseechingly. He sighed heavily when no saving grace seemed forthcoming. "The warning will sound something like 'Bell, bell, bell' and if you hear that, you can assume that I have already shaken my return bell."

"And will you send that to just one of us back at the fort, or—"

"This is stupid!" Nieve declared, cutting over Sage's quite practical question. "We shouldn't be splitting the party. If you three are going to the enemy camp, then we should all be going to the enemy camp together."

Hane faded back from the group, letting them rehash the argument they'd already had over breakfast. It was hard to slip away completely while the six of them stood alone on the rampart over the gate, but there was a small patch of shade cast by an observation tower that provided the illusion of slipping away. Hane eyed it wistfully, wondering if it was worth it to try to catch a quick nap.

They'd managed a few hours of sleep the night before, but even though Lani had offered to let them sleep in thanks to handling the assassination situation so succinctly, it had seemed more prudent to get up and actually act like a member of the team for once. The young kitsune's escort had taken longer than expected, and then upon completion, the village of kitsune hosted Hane for dinner and a night of rest, both of which Hane accepted gratefully. The kitsune also gifted Hane with a handsome reward: a fox-fur bedroll as plush and deep as a mattress, even though it folded up as small as a shirt. Hane usually took their cut of treasure in coins or gems unless they found something particularly useful, like their dimensional bag, but they were seriously contemplating keeping the fox-fur bedroll as part of their cut. Of course, they'd wait to bring it up until there was more of a haul than just what they had found in the lake after defeating the lake serpent.

It would have been nice if their first suggestion of how to work as a team hadn't been met with obstinate objections, though.

Attacking the enemy camp now, while they were all somewhat rested and between foreseeable attacks, truly was the wisest course of action for this scenario, but it was also prudent to leave behind a defense force to protect the ultimate objective, which was defending the fort. It should have been an easy decision. Most of the team agreed on that much, at least.

No, the part they couldn't seem to agree on was who should go and who should stay behind.

Hane had already offered their professional opinion, so all they could do now was wait for the rather spirited discussion to end.

"It isn't a matter of trust, Lani," Sage was saying, keeping his tone reasonable. "It's just that we all function better as a team. It would make me feel better if you weren't going alone with two new climbers." He cringed before adding: "No offense, you two. It's just that we've been climbing together for a really long time."

Hane wasn't bothered at all; in fact, they doubted that was actually the reason behind Sage's objection, but if it made him feel better to couch it like that, that was fine.

"Oh, by all means, take my spot on the advance team," Aldis said, waving graciously. "I would much rather stay in the nice, safe fortress with actual beds and regular meals. A Seer would be a much more valuable asset to a strike team, wouldn't you both say?"

Aldis looked first at Lani, realized that was hopeless, then turned pleading eyes on Hane. Hane said nothing, meeting the stare evenly until Aldis looked away, muttering darkly under his breath. It wasn't that taking a Seer was a bad idea, but if they took Sage with them, it left the team at the fort too blind for safety. For a strike team, Hane favored mobility over foresight. Considering the team they had to work with, this was the best division of skills.

"We're not wasting any more time over this," Lani said decisively. "You three"—she pointed to Nieve, Sage, and Emiko—"are staying here and holding down the fort. The rest of us are scouting out the enemy camp with the intention of reporting back what to expect. We are not going there to start a fight."

Hane noted that that, at least, took a little of the fire out of Nieve's eyes. She crossed her arms and turned slightly away from the group but didn't offer further argument. Sage was the one who still seemed anxious about the decision. Well, he and Aldis both, but for seemingly different reasons.

"We'll be fine here!" Emiko, the diminutive Cloudcaller, promised brightly. Initially, she had objected to splitting the party, but she'd been the first to see reason and the quickest to agree that this was the best division of the group's talents. Hane suspected it went deeper than simple tactics, though. Despite the others treating her a bit like a younger sister, Hane read Emiko as an old soul—like someone who saw much and listened more but only said what was necessary. It was good this group had someone like that; it was likely the reason they'd lasted so many years as a closed unit. Emiko latched onto Sage's arm and leaned her head against his shoulder. "It'll be a good little break for us. Nieve can train the soldiers, Sage can meditate, and I can rest my voice. Win-win-win!"

That only made Aldis pout all the more about being forced to go, but it seemed everyone had collectively agreed to ignore his poor mood. A solid tactic, in Hane's opinion. Why did the man even bother climbing if he valued safety that much? There was nothing safe about the spires.

"Good. I expect you to keep those two in line, Emi." Lani said it like she was joking, but Hane couldn't see it as such. They expected that Emiko would, in fact, be the one maintaining the peace between Nieve and Sage.

Nieve made a disgruntled noise. "You think the pipsqueak can keep me in line? You'd have better luck leaving the Seer in charge."

"Yes, because you've never done *anything* after Sage specifically told you not to do it," Emiko replied, rolling her eyes. "Like the time he clearly told you the food was poisoned and you ate it anyway."

"It wasn't poisoned," Nieve sniffed. "It had just . . . gone bad."

"You still could have avoided it," Sage muttered. "Would have saved the rest of us from having to deal with the fallout."

"Oh, you guys were uncomfortable?" Nieve asked, affronted. "I was the one who had to keep running to the privy every five minutes!"

"It was an open-trench privy," Sage shot back. "We all suffered for your mistake."

"If you had told me the food was rotten instead of lying about it being poisoned—"

Emiko grabbed Nieve by the belt and tugged her close enough to climb up onto her back, placing one elbow on Sage's shoulder to lean on him as well. "We'll be fine here, Lani! You three be safe!"

Some good-natured jostling and threatening grins were exchanged, hitting Hane with an unexpected wave of nostalgia—siblings who weren't siblings, arguments that were more laughter than ire. Children too young to be left alone inside a spire . . . Hane cleared their head with a deep breath, bringing their focus back to the present.

"Should we go?" Hane asked, looking to Lani. "Now is the best time to get into position to cause some damage before the enemy army starts mobilizing."

"Yes, we should go." Lani cast one final admonishing glare at her longtime teammates before turning and facing out over the gate. With a resigned sigh, Aldis stepped up beside her, bracing his hands on the low wall as he followed Lani's gaze with morose reluctance. "The enemy army always approaches from that direction, but we don't want to be too exposed. What about the hilly area over that way?" Lani pointed. "Can you place us right there and let us get our bearings?"

"If they're camped close to that spot, they could have lookouts anywhere through there," Aldis warned. "I might drop us right on top of a scouting party."

"Then you can always bring us right back," Lani countered in an overly sweet tone.

"Don't bother," Hane put in. "If there are scouts, we can just take care of them and move on. It doesn't matter if they know we're there, it can't change the next attack significantly."

"Unless they kill us," Aldis muttered.

"The hillock with the willow, please," Lani said, holding her hand out to Aldis. "Willows mean a water source, which is a good place to lay low."

Before Aldis could voice—or rather, mutter—another protest, Hane clapped a hand over his shoulder a bit more firmly than necessary. Aldis glowered sulkily but seemed to get the message. He set his hand delicately over Lani's, as if trying to touch it as little as possible, then cast the teleport spell to move them from the wall to the indicated willow-topped hill. Hane was moving before their feet even touched the grass, dropping into a crouch, one hand reaching back for their tonfa. Lani and Aldis dropped each other's hands immediately, looking around at their surroundings.

"Nothing here," Hane said, straightening from their crouch. "We're still too far to see anything of the camp. Give me a moment and I'll climb up to get our bearings."

They didn't wait to hear any protests or cutting remarks but sprang up lightly into the tendril-like branches of the willow. Rather than snap the branches, Hane extended their shroud out around them, suffusing it with transference mana in order to distribute their weight more evenly among the branches so they would hold. It was no use leaving broken branches to inform a clever scout that enemies were near. They peeked out from the leaves at the north-facing side of the tree, squinting into the distance, noting tracks and trails rutted into the earth from the movement of the war machines. There wasn't a true road from the enemy camp to the fortress, but there was a packed-earth trail formed by the march of hundreds of booted feet, giving them something to follow back to the source.

Hane dropped lightly from the tree, avoiding branches with taps and touches of transference mana and landing in a soft crouch. They were surprised to find only Aldis waiting at the base of the tree. He was peeling a tiny orange with his fingernails and looking particularly sullen.

"She went that way," Aldis said, pointing east along the trickling stream. "Scouting, she said. Seems a tad irresponsible, considering she's our healer, but that woman does not like listening to sense."

There was nothing to say to that, so Hane elected to ignore it. "The enemy scouts leave trails where they commonly patrol. There's a tall hill to the east that the patrols circle around. Lots of good cover and it looks out over the encampment. When Lani gets back, that's where we should go."

Aldis muttered to himself as he cupped the rind of the orange in one hand, then made it vanish. After popping a tiny section of orange into his mouth, he gestured with a hand, opening a small, circular portal in front of himself. "East, you said?"

"Yes." Hane moved to stand shoulder to shoulder, looking down over the terrain through Aldis's viewing portal. "That one."

"Hmph." Aldis ate another orange slice. "Should be fine. Once the Acolyte gets back." Aldis waved a hand and the portal disappeared. He glanced up, looking around as if searching for Lani. "Did you know she was a gambler before you joined the team?"

Hane shrugged. "I saw her hands during the interview. It doesn't bother me."

"Oh." Aldis toyed with his orange, looking somehow abashed. "Maybe she wore gloves to my interview. I didn't notice."

Again, there was no appropriate response, so Hane kept their silence. There were no citations against Lani in the climber registry for taking more than her fair share of treasure, and that was all Hane cared about. That, and the team's safety record. To have climbed so high without government sponsorship was remarkable, and even more so that it had been years since they'd had to invite new climbers to the team. Hane suspected they might be recruiting more often than they expected to. They were just about to begin the truly dangerous floors of the Tortoise Spire.

"Hey. Sorry." Lani emerged from the brush around the spring's bank, running a hand back over her hair to free a few leaves and twigs. "I didn't see anyone, but I think I found a patrol path that comes close to us here."

Hane nodded. "I found us a vantage point. Aldis says he can take us there."

Lani's lips formed a thin, straight line, but she nodded and came close enough to hold her hand out to Aldis. Aldis grimaced before taking both Hane and Lani by the hand and casting a teleport spell once more.

"We don't need to hold hands," Aldis grumbled, once again dropping Lani's hand as if it burned. "I can teleport each of us each individually rather than all at once."

"One teleport spell costs less mana than three teleport spells," Lani replied tartly. "At least, that's what our last Wayfarer said."

"It's true, but—"

Hane made a sharp gesture, waving them both into silence. They were close enough here that Hane could hear the distant sounds of the enemy camp: the low rumble of voices, the metallic sounds associated with blacksmithing, the beasts of burden calling to each other in pens. Hane motioned for the others to be silent and to follow them up to the crest of the hill so they could peer down at the camp below. Side by side, they pressed flat against the ground, lifting the lowest branches of bushes and parting grasses in order to look down without being observed.

The enemy camp appeared to be made up almost entirely of humans living out of simple A-frame tents pitched in orderly rows. Temporary shelters had been built to house supplies in the center of the camp. Cook fires were spaced about regularly among the tents. A foul stench on the air indicated that at least one privy had been dug somewhere nearby, which Hane decided to count as lucky: privies weren't generally areas guarded with great vigilance.

Most notable of the army were the massive pens of creatures held at the forefront of the campsite, near the trodden path leading to the fortress. It was difficult to make out any distinct species from this distance, but at least a few appeared to be bipedal, while most of the others were four-legged. The fences penning the creatures in were a joke: slim branches or saplings laid across Y-shaped posts weren't much for keeping anything enclosed, much less monsters intended to attack a heavily defended fortress.

"Must be a barrier keeping them in," Lani whispered, indicating the monster pens with a jut of her chin. "If it's an enchanted item, we might be able to break it. Think those fences are enchanted?"

"Could be," Hane replied. "Maybe an Architect could fashion a temporary holding pen like that, but I think it's more likely some sort of magical barrier."

"The monster pens?" Aldis asked, on his hands and knees but not lying flat as Hane and Lani were. His voice could have been softer, too, but at least no patrols were close enough to hear him. "It looks like a proximity teleportation field. I can see the perimeter runes etched into the fence posts."

"Are you sure?" Lani asked, though Hane could have told her that was the wrong question.

Predictably, Aldis bristled. "I may not be as well versed as Sage when it comes to general runes, but I make it my business to recognize any and all runes in relation to teleportation. Especially anti-teleportation runes, the bane of any Wayfarer's existence. So yes, I am sure."

Lani pursed her lips, no doubt restraining herself from further comment.

"You said proximity teleportation," Hane whispered. "Not anti-teleportation, right? Can you explain the difference?"

"Yes." Aldis looked a little more smug than necessary as he explained. "Anti-teleportation prevents teleportation magic from working at all. Proximity teleportation makes it so any being approaching the edge of the perimeter field—marked on the fence posts there—will be automatically teleported back to the anchor location, set somewhere in the pen's center. I'd bet those stone monoliths in the center of the pens hold the anchor to the spell."

Hane nodded, accepting this as a subject of expertise from the Wayfarer. "Can we bring the field down by destroying one of the runed fence posts from the outside?"

"If you broke it from a distance, with a spell rather than an object. You see the patrolling guards down there?" Aldis pointed, his finger following an armed soldier. "You can tell by the tracks that they're keeping the center of the walkways between the pens. Get too close, and the runes will teleport you to the anchor. Or anything you throw at the post to break it."

That was a lot of good information; even Lani looked mildly impressed.

"I can break the posts with transference mana," Hane whispered. "I don't have to get too close for that."

"What's the plan from there? Let all the monsters run around pell-mell, attacking each other as much as the enemy soldiers? And where are you in all of that? Getting eaten? Starting fights with an entire army?" Rather than wait for an answer, Aldis pulled back through the brush, muttering to himself as he cast a spell. Hane eased back to follow him, Lani just a beat behind.

Aldis created another viewing portal, this one hovering above the monster pens so they could look down from a bird's-eye view. He muttered as he counted, his portal moving slowly to scope out the terrain below. The pens seemed to contain only one type of monster in each of them, but each pen held between fifty to a hundred individual monsters. Hane could identify only a few of them from the distance of the viewing portal; most appeared more bestial than humanoid, but that wasn't necessarily a mark of intelligence among spire monsters.

". . . Eleven, twelve," Aldis finished, closing his fist and snapping the portal shut. "Twelve different pens down there with goddess only knows how many monsters. How many could you feasibly break before you'd get chased out of there, either by the monsters or the guards? And who's to say some of those monsters won't go running to the fort anyway?"

Hane considered the problem silently for a moment. Getting away wasn't the trouble, but Aldis was right: there was a limit to how many pens they could feasibly open.

"And what's your plan?" Lani asked directly. "Head back to the fort and wait for the stampede to trample us?"

"I think some form of sabotage is appropriate," Aldis replied defensively. "Perhaps we can poison the food they give these creatures so that they're in no state to attack when the time comes."

Lani looked to be considering that, but Hane shook their head. "The fact that these monsters are penned in means they aren't here of their own free will. We're not going to poison prisoners trapped in their cells, especially when they've done nothing to us first."

"You're right. It feels dirty." Lani tapped a belt pouch lightly. "If there was a way to direct any aggression away from the fort and focus only on the encampment, that would be best. Either that or . . . Hey!" She turned to Aldis so suddenly he leaned away. "Can you teleport the monsters out of the pens?"

Aldis gave her a withering look. "I could free about thirty of them that way before running out of mana. Portals are better for moving large groups, but they create natural choke points, which makes it easy for an organized army to defend against them. That's assuming one of the attuned officers of this army doesn't come and kill me first."

Another fair point. There had to be another way, one that didn't harm or kill innocents but also protected the fortress from a monster swarm.

"Let's try talking to them," Hane suggested.

"To the enemy?" Lani's brow furrowed. "If there was a way to negotiate with them, wouldn't this have been resolved already? I think they're far more likely to simply take us prisoner."

"Not the humans. The monsters."

"*Talk* to them?" Aldis asked incredulously. "You can't possibly expect to be able to reason with them. Nothing down there looked like kitsune or even oni, they're all practically beasts."

Hane closed their eyes and swallowed a sigh. Aldis's opinion was a common one, but in Hane's experience, it was dead wrong.

"Many spire monsters don't just speak, they can be reasoned with." Hane tipped their head in the direction of the monster pens. "They are clearly here against their will. If we can reach an accord, they may even fight for us rather than against us. If there's even a chance that we can keep the enemy from unleashing these monsters on the fort, we have to take it."

Aldis continued to hem and haw anxiously, but Lani nodded, her jaw firmly set.

"I think it's a risk worth taking," she affirmed. "But there are guards on those pens and it's broad daylight right now. Sage said the attack would begin in the late afternoon, so we can't just sit around waiting for nightfall."

"I don't think any of those guards are attuned," Hane pointed out. "No doubt there are attuned in the army, based on the runes on those pens. The trouble will be getting close enough to negotiate without being spotted and without triggering the teleportation runes that would pull us into the pens."

Aldis blew a breath through his nose, seemingly dissatisfied with the plan, but unable to come up with an alternative. "Well, if you do happen to get caught by the teleportation runes, I can pull you back out. It'd be best if I stay back here while you two go talk to the monsters."

"Good idea," Lani said, agreeable enough that Aldis regarded her warily. "This is a good vantage point for you to keep an eye out for the patrols. You'll take care of anyone before they spot us, right?"

"That depends on how many guards I'm teleporting and how much mana I keep in reserve to teleport us to safety," Aldis grumbled. "A safe number might be about three guards, and then you'll have to retreat and consider a new plan."

"Where will you send the ones you're teleporting?" Hane asked.

"I'll drop them outside the fort," Aldis said with a careless shrug. "Three soldiers can't do any harm and it would take them hours to get back here on foot if they aren't shot by archers on the wall."

"Do that, then," Lani said firmly. "But contact Sage first. Tell him to alert the archers that enemy soldiers will be popping up individually outside the walls and unless they surrender, they are to be shot. Hane and I will go down and talk to the monsters in the closest paddock."

"Just remember that if you start a fight, I'll be going into it at half strength," Aldis warned. "I'll keep enough in reserve to pull us all out if it gets to be too much."

"Fine, but let me make that call. You'll have the best vantage point from here, so keep us informed of any new developments." Lani tugged on each of her gloves before turning to Hane. "You ready?"

Hane nodded and beckoned her to the edge of the ridge. "Let's wait until just after the next guard comes around. Aldis, when I lift my hand, drop us at the bottom of this hill."

Aldis muttered something like "Your funeral," which Hane took as an affirmative. Hane marked the path the patrolling guard walked in order to steer clear of the teleportation runes and tried to make out the monsters in the closest pen. They didn't recognize what the creatures were, but they were bipedal, which was generally—but not always—a sign of intelligence. This would all be much easier if they could negotiate some kind of truce with an intelligent species.

Hane lifted a hand just as the nearest guard stepped around the far corner of the pen. They barely had time to get their feet under them before the teleportation spell took effect, setting them down in a crouch on the trodden footpath encircling the perimeter fence.

"Oof." Lani was still lying prone, seemingly startled by the teleport. Hane offered a hand to help her up. Lani climbed to her feet, brusquely dusting herself off. "Sorry, thanks. Do you know what those are?"

The last question was directed at the nearest monster paddock. There was no cover here at the base of the hill, which meant they had a clear view of the monsters, just as the monsters had a clear view of them. It also meant they had to be fast, as Aldis would only be teleporting away three guards before pulling them back.

"I'm not sure," Hane admitted, creeping closer to the paddock. The figures inside the pen walked upright and had a humanlike shape to their bodies, but most seemed a good deal taller than an average human. The biggest was about ten feet tall; the smallest looked to be about a head taller than Hane. As two of the odd creatures came closer to the edge of the paddock, Hane noted that their skin appeared more reptilian than fleshy, with bony protrusions around the knees, elbows, and shoulders. The skin-scales ranged in color from dull red to a rich green. All their clothing looked woven from leaves and natural fibers and typically only wrapped around the waist. Hane didn't see any weapons on them, save for thick, bony protrusions on the top of their heads, rounded more like bulbs than horns.

Hane stopped at the edge of the packed-earth path that the patrols kept to, wary of the teleportation runes on the fence post. The monsters stopped several paces back from the fence, too, proving they were at least intelligent enough to have noted the range and function of the spell keeping them fenced in.

"Can you understand me?" Hane asked, speaking in a natural tone. Whispering wouldn't be heard over the distance, but shouting would attract attention. Lani stepped up beside them, hands turned out to show they were empty. A gray-scaled monster eyed them suspiciously, turning and tilting their head in a birdlike manner.

"You magic humans?" they asked, lips peeled back from wide, flat teeth in a half snarl. "No fight for magic humans!"

"Apologies for the wrongs you have suffered," Hane said swiftly. There was no telling how much time they had before they were discovered. "My friends and I aren't with the magic humans who trapped you like this. We do not wish to fight you, nor make you fight for us. We would actually like to set you free."

"If we fight for you?" the creature asked sullenly.

"I won't lie to you, there is a strong possibility you might have to fight, but only so you might escape," Hane said honestly. "I saw beings that looked similar to you out by the lake to the west. Is that where you come from? Is your home near the lake?"

Other scaled creatures were beginning to gather, intrigued by the two humans attempting to converse with them. The gray-scaled ambassador turned away from the fence, saying something in a language that sounded like soft hisses and clicks to those gathered nearby. Hane looked around for the nearest guard while maintaining an outward appearance of patience.

"Aldis just teleported the first guard," Lani whispered, answering their unspoken question. "We have a little time to negotiate."

Hane nodded gratefully just as the creature turned back to face them.

"Some come from the lake," the creature admitted. "Many come from farther. Humans march us here like prisoners."

"Do you know if it's the same for the others?" Hane asked, gesturing to the other paddocks full of milling monsters. "Did the humans capture them nearby, or were they marched along with all of you?"

"Some." The creature shrugged. "Some someones."

"Someones?" Hane repeated, confused.

"Summons?" Lani guessed. "Is there a Summoner in the enemy camp?"

The ambassador for the creatures bobbed its head in something like a nod. "Someoner."

That was good information; if some of the creatures had been summoned, then defeating the Summoner might cut their numbers significantly.

"Would you like for us to free you?" Hane asked. "If you believe yourselves safer here, we'll respect your wishes. My friends and I don't want to cause you any further harm than you've already suffered."

Another softly hissed conversation, this time with more of the creatures joining in. Hane suspected more of them understood the language than were letting on, but that was fine. As long as the congregation of monsters didn't draw the attention of the guards, they could take their time in deliberating.

"If xin are freed, humans will hunt us." In context, Hane assumed that "xin" referred to these scaled, sapient creatures. "Many will be hurt or killed. Where will you humans be?"

"We intend to free as many of the others as possible, provided they don't attack the human fortress we mean to defend," Hane explained. "Perhaps you and the others can escape in the general chaos."

"Not good enough," the xin replied with a sharpness Hane hadn't expected. "You only free us to protect yourselves, but then who protects the xin? Better to take chances against other humans than the humans who herded us here."

"I respect that," Hane said, dipping their head and shoulders in a slight bow. "My friend and I will trouble you no longer. We will make the same offer to the other captives in these pens, though. I'll return here later, just in case you or other xin change your minds."

"Talk to others?" A different xin, one with pale scales bordering on pink, made a gesture to the other paddocks beyond their own. "Many others do not speak. You would free them only to see them slaughtered."

"That isn't our intent," Lani said, moving forward. "But we must protect our people somehow. I'm sure you all did everything you could to avoid capture and death. You understand that we must do the same."

The pink-scaled xin hissed something to the first xin, a conversation that spiraled outward from the two into the amassed gathering of creatures. Hane looked around again, double-checking that they hadn't drawn the attention of the guards or of the other captured creatures. It did appear that few of the other monsters fenced inside the proximity teleportation fields would be as easy to converse with as the xin. The nearest pen to this one held wolflike monsters with spikes jutting up from their spines, and another held what appeared to be floating balls of fire. Hane couldn't make out the creatures beyond the heat haze of the fireball-creature paddock.

"Second guard teleported," Lani hissed. "If we're not fast, we'll have to deal with a very ornery Wayfarer."

She probably meant it to be funny, but there was far too much truth in it to make Hane laugh.

"Xin have little magic," the first speaker said, somewhat reluctantly. "Not strong, but creates kinship with animals. Once free, xin can lead others away into hiding. Protect from fighting. No killing."

"But I thought you didn't want to be freed?" Lani asked, sounding confused. "Are you able to communicate with the other monsters from here and tell them to run away?"

"Xin can, but magic is . . ." The de facto leader, the gray-scaled xin, hesitated, hissing something to a companion. After a brief exchange, they finished by saying: "Tethered."

"Limited?" Hane guessed. "You're saying the spell has a limited range of effectiveness?"

"Yes." Another boblike nod. "Must be close to speak with animal-monsters. Cannot work from here for very long."

The pink-scaled xin snapped at the gray-scaled one, revealing rows of sharp, serrated teeth. The gray-scaled one flinched and hissed something back.

"Lives more important!" the pink-scaled xin declared, lifting their chin defiantly. "We take animals and we run! No fighting for humans. No dying for humans."

"Yes," Lani agreed quickly. "That's all we want: to let you and everyone else go so the humans must fight us themselves. If you stay here, these humans are going to lead you into a slaughter. We want to set you free so you can go peacefully and fight for no one but yourselves."

"Humans will slaughter us anyway!" the first xin countered. "These humans or other humans! Makes no difference!"

"But we protect animals!" the second xin pointed to the pens of monsters beyond this one.

"What if we protect you?" Hane asked, sensing the root of the problem. "You're right: if we break this teleportation field, the humans of this army will attack you and try to trap you again. But what if we brought down the teleportation fields around the other pens and let you flee with the other creatures, while we protect you from the humans?"

"Hane!" Lani hissed, clasping their shoulder. "There's only three of us here and Aldis just teleported the third guard! We can't make that promise."

"I'm not saying it wouldn't be entirely without risk to them or the other creatures," Hane explained. "But we can slow down regular human soldiers and we actually stand a chance against the attuned. Fighting here and now is better than letting a force this big reach the fortress."

Lani grimaced as she took in the pens ranged out along the packed-dirt road, more than could be seen just from this one spot. "If the fort can't handle them, what makes you think the three of us can?"

"We're not fighting the creatures in the pens, we're freeing them," Hane pointed out. "There's enough of them to threaten the camp here; it'll send these troops into disarray before they realize the captured creatures are fleeing instead of fighting. Once they do, it'll be too late for the soldiers to do much at all, except maybe fire a few arrows. Most likely, we'll just have the attuned to deal with."

"Oh, is that all?" Lani asked, more than a little skeptical.

While Lani debated Hane's suggestion, the xin spoke to each other in shushed tones, others joining in to voice their opinions to the two standing at the forefront of the negotiations. Hane waited until the susurrus of voices died down and the first xin to address them stepped forward again.

"If humans fight to protect xin and animals, we will flee to the lake." The creature pointed off in the distance. "We make no promise to stay there! Just hide to avoid the fighting."

"That's fine," Hane assured them quickly. "I'm sure you'd all like to return to your homes, and we don't mean to stop you. We just want to help you get to safety for now."

"Xin can't talk to all the animals here," the pink-scaled xin put in. They pointed, adding: "Fire does not hear the call."

Hane followed their gesture to the paddock of floating fireballs and nodded. That should be fine: if only those escaped to attack the fort, Aldis could let Emiko know to expect them. Any Cloudcaller worth their salt could drown out fire of that size. "Any others who don't heed the call?"

"Maybe some." The xin made a repeated bobbing motion with its neck, a gesture that looked like an odd shrug. "Xin don't know all the animals here."

Hane turned toward Lani. "Is that good enough for you?"

Lani's mouth twisted to the side thoughtfully before she answered. "Let's go back up and confer with Aldis, just to nail down a strategy. After that, we need to contact Sage and the others to let them know we'll be releasing the swarm early; some of these monsters might head to the fort all on their own. But yes, this is too good an opportunity to let it pass."

"Is that all right with you?" Hane asked, directing the question at both of the talkative xin monsters.

"When does freedom start?" the gray-scaled one asked.

"We'll send you a signal when we're ready," Lani said with authority. "One of us will come down and break the fence so you can pass. We'll try to open as many of the paddocks as we can before your captors realize what's happening here."

"Open far side." The pink-scaled xin pointed. "Closer to freed animals. We prepare until then."

"Very good." Lani nodded, hooking her arm through Hane's as she backed away from the pen. "The next guard is coming. If we can circle around and climb the hill without being seen, we'll conserve a few more teleport spells for Aldis."

"Good thinking. We'll need them for later."

Lani must have been in contact with Aldis, because he was waiting for them at the top of the hill, tapping a finger against his dueling cane impatiently.

"How exactly do you expect to break into twelve different paddocks all without getting attacked by monsters or guards, or letting the entirety of the army know that we were here?" Aldis demanded to know.

"The army is going to know we're here, that's a given," Hane replied calmly. "Part of our bargain with the xin is that we'll protect them as they run away."

"It'll be tough," Lani admitted, pacing as she considered. "The teleport locations are critical; Aldis, you'll have to send us where we can reach the maximum number of pens with spells that can break the runed posts. We've also got to time it so the xin break out first and use their magic to subdue the other monsters."

"Preferably without freeing the ones they can't control," Hane added. "Like the floating fireballs."

"Right, right." Lani chewed the thumb tip of her glove for a moment, her expression thoughtful. "Aldis, you'll have to take the friendly xin with you to the farther pens so she—"

"Absolutely not!"

"Sorry, *they* can tell you which monsters we're freeing and which ones we're leaving, and then you can tell Hane and me which pens to break."

"My objection was not based on your reference to the monster," Aldis barked.

"I should have thought to ask how they refer to each other," Lani said musingly, as if electing not to hear Aldis. "Would have been good to know."

"I will not—"

"*We*," Hane interrupted, silencing Aldis with a glare, "shouldn't risk offending the xin with accidental rudeness, so I think I should be the one who travels with the friendly xin. I can break the nearby pens, confer with my companion, and then Aldis can send the two of us to the farthest pens. From there, I'll ask the friendly xin to go to the center of the pens where Aldis will drop Lani, so the xin can tell her which pens to break open. That way, Aldis can remain up here as a lookout."

Lani gave Hane an exasperated look, but Hane knew when something wasn't worth the fight. Whatever lay between Lani and Aldis shouldn't jeopardize the mission, and in the end, Aldis was their exit strategy, as well as their only means of communication back to the rest of the team. Aggravating him would only end up hurting both of them in the long run.

"It's still not ideal, but I think that's a better idea," Aldis grumbled. "What about the army?"

"We're not going to get away without having to fight," Hane admitted. "But the excitement of the escaped monsters creates some cover for us. All we have to do is target the officers and any attuned to create chaos until the monsters get so far away, it isn't worth chasing them. Then Aldis can bring us back here—if it's still safe—and we can either hide out or head back to the fort, depending on how much mana Aldis has to teleport us."

"Okay, so Hane and I are breaking the posts with the runes on them, then fighting an army by assassinating the harder-to-kill targets, all while the Wayfarer hides up here," Lani said, almost sans inflection. She cupped her hand around the hilt of her cutlass and nodded to Hane. "Let's do it."

"I won't just be hiding," Aldis muttered sulkily. "There's a lot of spellwork that goes into portals and teleportation and mental communication and—"

"Let's get started," Hane prompted. "They won't wait forever to attack. Once we know which monsters can't be controlled by the xin's call, you should tell the others back at the fort what to expect in terms of monsters and numbers."

"Yes, yes, of course." Aldis sighed heavily. "You should go let the tender-hearted xin monster know to expect my teleport spell. Hopefully the Acolyte can stand my presence long enough to point out where it is I'm sending the both of you."

Lani scowled but motioned for Aldis to follow her through the brush to the top of the hill where they could look down. Leaving them to work out the details, Hane stepped off the edge of the steep-sided lookout, using a push of transference mana to cushion their landing at the bottom. A small group of patrol guards were congregating at an intersection several pens away, within sight, but clearly distracted: no doubt they had noticed the missing guards.

We have to move fast, Hane noted, creeping toward the xin pen. The pink-scaled xin stood nearby, clearing awaiting the promised signal.

"My friend on the hill is going to pull you out so you can come with me," Hane explained. "I need you to tell me which creatures will answer the call and which ones to leave inside the pens."

"And then you break open the pens?" the xin confirmed.

"Yes, but we won't be able to break many of the posts with the runes on them. Your people should expect to file through the opening in an orderly fashion, or else they'll get teleported back to the middle of the pen."

The pink-scaled xin gave the head bob that seemed to be a nod. "I am ready, then."

Hane motioned for the xin to follow as they circled the outer edge of the proximity teleportation field to an intersection of four different monster pens.

[About to start down here,] Hane sent to Aldis. [As soon as I crack these posts, drop me and my friend at the farthest four pens. The guards are already alerted.]

After Aldis confirmed the communication, Hane double-checked that the only nearby creatures that wouldn't heed the "call" were the floating fireballs, and at the xin's nod, they motioned for the xin to back up away from the invisible teleportation field. They were exposed out here; all it would take was one guard looking this way and they'd be seen. Not that that was a significant danger—Hane could move faster than any non-attuned person could—but the element of surprise was a necessary one. Marking the direction of the three pens Hane intended to break, they crouched down, putting their back to the fireball pen, and charged their shroud with transference mana. Focusing the radius of the spell outward, Hane set their hands on the ground, thinking one simple word: *Burst.*

The motion spell flew outward in an arc, tearing through the rune-marked fence posts and turning them into little more than splinters. It only gave the pens a narrow opening of about six feet, or else they risked getting teleported back to the anchors in the center of the pens, but it was the best Hane could do for them. The xin would have to take care of the rest. Hane scarcely had time to register that their spell had worked before the swirling magic of a teleportation spell whisked them away.

A scream like the hiss of hot metal plunged into water sent Hane sinking low into a battle stance, each hand freeing a tonfa from their harness, whirling them defensively almost without thought. Pointed nails sank into the meat of their upper biceps, and Hane very nearly dispatched of the creature before realizing it was only the pink-scaled xin, wide-eyed in terror after the teleportation spell.

"You're okay," Hane assured them, tucking their tonfa away again. "As quickly as you can, tell me which of these creatures will answer the call."

The xin cupped a claw-tipped hand to their mouth, as if warding away nausea. They took a breath, then pointed. "Those fliers. They will not answer the call. These others will."

"Good." Hane barely took stock of the creatures in the pens as they sank into the stance for their Burst spell. "You remember my friend from before, right? Head that way and let her know which barriers to break."

The xin nodded and took off, running in a zigzag pattern that was faster than Hane would have expected it to be. Once they were out of range, they charged their shroud and activated Burst, breaking three more barriers.

That's eight of the twelve pens, Hane thought, removing their tonfa from the harness hidden beneath their vest. A quick check showed that most of the monsters were cowering back from splintered posts, probably frightened of the noise. *We need to keep the army back while the xin use their "call" to control the monsters. It won't be long before they realize the barriers are down.*

Frantic shouts and the mournful cry of a horn were already alerting the army that something was happening at the monster pens. Coiling transference mana beneath their feet, Hane raced back between the paddocks, bent forward at the waist with the tonfa held back behind them. They skidded to a stop near Lani, who stood at the crux of four paddocks, two open while she worked on a third. She pointed with her attunement-marked hand and though Hane didn't hear her voice speak a spell, they saw the wooden posts marked with runes suddenly sprout branches and leaves, growing so quickly that the posts couldn't support the weight, causing them to topple over. A growth spell, then, most likely using life mana.

"They're going to be coming soon," Lani said, smoothing a hand back over her hair. "I'll stay back and make sure the xin collect the other monsters. Can you do something about the guards?"

Before Hane could answer, fire arced overhead like a comet, aiming to crash down in the dead center of the monster paddocks, where creatures were just beginning to emerge from the first broken pens, urged on by the xin. One of the smaller xin pointed up, eyes wide in fright, but Lani lifted her hand, tracking the fireball's trajectory, then conjured a jet of water shooting to intercept the fireball midflight. The opposing mana types were equal enough in strength that they exploded on contact, raining down harmless bits of twisting flames that died before they reached the ground.

"Yes, fire, that's what the prisoners need to remain orderly." Lani rolled her eyes. "Think you can do something about that before they start to panic?"

"On it!" Hane coiled transference mana in the balls of their feet before springing forward, running headlong toward the enemy camp. A high-arcing jump would have made them a target to whatever fire-flinging attuned was hiding among the enemy combatants, so Hane stayed low, bent at the waist as they ran, tonfa held behind them. Just as they reached the end of the paddocks, a line of archers from the camp sent up a ragged volley of arrows, arched high to land along the line of escapees. Hane shaped a weaker version of their Burst spell, releasing it like a wave to knock the arrows off course so that they tumbled uselessly to the ground. A glance back showed the xin splitting into groups, some staying behind to coax reluctant animal-monsters out of their paddocks, while others raced ahead, splitting off to assigned paddocks. The pink-scaled xin seemed to be directing the groups, shouting orders and pointing out targets.

Guess I can leave them to it, Hane decided, turning their attention back to the army. *The real dangers are the attuned.*

The ground trembled as more and more monsters began running free, kicking up a cloud of dust in their wake. As the dust rolled over the line of archers, Hane sank low to the ground, tugging a mask up from inside their collar to cover their nose and mouth. Whoever had thrown that fire-comet earlier had to be nearby, and while any common soldier had the potential to be attuned, Hane was willing to bet that someone with an attunement mark would stand out from the crowd.

There. Hane caught sight of someone wearing a bright red half cloak over their uniform. More telling was the hand they had raised, as if about to cast a spell. Hane didn't wait for confirmation but streaked forward into and through the ranks of enemy archers, slamming a shoulder into the fire-caster's chest to knock them flat. Before they could catch their breath, Hane whipped a tonfa sideways, slamming it across the spellcaster's temple. Hane was bounding away before confirming whether the spellcaster was dead or simply knocked out; either way was good enough. A few of the closer archers attempted to set arrows to their bows, but a quick Burst spell sent most of them staggering off balance, making them drop their arrows.

[Their Wayfarer is attempting to open a portal to the west,] came Aldis's voice inside Hane's head. [They're probably going to try to catch the monsters in a loop so they can be herded back to their pens. That's what I would do.]

Can't let that happen, Hane thought, half in response to Aldis and half to themself. They sweep-kicked the closest archer, using another blast of transference mana through their shroud to knock other soldiers away as they tore the archer's tunic off, pulling it over their black clothing even as they leapt away. The uniform wouldn't stand up to even the most cursory glance, but as quickly as they moved through the army, they thought it might be enough to make the archers think Hane might be one of their own just until they were out of bowshot.

They spotted another soldier wearing a half cloak over their uniform, but this one was edged in shining gold thread. A high-ranking officer, perhaps? They certainly appeared to be giving orders. As they turned to shout something at a pair of soldiers leading horses, Hane caught the glimpse of an attunement mark on their brow, though over the distance they couldn't make out exactly which mark it was.

Even if it wasn't the Wayfarer, one less attuned was one less thing to worry about later. Hane weaved their way through the throng of rushing soldiers, trying to look as unobtrusive as possible before springing forward to attack, intending to knock out this attuned just as they had the last one. Just as their left tonfa was careening for the side of the officer's head, the officer spun around, flinging a hand out toward Hane. A blast of wind slammed into Hane, knocking them off their feet and blowing them out of range for a strike.

Summoner attunement, Hane noted, rolling to their feet as the officer shouted for reinforcements. *A problem, but one I can handle after I find the Wayfarer.*

Hane used their Burst spell to knock over a stack of crates filled with weapons, distracting the Summoner and his reinforcements sufficiently enough to fade back into the crowd and slip away.

Finding the Wayfarer was proving difficult, especially as more soldiers were called up from the camp to create physical barricades along the avenues between the paddocks in an attempt to funnel the stampeding rush of monsters back into something resembling a single group so it could be caged. The portal Aldis had warned about kept flickering and failing: possibly too big for the Wayfarer to support from a distance, which meant they'd be hurrying to get closer to where they wanted to set the portal. A few groups of xin were well beyond the westernmost perimeter of the camp, but many others were still struggling to lead their charges while avoiding the barricades set by the soldiers. Lani was successfully deterring volleys of arrows with water spells, but if a soldier so much as shoved a monster toward a working rune-post, it was teleported back to the central pillar within the paddock, making for a significant amount of backtracking for the conscientious xin.

Hane darted from barricade to barricade, knocking out the cloak-wearing attuned officers as they found them, but none seemed to be the Wayfarer. After shooting a targeted blast of transference mana at a third cloak-wearing officer, knocking them into the teleportation runes surrounding the fireball paddock, Hane faded back to rethink their strategy.

The Wayfarer could be heading toward either end of the paddocks, Hane rationalized. *Either east by Aldis, or west toward the lake. Either way, they'd want to be moving fast, but probably not alone. They'd also want to conserve their mana, which means they won't teleport a large group. Then that leaves . . .*

The stampede of half-crazed monsters made it difficult to see anything through the kicked-up dirt and grass, but Hane wasn't looking for something small. No, they were looking for something large, and moving fast.

Aha!

Hane spotted a small two-person cart pulled by a single horse but surrounded by a vanguard of spear-wielding soldiers. While the driver directed the cart horse west, in the direction of the fleeing monsters, the second person in the cart stood with one hand braced on the driver's shoulder, the other hand extended out before them. A purple half cloak marked them as one of the attuned officers.

That has to be the Wayfarer, Hane thought, shoving a pair of soldiers into the teleportation runes. *Aldis, are you still connected to my thoughts?*

There was a slight pause, then: [Hane? Were you trying to reach me?]

[Yes. Please ask Lani if she can do anything to help separate the soldiers from that cart.] Hane sent a mental image of what they were seeing. [I'll take care of the Wayfarer.]

[Done.]

Hane worked their way closer to the cart, trying to stay out of sight while still moving fast. Anyone who caught sight of them was promptly blasted into the teleportation runes, regardless of whether the paddock still had creatures in it or not. They kept their eyes on the cart, awaiting their chance to strike. If they alerted the Wayfarer, Hane would likely find themself teleported somewhere quite far away, rendering them useless for the rest of the battle. At least they could survive being dropped from a very high height; that was a favorite way for Wayfarers to kill opponents.

The Wayfarer's cart was rolling steadily forward, but slowly, to ensure that the Wayfarer didn't topple over. Hane attempted to keep pace without appearing to follow. Suddenly, thick brown roots burst out of the ground, entangling the legs of the soldiers escorting the cart. The driver yelped and lashed the lines, driving the horse forward suddenly. The Wayfarer cried out in surprise, nearly toppling over backward before sitting down heavily and clutching the driver's shoulders. Hane took that as their cue and shed their disguise, bolting after the fleeing cart. Someone behind them shouted and they heard the stretch of bows, but a transference-aided leap carried them into the midst of the root-locked escort soldiers, where the archers would be fearful to shoot.

Hane ducked the swing of a sword and blocked another with their tonfa before diving and rolling clear of the entangled escorts, pelting headlong after the cart. The approach was dangerous, forcing Hane to keep their distance as the terrified horse juked first one way, then the other, attempting to wrest control away from the driver. When the cart appeared to be on a steady trajectory, Hane circled around to the driver's blind side and leapt, grabbing the back of the cart before vaulting over the bench to land lightly in front of both the Wayfarer and the driver. Without wasting a moment of movement—teleport spells took hold quite quickly in most cases—Hane slammed transference mana through their shroud, hitting the Wayfarer hard enough that she tumbled out of the back of the cart. The driver lashed out with a strike, but Hane was already jumping down from the cart, intent on the Wayfarer.

The Wayfarer was still rolling as Hane landed in a soft crouch. They circled around, trying to stay out of her line of sight, though that wouldn't always save them from being teleported unwillingly. They hoped the Wayfarer had landed poorly enough to knock herself out, but as she stopped rolling, the

Wayfarer fought to free herself from the half cloak that had fallen over her head. Rather than give her the chance to recover, Hane darted in close, swung back their tonfa, and cracked it against the side of her head. The Wayfarer collapsed, just one more crumpled body in the wake of a stampede.

Hane took a minute to catch their breath and slip their tonfa back into the hidden holster beneath their tunic. Most of the xin and other monsters were well beyond the reach of the main army, leaving only the three barriers they and Lani had intentionally left standing. There were a few straggling groups of xin appearing to struggle with leading their animal-monster charges. Lani was holding back the few guards moving in on them, but the army was regrouping and soon she would be overwhelmed. With a sigh, Hane charged back into the fray.

CHAPTER 12

&MIKO

Cloudcaller (lung mark), Sunstone

I still say that I should have gone with them instead of Hane," Nieve complained, lying on her stomach across a crenellation atop the wall over the gate. A block of ice the size of a boulder formed in the air in front of her, plummeting to the ground like a meteor.

"Maybe." Emiko watched the ice boulder shatter as it hit the ground, crushing the insectoid monsters below that were attempting to chew through the walls of the fort. She was similarly lying atop a crenellation just next to Nieve's, legs kicked up over her back, chin propped in her hands. A steady rain was falling—an earlier spell of Emiko's—but an air shield above the two of them kept them mostly dry. "But it's a little late to complain about it now."

"I should have challenged them to a duel," Nieve said thoughtfully. "Although . . . Do you really think they took out a lake serpent on their own?"

"No reason to think they didn't." Emiko touched the mana crystals fitted tightly into the strap across her chest. "They brought back enough water mana crystals to sink a ship. Unless you think they carried water mana crystals into the spire with them?"

"No," Nieve sighed heavily. "I don't think that. It's just . . . do you think I could take on a lake serpent on my own?"

"Oh, I definitely think you would!" Emiko beamed, tapping her heels together. "I can see it just like one of Sage's visions! You, running in all gallant and shiny in your ice armor. And then the serpent swallowing you in a single bite."

Nieve bellowed a laugh. "I'd at least get a hit in first!"

Emiko twisted her mouth to the side impishly, shaking her head as she considered it. "No, I don't think so. But! I bet you'd make the serpent real uncomfortable as it swallows you. Like the feeling when you swallow an ice cube? That would be you!"

Nieve flipped onto her back in order to laugh even louder, drumming her heels against the wall as mirth rolled through her. Her long jet-black hair dangled over the edge of the wall, threaded through with the long, red tails of her headband, just about the only color that glimmered through the rainy gloom. Emiko smiled to herself as her friend wiped tears from the corners of her eyes. It was good to see Nieve laugh. Before, Wyle had always taken it upon herself to keep the team's spirits up, even when the climbs got grim. Emiko had worried there would be far less laughter without Wyle, so Nieve's honest laughter was a sparkle of light against the gloomy rain.

Emiko held a hand out from under the air shield, taking a measure of her rain spell. It was still falling fast and hard enough for now, but she would likely have to renew the spell soon. She inched forward over the wall and looked straight down.

Aldis had sent a communication a while ago about the types of monsters they could expect to attack on behalf of the attacking army. It seemed Hane had convinced a large portion of the monster army to flee, but some few would not be swayed. At least none of the monsters in this wave could fly, which meant their methods for attacking the fort all concentrated on the lower portions of the wall, giving a hefty advantage to the fortress. The two main types of attackers were little floating balls of fire—currently kept at bay by Emiko's rain spell—and insectoid-looking monsters about as tall as humans who could chew through wood and stone. The insect-monsters were tougher to fight, but dropping heavy objects on them seemed to work, so Nieve mostly focused on dropping her ice boulders around the gate side of the fort, while fortress soldiers ferried rocks and crates up from the ground level to drop on the monsters from the walls. Luckily, there weren't that many, and they seemed to have a low intelligence, all attacking the fort head-on rather than spreading out to chew at the walls evenly.

"You're probably right," Nieve admitted, still grinning as she flipped over onto her stomach again. She pulled her head and shoulders over the wall, glanced down the length of the fort, and then conjured two new ice boulders to drop on the insect-monsters. "But how did Hane do it, then? Is a midlevel Citrine rank really that much stronger than a low-level Citrine?"

Is a high-level Sunstone really that much weaker than a low-level Citrine? Emiko wondered but didn't ask. She already knew the answer. "You and Lani interviewed Hane, right? There must have been a reason you picked them to join the team."

"Join the team . . . that's not exactly right," Nieve qualified. "Hane is an independent climber; they don't really join up. But it seemed like a really good opportunity to recruit a strong climber and help us break into the twenty-something floors, right?"

"Right." Emiko felt her stomach squeeze and churn. She didn't feel ready for level-twenty floors—she hadn't even broken into the Citrine rank yet! But Nieve focusing on ascension rather than attunement development was an old story by now. "Hey, and who knows? Maybe we'll climb so high that Hane will want to stay."

"I doubt it," Nieve said, drumming her fingers along the stonework. "Hane isn't all that interested in ascending; they've actually been to higher floors than this. And it's rare that they climb with the same team twice, and never on consecutive climbs. I think maybe they're more of a delver than a climber, really. Can't think of any other reasons to climb, other than treasure or . . ."

Nieve's gaze went fuzzy, staring off into the distance as she touched a spot on her breastbone: the spot where her locket lay hidden beneath her leather tunic. Nieve's only goal in climbing was to reach the top floor and meet the goddess: she had said so many times. But whatever that wish was, even Sage didn't know it. Emiko knew it had to be important, but whatever it was, it also made Nieve reckless at times: prioritizing ascension and combat challenges over growing her mana pool and learning new spells. Despite her mad drive to climb to the top of the spire, at least she listened when her team said they needed to slow down and build their skills for a while. But even then, she champed at the bit, urging everyone to develop faster so they could move on.

Are those the only two reasons to climb? Ascension or treasure? Emiko wondered. *Then . . . why do I climb?*

She knew the answer, it just didn't feel very satisfying: she climbed because Nieve and Sage climbed. She climbed because she could. She climbed because . . . because she had nothing better to do.

Emiko pinched her earlobe sharply, chasing away useless thoughts. "So will you and Lani have to recruit again for our next climb? Do you think you'll want another Wavewalker like Hane? Or another Soulblade, like Ren?"

"I'm actually really hoping Ren will be bored enough by then to come back to the team," Nieve admitted. Nieve tracked something moving on the ground, pausing as she conjured another ice boulder and dropped it. "I know Wyle was pretty much over climbing, even before we got started last time, but Wayfarers are easy to replace. It's hard finding someone to fight beside without worrying they're going to get in your way."

"You think Wyle will let him come back?" Emiko asked, musing. "She's not the type to just sit home and worry. And that last climb really got her upset."

"I don't think so," Nieve said with deep regret. "Not unless we can promise we won't run into any more Void Spiders."

"Maybe you could just promise not to charge headlong into garrote wire-webbing, so Ren doesn't have to risk himself to save you." Emiko reached over and poked Nieve's arm, pulling back when Nieve swatted at her. "You were lucky Lani was able to keep you in one piece long enough to get properly patched up when we got back."

"We were lucky Sage still had the presence of mind to grab the gate key before we hit our return bells. Would have been such a wasted effort otherwise."

Emiko jabbed Nieve in the arm again. "You mean you are grateful that we all made it out okay, and that getting the key was a nice bonus."

"I am grateful we all got out safe," Nieve said, for once looking morosely serious. "That's always the priority. I'd do anything to keep you and the others safe, Mi-mi. But it would have been disappointing to have survived all of that and not retrieved the key."

Emiko pursed her lips and reached out to feel the rain again. It was definitely lighter now, still falling but gently, like a gossamer veil rather than the downpour it had been earlier. She curled over the edge of the crenellation again, peering straight down. Far below, she could just make out the flickering forms of the fireball monsters. A simple rain wouldn't kill them, but it did prevent them from burning anything. It also tended to make them small and more compact, burning a sulky blue color rather than the usual vibrant orange and yellow flames. As Emiko watched, she saw sputters of red-orange light: the fireballs were attempting to re-ignite. Time to freshen up the rain spell.

Emiko pushed herself up to sitting, folding her knees beneath her as she pressed her palms together and drew a deep breath. The spell for rain was the first one a Cloudcaller learned, allowing her to chant effortlessly. She was good at coming up with spells in the proper format on the fly—a necessary skill for someone who mixed mana types as frequently as she did—but it was nice to use old familiar spells that always performed as expected.

The hiss and patter of the rain grew steadily, and when Emiko opened her eyes, it was falling in gentle waves. Before sliding out of her prayer stance, she renewed the spell on her air shield, widening it to keep the rain off. As she did, a figure holding a cloak over their head came trotting toward them over the rampart.

"I was hoping to make it before you renewed the rain spell," Sage laughed, shaking out his cloak as he stepped beneath the air shield. "Second phase is about to start. Ready to turn in, Nieve?"

"Just a moment." Nieve held her arms out in a wide gesture, a line of ice boulders appearing just over the side of the wall before gravity dragged them down to the earth below. The fortress wall shivered as they impacted the ground. "Now I'm ready."

Nieve rolled up to her feet, stretched her arms over her head as she yawned widely, and then sauntered off into the sheeting rain. Sage ducked beneath the air shield, still shaking out his clothing. Despite his friendly smile, Emiko felt a twinge of guilt: if she had waited until after the shift switch to renew her rain spell, her friends wouldn't have gotten so wet.

"How's it been?" Sage asked, leaning over the wall to look down. "Pretty quiet?"

"Whenever one of Nieve's boulders isn't impacting the side of the fort, it's pretty quiet," Emiko agreed. "If we hadn't reinforced the walls, I think Nieve's boulders would have brought them down already."

Sage laughed. "You're probably right. They'll have some construction to do after we leave."

"Do you think that's what happens?" Emiko asked, musingly. "After we move on to the next room, do the people here actually regroup and rebuild and wait for the next set of climbers? Or do you think the magic just kind of . . . goes away, then resets when someone else enters the room?"

"I'm not sure," Sage admitted. He tapped the side of his glasses as he continued. "The people we meet in scenarios like this one are the same people in previous challenges completed by other climbing groups, yet they seem to have no memory of the past. Obviously they're real enough, since Lani can heal them, but I guess I think it's a fresh version of the same simulacra every time the same scenario begins." After peering over the ledge, Sage turned around and sat down with his back against the wall, in the small, curved space where the air shield kept the walkway dry. Emiko slithered backward to sit beside him, folding her knees primly beneath herself and curling her hands together in her lap. Sage always sat more comfortably, legs crossed at the ankles, hands resting palm-up on his thighs. He took a deep breath, eyes closed behind his glasses. "Can you get your wind spell ready?"

"Yep! Just a moment." Emiko drew a breath, feeling the air mana stir inside her chest. "Wind who bows to none/I call upon our contract/Heed my every whim."

Rain blew in beneath the air shield, a cool, soft spray against Emiko's face. The wind tugged playfully at Emiko's sleeves and ruffled Sage's hair. He nodded, acknowledging the spell even though he couldn't see it with his eyes closed.

"The first one's approaching," Sage said, chin dipped almost to his chest. "Coming from the west, about a third of the way down the wall."

Emiko couldn't see anything against the blackness of the sky, but with her wind spell active, she was able to sense the puffs of air disturbed by massive wings in the direction Sage indicated. She could feel the monster's trajectory and speed by the way the wind moved around it. Rather than directing the wind into a jet to knock it away, Emiko drew a breath and focused her will.

"Here!" she shouted, drawing an outstretched hand back to her chest as a fist. Instead of air shooting away from her, a burst of air buffeted her, stolen from beneath the wings of the monster, sending it tumbling end over end until it crashed to the ground below.

"Nice," Sage commented, Seeing something that either had happened or would soon happen. "Looks like these are probing attacks. We'll have a lot more soon, I can See them marshaling for a big attack. But for now . . . One in the middle of the north wall."

Emiko sucked the air away from beneath the monster's wings again. She wanted to ask what creatures they were fighting; she'd been resting earlier when Aldis had contacted Sage about the upcoming attacks. She'd expected a wave of flying monsters but hadn't thought to ask what types of creatures they would be. They were big, whatever they were. Big and heavy. Odd, as most things that flew were light out of necessity. Even griffins had hollow bones to assist in flight. Heavier fliers often needed magic in order to stay airborne.

Sage called out a few more locations, one at a time, letting Emiko take care of them by dropping them out of the sky. Only once did one of the monsters draw close enough to be seen, causing a brief panic among the archers on the ramparts before the creature fell. Emiko could still see someone holding a torch over the edge of the wall and trying to look down.

At least that means the fireballs are too small to give any light down there, Emiko thought, wondering how the walls were holding up now without Nieve's ice boulders. Although, whatever these flying monsters were, dropping them on the monsters below was probably almost as effective anyway.

"They're coming," Sage said, voice low. "Can you slide over to the next merlon? Just until it's over."

Until what's over? Emiko couldn't ask, not while Sage had his eyes closed, but she shot him a dirty look all the same. Sliding over one space put her out in the rain, and she couldn't change the location of the air shield without breaking her wind spell. She did shift the winds to help blow rain around her, but it wasn't a perfect workaround and the ground was still wet beneath her.

"Nieve prepped the archers to use battering arrows, right?" Sage asked, his eyes flicking back and forth under his eyelids. "Yes, I See it now. It looks like all the arrows on the wall were replaced earlier. Perfect."

Battering arrows were flat-tipped, rather than pointy. They were also often heavier and more durable, used to knock down barricades or break windows from a distance. Enough of them could cave in weak doors or even walls, but they weren't exactly lethal. Emiko wondered what type of monster this was to warrant such arrows.

"Take down as many as you can once you see them," Sage advised, shifting so that he held his dueling cane point-up across his body. "And try not to scream."

Try not to— Emiko sucked in a breath to do just that as massive claw-tipped toes curled over the side of the wall right where she had been sitting before Sage told her to move. She looked up—and up and up—as a monster twice the size of a human spread batlike wings wide, back arching as it let out a long, keening scream that seemed to go on long after the monster hunched over, drool dripping through teeth that all looked like fangs. Its sloping brow, curled horns, and four arms would have identified it easily enough if its stone skin hadn't already given it away: a gargoyle. Lower intelligence than some other stone-skinned fliers, but not entirely mindless, either. Gargoyles had limited abilities to use magic—as if having the demeanor of a tiger whose tail had just been stepped on wasn't bad enough.

Emiko narrowly avoided screaming as the gargoyle whirled around, turning its face to snap at Sage. Emiko tried to get the words out for her wind spell but was still choking on her scream. Luckily, Sage seemed to have anticipated that. As the gargoyle hinged its jaw open to bite at him, Sage stuck the end of his dueling cane in its mouth and channeled a spell that made it go rigid before toppling over backward off the wall. Emiko placed her hand over her heart in an attempt to slow its frantic beat.

"Sorry, Emi. That one came up fast." Sage gave her a rueful look, head ducked in apology. "Most of them are coming straight for the gate. Can you handle them?"

Could she handle them? Of course she could! All she needed was a simple wind spell composed of air mana and nothing more. She could do this all day if she had to. Or at the very least: the remainder of the night.

Emiko scooted back under the air shield, squeezed water out of her long sleeves while giving Sage a very pointed look, and then pressed her hands against the low wall, looking out over the oncoming swarm of gargoyles. She swallowed to wet her throat, then drew in a deep breath.

"Here!" Emiko shouted, ripping the air out from under swaths of fliers. "Here! Here! Here!"

With the wind came the rain, splashing her with droplets every time a fresh wind zipped past her. Gargoyles fell to the earth screaming, sometimes clutching and clawing at others to try to stay airborne but only resulting in dragging down the others as well. While they were all grouped up, it was easy to yank away big fistfuls of air, leaving their wings no purchase to soar upon, but the gargoyles quickly began to scatter, flying every which way and making it difficult to strike down as many within a single command. Emiko stood at the rampart, waiting patiently for any to dare draw near. Only when they were within bowshot of the fort did she rip them down; otherwise she let them harry from a distance, or flee.

"We're doing okay on the ground, too," Sage said, his eyes once again closed, but it made Emiko smile to see droplets of water clinging to his hair. Despite the air shield, neither of them would be dry at the end of this. "Between the ice and the falling gargoyles, most of the wood-eating bug things have run away. The fireballs are still there, but there isn't much they can do with the rain. Probably one more cast tonight will leave everything too soggy to burn, so that's them out. Is there anything else coming tonight?"

Sage's last musing question was directed more at himself than at Emiko, so she didn't bother answering. She knew Lani and the others were softening the enemy from their own camp, but this still felt too easy. She hoped that didn't mean they were taking on a larger challenge than they should, just to make it easier on the fort. She didn't like the idea of any of her teammates being too far away to be of any help.

"Hey, Emi?" Sage's tone was meek, timid. He even looked smaller, more vulnerable, sitting on the walkway, so he had to look up to meet Emiko's eyes. "Do you think Lani left me behind because she thinks I'm no good in combat situations?"

Emiko could have laughed, but she was in the middle of ripping air away from beneath a swooping gargoyle. It crashed upon a distant rampart, sword and war hammer wielders rushing toward it to break it apart. After checking for any other close calls, Emiko signed her answer.

"No. If she was worried about combat, she would have taken you over Aldis."

"I thought the same thing," Sage said with a sigh. "Is it . . . do you think it's because she worries about me? You don't think she's trying to keep me safe, do you?"

Oh, this lovesick thing was getting old. Sage was reading way further into this than anyone else was.

"I think Lani made the most rational decision," Emiko signed. "Hane for quick and quiet combat, Aldis for fast transport, and Lani for healing, scouting, and planning. That's it."

"But I'm our best scout," Sage pointed out. "I worry that something might happen to them while I'm focused on the fort's future rather than theirs. What if I missed the moment when I could have saved La—one of them?"

"I'm sure you'd know," Emiko signed between casting spells. "Don't you usually get flashes of bad things before they happen?"

"Yes, there's a precognition spell that usually lets me know when someone's about to be hurt or killed, but only seconds before it happens," Sage pointed out. "I could see her—them—die and there'd be nothing I could do about it from here."

Emiko sighed and cleared her throat. The archers were shooting down the incoming gargoyles, so she let her spell fade as she crouched down in front of Sage, setting a hand on his shoulder.

"First, even if you couldn't do anything, I could," Emiko assured him, holding his gaze. "And second: you know Lani would ring out before she would die. She would trust you to See that and make sure that we rang out, too."

"You think so?" Sage's wide eyes were full of hope.

"Of course!" Emiko beamed. "That's why she didn't take you. She needs you here, to make plans and call out changes. Can you imagine what would happen if Nieve had stayed back while Lani picked you to go with her?"

Sage chuckled ruefully. "She'd pace around for about an hour, then come chasing after us. You're right, Emi, it was a solid decision. I guess I just . . . I guess I wouldn't worry about it as much if I knew how Lani felt about me."

Sage's shining eyes raised a question Emiko didn't want to answer. Whether she lied to spare his feelings or said what she really felt to be true, it wouldn't benefit the team at all. And false hope only led to broken dreams and a rift between teammates. Luckily, just then Emiko was distracted by screams and shouts from the soldiers posted along the ramparts.

"What is going on?" she asked, looking around.

"There shouldn't be any—" Sage started to stand up, then stumbled, staggering to one knee, a hand pressed to his forehead. He gave a pained groan as Emiko tried to help him up. "I missed it. How could I miss it? It's that big and I didn't See—"

"See what?" Emiko asked, her heart slowly speeding up to patter rapidly against her breastbone. "What is it? I don't see—"

She just barely caught a glimpse of something round and dark breaking through the clouds over the center of the fort when Sage tackled her to the ground, landing half on top of her, his eyes still squeezed shut behind his glasses.

"Don't let it look at you. Its spells can penetrate your shroud if it sees you."

Emiko felt her heart stumble in its dead run. Despite the warning, she pushed herself up onto an elbow, peeking over the wall of the rampart.

The slick, round body of some floating monstrosity descended on the fort like a looming specter of death. Even from behind, Emiko recognized it as something from the ocular horror species of monsters: a glare king, maybe, or an ocular destroyer. The "body" was covered in squirming eye stalks, which roved constantly in search of victims to afflict with paralysis, weakness, or sleep. Those spells wouldn't be deadly—not always, anyway. But there was a chance that someone hit with a paralysis or sleep spell might topple over the ramparts and die from the resulting fall. No, the little eyes weren't so bad on their own. It was the big eye of the central body that had to be avoided at all costs.

A sound like lightning cauterizing a wound made Emiko gasp and cower behind the rampart. The walls shuddered violently, hard enough that Emiko's teeth rattled against each other. The crash of falling stones and the wild, frantic screams of soldiers on the wall constricted her chest, making it hard to breathe. If they didn't do something soon, the monster would tear the fortress walls down from the inside.

Emiko dared another peek over the rampart, trying to assess the damage done. A glimpse of white sclera had her flattening herself to the walkway again, body trembling. The beam of ruination was turning this way.

"It's coming toward us," Emiko whispered, heart hammering in her chest.

"The weakness is the eyeball, have to hit it there," Sage murmured, eyes shut tight. "Archers have to see to shoot, but that opens them up to attack. Too far away for one of my spells. Lightning? But what about the chant?"

"Do the smaller eye stalks have to see us, or just look in our direction? Sage!" She elbowed him when he didn't answer. "Does it need line of sight, or do the little eyes affect a general location?"

"Ah, um, it's—" Sage was clearly in a panic, and Emiko hadn't directly fought any of these types of monsters on her own before: Nieve always created an ice shield and Ren sent one of his contracted summonses out to slay them. Sage was the one who studied monsters, spells, and runes, telling the others how to fight. But when Sage got panicked, that information center shut down.

"Sage." Emiko spoke soft and low, swallowing to keep the quaver out of her voice. "Get your head out of the future and concentrate on right now. Do they need line of sight, or are the spells location-based?"

Sage blinked his eyes open, looking lost for a moment before swallowing hard. "Sight-based. It's the ruler subspecies. All eyes need to see their targets."

"Okay, good." Emiko let out a slow breath and rolled onto her back, rain falling on her face. Out of the corner of one eye, she could still see the great body of the ocular ruler, rain-slick and turning a slow circle, eye stalks writhing in a chaotic, squirming chorus. Her hand shook as she felt along her belt for the appropriate mana crystal, clicking it into the mana diffuser as she drew a deep breath. Times like this made her glad she had so much practice with poetry.

"Creeping shadows writhe/Rise along the sky-borne mist/Midnight clouds gather."

She channeled water mana into mist, filling that mist with umbral mana from her diffuser. Her spell shaped the shadow-cloud into a veil that grew to cover the ocular horror like a second skin, blocking the sight of its central eyeball as well as its eye stalks. She peeked cautiously over the rampart, making sure her spell had worked before standing up and offering a hand down to Sage.

"Good thinking," Sage said, his voice still quavering. "That won't hold it for long, though. Eventually it'll shred your cloud and I still don't know how we're going to—"

"Hyaaaaa-ah!" A vicious battle cry broke through the fearful cries and the scraped-stone sounds of the still-fighting gargoyles. A figure on the eastern rampart took a running leap off the low wall around the walkway, a massive sword held high above the figure's head. The rain made the torchlight weak, but even so, it was easy to make out the reckless figure as Nieve, grinning as she plunged into the shadow-cloud, swinging her sword down just as her boots sank into the mist. Emiko heard a noise like a groaning keen, and then both Nieve and the ocular ruler were plummeting into the center of the fortress.

"Wind who bows to none/I call upon our contract/Heed my every whim. Billow!" Emiko shouted the words in a breathless rush, fearful that she wouldn't be fast enough, or that she hadn't put enough power into the spell. Wind gathered and swirled beneath Nieve and the monster, slowing and softening their fall, as well as directing them away from most of the buildings, but as large as it was, Emiko couldn't completely avoid collateral damage: an armory crunched beneath the monster's weight, the black shadow-cloud still swirling around it, though the tentacle-like eyes were seething toward Nieve. The abrupt landing had only dropped Nieve to a single knee, her sword pierced deep inside the monster's flesh the same way she so often used her pick in ice: for balance. With Emiko and Sage leaning over the rampart to watch, Nieve ripped her sword free and slid down the monster's side.

Emiko wasn't sure how she did it, but Nieve circled around the shadow-cloud-cloaked monster, then drove her sword forward in a vicious jab.

Another keening wail, and then the shadow-cloud started to break apart. Sage shook Emiko's shoulder, pointing to the stairs. She nodded and together they ran for the ground level. By the time they got there, Nieve had her boot braced against the massive eyeball in the central body as she tugged her sword free. A gush of clear-colored gore came spilling out just before the monster carcass faded, leaving a pile of mana crystals behind. Nieve shook the ice off her sword before leaning it back against her shoulder, grinning as she lifted her head to look toward Emiko and Sage.

"Did I surprise him?" Nieve asked gleefully. "Was he blind? Tell me he was blind, Mi-mi."

Emiko winced, shooting a look over at Sage, still pale and shaken. If he'd been a little sturdier on his feet, she might have been able to cover for him, but as it was, Sage answered Nieve's question for her.

"He wasn't . . . completely surprised," Emiko lied. Sage just looked miserable; he had to know that he'd distracted himself by worrying about what Lani thought of him. He'd punish himself enough for that without Emiko having to say a word about it.

"Ha!" Nieve sheathed her sword with a flourish. "That's one treasure out of Sage's cut for me. Come help me pick these crystals up!"

"What are you even doing here?" Sage asked, finally finding his voice. "You were supposed to go to the barracks and sleep. Tomorrow is going to be an all-out battle; what if you're too tired by then?"

"Pft." Nieve rolled her eyes. "Too tired for a fight? That'll be the day. And who could sleep anyway with all these rocks crashing down along the walls?" She gestured vaguely at the few gargoyles still attacking the ramparts. The appearance of the ocular ruler had actually driven them out of Emiko's mind for a while, but now that she was listening, she could definitely hear them scraping along the walls as they fell, shattering as they hit the ground. Nieve swiped her foot through the pile of mana crystals left behind by the ocular ruler. She picked one up and squinted at it. "What mana is this? I don't recognize it."

"Careful, Nieve." Emiko took the crystal from her delicately. It was the same shape as any other mana crystal, but the color was a sullen red that reflected no light, completely different from the vibrant red of a fire mana crystal. She shivered as she placed it inside a pouch, rather than her belt. "It's ruin mana. Looks like it dropped a lot of it."

"Some perception mana crystals as well," Sage pointed out, stooping to help scoop up the crystals. His hands were still trembling slightly, making his gathering attempts clumsy at best.

"Let me help." Emiko knelt down and gingerly picked up each crystal, setting them gently inside her pouch. The crystals were hardy—no reason to think they'd break—but it seemed foolish not to take care when handling ruin mana crystals. They would have to sell these as treasures: Emiko's mana diffuser was only a prototype and therefore only worked with the base mana types.

"Were you really surprised?" Nieve asked, nudging Sage in the ribs with her elbow. "C'mon, Sage, you're supposed to be this great Seer! How did you miss me?"

"It was actually quiet for once," Sage huffed, regaining a bit of his usual color. "Even gargoyles make less noise than you do, Nieve. No wonder Lani made you stay behind."

"I may be noisy, but I killed the monster!" Nieve countered, hooking her hand over her hilt. "What were you going to do? Offer to read its fortune?"

"We were just formulating a plan when you so recklessly jumped off the ramparts"—Sage pointed up at the walls, which did seem dizzyingly high now that Emiko focused on them—"attacking a monster that could have killed you with a glance! And in case you forgot: we don't have a healer right now!"

"I— Oh, yeah." Nieve's brows snapped together as if she hadn't considered that. "Well, I didn't get hurt, so—"

"That's not the point!" Sage ran his hands back through his hair, clearly frustrated. "Maybe you were fine this time, but that doesn't mean you will be every time you leap without looking!"

"Hey, I waited for you to make the first move, but you didn't—"

Emiko yawned widely, then rubbed at her eyes. "It's sleepy, isn't it? Is it shift-change time yet?"

She let her eyelids droop, watching Sage and Nieve through her lashes. It might be manipulative, but she couldn't yell at them like Lani could, or tease them until they laughed like Wyle could. She certainly couldn't glare as threateningly as Ren could. So instead she let herself sway on her feet as Nieve and Sage exchanged glances. She even touched her neck and cleared her throat for good measure.

"It has been a long day," Nieve allowed. "Why don't you go to bed, Mi-mi? Sage and I can watch the rest of the night."

"We'll take opposite posts," Sage told her, patting her on the shoulder. "Nieve can take north and I'll take—"

"Why do I get north?" Nieve demanded to know.

"Do you really have to turn everything into a fight?" Sage asked wearily, pinching the bridge of his nose.

Emiko leaned into Nieve's shoulder, yawning again. "Nee-Nieve, I forgot where the barracks are."

Nieve's twisted frown hinted that she knew what Emiko was up to, but she sighed anyway and wrapped an arm around Emiko's shoulders. "Any more surprises tonight, Sage?"

"I can meditate on it if you'll give me a little time."

"I'll be back after I take Mi-mi to the barracks. And then I want the south side!"

"Fine," Sage replied with an exasperated sigh.

Emiko curled her hand around Nieve's as they walked toward the barracks. "You don't always have to fight, you know. Sometimes it's nice to be nice."

"And sometimes"—Nieve tugged at one of Emiko's hair buns with her free hand—"you can put up a fight. You don't always have to be so nice."

I thought I was putting up a pretty good fight, Emiko thought. *I think I might have won, too.*

CHAPTER 13

SAGE

Seer (hand mark), Citrine

Sage yawned widely, jaw popping, eyes tearing at the corners. He'd gotten a little sleep at the end of the nighttime attack, but not as much as he would have liked. Aldis arrived at the barracks just minutes past dawn with an order from Lani to "muster up" as Aldis had put it. It was the final push and the team was united again, awaiting the final assault on the fortress. By noon this day, they would finally finish the first room of the spire.

If they survived.

"I agree," Aldis muttered in response to Sage's yawn. "Far too early for this, isn't it? We all could have been snug in beds all night, fresh for this fight while waiting it out inside the fortress. Why does your team insist on making the challenges harder?"

"Less damage to the fortress this way," Sage explained briefly, too tired to take issue with Aldis's criticism. "Less spire constructs on our side lose their lives or get injured, too. Should get us more options for when we move to the next room."

Aldis grunted, a noise that seemed to encapsulate both doubt and acceptance at once. He held a canteen of cold tea cupped in both hands, the only breakfast item anyone had thought to grab. Sage, of course, had gotten a canteen of tea for Lani, for which she had been immensely grateful (she had actually smiled!), and Emiko had insisted on bringing tea for Hane as well, though as far as Sage could tell, Hane hadn't had a sip of it. They were the only one looking fresh and alert for the coming battle; everyone else appeared weary and slightly haggard.

The ground chosen for the final stand was a low hill, surprisingly close to the fortress. Sage had expected them to stage their fight closer to the enemy camp, but Lani had already explained that they wanted the soldiers at the fortress to do some of the fighting, just to prove that their enhancements and reorganization had yielded some benefits; that supposedly this fortress could stand on its own next time it came under attack. It sounded like a good plan, but it left the team in a vulnerable spot outside the walls in the middle of what would soon be a battlefield.

"One more time," Lani announced, raising her voice, a half-empty canteen of tea dangling from her fingertips. "Hane, you've got the big bad, whatever that is and whenever it shows up."

Hane lifted a hand in acknowledgment. They were crouched on the edge of the hill, looking out toward the enemy camp, as if they might see the enemy approaching before Emiko did.

"And if you need help—" Nieve started with a sharp-toothed grin, but Lani cut her off.

"If they need help, they'll call Emiko in," Lani said sternly. "You need to be on alert for the secondary challenges."

"Fine," Nieve groaned, as if acquiescing were physically strenuous. "But if I finish all those fights, I'm going straight for whatever behemoth monstrosity Hane is fighting."

"Check with Sage first," Lani instructed, giving him a quick nod, which he returned. "Aldis, you'll be on transport and you'll also gather any of the minor challenges to Nieve so she doesn't get too far away for me to heal her. Emiko"—Lani pointed up to where Emi was riding on a cloud, on lookout for the approaching enemy forces—"will be calling out patterns as well as creating cover. Sage, you and I will cover Aldis so he can teleport without worrying about his safety during the battle."

That last part sounded suggestive of Sage and Lani making sure Aldis didn't run away in the heat of battle, and by Aldis's sniff, he heard it, too. Sage tried to give him a bracing smile, but Aldis ignored it, taking a long pull from his tea instead.

"Sage, any new information?" Lani asked.

Sage closed his eyes and cast the spell Divine Future. He must not have gotten enough rest last night, because the first few visions he Saw were scattered and diverse. He Saw a climber he recognized by sight but not by name fall into a pit trap and save herself by twisting shadows into a net to catch herself. He Saw Ren and Wyle on a picnic just outside the spire, laughing at something one of them had said. He Saw that curious flash of reflected light that almost seemed to ripple, but it vanished too quickly for him to be sure. He Saw a lake of molten lava so hot he could almost feel his skin burning.

Sage drew a deep breath and focused his Sight on his teammates and the fortress scenario, willing the visions into relevance. He Saw low waves crash against the fortress walls, one after another, the later waves higher than the first ones. He Saw Nieve standing within a pillar of light, her hand shielding her eyes against its brilliance. He felt the lightless chill of watery depths and heard a low, threatening growl. Both sensations gave the impression of monsters, but the first was cloaked in immense shadows and the second was wreathed in points of fire, making each one impossible to See in any detail.

"The main army will hit the fortress, just as planned," Sage reported, interpreting his vision out loud. "There's going to be a lake monster, or something similar—"

Nieve hissed a "Yes!" and pumped her fist.

"—but Nieve, you're going to be busy with a different challenger."

"Resh," Nieve cursed. "What is it? It better be good."

"There's a bright light, so I think you're fighting someone with an attunement." Blood splashed across the vision. "Someone strong."

"I hope it's Ana." Nieve sounded excited. "I was hoping to see her again."

"There's going to be some kind of quadrupedal pack monsters with some magic abilities and maybe one or two surprises, but nothing we can't handle." Sage cast his Divine Imminent Threat spell on each of his teammates, hoping, as ever, it wouldn't be necessary, then blinked his eyes open. "It's not the worst we've seen, but I doubt we'll come through unscathed."

"Okay, in that case, Aldis, if Sage shouts out a name suddenly—"

"Port them here to our little hilltop, where the Seer and the Acolyte can protect them," Aldis concluded, with no small amount of skepticism in his voice. "Unless it's one of the three of us, in which case, I'll drop you back in the fort for safekeeping."

"Aldis, we really don't need your—"

"Hey, Lani!" Sage stepped in front of Aldis, cutting off their argument before it could start. "Did you ever figure out the next part of the trading sequence? I meant to ask before you left the fort yesterday."

"No, I didn't." Lani set a hand over her belt pouch. "I don't understand how these sequences work. Was I supposed to go just waving it around, or do you know who wants it?"

"No, I was hoping it would be obvious whenever it happened," Sage replied, disappointed. "That's okay. After this, I'll take a better look at it and see if—"

"They're coming!" Emiko shouted from her cloud. "Setting down the fog barrier for the archers!"

"Thank you, Emi!" Lani shouted up. "Okay, everyone, check your cleats. Nieve, get ready."

Nieve smirked as Sage and the others checked the metal spikes they had lashed onto the underside of their boots. Neither Nieve nor Hane wore them, but Nieve was a confident ice skater and Hane . . . well, Hane probably wouldn't even touch the ground once the fight started. Sage unhooked his dueling cane from his belt as a wall of fog formed between the fortress and the approaching enemy fighters and monsters. Emiko imbued her fog with acid, not strong enough to seriously damage armor, but just enough to damage the fletching on arrows fired through it, as well as bowstrings. By the time the army broke through the fog barrier, they would be too close for arrows to be effective.

The idea wasn't to stop the army, though Emi's fog and Nieve's ice would certainly slow them down. The idea was to pick up the more dangerous elements and handle them before they could reach the fort. So the lake monster, the attuned fighters, and whatever other monsters this army brought would get rounded up and hopefully subdued so they couldn't cause any undue damage to the fortress. Nieve would pick up any obvious threats, but it was Sage's job to find the less obvious challengers amid the sea of charging soldiers. Luckily, talented warriors tended to stand out.

"The first ranks are breaking through the fog," Hane said, voice low as they maintained their crouch on the hill's edge. Emi's fog wall billowed outward before rank upon rank of armed and armored soldiers spilled through. Nieve grinned wickedly as she rolled her wrists, turning her palms out at her sides, conjuring ice to cover the ground in an outward radius from their hill. Sage pointed his dueling cane between his feet and channeled a small punch of gray mana through it, cracking the ice to step out of it. He crunched his cleats through a layer of unbroken ice, making sure he was steady before offering an arm to Aldis and helping him do the same. Lani stood just too far away to assist, and anyway, she'd balanced on one foot while Nieve laid the ice layer down, then twisted her trapped foot free of the ice. Hane, somehow, was still in their same crouched position, the ice smooth and unbroken beneath their boots. Sage hadn't even seen them move, which made the feat all the more impressive. Nieve shifted her weight from side to side, gliding effortlessly with the tip of her sword scraping along the ice in perfect arcs. She looked like a hunter waiting for her prey to come close enough for her to pounce on.

The first ranks of enemy soldiers had their ankles encased in ice the moment they stepped out of the fog barrier, sending them crashing to the ground. The second and third ranks tripped over the first, causing mass chaos and confusion. The few who did manage to avoid the pileup went skidding on the ice, fighting for balance in order to continue their charge. Nieve shaped ice walls around the team's little hill like a wedge, forcing the regular foot soldiers to go around, sending them on toward the fort. They needed to keep the area around them open for the real fight.

"I see someth—" Emiko was still shouting as Hane took off so quickly that it looked almost like they were flying over the ice rather than gliding. Sage gaped as a massive shape tore through the top of Emiko's fog barrier, weaving through the air the way a snake swims through water. A serpent? No, not just any serpent: an undead skeletal serpent, empty eye sockets black with shadows as it turned its head this way and that, as if searching for something.

"Seems a little out of touch with the setting, doesn't it?" Aldis asked critically, surprising Sage with his calm demeanor. "I mean, nothing else has been undead so far. Plenty of monsters, sure. A few attuned fighters, yes. But the undead?"

Sage didn't know how to respond: it seemed only a matter of time before the sinuous mass of clinking bones spotted Emi and snapped her out of the sky. Hane was speed-skating at a pace even Nieve couldn't match, likely aided by transference mana, but they were still on the ground—how were they possibly going to fight a flying serpent?

"Aldis!" Sage gripped the Wayfarer's sleeve in a white-knuckled grip. "Shouldn't you teleport them, or open a portal, or—"

Before Sage could finish the thought, Hane reached the fog barrier. They leapt, somersaulting at the apex, then *landed* on the fog barrier, running up the side of it as if it were both solid and level. Sage could only gape in astonishment.

"Well, fog is only water," Aldis pointed out unnecessarily, shaking Sage's hand off his arm. "Why are you surprised? Aren't you the one who knows when something's about to go wrong?"

"I . . ." Sage couldn't tear his eyes away from Hane racing up the vertical fog wall. When they reached the pinnacle of the fog, they kicked off, defying gravity in a flying arc, arms in tight at first, then stretching out, each hand gripping a tonfa. They twisted in midair, putting a rotation into their descent before getting their feet under them and landing on the spine of the flying, skeletal serpent. "I just . . . didn't expect that."

"Expect anything," Lani called over her shoulder. "And don't get distracted! We all have jobs to do, Hane's just doing theirs!"

It was impossible to look away from Hane's "job," especially as the serpent screamed and looped back on itself, snapping teeth as long as swords right where Hane had landed. Hane dropped from the spine, jumping from inner rib to inner rib, leading the serpent on a frantic, aerial chase. Sage had to shake his head and forcefully look away from the spectacle.

"Oh, oh!" Nieve's shout made Sage swing his dueling cane up defensively, but she was grinning as she pointed skyward. "That's the lake serpent they beat earlier in this scenario, isn't it! That's why it doesn't look like it fits!"

That did make a bit of sense, scenario-wise: an undead serpent bent on revenge. Maybe it had been looking for Hane in the first place. Either way, it was a rather difficult spectacle to ignore.

"Focus!" Lani called out. "Sage will predict it if Hane is going to fall, and Aldis will catch them. We have our own fights to worry about."

"If only," Nieve groaned, shifting her weight so she twirled a circle on the conjured ice. "When are the good fights going to—"

"There!" Sage's hand was up and pointing before he even realized his Foresight spell was showing him something that wasn't there yet. "Aldis, grab the girl in the headscarf. That's a dangerous one."

"Is it Ana?" Nieve looked giddy, like a child on their birthday. "Please let it be Ana!"

"Geez, Nieve, are you going to fight her or ask her out on a date?" Sage asked as Aldis cast the teleport spell.

"I mean, if it were the beginning of the scenario—" Nieve stopped herself as someone dressed in loose brown clothing with a bare midriff suddenly appeared in their midst, looking moderately surprised as she flicked her fists forward, long metal claws extending out over her hands. "Ana! I missed you!"

Spears of brilliant light made Sage take a step back, free hand coming up to shade his eyes.

"You again!" A snarling, unamused voice. "Fine. Let's finish this!"

"I finished it once before and I'll finish it again!" Sage could just make out Nieve's feral grin as she tugged her headband down over her eyes. "My only regret is that I won't get to see your blood bounce when it hits the ice."

Steel claws crashed against an ice-covered sword, and then Nieve and the assassin were circling each other at the base of the low hill. Sage kept the fight in the corner of his eye to keep the flashes of light from blinding him.

"She's going to toy with this one, isn't she?" Lani asked, ice crackling as she moved to stand closer to Sage and Aldis.

"She always toys with the cute ones," Sage replied, still scanning the hordes of enemies running past. "Keep your eyes open. There have to be more challenges than an undead serpent and an Illum—"

Insight moved Sage's body before he was fully aware of what he was doing. By the time the low growl resounded off the ice walls keeping the team relatively isolated, Sage had already pulled Lani back by her arm and knocked Aldis off his feet with a swipe of his dueling cane. A massive four-legged monster as big as a tiger landed right where the three of them had been standing.

"What is—" Aldis cut off abruptly as another shadow-colored beast leapt toward them. Aldis cowered, but Sage stepped over him, blasting the moving target with a powerful burst of gray mana from his dueling cane. Even with a direct hit, the monster was barely deterred off course. It landed far too close to the three of them, the scent of musk and brimstone alarmingly powerful. Thick, leathery skin encased the monster from snout to tail, save for a ruff of fur around its neck like a mane. Each paw was massive and tipped in long, black claws. The bony ridges down its spine looked almost like fins, except rigid, sharp, and tipped with venomous barbs. Flames frothed at the creature's mouth as fangs began to part, but then Aldis screamed and threw a hand out and the monster vanished from view.

"There's more of them," Lani called, turning her back to Sage's, cutlass held out by her side. "Four, by my count. What are they, Sage? Some kind of magical dire wolf?"

"Lahava," Sage answered automatically, recalling the page from a bestiary. "Not commonly seen below the twentieth floor of the Tortoise Spire. Pack animals, like wolves, only larger and able to breathe fire. Their skin is resistant to ordinary blades and their bones are resistant to cracking and breaking. They're also resistant to magic; you'll have to use a lot more mana in order to affect them at all."

"How in the name of the great goddess do you fight something like this?" Aldis squealed, jumping to his feet. "I can teleport them all away, but—"

"But then they'd just wreak havoc somewhere else on the battlefield," Lani concluded grimly. "Where did you send the first one?"

"I dropped it over the lake," Aldis replied, shooting a sidelong glare over at Lani as he unhooked his dueling cane from his belt. "Did you think I'd drop it inside the fortress?"

"Not the time, Aldis," Sage interrupted, keeping his voice low. "Nieve and Hane are busy, so this one is on us."

"The lake is really far away. Can't Aldis just—" Lani broke off as one of the lahava belched a fireball at her. She threw her hand out, conjuring an orb of water the same size as the fireball to block it. The magics hissed on contact, but the fireball overwhelmed the water orb, sending steam and chunks of flaming resin raining back on Lani, Sage, and Aldis. Before the steam could begin to blister his skin, Sage felt the cooling effects of a healing spell washing over him. He let out a controlled breath and tried to think through the fight.

"That should have worked," Lani gritted through clenched teeth. "The density of their magic is greater than what I can conjure."

"It may be part of their magic resistance," Sage suggested, focusing on the left lens of his glasses, where his Foresight spell showed him several seconds into the future. "Be careful making gestures to cast spells; they're intelligent enough to associate Aldis's hand motions with his teleportation spell now that they've seen it once. The best chance Aldis has to teleport them is when they stop moving to breathe out those fireballs. But they work together as a pack, so when one stops moving—"

The future he'd seen played out just as he was talking, forcing him to cut off the explanation. One of the smaller lahava dropped its head low into its shoulders, flames hissing and spitting as its jaw hinged open. As Aldis started to raise his hand to cast the teleportation spell, another lahava leapt at him, powerful claws extended, fangs flashing with carnal hunger. A high-pitched whine emitted from Aldis's throat as he pulled his arm back defensively, as if bracing for impact. Sage and Lani moved as one, Sage pointing his dueling cane, Lani conjuring a powerful jet stream of water from her hand, both impacting the monster's side and knocking it away at the apex of its leap. Of course, then the first lahava finished its fireball spell and they all had to dive to the ground to avoid it. Sage managed to land with his dueling cane outstretched, so when another lahava tried darting at them, he hit it full in the face with a beam of light mana. It didn't really hurt it, but it did force it to shy away from the bright light.

"We need one of our fighters here," Lani said, jumping back up to her feet. "Aldis, bring in—"

"No, don't," Sage interrupted, flinching as his Divine Imminent Threat spell flashed before his eyes, showing him a tender throat slashed by three parallel lines. He didn't bother looking any further to see who the victim was. "If we pull Nieve away, that Illuminator will kill one of us." It hadn't been a possibility before, with Nieve safely holding off the Illuminator, but if Lani called her over, there was a high probability of it happening. "We can handle this on our own, we just have to fight together."

"I'm all for standing and fighting, Sage, but how do we fight monsters resistant to blades, bludgeoning, and magic?" Lani demanded to know, holding her cutlass defensively across her body. "That also breathe fire for ranged attacks and have venomous spikes to counter close combat. Seriously, why are these monsters?"

"They developed those defenses to protect them from being eaten by serpents," Sage reported, still filtering visions, trying to find the winning scenario. His death mana might hurt them, but only if he got close enough to touch them, and even then, his death mana was new, his spells fairly weak. He would drain his mana pool quickly if he had to keep blasting these beasts with double the usual amount of power he channeled into his spells. Lani needed to save most of her mana to heal—and they were going to need healing. Nieve would encase these creatures in ice and let them suffocate; Hane would probably get behind them and find a weak spot to exploit somehow. But how was Sage supposed to defend against four deadly, quasi-intelligent monsters while protecting Lani and Aldis?

Sage hadn't even noticed the dark clouds gathering overhead until a searing flash of lightning struck the next monster to leap toward him. The lahava's eyes went wide, a belch of smoke erupting from its mouth before it fell hard to the ground, twitching in its death throes.

"Emi!" Sage looked up as the low black clouds rumbled ominously, making the remaining lahava monsters cower.

"Keep low!" Emiko shouted down from her cloud. "I can't control it completely. You should create a vacuum-shield to protect yourselves!"

"I can't—" Sage started, but was interrupted.

"I can." Aldis rocked back a step, putting himself between Lani and Sage. "Keep them off me while I cast it."

The moment Aldis lifted his hand to cast the spell, two of the three remaining lahava charged, the third hanging back to charge a fireball spell. Lani struck the first one with a water-jet spell hard enough that it knocked her backward into Aldis even as it repelled the lahava. Her cleats failed to break the ice on the ground and she stumbled, but Aldis caught her elbow in his free hand, helping her catch her balance even as he continued to cast. Sage fired off rapid bursts of light mana from his dueling cane, confusing and distracting the lahava that darted at him, keeping low to the ground. When it staggered, off balance and shaking its head, Sage lunged, jabbing the tip of his dueling cane into its eye. He channeled a spell called Touch of Death, making the lahava howl and reel backward, its black eye turning a sightless milky white. It staggered when it walked, but it was still alive and very much dangerous.

Aldis completed his vacuum-air-shield spell just as lightning cut the sky again. One fork of it danced along the air shield, leaving Sage deaf in its wake, but at least it hadn't broken through. The other fork struck the fire-breathing lahava that had hung back, making it spit its flames prematurely as it howled in pain. The lightning didn't kill this one, but Sage could see its muscles contracting violently beneath its leathery hide, as if it currently had no control over its body.

"Aldis, when they stop moving long enough to cast that fireball spell, teleport them away," Sage directed, a plan finally emerging from the slowly condensing myriad of futures. "Lani and I will cover you, just wait for your chance."

"Call out if you guys get injured," Lani added. "I'm going to have my hands too full to watch over you."

"Right." Sage chanced a glance over at Nieve, nearby but entirely absorbed in her fight with the Illuminator. Nieve was still grinning, despite the fact that her eyes were covered with her headband, but her leather armor sported several bloody stains, and the ice around her was all scratched and scarred from her opponent's clawlike weapons. Nieve would probably be fine even without Lani's healing, especially with her habit of covering wounds with patches of ice armor, but Sage was still leery about leaving her on her own for too long. Nieve could sometimes take poor risks, and any attuned opponent risked being stronger or smarter than they appeared at first blush.

Hane was still fighting on their own, too—or at least Sage hoped so, if the twining skeletal serpent was anything to judge by. Emiko's thunderclouds made it difficult to see more than the general shape of the serpent in the sky, but it looked as if the serpent was doubled back on itself several times over. Was Hane trying to tie it in a knot? Whatever the circumstance, at least the serpent wasn't attacking the fortress.

A flash of insight brought Sage back to his immediate problem: the encircling lahava. The one he'd partially blinded drooled as it growled, looking all the more dangerous for its sightless eye. The lightning-struck one was shaking itself off, looking a little scorched but recovering fast. Emiko often complained that combining mana types was difficult for her, so subsequent lightning strikes likely wouldn't be as strong as the first one had been. At least the first lahava Emi zapped wasn't getting back up.

Lightning continued to crackle and flash overhead, but as long as Sage, Lani, and Aldis stayed under the vacuum-shield, it wouldn't hurt any of them. While lightning might break a single-layer air shield, the vacuum-shield was a dual-layer shield with all air bled out from between the two layers, keeping heat and magic from passing through. Emiko was usually the one to cast such a spell, but she had probably rushed to cast the thundercloud first. Even as Sage looked for her, he caught only the tail of her cloud vanishing, likely gone to go help the fort, or possibly Hane if they needed the assistance.

One of the prowling lahava lunged low, teeth snapping at Lani's ankle. Lani cursed and stabbed down with the tip of her cutlass. The blade wedged between the creature's teeth; it bit down, viciously shaking its head in an attempt to wrench the blade from Lani's grasp. Lani gritted her teeth and held on, but she didn't have a lot of room to fight it off while trying to stay under the air shield. Sage longed to help her, but the other two lahava were watching him carefully as they prowled, making him worried that they would pounce at the first sign that he was distracted.

"Aldis! Can you teleport this miserable beast while it's right here?" Lani asked, still struggling to free her blade.

"Not unless you want to send your sword along with it," Aldis replied.

"I'd rather not be weaponless." Lani jerked her arm backward, jostling both Sage and Aldis. "I'm going to kick free on three; try to teleport it then. Ready? One. Two—"

Before "three," the other two lahava crouched low to the ground, then pelted toward Sage in a snarling, drooling rush. His dueling cane was poised to fire with double the usual amount of gray mana to fuel a blast, but Sage hadn't been expecting both of them at once—a double-strength blast wouldn't be enough to knock them both away. And with their bodies low to the ground, Emi's lightning wouldn't catch them before they got under the safety offered by the vacuum-shield. Sage gritted his teeth, preparing to physically fend off at least one beast when Aldis spun, holding his cane parallel with Sage's and firing off a burst of mana at the same time that Sage took his shot. Sage's target was knocked back, but Aldis managed to catch his target midlunge, tossing it up into the air, where Emiko's lightning caught it. Sage heard it yelp and howl, but a scream from Lani drew his attention before he could see if it was dead or not.

The lahava gripping her sword had yanked her off balance, and when she tried to get her footing, her cleats slipped on the ice. She fell with a crash, the lahava ripping the sword away from her, then snapping at her face. Sage only had enough time to think *But I didn't see this!* before Aldis vanished, reappearing just behind the beast's shoulder and laying his hand on its back. Scant inches remained between Lani's face and the lahava's teeth, and then the lahava was simply gone.

"You—" Lani gasped, one hand over her heart. "You could have done that this whole time?"

"Well, I wasn't going to try touching one unless it was suitably distracted." Aldis gestured with his hand, and Lani's fallen sword appeared in it. He handed it to her as she pushed herself up. "Those things are far too fast, even for a teleport."

There wasn't time for true relief to set in as the lahava Sage had blasted away regained its feet and leapt at him, drawing his attention from Aldis and Lani. Caught off guard, Sage swung his dueling cane at the beast only to have it ripped from his hand. In the instant where the beast turned its head to drop the dueling cane, Sage saw that it was the milky-eyed one that had caught his death spell earlier, so with a brazen last hope, Sage latched onto the beast's head with both hands, directing as much death mana as he could handle into the monster. With hope, he might paralyze it, or blind the other eye, anything that might give his companions an advantage to actually kill it. He redirected his shroud to protect his leg only seconds before teeth as hot as embers latched around his upper thigh while still channeling death mana into the beast's massive head. Something tore at his arm where his shroud was thinner, but he paid it no mind. Sage squeezed his eyes shut as he dug his fingers into the leathery scalp, pouring as much of his mana pool into his Touch of Death spell as possible. He felt the pressure increase over his thigh, and then slowly the lahava's jaw relaxed. It slid to the ground with a heavy thud, sliding over the ice, its single working eye darting around frantically as if confused as to why it couldn't move.

"Sage!" Lani sounded panicked. "Don't move!"

"I'm okay." Sage turned back, feeling giddy with relief. He grinned despite the fact that the fight was far from over. "It's only paralyzed, you should—"

Sage blinked and his vision tunneled, Lani and Aldis suddenly seeming much farther away though neither one of them had taken a single step. Strange colors washed over his vision as if he were looking through colored glass, first pale pinks and oranges, then deep reds and purples. The world seemed to be tipping onto its side.

Oh. Sage touched his arm, fingers coming away bloody. *The spines got me. I'm . . .*

Someone grabbed him by the shoulders, pushing him down to sit on the icy ground. He heard Lani's voice, both near and far at the same time, as if she had an echo. "Aldis, cover us! Call Emi in close if you can!"

"I've got her."

Sage's eyes closed, but that didn't stop him from seeing. Or maybe Seeing was more accurate. Suddenly, he was outside his body, watching as he slumped over on that cold hilltop with Lani placing both of her hands over his chest. He saw the threads of green magic leaking from her hand directly into his chest and felt the cool touch of healing magic.

I'll be all right, Sage thought, a feeling of peace settling over him. *Lani's the best healer ever, I'm sure she'll save me.*

Unless I'm already dead.

That was a grim thought, but one that begged considering. Nothing like this had ever happened to Sage before, and while it was a little disconcerting, it wasn't all that alarming. He'd heard that some attuned who specialized in mental mana were able to project a sense of their consciousness a limited distance from their bodies before, so he knew this sort of out-of-body experience wasn't completely unnatural. That, and he didn't feel dead. Whatever that felt like.

Putting aside the question of his own mortality for the time being, Sage looked around, wondering how much of this he would remember later. Aldis teleported the paralyzed lahava before stooping to pick up Sage's dueling cane. The thunderclouds still surged with lightning, but it was a mere crackle now, more light than lightning. Strangely, Sage couldn't hear much of anything in this vision: no voices, no tolls of thunder, no crash of weapons. The lack of sound stole the urgency from the raging battle, making the whole scene feel nonsensical, like watching a dream play out.

One of the lahava monsters Aldis poked with a dueling cane twitched, making Aldis recoil sharply, his expression so alarmed that Sage would have laughed had he been able. Half a wink later, the body of the lahava vanished, presumably teleported out to the lake with the others. After that, Aldis retreated to stand over Lani and Sage's body, dueling canes held out from his body protectively, though Sage predicted that if anything truly dangerous came for them, Aldis would likely teleport the three of them to safety rather than stand and fight.

Lani remained poised over Sage, a look of intense concentration on her face as green magic wreathed her hands. A single braid had freed itself from her bun, dangling forward of her face as she worked, making Sage wish he were corporeal enough to tuck it behind her ear while knowing full well he'd never have the courage to do such a thing if he were conscious. He would have been content watching her heal him until he revived, but curiosity about this new phenomenon drew his focus like a phantom itch. With a glance around the battlefield, Sage wondered how far from his body he could travel, and how much of what he was seeing was real.

Nieve was still battling the Illuminator nearby, though as Sage focused on her, it seemed she had lost a bit of her good humor. Her red headband had been cut away and lay half-trampled in the ice, one of the ends waving limply in the wind. Three parallel cuts marring Nieve's face—one of them perilously close to her eye—bled freely, the lines disappearing somewhere in her tangled mane of black hair. Her leather armor was scratched and scored, but from what Sage could see, the wounds on her face were the worst. Despite that, she kept her eyes closed as she fought, ignoring the lances of light that reflected off her icy pillars and ground cover. The Illuminator gained enough distance for a running start, dropping to her knees midslide, claws extended as if to cut Nieve's ankles out from under her. Fear for his friend's life made Sage try to cry out a warning, but he couldn't make a sound in this form. But even without a shout from Sage, Nieve seemed to know exactly where her opponent was: just before the Illuminator could land her deadly strikes, Nieve surged forward, slamming her knee into the

Illuminator's face. Sage was grateful he couldn't hear the crack and pop of cartilage, but he couldn't avoid seeing the spray of blood and saliva as the Illuminator reeled backward from the force of Nieve's kick. Nieve grabbed the shorter woman by the back of her collar, dragging her along like a chastised puppy as Nieve shouted something up at Aldis and Lani. The Illuminator struggled feebly in Nieve's grasp but seemed sufficiently dazed from the blow to her face.

A shadow rolled over the little hill, drawing Sage's attention skyward, where Hane still battled the undead serpent. Perhaps "battled" was too strong a term: Hane seemed to be doing more distracting than anything else. Part of the serpent's neck was stuck within its own skeletal rib cage, but that didn't stop it from coiling its body to bring Hane closer to its snapping jaws. Shadowy magic burned like black flames at each of its joints, which meant the undead construct was likely being held together by umbral mana. Sage felt especially useless just then: he was the only person on the team with light mana, the only one with the ability to burn away that umbral mana. Perhaps Nieve could "convince" the Illuminator to turn on the undead serpent, but that would take time. And Hane was moving slowly as they balanced on the rounded tips of vertebrae along the serpent's back.

The serpent's body writhed as it fought to free its head while also pulling a coil of its long body toward its snapping jaws, bringing Hane along for the ride. Hane somersaulted backward, landing precariously close to the narrow tip of the tail. Just as Sage was certain they would lose their balance, the tail snapped and Hane propelled themself in a leap over the serpent's head, traipsing now along the thicker spines above the rib cage. Was Hane injured? They appeared to be moving almost sluggishly. They couldn't be out of mana already, could they?

The serpent rolled its body, pitching Hane forward toward the skull, one shadowy eye socket watching as Hane rolled forward. They stopped their momentum by bracing their hands on the joint that connected the skull to the neck, then pushed off backward into a freefall. The serpent whirled to chase, most likely deeming Hane helpless while twisting in midair, but then, at a simple gesture from Hane, every joint they had touched or stepped upon along the serpent's back surged with an explosion of water, the largest splashing out from behind its skull in a great, wet X-shape. That in itself wouldn't have been enough to destroy the magic keeping the undead serpent animated, but the sudden flash of lightning that struck the X-shaped slash certainly was. The lightning leapt from joint to joint, shooting out sparks each time it hit the pocket of water Hane had left behind, hidden within the shadows. Sage could only imagine the beast's terrible scream as the shadows were rent apart, the pieces of its body tumbling from the sky to crash to the battlefield below.

Sage felt a tug at his chest but ignored it as he searched the sky, scanning each cloud until he found Emiko, eyes wide, shouting something frantically as she pointed at Hane, still falling at breakneck speed toward the ground. A pillowy white cloud formed around Hane, but they fell right through it, scattering the vapor into filmy tendrils. Another thick white cloud formed, then another, and another, all directly in the path of Hane's fall. Sage felt a cool wave of relief wash over him as he realized the clouds were slowing Hane's fall. Before they reached the ground, they appeared to be moving at a pace akin to walking, flipping around upright to land lightly on their feet.

Another sharp tug made Sage feel breathless—or whatever passed for breathless in this less-than-corporeal form. He caught the barest glimpse of Emiko streaking downward on her cloud, a nebulous trail of vapor spooling out behind her before his focus was forcibly snapped back to Lani, hovering over his body on the icy hilltop.

"C'mon, Sage, breathe!" Lani commanded, her voice distant and echoing, the first thing he'd heard since entering this state. "I converted all the poison, so why aren't you breathing?"

"Want me to hit him?" Nieve prowled nearby, still dragging the Illuminator along behind her, the other woman's hands and ankles bound by manacles of ice. "Hitting him usually gets his attention."

No, don't let her hit me! Sage tried to protest, but nobody seemed to hear him.

"I don't know." Lani shoved her braids back in a frustrated gesture, making Sage's heart ache. "Maybe a good shock to his system would wake him up? He's alive, he's just not . . . here."

Sage felt as if an invisible rope were drawing him closer and closer to his body. It was getting harder and harder to switch his focus, though through his periphery he could see both Hane and Emiko converging on their location. Aldis stood nearby, a worried expression on his face.

"Here, let me get a good crack across his face," Nieve said, though she lacked her usual good humor. If Sage didn't know any better, he'd think Nieve was concerned for him.

Sage relented as his focus shifted, making it so he could only look upward from the space between his body and Lani poised over him. As freeing as it felt to drift outside his body, it seemed that returning was the only thing that would keep Nieve from hitting him.

Sage's vision went entirely dark; the only sounds in his ears were the distant echoes of voices. He felt cold all over but burning hot at once. He gasped a breath into empty lungs, raising an arm defensively as his Sight warned him of an incoming blow. When his vision resolved, he saw only Lani, her brown eyes startled wide.

"Don't let her hit me," Sage gasped.

Then everything went truly dark.

CHAPTER 14

ALDIS

Wayfarer—Travel Specialization (hand mark), Sunstone

It was with deepest effort that Aldis kept himself from rolling his eyes and urging that they all simply get on with it. The final fight of the scenario was over and the part he was really looking forward to was up next. His nerves kept his impatience in check, but only just barely. In theory, his plan should work, but, well, theories had to be tested before they could be proven. He suspected this was half the reason this group had chosen to recruit him over all the other Wayfarer applicants, and if he failed to produce results, well, it was back to slogging through lower floors for a while.

The team stood in the fortress commander's office, with Lani giving a detailed summary to the commander who had greeted them upon first arriving in this scenario. Aldis didn't quite see why it was necessary to talk to a fake person at all, but it was a good respite. Sage was still recovering from the lahava's venom and . . . whatever else had happened to him while he'd been blacked out. He didn't seem quite right yet, muttering odd things and swaying on his feet. Nieve had his arm pulled over her shoulders to keep him upright, her face tight with concern. Emiko stuck close to Sage's other side, casting worried glances up at him and patting his hand consolingly. Hane alone looked calm and reposed, as if they hadn't just fought an undead serpent and fallen from a height that should have killed them.

Sweat drying on his skin made Aldis shiver. Nieve's ice had made the battlefield uncomfortably cold while fear and adrenaline made him sweat: not a pleasant combination. He tugged at the front of his tunic, feeling his clothing peel away reluctantly from his skin. His extremities—mostly his fingers, feet, and legs—were still cold-shocked and thawing slowly. In Aldis's opinion, it would have required but a moment's consideration to exempt the hilltop they'd used as a last stand from being covered in ice, but Nieve didn't strike him as particularly refined in the use of her magic. No, she seemed more likely to punch someone who tried offering her magic advice than take it.

Lucky Nieve hadn't been the gambler, or else Aldis probably would have gotten tossed off the spire gateway before they could even begin.

They'll forget all about that when they see what I can do, Aldis thought confidently. Then less confidently: *If it works.*

"Did Hane get down safely?" Sage asked, a little loudly, sharply drawing everyone's attention. His eyes were bleary as he shouted: "They were falling— We have to go back!"

Hane leaned around past Aldis and waved a hand to get Sage's attention. "I'm fine. No need to worry."

"How do you know Hane fell?" Emiko asked, her brow furrowed. "Weren't you knocked out from the venom by then?"

"I was . . ." Sage's eyes went in and out of focus rapidly. He lunged forward a step, making Nieve stagger for a moment before catching him. "Lani! Lani! It's now!"

"Sage— What's now?" Lani asked, concern in her eyes as she turned away from the fort commander. "Are you going to be okay? Do we need to ring out and have someone look at you?"

"No, I'm back now. I'm solid." Sage touched a hand to his chest as if to prove he was, in fact, solid. That made Aldis a little leery: could they really move on inside the spire with their Seer acting so loopy? "Lani, it's here! I remember now, the clue was the mother." He chuckled and shook his head. Everyone else exchanged concerned looks.

"What's here, Sage?" Lani asked, uncharacteristically gentle.

"They said their mother wanted them to be a commander." Sage laughed like a drunkard. "That means it's here, right? You still have it, don't you?"

Lani shot Nieve a confused look, but Nieve only returned a shrug. Lani pulled open a belt pouch, letting it hang open to reveal the contents. Aldis saw a few potion bottles, some rolls of bandaging, and a dark metallic gleam before Lani began sifting through the contents to show them to Sage.

"Do you need a potion?" Lani asked. "Or some bandages? Water?"

"Are those smelling salts?" Nieve asked, jerking her chin toward something in the bag.

"Yes." Lani held up a tiny corked jar. "Do you think that's what he wants?"

"No, I think it's what he needs." Nieve held her hand out and Lani dropped the bottle into her palm. Just as Nieve ripped the cork out with her teeth, the fortress commander exclaimed.

"Apologies, Captain Lani." He leaned over his desk, eyebrows nearly brushing his hairline. "But is that real?"

"Is what . . . This?" Lani drew a revolver out of her belt pouch almost as if she had forgotten it was in there. Perhaps she had: Aldis had forgotten all about it as well.

"Wow. We don't see very many of these." The fort commander touched the butt of the gun with a finger, the way someone might pet a snake. "This seems like it might come in handy in the future of this fort's defense. Is it possible I could tempt you with a trade?"

"Oh, I don't see why not." Aldis barely withheld a chuckle; it didn't seem as if Lani was as skilled a negotiator as Sage was when it came to trading sequence items. "What are you offering?"

"I'm not really certain if it's quite equivalent . . ." The fortress commander muttered to himself for a moment as he searched through drawers in his desk. "But I came across this key a while ago. Perhaps you'll find a use for it."

Aldis had seen plenty of spire keys before—one couldn't climb a spire without running across a wide variety of them; they were used for all manner of things: doors, chests, lifts, traps, once even a drawbridge. But this one was gleaming and golden, with a round, faceted diamond set into the bow. Was that normal for trading sequences? The key looked almost like a treasure itself!

"I think that's a fair trade," Lani confirmed with a nod, just as Sage began coughing from the smelling salts Nieve held under his nose.

"There you are, then." The commander handed over the key and Lani delicately placed the revolver in his hands. And Aldis learned a newfound respect for trading sequences; if he didn't get invited back to this group, he'd be sure to mention it in the next group he climbed with. "I suppose you all will be off on your next assignment from headquarters. Thank you for all you've done for us here."

"Just doing our jobs," Lani said formally, slipping the key inside her bag.

The fort commander gave each of them a formal salute, meeting each of their eyes just once. "I'm sure a communication from headquarters will reach you soon. I wish you well on your travels."

"Yes, thank you," Aldis said, the words lost in the discordant words of thanks from his other team members. Sage was gasping for breath and pushing away from Nieve by the time the fort commander left the room, closing the door behind him. Lani and Emiko caught Sage as he staggered away from Nieve, clumsy and off balance, but at least his eyes looked sharper than they had before.

"Goddess, that stuff stings!" Sage scrubbed at his red-rimmed eyes. "Did you get the key? Or did we miss it?"

"I have the key," Lani assured him. "Looks like a good one, too. Are you feeling better, Sage?"

"Yeah, I think . . . I think I'm feeling better now. Like me."

Well, that was a little more cryptic than Aldis wanted to contend with at the end of a scenario. Looking around, he caught concerned looks on the faces of Sage's longtime friends and guessed that this wasn't normal. Sage didn't appear concerned, however, getting his balance and adjusting his glasses quite calmly.

"I'm afraid I have a few holes in my memory. What happened with Nieve's Illuminator friend?" Sage glanced around the office, looking confused. "Did you kill her?"

"Ana? No, I just broke a lot of things she needed. Like her spirit." Nieve grinned as she cracked her knuckles. "She's locked up in the prison now. They're gonna ask her for some information on the enemy army."

"Oh. That's smarter than I expect from you." Nieve punched Sage on the arm and he returned the favor. He looked around again, face coloring slightly when he met Lani's gaze, then smiling as he tugged at one of Emiko's hair buns. "Are we finished, then? Ready to move on?"

"I . . . I'm still concerned that we might need to stop and get you checked out." Lani pursed her lips, watching him intently. "Are you sure you're okay? Not . . . damaged?"

"Yes, I'm fine," Sage insisted. "I think the venom may have affected my mental mana a bit, or maybe my mental mana saved me. I'm not really sure. I'll look into it after the climb, but I'm fine now. Really."

Lani's mouth twisted to the side. "Fine. But if you start acting funny again, I'm ringing you out. We need our Seer as grounded as possible."

As they talked, the fort commander's office had slowly faded out around them, like the fabric of a dream unraveling, leaving only the door behind. The room around them didn't seem nearly large enough to have encompassed the scenario—especially considering how high the fortress walls had been—but Aldis had long since stopped questioning the rules of what spire magic could accomplish.

"He says he's fine and he's not talking all goofy anymore." Nieve threw another punch at Sage, as if to prove he was fine, but he sidestepped it, glaring back at her. "See? All better. Let's go!"

"You need a better method of checking to see if someone's okay other than hitting them," Sage informed her.

Nieve grinned, showing more teeth than necessary. "I only use that method when it's you."

"Now that that's all figured out!" Aldis rubbed his palms together, grinning as he pivoted to face the doorway that remained. "Let's have a look at where we're going next."

"Looks like we unlocked all the possible routes." Aldis's heart jumped into his throat. When had Hane gotten between him and the door? They were pointing to a series of color-coded doorknobs placed along the right side of the door: blue, red, green, and finally gold. "The gold option is still locked, but we could choose to use that key here."

"Or we could use it on a door farther along," Nieve put in. "This is only the second room; it won't be much more difficult than the one we just completed. I vote for a combat room."

"I like the agility challenges," Hane put in lightly.

"Why don't we try something a little different and pick the exact challenge that matches our talents?" Aldis asked, recovering his grin. "Just because the spire is offering us four different choices doesn't mean we have to take one of them. Wouldn't it be nice to find a quick, simple challenge and move on from there?"

"That's not how it works, though." Emiko was holding Sage's arm in both hands, leaning into his side as if she were worried he might vanish if she let go. "We have to follow the path set by the goddess. Don't we?"

"Yes, but the goddess also encourages lateral thinking in her challenges." Aldis shooed Hane away from the door before bracing his attunement-marked hand against the frame. "And this is, quite literally, a lateral move."

"Aldis mentioned this in his interview," Lani informed the others. "It may not work, but he thinks he might be able to influence the portals enough to change the set destinations, allowing us to pick our next challenge."

"Really?" Emiko sounded conflicted. "Is that . . . really okay?"

"If it works, then it should be okay." Aldis grinned as his Detect Runes spell found the teleportation runes hidden within the door. "The spires are all different from one another, we all learn that in Judgment training. It's also commonly acknowledged that the Tortoise Spire has the longest, most time-consuming trials of any other spire but also grants some of the fastest attunements, like Wavewalker and Wayfarer. What if we're *meant* to manipulate the portals like this in order to ascend faster? I'm not suggesting that we avoid challenges entirely, that would certainly be against the teachings. But selecting the right challenges for our team? I believe that's exactly what Selys expects of us."

The doors in the spire weren't actually "doors" so much as they were portals, or magical gateways using the same type of magic that Wayfarers used in teleportation spells. And as someone who had grown up selling, demonstrating, and using enchanted items from Valia, Aldis had more than a passing familiarity with how runes worked. In his downtime between climbs, he read books about runes and visited Enchanters, mostly to stay current in case he could ever go back to Valia and work as a merchant. The more he studied runes and enchantments, the more he'd developed the idea that a Wayfarer should be able to cancel out teleportation runes on spire doorways.

Or, at least, it would if Aldis's spellwork was on par with these teleportation runes. Just as an Emerald-level fireball would overwhelm a Quartz-level fireball, Aldis's Sunstone-level spell couldn't hope to entirely cancel out whatever level spell these runes were.

But he could still influence them minutely. Just enough to change the predetermined path laid behind this doorway.

"Let's see where we were supposed to go." Aldis reached for a doorknob at random with his off hand, only to be stopped by Nieve.

"The red one! If it's a good fight, that's where I want to go."

Aldis rolled his eyes and selected the red doorknob. Ultimately, if this worked, it wouldn't matter which path they selected: his goal would be to find the room that contained the stairs that would take them up to the twentieth floor of the spire, and as that was generally a combat-style room, Nieve should have no cause to be disappointed. Nevertheless, he turned the red knob and pushed the door open, holding his arm straight out as a bar to keep anyone from passing through.

Nieve pressed close to Aldis's shoulder, peering past him into the room beyond. Aldis flinched at the blast of cold air that billowed outward at them.

"Ice and snow and those stalagtite things," Nieve said, frowning. "The preferred mana types for fighting any type of cold-weather monster would be fire and stone, and no one in our group has those."

"Looks like a cave," Sage commented, looking over Aldis's other shoulder. "And those"—he pointed toward the ceiling—"are called stalactites, Nieve."

As close as she stood to him, Aldis couldn't help but be caught by the very exaggerated eye roll that followed. "Whatever. Even I'm not into whatever fight this is going to be—"

"Yukinba." Aldis jumped and grabbed his heart in surprise. Why was Hane always sneaking up on him? They pointed to a trail of tracks in the snow. "All the prints are of the left foot."

Aldis hadn't noticed it before, but now that he looked, he felt a chill run up his spine that had nothing to do with the icy room beyond the doorway.

"Not the worst fight for us," Lani mused, touching something through her pocket. "Sage, can you tell if there are any broken shard pieces in this room?"

"Let me look," Sage said, touching the frame of his glasses.

"What's this?" Hane asked, curious. "Are you looking for something?"

"Oh, we meant to show you earlier." Lani shook her head ruefully. "It was late when you got back to the fort, and then we jumped right into the monster situation at the enemy camp. Sorry, Hane." She drew the crystal shard with the strange aura from her pocket and handed it to Hane. "I found it on the first day of the climb. It reacts strangely to water, and we think it might be a piece of something bigger. I wanted to ask if you'd seen anything like it at the lake."

"I didn't pick up anything that looks like this." Hane took the crystal shard, turning it over in their hands before conjuring a bit of water in their palm and pouring it over the shard. As interested as he was in testing his hypothesis, Aldis couldn't help but watch the shard with interest. Surprisingly, there was no hum of vibration from the crystal this time.

"Odd," Aldis commented. "It reacted differently to the bath water."

"Maybe there's not enough water?" Lani suggested with a studious frown. "We couldn't tell much about it, we're just hoping to figure out what it goes to."

"Interesting." Hane cocked their head as if listening to something. "Perhaps the water source matters? Should we test it in this new room's snow?"

"I don't See anything about the crystal shard in this room," Sage reported. "I'm searching for anything like the aura on that piece and I don't see anything like it here. And this room would be pretty challenging for us. The solution that gets us the best results from here would be to use fire and stone spells, which puts a lot of strain on Emi and her mana diffuser."

Lani shook her head, accepting the crystal shard as Hane handed it back to her. "Sorry, Nieve. I know you like a fight, but I'd rather find a room that allows Emi to take a short break."

"I agree," Nieve said, no small amount of disappointment in her voice. "If we can choose, let's look for something different."

"All right!" Aldis rubbed his palms together, excited to finally put his theory to the test. "Let's see where else we can go from here."

Aldis closed his eyes and cast Detect Aura, allowing him to see the faint runes etched into the doorframe. While each rune glittered with the potential for magic, only one was brilliantly alight. The rune wasn't familiar to him at all, so Aldis could only guess that the lit rune was linked to the portal's current destination. He set his attunement-marked hand overtop the glowing rune and concentrated on using only his transference mana, casting a spell he'd only ever practiced on basic enchantments before.

Drain, he thought, pulling the mana out of the rune. Slowly, he felt the rune's aura dim, then go dark. It would refill over time thanks to the mana-rich environment of the spire, so even after it felt empty, he kept his spell going, lest the portal reopen as the default path. Slowly, he cracked open his eyes, afraid of what he might see.

A wide grin broke out over his face as he looked through the doorway into an entirely different room, this one dark with leafy vegetation and a thick, wet heat emanating through the doorway. A quick scan of the doorway showed a new rune glowing brightly, proving his hypothesis correct.

"Whoa!" Nieve's eyes were wide with surprise and Emiko gasped audibly. Sage looked mildly concerned, and even Lani looked impressed. Only Hane appeared as they always did: cool, calm, and collected. At least they couldn't surprise Aldis now, not when he knew where they were.

"It worked." Lani looked impressed. "But how can we be sure you haven't opened a doorway to a room on the fiftieth floor, or some other impossibly difficult challenge?"

"That's unlikely for a portal on the nineteenth floor," Aldis explained, for once feeling in his element. "The teleport spells on each doorway actually have a finite number of destinations they can teleport to, and while it is theoretically possible for a doorway to send climbers up or down a level, it happens exceedingly rarely. Most floors seem designed to force climbers to find staircases in order to ascend, so jumping up any number of levels through a doorway isn't very probable."

"I'm not so sure about this," Emiko said, shifting her weight anxiously from foot to foot. "Aren't we supposed to follow the path the goddess sets before us? The teachings call it heresy to attempt to subvert the goddess's challenges."

"It's not really subverting," Nieve said, earning a soft grunt from Sage. Aldis understood: he was also surprised that the brutish warrior had used the word "subverting" correctly. "Just like Aldis said, we're choosing a path suited for us. I mean, there was an equal chance that this could have been the room revealed when we opened the door in the first place, right?"

"Ostensibly," Aldis agreed. "It would be heretical to attempt to alter the spire itself, or, say, batter our way directly to the floor above us. There's nothing in the teachings against changing the location of a portal: you can be sure I looked into that. But! There *are* a great number of stories where heroes are rewarded for unorthodox solutions and overcoming the goddess's challenges. That's all we're doing: choosing the right path for the team we have."

Emiko still looked conflicted. She rocked on her heels, then took Sage's hand, tugging lightly. "What do you think, Sage?"

"I'm not sure," Sage admitted, expression doubtful. "I don't put a lot of faith into the teachings, so I don't think there's anything wrong with changing the portal destinations. That aside, I have to say it does feel a bit like cheating."

"Okay, well, I do revere the goddess and the teachings, and I don't think this is cheating," Nieve declared firmly, crossing her arms belligerently. "If the goddess or our visage didn't want us changing the portal destinations, it wouldn't be so easy that a Sunstone-level Wayfarer could do it."

Aldis bristled but tried not to take offense. Nieve was on his side, after all.

"I tend to agree with Nieve," Lani put in, holding one hand in the other. Aldis couldn't help but note she was pinching her missing fingertips through her gloves. "I don't stand by the teachings, but Katashi is undeniably powerful. If he didn't want climbers to use the portals this way, then it simply wouldn't be possible to do. And since this gives us the option of climbing faster, I think we should do it."

"Yeah!" Nieve slung an arm over Lani's shoulders, giving Sage a taunting look. "But if you don't want to, Sage, Lani and I can go on ahead without you."

Sage scowled, but before he could come up with a retort, Emiko leaned around him and tugged at Hane's sleeve.

"What do you think, Hane?" Emiko asked. "You've climbed more than we have, right? Have you seen any other groups try this?"

"Not this exactly," Hane replied. "But I've been with plenty of groups who subverted challenges through means that might be considered cheating by most standards."

Aldis didn't like the silence that followed that statement.

"What happened to those groups?" Lani asked. "Were they punished?"

Hane shrugged. "Sometimes. More often than not, no. But if it comes to punishment, are we all willing to bear the consequence? I suggest we all agree before moving forward with this plan."

"Consequences?" Emiko asked timidly. "Like what? Did people . . . die?"

"Sometimes," Hane repeated. "But death isn't necessarily a result of cheating. The consequences vary when they do happen, but for the most part, a spire guardian appears as part of a challenge. Generally, if you can defeat or escape the spire guardian, you can continue on your way."

"We've beaten spire guardians before," Nieve declared boldly. She lifted a hand, calling for a vote. "I think this is a good idea. We can choose safer rooms and ascend faster. Isn't that what we're all here for? Climbing?"

Well, all Aldis really wanted was enough wealth to clear his family name, but the ability to choose challenges could only help with that. Apprehensively, Aldis lifted a hand. "As part of researching this hypothesis, I reviewed the teachings of Selys and I believe that this innovative technique is more likely to earn us a reward than a punishment."

Lani sighed heavily before raising her hand. "I have to say that I'm intrigued. This helps us collect treasure and climb faster, while still making safety our first priority. I can't see why we shouldn't at least try it."

That left three holdouts: Hane, Sage, and Emiko. Hane seemed to hold back, looking from Sage to Emiko as if waiting for them to decide first. Aldis observed a silent exchange between Nieve and Sage: a smirk from Nieve and a scowl from Sage. Lani seemed to miss the interaction entirely as she studied the new view through the doorway. Finally, Sage grimaced and lifted his hand in agreement.

"I agree that the point is to climb, and that this gives us a chance to do that faster." He paused, giving Nieve a hard look. "But the team's safety has to come first. No rushing in without checking the parameters first."

"Fine, fine," Nieve agreed, rolling her eyes. "What about you, Mi-mi? Are you coming with us?"

Emiko still held Sage's arm, almost halfway hidden behind him, but strangely it was Hane who set their hand on her shoulder. She looked up at them in surprise.

"You don't stand alone," Hane said in a steady yet soft voice. "If you choose not to proceed, I'll second your decision."

"Does that mean you're nervous about this, Hane?" Lani asked, surprised. "If you have a reason to think this isn't a good idea—"

"It's not that. I take the challenges as they come." Hane eyed the tropical setting beyond the doorway, then looked back to Emiko. "But that doesn't mean you should feel pressured to agree."

"I know. Thank you, Hane." Emiko beamed, then took a bracing breath before meeting everyone's eyes once. "I'm nervous, but I believe in our team. In us. So yes, let's try it."

Nieve whooped, pumping her fist in the air. "All right." She clapped her hands together and rubbed her palms. "So how do we decide where we're going?"

"That's my job." Sage shouldered his way between Nieve and Lani, touching one hand to the frame of his glasses, eyes going hazy as he stared into the junglelike mass of rustling bushes and dark-leafed trees. "This room looks like another battle challenge, just like the last room. Multiple enemies, likely some kind of pack monsters. Camouflaged to the environment. Considering the terrain, it would be a pretty tricky fight."

"And as hot as it is, Nieve's ice spells won't hold out for very long." Lani frowned, considering. "Do you see anything that looks like the crystal shard in there?"

"No," Sage said, shaking his head. "But it's possible that if the shard is meant to lead us to a secret treasure, it might be blocked from Sight. We should keep testing it to see if we can figure out more of its secrets, wherever we end up."

"That's a good idea," Lani allowed, her fingertips resting on the point of the shard that jutted out of her pocket as she eyed the junglelike setting. "If this is like the Tiles wheel, I think we should give it another spin and see where the needle lands."

"I agree," Nieve said, though she sounded grudging. "Try to find a room with stairs; I'll take ascension over a fight any day."

"Although, a room with stairs will typically provide a fight anyway," Hane pointed out.

Aldis moved his hand to the very next glowing rune along the doorway and drained it using the same spell as before. The view through the doorway changed once again, showing a very plain-looking stadium with people walking around with clipboards and colorful ribbons. Aldis frowned, squinting. "What is that? Is that . . ."

"A stadium-sized Crowns board?" Lani finished, sounding equally confused. "Sage, can you tell what this is?"

"Just a minute." Sage's fingertips rested on the side of his glasses, gaze hazy. "It's a living Crowns tournament. We'd compete as a team and try to win the championship. Each of us would take the place of a piece on the board and the other pieces would be filled in by illusions."

"That sounds kind of fun." Nieve grinned. "Are the exchanges settled by duels?"

"No, standard Crowns rules apply."

"Oh." Nieve crossed her arms and rocked backward on her heels. "That's not as fun."

"It doesn't sound hard, though," Lani mused. "Very safe if we don't have to fight anyone. And you're pretty good at Crowns, aren't you, Sage?"

"I'm good at Crowns," Aldis put in quickly. So far, this was the best challenge he'd ever seen inside a spire. "I placed second in a Valian—"

"It's not all that safe," Sage interrupted, shaking his head. "The matches are fair, but the competition is fierce. Like, poison-your-breakfast, or stab-you-while-you're-sleeping kind of fierce. We'd be watching our backs throughout the entire tournament. And it's a brackets-style championship: it would take at least a week to complete, maybe longer."

"I vote no," Nieve said loudly, holding her hand up. "Give me quick and violent over safe and boring any day."

"While I don't entirely agree with the sentiment, I also vote no," Hane added. "I'm not especially practiced in these types of challenges."

Aldis grimaced and cast a look over at Lani, hoping she would make the sensible decision and take a sure, safe win even if it took a little longer. She appeared to waver for a moment, then shook her head.

"That really is too long. Let's spin again and hope for something better."

It pained Aldis to pass on such a challenge, but with no one taking his side, he decided not to argue and looked around for the glowing rune linked to this destination. The first rune was already beginning to refill its magic; if it filled all the way, the portal would likely return to the first room they'd seen. Aldis made a note to drain the runes again before letting anyone pass through—better to be safe than risk splitting the team onto two separate paths.

By the blast of cold air that swirled around him, Aldis thought maybe that first rune had refilled faster than he'd expected, but one quick glance proved otherwise. This was no cave setting: this was a snowy mountaintop, with red pennant flags marching up to a distant peak.

"Survival challenge," Sage reported. "No monsters or battles to fight here. I don't even think we have to climb to the peak unless we want to make the challenge harder. Victory is decided on whether or not we're all still alive in ten days."

Lani shook her head at that, even as Nieve groaned her disappointment. "We didn't pack supplies for that type of challenge. We'd be dead in three days."

"One," Sage said grimly. "The first challenge is an ice storm. Spin again, Aldis."

At least we can all agree on that one, Aldis thought, already draining the next rune. A survival challenge sounded absolutely brutal, considering he'd have to spend all of it trapped with people like Lani and Nieve. Sage didn't seem so bad, though. And Emiko had an endearing charm about her. Hane . . . well, he could do without ten days of Hane startling him with their every word.

The next room was entirely underwater (or, perhaps, under-acid), which was a very easy skip. One room appeared entirely empty until they realized the center of the room was taken up by a clear slime so large that there was almost no room in which to wield a weapon. Another room appeared to be the inside of a beehive, complete with waxlike comb, dripping amber liquid from the walls and bees the size of cart horses. Aldis nearly screamed when he saw that room; he didn't even want to wait around for the team to vote no. Which they did, like the sensible people they were.

Aldis drained the next rune, feeling a little dismayed at how many options there truly were within this doorway. Maybe he should have had someone writing down which rune corresponded to what challenge, in case they wanted to go back to one they had seen earlier. It was a little late for that now, though. Just as Aldis was resigning himself to settle on something horrible, the view through the doorway changed, making his jaw drop in surprise. He looked around the group to make sure they were all seeing what he was seeing.

"Yes," Nieve hissed. "This is it. This is the room."

"So . . . many . . . treasure chests!" Emiko sounded awed. "Is this . . . the fabled lost treasure repository?"

Every climber knew the rumors: that somewhere inside each spire was one room dedicated to all the treasures, gear, and equipment lost on climbs. Whether it was pocket money or a sentient weapon, all the lost articles from decades of climbers had to end up somewhere—why not in one central repository where a lucky climbing group might stumble upon it one day?

And this certainly looked to be exactly that. Treasure chests were stacked neatly one on top of the other, extending up toward the unseen ceiling, forming a long corridor straight ahead of the door. Small mounds of gold coins and jewelry featuring sparkling gems glinted on the floor enticingly. Just one of those chests looked enough to pay off the bounty on his parents' heads, with enough left over to set himself up well, once he could use his old family name again. It was enough to make him drool just a little.

"I vote yes!" Nieve surged up on her toes, as if to dart into the room. "I don't care if it doesn't have stairs, this is good enough to stuff our bags full and ring out with—"

"Wait." Sage caught Nieve's collar from behind, mouth set in a grim line. "Those are mimics. Each and every one of them."

The atmosphere of anticipation visibly deflated, shoulders slumping, smiles fading. Of course it was too good to be true. Why couldn't he have gotten lucky just this once?

"What kind of challenge is it?" Lani asked, curious. "Mimics won't attack unless we bother them, right? So if we don't touch a single mimic, what happens?"

"I think the walls of mimics are arranged in a maze pattern," Sage explained. "The challenge is just making it to the exit without waking up any of the mimics." His eyes narrowed slightly as if something had only just caught his attention. "Oh, and there is one real treasure chest in there somewhere. But its location isn't fixed until we cross the threshold and it'll be protected by anti-Seeing runes, so I won't be able to find it. But the challenge itself isn't all that hard."

"It's quick, too," Nieve said slowly. "Just finding a way out? That's easy, isn't it?"

"We'd have to be exceedingly careful not to touch anything that could be a mimic," Hane pointed out. "That doesn't just mean the treasure chests, but anything in a room like this one might be a mimic trying to catch us off guard. There will be traps, too. There always are in challenges like this one."

"Yes," Sage agreed. "Traps designed to startle or scare us into crashing into the wall of mimics. And if we wake up one mimic . . ."

"The whole wall will come down on us, won't it?" Lani asked grimly. She blew a breath out, still studying the room beyond. "I don't think it would be that difficult to find the correct chest, even in all of this. I can use a Sense Life spell and look for the void space. But I don't know how we'd extract it from the wall of mimics without waking them all up."

"I could freeze them," Nieve suggested, though she sounded doubtful. "It would work for a little while, but not too long. Maybe if we already had an exit strategy, we could book it to the door."

"I can try to find the exit," Emiko suggested, slightly wary. "Challenges like this typically don't allow climbers to go over the maze walls, but I can float up and try to map it from above."

"There are a lot of traps in there," Sage warned. "I'm Seeing pit traps, pendulum traps, poison darts, triggers that set off jets of flame and arcs of lightning. This isn't going to be a leisurely walk along a corridor lined with monsters; we're going to have to stay on alert the whole time."

"What about stairs?" Nieve asked. "Are there stairs at the end of this room?"

Sage's unfocused eyes shifted from side to side, following something Aldis and the others couldn't see. "No. No stairs, just standard doors with the standard choices to proceed. The only challenge is getting to an exit."

"It's potentially a very short challenge," Lani mused. "We could probably finish it in less than a day. That's less time than any of the other options we've seen so far."

"Should we keep looking?" Emiko asked. "Maybe we'll find the combat room with the stairs instead?"

"Actually," Aldis said, considering the runes he felt powering the doorway portal. "It seems this doorway has limited options for where it can send a team. It's very possible that the first doorway inside a spire isn't directly linked to a room with ascending stairs. It doesn't seem as if the goddess intends to make it that easy for us."

"All right, so if we can't jump straight to a stairway from here, we need another doorway with a different set of choices," Nieve said. "This isn't a bad challenge for us. We can handle traps and avoid anything vaguely mimic-shaped. Even if there's no combat element, it's not a bad choice overall."

"I agree." Lani nodded firmly, smoothing a hand over a belt pouch. "Any objections?"

Personally, Aldis would have preferred the relative safety of the living Crowns tournament, but it seemed he was in the minority for that particular vote. The others voiced their approval for the room ahead of them, so with great trepidation, he agreed. It couldn't be that bad, right? At the very least, it wouldn't take three days to reach the next door, and that was something Aldis could appreciate.

"Any traps right inside the doorway?" Lani asked, directing the question at Sage.

"No," he said slowly, thoughtfully. "I think the idea is that we're supposed to rush in and start grabbing treasure, thereby waking up all the mimics. The traps start a little farther in."

"Okay. No one touch anything, not even the bait-treasure lying on the floor." Lani spoke with unquestioning authority, giving each team member their marching orders. "Sage and Hane, you'll take point and keep an eye out for traps. Nieve and I will follow second, and I'll be using my Sense Life spell to try to locate the real treasure chest. Emiko and Aldis, follow behind. Aldis, be ready to teleport anyone who gets too close to the mimics or falls into a trap. Emi, fly up and see if you can get the shape of the maze once we're inside."

"Not too high up," Sage warned. "I'm seeing lightning bolts if you try to go too much higher than the tops of the highest mimics."

"Good call. Okay, is everyone ready?" Lani asked bracingly.

"You'll have to squeeze past me," Aldis informed the group. "I have to make sure none of the other runes refill, or else the doorway could change as we're passing through. I'll go last to make sure I hold on to the correct location."

"Okay, then, Hane? You first," Lani ordered.

Hane gave a stoic nod, then slipped past Aldis and through the door. They stepped lightly, head swiveling for a tense, silent moment, and then they turned back and beckoned to the others. Sage went next, his attunement-marked hand still touching his glasses, eyes unfocused like he was seeing something else entirely. Nieve went next, followed by Lani.

Emiko clasped Aldis's free hand, giving it a gentle squeeze as she smiled up at him. "This is really clever, Aldis. And thank you for checking the teachings first. I feel a little better about it knowing that you looked into it."

"I wouldn't have tried it without considering the teachings," Aldis admitted, grinning briefly before Emiko hopped through the doorway. Aldis edged around the frame, leaving his hand in place for as long as possible to keep the portal from shifting. All in all, he was just happy it worked.

He'd be happier still if they managed to avoid running into a spire guardian.

CHAPTER 15

NIEVE

Champion (mind mark), Citrine

"Careful, Emi, not too high!" Sage called up, visibly fretting by the way he fussed with his glasses and squinted at a distant object that was most certainly not Emiko.

"Ooh, I can see the traps!" Emiko called down from her puffy cloud. "You were right, Sage, it looks like a lightning net would zap anyone who tries going over the walls of the maze."

"Okay, just—be careful!"

Nieve swung the back of her hand into Sage's chest. Not hard, but it still made him huff in surprise, eyes blinking into sharp focus for a glare.

"She's not a first-time climber, Sage, you know she's being careful," Nieve informed him tartly.

"I know that. I do." Sage exhaled a breath as he ran a hand back through his hair. "This maze is littered with anti-Seeing runes. I'm not completely blind, but I'm afraid I won't be very helpful in this challenge. I'm trying to See as much as I can to keep everyone safe."

"We're all seasoned climbers, Sage." Lani said, giving him a steady look. "It's not your job to protect us. We protect each other."

Sage blushed as he ducked his head. "You're right, Lani. I'll just look ahead for traps for now."

Nieve rolled her eyes and looked up to where Emiko hovered on her cloud. If Sage was going to make a move on Lani, could he hurry up and just do it already? It would be so much easier to consider Lani off-limits if she seemed even moderately interested in returning Sage's affections. All the shy smiles and longing looks got on Nieve's nerves. If Lani hadn't noticed them by now, that was a pretty clear indicator of disinterest, wasn't it? And the sooner Sage realized that for himself, the sooner Nieve could make Lani a different sort of offer.

Feelings and relationships were overrated; why not skip that part and jump right into the fun stuff?

Emiko's cloud descended, looking a little darker for her drawn frown.

"I can't get high enough to search for an exit," she explained, pouting. "I can't even see the edges of the maze, it looks like it just goes on and on in every direction forever."

"It's possible the exit is built into the maze, rather than the wall of the room," Hane pointed out. "There's also the strong possibility that there are multiple exits hidden in here. Normally, I'd say we might not want the first one we find, but with Aldis's doorway trick, that's not necessarily the case."

Aldis's smug face looked incredibly punchable just then, but Nieve couldn't be angry for any trick that helped her climb the spire faster. She wished Wyle had thought to try it sooner, but then again, Wyle wasn't really the type to study and tinker around with runes.

"Emiko, can you try using the spell Cloud Cover?" Hane continued. "I've seen it used to great effect in challenges like this one."

"Er, that's a Citrine-level spell." Emi wrapped her arms around herself, looking abashed. Hane probably didn't know she was only Sunstone level, but Nieve still resented the question on Emi's behalf. "I have a few perception mana crystals, but I've never tried that spell before."

"One of our former teammates was a Soulblade," Nieve explained in Emi's defense. "In challenges like this one, he'd send his minions on ahead to find the exits for us." She paused, grimacing. "I didn't really consider that before we decided on the maze room."

"Well, if there are multiple exits, then chances are good that we'll stumble on at least one of them," Lani said. "I know Sage said there are interference runes in here. Aldis, can you share anything about teleportation in this room?"

"There are a few void spaces that I can't teleport directly to," Aldis confirmed. "And knowing how trap-filled these types of challenges are, I'd be wary about teleporting anywhere in here without absolute confidence in where I'm landing."

"Not to harp on this," Hane said, voice as even-tempered as ever. "But a Cloud Cover spell would give us a top-down view with the benefit of a traced trail to follow. If perception mana and experience are the only holdbacks, I'd be willing to assist in a joint cast with Emiko."

"Are you sure?" Emi asked, hesitant.

"You don't have to if you don't want to, Mi-mi," Nieve assured her. "If you're not ready, you're not ready."

"No, I've been studying Cloudcaller perception spells," Emi assured her. "And Cloud Cover is a standard one, so I have a chant already. I just . . . haven't been able to use it yet."

"I'll help," Hane said, holding out a hand. "I have a Sense Water spell that's similar, it just works best in deep water, rather than clouds or mist."

"I don't know if it'll work," Emiko admitted, her little cloud carrying her closer to Hane's outstretched hand. "But I'll try. Just a moment, everyone."

Lani motioned everyone in close as Emiko clasped Hane's hand. Nieve pressed in against Emiko's opposite side, lending some moral support. She couldn't help with the spell, but she hoped Emi knew it would be all right even if the spell failed. Even if this challenge dragged on for a while, Nieve had confidence that they'd get through it as a team. It would just take a little patience . . . for all that wasn't a strong suit of hers.

Emiko drew a deep breath and began a chant. "Restless clouds drift by/ Looking down on all below/Show me what you see."

Nieve felt a chill in the air before she noticed the ambient light dim slightly. Clouds gathered above the mimic walls of the maze, and as she stared up at them, Nieve could make out tiny flashes of purple lightning against them. Emi's spell shouldn't set off the lightning traps above the maze, but perhaps the moisture in the expanding cloud was enough to react with the traps. She shifted her weight from foot to foot, trying to rein in her impatience. She knew that following a path was faster than blindly stumbling through a living maze of monsters, but she couldn't entirely quell the urge to forge ahead and let the challenge unfold as it would. Especially since there was no guarantee Emi's spell would work.

The clouds continued to spread over the top of the maze, churning and mixing as if caught in wind currents, though Nieve suspected it was all magically driven. Hane stared up at the clouds while Emiko ducked her face, eyes closed as she concentrated on the spell.

"It's . . . it's working!" Emi sounded surprised. "I can see what the clouds see. Well, sort of."

"Can you find a doorway?" Aldis asked eagerly. "Any door will do. The closer the better."

Nieve agreed with her whole heart but was grateful someone else had said it so she wasn't the one pressuring Emi.

"I think . . . I think . . ." Emi furrowed her brow, grip tight on Hane's hand. "There! Hane, is that—does that look like a doorway to you?"

"I can't see the way you do," Hane admitted. "Mist is too thin for me unless it's actually touching something. Trust yourself, Emiko. If you say it's a door, we'll follow you to it."

"Follow . . ." Emi went quiet, eyes zipping along a trail only she could see. "I don't think I can remember it all. The twists and turns look different up here than they do from inside."

"Pull a vapor trail down," Hane suggested. "It doesn't have to be very much. Anyone with Water Sense can follow a vapor trail."

"Okay. Okay, I see it." Emi giggled unexpectedly. "It's so weird looking down at myself! I mean, I look down on you guys all the time, but seeing myself from above is a first."

Nieve snorted and Sage laughed. Even Lani smiled a little. Aldis looked up, as if expecting to see Emi's face in the clouds above.

"Okay, I've got the path," Emi said. "I'm tracing it out now."

As the minutes grew longer and longer, Nieve felt her spirits sink. If it was taking this long just for Emi to draw them a map to an exit, how much longer would it take to actually get there? Especially with all the traps in the way and the runes preventing Sight and teleportation, not to mention looking for the one real treasure chest out of the thousands of treasure chest look-alikes making up the walls of the maze. It looked like this was going to take longer than she'd originally thought it would.

Fighting the urge to pace or stomp her boots, Nieve reached for her locket, fingering it beneath the layers of her clothing. She knew that rounded-edged diamond shape better than even the hilt of her own sword. Her fingers had traced the four knots on its surface so many times she could draw the pattern with her eyes closed. It didn't hold a memory, it held a promise. It was that very promise that kept her climbing, kept her racing to reach the top of the spire, to see the face of the goddess. She had some time to get there, but how much? Without any way to know, the only thing she could do was keep moving.

She hated standing still inside a spire; she felt like she could feel every passing second like an added weight upon her shoulders. How much more weight could she carry while continuing to climb?

Nieve only realized she'd been drumming her fingers on her sword hilt after Sage shot her an exasperated look across their little team huddle. She rolled her eyes, but she stopped. She wasn't sure if Emi could hear her while she was working the spell, but she didn't want Emi to think Nieve was rushing her.

"I can sense it ahead," Hane said suddenly, head turning to track something Nieve couldn't see. "I can follow it from here. Good work, Emiko."

"Thanks!" Emi's cheeks flushed with pride as she let go of Hane's hand. "Thank you for helping me with the spell! That was new for me."

"Hopefully that makes it easier for when you're ready to do it on your own," Hane said, almost kindly. They spoke with the barest inflection, making it hard for Nieve to discern tone, but at least they didn't come across as rude. No one was allowed to be rude to Emiko.

"Did you see? Did you see?" Emi's cloud shimmied as she danced excitedly. "I used perception mana in a spell! And it worked!"

"Yeah, yeah, you did great, Mi-mi." Nieve grabbed one of Emi's hair buns and twirled her around in a circle. "We're done standing around here now, right? Let's look for that treasure chest on our way through the maze."

"You mean, let's go look for that needle in a haystack?" Lani asked, arching a brow at her. "My Sense Life spell is showing a living aura around everything in here. I'm looking for a negative space among all these monsters." Lani waved a hand at the stacks and stacks of mimics that created the walls of the maze. "If we go too fast, I might miss seeing it."

"Going too fast won't be a problem." Hane sounded far away. Nieve scanned the corridor of mimics, surprised to find Hane halfway to the first intersection of the maze. "The walkway is littered with traps. Don't let your guard down just because we have a trail to follow."

"And those of you with Detect Aura spells, keep your eyes open for anything that looks like the shard's aura." Lani tapped her pocket, looking from Sage to Aldis. "Call out if you see anything worth stopping for."

Despite having Detect Aura herself, Nieve elected to cast Detect Water, making Emi's vapor trail visible as a thread of mist to her eyes. Sage and Aldis were better suited for seeking out magical auras and determining if they were relevant to the shard or not. Nieve was best suited for keeping her eyes on the way ahead, in case this maze hid more than just traps.

"Hey." Sage faced forward, probably scanning for traps or strange auras, but he tapped his elbow against Nieve's. "How were you tracking that Illuminator in the last room? I've never seen you do that thing with your headband over your eyes before."

Nieve fingered the shortened tail of her headband. Ana had managed to cut it off her head in their last fight; luckily, Nieve had been able to salvage the longer portion of it to tie her hair back from her face. "I was using one of the mental mana spells you taught me. The Detect Mind one."

"And that worked even with your eyes closed?" Sage asked.

Nieve shrugged. "You See with your eyes closed all the time."

"I See the future with my eyes closed," Sage explained. "And only when I'm trying to look way ahead. I don't think I've used Detect Mind with my eyes closed. That was actually really smart thinking, Nieve."

"Don't sound so surprised," Nieve snorted, bumping her shoulder against Sage's. "What about you? The poison knocked you out for a while, but you still knew everything that happened while you were out. How'd you manage that?"

Sage frowned, looking pensive. "Something strange happened. Maybe a new aspect of my attunement, I'm not sure. I'll look into it after the climb."

"All right." Nieve rolled her shoulders in a shrug. "As long as you don't go all comatose and expect me to carry you through this climb. I'll just leave your dead weight behind, see if I don't."

"Don't worry, I won't." Sage rolled his eyes. "And you wouldn't leave me behind. You'd use me as a projectile to throw at enemies for crowd control."

Nieve barked a laugh. "I would, too! That sounds fun, we should try it sometime."

"Ow, let go!"

"I'm just trying to see how heavy you are." Nieve threw an arm over Sage's shoulders and squeezed, squishing him against her side.

"Knock it off." Lani gave each of them a pointed look. "We're supposed to be keeping an eye out for traps, remember?"

"Isn't that what Hane's doing?" Nieve let go of Sage to gesture ahead. Hane was still out in front of the group, a single tonfa held akimbo and their head on a swivel. "They'll see anything coming before we will."

"At least refrain from wrestling with each other like pit fighters," Lani demanded. "The walls are made of monsters, in case you'd forgotten. One wrong move and this whole maze comes to life and we get buried in an avalanche of teeth."

Emiko made a fearful noise, her cloud floating up so she could clutch the back of Nieve's collar. "Please don't wake them up, you guys. I'd hate to have to watch you all get eaten."

Nieve snorted. "Don't worry about that, Mi-mi. I'd drag you down off that cloud so you get eaten, too."

"So mean, Nee-Nieve!"

"Hey." Hane's voice wasn't loud, but it carried a hint of impatience along with it. "I'm activating a pit trap here. Is everyone ready?"

"Why activate it? Can't we just go around?" Emiko asked.

"The sides of the trap are narrow. You'd risk walking far too close to the mimics." Hane pointed, indicating the width of the walkway that would remain after the false floor fell. "With the parameters of the trap exposed, we can best avoid any accidents."

"I agree, but wait just a moment." Lani held out a hand toward Hane and turned toward Sage. "Anything we should be wary of?"

Sage was silent a moment, then shook his head. "I think it's a standard pit trap. Nothing too nasty unless we fall in."

"All right." Lani nodded to Hane. "Go ahead and trigger it."

Hane pointed the tip of their tonfa at the floor and fired a punch of mana through it. Even with the forewarning, Nieve was surprised when the floor bisected neatly down the middle, the halves swinging on a tilted hinge as they snapped open. Not all pit traps opened like that: most crumbled.

"I'll go on ahead," Hane said, looking back. "But perhaps an ice bridge could help get the others over?"

Nieve glared at the back of Hane's head as they took two quick steps and leapt lightly over the ten-foot-wide gap that had opened in the floor. She didn't need Hane telling her to make an ice bridge. That was Lani's job.

"Try to make it as dry as possible," Lani suggested as Nieve stepped up to the edge of the pit. It was empty and dark, with no discernible floor: one of those "fall forever" type of pits, then. "I don't want anyone slipping off."

"I can do that. I'll make edges, raised, too." Nieve pictured a flat ice bridge in her mind, with raised lips along the edges, long enough to reach the far side of the pit. When laying down a field of ice before her enemies, Nieve liked her ice just a touch slick beneath her feet: not only was it easier for her to move, but it also caused most of her opponents to lose their footing and fall. But here, a little water on the bridge could send one of her teammates to their death. When she was sure she had the bridge shaped just the way she wanted it, she let the spell roll down through her chest and out through her arms, placing it in the center of the pit trap.

Nieve crossed her bridge first, looking back at the others as they began crossing. Aldis had been lurking silently at the back of the group ever since entering the mimic maze. She had to wonder if he wasn't sulking: he'd seemed really excited for that living Crowns tournament. Honestly, if the exchanges were settled by duels, she might have been tempted to choose that room, too. A challenge as long as that one usually brought climbers to a mana fountain, which typically preceded a room with ascending stairs. And fighting in the tournament and espionage outside it sounded like a good time. Too bad the tournament was set up to be a fair game.

Sage and Lani crossed behind Nieve, moving more cautiously on the ice than Nieve had. Lani lost her balance, skidding toward the edge with Sage reaching out to catch her, but she recovered and pushed off her back foot, gliding forward rather than walking, which was the best method for moving on ice anyway. Emiko floated alongside the bridge, moving at the same speed as Sage and Lani, as if providing moral support. Just as Lani got close enough for Nieve to reach out and grasp her hand, Aldis vanished from the far side of the pit trap and reappeared beside Nieve.

Nieve cocked an eyebrow at him. "Couldn't you have done that from the beginning?"

Aldis shrugged. "I wanted to make sure this side was safe first."

"Always thinking of your safety first, huh?" Lani sniped, turning back to offer a hand to Sage.

"I don't see why that should offend you," Aldis said archly. "If I'm not safe, how am I supposed to save anyone who falls?"

"You could have teleported all of us," Sage pointed out. "Or at least just Lani, Nieve, and me."

"There was still the possibility of an undiscovered trap on this side. I knew that side was safe." Aldis grimaced as he looked up at the towering stack of mimics. "Relatively, at least."

"It's better to save mana, anyway," Lani put in, though she sounded cool as she said it, not quite agreeing with Aldis, but not disagreeing either. "Let's catch up to Hane, but stay alert in case they missed anything."

"Why can't we pick up treasure as we go?" Emiko asked, once again clinging to Nieve's belt as she floated along behind her. "A mimic's greatest attack is in the element of surprise, right? If we don't let our guard down, what's wrong with grabbing a few shinies?"

Nieve couldn't help but eye the glittering trail of coins, gems, and other small treasures that lined the edges of the corridor, as if they had been spilled over by the "treasure chests" that formed the walls of the maze. If even half of it was real, it would topple her climbing team's highest yield return of all time, but as tempted as she was to sweep it all up into a pile and swim in it, she knew it wasn't worth the risk.

"We'd have to get too close to the mimics to gather the treasure," Nieve said, sighing woefully. "And since mimics are typically pretty cowardly, I'd guess that it isn't the closest one you'd have to worry about. A mimic might leap at you from behind, or fall from above the moment you're distracted. It might be possible to gather some of the treasure carefully, but it would slow us down more than it's worth."

"That and you can't be entirely certain what's real and what's not." Sage had paused, staring down at a book with conflicting emotions written all over his face. Nieve recognized the book as one Sage had read a hundred times back when they were taking Judgment classes together, the one about the Blackstone Assassin. The cover looked ancient, with peeling leather and a title that simply read "Blackstone." He'd read the book before, multiple times if memory served, so Nieve wasn't sure why it was slowing him down until she noticed the gold-foil stamp proclaiming it a first edition. "While the treasure-chest mimic is the one most commonly talked about in climbing circles, those aren't the only types of mimics. In fact, I'd guess the treasure chest mimics are the least successful hunters, since that's the type that climbers know to look out for. The farther we go into this maze, the more likely it is that the treasure chest mimics are just the distraction and the treasures are the real traps."

"Are you implying that any of these little gold coins might be a mimic?" Aldis scoffed. "What's the harm in that? Losing a fingertip?"

As soon as he said it, he flinched. As if he couldn't help himself, he looked over toward Lani, who leveled a long, icy stare back at him.

"The coins might be safe, but just because I've never heard of a mimic coin, that doesn't mean they don't exist." Sage sighed as he walked past the book he'd been staring at longingly, seemingly having missed the silent exchange between Aldis and Lani. "For safety's sake, we should suspect anything in this room of potentially being a mimic. That means any stones or benches or even treasures. It's just not worth the risk."

"I had no idea mimics were that versatile." Aldis frowned down at the book as he stepped past it. "They can really be anything?"

"According to the most recent bestiary, yes. Although, I recommend you don't try looking it up in the Mimic Book of Mimics." Sage chuckled, making Nieve wonder if that was a joke or not.

Aldis shuddered. "Is there a way to tell definitively if something is a mimic or not? I'm worried the next floor tile I step on might be a mimic now."

"The floor has no life signature," Lani supplied. "But all the coins and gems are too close to the walls, so the life aura from the chests spills over them, making it difficult to tell if they are or aren't mimics. As Sage says, it's better to be safe."

"Life spells are the best way to be sure," Sage agreed, smiling at Lani. "But there are a few other methods that can help tell a mimic from an inanimate object."

"Oh, oh!" Emiko raised her hand, cloud floating up another several inches. "I know one! Poke it from a distance!"

Nieve laughed along with Sage, and even Lani chuckled. Nieve poked Emiko with her finger, pushing her floating cloud farther behind her.

"Poking works if you're ready to fight the mimic when it lunges at you," Nieve continued. "That first lunge is always faster than you think it'll be."

"It's not so much that they're sleeping as they're just in a dormant state. It's almost like a hibernation, except—" Sage was starting one of his super long, very annoying lectures about boring monsters, so Nieve gave him a shove. He missed his step and nearly tripped, and for one fearful moment Nieve thought she might have to grab him before he fell into the wall of mimics, but then he recovered and shot her a nasty glare.

"No one cares," Nieve informed him. "The question was about identifying mimics, which is a lot more important than explaining the difference between hibernation and dormantness."

"Dormancy," Sage snapped, clearly irritated. Nieve snickered when he turned away from her to talk to Aldis directly. "There's a general rule of thumb to keep in mind regarding mimics, but it's by no means universal. An object that opens—like a chest or a book or even a door—is more likely to be a mimic than something that can't be opened."

"Ah. That does make a certain amount of sense," Aldis admitted, nodding thankfully. "And it's easy to remember. I'll keep it in mind."

"There are exceptions, though." Emiko's tone was serious enough that Nieve recalled the exact incident she was talking about. By the way Sage turned his face away, he remembered, too. "There was one that looked like a stone bench in one of the early levels, before we started climbing with Lani and Ren. Remember?"

"How could we forget?" Nieve shook her head. They'd gone to school with that girl, and while she hadn't died, she wasn't a climber any longer. She wasn't even attuned anymore. It seemed viciously unfair to put such a nonstandard mimic in a level below the tenth floor, but maybe that was what it took to forge a true team: a shared trauma that hadn't broken their will to ascend.

Aldis turned visibly pale. "No, don't tell me. I'd like to think what I'm imagining is the worst that could possibly have happened. I've been fortunate enough to run into the very standardest of mimics, with teams equipped to handle them efficiently. But you can be sure I'll watch where I sit in the future."

"Or open," Sage reminded him. "Doors, windows, pianos. The boxes that hold the little Crowns board pieces."

Aldis recoiled sharply, eyes going wide. "How dare you! I'll never be able to look at a Crowns set the same way again. I thought we were friends, Sage!"

Sage seemed to find that funny, but then he got a shock himself as he turned around to face forward and nearly ran directly into Hane. He stumbled back, uttering an obscenity while cupping his hand over his heart. Nieve cackled; she'd seen Hane stop and circle back toward them, a blandly chastising expression on their face.

"The first intersection is up ahead," Hane said, pointing. "There's a pendulum trap meant to scatter us in different directions, or drive us into the mimic wall. The vapor trail turns to the left."

Nieve cracked her knuckles as she surveyed the intersection ahead. It was a four-way intersection, which meant that if the pendulum dropped, it could swing in any of four different directions. The trick would be activating it to go either straight ahead or right, if they couldn't simply avoid activating it entirely.

"It's probably connected to floor switches, since we can't really touch anything else in here," Sage guessed, touching his glasses, though Nieve thought he'd turned the enchantments off earlier. "In theory, the pendulum should swing in the direction of the activated switch."

"Blah, blah, theory, whatever." Nieve crossed her arms. "We can just skip past it. Aldis can open a portal down the left corridor and—"

"Ah, no, I think that's a terrible idea." Aldis spoke up, shaking his head. "I can't see what's over there and I don't want to risk setting the portal too close to the mimics, nor do I want to drop someone on top of the switch that brings that pendulum swinging toward us. Can't we just inch around and try to avoid the switches?"

Sage hummed studiously. "I'm seeing a lot of magic runes on the floor up ahead. Most are probably harmless, it's just meant to confuse us as to which ones activate the trap."

"All right, then." Lani clapped her hands once. "We'll send someone ahead to activate the pendulum trap to the right. Once we see it swinging down, the rest of us will run through and turn left. The pendulum will keep swinging, but at least we won't have to watch our step when clearing the corner, we'll just have to keep moving."

"But who would be so suicidal as to go out alone to knowingly set off a trap?" Aldis asked, as if the suggestion was ludicrous. His laughter died as he realized everyone was staring at him. "Ah, no. No, no. There could be monsters—not just the mimics, I mean—and as I said before, I can't see—"

"The intention is to activate the trap," Lani said, almost sweetly. "It doesn't matter if you land on it. Once you trigger it, you can teleport away again. You're the best person for the job."

"I—I—" Aldis sputtered, then shook his head. "Well, I am most certainly not going alone! Not when there's no assurance that I won't get eaten by some horrible monstrosity."

"I can—"

"I'll go!" Nieve shouted over Hane's offer. "I love horrible monstrosities. I'll go with Aldis to activate the trap and make sure he doesn't get eaten."

"Fine," Lani agreed, tugging at the cuff of her glove. "Just be careful once you activate it. We're only assuming the pendulum will swing in the direction of the triggered switch. You'll have to react quickly if it goes in an unexpected direction."

"We'll be fine," Nieve replied, slinging an arm around Aldis's shoulders. "Aldis is a rune-nerd like Sage. I'm sure we'll figure out the right switch to hit."

"The rest of us need to be prepared to run," Hane said. "The pendulum's second swing will likely follow us down the left corridor."

"We'll go as soon as we get Aldis's confirmation that they hit the switch," Lani affirmed. "You two should go."

Aldis sighed heavily, casting a sulky glare over at Sage. Sage pretended to ignore him by touching the side of his glasses and moving his eyes like he was Seeing something. It was a common enough tactic of his that Nieve recognized it, but perhaps it fooled Aldis. The Wayfarer couldn't possibly have wanted Sage to go with him, could he? Sage was fine as far as fighting went, but he didn't enjoy it nearly as much as Nieve did.

"Let's go!" Nieve flexed her arm around Aldis's shoulders. "I'll create a platform under our feet so we don't trigger a switch when we land."

"If I must," Aldis said with another heavy sigh. "I'm going to drop us a little above the floor to leave space for your platform. Try not to fall."

Nieve rolled her eyes but held back a cutting remark; Aldis hadn't been on the team long enough to know that Nieve never slipped on her own ice.

The teleportation spell was over in the blink of an eye, but even with the warning about dropping them above the ground, Nieve felt disoriented as she created the ice platform for them to land on: wide and flat, with legs angled to the edges of the walkway, where they were less likely to trigger a switch. Her boots slid as they hit the ice, but she would have recovered herself if not for Aldis missing his footing, too, becoming little more than dead weight that pulled Nieve down. She fought it for a moment, then gave up, dropping hard onto her backside while being careful not to land on her hands. Aldis would have slid off the edge and into the wall of mimics, but Nieve maintained her grip on his collar, yanking him down so that he landed on top of her. Her breath burst out of her all at once and the ice platform cracked beneath them, dropping them a short distance to the ground and earning Nieve a bruise for her trouble.

Aldis pushed himself up, muttering something that sounded a lot more like blame than an apology as he dusted himself off. He reached down a hand to help Nieve up, but as he shifted his weight backward to haul her up, Nieve heard something click. By the sudden pallor of Aldis's face, he'd heard it too.

"What was that?" Nieve asked sharply, freezing midway in getting to her feet.

"I, um—" Aldis swallowed hard. "I stepped on something."

Nieve swore as she leapt to her feet, shoving Aldis out of her way. The enormous brass pendulum was descending, dropping straight down and gleaming with malicious purpose. Which way was it going to swing? Toward them? Away from them? Down the empty corridor or the one with their teammates in it?

Please, goddess, Nieve begged in her moment of helplessness. *Please let it come this way!*

At first, it looked almost as if the pendulum would descend straight down and crack the floor stones of the maze. At the last possible second, the pendulum began to swing—only it wasn't swinging toward Nieve and Aldis. It was swinging down the entry aisle where they'd left the rest of their team.

Nieve's breath caught in her chest as it contracted with fear. She had just enough time to visualize what she wanted, throw both hands out, and think: *STOP!* Just as the heavy brass ball would have swung out of sight down the other aisle, ice formed around it, growing and spreading quickly, rooting itself to the floor and cradling the pendulum midswing. Nieve exhaled a relieved breath, grabbing Aldis's shoulder for support as her head swam.

That had been far too close.

Beside her, Aldis drew a breath that shuddered. When she looked over, he was still clutching his chest. He swallowed hard and tried to recover, smoothing his dueling tunic and hitching up his belt.

"That was some very quick thinking," he said, head jerking in a nod of approval. "Will it hold?"

"I don't know," Nieve replied honestly. "We should try and get everyone past it as quickly as possible."

"Yes, right." Aldis tugged at his collar as if he were hot, then placed a hand on Nieve's shoulder. "I'll take you to the far side, then go back for the rest of the team."

"Uh-huh." Nieve's heart was still hammering in her chest. She wasn't sure if her sudden dizziness was from relief or from the sudden, unexpected spell that trapped the pendulum. "Wait, wait! What about the floor traps? Can we still activate them?"

Aldis paused, eyes narrowing at the floor ahead of them. "Most of the runes are dark now that the trap's been activated. You can see auras, can't you?"

"Yeah. Wait." Nieve squeezed her eyes shut, thinking *Detect Aura* to activate the spell. She couldn't read runes the way Sage could, but she could at least avoid stepping on any of them. "Okay. Okay, I'm ready."

Another rapid teleport spell, then Aldis stepped away from her, vanishing in a breath. As Nieve attempted to slow her racing heart, a shadow vaulted lithely over the ice-ensnared pendulum. Nieve was reaching for her sword before she recognized Hane, landing in a neat crouch. They didn't say anything, but they did glance back at the pendulum, then lift an eyebrow questioningly.

"Shut up," Nieve grumbled. "It wasn't my fault."

"I didn't say it was," Hane said easily. "But you might consider that sometimes patience is the better part of courage."

Nieve gritted her teeth and turned away. Yes, it probably would have been better to let Hane go with Aldis rather than insisting she go herself, but she hated waiting around when she could be moving forward. Every minute wasted was one minute gone in her quest to climb to the top. And though she never wanted to be the reason one of her friends was put in danger or hurt, she couldn't help but feel that a minute spent waiting was a minute lost forever.

CHAPTER 16

LANI

Acolyte (hand mark), Citrine

Lani's heart was still hammering in her chest when Nieve and Sage resumed bickering like children. Seeing the pendulum descend and begin its swing up the corridor was nothing short of a nightmare played out in slow motion. Her plan, in its entirety, had been to throw herself flat against the ground and hope the pendulum swung over her without actually hitting her, but there hadn't been time to articulate that to the rest of the team. Her biggest fear was someone running into the wall and waking the mimics, but it seemed instead that everyone had been paralyzed with the same fear and indecision that had kept her own feet rooted to the floor.

Luckily, Nieve had reacted fast enough to freeze the ball of the pendulum in place.

"Let's argue somewhere else," Lani urged, stepping between Nieve and Sage, grabbing one ear from each of them. "That ice might not last very long and we don't want to be here to find out if the pendulum can swing in another direction."

"This way," Hane called, already a few steps down the corridor. "Did you two see anything from the opposite side of the corridor?"

"Nothing of any more note than the trigger runes," Aldis said, tamping sweat from his brow. "Of course, we wouldn't have noticed something as subtle as a real chest among the fakes."

Hane nodded, skipping ahead several more paces. "Lani, please call out if you happen to notice that dead space in your Sense Life spell."

"I will." Lani released Sage first, waving for him to go on ahead with Hane to look for traps. She kept hold of Nieve's ear as she whispered: "I'm glad that was only nearly a disaster, but try not to let it happen again. We didn't even get a warning before you set off the trap."

"It was an accident," Nieve said defensively, tugging her ear free of Lani's grip. "It happened too fast. You know I wouldn't put you guys in danger on purpose."

"I do know. But my heart doesn't seem to understand that." As Lani waited for her heartbeat to return to normal, she double-checked her teammates, looking for anyone exhibiting signs of pain or injuries that needed to be healed. Neither Nieve nor Aldis appeared to have been hurt, though Aldis did look rather pale. Emiko's eyes were still wide as she trailed along behind and above the rest of the team on her cloud, but otherwise she looked fine. Sage had appeared every bit as paralyzed as Lani, possibly shocked that he hadn't foreseen the trap's release. Seemingly he'd recovered if he'd been able to snipe at Nieve for her mistake. Hane alone seemed unshaken, but then again, Hane had looked prepared to try something just prior to the pendulum being frozen in place. Precision spellwork like that wasn't normally Nieve's forte, so it had likely taken quite a bit of mana. Nieve would probably need a little time to recover fully.

I wonder if it's too early to find a mana fountain, Lani thought, fingers toying with something poking out of her pocket as she scanned the walls for an absence of life. A hazy green aura hovered over everything as far as she could see, indicating that each and every one of the treasure chests was actually alive. It was a strange life-signature, though. It wasn't the vibrant sprout-green that plants gave off, nor was it the dark, thrumming green that most beings with a heartbeat had. The green haze over the mimics was almost muddy-looking, sullen, and stagnant. Perhaps that was simply a quirk of mimics, or maybe it was because of the state of dormancy they were in, or perhaps it was just a function of a mimic's adaptability. That muddy-green aura might be easy to miss if she were checking a lone chest in a dark room, but in this maze with so many mimics gathered together, it almost seemed as if Lani were peering through green-tinted glasses.

Even if we find the real chest, how would we extract it? Lani wondered. *There's no point if we have to ring out right afterward, but it's not enough to complete a challenge without earning a reward. Unless there are other treasures hidden in this maze?*

She found herself wondering about all the turnoffs they passed as Hane followed Emi's vapor trail. Was it worth exploring a few of them? Or was it too hazardous considering the anti-Seeing and anti-teleportation runes hidden within the maze? Her fingers twitched, anxious for the feel of a pair of dice, or the velvet of a betting table. To distract herself, she toyed with the crystal shard jutting up from her pocket, tapping her thumb against the pointed tip. She liked keeping it in her pocket rather than her satchel so she would be sure to feel it if it began vibrating again, as it had in the first room.

Hane found another pit trap, this one filled with metal spikes rather than simply empty air after they triggered it. Nieve created another ice bridge and Lani watched her footing before looking around at the mimics again.

It would be luckiest for us to find the chest near the exit, Lani thought, tipping her head back to check the chests along the tops of the walls. *But even I wouldn't bet on those odds. Part of the challenge is probably getting the treasure to the exit.*

Surprisingly, it was Sage who suggested that they check out a few of the alternate paths through the maze, pausing to look back over his shoulder at the rest of the team. "We don't have a time limit in here, which gives us a little leeway to explore," Sage pointed out. "We can't trust that the lone real treasure chest will be along our path; we should check out some of the other corridors, too."

"The vapor trail won't last forever," Hane cautioned. "The longer we take, the more it breaks apart and becomes harder to trace."

"We'll probably end up having to recast it anyway," Sage said with a shrug. "We'll likely end up camping somewhere in here for the night, and the spell was never going to last that long. Might as well make the best of our time and search for the real treasure."

Hane tipped their head to the side, then nodded. "I can agree to that. Should we take this turnoff, then?"

Hane indicated a branching corridor, which even Lani could see curved away, rather than continuing on straight, as all the corridors had so far. Something about that curve, hiding what lay ahead, made Lani's guts roll like a pair of tossed dice.

"Let's check it out," Lani said, giving in to a gambler's temptation. "Emi, do you see anything down the way?"

"Not from here." Emiko floated up a little, moving to the side as she tried looking down the corridor. "Nothing obvious. Are there any other monsters in here aside from the mimics? Because I think we should avoid them if there are."

Fighting a monster within these tight confines with traps littered about like chips on a betting table would be utterly disastrous.

"If we do find a monster, let's try talking to it before we start a fight," Lani ordered, catching and holding Nieve's eye. "I can't see that we were meant to actually fight in a place like this, so the challenge is probably to avoid a fight."

"What are we supposed to do if the monster doesn't want to talk?" Nieve demanded to know. "Pat it on the head and send it on its way?"

"Many lone monsters will accept food in lieu of a fight," Hane suggested softly. "Or a piece of treasure might buy them off. I can do that talking, if you prefer."

"Is that how you beat the lake serpent?" Nieve asked skeptically. "By talking to it?"

"Serpents don't typically converse with their food," Hane replied blandly. "Watch out for the tripwire trap ahead."

"More than one. Look." Sage held his hand out toward the empty-looking corridor and slowly three thin lines that Lani had mistaken for shadows glowed brightly with golden light. "Low enough to step over, just watch you don't catch your boots on them."

Hane, of course, sprang over all three tripwires neatly, and Emiko merely floated over them. Lani, Sage, and Nieve had to pick their way over cautiously, once again getting halfway through the trap before Aldis appeared on the far side of the tripwires. Lani bit back a comment about teleporting more of them across the trap, reminding herself that it was better than having to watch him lumber across the tripwires without the use of sorcery. Just the thought of him wobbling precariously over a tripwire was enough to unsettle her stomach. Better to let him continue in a way that was safe than berate him for not being more helpful to the rest of the team.

The corridor curved around and around, as if spiraling in on itself, terminating eventually in a dead end without resulting in a single dead space in Lani's Sense Life spell. At least backtracking gave her the chance to double-check, just in case she'd missed it.

Following the vapor trail once more, Hane and Sage revealed more traps, setting some off, alerting the team to others. Emiko continued to float overhead, calling out if she found anything lurking in the shadows of the ceiling but never going any higher than the tops of the walls. With Nieve keeping a close eye on her, Emiko scouted ahead down alternate routes, returning to report that she'd seen nothing out of the ordinary. Sage paused every so often to check his Sight, pointing out corridors that were dead zones to him. It seemed equally likely to find monsters or treasures hidden in those dead zones, and after some discussion, the team decided to carefully check each one. When each one turned up nothing, Lani began to wonder if they were missing something, or if the anti-Seeing runes were scattered about randomly just to lead climbers off-track.

The team picked a few more corridors at random before stopping in a place Hane declared safe to sit for a small rest. The silence was strangely disquieting, broken only by calls to look out for this trap or that. It felt cathartic to sit down and break out a few snacks, cautious chatter creating a temporary barrier against the funereal-like silence. Lani blinked away her Sense Life spell, hoping to avoid the headache she usually got after prolonged use of an aura spell. A warm drink like tea usually helped, but they weren't stopping for so long that they could brew any. Instead, everyone sipped from canteens and passed around snacks from their rations. Emiko offered everyone small bunches of grapes while Sage tore chunks off a loaf of bread that was still soft and passed them around. Nieve tossed down a small pouch of salted nuts to share and Aldis peeled an orange, offering sections around in a small circle. Hane politely declined any offerings of food but instead hugged their knees to the chest, lowered their head, and, to all appearances, fell instantly asleep. Lani found herself envious of the ability to simply sleep anywhere at any time—she'd even had trouble falling asleep in the moderately comfortable bed back in the fortress scenario.

"Has there been any change in the crystal shard?" Aldis asked, using a section of orange to point to Lani's pocket. "Any humming or something of the sort?"

"No." Lani drew the crystal from her pocket, holding it out flat on her palm. "I wish I understood why it reacted to the bathwater but not conjured water. It hasn't made a peep since then."

"Maybe it needs to be submerged?" Sage suggested. "Or maybe it was a characteristic of the bathwater. The soap, maybe, or the original source."

"Have you tried putting it in other water?" Emi asked. "It's a shame we didn't take it to the lake before the scenario ended."

"I still think that if it's missing pieces of itself, they wouldn't have all been within the same room," Lani pointed out. She blinked on her Sense Life spell, squinting at the amorphous shadow that she could barely discern. "I think it might be able to point us in the right direction of its missing pieces if we could figure out how to activate it."

"I could try a few spells on it right now, if you'd like," Sage offered kindly. "May I see it?"

Lani held out her hand and Sage plucked it from her hand, holding it pinched between his fingers, and touched his attunement-marked hand to his glasses.

"Detect Mind," Sage said, brows knitted studiously. Next to him, Nieve narrowed her eyes as well, as if also casting a spell. If she was, however, it didn't stop her from chomping through a handful of nuts. "There's something there, but it's . . . it's not like any mind I've sensed before." He twisted his lips to the side as if considering something, then tried a few more spells. "Detect Enchantment." A beat of silence, then: "Divine Purpose."

"Did you try that one already?" Nieve asked, picking something out of her teeth.

"No, I think he tried Divine Future," Emi said, correcting her. "I think Divine Purpose is different."

"It is, but it didn't show me anything," Sage groused, seemingly giving up. "Divine Purpose helps in puzzle challenges, usually on things like switches or keys. This thing isn't showing me anything."

"Let me try." Aldis wiped a hand on his leggings, then held his palm out, letting Sage drop the shard into it. "If it has a mind, maybe I can communicate with it."

Aldis's face took on a studious expression, as if concentrating very hard. Lani finished off her heel of bread and took a long pull from her canteen. Water would help stave off the headache the use of her Sense Life spell would eventually give her.

"Well?" Lani asked after a long-enough silence. The snacks were mostly finished and they'd have to be moving on shortly. It was still too early to set up camp, and Lani was hoping they'd find a better spot for it than a simple maze intersection.

"It's very odd," Aldis said finally, rubbing at his eyes. "There's no voice at all, no humming or any response at all. But I can establish a connection to it, which means it has some level of awareness. It almost feels like it's asleep, or dormant, perhaps."

"Oh, like the mimics?" Emi asked brightly.

Sage held up a hand as if alarmed. "Please do not attempt to communicate with the mimics! It's possible that might be interpreted as an attack, which would wake them up."

Aldis cringed slightly, looking warily at the walls as he held out the shard to Lani. "Yes, I think I'll avoid that for now. But I think the place to start with this is in waking it up. Perhaps that's what the bathwater did: rouse it in some way."

"Water always wakes me up," Nieve grumbled darkly, shooting a glare at Sage. "Even without having it splashed in my face."

"You were out cold," Sage retorted, starting to pack his shared supplies away. "And by the way: splashing someone's face with water is a *much* better way to wake them up than hitting them."

"I remember that one!" Emi laughed brightly. "We had to ride horses and Nieve wasn't looking and a branch got her right across the face!"

"Was that broken nose three, or broken nose four?" Lani asked mildly. "I often forget."

"Yeah, yeah, it's funny when the frontline fighter gets hurt," Nieve said, rolling her eyes. "What about waking up that thing? If the bathwater didn't do it, what else do we try? Fire? Lightning?"

"Hitting it?" Sage suggested, his tone overly innocent.

Nieve looked ready to hit something—or someone, rather—when Emiko scooted into the middle of the circle, peering intently at the crystal.

"Should we try casting some spells on it?" she asked quizzically. "If it's just lightning, I could fly it up to the traps above the maze and see if that does anything."

"Its aura isn't right for lightning," Aldis pointed out as he secured the flap over his satchel. "By the colors, I think it's related more to water, or a mana source close to water. Most likely a compound mana type, considering that purplish color."

"Poison?" Emi suggested, leaning back on her hands to put some distance between herself and the shard.

"Unlikely. I would expect to see black and purple if that were the case, but the blue is quite bright." Aldis squinted at the shard again, as if refreshing his memory of the aura. "Ice, maybe. Or rain. Any magic related to water would be my guess."

"Blood?" Lani asked, peering into the prismatic facets of the crystal. A beat of silence made her blink and look up. "What? Blood magic *is* related to water mana."

"Yes, but suggesting we submerge the artifact in blood is a bit morose, don't you think?" Aldis asked, face twisted in disgust.

"That's not what I— Ugh." Lani pushed herself up, slipping the shard back into her pocket. "Let's push on. We can ponder ways to wake the shard up later when we make camp."

The grunts, grumbles, and general shuffling must have alerted Hane, because they picked up their head, blinked once, and asked: "Are we ready to move on?"

"I think we are," Lani replied, checking her hair to make sure it was still secured in its bun. Almost without meaning to, she set her fingers on the point of the shard again. "Is everyone ready?"

A chorus of grumbled affirmatives joined the scrape of bags and boots as everyone picked themselves up. Hane took a quick quaff from their canteen before taking point again, orienting on the vapor trail that would take them to an exit. Lani reluctantly reactivated her Sense Life spell, once again scouring the towering walls for a space void of the muddy-green aura surrounding the dormant mimics. After a few twists and turns along corridors that all looked roughly the same, Lani began to doubt that her spell would even accurately find the chest, seeing how each mimic's aura extended a few inches outward from the core of its body. It seemed possible that if the real chest was surrounded on four sides by mimics, the auras might overlap enough to make her miss the tiny window void of life mana. But as Sage couldn't See where it was, this was the only other option their group had to find it.

It's not like we're desperate for treasure, Lani consoled herself. *The goal was to make it to the twentieth floor or higher on this climb, and with Aldis's spell, we'll probably get there sooner than expected. There's going to be plenty of treasure once we get to the twentieth floor and beyond.*

It was an honest thought, but it set the tips of her missing fingers to throbbing. If she didn't end the climb with a substantial haul, she'd have to take out another loan in order to hit the casinos, and that hadn't worked out so well for her last time.

I'm sure it'll be fine, Lani thought, opening and closing her hands a few times. *I'm overdue for an uptick of luck soon anyway. And it's not like we ever leave a spire empty-handed.*

Even when the climbs turned rough, they'd never lost their entire haul. Not that Lani wouldn't sacrifice everything just to save one of her friends, but they had a system for maximizing treasure returns: usually after a particularly lucrative find, the treasure would be packed up in a bag marked with Nieve's name and climber team identity, and then a delayed-return bell would take the bag away for storage while the team continued to climb. The storage service cost a little money, but it was worth it to ensure they wouldn't end up dropping priceless treasures down a bottomless pit accidentally.

So far, there really wasn't enough treasure to be worth sending back just yet. First-room scenarios were usually a little treasure-bare, though Hane had gotten a few things from the serpent they'd killed. Lani had the golden key from the finished trading sequence, and Nieve had claimed the Illuminator's metal claws as a treasure. Aside from that, their rewards were mostly mana crystals, with all the Class Three mana crystals donated to Emiko for use in her mana diffuser. The rest of the mana crystals had been divided up among Lani, Nieve, Sage, and Aldis so that everyone carried a roughly equal weight of treasure. Hane's dimensional bag was probably carrying significantly more than the rest of them, but that didn't change the bag's weight at all.

More than once, Lani had considered investing in a dimensional bag for the team, but Nieve had always railed against the expense. If they found one on a climb, Lani would argue to keep it, rather than sell it, but so far they hadn't been that lucky. And besides, Lani liked having important items, like healing potions and her canteen, close at hand, rather than having to summon them from the depths of a dimensional bag.

Realizing she'd let her thoughts stray, Lani refocused on the task at hand: trying to pick out the sole real treasure out of the slew of false ones.

The hours passed slowly, trudging by sullenly as the scenery remained unchanging, often giving Lani the impression that they were walking in circles, with new traps being the only indicator that they were moving forward. Aldis began pointedly checking his watch and sighing theatrically, which only made Lani want to continue forging on even more, but when she caught Emiko stifling a yawn, she ruefully considered that it might be about time to pick a campsite for the night. Before she could tell the team to look for someplace relatively safe to set up camp, Emiko made a soft noise of surprise.

"What is that?" Emiko asked, drifting upward on her cloud. "Is that a trap, or—"

Lani looked up in time to see what looked like a vast, fast-moving cloud of dark green descending from the shadowy ceiling. It took a moment for her to realize that it wasn't a poison-gas cloud, but a life aura surrounding many small, black creatures. She started to shout for Emiko to come down, but Emiko's sudden shrieks cut her off. A cloud of bats surrounded her, flying around her and hiding her from view so suddenly it was almost like a spell.

"Drop down, Emi, we'll catch you!" Nieve shouted, shoving past Lani to stand beneath Emiko. "Just drop, I'll get you!"

Hane took a running leap and somersaulted just over the cloud of bats, drawing a few of Emiko's attackers away while reaching through the chittering mass to grasp Emiko's shoulders and shove her down roughly. Her cloud spell must have failed her, because Hane's push sent her flailing as she fell. Lani forgot to breathe as Emiko tumbled end over end: the distance was short and Nieve was right there to catch her, but she was falling so close to the mimics! If one frantic kick managed to hit that wall, it would be over for them.

A burst of air blew past Lani's face, gusting up and around Emiko, putting just enough distance between herself and the wall as she dropped into Nieve's arms. Lani spun around in time to see Aldis lowering his hand, fear still evident on his face. She managed a brief nod before she rushed to Nieve and Emiko. Emi was bleeding from bites and scratches all over her face, neck, and arms, but she looked more frightened than hurt. She shrieked as the cloud of bats turned around to descend on all three of them, but Nieve snapped up an ice dome around them, shutting out the bats.

"Shouldn't you go out and fight?" Lani asked as she placed her hands on Emiko's shoulders.

"Leave it to the others," Nieve growled. "I'm not going anywhere until I'm sure Emi is okay."

Lani exhaled and cast Sense Injury and Sense Toxin, both passive diagnostic spells rather than healing spells. Anything and everything here could be venomous, and Lani wasn't going to take the chance of Emi dying just because she hadn't been cautious enough. A healing spell would only circulate venom faster, so Lani kept her spells probative until she confirmed that there had not been venom in the bats' bites.

"Okay, Emi, hang on," Lani said. "Just a few small wounds, you've been through worse."

"It happened so fast!" Emiko's teeth chattered as Lani cast a regeneration spell. "I barely saw them until they were already on me."

"We must have activated a trap or something," Nieve said, still cradling Emiko in her arms. "Why didn't Sage See this?"

"Probably because of an anti-Seeing rune," Lani replied. "And these injuries aren't all that bad. He might get a warning if something truly dangerous is—"

Something slammed against the ice dome, making all three women gasp and jump. Lani checked to make sure that Emiko was all healed up, then scowled through the opening Nieve created in her ice dome.

"We have to run," Sage said, unapologetic and breathless. "Something worse is coming and if we don't run right now, the fight is going to wake up all the mimics."

Well, as far as excuses for interrupting a healing, that one was pretty good. Nieve's ice dome melted down into a pool of water and Lani helped Emiko to her feet. The bats were still chittering excitedly in a flickering cloud nearby, but Aldis had his dueling cane out, channeling wind spells that tossed the bats away when they flew too close. His face was red, his breath coming fast, and he was already inching past the pool of melted ice, as if eager to move on. Hane was up ahead, waving back to the rest of them.

"Follow me! I'll try and expose the traps as we go!"

That was all the warning they gave before turning and bolting off into the maze. Lani swore as she sized up the others. Everyone else looked ready to run, but Emiko was still swaying on her feet.

"Can you cast a levitation spell?" Lani asked her.

"I'll do it." Aldis switched his cane to his opposite hand and pressed his palm to the top of her head. "Chanting takes too long."

"Put her on my back," Nieve insisted, crouching down. "I can run with her."

"That's a bit foolish when you can give her to me," Aldis said, sending another blast of air at the bats before hooking his cane to his belt. "I can catch up to Hane the easiest, and with a levitation spell on her, even I can carry her. The rest of you need to go!"

"He's right. Don't argue, Nieve." Lani made sure Emiko was pressed tight beneath Aldis's arm, then turned to run. The moment Aldis vanished, the bats swooped to attack. Lani was already running, but she sent a wave of conjured water over her shoulder, hoping bats couldn't fly with wet wings. "Which way, Sage?"

"Here!" Sage pelted along after Hane, Lani running beside Nieve as they followed. Sage must have been able to predict Hane's path in order to follow, because of course this was exactly where the maze branched off into twists and turns, the aisles becoming narrower and narrower the farther along they went, forcing them to run single file. Running close behind Sage kept Lani's field of vision narrow, but her passive Sense Life spell was still working, showing the green haze over the rows and rows of mimics narrowing the path. She considered turning the spell off but decided against it, since it might just help her spot whatever it was they were running from.

The traps didn't stop just because the corridors were narrower now. In fact, they almost seemed to sneak up out of nowhere, forcing Lani to watch Sage's every move, dodging when he dodged and jumping when he jumped. Sage called out over his shoulder when he needed an ice bridge, and Nieve conjured one to cross a pit trap. Lani's side was beginning to burn, her breath starting to flag when she saw it: the square of dead space in her Sense Life spell.

The treasure chest. The real one. About ten feet up the left-side wall of mimics.

Lani stopped so fast that Nieve ran into her from behind, bowling them both over. Sage skidded to a halt and turned back, anxiously pulling them both back up to their feet.

"Come on!" Sage clasped Lani's hand and tried to urge her to a run, but she pulled it away from him, pointing up at the dead space in her Sense Life spell.

"There! That's it! That's the real one!"

Sage and Nieve's heads tracked upward, expressions of longing mixing with trepidation. Was it worth stopping here and trying to figure out how to get the chest? Or was it better to keep running and make sure they lost whatever monster was on their tail?

"What are you doing?" Aldis called from farther up the corridor. He still had Emiko tucked under one arm, but her color was better now than it had been earlier, like the surprise of the bats had worn off. "There's a big opening just ahead; Hane figures we can lose the monster there if—if—"

Lani heard the tremor of fear in Aldis's voice and turned slowly, facing the direction she and the others had run from. A shadow rose up from the floor, looming almost as high as the stacks of false chests, silent and ominous until a pair of brilliant green eyes with vertical slits down the center opened, fixing on the trio stopped in the center of the corridor. Lani felt paralyzed by those eyes, unable to take a single step, even as jaws as wide as a wagon cart hinged open, revealing needlelike venomous fangs.

Sage managed to move first, throwing his hand out toward the real treasure chest and casting a soft, golden glow over it. Nieve caught his momentum and for once, she didn't turn and fight: instead, she grabbed Lani's arm and threw her over her shoulder before bolting away from the black-scaled cobra. Hanging upside down over Nieve's shoulder, it was all Lani could do to not scream as the hooded snake lunged after them, twin droplets of thick, green venom clinging to its fangs, but Nieve must have enhanced her body with a spell, because she outpaced the lunge faster than Lani ever could have on her own.

Sage raced along behind Nieve, but Lani couldn't tear her eyes off the cobra, spitting angrily after missing its meal, then flattening its body not just to the floor but *into* the floor, as if the snake were little more than a shadow. It had certainly looked solid enough when it was looming over them, but now Lani noticed that it didn't make a single sound as it slithered along after them, as silent and deadly as a riptide. Would they even have known it was sneaking up on them if not for Sage's Foresight?

The corridor ended abruptly, opening into something like an atrium around a merrily splashing fountain, multiple corridors branching off like they were at the center of a wagon wheel. Lani only had a second to take that all in before her view flipped, giving her a sense of vertigo that wasn't helped at all by Nieve's rough handling.

"Let me down!" Lani rolled in Nieve's grip, getting her feet beneath her but collapsing to her knees as the dizziness overwhelmed her. She was dimly aware of Nieve and Hane squaring up, weapons in hand, before soft hands gently clasped her wrists.

"Lani?" Emiko's voice, warbling with concern. "Are you okay?"

"Yes, I just—" She blinked, disoriented by her position in the room. The fountain she had seen at a distance was now between her and the ink-black snake. That monstrous beast couldn't teleport, could it? But wait, did that make sense? "What happened?"

"Aldis opened a portal and you all ran through it," Emiko explained. "We're on the far side of the room now."

"Thank you," Lani breathed. "That helps."

Now oriented, Lani stood up, turning to face the shadow-snake, its black tongue flicking out silently as it tasted the air. A hood of shadows flared around its head, making it look even bigger.

"Shadow-cobra," Hane said, voice as low and calm as ever. "Normally they can levitate, but I think this one is limited by the lightning grid above, just as we are. Venomous and occasionally incorporeal."

"Traps?" Lani asked.

Hane shook their head. "This appears to be a rest area built into the maze. But I haven't checked the fountain yet, so stay clear."

Lani glanced over at the fountain, her Sense Life spell still active. The fountain itself possessed no aura, but that didn't necessarily mean it was safe. As Lani set her hand down on the hilt of her cutlass, she felt a humming vibration run up through her hand, like the heartbeat of a frightened bird. The crystal shard again? Strange, but she couldn't let it distract her now. "Hane, we found the real treasure chest. It's down the hall that snake is blocking."

Hane's grunt of acknowledgment seemed surprised, as if they hadn't expected to find the real chest. They glanced sideways at Nieve, who gripped her sword in both hands. She nodded minutely, then charged at the shadow-cobra, her sword blooming ice crystals to change its shape into that of a zanbatou as she ran. Hane leapt away, a shadow disappearing among shadows. Emiko chanted softly under her breath, a cloud forming beneath her to carry her up above the battlefield.

"Aldis, pull anyone back if it looks like they're about to get bit." Lani could purify most venoms, but she didn't want to take any chances against a shadow-cobra. Some venoms were too fast-acting for her to heal. She drew her cutlass, ignoring the thin vibration from the crystal shard tucked in her pocket. "Sage, stay back and tell Aldis who he needs to teleport. I'm going to support."

"Lani, wait! Let me go instead, we're going to need you if anyone gets bitten!" Sage protested.

Lani shook her head. "There isn't time. Better to be close by than too far to be of any use. Stay here, Sage."

Sage continued to argue, but Lani was already racing forward, her cutlass held out wide. That monster was separating them from the first real treasure they'd found on this climb and Lani would be damned before she let that slip through her fingers. And if this area truly was a safe zone, then it was the perfect spot to set up camp and rest for a few hours. All they had to do was defeat this monster first.

But even Lani could see it wasn't going to be that easy. Nieve conjured ice to try to trap the monster, but it simply slithered straight through the ice the same way it had slithered through the floor. Hane dove at it from above, tonfa crossed in front of them to strike, but the weapons only passed harmlessly through the serpent like it was no more substantial than a shadow. Emiko was trying to chant something, but the serpent kept striking at her, making her dart and dodge about on her little cloud, chanting again whenever she had the breath for it. And after hours of walking through the maze, everyone's exhaustion was showing.

If this goes on too long, someone is going to get bitten, Lani rationalized, flinching as the snake snapped at Emiko once again. *We can only hurt it when it's corporeal, but it changes forms so quickly. What can hurt it while it's incorporeal?*

A bead of venom dripped off a fang, giving Lani an idea.

I just need to touch it long enough to change its venom into something else, Lani told herself, stepping carefully over Nieve's chipped and broken ice. *Water would make its bites a little safer, but converting it to acid would eat it up from the inside, in both its corporeal and incorporeal forms. All I need is a little time . . .*

She took her chance as Hane kicked off the shadow-cobra's nose, enraging it into chasing them as they leapt away. Lani jammed the tip of her cutlass into the ice and braced her foot against it as she slapped her hands down against the inky dark scales along the cobra's skin. She followed the green tendrils of flowing life mana through the cobra's body until she traced them up to the venom sacs, heavy and engorged in the serpent's throat. There wasn't much of a difference between converting venom to water and converting it to acid, but Lani had far more experience making venom safe than making it more dangerous. But since the cobra carried its venom sacs with it whether it was solid or not, then converting the venom was the best way to ensure the creature's death. She felt the powerful body of the cobra moving beneath her hands but maintained her focus on the spell. Just when it seemed like it was beginning to take, the cobra darted forward and the coil Lani had her hands pressed against shot out toward her, tossing her up and backward off her feet. She had just enough time to pray that she wasn't about to hit a wall of mimics when she slammed into something cold and wet: one of Nieve's ice walls. While far from gentle, at least it had kept her from crashing into the mimics.

On instinct, Lani pressed a hand to her chest, casting a regeneration spell before checking her own condition. Her ears were ringing with the impact of hitting the wall; her vision blurred in and out. As she fought to remain conscious through her spell, she saw Sage place himself between her and the shadow-cobra, but then the room spun dizzily and all she could think of was the fact that the crystal shard wasn't vibrating any more.

HANE

Wavewalker (leg mark), Citrine

The trouble with shadow-cobras was that they never stayed solid long enough to take a decent hit. And often it was difficult to tell when the overgrown snake actually was solid or not, which made all of Hane's midair jumps and twists that much harder with nothing to push off from. While it was certainly possible to push off from thin air and change direction, Hane always felt that transference-aided pushes were stronger when pushing off from something solid. Liquids worked well, too, though they tended to feel a little more flexible, like jumping off a springy mattress. Every time Hane calculated a push off the shadow-cobra, it turned incorporeal, making all their attacks feel slightly mistimed and making it harder to get back into position for an attack. Even when they were in the right place at the right time, the snake would shift and their attacks would pass harmlessly through its shadow form.

Frustrating.

Nieve didn't appear to be having any more luck than Hane was. Worse, perhaps, since her usual ice traps weren't restricting the cobra's movement at all, Nieve couldn't seem to find the right timing to take her swings at the beast. And Hane wasn't sure what Lani was trying to accomplish, but it looked like she'd hit that ice wall pretty hard. Hane had an idea of what might work but didn't have the right mana to pull it off. If they could get to Emiko, perhaps her handy little device could whip something up, but as the cobra seemed to be targeting her specifically, she wasn't able to remain still long enough for Hane to tell her the plan.

Nieve backed off her assault on the ground, snarling curses as she looked for an avenue of attack. Hane completed a midair twist to avoid the cobra's snapping fangs and landed in a crouch beside her. Nieve glanced over at them, a sardonic twist to her lips. "Should we try offering it some food, or some treasure?"

"That's not helping," Hane informed her. Food might work if they had anything big enough to offer a shadow-cobra, but it seemed that nothing less than an adventurer or two was going to satiate the beast now, and Hane doubted something of this size would be deterred from a meal for a mere trinket or two. "What we need is to force it stay corporeal long enough to—"

A burst of light flared from behind them, making Hane flinch at the suddenness of it. They had to squint in order to see that it was Sage, holding his dueling cane pointed at the cobra, light mana emanating outward in an aurora of brilliance. The serpent hissed and drew its coils in tight, shying back from the light. Hane noted the moment it switched from its shadow form to its solid form as little burning tendrils of smoke stopped drifting off from it. The light couldn't hurt its solid form, but it could burn away its umbral form. At last! They had it contained. As Nieve cast an ice spell to trap it further, Hane leapt straight up, seeking Emiko on her little cloud.

"Emiko." The little Cloudcaller's head whipped around, wide-eyed and breathless as she met Hane's gaze. "The snake is contained by the lightning barrier above us. Lightning can hurt it."

She nodded sharply, breathing fast as her fingers danced along her bandolier to select a fiery red mana crystal. Hane dropped to the ground as Emiko began chanting, taking up a flanking position beside Sage as he continued pouring light mana through his dueling cane. Nieve had fallen back to Sage's other side, casting glances back over her shoulder at where Lani lay against the ice wall.

"Is she okay?" Sage asked without letting up his light spell.

"She's fine," Nieve said, glancing back again. "Looks like she's healing herself. Shroud probably protected her."

Sage grimaced. "Ice isn't always the best idea, Nieve. She could have been really hurt."

"Yeah, next time I should let her hit the wall and wake up a thousand mimics while we're still fighting a shadow-snake."

"That's not what I'm saying! Sometimes, you could just—"

A sharp flicker of light cut off Sage's rebuttal, drawing all eyes upward as lightning jumped from black cloud to black cloud. The following boom of thunder left Hane feeling mildly deaf. The snake hissed and lunged for Emiko, who suddenly plummeted as if she'd canceled her levitation spell, then caught herself once she was far enough away from the venom-dripping fangs that nearly had her.

"I have an idea but I need help." Hane leaned around Sage to talk to Nieve. "Can you hit it from the left with a wave spell?"

"Yes," Nieve said, brows knitted. "But anyone caught too close would get caught by the lightning."

"Then get back. We need the water to make the lightning catch."

"What about you?" Nieve asked. "Isn't yours a leg attunement? You'll get too close just to cast it."

Hane shook their head. "Don't worry about me. I can get out of the way fast enough."

Nieve looked doubtful but resolved it quickly as the shadow-cobra snapped at Emiko again. The dark clouds were flickering with blue-white light, building up to a second lightning bolt. Hane bounded away as Nieve's expression settled into one of concentration. From what Hane had seen so far, Nieve tended to cast large, rough spells fairly quickly, so even as they got into position for their wave spell, Nieve had already sent a wave of conjured water surging up and over the serpent's coils. Hane took a position opposite Nieve's wave and cast a spell called Tsunami, sending it rushing out toward the snake. As the two waves met, splashing high enough to make the serpent writhe and hiss, lightning arced down from the clouds, but Hane was already leaping clear in a sideways, transference-mana-aided jump. They rolled once, then popped back up on their feet once they were clear of the water. The shadow-cobra keened in pain, but the fight wasn't over just yet.

"Fury of the storm/Unleash upon my command/Strike that cobra down!" Emiko's chant rose above the crash of the waves and the resounding boom that rolled down every mimic-made corridor. The lightning flashed furiously, bolts striking one after the other, the resulting thunder driving Hane back and making them cover their ears. The snake went rigid after each strike, keening soundlessly until it finally collapsed hard enough to make the floor shudder. Hane dropped into a crouch, ready to spring away at the slightest movement from the mimic boxes, but even as they turned a slow circle, they saw no movement from the walls. Perhaps the boxes required a certain proximity to awaken, and lacking that, they would remain dormant. At least, that was what Hane hoped.

Sage didn't drop his light spell until the shadow-cobra dissolved into a puddle of mana crystals, and then he spun away to rush to Lani's side. Nieve seemed conflicted between Lani and Emiko, then settled on waiting for Emiko as she drifted down from the ceiling, her storm clouds already breaking apart. The whole room felt damp, the conjured water spreading into pools and puddles, giving off the smell of petrichor. Hane waited long enough to be certain that the conjured water wasn't about to wake up the encircling mimics, then circled back, exchanging a quick glance with Aldis. A jerk of their chin indicated that Aldis should check one side of the open space surrounding the fountain and Hane would check the other. Aldis looked almost relieved to be given an order, hurriedly moving to comply. Hane circled opposite the direction he went, stepping carefully and cautiously despite already having checked this area for traps. They couldn't be certain that this maze was immutable, which meant traps might spontaneously manifest even after an area had been checked.

Sensing the thin vapor trail left behind by Emiko's earlier spell, Hane took a piece of chalk from their pocket and marked the floor with an arrow. The trail had already thinned out significantly, and if the group was stopping to rest here—which seemed prudent, considering how much energy and mana they had spent in that last fight, as well as how long they had been wandering the maze so far—then at least they knew which direction to start off in before Emiko recast her Cloud Cover spell.

Aside from traps, what Hane was really looking for was any sign that the mimics had moved. When they'd first entered this open area, they hadn't thought to be staying long and had only had time to look for obvious traps, but they hadn't put in the time to measure how much space lay between the fountain and the mimic walls, so they walked a full circuit now, then counted their steps from the end of a corridor back to the fountain, then repeated the process to see if the number of steps matched up. The count did add up, which meant all the corridors were equidistant from the fountain. For now.

Hane joined the rest of the team at the mana fountain, which Sage was heroically poking with his dueling cane, as if to ensure that the fountain was not, in fact, a mimic. The instincts were good, but Hane had been less worried about the stonework and more worried about finding out if the water was actually water. When the fountain failed to attack Sage for poking it, Hane held their hand over the surface of the pool, using the spell Sense Purity to test the safety of the water.

"It's actual water," Hane announced, dipping their hand into the fountain. The temperature was tepid, but even that was a relief after a long run and an intense fight. "This is probably a built-in rest area, based on the lack of traps within the circumference of the fountain."

"I think we could all use a little break," Lani suggested, still rubbing the back of her head. She looked weary, her braids all pulled out of their bun and straggling about her face and shoulders. She shoved a handful of hair behind herself and sat down on the fountain's edge. She jumped up a moment later, holding the splinter of crystal from earlier in her hand. "Does anyone have any guesses as to why this thing started vibrating just now? Is there a broken piece nearby, or is it something else?"

"Is it the fountain?" Sage asked. "Try dunking it and see if anything happens."

It seemed as harmless a way as any for everyone to catch their breath. Hane lingered nearby, watching along with everyone else as Lani peeled the glove off her hand and dunked the crystal shard beneath the water. While Hane hadn't been able to confirm that the piece had been vibrating in Lani's hand, they could now see the ripples caused by the crystal's movement beneath the water.

"How odd!" Aldis kept rocking forward, then drawing back, expression alternating between curiosity and disgust. It took Hane a moment to realize why: without her glove, it was impossible not to notice Lani's missing fingertips. It seemed a strange thing to fixate on: Hane had climbed with plenty of people with varying physical challenges. Missing fingertips barely even registered to them. "Is it trying to give us directions? If you release it, does it point a certain way?"

Releasing the shard only seemed to make it sink to the bottom of the fountain, where its shivers continued to disrupt the surface. Lani had to reach in past her elbow to pull it out again.

"We could try hitting it with some other spells while it's active," Sage suggested. "Nieve, can you freeze it?"

"Here, Sage. You can play with it." Lani dropped it into the Seer's hand, then set her hand on her chin and cracked her neck. "We need to go back for the treasure chest, but before that, does anyone need any healing?"

"I'm fine," Hane said, waving off Lani's offer of a healing spell. "I'd like to go take a look at the chest you found. You said it was back the way we came?"

"Sage marked it with a light spell," Lani explained, beckoning Emiko closer. "If you're going down that way, please take care of yourself."

"I'll come with you," Aldis offered, somewhat surprisingly. "I didn't get a look at the chest either. We should gather up those mana crystals, too."

A good point: Hane nodded their agreement. They turned to walk back toward the pile of mana crystals, only to find themself blocked by an outstretched arm. They tracked it back to Aldis, giving him a questioning, even look.

"I know you're already fast, but I'm just a bit faster," Aldis huffed. "And I'm fairly sure you used more mana than I did in that fight."

That might be true, but Aldis had been teleporting himself and Emiko constantly during the frantic flight from first the bats, then the snake. That was no small amount of mana, but it was probably easier for Aldis to teleport than it was for Hane to cast a wave spell or check the purity of the water in the fountain; they vastly preferred the use of transference spells rather than spells based on water mana or multiple mana types. Hane accepted Aldis's help and allowed him to teleport them closer to the mound of mana crystals.

"Nice of you to offer to help," Hane said, scanning the pile of crystals. It wasn't as big as the pile they'd gotten for killing the lake serpent, but it was still a good amount. Lots of umbral mana crystals, but also a few enhancement and death mana crystals as well. According to the loot-split contract Hane had signed to join the group, a portion of mana crystals gathered during the climb would be retained by the team to replenish Emiko's supply, with the remaining percentage set aside to be sold and the profits split evenly. Death mana crystals didn't sell all that well, but umbral usually got a decent price, and enhancement mana crystals sold for a premium. Hane wasn't entirely certain what types of crystals Emiko had used up until this point, though, so it was impossible to calculate what their cut might be.

"Yes, well." Aldis flipped open the top of his bag and held a hand out over the crystals. Large swaths of the glittering gems vanished, reappearing inside his satchel. "I wasn't able to do very much during the fight, so I wanted to be seen doing something." Another wave of mana crystals vanished from the floor, leaving only a few scattered crystals behind. Aldis groaned as he knelt down to pick up the remaining crystals one by one. Hane kicked a few closer to Aldis, then turned down the corridor the team had emerged from earlier. Aldis called a protest but didn't actually try to stop them. Probably something about safety, but Hane's perception spells would alert them to anything long before it got close enough to be harmful.

The gold-marked chest was easy to find among the stacks of mimics but not so easy to get to. Hane could jump high enough to grab it, but doing so would put them far too close to the mimics, and even if they took a chance on speed, how were they going to remove it without bracing their hands or feet against the mimics surrounding it? Maybe it could be punched out through the opposite side of the wall? Although, more than likely, this chest was backed up against a mimic to make up the opposite wall, so that wouldn't work.

Nieve had said she could freeze the mimics in place while they pulled out the chest, which was looking more and more like their best option. Hane could brace against an ice wall while working the chest free and it would certainly give them a little time to get away, but that still ran the risk of waking up the mimic next to the chest. And if one mimic woke up, did that mean *all* the mimics would wake up? If this entire maze came to life, they would certainly lose a few team members before they reached an exit. Of course, they could always grab the treasure, hide behind an ice wall, and use their return bells to ring out, but a short climb wasn't what Hane had signed up for. This team was known for spending weeks inside the spire, as long as they had the supplies to last, which was what had piqued Hane's interest in them.

As a rule, Hane preferred to be inside a spire rather than outside one.

Though, as of yet, they hadn't had the chance to travel anywhere other than the Tortoise Spire.

As Hane stood examining the treasure chest, Aldis silently popped into existence at their side, also looking up at the gold-marked box. "We can't be sure that's the right one, can we?"

"I think it is." Hane pointed to a box that was eye-level with them. "The mimic boxes all look very much the same: equally weathered and worn with the same pattern on the wooden boards. The marked one has minor differences, like the chipped brass on the corner and the water stain on the lowest boards."

"Ah." Aldis looked impressed. "I wouldn't have noticed that. Is that another way to tell a real object apart from a mimic object?"

"Not normally. It really only works in a situation like this one, where you have so many mimics to compare. A chest all on its own will just look like a solitary chest."

"Ah, true." Aldis clapped his hands once and rocked back on his heels. "So. Any ideas?"

"No good ones," Hane admitted. "You couldn't teleport it out, could you?"

Aldis made a face and actually shuffled back half a step. "My teleportation spells aren't quite so refined: I put a lot more effort into practicing my portals, you see. Unless I'm directly touching something, my teleport spells tend to work in an aura around a person or object—you know, so pieces don't get left behind." Hane nodded, though that was a gruesome visual in regard to teleporting people. "I've come to understand it's easier to refine a teleportation spell for an individual at the Citrine levels, or through fine practice, but I'm afraid my current spellwork is a little rough for what you need."

"If you touched it directly, would the spell work?" Hane asked.

Aldis shrugged. "It's possible, but that puts me far too close to the other mimics, doesn't it? And the walls are so narrow here."

That was true. Even just drawing the chest straight out risked backing into the wall of mimics behind them. And someone as twitchy as Aldis was as likely to jump at a shadow as much as he was to jump at a mimic licking its lips.

"We'll work it out as a team," Hane finally pronounced. "Sage said its location would be fixed upon entry, so at least we know where to find it."

"As long as the walls are set in a fixed configuration," Aldis muttered as he placed his hand on Hane's shoulder.

A fair assessment, considering the living maze surrounding them, but not one Hane had much time to put any thought into as Aldis teleported the both of them back to the group at the fountain. For a moment, Hane didn't know what they were looking at: Lani, Sage, Nieve, and Emiko were huddled around a tiny gray rain cloud that was dripping with rain. Then they realized that the others were performing more tests on the crystal shard.

"Has it done anything else?" Aldis asked with interest. "How did the ice test go?"

"It stopped vibrating." Lani sounded disappointed. "It won't even shiver in the fountain water anymore."

"Why are you only testing water spells on it?" Hane inquired.

"Mostly because the first time it started humming was in the bathwater," Lani explained, grimacing as she straightened her back, then twisted from side to side. "Its aura is a mix of bright blue and blue-purple colors, which probably means it's tied to a compound mana type, possibly tied to water, but we can't be certain. Got any ideas?"

Hane considered a moment, then shook their head. "If it's something like the key to a vault, it's possible the aura is only meant as an indicator of sameness, rather than a particular enchantment or mana type. If the aura does indicate a specific type of mana, I'm afraid I don't know enough to be of any help."

"It was worth asking," Lani said with a shrug. As Emiko's rain spell ended, she scooped up the crystal, holding it loosely in her hand as she addressed the team. "We'll set up camp here tonight. Make sure to eat and drink and do whatever you need to do to relax and recharge. Unless you two figured out a way to remove that treasure chest before we make camp?"

Hane shook their head. "I believe it's a matter that requires some reflection."

Lani's nod was sharp, authoritative. Interestingly, the water in the fountain rippled outward from the hand holding the crystal shard, though the crystal didn't seem to be vibrating. Did that make it more likely to be connected to a compound mana that included water? Or was it more likely to be something that affected water instead? "Nieve and Sage are on the first watch, Emiko and I are on the second. Hane and Aldis, can you handle the third watch?"

Hane nodded, accepting the assignment. "My preference is to sleep now anyway. We can make a plan to remove that treasure chest once we've rested."

Lani nodded as she tucked the crystal shard away in her pocket. As the others began unpacking bags of food, clothing, and bedding, Hane sat down with their back against the fountain and drew their knees up to their chest. They considered the fox-fur bedroll they had earned in the first challenge and briefly considered using it but decided against it: they wanted to be able to jump to their feet at the first sign of an attack, and the fox-fur bedroll would likely lull them into a deeper sleep then they preferred. Hane ignored the voices of their teammates as well as the smell of food cooking and put their head down on their knees, falling asleep almost instantly.

Hours later, Hane woke up just as Emiko was reaching out to tap their shoulder, making her gasp as they lifted their head from their knees. They made the hand sign for an apology, then waved her off before she could rouse Aldis. Once Emiko and Lani were curled up again, Hane stood, stretched, then walked a circuit around the fountain, eating from a pouch of dried rations as they checked for traps, monsters, or shifted walls. Suspecting that Aldis would only huff and complain if awoken, then fall back asleep, Hane elected to leave him sleeping. Instead, they measured the distance between the fountain and two randomly selected corridors by counting their footsteps, finding it to be the same distance as before. But even so, something about that felt . . . off. Using a perception spell to enhance their sight, hearing, and sense of smell, Hane walked a circuit around the fountain again, pausing when they found the chalk mark they'd left indicating the direction of the vapor trail they had been following. Where once the arrow Hane had drawn pointed directly down the center of an aisle within the maze, it now pointed at a wall between two aisles. Which had to mean that the walls of the maze had shifted as the team rested.

Shifted, but not crept closer, Hane thought, working the problem through slowly. *Is this area meant to be a respite for weary climbers? Does that mean there are other such safe zones within the maze? It didn't stop the shadow-cobra from following us in here, but if the mimics can move subtly enough that no one else noticed it, why didn't they creep closer as everyone slept?*

Maybe because they couldn't? But why? Hane had spent enough time inside this particular spire to know that such things didn't happen by accident: there was a reason this area was kept immutable. With that thought in mind, Hane performed a more intense inspection, bolstering their senses with a stronger perception spell, one that enhanced their sense of touch to the point that they could feel magic as little tingles along their skin. The sensation of hidden magic was strongest around and within the water fountain.

Hane wasn't sure how much time passed, but perhaps an hour or so later, Aldis sat up yawning and rubbing his eyes.

"Is it our watch?" he asked blearily, squinting at Hane standing atop the fountain water.

"It was," Hane replied. "I expect the others may wake soon."

"Oh." Aldis checked a timepiece kept inside his vest. "Well, then. Guess I'll start some tea."

Not a single thanks for allowing him to sleep in, but Hane hadn't expected one. They maintained their focus on shaping the fountain water out of their way as they inspected the bottom of the fountain.

"What exactly are you doing?" Aldis asked as he approached the fountain with a metal teakettle. Beyond him, Hane noted an enchanted hot plate, as well as an open pouch of food.

"Looking for something." Hane gestured to the kettle. "Here."

Aldis held the kettle out and Hane conjured enough water to fill it. Aldis muttered his thanks and returned to the hot plate, setting it to boil while he selected tea leaves from a tin. It was oddly peculiar but not the strangest thing Hane had ever seen anyone do inside a spire.

Not long after, Lani groaned as she sat up, pushing her braids out of her face. "Do I smell tea? Hane, what are you doing? Is there something in there?"

"Not yet." Hane used a touch of transference mana to glide forward on the water. "I think we might need to remove all the water from it first. I thought that would be rude with you all still sleeping."

"Wh-wh-where is Aldis?" Lani asked through a yawn. The others were beginning to roll and stretch, churning beneath the cloaks they had used as blankets.

"Making that tea you smelled," Aldis retorted gruffly. He poured the steaming water through a strainer into a small tin cup with no handle, intended to be nestled among other similarly sized cups for easy storage. He grunted as he pushed himself up, hand-delivering the tea to Lani while managing to look ever so put-upon for someone who had slept the most out of everyone. "I don't know how you take it, so it's just a green tea."

"Green tea is perfect. Thank you." Lani sipped from the cup, then set it aside to gather her hair back behind her head. "Why do you want to drain the fountain, Hane?"

"I think it's hiding a secret." Hane placed their hand down in the spot they had pushed the water away from. "Maybe more treasure, or a key, or something else. I can sense a secret, but I can't see what it is."

"Are there runes?" Sage squinted dolefully as he cleaned the lenses of his glasses. "I have a passing familiarity with most runes, and a pocket guide for the ones I don't recognize."

Hane shook their head. "I can't see them, I can only sense them. Perhaps you have a spell that can look deeper than my perception can?"

"Yeah, give me a minute." Sage yawned, stood, and then fastened his cloak around his shoulders once more. He accepted a cup of tea from Aldis before he touched his glasses and squinted at the fountain. "I see water-conjuring runes, and the runes that make the fountain run so the water doesn't go stagnant. I'm not really seeing anything unfamiliar or unexpected."

"I didn't sense anything strange until I looked beneath the water," Hane explained. "That's why I think we need to empty the fountain."

"Well, let's start with breakfast first, refill our canteens, and then we can empty the fountain," Lani decreed, stuffing her cloak back into her satchel. "Did anyone come up with a plan for removing the treasure chest from the wall of mimics?"

After a grumbled round of "No," Hane explained that the walls had shifted somewhat as they'd slept, so the chest might not be exactly where they'd left it. They would also need to cast another Cloud Cover spell to create a vapor trail to the exit, which Emiko acknowledged with a bleary-eyed nod.

"We could take a chance on freezing that portion of the corridor," Nieve suggested, elbowing her way into the circle that had formed around the kettle and helping herself to a cup of tea. "If the corridors just shifted to the side, we're still going in an almost opposite direction from where the chest is. We'd be long gone by the time the mimics started waking up, so they might just fall back asleep without waking up the entire maze."

"But if you're wrong, we'll have to ring out," Sage pointed out. "If the whole maze comes alive, there's no way we'll make it to an exit before they attack us."

"So then, what's your plan?" Nieve asked.

Sage shrugged. "I don't have a better one, I'm just pointing out what could possibly go wrong. That's my job, isn't it?"

"It is good to be prepared to ring out if we have to," Lani said, sounding a little more awake by now. "But we should try to come up with a plan where we won't have to. All right, everyone who's finished eating: refill your canteens and pack up. Once the canteens are full, let's drain this fountain so we can see if there's anything underneath it."

There were spells that could make conjured water vanish, as well as spells that could evaporate water rapidly. Hane didn't know any of those spells, but making water move was a specialty of theirs. Once the others were clear of the fountain, all it took was a firm punch of transference mana into the pool to send it all sloshing out over the sides. Hane swept aside the water that remained, scooping it up over the rim and letting it dribble down to the rest of the displaced water. With the water gone, the tickle against Hane's perception was even stronger; one section of discolored stonework stood out starkly without the water covering it, hinting at a hidden secret.

"It's here," Hane said, getting down on their hands and knees. "Look, there's an odd crack right here that looks deliberate."

"There are runes, but they're hard to make out. The magic is dense." Sage stood on the rim of the fountain, staring down at the section Hane pointed out. "I can see air and transference mana . . . and mental, I think."

"Air, transference, and mental?" Aldis perked up. "That's teleportation magic. You must have found a secret exit!"

"Really?" Lani, Emiko, and Nieve crowded around, as if there were anything to see but stone.

"So we can exit the maze right here?" Nieve confirmed. "We don't have to spend another day inside this maze?"

"A moment," Hane cautioned. "This crack looks to be a keyhole. Most likely there is a key hidden somewhere in the maze. In order to open the door, we'd need that key."

"Unless!" Lani rooted around in her satchel, grinning as she produced the golden key they'd earned in the first scenario. "A gold key should work on almost any lock, right? We can open it!"

"Oh, oh!" Emiko shimmied in a cheerful little dance. "And this exit is close to the treasure chest! Nieve's plan to freeze the mimics just might work if all we have to do is jump through this doorway!"

"Wait. Do we really want to spend our key here?" Sage asked. "It's just as likely that the treasure chest will need a key. If we can't get it open, we'll have to lug it around with us until we find another key."

"That's a good call, Sage, but don't forget: we get to pick where we land now." Lani flipped her grip on the key and held it out to Aldis. "What do you think? Can we find a nice safe spot to land in and figure out what to do with a locked chest?"

"I should think so." Aldis's lips curled up at the corners as he accepted the key. "A gold key often yields better choices, right? With a little scanning, we should be able to land somewhere nice enough to give us a little breathing room."

Hane backed up as Aldis turned the key in the lock. A square of solid stone vanished as if it had never been there at all, revealing an opening in the base of the fountain. Sage knelt down for a better view, one hand on his glasses as he squinted down into the portal they would all have to drop through.

"Find me something with a fight!" Nieve demanded, tightening the knot on her headband. "I'm tired of all this treading lightly stuff, I want to crush a few monsters!"

"But also check for any auras that match the crystal," Lani advised, her fingers toying with one pointed end of the shard protruding from her pocket.

Hane had seen enough monsters already and wouldn't mind an agility challenge but didn't bother to say so out loud. The crystal shard was intriguing enough that they wouldn't mind any challenge that solved that particular mystery.

"Not this one," Sage said after a moment of staring into the doorway. The light through the portal shifted, though from their vantage point, Hane couldn't catch a glimpse of the view. "Not this one, either." Another flicker of light and Sage hedged. "Maybe? It's an escort quest. We'd be protecting a caravan for either four days or seven, depending on the route we choose."

"Pass," Nieve said loudly, cutting over the other responses. "Find a room that lets me fight something big, so when I win, we can just move on." Nieve considered for a moment, then added: "Or stairs. Any room with stairs is fine."

Sage looked to Lani for confirmation, then sighed heavily as he adjusted his glasses. "Fine. Next room, please."

Hane waited patiently as Aldis worked his magic to change the portal every time Sage reported "Not this one," then stared unblinkingly through the next portal, peering into challenge after challenge. By the time Nieve became restless enough to begin pacing, Sage sat back on his heels and pinched the bridge of his nose.

"Okay, Nieve, I think I have something for you. It's not exactly what you wanted, but it's a lot of fighting and a chance for treasure if we do it right." He paused to yawn, ignoring Nieve's overly excited expression. "Instead of one big bad monster, we'll be fighting swarms of smaller monsters. Once we start the challenge, one swarm of monsters will come at us, and then after a five-minute timer we'll get another swarm, then four minutes a swarm, and so on until it's one minute between swarms. There are platforms and switches around the room that will either increase the timer between swarms, reveal treasure, or open the exit. The swarms won't stop coming until we find the sequence of switches that opens the door."

"Stairs?" Nieve asked.

"No stairs." Sage shook his head. "I didn't see a single room with stairs. You know it usually takes a week of climbing to find stairs; we might not be deep enough in yet." To Lani, he added: "Sorry, but I couldn't find that aura, either."

Nieve's mouth twisted in a moue, but she nodded. "I can handle swarms easily enough. I'm fine with this room."

"If the switches are on platforms, I'm good to help with that," Hane put in. "Unless you need me on the ground."

"Nah." Nieve's grin sharpened. "I'm good."

"And I like the possibility of collecting more treasure," Lani said with a firm nod. "And to that end, we need to grab the chest in here and make a run for it. I'm thinking Nieve freezes the corridor and pulls the chest free, then Aldis teleports both her and the chest—"

"Can't, sorry." Aldis shook his head, his hands still braced against one side of the opening in the fountain. "I can't move from here or else we lose the room. I have to keep the runes drained in order to hold this particular portal open, which makes teleporting anything extremely difficult for me right now, especially something that's out of sight."

Lani seemed to accept the answer with good grace, looking instead to Hane. "Any ideas? After Aldis, you're probably the fastest."

"A few, but moving a chest that big is going to be cumbersome." Hane looked back toward the corridor containing the chest, thinking through several scenarios. "I have an idea, but it will take three of us: Nieve, Emiko, and me. Aldis stays to hold the portal with Sage and Lani standing guard in case our expectations are incorrect and we awaken all the mimics at once."

"Me?" Emiko asked, pointing to herself. "What can I do to help?"

"We just need you for one spell. It's an easy one, and then you can fly back to the doorway," Hane assured her. "We'll have Nieve ice both sides of the corridor, as well as a pathway back to the fountain. You'll need to be precise enough so the ice doesn't cover the real chest, because we're going to have to slide it out of the wall together."

Hane expected Nieve to scoff and say "No problem!" but she actually glanced away, rocking back on her heels as she crossed her arms over her chest. "Yeah, I can do that."

Well, that's not her usual confidence, Hane observed. *It doesn't exactly fill me with confidence either, but it'll have to do.*

"Emiko, once we have the chest out, you need to cast a levitation spell on it so it isn't too heavy for us to carry."

"That's easy!" Emiko beamed. "So I just make it weightless, then fly back to the others?"

"And call out anything that goes wrong," Hane added, though that was probably unnecessary: surely Emiko knew to warn her team if something terrible occurred while pulling the chest free of the wall. "Nieve and I will each take up opposite sides of the chest: Nieve out front to guide and I'll push us with transference mana so we slide along the ice path all the way back here. Hopefully that gets us through the portal faster than the mimics can break Nieve's ice."

"Good, got it, I love it!" Nieve clapped her hands, an enthusiastic grin on her face. "Now which corridor was our chest in?"

"That's the other thing," Hane admitted with a sigh.

At least it could only really be down one of two corridors directly next to each other, and Emiko easily scouted both on her cloud, finding the treasure chest with the minute differences that marked it as genuine amid the dross. Nieve took a much longer time laying down a path of ice from the fountain to the correct corridor, making it curve gently to the right and down the corridor Emiko indicated.

Hane had seen Nieve coat the floor with ice a few times before, but this was different: she was actively keeping the layer of ice thin and smooth, without the usual cracks and crags that tripped up her foes. And upon entering the corridor, she kept the path narrow enough so it didn't touch the mimics resting along the floor. The amount of effort it took had her sweating by the time she stopped in front of the marked chest, her breath coming just a little hard. Hane could only guess that precision was not her forte when casting ice spells.

"A minute," Nieve requested, drinking heavily from her canteen. Hane glanced up at Emiko, who waved cheerily down at them. They assessed the height to the chest and the length of the ice path—the portion of it they could see, at least. It wasn't exactly a straight shot back to the fountain, but it would be close enough. And with the weightless chest, it should be easy to shoot back along the path and leap down the portal into the next room.

In theory.

"Ready?" Nieve asked, shaking out her hands and bouncing on the balls of her toes.

"Ready!" Emiko called down.

"Ready," Hane affirmed. "After you freeze the walls, lift us up on an ice platform so we can reach the chest."

Nieve nodded, fixing her gaze on the marked chest above their heads. As she bit her lower lip, a chill filled the air. Her eyes narrowed as she lifted both hands, her jaw tightly clenched. Slowly, starting from the edges of the real treasure chest, ice grew outward, rapid and thick, spreading to encase the nearest mimics making up the wall in front of them before growing up the wall behind Nieve like vines of ice that quickly grew and merged into one solid sheet of ice. Before Hane could offer any words of praise, the ice rumbled beneath their feet and shot upward, a platform of ice raising both Hane and Nieve to the one chest left uncovered by ice.

"Ha!" Nieve looked tired but triumphant as she smacked the chest once with her bare hand. "Not bad, right? Told you it was no problem."

Actually, she hadn't, but despite her supposed doubts, she had accomplished exactly what they needed. As Hane and Nieve worked to find places to grab the chest, Emiko floated down just behind them, beginning her chant.

"Come soft, gentle— Ah!" Emiko screamed as the mimic to the right of the treasure chest snarled and lunged, teeth just visible where the lid met the top of the box. It couldn't move very much, not with Nieve's ice wall trapping it, but others were starting to twitch and stir, and enough of them lunging at the ice might just be enough to break it.

"The spell, Emiko," Hane urged, struggling to pull the chest free of the wall without letting their fingers get too close to the mimics surrounding it. "The chest is heavy, we need the levitation spell."

Emiko trembled, but started again. "Come soft, gentle bree— Eee!" The ice over Nieve's shoulder splintered outward, a thick, red tongue questing toward the opening in the ice as the chest slid halfway out of the wall. Emiko's cloud floated backward so fast, she hit the opposite wall, screaming again as the mimic boxes behind the ice started to shift and move. The real chest slid out by another few inches, but the mimic below it popped its lid up slightly, pinning the chest to the top of Nieve's ice window. Looking down the corridor, Hane could see a sort of ripple rolling outward far beyond Nieve's ice wall.

"Emiko." Hane kept their voice low and even. "You either need to cast the levitation spell, or we all need to run and leave the treasure behind. It's up to you."

The little Cloudcaller drew in a shuddering breath. Her chant came out weak and stuttered. "Come soft, gentle breeze/Lift my burdens with your touch/A leaf on the wind."

The treasure chest became lighter, but the levitation spell was weak, so it still took a lot of pulling and wiggling to free the chest from the ice wall. When Hane and Nieve hauled it to the ground, it thudded down heavily, listing from side to side to rest on its edges, floating only lethargically.

"I c-can c-cast it again," Emiko stuttered, her face pale and bloodless, the moving boxes behind the ice holding her attention hostage.

"No, this is fine." Hane had no reason to believe a recast would fix the problem. "Go ahead and tell the others—"

The mimic box above the chest they had just pulled out dropped into the empty space and lunged through the opening, the chest lid opening to reveal a row of teeth and a slobbering tongue. A spear of ice angled up from the floor, piercing the mimic through and through before it could get entirely clear of the empty space. Even with that, the mimic twisted and writhed, snarling menacingly. Emiko's scream reverberated along the ice walls so that they almost seemed to shiver from the sound, although that was probably due more to the mimics waking and stretching just beyond it.

"Emi, go!" Nieve commanded, grabbing the narrow side of the chest. "Go now, go fast!"

Words to live by, Hane thought, grabbing the opposite end of the treasure chest. They angled their feet, infusing their shroud with just a hint of water mana to slide better over the ice. "Tell me when you're ready, then brace yourself."

Nieve turned so that she held the chest behind her with each hand grasping a corner. Hane couldn't see her legs, but she leaned forward slightly in that speed-skater stance they'd seen her use the other day. "Ready!"

Hane took her at her word and sent a burst of transference mana through their legs and feet, pushing the box into Nieve's back so they all moved as one. Nieve cursed and nearly lost her balance but caught it quickly, turning the jolt into a strong, purposeful glide. When Nieve adjusted to the speed, Hane used a second burst of transference, pushing them faster along the ice path. Nieve didn't stumble that time but kept her shoulders and center of balance low as she rode out the speed burst.

The ice along the corridor walls was beginning to splinter, and though they kept their eyes straight ahead, Hane couldn't help but catch glimpses of mimics moving, mimics lunging, mimics baring their teeth as they raced along with the treasure chest. It was lucky they didn't have to continue through the remainder of this maze because there was no way they would have made it through with the treasure.

Just when the corridor seemed unending, Nieve and Hane broke through into the open space surrounding the fountain. An ice wall sprang up from the ground, blocking off the entrance to the corridor completely. It was rough and unpolished, like most of Nieve's spells, but it appeared strong and functional—for now. Hane doubted it would hold the mimics for long.

Up ahead, Sage and Lani stood on opposite sides of the ice path, Emiko hovering just behind them. Sage held his dueling cane at his side as he urged them forward with his free hand. Lani held her cutlass out to one side as she cupped a hand to her mouth, shouting for Nieve and Hane to hurry up. Hane was using controlled bursts of transference mana to boost them along the ice path but didn't want to use much more just in case it overbalanced Nieve. If the chest was lighter, maybe they would have chanced more speed, but their pace was reckless as it was.

Hane heard the sound of ice cracking and breaking behind them but didn't chance a look back.

That became harder to resist when the wall shattered, sending big chunks of ice crashing into the ground all around them.

Nieve turned to look over her shoulder just as a falling ice chunk landed on the thin, icy pathway, cracking it beneath their feet. Nieve pitched forward, dropping her side of the trunk to try to catch her balance, but it happened so fast that Hane stumbled right over her, the partially levitated treasure chest spinning off in an odd direction as Hane tumbled, rolled, and then leapt to their feet. They spun around to offer Nieve a hand up but instead were transfixed by the sight of dozens, if not hundreds, of mimics leaping down from the places on the walls and charging forward in lunging, drooling jumps. They had fought mimics before, but never on this scale. Like this, the mimic boxes looked almost like hungry, pygmy crocodiles, determined to swallow each team member whole.

Nieve cursed and pushed herself to her feet, looking back only once before she kicked the side of the treasure chest, sending it skidding forward. "Let's go!"

Hane turned and ran, catching the side of the chest as it spun toward them. Nieve grabbed the opposite side and ran full-tilt toward the fountain. Sage fired off a blast from his dueling cane as they ran between him and Lani.

"Emi, go through the portal!" Lani ordered, pitching her voice over the snarls and growls of the mimics. "Everyone, go! Quick, quick!"

Emiko looked terrified but determined as she streaked through the portal in the base of the fountain. Nieve climbed up onto the rim and turned back, catching the lightened treasure chest as Hane tossed it to her. She jumped feet-first through the portal, hauling the chest along with her. Hane climbed up next to the portal, catching the bloodless tremble of Aldis's hands as he held the portal open, completely vulnerable until the last.

"You'll be fine," Hane assured him as they removed a tonfa from its harness on their back. "I'll make sure of it."

Sage and Lani were retreating to the fountain, firing blasts of mana at the mimics as they approached. Sage was sweating, but his aim was true as he sent mimics tumbling over backward, some landing on their heads so they had to struggle and flail to right themselves. Lani sent the mimics skidding away with blasts of conjured water from her hand. She slashed sideways with her cutlass, sending one mimic slamming into another so that they began to fight each other. Hane grabbed Lani's arm when she got close enough. She started to ask a question, but it turned into a scream as Hane tripped her backward into the portal, holding her long enough to make sure she didn't hit her head on the edge. Sage looked back, alarm and a question on his face.

"Go," Hane insisted. "I'm going to get Aldis through safely."

Sage bit his lower lip but nodded, stepping back into the portal and dropping through. Hane moved to the point of the fountain closest to the onrushing mimics, braced themself, then charged their shroud with transference mana and *shoved* it outward in an arc from their body. That effort always left them a little unsteady on their feet afterward, but the effect was undeniably powerful: the mimics were flung backward nearly fifty feet, giving Hane and Aldis just enough time to get through the portal.

"I've got you," Hane said, gripping a handful of Aldis's tunic. "Try not to let go until the last second."

Aldis stuttered a response, eyes wide, face pale, as Hane stepped through the portal, pulling Aldis through after them.

CHAPTER 18

&MIKO

Cloudcaller (lung mark), Citrine

 miko waited, breathless, staring up at the portal cut into the ceiling of the room she'd landed in. Her teeth chattered, her hands shook even as she hugged herself. She had been feeling anxious even before this plan got underway—to be honest, she'd woken up feeling anxious—and it had only gotten worse the longer she remained alone in this torchlit, gray-stone antechamber.

I can just go back, Emiko told herself, cloud shifting back and forth near the portal. *I can just go back and see if they need—*

Emiko yelped in surprise when Nieve suddenly tumbled through the portal, landing hard on the ground below. The treasure chest she'd pulled through with her landed on her stomach, blowing the air out of her chest. The lid hit the gray stones of the floor hard enough that it popped open, spilling coins, gems, and other treasures across the floor. Emiko dismissed her cloud and ran to Nieve's side, helping her carefully dislodge the chest without hurting herself further and making sure she got her breath back.

"Wh-where are the others?" Nieve gasped, one hand pressed to her chest.

"Coming soon," Emiko said hopefully. "Are you hurt? I have some life crystals if you need a healing spell."

"No, my shroud took most of the impact." Her grimace, as well as the arm wrapped around her middle, said otherwise, though. She stared up at the portal, eyes hard, jaw clenched. "Mi-mi, if no one comes through, can you get me—"

Just then, Lani fell through screaming, landing on the upturned bottom of the treasure chest, which softened her fall. Emiko let out a relieved breath as Nieve helped her to her feet.

"Hane dropped me!" Lani said, looking torn between impressed and distressed. "They dropped me straight through the—"

Sage dropped through next, looking prepared for a fall but not for the upside-down treasure chest in his way. He hit it feet-first, then fell sideways onto his elbow. As he hissed in pain, Lani flicked a healing spell at him.

"Was everything all right up there?" Lani asked as Sage stood up. "Did they need help?"

"Hane didn't seem to think so," Sage replied. "They said they'd make sure Aldis got through."

Emiko wrung her hands as the four of them stared up at the ceiling, waiting. The sick dread churning in her stomach made it feel like it took forever, but in reality, it was probably only a handful of seconds. Hane fell through first, clutching Aldis's shirt so Aldis tumbled after them. By some trick or magic, Hane managed to slow their fall and even get Aldis turned around right side up, so he only stumbled when he landed on his feet. Hane landed in a crouch on top of the treasure chest.

"That looks lucky," Hane commented, rapping their knuckles on the chest. "Do we have time to sort it out before the next challenge?"

Emiko hadn't even bothered taking in her surroundings yet, a potentially dangerous oversight while within a spire, but her fear for her friends had her sufficiently distracted. She turned around now, half afraid of what she might find.

The six of them were in a square alcove off a much larger room, the details of which Emiko could just barely make out, like shadows in the night. An unlit torch stood sentinel just beyond the antechamber, begging to be lit by one of the merrily burning sconces in the antechamber. Beyond that, Emiko saw great stone pillars stretching toward an unseen ceiling in a room that appeared to be shaped like an underground cavern. Something prickled at the edge of her awareness, like the feeling of being watched, or the uncomfortable sensation of someone reading over her shoulder. The looming darkness made her feel wary, as if it might creep up and engulf her entirely. But that made no sense. Right?

"It looks like the starting mechanism for the challenge is—" Sage stopped himself, head turning sharply to look at Emiko. "Emi! Your shroud!"

"What about it?" Emiko hugged herself, shrugging her shoulders up defensively. "Is it broken? Is there interference magic in here or something?"

"No, it's—" Sage broke off, laughing. "Your shroud changed color. Did your attunement reach Citrine?"

"No, I just— Oh!" Emiko stared into the dark room beyond the torchlight again, understanding coming upon her all at once. She wasn't *seeing* the objects in the room ahead, she was *sensing* them with an entirely new mana type! That explained why she'd felt so anxious since waking up: her perception mana must have developed while she slept, slightly altering the way she saw and felt things around her. She should have realized earlier!

"That does appear to be a Citrine shroud," Aldis confirmed, the hand bearing his attunement held aloft. "Congratulations, I'm officially the only Sunstone climber in this group now."

Emiko laughed and hopped from foot to foot in a little dance. "I didn't even realize it! I have perception mana now! Huzzah!"

"Great job, Emi!" Sage caught her around the shoulders and gave her a quick squeeze.

"Yay, Mi-mi!" Nieve pumped one fist in the air, still holding her midsection with her other arm.

"Did you study any perception spells before the climb?" Lani asked, direct as always. She was seated on her knees in front of the mound of treasure, sweeping her hands through it and plucking out items from the mass of coins and gems.

"Um, a little bit." She had tried, but she'd always had trouble learning spells from books. Emiko had hoped that if she achieved the Citrine rank during the climb, it would be toward the end so she could study perception spells with Lani during their next break. And if such lessons kept Lani from losing her cut of the treasure at gambling dens and casinos, then so much the better.

Lani sighed heavily as she looked up from the treasure. "Do you need me to show you how to work with perception magic?"

"I can show her," Hane said softly, picking their way over the spill of treasure. "The challenge starts when we light the torch, right? Then there should be enough time for her to get a feel for it."

"That's fine." Lani turned her attention back to the mound of treasure. "It seems like your perception mana is stronger than mine, anyway."

That was probably true, but the dismissal still felt a little harsh. Emiko fidgeted with her hands as Hane steered her to the edge of the gray-stone antechamber, right before the light gave way to shadows.

"She's not really greedy or treasure-obsessed or anything," Emiko said, feeling defensive of her longtime teammate, even though Hane hadn't said anything. "She just likes to make sure we all share carrying the treasure so we get out with something in the end."

Hane nodded. "A wise policy, but I'm not worried about the treasure distribution. I am a little troubled that she didn't ask if anyone needed to be healed."

Emiko cringed and glanced back at Nieve, who was still holding her side as she sat down to help sort the treasure into piles. "She can get a little narrow-minded sometimes. Sorry. Do you need any healing?"

Hane shook their head, turning to look into the empty room. "I'm fine. If your perception mana came in, you're probably already seeing things a little differently, aren't you?"

"Just a little. Like outlines of things." Emiko hesitated, then pointed. "Those are pillars, right? Or big stone columns? I think . . . six of them?"

Hane nodded. "Perception mana on its own enhances your normal senses, like sight and sound. After a while, it'll become second nature and you won't even think about it anymore. For Wavewalkers, perception mana helps us see underwater just by touching it. For you, perception mana should enable you to see or sense things inside your cloud spells."

"Like the Cloud Cover spell we cast together in the last room, right?" Emiko confirmed.

"Right," Hane agreed. "You should try it out. Tell me about the room ahead of us."

"Okay." Emiko's heart fluttered nervously. Her first breath felt shaky, so she let it go and tried again. The second breath felt stronger, powerful, allowing her to breathe out power as she chanted. "Restless clouds drift by/Looking down on all below/Show me what you see."

She couldn't quite see the clouds that formed over the pitch-dark room ahead, nor did the room become any lighter. She didn't "see" the room, not in the way Sage described his visions, anyway. It was more of a sensation, as if the shape of the room was something she could feel, touch, and examine. It was an odd sensation, different from looking down on the maze, but not in a way she could put into words.

"The pillars are all different heights," Emiko said, speaking aloud for Hane's benefit. "There's an activation switch on top of each pillar, but I can't tell what they do. There's also a lot of air flow and . . . water, I think? Up above that pillar—" She pointed, then realized Hane probably couldn't see which one she meant. "The central pillar on the left. Maybe a secret passage or treasure?"

"Possibly," Hane said mildly. "I think the presence of water there might indicate a trap instead. It's hard to know for sure without checking it out. My guess is that whatever it is would be revealed by activating the switch directly beneath it."

"So we should be careful with that one," Emiko suggested. She felt a warmth in her chest at Hane's nod. "There's also something . . . I don't know, kind of sparkly? It's directly across the room from where we're standing."

"You're probably sensing the exit. The magic on doorways is usually pretty strong." Hane considered, then added: "I should say obvious doorways.

Hidden doorways, like the one in the fountain, are often harder to detect using perception. Can you sense anything else?"

Emiko "felt" the room with fingertips made of cloud vapor. "I can tell how tall each of the pillars are, and that the tallest is under that secret opening. I think there's something on the floor between two pillars on the right . . . It's faint, just like air stirring the clouds a little."

"Possibly treasure, but more likely a pit trap," Hane guessed. "It's positioned where someone would step on it while attempting to scale a pillar."

"Oh, I think you're right!" Emiko blinked into the darkness beyond the lit antechamber, as if she could actually see the stretch of floor they were talking about. "I wouldn't have guessed that on my own."

"That's fine. The important thing is calling out everything you find so your team can be aware of it." Hane's gaze was wandering over the dark room as if they could see it just as clearly as Emiko could. "No one expects you to be an expert right away. For now, it would be good for you to practice using it and calling out what you find. As you develop your perception mana, you'll find yourself able to distinguish between exits and secrets and traps all on your own."

"I'll practice," Emiko vowed, nodding once. She looked up at Hane, watching them silently assess the room ahead of them. "Is it true you won't climb with us again? We could really use you, and you seem really nice."

Hane gave her a strange look before resuming their careful scan of the room. "I'm a climber for hire. I'm not looking to join a team."

"But you could," Emiko insisted. "Isn't it nice when you know what to expect from teammates, instead of learning about five new climbers every single time?"

Hane was silent for a moment, staring into the darkness of the room beyond the antechamber. "I already know what to expect from people climbing the spire. More importantly, I know what to expect from the spire itself. Once you reach the twentieth floor and above, you'll understand why it's important to have a climber who isn't your friend on the team."

Emiko stared, puzzled. "But everyone I climb with is a friend. You're my friend, Hane."

Hane shook their head with slow purpose, not glancing down to meet Emiko's eyes. "I'm not here to be a friend. I'm here to make the hard calls if and when your team needs me to."

Emiko set her jaw stubbornly. "The only hard calls we make involve getting everyone out safely."

Hane looked over at her, but Emiko refused to meet their gaze. "You're not a child. You know that's not possible every time."

"It is if everyone tries hard enough," Emiko insisted. "Last time . . . On our last climb, someone like you would have left Ren behind. We got Ren out. Alive."

"I'm glad," Hane said, sans inflection. "But as the challenges get harder, you won't be able to rely on that every climb."

Emiko decided she didn't want to pursue that line of discussion any further. The last climb had gone badly—very badly—but everyone had survived. That was the important part, right? Not leaving anyone behind? Whatever "hard calls" Hane had made on other teams wouldn't be necessary here.

Emiko drew a shaky breath, determinedly searching the large, dark room once more for anything she might have missed, but just then, Lani called out: "Come pick up your portion of the treasure! After we finish this room, we'll bundle it all up in one pack and send it back for storage until the climb is over."

That was easy enough. Emiko could do that. The others were already sweeping piles of gems and coins into their bags and satchels, Nieve's movements looking easier and more relaxed, indicating that she'd been healed while Hane instructed Emiko on the basics of perception mana usage. Emiko helped herself to an unattended pile of treasure, grabbing handfuls to stuff inside her treasure pouch. Three objects sat alone in the middle of the roughly divided piles of loot: a red pearl, a beaded necklace, and a dagger with a translucent blade.

"Enchanted items?" Hane asked as they stooped to one knee to gather up their portion of the loot.

"Two of them are," Sage explained. "The necklace looks like an anti-poison, anti-venom charm. We're probably going to use it for this climb and see if it's worth keeping. I can't tell what kind of enchantment is on the pearl; we'll have to take that one to an Enchanter to find out what it is. Something to do with fire and stone mana, I think. The dagger isn't enchanted, but it's meant to be a vessel for something. It would be a perfect weapon for a Soulblade."

"Oh! Ren would love that!" Emiko said, forcing a bright smile. Her conversation with Hane had affected her mood more than she'd realized. "It looks like just the sort of thing he'd use for a contract."

"Well, if Ren wants it, he's going to pay a fair market price for it," Lani said firmly. "He's not here, he doesn't get the climber's discount."

"Ouch, harsh, Lani." Nieve chuckled. "He climbed with us for years. I'm sure none of us would mind if you cut him some slack."

Aldis made a grumbling noise that sounded as if he didn't quite agree, but he didn't actually voice an objection.

"Ren isn't a climber anymore, so he doesn't really need it," Lani said decisively. "Now, if we get back and he says he's thinking about rejoining the group, that's a different story. Let's see . . . Sage, you carry the dagger and Emi can carry the pearl." Lani held up the beaded necklace. "Which one of our frontline fighters wants to try this out?"

Nieve snorted and shook her head, refusing the trinket. Hane shrugged and let Lani drop it into their open palm. Rather than wear it around their neck, Hane looped it twice around their wrist and pushed it up their arm so it didn't drape at all.

"Okay, Sage— No, Emi." Lani shouldered her satchel as she stood up. "Tell us what you saw."

"It's a big room, like a cavern," Emiko explained. "There's six pillars, three on each side, all with switches on top of them. There's something like a trap above the tallest pillar, and maybe a pit trap, but maybe not, between the two farther back on the right side. The exit is straight ahead, but I don't think it'll open."

"The exit will open when we find the correct sequence of switches," Sage said, stepping smoothly into the explanation. "That torch just in front of us starts the challenge and releases the first swarm of monsters, while also allowing us to activate the switches. The switches will also add or subtract time between swarms, reveal treasures, or activate traps, so shout out before anyone hits a switch."

"Sounds good!" Nieve grabbed a torch off the wall, swinging it in front of her like a conductor's baton. "Everyone ready? I've been itching for a good fight."

"Nieve, maybe we can discuss a plan before—"

"Planning for swarms is always the same," Nieve proclaimed, cheerfully cutting over Lani. "Everyone stick close to me, call out strays, and watch my back. Sage can't predict the monster swarms, but he can call out if something's about to go really wrong, and that's all we need for now."

Emiko looked at Sage, who shrugged slightly. "That's about the shape of it, yeah."

Hane raised a hand. "Do you want me on the ground helping with monsters, or should I focus on the switches?"

"Emiko and Hane both on switches," Lani declared. "Everyone else, stick close to Nieve. But watch out for her backswing."

Nieve chuckled as she strode off into the darkness, the torch held down casually at her side. Shadows fled before her as she strode toward the unlit torch.

Emiko tugged Hane's sleeve lightly. "Do you need the room filled with mist? For, like, wave walking?"

Hane gave her a small smile and shook their head. "Thank you, but no. The residual cloud vapor from your Cloud Cover spell is enough for me."

"Okay." Emiko let the others get ahead of her as she chanted a levitation spell, vapor and air whirling around her to lift her off her feet. The cavernous room ahead was still too dark to see anything, but Emiko's earlier spell was still active, showing her shapes that would normally be lost within the darkness. Had she missed anything important? If she had, would Hane call it out? Hane was the one with the actual experience in interpreting anything revealed by a perception spell, but they had admitted that vapor wasn't as clear to read as a pool of water. She tried telling herself that Sage would call out anything truly dangerous, but she still hovered fretfully close to Nieve and the others, waiting to make sure they didn't tumble into a trap she had missed seeing.

Nieve swung her torch in an arc, tossing it off into a corner the moment the grounded torch caught. The torch roared and flared far higher than it should have, burning hot and bright enough to illuminate the entire cavern. Emiko blinked away the light scars hurriedly as monstrous wails sounded from every corner of the room. She took just enough time to orient herself, then jerked her cloud up toward the ceiling, glancing down once to make sure the monsters weren't about to overwhelm her team.

The monsters looked like some kind of lizard-scorpion hybrid: long, lithe lizard bodies with clawed forelimbs and colorful frills around their necks that fanned out when they screamed—which they seemed to like to do a lot. Their long tails were curved and hooked over their backs, ending in wicked points. Emiko thought she could see venom beaded at the tip. These things were probably venomous from both ends, but if they were anything like most reptiles, they weren't going to last long against Nieve's ice.

Satisfied that at least the first wave of monsters would be handled, Emiko turned a circle, looking around the room for the aforementioned switches. Her new perception spell tugged annoyingly at her vision now that she could see the room clearly, drawing her focus more than the search for switches. It was more distracting than she had thought it would be.

"Emiko."

Emiko shrieked; she hadn't even seen Hane leap away from the rest of the group, never mind land on the room's ceiling right above her head. They were crouched on the ceiling as if gravity had no particular hold over them and sitting upside down were normal.

"We should take turns hitting the switches around the room," Hane explained briefly. "When one of us hits a switch, the other should try to look out for what it does. Make sure to call out, so we don't hit too many at once."

"Ah, okay." Emiko was unnerved by how naturally Hane perched on the ceiling like a bat. "Um, you want to hit the first switch?"

Hane shook their head. "You'll get to a switch before I will. Be careful on the highest switch, though. It's most likely a trap, based on what you sensed from it."

"Oh, right." Emiko sized up the tallest pillar. She didn't notice anything out of the ordinary about the space in the room's ceiling above the pillar, but her Cloud Cover spell had definitely sensed wind and water in that location. A trap seemed likely. "I'll hit it from a distance, but let's start in order from the front pillars and work our way back."

Hane nodded. "Sounds good."

A shift of Emiko's weight sent her cloud scudding sideways, with Hane leaping off the ceiling behind her. A quick examination of the orb-switch on the front left pillar showed that all it required to activate was contact, meaning a light touch would do. Emiko looked down over the edge of her cloud, checking on her friends before she hit it, making sure they could handle whatever challenge this created for them. Nieve's sheet of ice on the floor was littered with scaly green lizard limbs, and it looked like the team was just picking off stragglers. She wasn't sure how much time had elapsed of their five-minute window, but it looked like a safe time to activate the first switch and find out what it did.

"First switch!" Emiko shouted, cupping a hand over her mouth to be heard.

[I hear you,] came Aldis's mental voice along with the bell-like toll inside her head. [I'll tell the others.]

Emiko sent along her thanks before shifting her weight forward to shoot past the gray orb. She held her hand out wide, slapping the switch as she passed it, then zoomed on past, looking for the reaction it had caused.

The orb turned a luminous blue color, an echoing tone following Emiko as she flew a circuit around the center of the chamber. A switch could activate anything, from opening a door, to unleashing more enemies to fight, to tripping a trap. Whatever this orb had activated, though, Emiko couldn't find it.

[The torch flickered,] Aldis's voice said inside Emiko's mind. [Sage says we lost a minute on our timer. He's going to mark that switch with a light spell.]

Ah, that would be why Emiko hadn't noticed a difference: she was too far away to have seen the distant torch flicker, but her friends standing right on the torch certainly would have. She looked back toward the orb she had activated and saw a red ball of light hovering over it, cast by Sage down below.

"Second switch!" Hane shouted, waving an arm to make sure the group took notice. They stood on the narrow platform with the orb, though by the time they hit it, they were already midleap over the empty air between the first platform and the second. Unlike Emiko's fifty-foot-high platform, Hane's second switch platform was lower, so it was an easy somersault down to land next to their second orb.

This time, Emiko saw the central torch flicker rapidly twice in succession. Sage adjusted his glasses, said something to Aldis, and then cast his hand out toward the second switch.

[The switch gave us an extra minute of fighting time,] Aldis reported as an orange orb of light glowed over the second switch. [But those two switches don't go in that sequence.]

Emiko looked back at the first orb and realized that the luminous blue light had gone out and the orb was a dull gray again. Hane's orb had flicked to blue only for an instant before flickering out again. Hane waved to her, beckoning her close for their position next to their middle orb.

"Don't worry about the sequence just yet," Hane instructed. "I'm certain there are more than six switches in here; just figuring out what the switches do and marking them for later is enough right now. Let me hit this switch first, and then I'll be on guard when you hit the switch beneath the trap."

"Okay!" Emiko zipped away, spiraling up the column that held the middle right switch aloft. She missed Hane shouting out as they hit their middle switch, but this time the effect was noticeable: each monster still alive on the ground below glowed with a white light, then split into two monsters, doubling the number of monsters left to fight.

"Thanks, Hane!" Nieve shouted, sounding bemused. "I was just getting bored!"

"You're welcome!" Hane called back, skidding sideways down a column before pushing off and flipping in midair to kick off the wall. True to their word, they were moving to be close by when Emiko hit the supposed trap switch.

She didn't think she would need the support, though. Emiko didn't normally use weapons—she preferred to rely on magic and mana crystals—but that didn't mean she was completely unarmed. She loosened the drawstring on a belt pouch, then pulled her slingshot from its hard leather case. Her little ammunition balls were mostly inert—little more than marbles, really—but they held the potential to be charged with mana at need. For hitting a switch, though, a plain marble would be enough.

Emiko hovered a wide distance away from the switch, keeping her cloud still as she lined up her shot. A long, slow exhale, then she released, shifting her weight backward to carry her out of range of whatever trap effect occurred.

She was lucky she had been forewarned: if she had tried slapping the orb with her hand, as she had the first one, she would have been caught up in the sudden roaring downpour of water that burst through the ceiling. Not even her levitation spell would have saved her from being dragged along in the current to crash into the ground below. She might have survived the fall, but it would have been a climb-ending injury at best. Luckily, her slingshot had kept her far enough away from the downpour to remain safe.

Unfortunately, the same couldn't be said of her teammates on the ground.

Screams and shouts of surprise sounded from below as water swept over the ice-covered floor, creating a hazard that even Nieve couldn't withstand. At least it swept up the monsters too, making it difficult for them to attack, but most managed to leap free of the water, walking sideways on the walls as lizards were wont to do. Nieve created a pillar of ice and jabbed her ice pick into it, catching Lani around the waist as she pulled herself back up to her feet. Emiko never saw Aldis work his teleportation spell, but when the sound of loud, hacking coughs tugged at her ear, she found Aldis and Sage atop the red-light-marked switch platform, both looking soggy and unhappy.

Emiko spun on her cloud, looking for Hane. "We have to turn it off!"

"I already hit the next switch!" Hane hung off the side of their third platform, pointing up at the translucent blue orb. "Breaking the sequence doesn't stop the trap! We need to find another way."

Emiko bit her lip, looking for something that would stop the flow of water. Down below, Lani and Nieve were shaping the water away from themselves, creating a small space for themselves as the water rose higher and higher. Shaping wouldn't work for long—there had to be a way to stop the waterfall, or at least create a place for the water to go.

"One of the traps is a pitfall!" Hane shouted over the roar of the water, once again balanced on the ceiling. "I'm going to activate the pit trap and hope that sends the water somewhere. See if you can stop the water!"

"Um, but—" Hane was already gone. Emiko shivered, the spray from the waterfall landing on her arms and clothes like dewdrops. How was she supposed to—

Emiko blinked, her breath catching even as her fingers trailed along her belt, selecting two of the same mana crystals. Her hands shook, but she managed to get the first one slotted into the mana diffuser before she drew the breath for her spell.

"Soft now, rushing stream/The winter winds are calling/Water falls no more."

Emiko shaped her winds to encircle the top of the waterfall as she released enhancement mana from the diffuser on her hip. The wind burned cold enough to bite, but she was sure-fingered in slotting in the second enhancement mana crystal after the first one finished pouring itself into the spell. Creating a sheet of frozen water or even snow was easier than attempting to freeze rushing water, but with the cold wind and the enhancement mana combined with her own water mana, slowly the edges of the waterfall began to freeze, growing inward until the opening in the ceiling of the room was sealed shut with ice. Unfortunately, that also ended up encasing the switch inside the ice, too. Even less fortunate: aside from activating the waterfall, Emiko wasn't even sure what it did.

"Emi, help Lani and Nieve!" Sage shouted, casting glowing light spells over the last two switches activated. Hane's final switch was still glowing blue, but just as with the trap switch, Emiko had no idea what it had done. It seemed that Hane had been successful in activating the pit trap, though, because all the water that had collected within the room was rushing toward it, dragging Nieve and Lani along in the current. The obvious question was why wasn't Aldis teleporting them to safety, but a quick look showed Aldis firing blasts of mana through his dueling cane at lizard-monsters swarming up the sides of the platform he and Sage stood on, giving him more than enough to deal with at the moment.

Emiko shot forward, sweeping low over the raging current, heart stuttering every time either Lani or Nieve dipped beneath the surface of the water. She stretched her hand out, reaching as far as she could, and finally caught Lani's cold, clammy hand. She didn't have the strength to pull Lani up, but leaning her weight backward, she was at least able to keep Lani from being dragged toward the pit trap.

"Thanks," Lani gasped, coughing on a mouthful of water. She looked around, pushing her braids back off her face. "Nieve! Where's—"

She cut herself off as a figure wearing all black walked along the surface of the water and plucked Nieve out of the current like a bear catching fish swimming upstream. Hane had only taken hold of her wrist to draw her out, but Nieve snarled as she coughed, demanding, "Let me go!"

Hane looked confused, but they complied. Nieve dropped onto an icy raft that was immediately caught up by the current, but as she passed one of the earthen pillars, the ice from the raft latched onto it, creating a thick platform of ice on top of the water. Emiko towed Lani over to the ice platform, where Nieve hauled her up out of the water. Lani hugged herself and shivered, leaning into Nieve's chest for warmth.

"It should all drain out in another minute or two," Hane said, gliding over the water just as easily as if it were ice. "Any idea how much time is left on the timer?"

"Not with the torch underwater." Nieve gestured toward the front of the room. "Did that switch only activate the waterfall, or did it do something else, too?"

"I didn't see an effect," Hane admitted. "It could just have activated the trap. I hit a fifth switch, but I can't say what that did either."

"Some of them might just be sequencing switches without causing effects," Lani suggested, teeth chattering. "Where are the others?"

"Aldis and Sage are at the first switch, fighting the lizard-monsters." Emiko pointed, but from the angle, it was impossible to see them. "I'll go and see if they need any help."

"Wait, Emi, do you need any healing?" Lani asked, hand trembling as she reached out. "It must have taken a lot of mana to freeze all that water. We can cover for you if you need to get to a safe place and recover."

Emiko paused, surprised by the question, then surprised by her surprise. She felt her cheeks stretch in a wide smile.

"I'm actually fine," Emiko replied, truly and honestly. "But thank you for worrying about me, Lani."

CHAPTER 19

SAGE

Seer (hand mark), Citrine

"This is the end, isn't it?" Aldis shouted, firing another blast of mana through his dueling cane. Sage could feel him trembling as they stood with their backs pressed together, shooting down scorpion-tailed lizards that crested their safe haven atop the switch platform. "We're ringing out, right? Want to count us down, or just go?"

"We're not ringing out," Sage called back. With lightninglike agility, a lizard-monster avoided the tip of Sage's cane, crouching right beside his boot as it hissed and flared the brightly colored flap of skin around its neck. He jabbed his dueling cane into its mouth and blasted it with a burst of gray mana. The lizard flew backward, crashing into two other monsters just cresting the edge of the platform. It hit the first one hard enough that both tumbled off the side into the rushing water below, but the other managed to cling to the pillar, neck frill flaring as it hissed. Aldis whimpered and cringed before teleporting the monster away. Sage took the brief moment of calm to rub the sting of sweat out of his eyes. "The others are fine; my Imminent Threat spell would have warned me if they weren't."

"They would also be fine if they rang out already!" Aldis cried. "They got swept away and that water looks violent!"

"They have enough water spells among them to keep themselves safe," Sage said, projecting as much confidence as he could into the statement. "And if you're that worried, why don't you try contacting them?"

"You expect me to concentrate with all this— Ah!"

Sage managed to spin and knock Aldis's dueling cane down before he could fire raw mana at Emiko, floating on her little cloud.

"The others are safe!" she declared cheerily, unconcerned about Aldis's knee-jerk reaction to her sudden appearance. "Hane found a way to drain the water, so the floor should be safe in a minute. If you guys hold on to the pedestal of the switch, I'll try and blow all the lizards off the column for you."

"That would be wonderful, Emi," Sage said with relief. He'd been certain that Lani and the others were safe, but it was nice to have that confirmation. He looped one arm around the pedestal, taking care not to activate the switch itself. If he remembered correctly, this switch was the one that subtracted a minute between monster swarms, which would only add one more stress factor to this already taxing situation. He looped his other arm through Aldis's and held on tight.

Emiko floated backward, her chant lost by the sound of rushing water below. A vicious wind encircled the column, plucking a half-dozen lizard-monsters off and tossing them to a distant corner of the room—a distant corner where Sage could now see a whirlpool of water funneling down through an opening in the floor. He watched as the last of the water drained through, sucking a screaming lizard down with it.

"Well, that was a little more harrowing than it needed to be," Aldis said, straightening up and adjusting his belt. Sage held his tongue and said nothing; it didn't pay to agitate the Wayfarer, especially when he could easily be left stranded on this platform with no way down. "Shall we go find the others?"

"Yes, let's—" Sage started to place his hand in Aldis's for a teleportation spell but stopped when a flare of light caught his eye. He had to lean over the edge of the platform to see that the torch that began the challenge had sputtered back to life spontaneously, the flames shooting higher than a person's height before receding to normal torch flames.

"What does that mean, do you think?" Aldis asked warily.

Sage sighed. "I think it means the second wave is coming. Let's regroup quickly."

He clasped Aldis's hand, and a blink later he stood on the wet stone floor in the center of the cavernous spire room. From here, he could see the exit they were attempting to unlock via the switch sequence but so far no monsters. Nieve was helping Lani down from an ice shelf attached to a rocky column at about shoulder height from the ground, possibly marking where the water had been when Nieve had created the platform. Lani shivered, tossing the wet tendrils of her hair over her shoulder before crossing her arms and rubbing them to warm herself.

Sage's hand dropped to his side pouch, touching the circular object through the canvas. She wouldn't thank him now, but she definitely would have appreciated having it in a situation like this. Maybe he should just hand it to her the next time they had a brief respite and forgo all the ceremony of giving it as a gift. But then, would she think it was a spire treasure? That defeated the purpose entirely, but the longer he waited to give it to her, the more annoyed she would be about not having it at the beginning of the climb.

I can't think about this now, Sage thought, letting his hand fall away from the pouch. *There's about to be another wave of monsters any second; there isn't enough time for her to use it right now.*

"D-do I have t-time to put on my cloak?" Lani stuttered, bouncing on the balls of her feet, hands chafing her arms.

"We just saw the torch at the entrance flare up," Sage said apologetically. "I think the next wave is due to start any moment."

Lani swore, stamping her feet to warm them. Nieve rubbed her back absently as she kept her head on a swivel, sword held out to her side.

"I figured out what one of those two switches activated." Hane trotted up to the group from wherever they had just been. "There was a false floor in the far left corner of the room. When we activated the switch, the section of floor vanished, revealing a treasure chest underneath. I bet there's a key hidden somewhere, too, if we keep hitting switches."

"How many switches are left to activate?" Sage asked.

Hane shrugged. "We've hit five already, but I think there are more switches than we're seeing. And even with the six visible switches, finding the right sequence is a one-out-of-sixty-four chance."

"Should we ring out and try again?" Aldis asked, wiping his face against his shoulder. "I'll join you on another climb, see if we can find a better path using my doorway trick."

Lani shook her head even as she rubbed her arms for warmth. "We're deep enough now, we have to continue. And we still need to find the key to that treasure chest before we can consider—"

A skittering sound sent chills racing up Sage's back, making the little hairs on his neck stand on end. On instinct, he turned his back toward his teammates, holding his dueling cane out in front of him. He felt Hane's shoulder settle against his, and then a moment later, Aldis fell into the circle, swallowing hard as he held his dueling cane in a trembling grip.

"Bugs bugs bugs!" Emiko zipped around a column, almost shooting past the group in her hurry to get away from . . . bugs, apparently. Her cloud lifted her well above the group's collective heads so she could call down: "Big bugs! Lots and lots of big bugs!"

"Great," Lani groaned from somewhere behind Sage. "And we're down to a four-minute window before the next wave, right?"

"Should be," Sage confirmed. "If you can see the torch, it gives a deliberate flicker for each minute that goes by."

"We can add a minute," Hane suggested. "If we hit the right switch."

"Okay. Emiko, Hane, get back to finding switches and figuring out what they do. If you can, handle that treasure chest." Lani tossed her head, flinging her braids, like the many tails of a whip, over her shoulder. "Anyone have a plan for figuring out the sequence of the switches to open the exit?"

The skittering sound drew closer. Sage felt his guts turn to water as a bulbous, oblong-shaped head peeked around an earthen column. It edged around the column, tilting its head to the side almost inquisitively, revealing a brown body resembling an eight-foot-tall praying mantis—if praying mantises had blades on their forelimbs. And by the looming shadows behind it, it wasn't alone.

Nieve uttered some choice words as she shoved her way between Sage and Hane. "When you said 'monster swarms,' I was picturing much smaller monsters."

"Oh, like you're not excited to fight a pack of giant bugs," Sage retorted.

Nieve's grin was lopsided. "You're right: I am."

"I could teleport each of us to the top of the columns," Aldis suggested, voice warbling slightly. "Stay above the monsters and just keep hitting switches until we hit the right sequence to open the door?"

"I don't think that would work," Hane said, sounding thoughtful.

"Why not?" Aldis whined.

"Because—"

The lead mantis took a sudden, bounding leap before translucent wings flickered open on its back. Emiko screamed and bolted away as the mantis streaked after her.

"—that," Hane finished, before crouching low and springing away almost too fast for Sage to track.

Nieve swore right before she covered the floor ahead of them with a sheet of ice, trapping the insects' legs to keep them from following after the first.

"We stay tight and keep them right here," Lani ordered. "Nieve and I will charge; Aldis and Sage, cover us with—"

"Wait!" A spark of inspiration struck right as Lani shared her plan. "I think I can predict the switch sequence. I just need a minute to meditate."

Lani hissed a breath through her teeth. "Fine. Aldis, send him—"

"To the orange-marked column." Sage pointed. "Aldis can tell me if you want me to hit the switch for more time."

"I can go with him," Aldis suggested hopefully. "To watch his back?"

"We need you watching our backs," Lani said sternly. "Send Sage where he wants to go, then cover us."

Aldis shot Sage a miserable look. Sage shrugged an apology back at him. He wouldn't have minded staying and fighting, but someone had to figure out the sequence to open the exit, and his divination seemed like their best bet.

An eye blink later, Sage stood on the central earthen column on the left side of the room, his orange orb of light hovering just over his head. It was a good spot to observe from, especially as Nieve, Lani, and Aldis were fighting in the center of the cavernlike room. Nieve charged the ice-trapped mantis-monsters with Lani just behind her. Aldis stood at the edge of the ice, shooting a blast of mana at the mantis that raised its bladed forelimbs over its head to slash down at Nieve. The mana didn't hurt it too much, but it surprised it enough that Nieve was able to crunch it with the broad side of her ice zanbatou. Lani skidded on the ice, sinking low enough that one knee touched down, her momentum carrying her beneath the abdomen of a different mantis as she sliced its legs out from under it. It fell hard, wings buzzing as it fought to right itself. A carefully aimed slash of her cutlass severed its head from its neck, but even after that, it continued to buzz and struggle for long moments before slowly going still.

A shrill sound slowly grew louder, making Sage wonder if these mantis-monsters could scream, only to realize that it was Emiko screaming as she streaked past. A dark blur darted out of seemingly nowhere: Hane landing a kick in the middle of the insect's back, breaking its thorax before using a transference-aided push to flip backward and land beside Sage on the platform with an easy poise that made Sage just a little envious.

"The only visible switch we have left is that one." Hane pointed to the third switch on the right side of the room. "I suspect there's at least one more hidden switch we'll need to find to complete the sequence."

"Is it too much to hope that triggering the sixth switch will make the final one appear?" Sage asked, casting an orb of purple light over the indicated switch.

"Possible, but equally possible we'll need a sequence of these switches to reveal the final one."

"Great. More sequences." Sage massaged his eyes behind his glasses. "And one of the switches starts that waterfall again."

"Another switch might halt the waterfall," Hane offered with a shrug. "After Emiko hits that last switch, I'm going to search the room for secrets and see if I can find the key to the chest. That should give you some time to contemplate the first switch sequence."

Sage nodded. "Check in with me when you're finished."

Hane hopped away as Sage settled down with his back pressed against the switch's pedestal, his dueling cane balanced across his knees. The Divination glasses that allowed him to See challenges before they began weren't going to help him with this, but even a low-level Seer could predict the correct sequence of a series of switches. The trouble was that it took time and concentration, two things that were often hard to come by in these types of challenges. He closed his eyes and pinched the bridge of his nose beneath his glasses, breathing out slowly as he pushed the sounds of the battle below into the background. He couldn't focus on that now.

Divine Desired Future, Sage thought, holding an image of the room, the switches, and the exit in his mind. The team didn't have time to attempt sixty-four different combinations of switches while fighting swarms of monsters, but if Sage could find the correct sequence through a vision, they could end this trial quickly, before anyone got hurt.

The vision slammed into Sage like a heat wave, forcefully expelling the air in his chest. His vision burned a brilliant, searing red—not so much flames as heat. The kind of heat that melted metal and set fire to the very air one breathed. He could feel it like sunburn on his face, tightening his skin, licking at his boots, creeping closer and closer . . .

Sage drew in a hard breath, shaking his head to cancel the spell. He blinked, surprised to find that his eyes were already open. What was that? Certainly not a "desired future" by any means. Was it a prediction for the next wave of monsters? Some sort of fire elementals, or something that attacked with fire?

That shouldn't have happened, Sage thought, rubbing his brow. *I must not have been clear enough in directing the spell.*

Sage tried holding an image of an activated switch in his mind's eye but couldn't quite clear the image of red heat from his head. He drew breath after breath, attempting to clear his head, but the first vision had sparked a flicker of fear in his chest, and the clash of metal and shouts of his teammates didn't make it any easier to concentrate. He pressed his knuckles to the center of his forehead and blew out a breath.

Okay, time for a different spell, Sage told himself, forcibly breathing in and out to a four-count beat. This spell was going to cost him later, but it would be worth it as long as it worked. He fixed his gaze on the switch across the room, the one marked with a red orb of light, and thought: *Divine Outcome.*

In his mind's eye, the dull orb atop the switch turned a hazy blue. He flicked his gaze to the next pillar, imagining activating that switch as well, only to have the first orb go dull again. He started over, activating the red-light orb, then skipping to the third switch across the room, only for that to fail as well. Sage tried all five sequences beginning with the red-light-marked switch only to have them all fail. A deep breath, and then he started again with the orange-marked switch.

It was a brute-force method and a costly one at that, requiring Sage to cast the same spell over and over in an attempt to find the right pattern. It wasn't at all elegant or refined, but it was almost guaranteed to work—in time. After a few tries, Sage was able to close his eyes and hold a perfect vision of the room in his head, flicking switches on and off even faster than even Aldis could using a teleport spell. He played through several iterations at a rapid pace before one finally triggered a reaction from the room. Sage replayed the sequence in his head, examining the result and considering the order of the switches. There was a pattern there, like a zigzag across the pillars. Rather than immediately alert the team that he'd found one correct sequence, Sage envisioned the same zigzag pattern but starting from a different switch this time. The prediction played out with a different result but still a desired one. Sage sighed in relief, then blinked the visions away before crawling to the edge of his platform to check on the status of his team.

Nieve was still fighting, but it appeared the mantises hadn't fared well against her ice. Sage could only see two monsters still standing, though the pieces of many more littered the icy floor. Aldis was catching his breath, standing with his back against a pillar while Lani held her hand extended toward Nieve, possibly healing her. Perfect timing to discuss a plan.

Sage channeled light mana through his dueling cane, not as an offensive spell but simply as a beam of ordinary light. He shone the beam down at Aldis, attempting to attract his attention by zigzagging the light over his chest, and when that failed, he shone the light directly into Aldis's eyes. Aldis flinched, shielding his eyes as he tracked the light back to its source.

[My retinas don't appreciate you right now,] Aldis sent, opening a channel within Sage's mind. [What is it?]

[I have a solution, but it's going to get rough before it gets better,] Sage advised. [Do you know how much time you have before the next wave?]

[Perhaps another minute. I rather lost track some time ago.]

Sage grimaced. It would be best to attempt this between waves, but their timers were getting shorter and he still had to check in with Hane and Emiko. [Let Nieve know that the first sequence of switches will both shorten her timer and double the monsters. I'll try to get it done before the timer ends on this round, but I can't promise anything.]

Aldis sent the mental equivalent of a nod. [Next time, pulse your light spell. I'll notice that faster.]

Sage would have sent back an affirmative, but just then a shadow dropped down from the ceiling, stopping his heart as he swung his dueling cane around. Hane diverted it to the side with an easy wave of their hand.

"I can't find a way to access any of the secret alcoves, but I think I know which one holds the key," Hane said, undeterred by Sage's near-attack. "What have you figured out?"

"The sequences to reveal the key, as well as the final switch." It would be easier to meditate on the exit sequence after the final switch was revealed. "The sequence to reveal the switch is going to be difficult. We'll need to hit the switch under the waterfall."

"I think the purple switch might be the one that turns off the waterfall. Nothing happened when Emiko hit it, but I thought I heard a sound like grinding stone."

"That's helpful, but we'll still have to prepare for the room flooding at least a little bit. With that pit trap open, I'd rather play it as safe as possible."

Hane nodded. "Then before we try that sequence, we'll have Aldis bring everyone up onto a platform. Maybe the water will even sweep away the monsters and make the fight easier."

"Maybe." It was possible, but Sage doubted it. And even if it did work that way, Nieve would be upset about missing the fight. "You know where the key alcove is, right?"

Hane pointed, though Sage couldn't see what they were pointing at.

"Either you or Emi should be ready to grab it. It will only open for a moment, then snap shut. Then, I guess you'll have to gather the treasure before we activate the second sequence."

"Shouldn't be hard. If you and Emiko hit the switches, I'll grab the key."

"Right." Sage channeled light through his cane again and held it above his head, waving it in a circle. Emiko zipped over on her cloud, looking cheery for all she had just been chased by a praying mantis out of nightmares.

"We hit all the switches! I think the last one—the one you marked with purple light—might turn off the waterfall trap," she chirped, beaming brightly. "Do you need me for something?"

"Yes, if you can spare the time." It was unusual to see Emi looking so cheerful while the rest of the team was fighting; perhaps she was even more relieved to have broken the Sunstone wall than she let on, even if it didn't change her abilities to cast spells by all that much. "I need you to help me hit the switches in a specific order to reveal the key we need. After that, we'll have to activate the waterfall trap, so hopefully we can confirm if the purple-marked switch actually does turn it off."

"Okay!" Emi looked excited, but ready, as if she had been waiting to be given a task she could do. It was a nice change from seeing her worry and fret over her teammates. "What's the sequence?"

"The first sequence reveals the key to the treasure, and then the second sequence reveals the final switch to open the door," Sage explained. "Emi,

I need you to hit the purple switch, then the yellow switch. I'll hit the red switch from here. As soon as the red switch activates, the key alcove will open for a short window. I've already warned Aldis and the others about the consequences."

"I'll grab the key and take it to the treasure chest." Hane looked to Emi. "Meet me there and help me gather it?"

"Yep!" Emi beamed. "What's the next sequence after that?"

"We'll want to get Lani, Nieve, and Aldis up on platforms before we start that sequence, so they're out of the way of the waterfall. I'll call out the order once everyone's safe."

"Go fast," Hane advised. "The torchlight is almost out, so the next wave will be coming soon."

Emiko zipped away on her cloud as Hane vaulted off the top of the platform. Sage readied his dueling cane, pointing it straight across at the unlit orb on the red-marked platform. He hoped they would make it in time. Better to double the number of mantis-monsters remaining than double the next wave of unknown monsters.

Sage had thought the key alcove would be inside one of the walls, but instead, Hane clung to the side of the room's tallest earthen pillar, the one beneath the waterfall. They held on to an outcropping above their head and simply waited, watching for Emi to begin hitting switches. She buzzed past the purple-marked switch, slapping the orb with her hand, then zoomed to the yellow-marked switch, not slowing down as she struck the orb, making it glow with a soft blue light. Sage fired off a concentrated ball of gray mana at the red-marked switch, cursed when he missed, and then fired again. The second shot hit home, and the orb turned blue. Sage whipped his head around to find Hane, who had already kicked off the earthen pillar, something small and shiny gripped in one hand.

One down, Sage thought, relieved. *One to go.*

He crouched down at the edge of the platform, checking on the others down below. Just as he looked down, the torch flared high and bright, signaling the next wave of monsters. But at least it looked as if all the mantis-monsters had been defeated, as Nieve, Lani, and Aldis were all standing in an alert yet calm cluster. Sage didn't even have to wave, as Aldis was already looking up at him.

[Is it done?] Aldis sent.

[The first sequence, yes. Hane and Emi are gathering the treasure now. We have to activate the switch on the waterfall pillar for the next sequence, and Hane suggested we get everyone up on a platform so they don't get swept down the pit trap.]

[All on one platform, or one on each?] Aldis asked.

[Whatever is easiest for you.] Sage considered a moment, then added: [Blue is the important one. We can't put anyone on green for the ice and I'm already on orange.]

The first sequence had been a zigzag pattern: back right, middle left, front right. Sage had noted it when scanning all possible sequences. Based on that, he'd used his prediction spell to show him if the opposite zigzag pattern—back left, middle right, front left—also revealed a secret and found it to be the sequence to reveal the final switch. And with everyone off the ground, they should be safe to find a way to hit the waterfall switch.

"We got it all!" Emi sang, flying a circle around Sage's platform, looking pleased with herself. "What's the next step?"

"You might have to melt the ice around the green—" Sage stopped as a voice inside his mind cut him off.

[I can open a portal to the green switch.] Sage looked around for the others and found Aldis, Nieve, and Lani crowded around the blue-marked switch two earthen pillars away. [What's the sequence?]

"Don't start until we know Hane is clear of the ground," Sage warned, both verbally and mentally. "It goes blue, green, orange, and then the final switch should appear. Hopefully the waterfall washes whatever the new monsters are down the pit trap, because I'll need more time to meditate when the final switch appears."

"I'm clear." Sage tried not to flinch at the sound of Hane's voice so close by. He hadn't even seen Hane as a shadow that time; they must have approached from behind. "Emiko, would you go be ready to hit the purple switch? That should turn off the waterfall when we're ready to climb down."

"Right!" Emi replied cheerily, floating away.

Sage scanned the ground briefly as he gave Emi time to get into position. He didn't see any new monsters, though the new wave should have appeared by now. Was the ground a little darker than before, or did it just look that way because it was still wet? Strange, he'd thought by now the new wave of monsters would be on them, especially now that the timer had gotten shorter between waves. But even as Emi took up her position by the violet-marked switch, Sage saw nothing down below.

"Okay!" Sage shouted, holding up his hand, ready to hit the orange switch. "Blue first! Go!"

Nieve slammed a fist back into the dull gray orb on the platform she shared with Aldis and Lani, hitting it a bit harder than was absolutely necessary, but it shimmered with a ghostly blue light all the same. Sage didn't really see Aldis hit the green switch within the waterfall, but the sudden rush of water cascading over the switch as well as the room's tallest earthen pillar clearly indicated that he had. Sage slapped the orb on his platform just as water began to rush and run along the cavern's floor. A tone like the tinkle of wind chimes sounded, and a floating platform in the center of the room shimmered into existence. Sage marked it with a white ball of light the moment it finished solidifying.

"Emi, don't hit the switch yet!" Lani shouted, her hands cupped over her mouth. "Let's see if we can flush the new monsters out of hiding before we stop the waterfall!"

Emi saluted her rather than shout across the room. Her little cloud hovered right over the violet switch, hand poised over the orb to hit it at a moment's notice.

"Want to meditate on the solution?" Hane asked, voice soft. "Or should I go hit the new switch to see if it does anything?"

"It won't do anything." A flash of insight played out within Sage's mind's eye. "That switch is the final one in the sequence; its only purpose is to end the wave of monsters and open the exit. But that's the only part of the sequence I can See."

Hane nodded. "I wanted to ask earlier, but can this switch be used to add time infinitely to a timer? Or is there a limit?"

Sage squinted at the pedestal, the orb already turned dull and gray again after the final switch revealed itself. "It only works once per wave. And using it in that sequence added the only extra minute we'll get."

Another nod. "Makes sense. I'll help the others fight the monsters until you come up with the final sequence."

"Sounds good." Sage sat down, putting his back to the pedestal, massaging his temples before closing his eyes. Using his Divine Outcome spell over and over chewed through his mana pool fast, leaving him feeling weary and thin. "Have Aldis contact me if you guys need me to hit the orb during the next wave. This might take a while."

CHAPTER 20

ALDIS

Wayfarer—Travel Specialization (hand mark), Sunstone

I'm not seeing any monsters," Lani murmured, watching the water flow past their pillar. "Are you guys seeing anything?"

"No." Nieve looked disappointed. "I'm not even seeing anything with my Detect Mind spell. Maybe hitting the switch sequence messed up the monster wave somehow?"

"Maybe . . ." Even to Aldis, Lani didn't sound entirely convinced.

"The water is still rising," Aldis felt the need to point out. "Maybe we're fine here, but Sage and Hane are on a lower pillar."

Lani shot him an irritated look, which made no sense because he was right, then cupped her hands around her mouth to shout, "Turn it off, Emi!"

Aldis covered an ear and winced. There was absolutely no reason to shout: he could have very easily sent the message directly to Emiko without shouting. Perhaps it didn't matter as much, since there didn't seem to be any monsters this time around. Maybe they had skipped a wave of monsters as a result of that last switch sequence? Aldis looked over toward Sage, hoping he had an answer for them, but Sage was already seated with his dueling cane across his lap, head tipped up as if he were staring at the ceiling.

Probably already meditating on the next sequence, Aldis guessed. *Better not bother him just now.*

The water drained rapidly from the cavern-style room, swirling around the pit trap Hane had punched open earlier. Aldis squinted, trying to catch a glimpse of any current-caught monsters getting sucked down with it, but by the time the water drained down all the way, he still hadn't caught sight of a single one.

"Aldis, could you take us down, please?" Lani requested, primly proper. Aldis held his hands out toward Lani and Nieve, teleporting them all down to the cavern's floor at once. He dropped Lani's hand at once but stayed close to Nieve's side, just in case the monsters were invisible and had somehow avoided getting swept up by the current. The current must have broken chunks of rock off the giant stone pillars because little round stones littered the floor, where before the floor had been clear.

"Ugh, what are we supposed to do?" Nieve asked, stomping around in a circle, her sword flashing in her grip. "Just sit around and wait for the timer to run out, or—"

Crunch.

Aldis clapped a hand over his mouth, swallowing back his rising gorge. That crunch had the distinct sound of brittle bones snapping—a sound he had heard before on previous spire climbs—and the way Nieve lifted her foot up and shook it brought back a visual that was best left forgotten. But even as he searched for what she'd stepped on, he saw nothing but the small, rounded stones.

"What was that?" Lani asked, similarly confused by the sound. "What did you step on?"

"I don't know. A rock, maybe?" Nieve scraped the sole of her boot along the floor. "A fragile rock, to shatter like that. The waterfall must have dropped all these rocks here, or—"

Nieve backed up a step, trying to find what she'd stepped on when another heart-stopping crunch sounded from beneath her heel. But this time, she howled in pain and lurched forward, hopping on one foot to crash into Lani's arms.

"What was that? What got me?" Nieve asked, shaking her foot as if she were trying to kick it free of her leg. "Get it out! Get it out!"

"Get what out?" Lani was staggered just helping Nieve balance on one foot. "Did you step on something sharp? What happened?"

"Even if she did, it should hardly have gotten through her shroud," Aldis responded, as bewildered as Lani looked. Nieve didn't answer as she slung one arm over Lani's shoulder in order to reach back and yank at the heel of her boot. With a pained moan, she loosened the boot around her calf and pulled it halfway off, sighing in relief.

"What could possibly have . . ." Aldis left the question unfinished, squinting at the rocks littering the floor. The rocks hadn't drawn closer to the three of them . . . had they?

"Look what I found!" Emiko floated down on her cloud, cupping something in her hands and smiling brightly. "Isn't it cute? It looks like a sea urchin!

I think it came down with the waterfall. Do you think sea urchins live inside the Tortoise Spire? Do you think I can take it—"

"Wait." Lani grew visibly pale as Aldis inspected the creature cupped in Emiko's hands. Urchin was a popular dish in certain restaurants, but he'd never seen a live one before. It was bigger than the dried-out, spiny husks he'd seen on display before, but perhaps that was because this one was alive? He'd never seen one look so black that it almost seemed to exude a shadowy aura. Were urchins magical creatures? He'd always thought they must be mundane animals, like fish or crabs. "Emi, drop that at once!"

"What? Why?" Emiko pouted, drawing the creature closer.

"That's not a sea urchin." Lani started to step backward, then stopped, looking behind her. Aldis looked around again and suddenly realized what he was seeing. Those weren't rocks on the ground at all. They were spiny little creatures, inching forward from all sides. "Hurry, Emi, toss it away, it's a—a—"

"Shiuni!" Hane shouted right before several magical blasts resounded from the orange-marked platform. "Look out, they're everywhere!"

Emiko shrieked and tossed the tiny monster away from herself. She started to float higher, but then her cloud faltered and broke apart. She fell with a scream. Luckily, she wasn't that high up, so Aldis was able to catch her by taking a sliding step, not daring to lift his feet. Nieve was still struggling with the spines stuck in the bottom of her boot as Emiko wrapped her arms behind Aldis's neck.

"Don't put me down! Don't let them get me!" She pressed her face into his shoulder, one of her hair buns jabbing the side of his face.

"That makes it rather difficult for me to do anything at all," Aldis blustered, off balance but unwilling to take a step. He felt something nudge the side of his foot and he lurched away from it so suddenly that he stumbled, nearly falling but for Nieve and Lani each catching a sleeve and pulling him back to a safe place to stand—though those were getting harder to come by with each passing second.

"Can't we fight them?" Aldis asked, struggling to maintain his balance as Emiko climbed around onto his back, clinging to his shoulders. "Or are they harmless unless stepped on?"

Lani sucked in a cheek, making a weird face as she thought. "We haven't seen these before. Sage is usually our walking bestiary, so I don't really know."

"I don't feel good," Nieve moaned, Lani trembling under her weight. "'M all weak and shivery and I think I might throw up."

"Lani, my hands," Emiko moaned. As she held one palm out, Aldis felt his gorge rise, fighting the urge to shove her off his back. Her palm was mottled with gray and black spots, the color of her skin gone ashen. "It hurts, it hurts so much!"

Lani's face hardened as if she had just come to a decision. "Aldis, carry us up to a platform. I'll need you to defend us while I heal Nieve and Emi."

With Emiko on his back, Aldis had his hands free to grab onto Lani and Nieve before casting his teleportation spell. The shiuni were obviously able to climb the pillars, as evidenced by Hane firing blast after blast of mana while dancing a circle around Sage, but hopefully it would take them a while to climb up, which would allow Lani to heal both Nieve and Emi to get them back into fighting condition.

"Okay, that should bottleneck their approach," Lani said, helping Nieve sit down against the pedestal. "Aldis, keep an eye out, okay?"

"So these are poisonous urchin-monsters?" Aldis asked, heaving a sigh of relief as Emiko climbed down off his back to go sit beside Nieve.

"Only if you're dumb enough to eat them," Lani replied, tone clipped as she set a green-glowing hand against the center of Nieve's chest. "They do seem to be venomous, though."

Aldis rolled his eyes. "That's a bit of a pedantic distinction, don't you think?"

"No, it's a precise distinction." Lani frowned at whatever her magic was sensing. "Necrotic tissue around the puncture. That's going to take me a bit longer to heal." She looked over at Emiko's hands, her countenance darkening. "Can you cast like that? Is your magic affected?"

"I don't know, it . . . it's hard to concentrate on getting the words out," Emiko admitted, her hands shaking. "I could try if you need me to."

"No, try to stay still," Lani encouraged, voice gentler than Aldis had yet heard it. "Nieve, can you use your water form to thin out the toxins? I need to see to Emi's hands before they get any worse."

"Flood Form, right." Nieve's voice was a pained moan, her eyes half shut. Her lips moved as if she whispered the spell to herself, her chest rising and falling as she breathed through what Aldis could only imagine was a tremendous amount of pain if it felled the fearsome Nieve.

Lani clasped Emi's hands, warm green light bathing her black-and-gray-mottled palms. Aldis shivered, briefly checking his own palms for dark splotches, then tugged at his collar for air. He kept his eyes out for the little urchin-monsters, praying fervently that they couldn't climb very fast. Lani worked quietly over Emi's hands for a few moments, the dark spots getting lighter and lighter, though Emiko's face remained ashen.

"Aldis." Lani spoke without looking up. "Could you ask Hane if they know—"

"Need some help over here!" Hane shouted. "I'm trying to give Sage time, but the shiuni are almost on us!"

"What? Something the Wavewalker can't do?" Nieve chuckled darkly. She tipped her head forward from where it had been resting against the switch's pedestal, her demeanor seeming less solid than usual somehow. "I think I can get them from here."

Nieve closed her eyes and drew a deep breath, extending both arms out toward the pillar where Hane was fervently defending Sage. Looking down on the shorter pillar, Aldis saw vines of ice grow up from the floor, expanding to cover the pillar in a solid sheet of ice. The ice stopped growing just as it reached the peak of the pillar, Nieve collapsing back against the switch's pedestal as her arms dropped heavily to her sides.

"Good job, Nieve." Lani glanced briefly over her shoulder before returning her focus to Emiko's hands. "When you can, do the same thing to—"

"Uh, guys?" Aldis said, pointing. "I don't think that worked as intended."

Nieve's thick layer of ice encircling the pillar was already fracturing, huge chunks of ice falling off to crash to the floor with the little specks of shiuni all but unimpeded, continuing their relentless climb upward.

"What? That should have worked." Frustrated, Lani shoved a strand of hair behind her shoulder, looking from Emi's nearly healed hands to Nieve breathing slowly and deeply in her half-reclined position. "Sea urchins don't survive being frozen."

"I thought we established that these aren't sea urchins," Aldis pointed out. "What, exactly, are shiuni? What's their primary mana type? Aside from venom and their pokey little spines, what do they do?"

Lani's jaw tightened, a muscle ticing as she shook her head, indicating she didn't know the answer to the question. She released Emiko's hands once they were smooth and pale once more, then turned to focus her attention on Nieve. "Good job thinning the toxin, that'll make it easier to remove. Just a moment and I'll heal your foot."

"Thanks, Lani," Nieve said weakly. "I hate Flood Form. Everything feels all . . . wobbly."

Aldis swallowed tightly as the first few spiny monsters crested the top of the pillar, inching silently forward. He shuffled backward, pointing his dueling cane at the closest one, firing off a blast of gray mana. The creature seemed to shrug, its little spines all pinching into a convex point, which the blast of gray mana shattered against. A small whine of fear catching in Aldis's throat, he shot a look over at Hane, who was successfully flinging shiuni off the top of the pillar with blasts of some type of mana. Transference, perhaps? Aldis could do that too: he took aim again, this time using a focused blast of transference mana through his dueling cane. The little spiked creature went flying.

That's going to get exhausting soon, Aldis realized, counting another four shiuni cresting the pillar's edge. *I'd rather just run away to a different pillar, but . . .*

A quick glance back at Lani still kneeling protectively over Nieve proved that wasn't quite possible. He blasted another three shiuni off the platform, sending a message to Hane in the hopes the Wavewalker might have a plan.

[Hane, what are these things? What do they do?] Aldis sent, trying not to take his concentration off the encroaching shiuni.

[They feed off shrouds,] came the chilling, if brief, response. [The spines are also venomous.]

Aldis instinctively checked his shroud, panicked until he confirmed it was still there. He chanced a glance sideways at Nieve, using Detect Aura to check her shroud. Instead of the bright yellow color a Citrine shroud should be, it looked pale, watery, closer to a red-orange, as if she were still Carnelian or Sunstone. Emiko's shroud looked even worse, like a thin layer of pinkish red.

"Hane says these things eat shrouds," Aldis announced grimly. "Nieve and Emiko both look like they've had their shrouds diminished."

Lani sighed heavily. "That must be how one managed to stick Nieve through her boot."

"I only just got my shiny new shroud," Emiko groaned despondently. "So stupid to pick that thing up!"

Aldis couldn't argue against that, but it didn't seem helpful to agree. "We're losing ground here. I can take us to another platform, though I suggest someone go and help Hane protect Sage."

"How am I supposed to do that without a shroud?" Nieve growled fiercely, sounding a bit more like her normal self. "Even *with* a shroud, I'm barely any help in a fight like this."

"How much more time do we have on this fight?" Lani asked, sitting back on her heels and swiping a hand across her forehead. "Was anyone paying attention?"

Oh, that was a grim thought. If they kept running away from these things, that meant when the next wave of monsters came, they'd have to contend with both the shiuni and whatever new horror the spire could concoct. And with weakened shrouds, Aldis didn't want to imagine how badly that might go.

"Ugh, fine. Send me over to Sage and Hane," Nieve said, climbing to her feet and adjusting the boot she'd pulled halfway off earlier. "Ice doesn't hurt these things and they don't have enough of a mind for me to affect them in any way. Our best hope is that Sage figures out the sequence quickly."

"Be careful," Lani advised. "Your shroud is already damaged. Try not to get too close to them."

"As long as I don't step on one, I should be fine," Nieve said with a careless shrug. "Just try and figure something out, okay? We can't go into the next fight without dealing with these things one way or another."

At Lani's nod, Aldis teleported Nieve to the orange-marked platform. The first thing she did was hit the orb, but the torch didn't flash to indicate an added minute. Resh it all, that probably meant they'd already used their extra minute for this wave of monsters and they still didn't know how to fight the shiuni.

"Are you all right, Lani?" Emiko asked, face tight with concern. "Sorry to make you heal so much in the middle of all of this."

"That is my job, you know," Lani said with a weak smile. She accepted Emiko's hand to pull herself up. Her expression turned grim as she noted the tide of shiuni inching closer and closer. "Emi, can you do anything to help us out here? Any spells that might kill wide swaths of these things?"

"I can try a light spell," Emiko offered, her hand running along the mana crystals slotted into the bandolier across her chest. "That should help, right?"

"It's worth a shot," Lani agreed. She drew her cutlass, using it to flip shiuni off the platform using just the tip.

"Maybe we should try moving to a different pillar?" Aldis suggested. "Or anywhere with a smaller concentration of these things?"

"Right." Lani shuffled her feet, shoulder bouncing off Aldis's as she knocked a shiuni away. "The purple platform, maybe? It's low, but none of the other switches are safe enough to fight near."

Aldis hoped she was right; quite frankly, he'd forgotten what most of the switches did, except for the orange one near Sage and the one beneath the waterfall. Making sure he was in tight contact with both Lani and Emiko, Aldis teleported everyone to the violet-marked pillar. He leaned over the edge, then quickly straightened up.

"They're already climbing up this one," Aldis said, swallowing tightly. "What's the plan?"

"Try light, Emi," Lani said calmly. "As bright as you can."

Aldis heard Emiko draw a shaky breath as she pressed a mana crystal into her little belt device. "First light, pure and strong/Gold and bright, rise up the dawn/Soft within the clouds."

A gray foglike cloud encircled the pillar, closing around Aldis, Lani, and Emiko clustered around the switch. Slowly, the cloud began to glow with soft, yellow light. It wasn't the day-bright beacon Aldis remembered from the first scenario, but it still brightened the room considerably. He had to shade his eyes to peer over the edge of the platform again.

"I think . . . Yes, it looks like the light stopped them. I don't see any of them moving anymore."

"But they're not dying, are they?" Lani leaned over the edge, chewing on her lower lip. "Emi, can you make it any brighter?"

"Not without using another light crystal," Emiko said, her voice weary, heavy. "I'm afraid I'm down to my last one. Want me to use it?"

"No, if that's all you have left, it would be best to use it on the orange pillar," Lani said, a note of disappointment in her voice. "I guess we really didn't collect that many light crystals this climb, did we? Maybe we'll look for a room that might have some for you later."

Emiko fit another crystal into her diffuser, then folded her hands and repeated her chant, her voice strong as she spoke, but she sagged noticeably at the end of it. Lani steadied her with a hand on Emiko's shoulder while a yellow-gold cloud enveloped the distant pillar, making it impossible to see anything beyond it.

"Hopefully that helps them," Lani said, sighing. A flicker of light beyond their cloud caught her eye at the same time it caught Aldis's: the torch near the entrance was guttering low, sullen blue flames barely licking higher than the torch's core. "That means we're on our last minute before the next wave of monsters. Got any ideas, Aldis?"

"Nothing good," he muttered, staring straight down the side of the pillar. He cleared his throat, then straightened up, stepping back to the center of the platform, pressing his back against the switch. "I have a spell I've been working on, but I'm not sure if it'll kill any of them. More likely it'll simply shake them off the sides of the pillar."

"Give it a whirl," Lani suggested, almost encouraging. "If we can at least keep the shiuni at bay, then maybe we stand a chance of fighting whatever the next wave of monsters is."

Aldis nodded, releasing a slow breath. He placed the tip of his dueling cane against the rough stone of the pillar, not the shaped platform that held the switch's pedestal. He didn't often use transference mana on its own; more often it was merely a component in his teleportation and portal spells. When he did use it on its own, it was usually for delicate work, like draining mana out of enchanted items and runes, but he had seen Wayfarer duelists use transference mana in offensive spells, or even to assist them in movement, similar to how Hane moved. Not that Aldis intended to go flitting about the room the way Hane did, but a modified transference spell might be enough to dislodge the paralyzed shiuni.

Aldis closed his eyes and very carefully channeled a thin stream of transference mana directly into the earthen pillar. Too much at once, and the recoil would send the dueling cane flying out of his hand. Finesse mattered here. It was a delicate balance: too little mana and the shiuni would be unaffected, but too much mana could potentially crumble the earthen pillar. When he felt he had the feel for the correct amount of transference mana, he channeled the spell: Shiver Burst.

The pillar rumbled, trembling beneath their feet as the transference mana Aldis had channeled through its core burst outward all at once. Little spiny shadows popped off the sides and tumbled end over end, hitting the floor with soft little plops. Aldis waited for the trembling to stop before lifting his dueling cane and peering over the side.

"Not bad." Lani actually sounded impressed for once, which, actually, was rather insulting. This wasn't the first good idea Aldis had had this climb. "Hane should be able to manage that spell, too, right? Can you tell them to try it?"

"Tonfa have different channeling enchantments than dueling canes," Aldis explained. "I believe most models are designed for bursting damage, rather than trickle-and-saturate spells."

Emiko coughed and cleared her throat. "Can we do the same thing for the pillar Sage and the others are on?"

"Good idea." Lani turned to Aldis. "Do you have to be on top of the pillar for that spell to work, or just touching it?"

"Touching it should be fine." Aldis thought he understood where this was going. "But if I'm standing below the pillar, then the shiuni are going to fall on me, and I'd like to keep my shroud intact, thank you very much."

"Emi can place an air shield over us." Lani sounded confident. "We have to hurry, or else we'll get caught by the next wave of monsters. Drop us near the base of Sage's pillar."

Aldis sighed. "Fine. Would have been easier to just clear one pillar, but let's go protect the frontline fighters, shall we?"

He ignored Lani's glower and used yet another teleportation spell. He dropped them several feet above the floor, giving him the opportunity to fire off a blast of transference mana straight down, clearing the ground of shiuni as they fell. Emiko staggered as she landed, but Aldis and Lani each steadied her by her shoulders. She signed a thank-you that even Aldis understood.

"Let me know when the air shield is up." Aldis looked for a likely place to set the tip of his cane against the pillar. The nebulous cloud surrounding it still shone with golden light, which meant the shiuni should be paralyzed, but he still didn't want to take the risk of a shiuni falling on top of him and leeching away his shroud. He couldn't shake the image of Emiko and Nieve's shrouds, how watery-thin they had seemed; couldn't help but wonder how neither of them had suggested ringing out of the spire after the most important part of their armor had been so weakened. And with the lowest-level shroud of the group, Aldis felt particularly vulnerable.

Emiko chanted solemnly, then signed something to Lani. Lani's jaw tensed as she looked up along the earthen pillar infested with the little spiky monsters. "Ready when you are."

This still seemed like a terrible idea to Aldis, but in lieu of anything better, he channeled his Shiver Burst spell through the pillar. It was a little easier this time, as the composition of this pillar was nearly the same as the first one. However, instead of violently shaking all the shiuni off, he tempered the release of the mana to vibrate more than reverberate. He could make the argument that this was less likely to disturb Sage in his meditation, but really it was more about protecting himself from the shiuni that would get shaken off nearby. The shield would protect him from any dropping off his head, but he didn't want the ones in front of him to pop off and roll beneath the shield.

Aldis couldn't help but flinch as the first few shiuni began to rain down on Emiko's air shield. The good news was that most of the ones that fell from near the top of the pillar landed hard enough to kill them, their spiky little forms dissolving and leaving behind a few small, dark mana crystals. Unfortunately, the ones close to Aldis's dueling cane weren't falling far enough to harm them. Just as he predicted, they hit the ground and rolled, making him shuffle nervously while still holding his cane to the pillar.

"At least they're still paralyzed by the light," Lani observed, using her cutlass like a broom to sweep the urchins away from their feet. Her free hand toyed with the end of the crystal shard, just peeking out from the top of her pocket. At least that was better than her habit of jingling her coin purse. "When the next wave comes, we should retreat to—"

Aldis was looking up along the pillar when it happened: he sidled back just a single step when his heel struck something round and hard. That alone wouldn't have been enough to trip him, but he panicked and threw himself backward, dropping his cane as his arms wheeled around for balance. The ground was littered with shiuni in an almost perfect ring around the air shield, and in the moment when Aldis realized that falling was inevitable, he began casting a teleportation spell. But where could he safely teleport to? If he landed on the top of the closest pillar, he could disrupt Sage's meditation. The violet-marked pillar was still encased in the golden-light cloud, but it was so far away and the next wave of monsters was due to start any moment. The safe space under the air shield was too small, and anyway, he'd just stepped on a shiuni there, so his shroud might already be compromised, and—

Aldis squeezed his eyes shut. Maybe he could reach his return bell and ring out before the shiuni did too much damage to him and his shroud.

A brilliant flare of green light blazed against Aldis's eyelids as he braced himself for the fall. He hit the ground hard, but the pain of landing left him almost as soon as it registered, and the lumps beneath his hands didn't feel prickly at all. Cautiously, he opened his eyes and looked for the source of the light.

Lani stood with her hand extended, a cone of green light emanating outward from it. She turned a circle, holding the cone of green light out like the beacon of a lighthouse.

"I wasn't sure it would work," she admitted, a relieved smile on her face. "But if these things can affect shrouds, they must primarily use death mana, so life mana should be able to hurt them."

As she swept the green light over the scattered urchin-monsters, they didn't just die, they exploded in puffs of inky smoke. Aldis lifted his hand and found tiny, black mana crystals stuck to it. He exhaled a shaky breath, almost dizzy with relief. After regaining his senses, he took Emiko's outstretched hand and allowed her to help pull him to his feet. Lani stepped past him and cast her life spell over the shiuni clustered around his dueling cane, melting them all away so he could stoop and grab it.

"Thanks for that," he said, swiping sweat off his face with his sleeve. It was with both relief and embarrassment that he noted that a simple rock had caused his fall, rather than a shiuni. At least his shroud was still intact, even if his pride wasn't. He kicked the stone away and brushed mana crystals off his skin and clothing. He paused a moment later, offering one to Emiko. "Can you use these?"

She shook her head and made a gesture Aldis took to mean "too small." He finished cleaning himself up just as the torch at the head of the room roared with red-orange flames that nearly licked the ceiling. The next wave of monsters was upon them.

Lani turned on her heel, face determined. "I can't kill all of the ones on the floor before the next wave of monsters hits us. Should we retreat to the other pillar Emi lit up, or is that too far—"

"He's got it!" The triumphant shout made Aldis jump and clasp his chest to keep his heart from leaping out of it. Nieve's voice echoed off the pillars, hitting every corner of the room. "Sage knows the sequence to get the resh out of here!"

"Thank the goddess," Aldis breathed, grabbing Lani and Emiko each by a shoulder. "Make room! We're coming up!"

Aldis teleported to the top of the orange-marked pillar, nearly losing his footing at the edge of the switch's platform. It was a tight fit with all six of them huddled around a single switch, but it was good to see Sage on his feet, even if he swayed slightly.

"If we go quick, we can avoid the next monster wave," Sage explained, pinching the bridge of his nose beneath his glasses as if relieving some pain. "Or at least, we won't have to fight them for long. It goes green, orange, red, yellow, blue, purple, with the white switch last." He pointed up at the platform hovering over empty air. "There are seven switches and six of us, so someone will have to hit two switches."

"We can't split up among that many pillars," Lani said quickly. "Those shiuni are everywhere. If they're clustered at the top of the pillars, we'll lose our shrouds before we can finish the sequence."

"And then we'd have a monster to fight," Nieve groaned, for once not looking excited by the prospect. It was nice to know she wasn't reckless to the point of self-destruction, at least. "My shroud feels like a wet tissue right now. I can take a few hits, but I'm not really in fighting condition."

Emiko signed something that made Sage's expression turn grim: it seemed her shroud still wasn't functional either.

"We don't need to be on the pillars to hit the switches," Aldis pointed out. "I can open fist-sized portals to each one from here."

A low, spitting growl echoed off the corners of the cavernlike room, making Aldis shudder. The sound of stone scraping against stone filled the room.

"As long as whatever that is doesn't interrupt me," Aldis added anxiously.

"I'll take care of it," Hane said, rolling their shoulders. "Anything is better than shooting shiuni with mana."

"Wait, I need someone to—" Aldis stopped as Hane somersaulted off the top of the pillar. He sighed heavily, the opportunity missed. "I need someone to hit the last switch. I can't see it from here, so I don't know how to place the portal."

"You can still send someone up there, right?" Lani looked up at the platform hovering just high enough that the switch wasn't visible from where they stood. "Send Nieve. You can tell her when to hit it."

"I'll know when to hit it," Nieve grumbled, seemingly grumpy that Hane was stealing yet another fight from her. "It's last after the purple switch, isn't it?"

"It has to be quick," Sage explained. "If the switches aren't struck fast enough, we'll have to start all over again, and depending on where we lose the sequence, we could end up with less time, or double the monsters."

"Right, fast then." Nieve reached out and Aldis clasped her hand, teleporting her up to the floating platform with the last switch. He waited to make sure Nieve landed safely before drawing a shaky breath. Opening one portal, even a small one, required a great deal of mana. Holding open five portals at the same time was going to be a strain, especially after all the transference mana he'd already spent on this fight.

"Say the order one more time," Aldis pleaded, getting ready. "And call out who is hitting which. I'll have my hands full with the portals and warning Hane of the waterfall."

"Green, then orange," Lani replied promptly. "I'll get those two and I'll watch the purple pillar so I can shout to Nieve."

"The next two are red, then yellow," Sage said. "I can get those two. Emi, can you handle blue, then purple?"

At Emiko's nod, Aldis drew a deep breath, letting it out slowly as he concentrated. He opened the portals in reverse order so the first one couldn't be struck before he was ready. About halfway through the sequence, his heart juddered to a stop as something vaguely snakelike with webbed ridges along its spine spiraled up a distant pillar, undulating through the stone as if it were water. With sweat running down the back of his neck, Aldis focused on opening the rest of the portals.

"Steady," he said out loud, pausing just long enough to warn Hane about the waterfall. Upon receiving acknowledgment of his warning, Aldis declared: "Now!"

Lani reached through the portal ahead of her, smacking the gray orb with gusto. She then wheeled around and slapped her palm down on the switch in the center of the platform. Sage reached out to both his portals, hesitating just a second before hitting the red-marked switch, then the yellow-marked switch.

A hiss that turned into something like a keening scream at the end made the earthen pillar shudder. Aldis felt his knees shake as the sound of stone grinding against stone grew louder—he didn't have to be a gambler to place good odds that one of the monsters was currently climbing the pillar they were all on.

Emiko cried out sharply as the pillar trembled, but she still managed to hit the blue-marked switch. She bit her lower lip as a tremor rumbled through the pillar, keeping her balance as she hit the final violet-marked switch.

"Nieve, now!" Lani shouted, echoed by Sage and Aldis.

A great reptilian head crested the top of the platform, rising higher and higher, baring fangs as long as swords as well as a flickering, forked tongue. Its beaded hide was mostly made up of grays and blacks, but with shockingly brilliant orange chevrons pointing back along its ridged spine. He'd thought it a snake at first, but then two claw-tipped forelimbs grasped the edge of the platform, the immense lizard cocking its head to the side as it eyed them hungrily. His hand was already reaching for his return bell when Lani and Emiko flanked him, Lani rolling her cutlass in her grip, a determined expression on her face as Emiko drew a deep breath, her fingers dancing over the mana crystals slotted into her bandolier.

Aldis started to raise his dueling cane, wincing with his eyes half shut, when a loud, clear tone resounded through the room. Just as the lizard-monster lunged, jaws gaping wide, it vanished. It didn't dissolve into mana crystals as the defeated monsters did but simply ceased to exist, as if banished. Perhaps that was what the tone did: banish all monsters remaining once the challenge was ended. Aldis's knees wobbled, nearly giving out beneath him. He leaned back against the switch, sucking in a breath of thin air. Goddess, but a break would be lovely right now.

"Hey!" Nieve was leaning over the edge of the floating platform, waving down at him. "Is it over? Can I get a little help?"

Yes, down. Getting out of here was the next logical step. Aldis started to cast a teleport on Nieve, then stopped himself.

"Are all—" His voice cracked. He cleared his throat, coughed, then tried again. "Are all the shiuni gone?"

"Yes." Hane landed in a crouch right in front of Aldis, weakening that last bit of resolve in Aldis's knees, making him fall heavily on his backside. "The exit is uncovered, too. We can move on."

"Do you need healing?" Lani asked, sheathing her cutlass.

Hane thought about it, then nodded. "I'm not greatly injured, but something for small aches and pains would be welcome."

Aches and pains, Aldis thought in an internal voice that sounded like a grumble. *How about something for my heart, which you keep stopping?*

After teleporting Nieve down safely, Aldis offered the same favor to the others. Hane declined after receiving a minor healing from Lani. Emiko, Sage, and Lani gripped Aldis's arm, and he teleported them all down near the door. Nieve was already there examining the symbols carved into the door's surface.

"No key required," she called out. "That's good because I didn't want to start this all over again."

"I don't think I could start all over again," Lani admitted, shaking her hand out. "I don't think I've ever channeled that much raw life mana before. It hurts more than conjuring water does."

"Yeah, we'd definitely have to take a long break before attempting that again," Sage confirmed, rubbing his eyes. Even blind, he was able to hook an arm around Emiko's shoulders and give her a quick squeeze. "Not to mention finding a way to fix any damaged shrouds. Either of you recover yet?"

Emiko shook her head while Nieve glowered.

"It feels like trying to talk after losing my voice," Nieve explained. "I hate it."

Aldis looked to Hane, expecting them to say something along the lines of "I could go again," but even they looked unenthused at the prospect of having to do the room all over again. Perhaps even Hane the Great had their limits.

"Aldis, can you try and find us a mana fountain?" Lani asked, frowning as she set a hand on Emiko's shoulder, green light shimmering around her fingertips. "I think we all need a little time to recuperate."

Finally, something we can agree on, Aldis thought in deepest relief. He took a moment to shake out his hand, quickly massaging the stiff muscles of his wrist and forearm. The strain of using so much transference mana, on top of simultaneous portals, had almost been too much for him. He'd certainly need some healing and a break after this. Placing one hand on the side of the door, Aldis selected a doorknob and swung the door open. A blast of dry heat just about punched him in the face before he caught a glimpse of a goddess-forsaken fire-and-brimstone landscape beyond it. Even as exhausted as his mana felt, he gladly drained the first location rune of mana, switching the view through the portal to a new location.

"Maybe that's what that was," Sage murmured, seemingly to himself. He shook his head, touched his glasses, and then swayed woozily from side to side. Emi grasped the arm slung over her shoulders as if afraid he might fall over. "I guess if we're just looking for a mana fountain, you don't really need me to look at each room we pass."

"No, but when I do find a mana fountain, I'd appreciate you confirming that it is, in fact, a mana fountain, and not, say, a giant mimic," Aldis said, only half joking.

Sage snorted, blinking as he lifted himself off Emiko's shoulders. With all the energy of a shambling corpse, he shuffled over to Aldis and hooked an elbow over Aldis's shoulder, leaning against him as he squinted through the flickering doorway. Even as tired as Aldis was from all the spellcasting, he didn't mind Sage's weight against him so much. It felt comforting: like camaraderie. After only a moment, Sage lowered his forehead against his own forearm, apparently too tired to even keep his eyes open, as Aldis searched the runes to find a mana fountain.

The rooms flickered past one after another, showing desert landscapes, verdant forests, a strange-looking city, crumbling ruins, and even a village inhabited entirely by bearlike monsters before finally a classic mana fountain room appeared beyond the doorway. Aldis sighed in relief but nudged Sage awake just to be certain. He didn't think the goddess would be cruel enough to let a mimic take the shape of a mana fountain, but all the same, he didn't want to take the risk.

"What? Oh." Sage squinted through red-veined eyes, touching his glasses as he checked the room beyond the doorway. "It's safe. We can camp out here for a while and recover."

After a round of muttered "Thank the goddess" from just about everyone, Nieve plucked Sage off Aldis's shoulder, pulling his arm over her neck and half carrying him into the fountain room. Emiko followed close behind, already tugging her canteen off her travel bag. Hane waited a beat, then followed. Lani pushed a loose braid back off her face, then sighed in frustration when it dropped right back where it had been.

For a brief second, their eyes locked and Lani offered a weary smile. She didn't say anything, but she made a fist and pressed her knuckles lightly against Aldis's shoulder before passing through the doorway. It wasn't a spell, but somehow that show of camaraderie felt better than a healing spell. Wearily, Aldis trudged through the doorway after her into the relative safety of the mana fountain room.

CHAPTER 21

NIEVE

Champion (mind mark), Citrine

Nieve stumbled into the mana fountain room, shivering as the adrenaline-fueled sweat on her skin seemed to crystallize by the sharp drop in temperature as well as danger. She felt naked without a functioning shroud, but at least she wouldn't need one here. Hopefully her shroud would recover soon so her team could move on; otherwise they'd have to call the climb here and return home before they made it to the next level, which would make this entire excursion feel like a wasted effort. Not to mention the expense of trying to buy another gate key close to this level.

Sage's weight was still draped over Nieve's shoulders, his steps shaky and unsteady as he pressed his free hand to his forehead, covering his eyes. Nieve lowered him carefully to his knees beside the mana fountain, holding him steady when he would have pitched face-first into the icy pool. His hands shook as he reached out to cup a handful of water and bring it to his mouth to drink. Nieve sank down beside him, submerging her arms beneath the water up to her elbows. She reveled in the icy coolness for long moments, allowing herself to get her breath back and release the tension coiled throughout every muscle and limb. Only after the rest of the team shuffled past her to claim their own space around the fountain did she bring a cupped handful to her lips to drink, water running down her arms to drip off her elbows. Her next exhale tasted like ice.

"I'll come around and give everyone a quick healing," Lani called out over the sound of a bag being slung down onto the ground. "Unless anyone's in danger of bleeding out right now?"

Nieve's foot was still sore from stepping on the shiuni, but she wasn't in any dire need of a healing spell. Dangling her arms in the pool, Nieve slouched over the rim of the fountain, watching the ripples and reflections on the water. Knowing that the team couldn't move on until her shroud was back to full strength soothed her usual impatience, allowing her to fully let go and relax. She let her vision go hazy while watching light play beneath the water's surface.

She heard steps and voices but didn't bother to pay them any attention. If someone needed her, they'd call for her. Sage jostled her as he shifted, turning around to put his back against the fountain. In her periphery, she could just see him slouch down and tip his head back against the stone rim of the fountain, his eyes closed, his breath coming slow and deep. He'd probably fall asleep like that: he'd done it often enough in the past.

Nieve startled at a sudden touch, someone's hand light on the crown of her head.

"Just me," came Lani's soothing healer-voice. "Let me get that pain in your foot. Is there anything else? Any lingering effects from the shiuni toxin?"

"I don't think so," Nieve grumbled. Nothing more than her shroud's erosion, anyway. "You should get Sage. I think he overdid it back there."

"I'll get him," Lani assured her. Nieve didn't look back, but she felt the cooling tickle of healing magic flowing through her, healing a few scrapes and bruises, soothing a few aching muscles. The healing combined with the mesmerizing patterns of the light through water had Nieve feeling sleepy and dull. Even though Nieve's hands were entirely still in the water, a constant ripple emanated out from the edge of the pool. Her breath, maybe? Strange that she hadn't noticed it earlier.

Lani took her hand back and moved a step to the side, crouching down in front of Sage. Nieve rolled her head onto her shoulder, watching from the corner of her eye. Sage smiled weakly as Lani touched her fingertips to his temples. Though Lani looked intent and professional in her manner, Nieve couldn't help but grin: Lani had already kicked off her boots and changed her socks to fresh ones. She always looked so cute, sliding over the mana fountain room's tiles in her socks.

"Don't fall asleep just yet," Lani cautioned, rocking back on her heels as she dropped her hands from Sage's head. "We need to consolidate the treasure and send it to the depository. You should both eat something, too."

"Yes, Lani," Nieve replied as Sage mumbled something incoherent. As Lani stepped away, Nieve pushed herself back and up, stretching her arms over her head and drawing herself up on her toes. She had to move, or else she'd fall right to sleep.

Nieve nudged Sage with the toe of her boot. He only grunted in response. "Hey. Want me to take your treasures over for you? Or I could stand here and keep kicking you until you get up."

"Ugh. Take them." Without opening his eyes, Sage grabbed at the satchel strap over his chest and started to lift it but seemed to lose his willpower before taking it fully off. Nieve curled her hand beneath the strap and lifted, shouldering its weight along with her own.

"Got anything else tucked away?" Nieve pressed, more to pester than to help. Sage owed her that much for being so nice and taking his treasures over for him. "Stuff any mana gems into your pockets? You holding anything back from the share?"

Sage slitted his eyes open just enough to glare up at her, then patted down his pockets in a halfhearted manner. Nieve knew he'd never willfully hide a treasure earned on a climb, but sometimes things could be forgotten. Like a handful of gold coins tucked in the wrong belt pouch, or a weapon clipped to a belt. Sage paused in his search as his hand closed around a belt pouch that Nieve didn't recognize. It wasn't his purse and it wasn't the bag that kept his return bell. Rations, maybe? But Sage usually carried those in his satchel.

"No," Sage said finally, shoving the little pouch a bit behind himself, as if to hide it. "Nothing else. Gonna sleep now."

"All right." Nieve shrugged the satchel higher up on her shoulder and strode away. Lani had left the large collection pouch open on the ground on the opposite side of the fountain, probably so that anyone who wanted to could sleep without being disturbed by the sounds of sorting treasure.

"Load up the coins and gems, but leave everything else out, please," Lani called, casting a healing on Aldis's right arm. Probably mana strain: Nieve hadn't seen him take an injury in the last room. "I want to get an idea of how much we've collected so far."

You mean you want to calculate your cut so you know how much you can lose at the casino, Nieve thought, dropping both her and Sage's bags down beside the collection bag. Of course, Lani had the right to do whatever she wanted with her share of the treasure. Nieve just hated the idea of her losing yet another fingertip. Hopefully they would only need to hire one new climber for next time, rather than two. A shorter downtime between climbs meant less time for Lani to lose more than she could afford to.

Nieve dumped out Sage's satchel first, careful to keep the spill of collected treasure contained so she didn't have to chase it across the tiles. She had to shove Sage's personal effects—like his clothes, food supplies, and books (why did he even bother climbing with *books* of all things?)—back into his bag before adding her own collected treasures to the pile. As she began sorting through the resulting mess, Emiko came over to join her, smiling sweetly as she started her own pile.

"How are you feeling, Mi-mi?" Nieve asked, dropping a handful of gold, silver, and copper coins into the collection bag.

"Still pretty foolish for picking up that shiuni." Emi shook her head at herself. "How about you? Is your shroud working yet?"

Nieve sent her senses questing into her shroud, feeling its limits. She grimaced at what she found. "No, it's still terrible. I should eat something and maybe take a nap." She reached out to tug at one of Emi's hair buns. "You should, too, Mi-mi."

"Aldis is setting up a kettle on a hot plate," Emi said, pointing over to where Aldis had set up a tidy little camp for himself, complete with his bedroll folded into a cushion to sit on. Nieve smirked; he'd be disappointed to learn that they didn't plan on camping here very long. It should take only an hour or two for Nieve's shroud to recover.

Hopefully.

Lani joined them with a quick smile before she popped in her aura-detecting monocle and began swiftly sorting through the treasure, creating a separate pile of possibly enchanted items. Nieve considered helping her by using Detect Aura, then decided against it: spending time with Lani was great and all, but if she offered to help this time, Lani would expect it of her in the future, and sometimes Nieve just liked to collapse in fountain rooms.

"Did you see the treasure Hane and I scooped up in the last room?" Emiko asked cheerfully, pulling something out of her bag. "Look, look! It's a little statue. Think it's some kind of reliquary?"

Lani plucked the statue from Emi's hand as Nieve leaned in closer for a look. She frowned as she turned it in the strange light of the mana fountain.

"Not sure," she admitted finally. "Ren would be able to tell. I can ask him to take a look when we get back. Good find, Emi."

"There were also weapons." Nieve jumped, hand reaching for her sword before she realized it was just Hane, approaching the group from an odd angle. Had they just finished a sweep of the room? Why? It was a mana fountain—traditionally the safest place to be inside a spire. Had they even taken a moment to refresh themself at the mana fountain at all? Or were they just always trying to pop out of nowhere to scare their teammates?

Hane knelt down, flipping back the cover of their dimensional bag. "I'll lay the weapons out in case there's something anyone needs. Let me know if you need help lashing these together later, Lani."

"Thank you," Lani said absently, holding a large gold coin above her head and squinting at it through her monocle.

Nieve grinned as she pulled the matched set of metallic claws she'd taken from the first room out of the pile of treasure. "Need some new gloves, Mi-mi? I think these would look adorable on you."

"Hm, I don't know." Emi took one and tried it on. It was only two sizes too big for her small hand. "I feel like it would get in the way when I'm reaching for my mana crystals."

Nieve chuckled and continued scooping up the smaller items to drop into the collection bag. Lani liked to wrap anything sharp or delicate before stowing it with the rest of the treasures to be sent back for storage in the depository. Nieve thought it was mostly a waste of time to be so meticulous, but then again, on more than one occasion she'd cut her hand reaching into a loot bag full of blades and daggers.

It was hard not to watch Hane drawing out weapon after weapon from their dimensional bag, each far longer than the bag looked to be able to hold. Nieve wasn't sure whether Hane's bag was a treasure they'd found while climbing or merely an enchanted item, but either way, it looked to be fairly expensive by the sheer volume it could hold. It must have had "pockets," or at least something similar, too, because after Hane finished laying out the weapons, they reached into the bag, fiddled with something, then upended the entire thing over Lani's collection bag, a spill of coins and mana crystals pouring out in a jingling mass. For years, Lani had wanted such a bag to add to the team's climbing gear, but if they ever did find one as substantial as Hane's, Nieve would rather sell it for coin.

"Interested in a polearm?" Hane asked, noticing Nieve watching them as they shook out their dimensional bag. "I believe that one on the end is imbued with ice magic. Might be of use to you."

The indicated polearm was an ornate glaive, capped with a half-moon blade and a pattern like snowflakes down the haft. The end terminated in a sharp spike, like an ice pick. Nieve scooted over to set her hand on it, the metal cold to the touch. With a groan, Nieve surged to her feet, taking the glaive up with her. She practiced a slash, a jab, and a whirl before laying it back down with the other weapons.

"It'll fetch a good price," Nieve said with a shrug. "But long weapons are harder to carry, worse to swing in tight spaces. I like my sword better."

Hane shrugged, sitting next to Lani as they added daggers, pieces of armor, and odd little trinkets to her tiny hoard. Nieve glanced at the bits of armor but didn't see anything that really appealed to her.

"Thank you for carrying all of this, Hane," Lani said absently, wrapping the translucent dagger blade in a cloth before setting it inside the treasure sack. At her knee was a stack of cloth about as large as handkerchiefs, though most were little more than rags. She selected a new cloth to wrap one of the metallic claws Nieve had passed over to her. "I'll lash all the big weapons together and tie them to the bag before I send it. Does anyone want to claim anything before I ship this all to storage?"

"Hang on, hang on, I haven't taken a look yet." Aldis hustled over, letting his satchel drop hard enough to spew out a few coins in his haste to look at the pile of treasures in front of Lani. "Do we know what any of this does? What about these? Do these bracers reflect lightning? Or do they shoot lightning? That is the rune for lightning, isn't it?"

"Only Sage really reads the runes," Emi said, pinching a ruby ring between two fingers, not wearing it, but holding it up as if admiring it. "You can set the bracers aside and ask him later if you want."

Aldis hedged, then set the bracers down, something else catching his eye. As he muttered and pondered aloud, an enticing scent caught Nieve by the nose, making her stomach gurgle and rumble.

"Are you cooking something?" Nieve asked, blotting the corner of her mouth with her sleeve.

"Yes, just some chopped vegetables in chicken stock, nothing remarkable," Aldis said flippantly. "And some water for tea. I don't have enough cups for everyone to have soup and tea, though, so you'll have to bring your own over, or else wash your cup after you use it. Is there a pair to this boot? Or did we really find a single boot in one of the treasure hauls?"

"Here." Lani handed him the boot that had been hidden from sight by the collection bag. "There's a levitation enchantment on them, but it looks weak, like there's a time limit, or a weight limit."

Aldis pouted and set the pair of boots back down. As he reached out to pick up something else, Lani tapped the back of his hand lightly with the hilt of a dagger.

"Can you add your treasures to the stash, please?" she asked, not unkindly. "You'll have a chance to look at this all again when we collect it after the climb."

"Yes, yes," Aldis grumbled impatiently, jostling his bag a bit and drawing out a few of the larger items before emptying the coins and gems into the collection bag. "I can't stay long; I have to get back to stir the soup. How does everyone take their tea? I have sugar, cinnamon, and mint."

"Oh, I have buttermilk!" Emi rocked side to side in a little dance. "I'll bring it over once we're finished here."

"You can leave as soon as you've turned over all your treasures," Lani assured him. "We rarely ever put any treasures to immediate use, except things like those anti-poison and anti-venom beads Hane's using." Lani gave Nieve a pointed look, her one eye appearing disproportionately larger through the monocle. "That would have been a good thing for you to have when you stomped on that shiuni."

"Blame the Seer," Nieve replied with a casual shrug. There was no way she could have predicted that something so small would have penetrated her shroud to envenom her. "Did Hane even find out if those beads worked?"

"No, Hane was not so foolish as to step directly on any of the shiuni," Hane said, pulling something thick and furry from their dimensional bag.

"Ooh, what's that?" Emi asked, crawling over the diminished piles of treasure to touch the odd-looking treasure. Nieve couldn't help but go and take a closer look herself. Whatever it was, it felt far warmer and deeper than it had any right to feel.

"It's an enchanted bedroll imbued with kitsune magic," Hane explained, laying the bedroll down on the floor. Aldis scrambled up from the pile of enchanted treasures in order to inspect it. Lani squinted through her monocle. "I got it from an escort quest by the lake in the first room. I thought I might claim it, but I don't often use bedrolls when I sleep."

"Ooh, it's so soft!" Emi plopped on a corner of it, digging her fingers into the fur. "It's warm, too! This would be great for some of the cold location challenges."

"It would also sell really nicely," Nieve observed, pressing her hand down into the bedroll to find resistance similar to a real mattress. "It's rare to get even a handful of kitsune fur out of a spire, and here's a whole clutch of it."

"Hane does have right of first refusal," Lani called out, groaning as she pushed herself to her feet. Apparently, they'd made such a fuss over the bedroll that she had to come see it for herself. "That's a treasure they earned on their own, they can choose to make it part of their cut."

"I haven't decided yet," Hane admitted. "There are challenges where it would be useful, but someone else might get more use from it than I would."

"Well, put me down as interested if Hane passes," Aldis said, a corner of the bedroll pinched between two fingers. "Although, I daresay this one piece might make a full share of our current treasure haul."

"We'd be better off selling it," Nieve said, stooping to grab her satchel by the strap. It felt far lighter now that it wasn't carrying any treasure. "Money splits more evenly than luxury bedrolls."

"Aw, I'd share with you, Nieve!" Emi said, taking Nieve by the hand and nuzzling her cheek against it.

"You're a sweet piece, Mi-mi, but you're not the type I usually take to bed," Nieve retorted with a risqué wink.

"Ew, now I'm thinking about Ren and Wyle." Emi made a face and pulled herself up using Nieve's hand. "I don't think I want anything just now, Lani. I want to know what a few of these do before I decide."

"Will I be able to choose a few pieces after an Enchanter looks them over?" Aldis asked, a thick leather belt tucked against his chest as he ran a chain of golden links through his fingers, letting it fall back into the pile outside the treasure sack.

"Yeah, that's how we usually pick our pieces," Lani explained, cleaning her monocle lens on the edge of her tunic before setting it against her eye again. She was looking at a tiny, wickedly curved dagger, almost like the talon of a bird.

"We usually leave our haul in storage until we can get an appointment with an Enchanter to come and evaluate it," Emiko explained to Aldis. "Once we know what everything does and what it's worth, we split it up to either sell or use. Except the mana crystals." Emiko nudged the collection bag, gleaming with the light of dozens of mana crystals. "I keep the Class Three ones for my mana diffuser."

"We consider those team property," Lani said without looking up from a talonlike dagger. "Emi only uses the crystals on climbs, and we couldn't have ascended so high without her diffuser."

"I wanted to ask about that." Aldis reluctantly set down the belt he'd been holding with the other pieces of armor. "I've never seen anyone else with an enchanted item quite like that, and I used to travel with merchants from Valia to Dalenos. Where did you—"

"Uh-uh, nope." Lani grabbed the monocle from her eye in order to glare at them. "If you're going to get chatty, go do it by the food. You're distracting me from calculating an estimate on this haul."

"You don't have to tell me twice." Nieve's stomach was already leading her over to Aldis's hot plate. "C'mon, Mi-mi, I'm starving."

"The soup!" Aldis gasped, stumbling to his feet so fast that Nieve and Emi had to grab his arms to steady him. He rubbed his leg, complaining about it falling asleep under him, then limped over to his hot plate in order to stir the soup. The kettle was steaming but not whistling yet as Nieve took a seat opposite Aldis with Emi sitting down beside her. Nieve's stomach rumbled ominously as she dug through her satchel for her cup and utensils.

"Wow, Nieve, it sounds like you haven't eaten in days!" Emi teased, poking Nieve in the side. "Or did you eat a monster and that's what I'm hearing?"

"I'm going to eat you if you don't stop poking me," Nieve said through a wolf's grin. She fished a pouch of food from her bag and tossed it down as a group offering. "I brought some mild jerky this time, since you didn't like the spicy stuff last time."

"Oh, good!" Emi rooted through her satchel and produced a metal canteen. "I brought the buttermilk just in case you had that face-melting jerky again!"

Nieve snorted. "I do have some of the spicy stuff, in case you want to try your luck again."

Aldis squinted through the steam over the hot plate. "Is that an enchanted canteen? Does it keep the milk cold?"

"No, just fresh." Emi set the canteen down between herself and Aldis, sitting neatly on her knees. "I like buttermilk warm, especially when adding it to tea." She looked up at Nieve with a bright smile on her face. "Besides, if I wanted something cold, I'd just ask you!"

"Be grateful I don't freeze you into a solid block of ice," Nieve teased, sitting down next to Emi. She covered a yawn, then tugged open the pouch containing her jerky. She snapped a stick in half with her teeth, enjoying the burn on her tongue. Emi made a face as she picked through the pouch for the less-flavored variety of jerky.

Sage was still asleep on the far side of the fountain: Nieve could just hear his deep, even breathing over the tinkling of the fountain water. Lani wouldn't leave the treasure pile until everything had been properly stowed in preparation of sending it off to the storage facility. Most climbing teams used the Safe Haven storage facility, owned and operated by Haven Securities, which was known to be the safest place to store spire treasures, but they also took the most expensive cut from recovered treasures. Lani had found a smaller depository that had some decent protections in place and charged a lot less, but it wasn't unheard of for people to try to rob the smaller storage facilities: breaking into a vault was safer than climbing a spire, after all. So far, they'd been lucky enough that nothing recovered had been stolen from them.

If Sage was sleeping and Lani was counting treasure, then where was Hane? Nieve scanned the room until she found them, a shadow against the darkened edges of the room.

"Hey, Hane!" Nieve called, waving her half stick of jerky. "Come eat with us. We've all got some food to share."

Hane lifted a hand in acknowledgment of the offer, coming close enough so they didn't have to shout. It was polite, considering that Sage was asleep, but Nieve knew a little shout like that wasn't enough to wake him now.

"Thank you, but I'll eat later," Hane assured her. "I think I'm going to copy Sage and catch a nap instead."

"Suit yourself," Nieve said with a shrug. She crammed the second half of her jerky into her mouth, watching as Hane sunk into the shadows, drawing their knees up tight to their chest and putting their head down. That was strange, wasn't it? This was the perfect opportunity to use that fox-fur bed-roll, and yet they chose to sleep sitting upright. Oh, well. Every climber had their quirks; Nieve supposed Hane was allowed theirs. At least napping was a better use of time than prowling around the perimeter of a safe room.

"Okay!" Aldis rubbed his palms together, having finished setting out baskets of food in the middle of their little gathering, looking happier than Nieve had ever seen him appear. Even she had to admit that it looked like a clever arrangement: Aldis's large food basket was actually a series of separate containers, making it look more like a picnic than a respite during a treacherous spire climb. "I have some fresh fruit, vegetables, and hard-boiled eggs here and I have this wonderful tea blend with cinnamon and dried cranberries. It'll taste excellent with some buttermilk. Unless anyone has a specific tea blend request?"

"Wow, you came prepared!" Emi leaned forward on her hands, peering into the round tin Aldis had carefully pried open. The tin looked to be divided into about a dozen different sections, each containing different types of tea leaves. The center of the tin held strainers and pouches of sugar and cinnamon. Altogether, it seemed a little decadent for climber gear. "I want to try the cranberry blend like you suggested, but do you have a lavender and cardamom blend?"

"I do," Aldis said proudly. "It's perfect for those nights when you just can't fall asleep."

"I could fall asleep just listening to you talk about tea," Nieve retorted, helping herself to an orange from one of Aldis's baskets. "You should save some for Sage, though. He likes a cup of green tea when he wakes up."

"Aw, you're only sweet to Sage when he can't hear you," Emi said, shaking her head sadly. "Why must you always hurt the ones you love, Nieve?"

Nieve grinned, cracking her knuckles against her palm. "Sounds like you want a bath, little Emi."

"No!" Emi shrieked, cowering away. "Don't toss me in the fountain, Nieve!"

"If you do, don't get the food wet," Aldis protested, moving to shield the hot plate.

"Can you three quiet down?" Lani demanded, sending a harsh glare their way. "I just lost count of my estimate for the treasure collected so far." A pause, then: "And Sage and Hane are trying to sleep."

Aldis looked affronted, but Emiko ducked her head ruefully. Nieve grinned as she peeled her orange, holding Lani's gaze as she popped a section of the fruit into her mouth. Lani rolled her eyes and resumed cataloging her dragon hoard of treasure.

"Don't mind her," Nieve counseled lazily, sprawling a little to sit with one knee bent, the other curled beneath her, hand holding the orange dangling over her knee. "This is Lani's favorite part of the climb: evaluating the treasure."

"It's the whole reason she climbs," Emiko confirmed cheerfully.

"Is it?" Aldis asked, a hint of disapproval on his face, no doubt thinking of her gambling habit. His expression softened a moment later, shoulders rolling in an almost-shrug. "I suppose I can't truly blame her: isn't treasure the reason we all climb?"

Unconsciously, Nieve touched the locket beneath her leather armor. "No. It's not the only reason."

"Nieve's going to make it to the top," Emi proclaimed proudly. "That's why we're always trying to ascend."

"Truly?" Aldis asked, sounding intrigued. "You actually believe the goddess awaits climbers at the top of each spire in order to grant a wish?"

"Why not?" Nieve said, rolling her head back to look up at him. "It's not like anyone's ever gotten there and said she *wasn't* there."

"It's not like anyone's ever really gotten there," Aldis countered. "Outside of Tarren Tales, I mean."

Nieve rolled her shoulder back in a shrug as she tore another section of orange off with her teeth. "Someone's got to be the first."

Aldis shifted his weight for a moment, making Nieve dread the common follow-up question: *What do you want to wish for?* Instead, he began setting tea strainers over four small cups, fastidiously adding pinches of tea leaves to each one. The kettle had just started to whistle when Aldis whisked it off the heat.

"It's a nice thought, meeting the goddess," Aldis said mildly. He cast a look back over his shoulder at Lani before lowering his voice. "If you're a believer, doesn't it bother you to climb with a . . ."

A gambler. He didn't say it, but the implication was clear. Nieve glanced up at Emi, who was determinedly rooting around inside her satchel for something and ignoring the question.

"Everyone's got their own thing," Nieve replied lazily. "She's good at what she does and that's good enough for me. If the goddess cares so much, she can refuse to grant her wish when we get to the top."

"Do you each have a wish, then?" Aldis asked, adding water to each of the cups. He set small saucers over each cup, allowing the leaves to steep. "Has it always been a group goal to make it to the top of the spire?"

"Always been my goal." Nieve shrugged. She dropped her empty orange peel into a handkerchief, then lurched forward to grab a handful of snap peas. "What about you, Mi-mi?"

"Me?" Emi beamed as she shook a hard-sided canteen in her hands. She usually mixed flavored sugar into her water on breaks. "Seems a little rude to ask me about my wish when you won't tell anyone about yours, Nee-Nieve."

"No, I mean . . ." Nieve chewed over the question before blurting it out: "Why do you climb?"

It was a question that had been with her for a few climbs, even before Wyle and Ren quit climbing. It had been a relief to have to replace only two climbers instead of three, but it had been nagging at Nieve ever since. Emi had no reason to climb: she was close enough to the nobility not to need treasure, and she wasn't particularly driven to ascend. She didn't participate in duels, didn't work on her magic outside the spire save to practice chants and poetry. If there wasn't something driving her to climb, then why do it at all?

Emi's face drew in on itself, her lower lip trembling as her eyes grew big and watery. "Nee-Nieve doesn't want me climbing with her anymore. So mean!"

"Oh, knock it off or I'll turn that tea into an ice cube." Nieve tossed a snap pea at Emi. Emi tried catching it in her mouth, but it bounced off her nose. The three of them laughed, earning them a pointed glare from Lani. "I was just wondering, that's all. It's not like you need to climb for anything."

"I like climbing," Emi said defensively. "And I'd miss you and Sage if I stopped. Would I even see you guys if I retired from climbing?"

Nieve hummed thoughtfully. She and Sage had visited Emiko at her family's home before, but it had been uncomfortable: the nobility had so many rules and expectations that Nieve often lost track and ended up embarrassing herself. Even Sage had been uncomfortable, and he had actually researched rules and customs beforehand.

"It's not like we'd never see each other," Nieve replied. "I'm sure we're going to see Ren and Wyle again after this climb. Catch up over drinks or something. It would be the same."

"It wouldn't be the same," Emiko insisted. "I'd be listening to your climbing stories instead of sharing in them. And I'd be worried. Do you know how hard it is to worry? I'd rather be here, in the same danger as you, than be safe at home worrying about all the ways I can't help you because I'm not with you."

"Aw, Mi-mi, we'd be all right," Nieve insisted, rocking her shoulder into Emi's. "Even Sage is pretty reliable most of the time. You shouldn't feel like you have to keep climbing just because of us."

"I like climbing with you," Emi declared with a sniff. "And until you replace me with someone else, I'm not going anywhere."

"Well, you are certainly the most capable Cloudcaller I have ever climbed with," Aldis put in, blowing steam off a spoonful of soup as he raised it to his lips. He deactivated the hot plate and added a sprinkle of some type of green herb to the soup, mixing it slowly. "Do you mind if I ask about your mana diffuser? My family used to trade enchanted items from Valia, but I've never seen anything quite like that."

"It's a prototype!" Emi's good humor returned as she spoke about her handy little mana crystal device. Nieve finished her snap peas and grabbed a few sticks of jerky as Emi twisted her belt around to show Aldis her mana diffuser. "The Enchanter who made it was petitioning for a loan through my family. They have a patent but can't mass-produce it yet. So far, they've only been able to make it efficient for heart and lung attunements, which was why my family gave it to me. I'm the only active climber who can use it."

"I see." Aldis scooted forward, examining the device the same way Sage had when he first saw it. "And when you say it's only efficient for heart and lung marks, does that mean it's of limited use to arm-, leg-, and mind-marked attuned?"

"Something about mana leakage?" Emi shrugged, then demonstrated fitting a mana crystal into the diffuser. To Nieve, it had always looked like a little box with a vent on the front, though Sage had taken the time to study the runes, looking up what each one did. Mana crystals popped into the box with a sharp "snap" and began bleeding mana through the vent when Emiko chanted her spells. The released mana was woven into Emi's spell by her chant, usually using a cloud or some form of vapor as a vessel for the spell. In the beginning of their climbing career, Emi had only been able to use base mana types, like adding light mana to a cloud so that it would glow. But as she practiced climb after climb, she'd taught herself to fuse fire mana to her natural air mana and create lightning storms. It used to take a lot out of her, mixing mana types like that, but now it seemed almost easy. What no one ever seemed to realize was how heavy the mana crystals were, which Emi had to carry with her throughout every single climb. The crystal-laden bandolier weighed more than the glaive Nieve had tested out earlier, which was actually the entire reason Emiko chose to float around on a cloud rather than walk. "It's something about how the mana gets shaped, but I don't really understand it. I know the Enchanter is working on a version that works with all attunement marks; it's just taking them a long time to get it right. That's why they needed an investor: so they could create more prototypes."

"Did your family choose to support them?" Aldis asked, eyes narrow as he studied the box. The look was a familiar one: Sage often wore that look when examining something new. Nieve assumed he was using a spell to see the runes. "I'd be interested in knowing how the Enchanter's research is coming along."

"They did," Emiko confirmed. "I can get their information for you after the climb. I believe their workshop is in Valia, though, so it'd be kind of a long trip."

Aldis went still a moment, and then a little of the light faded from his eyes. He sat back heavily with a muttered "Oh."

"What?" Nieve asked, curious. "You seemed pretty happy when you thought Sage was Valian. Don't travel well?"

"Valia and I . . ." Aldis hedged, his gaze darting around elusively. "Well, it's not really me, per se, just . . . it's complicated."

"Ooh! Are you a bandit?" Emiko leaned forward, bracing herself on her hands. "But not like a mean one, like someone who stole from the nobility to help feed the poor? But then someone figured out your identity and you had to flee the country before they could exact vengeance? Oh, oh! Are you running away from a loveless marriage? Or a forced betrothal? Or the person you loved fell in love with someone else and you couldn't face them any longer?"

Aldis looked confused and aghast as Nieve barked a laugh. When Lani glared at her, Nieve tried inviting her over with a tip of her head. Lani pursed her lips and resumed counting her treasure.

"You've spent way too much time at the theater lately, Mi-mi." Nieve jostled her with her shoulder. To Aldis, she said: "Emi's a drama junkie. She says it helps with her poetry for chants and stuff, but I think she's actually a sticky, gooey romantic at heart."

"Better to be a romantic than a curmudgeonly oaf." Emiko sat up on her knees and planted a kiss on Nieve's cheek. Nieve laughed and swiped at her, but Emiko had already dodged, stealing a snap pea from Aldis's basket. She grinned up at Nieve before turning her attention back to Aldis. "So? What's complicated about Valia?"

"I'm . . . not supposed to say." Aldis rubbed the back of his neck, looking distinctly uncomfortable. "It wasn't my doing, though, it was entirely my parents. They just worry that if I go back to Valia, then . . . the people who are looking for them might use me to draw them out."

Nieve exchanged a look with Emiko, who looked both shocked and pleased.

"This does kind of sound like some sort of bandit story," Nieve admitted.

"Right?" Emiko squealed, inching closer to Aldis, lifting a hand as if to whisper. "Can you give us a hint? What kind of people are after your parents? They didn't anger Visage Tenjin, did they?"

"Goddess, no!" Flags of color appeared on Aldis's cheeks. His eyes darted around, no doubt looking for a diversion. Just then, the fountain chamber echoed with a snort and a snore from Sage, sleeping on the far side of the fountain. "What about him, hm? Do either of you know his reason for climbing?"

It was an obvious change of subject, but Nieve got the hint: they were prying, and Aldis didn't want to share. That was fair: she had things she didn't share, either.

"Sage always wanted to climb," Emi said, smiling fondly. "He likes discovering new things and solving puzzles and he loves the historical scenarios, or anything based on a book or story. He's just always loved climbing."

"It's a job," Nieve countered, pointing out the practical nature of climbing. "He'd rather climb than work in his parents' trade shop, like most climbers. Gotta do something to pay the bills."

"Yes, but shop work is generally a very safe profession," Aldis pointed out. "It takes more than a desire to pay bills routinely to climb a spire, wouldn't you say?"

"Depends on what you want." Nieve wiped her fingers on a handkerchief before freeing her canteen from her belt and taking a long pull. "Sage gets all that technical stuff about runes and enchanted items, and he's pretty good at explaining it to people, but it'd be a waste of his talents to sit behind a counter all day. He's a really good Seer and an almost decent fighter, and he couldn't put those skills to use anywhere else but a spire."

"Aw, Nieve." Emi glowed. "You said something almost nice about Sage!"

"Yeah, well, if he was completely useless, I wouldn't climb with him, would I?" Nieve bared her teeth in a grin. "I only give him a hard time to help him get better."

"Strange he isn't more grateful," Emiko teased airily.

"I know, right?" Nieve chuckled. The smell of soup was enticing, but it looked too hot to eat at the moment. She was considering risking it anyway: fruits and vegetables only made her feel so full. A hearty soup was exactly what she needed to keep pressing on in the spire.

Well, that and a fully functioning shroud.

"Why do you think—" Aldis hushed himself hurriedly before casting a furtive look around and lowering his voice. "Why does Hane climb, do you suppose?"

"I dunno. Probably to save baby kitsune from serpents, or something heroic like that." Nieve scooted forward with the carved wooden bowl she used for spire climbs. Aldis didn't protest as she stirred the soup and poured some of it off into her bowl. The smell rising off the steam was enough to make her drool a little. "I bet Hane isn't even a climber, really. They seem more like a delver, searching for legendary treasures; why else would they revisit floors they've already been to instead of climbing higher?"

"Not everyone's in such a rush to ascend, Nieve," Emi pointed out, accepting a cup of tea from Aldis. She added a bit of her buttermilk and a spoonful of sugar, blowing across the surface once before taking a sip. Her face lit up, eyes gleaming as she shimmied from side to side. "Mmm, this is so good! Thank you, Aldis!"

"Well, I'm certain your buttermilk makes quite a difference." He looked like he was trying to hide a pleased smile even as he demurred. Nieve found it hard to resist telling him that Emi was just like that, endlessly cheerful and uplifting, but a sip of the soup gave her pause. It seemed Aldis actually had quite a talent for assembling good food during a spire climb. It almost made up for all the times he tried running away during combat.

Almost.

"There isn't very much of the soup, I'm afraid," Aldis pointed out as he scooted one of his tea cups over to Nieve. "We'll have to be sure to save some for Sage and Hane when they awake."

"I dunno. Do we really like them that much?" Nieve asked.

"Rude, Nee-Nieve!" Emi swatted her knee before twisting around to look back at Lani. "Come eat something! The treasure will be there later."

"I'm almost finished," Lani called back, keeping her voice soft for the sleepers. "I'll just be another minute."

"But the tea is hot now," Emi protested. "It'll taste different if you wait to add the milk."

"I'm sure it'll be fine," Lani assured her without looking up.

Nieve set her bowl of soup down, deliberately scraping her boots across the tiles in order to draw Lani's attention. "Don't make me come over there and drag you away from the hoard, Lani," Nieve threatened with a grin.

Lani gave her a pedantic stare. "How much of your shroud have you recovered, Nieve? Because I have a plethora of pointed objects over here with which to stab you."

Nieve snorted, then gave her shroud an experimental push. It felt stronger than it had before, though certainly not fully recovered. Was it worth the risk of disturbing Lani to pick her up and carry her over to the food? Lani had a bad habit of getting lost in her calculations, sometimes forgetting to eat until after everyone else was ready to move on to the next trial. The treasure could wait; the food was ready now.

"What about that mysterious shard from earlier?" Aldis asked, fixing his own cup of tea with milk and sugar. He inhaled the aroma of it, smiling warmly before taking a sip. After a contented sigh, he added: "Did we collect anything that might react with it to wake it up? Have you already tried swishing it through the mana fountain?"

"Oh, I forgot about that." Lani took the monocle from her eye and rubbed the red mark it left behind on her cheek. "I felt it vibrate once or twice in the last room, but I forgot until now."

Nieve and Emi exchanged a silent raised-eyebrow look. It was no surprise to them that Lani had forgotten such an intriguing mystery while calculating an estimated value for the treasure. Lani was a great team leader and an even better healer, but when it came to treasure, she could have a one-track mind.

"Come eat with us, La-la-ni-ni!" Emi patted the floor beside herself, inviting Lani over. "Or else Nieve will eat all the soup."

"She's not even making that up, I will eat this whole pot of soup," Nieve assured Lani. She raised her bowl to her lips, taking a long drink of the broth. As curious as the crystal shard was, Nieve found herself wondering when Aldis had cut all the vegetables down so small. Were they precut to be cooked like this? That was more planning than she usually put into her own spire rations. If the scenarios didn't provide food, like the fortress in the first room had, Nieve survived on jerky, nuts, and water.

Aldis hurriedly poured off some soup into one of his empty cups after shooting Nieve a wary glare.

"Fine, I'm coming," Lani said, rubbing her eyes before standing and stretching. Nieve stared a respectful amount: there usually wasn't enough time for staring during combat, so she had to take her chances where she could. She dropped her gaze as Lani turned toward the fountain, tipping the bowl up to finish the last of the vegetables.

"No, Nieve." Emi slapped Nieve's wrist as she reached out to refill her bowl. "We're saving some for Sage and Hane."

"It'll be cold by the time they wake up," Nieve pointed out. "And they have their own rations."

"I pray they carry better rations than you do," Aldis commented, eyeing her pouch of jerky doubtfully. "I have to ask: Have you ever come down with a case of scurvy?"

"Only when I drink ale on a boat," Nieve replied with a grin.

"That's not—I don't even—" Aldis sputtered, clearly at a loss for how to respond. Nieve grinned, glad that Aldis was so fun to tease. Lately, Sage had been getting a bit testy about her teasing, probably in response to their mutual affection for Lani. It would be nice to have another outlet for her humor while climbing.

It felt a little like betrayal, accepting Aldis as a teammate so soon after Ren and Wyle retired. Of course, Ren and Wyle had known that the team would continue climbing and that they'd recruit new people to the team. They had decided to leave on their own; no one had forced them out. They'd probably get married soon and start a family, so it was better that they didn't climb anymore.

It wouldn't be right if the two of them died on a climb, leaving children behind.

In any event, Nieve was already thinking of Aldis as a permanent addition to the team and finding that it wasn't such a disagreeable notion. Hopefully he'd get over Lani's gambling habit quickly and really settle in as a teammate. Nieve wouldn't mind more meals like this one in future climbs, and his portal technique just about made him her new favorite person.

They would still have to recruit at least one new person after this climb: Hane almost never climbed with the same team twice, and never for consecutive climbs. It was almost a shame, though. Nieve hadn't had a good opportunity to fight alongside them yet, the way she used to fight shoulder-to-shoulder with Ren. She missed that feeling of absolute trust in a fellow warrior. It was sad to think she might not ever have that again, no matter who they recruited to fill the role.

"Sage and Lani make sure Nieve eats like a civilized person," Emi explained to Aldis. "Well, nutritionally, anyway. They can't do anything about her table manners."

"They could try," Nieve challenged. "But all it would get them is—"

"Do you hear that?"

Nieve's hand jerked, spilling her tea over her leggings while Emi yipped in surprise, her hand crushing the pouch she'd just drawn out of her satchel. Aldis huffed and covered his chest with a hand, muttering oaths under his breath.

Nieve scowled up at Hane, standing just behind her shoulder. "I didn't even hear *you* until just now. Why are you always—"

Infuriatingly, Hane held a finger up to their mouth in the sign for quiet, eyes narrow as they scanned the room. "What is that?"

"Did you hear Sage snoring?" Nieve growled, mopping at the tea on her leggings. Luckily it wasn't scalding hot anymore, but the spill was upsetting regardless: that tea had been really good! "Or maybe you had a bad dream."

"No, I hear it still." Hane cocked their head to the side. "It's a whisper. Emiko, do you hear it?"

"No, I—where's Lani?" Emi looked back toward the treasure, then spun around the other way, searching for Lani.

"She was just here, wasn't she?" Nieve asked, rising to her feet. "She said she was—"

Nieve cut herself off, frowning as she caught sight of Lani standing stock-still at the fountain, half bent over and staring intently at something in her hand. She looked transfixed, as if caught by a spell. Alarm, already close to the surface thanks to Hane, welled up quickly within her chest.

"Lani?" Nieve called cautiously. She glanced around the room for threats but found only her team members. Hane stood close by, almost shoulder-to-shoulder with Nieve, staring intently over at Lani. Emi and Aldis looked bewildered, still sitting on the floor by the hot plate. Sage still slept on, undisturbed by whatever whispering had awoken Hane and whatever force held Lani enthralled at the fountain's edge.

"Lani?" Emi called softly. When Lani remained unmoved, Emi started to stand.

"Wait," Hane instructed, their movements fluid and silent as they placed themself between Emi and Lani. "She's holding something."

"Is it the crystal shard from earlier?" Aldis asked, looking surprised and confused. "I suggested she dip it in the mana fountain. Perhaps it finally activated?"

"Can she hear us?" Emi asked, clasping her hand around Nieve's lower leg, eyes wide as she looked up. "She's okay, right? Sage would have told us if the shard was dangerous."

"Yeah," Nieve replied, though her hands dropped to the hilt of her sword. "Of course. Sage would have told us if it was dangerous."

Except that Sage hadn't been able to See very much at all about this shard; he'd said as much when he tried divining its future. What if it was protected from Sight?

What if it *was* dangerous?

Hane crept closer, circling around Lani where she leaned, unmoving, over the fountain's rim. She stood with one foot on the ground, one knee on the fountain's edge, water still gleaming on her wet hands. Her mouth was slightly open as she stared at the broken shard cupped in her hands. Hane waved a hand in front of her eyes, and Nieve was relieved to see Lani impatiently swipe their hand away, so at least she wasn't locked in some kind of stasis spell.

"Should we wake up Sage?" Aldis suggested, voice meek. "Perhaps he'll have some insight on all of this?"

"Good idea," Nieve agreed, remaining stalwartly between Lani and the others. She couldn't discount the possibility that the object might have mind-control powers, and if Lani attacked, she wanted to be ready to defend. She didn't feel especially great about how close Hane was to the mysterious artifact, either. Fighting an Acolyte would be bad enough; she didn't know how she'd fight a Wavewalker like Hane. "Emi, go wake up Sage."

"Okay." Emiko scrambled to her feet, taking the long way around the fountain to avoid passing Hane and Lani. Nieve kept Emi in the corner of her eye as Hane set a hand on Lani's shoulder, giving her a slight shake.

"Is that safe?" Aldis asked, attunement-marked hand partially outstretched. That was good: if Hane did attack, Aldis could teleport them away faster than they could move. Probably.

"It's talking," Hane said, sounding surprised. "I can hear it, like it's whispering."

Nieve drew her sword as Hane touched a finger to the shard cupped in Lani's hands. Lani gave them a surprised look before shifting a step backward, as if making space for them beside her. Nieve gritted her teeth as she sank into a defensive stance, silently mapping the room as a battlefield.

Sage startled with a grunt, followed by a yawn. In a sleep-drenched voice he asked: "Are we ready to move on? Can I eat something first?"

"Wake up, Sage!" Nieve ordered, voice ringing off the shadowy corners of the room. "We have a situation developing."

"Wuh?" Sage rubbed his face, obviously groggy. Emi crouched in front of him, speaking quickly and softly, likely filling him in as he woke up. Nieve kept her eyes on Hane and Lani.

Seemingly sensing Nieve's intent to freeze first, ask questions later, Hane lifted their hand from the shard and turned back to face her. "From what I can tell, it's nothing sinister. I believe it's a piece of something larger."

"And it's talking?" Nieve asked, not dropping her stance.

"Yes," Hane confirmed, holding both hands up in a placating gesture. "It doesn't seem dangerous, which may be why Sage couldn't foresee this eventuality."

"Objects that speak aren't exactly safe, either," Nieve retorted. "If that thing mind-controls either of you, I won't be gentle in holding you both down."

"Nieve's not wrong about talking objects being dangerous," Sage suggested, taking a bracketing position on Lani's far side. "It could be a trap that was biding its time to spring, or it could be a trial sent by the goddess. Either way, we need to confirm that it's not placing anyone under a mind-control spell."

"Wait, I'm confused," Aldis admitted, one hand still held out toward Lani and Hane. "Haven't we been trying to wake that thing up? Isn't this what we wanted in the first place?"

"I thought it would act like a compass," Nieve countered. "Like, after we figured out how to turn it on, it would point us to a hidden treasure. If it talked, I was expecting a riddle, or instructions. And why can't we all hear it? Hane said they could hear it before they knew what it was."

"She touched it to the fountain water, didn't she?" Hane asked, touching a finger to the shard again, then holding up a droplet of water on their fingertip. "My passive perception is strongest around water sources. It's likely Emiko's will be the same with practice."

"That would probably be more reassuring if I were certain you weren't being compelled to say that," Nieve countered harshly. She didn't want to fight Hane or Lani, but she would if either of them became a threat.

Hane looked back over their shoulder toward Sage. "Would you be able to tell if I'm under a compulsion or not?"

"Er, I should be able to?" Sage started to move forward, then stopped. "But you come here. I don't want to get closer to the crystal shard in case it's dangerous."

Good move, Nieve thought approvingly. It didn't fill her with confidence that Lani didn't seem to be aware of the events unfolding around her. Hane walked slowly over to Sage, extending a hand out for him to touch. Sage clasped it as if in a handshake, his eyes going misty as he cast a spell. The room held its breath as they awaited the verdict.

"I don't think they've been compelled," Sage said finally, releasing Hane's hand. "I can't confirm it definitively, though, since I don't know Hane all that well."

"But you do know Lani," Nieve said, holding her defensive stance.

Sage nodded. "I'm more worried about her, to be honest."

Nieve agreed: Lani's eyes were wide, her mouth slightly open. She was staring at the crystal as if she were seeing the face of the goddess. No, probably even more reverently than that.

Hane cupped Lani's shoulder and gave her a firm shake. She blinked, looking surprised to find herself still curled over the fountain with Hane right beside her.

"Your team is worried that the object is placing you under a compulsion," Hane explained.

"Oh. No, no!" Lani whipped her head up, looking from Nieve to Sage to Emi. "I'm not— This is— It's—"

"You'd say the same thing if you were being compelled," Nieve pointed out, her ice-trap spell in the forefront of her thoughts.

"Sage, come check me," Lani invited, waving him over.

"You should put that thing down first," Sage cautioned, maintaining his distance. "We don't know its properties and it isn't worth the risk of more of us getting compelled."

"Oh, but—" Lani grasped the slivered shard closer to herself, bowing her head over it. "I'm sorry, friend. Give me a moment and I'll explain it to my team." This version of Lani was new to Nieve: she'd never seen that look of wonder on her stalwart leader's face. Lani usually read like a closed book with blank binding. Seeing her so reluctant to set something potentially dangerous down seemed a clear indicator of a mind-control spell. Nieve held her ice-trap spell close as Lani very cautiously set the object across Hane's open palms, refusing to turn away as she reached her hand out toward Sage.

For his part, Sage cast a wary glance over at Nieve before taking Lani's hand. She gave him a grim nod, letting him know she would handle any fallout, and then, almost timidly, he lifted his attunement-marked hand to cup Lani's fingertips. Sage's eyes went blank for a moment as he quested inward, using a mental mana spell to make sure Lani's mind was her own. It was a spell that Nieve could, perhaps, learn one day, but not one she had put any focus into learning since developing her mental mana. At least her Frost Form spell made her more resistant to falling victim to mind-control spells; that was probably better than trying to resist a compulsion after the fact.

"She's fine," Sage concluded, his hand lingering on Lani's a moment longer before he let it drop. Facing Nieve, he added: "Blue rabbit wings."

Emi released a pent breath so quickly that she collapsed onto the edge of the fountain, cradling her head in her hands. Nieve released a breath slowly as she sheathed her sword but kept one hand hooked over the hilt. She never minded dueling a friend, but genuinely fighting a teammate was something she'd rather not experience.

"Blue rabbit—what?" Aldis asked, confused. "What does that mean? Is—" Aldis gasped, drawing back a step. "Is Sage compromised as well?"

"No," Nieve said, not exactly relieved, but perhaps a little less wary. "It's a code phrase we use for checking compulsion. It means his mind isn't taken over."

"Well, not necessarily," Sage said with a shrug. "If the caster is clever, a compulsion spell could be worded as 'Convince your friends you're not under a compulsion,' in which case I would have spoken the code phrase anyway. But most compulsion spells aren't so thorough."

"Thanks, Sage," Nieve said bitterly. "Now we all have to question whether half our team is under a mind-control spell or not."

"We're not being mind-controlled," Lani said, taking the broken shard from Hane's hands. She held it out, as if Nieve would be stupid enough to touch it. "She's a— They— Sorry, how are you called?" Lani was quiet for a moment, clearly hearing something that Nieve wasn't. "They're a piece of a sentient crystal, taken forcibly from their shrine in the Unclaimed Lands. The mana fountain woke them up and they were just explaining how they came to be here. I think they need help."

"Uh-huh." Nieve remained unconvinced. "What took them so long to wake up, then? We've been dunking that thing in every water source we could find up until now."

"It's a mana fountain, Nieve," Lani said, slightly exasperated. "It's a concentrated source of magic. This isn't their entire form, they've been asleep or dormant or something. If we listen, I'm sure they'll explain it all to us."

"Have they said anything about treasure?" Aldis asked, peeking around Nieve's shoulder. "Or a reward, or anything of that nature?" He frowned and peered over at Sage. "How does a shrine crystal come to one of the Soaring Spires, anyway? The ancient crystals are not of the goddess."

"A question we could ask if we'd let them speak," Lani replied with obvious irritation. "Look, the strange aura finally makes sense now that we know we're dealing with pre-attunement-era sorcery. Even if they did intend us harm, they don't even have enough strength to speak to each of us mind-to-mind without physical contact, so really, what's the harm?"

Lani pivoted on her heel, turning from Nieve and Aldis toward Sage and Emi.

"I think they need our help." Once again, that didn't sound like Lani. Not the Lani that Nieve knew.

Nieve flicked her gaze over to Hane, still hovering near Lani and the crystal. They lifted their eyes, noting Nieve's scrutiny.

"They are not of the goddess," Hane confirmed. "In all my years as a climber, I've never come across anything like this. I'd like to listen to what they have to say."

"What do they need?" Emiko asked, peeking out from behind Sage as if she might edge closer.

"Stay back, Emi!" Nieve commanded, the crack of a whip in her voice. "If that thing really is capable of mind control, or it's a cursed object of some kind, it could already have affected half of our team. Everyone else stays back." Nieve calculated that she could win a fight against Lani and Hane. She could probably beat Sage, too, if his brief connection with Lani's and Hane's minds had affected him. But adding either Emi or Aldis to the mix substantially lowered her odds of winning a fight. She didn't draw her sword but kept her hand over the hilt as a precaution, pursing her lips before looking over at Sage. "What do we do here? What happens next?"

Sage shook his head, looking perplexed. "I don't know, Nieve; I have the same information that you have. I glanced ahead and I didn't see any immediate threats." He shrugged unhelpfully. "Has your shroud even recovered yet? Emi, how about yours?"

Nieve pushed a little mana into her shroud, feeling it stronger than it had been before but still weaker than she liked it to be when going into a fight.

She'd forgotten to take that into her calculations when considering a fight with Lani and Hane.

"Mine isn't recovered yet," Emi reported, sounding disappointed. She had inched around Sage, getting closer to Lani than Nieve liked as she stared at the crystal shard with curious interest. "If they want to talk to us, can't we just listen? We were only taking a break anyway."

"Does listening require us all to touch it?" Nieve asked, a bit of a growl in the back of her throat. "Because that sounds like a trap to me."

"It sounded like it was going to be a long story," Lani said slowly, cupping the shard close to her chest. "And I'd rather not stop to explain it, or interrupt them with your questions." She was silent for a moment before adding: "They said they don't have enough magic to perform any spells while in this form."

"And strange, sentient items never lie," Nieve shot back.

Lani lifted her warm brown eyes, meeting Nieve's with that stubborn defiance she admired most of the time. "I am going to listen to them. That's the choice I'm making. You can choose to listen, or you can choose to stand around posturing, Nieve. Everyone is free to do as they like right now, especially since we can't progress until your shroud fixes itself."

Nieve wavered as Lani sat down on the floor with her back against the fountain, settling in as if she intended to be there for a while. Hane cast a look around, shrugged, then sat down facing Lani, touching a fingertip to the point of the shard.

Nieve hedged, biting her lower lip. It wasn't unheard of to find sentient items hidden within the spires. In fact, many climbers dreamed of finding sentient swords, or objects with spirits hidden within them, giving them powerful qualities. But usually those items were recognizable as weapons, enchanted gemstones, or perhaps vessels that possessed a magical aura; she had never heard of anything that looked like a broken shard of crystal possessing sentience, much less a sliver of an ancient crystal needing the help of a passing climber team.

A glance at Sage showed the same internal debate. Sage's not-knowing made Nieve skeptical: there wasn't much he didn't have a clear-cut opinion on, especially when that opinion could happen to fall in Lani's favor. Indecision was written clearly on his brow and in the bloodless pinch of his lips. As he looked back to Nieve for her opinion, Emiko firmed her jaw and sat determinedly down next to Lani, folding her legs neatly beneath herself before reaching out and laying a finger against the broken shard. It took only a moment for her eyes to widen and her jaw to drop.

"It really is talking!" Emi breathed. "Sorry, sorry! *They* really are talking."

"May I ask something?" Hane spoke aloud, though the question was clearly addressed to the shard. "Which shrine did you say you were from?" A moment's pause, then: "The Shrine of Singing Waters? That's not one I've heard of."

If the crystal shard responded, Nieve couldn't hear it. The room lapsed into silence but for the gentle lapping of water within the fountain. Nieve held her stance, teeth gritted tightly, though she wavered as looks of concern and pity showed clearly on Lani's and Emi's faces. Uncertain, Nieve cast another questioning look at Sage. He appeared racked with indecision, one moment shuffling toward the seated group, then alternatively backing away.

"Can't say I'm not curious," Aldis admitted, stepping around Nieve. He inched forward as if he expected the broken shard to reveal a mouth full of teeth and snap at him, casting a wary look back at Nieve, then over at Sage before kneeling down and reaching out to touch the crystal. He drew his hand back several times before sucking in a breath and jabbing his finger at its side. He stiffened, and then very slowly he relaxed, making his seat more comfortable. "I'm sorry, I missed what was said at the beginning. How did something from the Unclaimed Lands come to be found inside the Tortoise Spire?"

"Wait, this is ridiculous," Lani said through an irritated breath. Her eyes snapped up, looking between Sage and Nieve. "I don't want to keep starting over, so either come in and touch the crystal now, or forever hold your peace."

Sage still hesitated, grimacing as he looked from Lani to Nieve, shrugging helplessly. "They haven't hurt anyone yet. And I know they didn't place Lani under a compulsion. I'll keep my Foresight spell active, in case anything happens, but I guess I don't see the harm. We can't go anywhere until your shroud recovers, right?"

"I guess not," Nieve admitted grudgingly. She watched as Sage took his place in the circle, touching a finger to the crystal shard. His expression didn't change from one of grim expectation as he listened to whatever the shard had to say. Nieve scowled, stymied by indecision. If this all went badly, shouldn't at least one of them remain untainted by whatever that thing was? Or was it possible that she'd miss out on some fantastical reward if she held back? How could she know which choice was the right one?

She held off a few moments more when Lani lifted her eyes, seemingly surprised to see Nieve standing alone, outside the circle that sat touching the glinting shard.

"Please, Nieve," Lani said, voice soft, cajoling. "I just have this . . . feeling. We're supposed to help them. I know it as much as I know that we can't do it without you."

"Fine," Nieve said, throwing her hands up. "If it kills us all, at least we all die together."

Her statement made Emiko giggle nervously while Sage and Aldis shifted uncomfortably. Hane looked nothing but endlessly calm, yet that did nothing to soothe Nieve's nerves. She sat down between Emi and Sage, reaching out to finally touch the sentient shard of crystal.

CHAPTER 22

LANI

Acolyte (hand mark), Citrine

It was not my intention to cause such discord.> The voice inside Lani's mind was resonant and melodic, like the hum of a bell after it had been rung. <I am not used to speaking to so many at one time, and without my true form, my capability of speech is limited. I have come to comprehend the design of the structure we are all within, and thus, I understand your reticence to converse with me.>

Lani glanced over at Nieve, her expression sour as she held herself as far away from the crystal shard as possible while still touching it.

"What are you?" Nieve demanded to know. "How did you compel Lani to pick you up at the start?"

Lani bristled but pinched her lips shut to hold back a protest. She hadn't been compelled at all; she'd only thought the shard a curiosity, then later a possible treasure. There had been no nefarious act that compelled her to pick up the crystal shard.

<I did nothing to your companion,> the voice of the crystal replied. <It was her choice alone that has brought me here. I have no power as I am right now, and without my full form or power, my consciousness falls dormant for long stretches of time. I thought myself to be dreaming as this human carried me, and I am only awake now from the shock of the mana density contained within this water.>

"I'm sorry to ask you to repeat yourself," Lani said gently. "But would you mind starting over from the beginning?"

<Not at all,> the crystal responded in its melodic hum. <I am a gateway crystal. Or I was when I was whole. The form you see before you is only a piece of my true self, delivered here through great misfortune.>

"Dramatic," Nieve muttered under her breath. Lani shot a glare over at her. She made a face but pressed her lips together tightly in an effort to keep quiet.

"Is there some name we can call you?" Hane asked. "Or a way you prefer to be addressed?"

<I have never spent much time in the presence of humans, save for the one who brought me to this place,> the crystal intoned. <I do not care for any form of address that includes gender, as I have none. As for my name, it is not one any human has ever been able to speak, but I shall attempt it for you.>

Lani heard the sound with her whole body: an intense rhythm that made her heart thrum, clear resonant tones that made her ears sing, a vibration she felt deep in her bones. It wasn't a name so much as a song, but one Lani couldn't replicate with an entire orchestra at her disposal.

"I'm sorry," Emi said once the sound ended. "Can you repeat that once more?"

Lani felt the vibrations of the sound through her teeth, tickling her sinuses and making her ears itch.

"You're right, we can't say that," Emi continued, as if she hadn't realized that the first time. "But if you're not offended, we can try to come up with a nickname based on the sound of your name. It sounds like bells to me. Or maybe chimes?"

"Chime?" Hane tried, cocking their head to the side as they tried it out. "Would that be an acceptable nickname for you?"

<I suppose that if you wish to call me something, that is acceptable,> the crystal replied. <I have known other gateway crystals to take human names. While interacting with humans, I suppose it is the only proper thing to do.>

Nieve grunted as she shifted, likely holding back a comment of how "Chime" wasn't actually a human name. She caught Lani's glare and fell still again.

"Chime was just telling me how they came to be here," Lani explained to the others. She'd heard only part of the story before she'd been interrupted and forced to prove that the helpless crystal shard hadn't placed her under a compulsion. "They said they need our help."

<Yes,> Chime agreed. <I was brought here against my will and wish only to return to my shrine, but I cannot do so without the other pieces of myself. I am not able to move on my own or use the magic of the stars in this weakened state. But once I am whole again and returned to my shrine, I will have the power to grant boons to any who aid me in this time of need.>

Lani saw interest pique on the faces of her teammates at the mention of a reward. Aldis leaned in closer, his breath quickening in a way that reminded Lani of someone watching a pair of dice roll on a table. Hane's eyes sharpened as if considering whether the unknown task would be worth it. Even Nieve lifted her eyebrows in interest, though Lani read caution on her features: Nieve would be a hard sell on anything that didn't involve climbing higher within the Tortoise Spire. Sage seemed more focused on a scholarly study of the crystal, removing his hand from the shard, then touching it again, as if testing the range of Chime's "speech," but then Sage always had the lowest interest in treasure unless it was interesting in some way. Emi seemed eager, though.

"How can we help you?" Emi asked. "And how did you get here? I've never heard of a gateway crystal being moved before. Aren't the crystals in the Unclaimed Lands super powerful?"

The last question she addressed to the team rather than Chime. A few looks were exchanged, and then everyone turned to Sage.

"Er, I suppose it depends on the crystal?" Sage shrugged. "I've only ever seen the Water Temple from a distance; I've never gone to a shrine in the Unclaimed Lands. I know a little about crystal marks but only what I've read in books."

"The crystals were the main way to earn magic before the goddess created the spires, right?" Aldis confirmed. That sounded right to Lani, but then again, she'd never been particularly studious when it came to ancient history. "I haven't met too many people willing to venture into the wilds when going to a spire for a Judgment is so easy."

<It is true that fewer and fewer humans have come to visit my shrine of late,> Chime agreed in their emotionless voice. <I am afraid the story of how I came to be here and what I require will take some time to tell. I wish to be respectful of your short life spans, but it may take some time to tell my tale and answer all your questions.>

Lani glanced around the group, meeting each person's eyes, reading both doubt and interest in each of them.

"We have a little time right now," Lani said firmly. "At least until Emi's and Nieve's shrouds recover. I intend to sit here and listen to Chime, but anyone who wants to walk away is welcome to leave right now."

Sage tested that by withdrawing his hand, then slowly reaching out to touch the crystal shard again. He frowned, then flicked his hazel eyes up to meet Lani's. "I'm interested enough to listen, but I won't make any promises past that."

"I want to help," Emi insisted. "This sounds like a story I'd like to be a part of."

"What kind of reward would we get for helping?" Aldis asked eagerly. "Do we get to choose our rewards? What about favors? Can you grant those as well?"

"I wouldn't mind something that could help me climb the spire faster," Nieve admitted, folding her legs into a more comfortable seated position. "I'll listen, but only because there's nothing better to do right now, anyway."

"I think the time frame it takes for Emiko's and Nieve's shrouds to recover is an acceptable amount of time to listen to Chime and decide if there is something we can do to help them," Hane said, also settling in. "Though like Sage, I will promise nothing until I hear more of what needs to be done."

"So no one's backing out?" Lani confirmed, looking around the circle again. Nieve still looked doubtful, but her shrug combined with the way she shifted closer to the crystal seemed to indicate her willingness. Lani nodded and addressed the crystal shard once more. "Please tell us how we can help you, Chime."

<I thank you for your consideration,> Chime intoned in their bell-like voice. <You already understand that I am not of this spire, nor am I of your goddess. I am from before. Long before. Before I became what you see now, I was a gateway crystal within my own shrine, hidden in the deepest wilds. My purpose was to create trials for other beings to challenge within my shrine and grant those who passed my trials a boon of their choice. I do not judge the passage of time well, but I have been testing people and granting such boons since long before your goddess raised the spires that now grant the ability to use magic. Over time, the frequency of humans visiting my shrine lessened. It came to be that administering a trial was a rare and unexpected event, one that I . . . enjoyed.>

Lani sensed hesitation in the crystal's words. Was joy not something the crystal was used to experiencing? Or had it merely struggled with the word?

<Some time ago, I have no bearings to say as to how long ago this transpired, a challenger passed all of my trials and stood before me to receive my boon. The request was a simple one, but one I was unable to grant. You see, my shrine was once home to a powerful amulet, one associated with a sword of tremendous power, but that prize had been claimed long before, so I did not have the amulet that was sought. The challenger then asked for the sword of great power, or any sword with the ability to create a spirit bond with its wielder, but again, I had no such prize in my possession to give. It felt . . . unfulfilling to be unable to give the powerful challenger that which had been rightfully earned by completing my trial.>

"What kind of trial was it?" Emi asked, eyes wide as she listened to Chime's story. "Do you know what attunements they had? Or how strong they were?"

<I am sure I knew the answers to those questions once, but this form does not recall those memories.> A low, long tone made the backs of Lani's eyes sting. The crystal didn't speak with emotional inflection, but somehow the notes still sounded hauntingly sad. <Perhaps if I were reunited with more of my pieces—but that is a part of the story I will come to in time. When I again denied the challenger the desired reward, I was asked what magical abilities I might bestow by means of a bond.>

"I've read about crystal marks and gateway crystal bonds like that." Sage touched the side of his glasses, a habit he had when attempting to recall something he had studied. "Even after the spires began granting Judgments and sharing the gift of the goddess's magic, climbers could still visit the shrines in the Unclaimed Lands for additional spells, or even weapons and climbing gear they could use inside the spires. Supposedly, the shrines were easier with even a low-ranked attunement than challenging the spires without proper gear."

"Shrine challenges are all individual challenges, aren't they?" Aldis asked, sounding uncertain. "Some attunements just work better as part of a team, so I can see how that fell off."

"It depends on the challenge," Sage replied. "I hear the bigger temples, like the Water Temple, allow six-person teams, just like the spires."

"But the temples and shrines have been around for longer than humans could earn attunements," Hane put in. "Meaning magic isn't necessary to complete a gateway crystal's challenge."

<Precisely,> the crystal shard intoned. <And while the principal attributes being tested do not change, the scale of the challenge can be altered. For a human with no magic and limited armor or weaponry, I would present a slightly simpler challenge. For those with considerable power and resources, such as the last human to attempt my trials, I would increase the complexity and duration of my challenge. In order to create a proper challenge, I created a labyrinth requiring great skill and ingenuity to overcome. At the end of it all, we were both quite frustrated that I did not possess any of the desired rewards.>

"I bet if they were powerful, they didn't like finding out their efforts were for nothing," Emiko guessed drily.

<No,> the crystal shard agreed. <But as I explained that my original boons were gifts of magic that harkened to my own powers, they became intrigued once more. After a great deal of questions, the challenger requested that I grant a spell mark linked to my source dominion: the dominion of sound."

Lani felt her stomach twist: she sensed that the crystal was nearing the crux of its story.

"Would that be like a Spellsinger?" Emiko asked, looking over at Sage. "They use sound magic, right?"

"Yes, but I've never met a Spellsinger, so I'm uncertain how their magic works." Sage looked over at Nieve. "Have you ever dueled one?"

"No. Or at least, if I did they didn't use sound as part of their attack." Nieve shrugged. "I don't think it's used as a combat attunement."

<The applications of sound manipulation are limitless,> Chime intoned, the notes stringing together in a way that evoked feelings of resentment to Lani's ear. <The challenger seemed to understand this intrinsically. They stayed at my shrine for a time, learning the nuances of sound magic and crafting spells in ways that interacted with the magic of your goddess. This human seemed quite gifted: innovative in ways I rarely associate with beings who attempt my challenges. And perhaps I granted access to more of my magic than was wise; I believe I felt chagrined for not being able to grant that which was most desired and wished to make up for it. Few humans have appreciated the magic that is sound as well as they, and I was joyful that someone so strong was able to understand the depths of that magic. And in that, my pride proved my downfall.>

"That's how you were changed, isn't it?" Lani asked bluntly, cold horror gripping her guts. "That challenger used your power against you."

Emiko gasped. Hane dipped their head almost imperceptibly. Sage shifted uncomfortably, but both Nieve and Aldis looked strangely contemplative. Lani shifted her attention back to the crystal.

<It should not have been possible,> the crystal shard said, something in its mental voice affecting an incredulous tone. <My form and power were ancient. My will to exist had always been greater than that of any human, monster, or new-come god. I should have been unyielding, and yet, all I can recall is assisting with the creation of a spell, and the next moment I felt such a rending of my self and my spirit that I found myself outside the crystal that was my body. I remember attempting to return, but somehow I found myself inside a new vessel, a crystalline bladed sword that the interloper carried. I was so disoriented that I lost myself in blackness for a time, perhaps what humans would call unconsciousness. When I came back to myself, I found I was no longer within my shrine, but somewhere new, somewhere I had never been before, trapped within the void space linked to the crystal-bladed sword. I begged to be released, to let me go back to the crystal that served as my vessel, but the human refused. Through our bond, they imbued the crystal-bladed sword with sound magic, even against my will. I was to serve as the base of the new sacred sword, a sword of intelligence and power. They told me that I was . . . better that way.>

The hand cupping the sliver of crystal began to tremble; Lani braced her wrist with her other hand, only to find that it, too, was shaking. How dare this person inflict their desires upon another person? What gave them the right to rip a being's sentience out of their vessel—their body—and then claim to have improved them? Why did humans insist on forcing others to change themselves into what they felt was "right," or "useful"? What would it take for people to learn that what was "right" for one was not "right" for all?

Her gaze fixed on Aldis as she asked herself those questions. She caught it as Aldis's eyes flicked up to meet hers, then abruptly skittered away.

"Is that—" Emi stopped herself with a sniffle. "Does that mean the challenger was a Soulblade? If they were able to bind a being to a weapon?"

"I don't think so," Sage said, frowning studiously. "Soulblades have to honor the contracts they make with other entities. If they don't, the entity can just leave. By Chime's story, that doesn't seem to be the case."

"You're right," Lani confirmed. "No being can be forced into a contract. Not normally, anyway."

<I do not know how it was done,> Chime said with morose, tuneless notes. <I only know that I hated that existence. I was powerless on my own, forced to use my powers at the wielder's command, to wake when ordered, and wait in darkness when I had no use. My power was perverted into that hateful spell in order to capture more innocent beings into becoming weapons. I felt . . . violated.>

Lani tasted blood in her mouth. It took longer than it should have to realize she'd bitten her lower lip until it bled. She moved to heal it, then stopped herself: she would probably only bite it open again.

Emi looked similarly affected as she turned her face into Nieve's shoulder, scrubbing her cheeks against the worn leather of Nieve's sleeve. Nieve patted Emi on the knee consolingly, her eyes still sharp and critical. No doubt she was still wondering what Chime wanted of them; Lani was still waiting on that part of the story, too.

"What happened next?" Aldis asked, seemingly entranced as if the crystal shard's story were an epic bard's tale.

<We traveled for a time,> Chime continued. <With the missing spaces within my memory, I cannot say as to how long, but we spent much time inside these spires. Not just this one, but others like it. I watched helplessly as my magic was twisted into something ugly, something repulsive. I was afraid that if I remained a captive, I would become corrupted, twisted, and ugly, too. So I did the only thing I could do. I began to . . . break myself.>

"Break off pieces of the sword?" Nieve clarified, squinting at the shard at the end of her fingertip. "Is that what this is? A piece of the crystal blade?"

"But breaking an item isn't enough to harm a spirit bonded to it," Sage protested. "Unless it's something specifically meant to protect the entity, like a reliquary."

<It was not an easy process,> Chime admitted, the tolls within Lani's mind softer, as if they didn't wish to speak of this. <I had to wait until my power was invoked so I could bind a portion of my consciousness inside the piece I broke away. The pain was . . . unimaginable. But I could not remain a part of coercing innocent spirits and beings into objects of power, so I kept on breaking off pieces of myself until the whole of my being was able to leave the sword and dwell inside the broken pieces, such as the one you see before you.>

"So you've just been . . . waiting?" Emi asked, her face pinched, eyes watery. "How could you know anyone would ever find you?"

<I did not know,> Chime replied. <I only hoped. But even the endless waiting and hoping is preferable to being put to a corrupted use. I thought one day someone might find me and restore me to my rightful shrine. I decided that anyone kind enough to help me must truly be worthy of any gift I have to bestow.>

"About those gifts—" Aldis started, but Nieve spoke over him, cutting him off.

"Is that all we need to do?" Nieve asked. "Just follow your directions to your shrine and drop you off there? Or do we have to fight our way through a challenge to arrive at the gateway crystal?"

<Without me there to control it, my shrine is little more than an empty husk,> Chime explained. <No challenges will occur, save for any beings that may have come to inhabit the space while I have been absent. But unfortunately, it is not so easy as simply taking this piece of me back to my shrine. There isn't enough of me here to use the magic required to move from this vessel back into my original body.>

"You need us to find your missing pieces," Hane guessed. "Other shards broken off the same sword."

<Yes,> the crystal shard agreed as the humans exchanged grimaces around the story circle. <Only when my fragmented consciousness is complete again will I be able to use enough power to transfer myself from these broken bits into my former vessel. Any who aid me in returning to my true form will be granted the boon of their choosing, just as if they had triumphed over the challenges of my shrine.>

"We need to—" Emi was waved into silence by Sage, his lips pressed together in a thin, grim line.

"Your other pieces," Sage started, his tone tight. "Where would we look for them? Are they here, in the Tortoise Spire?"

<No,> Chime intoned. <My other pieces were all broken off in various structures like this one, but no more pieces of myself reside here. I can sense the pieces of my fragmented consciousness, and I can direct you to one if one is close. But there is no more of me here in this place.>

"Other spires," Sage said grimly, looking around the group. "That's not an easy trip. It's costly to climb other spires, even in nations friendly to Dalenos. And some spires are as good as closed without going through proper channels. I'm not certain this is something we can do."

"I'm not certain it's something we *should* do," Nieve countered. "I mean, a reward would be great, but even if we could get into every single other spire on Kaldwyn and find pieces as tiny as this one, it would take way too much time away from climbing. I'm sorry, but I'm not interested."

"How can you say that?" Emi asked tearfully. "All they want to do is go back to their home. We have to help them!"

"It isn't a question of wanting to help," Hane said gently. "It's about being able to help. Even with the means to travel and the ability to enter the other spires, the paths within the spires are variable. How would you reach the right floor, or navigate to the correct room? This task is too big for one team."

"Not for this team," Aldis argued. "My doorway trick should work in any spire. We have the ability to choose where we go once we're inside a spire. And Sage can keep us on track and out of trouble, right, Sage?"

"Well." Sage hedged, touching his glasses. "My glasses are only enchanted to work within the Tortoise Spire. I wouldn't be as much help anywhere else. My Foresight spell would still warn me before anything goes tragically wrong, but I wouldn't be able to See the parameters and rewards of challenges the way I do here." His shrug looked like a surrender. "I'd like to help, but I agree with Nieve and Hane. That doesn't mean we do nothing: we can always turn Chime over to the Soaring Wings and let them assemble teams to find the missing pieces in the other spires. They'll have the easiest time getting through bureaucratic barricades and successfully navigating the spires."

Emi worried her lower lip, shrugging her shoulders up to her ears. "I guess that's one way to help them. It's just . . . I want to do more. I want to be there to say 'welcome home' when Chime returns to their shrine."

"I'm helping them," Lani said determinedly, meeting Emi's eyes first, then Sage's, then finally Nieve's. A muscle ticced over Nieve's jaw before she looked away, a sour look to her pinched lips. "I'll petition the government and the Soaring Wings for help, but I am going to be part of the team that finds Chime's missing pieces, and I am going to restore them back to their shrine. I'm going to do it because a human inflicted this horrific wrong on Chime, forcing them to be something they didn't want to be, something that made them dislike themself so much that they deliberately tore away parts of their body and their mind to escape it. I'm going to help restore Chime back to their original form because evil that was wrought by a human should be undone by a human." Her gaze lingered on Aldis's before he turned away, shamefaced. "Everyone deserves the right to be themself. No matter what others try to force them to be."

Aldis wasn't the only one who averted his gaze at that pronouncement. It seemed Lani wasn't the only one thinking of her gambling habit and how people seemed determined to "fix" her when all she wanted was to enjoy her free time. Hane alone seemed unaffected, canting their head to one side as they considered something.

"How long ago did all of this happen?" Hane asked delicately. "An estimate will suffice. For instance, a few months ago to several hundred years ago. It makes a great deal of difference to those of us with limited life spans."

<Truly, I cannot say,> Chime replied in clear, resonant tones. <My perception of time continues to slip, especially when I am lost in the darkness. Sometimes it seems as though this all happened many lifetimes ago, and other days it is as fresh as if it happened scant moments ago. I am too often lost in dreams to accurately answer such a question.>

"Are there any other ways to return you to your original vessel?" Hane continued. "Perhaps an Enchanter or someone similarly attuned could forge a bond between this sliver of consciousness and the original gateway crystal's form."

<Even if that were to work, my magic is bound to these broken shards,> Chime pointed out. <Without all my pieces, any magic I had would be thin. Diluted. And my memories would remain lost to me. I wish to be whole in both physical form and spirit.>

"I understand," Hane said sympathetically. "But I feel I must point out a further concern in collecting your missing pieces: the wielder of the crystal-bladed sword must surely have realized that their sentient weapon is no longer sentient. Someone with enough power to forcibly bind the spirit of a gateway crystal would be a formidable opponent to meet inside a spire."

"But by the crystal's—sorry." Aldis rubbed his nose with his free hand. "By Chime's own admission, this all could have occurred hundreds of years ago. We're not likely to run into anyone bearing a crystal-bladed sword still searching for its broken pieces. By the goddess, that sword has likely been added to some spire's lost-treasure repository by now, if not handed down to descendants."

"They wouldn't know the blade had lost its spirit until they tried to call on Chime's power," Nieve pointed out. "They probably ran into a challenge they couldn't defeat without Chime's magic and died."

"Does that mean you're going to help?" Emi asked her hopefully.

"No," Nieve said with a snort. "If anything, that makes me less interested in helping. A strong opponent is something I can get excited about."

<I do not know whether the wielder of the crystal-bladed sword still lives,> Chime informed them. <But if they do, they would be easily identified by the crystal mark I placed on their left hand.>

An image appeared inside Lani's mind, startling her before she could focus on it. It certainly looked distinct from the attunement marks she had seen before, but she was by no means an expert. Knowing the mark was on the villain's left hand was more telling than the mark itself just then. By the way Emi shook her head and by Nieve's drawn brow, Lani guessed her teammates had seen the same image she had.

"Wait, wait, let me write that down," Sage begged, pulling his hand away from the crystal shard to pat his pockets for some paper and a pencil. When he found them, he touched the shard again and requested to see the image once more. A moment later, he sketched the crystal mark on a piece of paper, holding it out so the others could verify he'd gotten it right.

"Okay, look," Nieve said as Sage tucked the scrap of paper inside his dueling vest. "I agree it would be very noble of us to set aside our careers and help Chime find all their missing pieces so they can go home again, but we need to be realistic. We don't have the funds or resources to visit all the spires, and we have no guarantee that the boons they can grant would make up for the possible years we'd miss on climbing this spire. I say we bring Chime out of the spire with us and give them to the Soaring Wings so they can find the missing pieces and collect the reward."

"You can do whatever you want, Nieve, but I'm going to help look for Chime's missing pieces, even if that means joining a Soaring Wings climber team." Lani tightened her grip around the crystal shard. "We all know you want to make it to the top of the spire, so if that's your objection, why not just say it?"

Nieve's face went hard, a muscle ticcing over her jaw. Lani hadn't meant to snap, not really, but anyone could see that reassembling Chime was a far more achievable goal than actually reaching the top of a spire. More achievable, and more worthy than any selfish wish.

"Have you considered that by reaching the top of a spire, you could just ask Selys to make the crystal whole again, restore their former power, and send them right back to their shrine?" Nieve asked, her temper barely withheld. "We could actually do it, Lani. We could make it to the top if we keep using Aldis's trick on the doors and Sage's Sight to find floor keys. We might even make it to the top faster than we could travel to all the spires, even if we had the money for such a trip. I'm not saying we shouldn't help, I'm saying there are different ways to help."

"Have you considered that there may be easier spires to climb?" Lani challenged her. "Tortoise Spire is said to have the slowest progression among all the other spires. This could be an opportunity for you to find a more suitable spire to climb—you know it doesn't matter which one you get to the top of, right? Any one of them will grant your wish." *If that part of the legend is even true*, Lani thought but didn't say out loud. While she and Nieve generally got along well, neither of them liked having her beliefs questioned.

"This isn't a simple matter of picking a new spire to climb and relocating the team there," Nieve argued. "You're talking about days or weeks of travel, of researching and studying new spire challenges, and then we have to actually find more shards that look like this one"—Nieve gestured to the splinter-thin, nearly see-through crystal shard—"and then do it all over again. How are we even supposed to get to these crystal pieces? It's not like there are straight paths through the spires. Even if we find a way to enter on the correct floor—which will be immensely expensive if we're buying gate keys—that doesn't necessarily mean our paths are going to intersect with the crystal piece."

"As you already pointed out, we have the perfect system for that." Lani looked pointedly over at Aldis and Sage. "We can forge our own path through the spires if need be. Look, Nieve, if you don't want to help, then that's fine. I know you have your own reasons for climbing, but I'm doing this." Lani's hands trembled beneath the crystal. "Even if it means I have to assemble a whole new team in every nation, I'm doing this."

"You won't have to." That surprisingly assured statement came from Hane. They shrugged nonchalantly as all eyes turned on them. "I have no reason to stay in Dalenos, and I've long thought I'd enjoy challenging other spires. If you're going on this journey, I would be happy to accompany you."

"I can talk to my family about sponsoring us," Emi offered meekly. "We might have to agree to certain stipulations—like hiring on an Emerald guide for protection, or letting my family choose a portion of the recovered treasures. But I'm sure they would cover travel fees and accommodations, at least."

"Emi." Lani felt a bubble of warmth bloom in her chest and lodge itself in her throat, making it hard to swallow or speak. "That would be a tremendous relief. I would honor any agreement your family would make with me."

"But you have to bring me along, too," Emi said stubbornly, her jaw set. "I want to help Chime, but I also want to be there for you, Lani. And whoever else decides to join us."

That last was spoken almost like a question. Lani looked up in time to see Sage and Nieve exchanging a wordless glance, both of their expressions tightly grim. A small cough from Aldis drew her attention away from their silent exchange.

"I'm interested in joining, if it's an open offer." Aldis managed to look both hesitant and determined at the same time. "I know we didn't exactly get off to the best start, Lani, and I accept the fault of that. But my skills and my travel specialization are made for a quest like this one, and I do believe I'd be an asset in navigating the spires to find Chime's missing pieces." A small pause, then a grimace: "Except the Serpent Spire. I can't be of any help to you anywhere in Valia."

"I welcome your assistance, Aldis." Lani nodded cordially. "You're right: it will be much easier to move through spires using your expertise in manipulating doorway portals." She would have placed a large wager on the boon being the determining factor to Aldis's offer of help, but his reason didn't matter as much as his skillset did. It did her no good to question his motive.

The support from Emi, Hane, and Aldis gave Lani hope, but there was something else she needed: companions she could trust to be stalwart and steady when the tides of battle turned against them. Companions who didn't lose their focus or determination in the face of overwhelming odds. Companions who had been through the fire with her and come through stronger on the other side.

She needed Nieve and Sage.

But as she looked from one to the other, it seemed less and less likely either one would agree.

"I really want to help, Lani," Sage said, his eyes beseeching. "I just think there may be better ways to help. It would be different if we were looking for these pieces all within the Tortoise Spire. We know the Tortoise Spire, we know what to expect, and we know we'll be safe after we leave the spire, no matter what condition we're in. And maybe that's true of the other spires, but we can't know that for sure. You really want to go to Edria? To East Edria?" Sage shook his head. "We don't speak the language, we'd have to convert our currency, we'd have to trust that the storage depository isn't ripping us off, and I just . . . I think there are teams better suited to this type of thing than we are."

"Sage is right," Nieve declared in a rare show of solidarity with the Seer. "Even if we had the funds to travel and hire translators and used all the best resources, we still have no guarantee that we'd find even one of these shards. Who knows how long *this* shard waited to be found? Oh, and what happens if one of their pieces *was* found by a climber team, but they never thought to dunk it in a mana fountain and wake it up? There are way too many variables, Lani. We'd miss out on *years* of climbing with no guarantee that we'd even find all the pieces, never mind earn Chime's promised boon."

"What if Chime could grant your wish, Nieve?" It was a dirty play, like a card hidden up her sleeve, but Lani couldn't afford to lose this hand. Since the beginning, Nieve had climbed for a singular purpose: to make a wish of the goddess. Surely something as powerful as a gateway crystal could grant her whatever it was that made her risk her life on climb after climb within the spire. "You could ask them, you know. Tell them your wish and see if it's possible."

"No." Nieve's tight-lipped refusal made Lani blink in surprise. "I'm sure it couldn't give me what I want, and even if it could, it means nothing without reaching the top of a spire."

That was more than Lani had ever learned about Nieve's wish to date. She saw curiosity on both Emi's and Aldis's faces but didn't pursue the subject any further: she knew a closed door when she saw one.

Lani heaved a sigh and glanced over at Sage one last time. "Are you sure you won't help us? We can do it without you, but you're always so knowledge-able about runes and monsters, and your Sight keeps us safe."

"Lani . . ." Sage's eyebrows pinched together, emotions warring on his face. "Can we just—can we talk about this some more? Maybe after the climb, or even just a little later on? This is a huge decision and I think maybe we all need some time to consider it before making a decision."

Lani felt her heart sink, her gaze dropping to the crystal shard cupped in her hands. "You're probably right about not rushing into this, but . . . I just can't help but think of Chime being forced into a form they never asked for, being put to a use that imprisoned other beings against their will, and then *breaking* themself to escape . . . I want to restore them as soon as possible. I want this nightmare of a life to be over for them. Wouldn't you?"

Sage looked to be wavering, his lower lip pinched between his teeth, his eyes dropping to the crystal shard.

Nieve shifted her seat, the bottom of her boot scraping loudly against the tiles. "Look, we at least have until the end of the climb to think about it.

As Chime said, there aren't any other pieces inside the Tortoise Spire and we've barely gotten started here. There's nothing we can do until after we ring out."

"I was actually thinking of stopping here," Lani admitted. It hadn't even occurred to her to finish the climb: Chime's plight came before everything, even Lani's desire to collect more treasure to feed her gambling habit. For now, at least. She wouldn't be able to stop herself from visiting foreign casinos, where the card dealers wouldn't know her tells or her bluffs. "I want to start making plans for the journey. Figuring out a route, travel costs, permissions for climbing other spires. I don't want to wait, Nieve. I want to get started right away."

"We said we were reaching the twentieth floor or higher," Nieve reminded her in a tight voice. "We already used our gate key; if you leave now, this whole climb will be for nothing."

"I'm against forcing anyone to climb who no longer wants to," Hane put in. "But I actually do agree with Nieve on this. It's a waste to cut a climb short, especially without any means of returning to the same floor or higher. Chime, would you begrudge us a little time to finish up here before assisting you?"

<Time is of little meaning to me, especially as I am.> Was Lani imagining it, or did Chime's tones sound resigned? <I appreciate your willingness to aid me, whether through direct or indirect means. I am currently at your mercy, so if you ask for time I have no choice but to grant it. I feel I must warn you that if I lose consciousness again, you may have to awaken me in a similar method to this mana-water. And the longer I am away from areas of high mana concentration, the weaker I will be. I may not even be able to speak to you like this once we leave this place.>

Lani pressed her lips together, barely holding herself back from chastising her teammates. Couldn't they see that Chime was suffering? Were they heartless not to hear those pleading tones, even as the shattered crystal granted them their request? How could any of them even consider continuing at a time like this?

But as she looked around at her seated teammates, she saw that they understood. From Emi's trembling lower lip to Nieve's sharply averted gaze. They heard it. They understood. Perhaps all they needed was a little time to make the right decision.

"Fine," Lani said with a sigh. "We'll continue. But just until we find another gate key, okay? That way, anyone who chooses to stay has the means to continue climbing. Is that acceptable?" Sage nodded, but Nieve wouldn't meet Lani's eyes. "Nieve?"

"Fine," Nieve grumbled. "We find a gate key first. And the treasure distribution is the same as always: you don't get to take more to help fund your travel."

"I agree to those terms." Delicately, Lani drew Chime away from the outstretched hands of her companions, cradling the shard close to her heart. "Are we prepared to move on? I can have the treasure packed and ready to send back in the time it would take to break camp."

"Wait, please, I haven't eaten yet," Sage begged, one hand over his stomach.

"I don't think my shroud's at full strength just yet," Nieve added, stretching before pushing herself up to standing. "I think all the food's gone cold by now, though."

"It's a simple matter of heating it back up," Aldis assured her. "My enchanted hot plate has different settings, so you can warm a cup of tea instead of a full kettle."

"Oh, good! I wanted to try the soup." Emi bounced to her feet, then clasped Sage's hand, pulling him up. "You have to try Aldis's tea! It's so good!"

Hane lingered even after Emi, Sage, Nieve and Aldis moved away to return to the makeshift campsite and the shared offerings of food. They appeared to be studying Lani's face, making her fear that a deep question might be forthcoming. Instead, all they asked was: "Will you come eat?"

"In a minute," Lani promised, relieved it wasn't anything personal or provocative. "I have a few more questions for Chime."

Hane nodded once and turned away, their boots silent over the floor tiles as they followed the others over to the food. Lani smiled fondly at all of them before lowering her gaze to the slim sliver of crystal held clasped between her hands.

Can you hear me when I speak to you like this? Lani asked, thinking the words "loudly" inside her head.

<Yes,> Chime replied promptly, sending a small thrill through Lani. <Though your voice sounds weaker to me than before. I think more than one voice like this would become distorted, but for one voice, this works well.>

Perfect! That meant they could speak privately. Not that Lani wanted to hide anything from her team, but what she had to say felt personal.

I'm sorry about before, Lani thought, thinking shamefully about how she'd toyed with Chime throughout the climb, even dropping them back at the bath. *I've been treating you like an object. I thought you were a means to a treasure and I intended to use you. I'm so sorry; I want you to know that I regret my actions.*

<It is not surprising,> the crystal assured her. <This form hardly evokes a sense of personhood. I can hardly blame you for thinking me nothing more

than an oddity. In fact, I am quite grateful that you kept hold of me, even when I was silent. And I greatly appreciate your support of me and my request. I sense it will be quite an undertaking, though I admit I do not understand all the logistics that were discussed.>

I'm sorry this happened to you, Lani told them, meaning everything that had led Chime to this end. *It wasn't fair to you. That human shouldn't have been able to do what they did. If they're still alive, I hope they're paying for it.*

<I hope one day to understand what it was that was done to me,> Chime admitted. <If only to warn others so they might resist. I cannot stand the thought of this being done to any other beings.>

Lani shuddered: it was horrifying to think someone might be searching the Unclaimed Lands, converting sentient crystals into unwilling servitude. *But you said they used the magic you gave them, right? Even if they're alive, they can't use that magic anymore, can they?*

She sensed an edge of hesitation before the crystal shard replied. <Through me, that human was able to wield the full extent of my powers, even despite my unwillingness to aid their quest. Since breaking free of the sword, that human would no longer have access to my breadth of power, but the crystal mark could still be used to cast spells associated with the dominion of sound.>

That was both good and bad. This villain—whoever they were—hadn't needed Chime's full power to trap and bind them in the first place, so it was feasible it could be done again. Lani preferred to think that the shrine's challenger was already dead, possibly from attempting a fight they couldn't hope to win without Chime's powers. It seemed justified, if not entirely probable.

What was your shrine like? Lani asked, changing the subject to something more pleasant. *Do you know where you were located in the Unclaimed Lands?*

<My shrine was my home. To me, it was comfortable, though I am sure those who challenged my trials would not say it was so.> Lani sensed a hint of pride from Chime. <I could find it again, much in the same way that I can find my missing pieces, but I have no way to describe to you where it was located. Prior to my abduction, I had little knowledge of the world outside my shrine. In a way, I could almost appreciate my indenture, as it has given me new experiences to draw upon in creating obstacles for challengers to overcome. But even so, I wish it had not come to pass.>

I think I understand you, Lani thought back. She couldn't help but look over at her friends and teammates, clustered around the hot plate, jostling each other as they fought for food, playfully teasing and taunting each other. Emi was trying to get Hane to eat another cookie, despite their polite declination. Aldis was pouring out portions of tea while Sage and Nieve bickered over a piece of jerky. *I love my friends, but there's . . . something about me they'd like to change. I know their intentions are good, but I still wish they could just accept that part of me and leave it alone.*

<That would be a difficult boon to grant,> Chime replied. <My boons are not designed to affect anyone other than the challenger who earns them.>

Oh, no, I didn't mean to make that sound like a request. Asking for such a thing would be just as bad as one of them asking me to give up gambling. Watching her team through her eyelashes, Lani added: *I guess I am hoping they'll make a connection between their offer to "help" me and what that villain did to you, but I think if I can convince them to help me collect your pieces, that will be good enough.*

<I surely appreciate the assistance that you offer.> The shard's tone didn't change or offer any inflection, but Lani felt a rush of gratitude all the same. <I can't entirely understand the burden of what I am asking you to do. I can only hope my boons will suffice as repayment.>

No need to worry about that. I would have been willing to help for no reward at all.

Although, visiting a few new casinos where the staff and loan officers didn't know her face had a great deal of appeal in addition to climbing different spires.

"Hey." Lani jumped at the closeness of the voice. She looked up from Chime, surprised to see Aldis standing in front of her. "We've started cooking up some of the rations. I know we're planning to ring out soon, but I noticed you didn't eat earlier."

He held out a bit of toasted flatbread wrapped in a handkerchief. It had been folded over twice and heated up to melt cheese inside it. Upon closer inspection, Lani could see fish flakes and bits of pepper and mushrooms cut up into it as well.

"Thank you." She shifted Chime into one hand to accept the offered food. "You didn't have to bring it over. I would have eaten before we moved on."

"Yes, well." Aldis shuffled anxiously. "I felt I owed you for our . . . misunderstanding. And for saving me from the shiuni, too. It was clever of you to think of using a life spell that way."

"Oh, that." Lani chuckled. "I was just paying you back for teleporting that lahava that almost ate my face in the first room."

"Did I do that? Doesn't sound like me." Aldis shrugged, half a smile on his face. Lani understood: when combat got intense, it was sometimes easy to forget your own heroisms. "Anyway, I just thought . . . Well, sorry. About how things started between us. I just . . . wanted to be helpful."

"I understand your intention, but I'm fine as I am," Lani said, injecting a hint of insistence into her voice.

"I see that now." Aldis shrugged, shuffling back a step. "I'll try not to make such assumptions in the future."

That was a little better than the apology was. Lani decided to accept it. "Thank you, Aldis. And thank you for the snack."

He made a gesture like an offhanded salute before walking back to join the others around the hot plate. Lani found herself watching as Sage and Nieve battled over what had to be the last of Emiko's cookies. Sage threatened to crumble it if Nieve tried taking it by force. In the end, Emi bit it out of Sage's hand, looking immensely pleased with herself as Sage and Nieve cried foul. Aldis told them he had more fruit if any of them needed it, and Hane looked on with silent interest, something shadowed in their eyes.

<You have a good team,> Chime murmured inside Lani's mind.

Lani smiled. *The best.*

CHAPTER 23

HANE

Wavewalker (leg mark), Citrine

Emi, how's your shroud?" Nieve asked, interlocking her fingers and cracking her knuckles. The shared food pouches in the middle of the seated circle were crumpled and empty-looking, the hot plate and kettle long gone cold.

Emiko whispered something rapid under her breath, no doubt testing her shroud with a spell. She beamed when she looked up. "It feels stronger than ever! I think I like being Citrine."

Nieve chuckled, tugging on one of Emiko's hair buns as she stood up and stretched. "I feel like I can take a hit or two, too. I hope we can find a spire guardian ready to lose a fight."

Hane picked their head up from where it rested on their knees. They'd caught a quick power nap after eating a few bites of shared food, but they'd been awake for a while, simply listening to the others talk. It seemed prudent to be aware of the team's dynamic, since Hane might be climbing with a few of them for a while. Normally climbs that ended short vexed them, but they found they didn't mind so much this time. Finally having a reason to travel and visit other spires was a worthy ambition, and the thought of navigating foreign spires to find slivers of a sentient crystal seemed an excellent challenge. Hane was actually looking forward to it, even with the uncomfortable notion of climbing with the same group of people over and over. Maybe by the time the quest was over, they'd find a new spire to climb and a new place to settle. Anywhere far away from Dalenos would be nice.

Hane shook their hair back out of their eyes as Aldis, Sage, and Emiko packed up the food pouches, the utensils, and the enchanted hot plate. There had been enough food available that Hane hadn't broken into their own supply of rations, but they tugged at the strap of their dimensional bag to confirm that it was still there, just to be certain. A glance around found Lani securing the weaponry across the loot bag, lashing the polearms and longswords beneath the satchel's flap by looping a rope around them a few times. She had joined them to eat at some point, but she hadn't lingered long. She had seemed impatient ever since the discovery of Chime's sentience as well as their plight. Even more impatient than Nieve had seemed up until now.

It seemed as if the two women had swapped roles, with Lani's actions silently urging the team to hurry up while Nieve lounged over the food, counseling "safety first" as she waited for her shroud to recover fully. Hane found the reversal jarring.

"Does anyone have any more treasure to add to the loot bag before I send it back?" Lani called as she finished securing the team's identity tag to the front of the bag. As she straightened, Hane caught sight of Chime, tucked neatly into a corner of Lani's belt pouch. The crystal shard's tip jutted up between the side of the pouch and the tied-down flap, as if to allow Chime a view of their surroundings. Hane doubted the bag would offer any obstruction to such a magical entity but found the gesture endearing all the same.

"I think we dumped it all out earlier, Lani," Nieve called back. "Unless Hane still has something?"

Hane rolled their wrists, linked their fingers, and stretched their arms long in front of them, uncoiling their body from the stiffness of sleep. "No. I handed over everything but the anti-venom beads I'm wearing. Unless you would like those, too?"

"You should keep them in case we run into any more venomous monsters." Lani checked her belt pouches one final time, then grasped the return bell attached to a metal ring on the loot bag. She gave it a firm shake, then counted off four paces as she swiftly backed away. Half a minute later, the loot bag vanished, whisked away to the storage site outside the spire to await collection at the end of the climb.

Hane silently approved. Other team leaders might have thought that since they were hoping to end the climb after finishing another room or two, they might as well continue carrying their treasures and avoid the storage fee altogether. It spoke to Lani's experience that she'd rather pay the storage fee than risk everything in the next challenge. Or maybe that was a gambler's instinct, protecting certain gains against uncertain risk. Whatever it was, Hane thought the action wise.

"Are we ready to search for our next room?" Aldis asked, groaning as he pushed himself to his feet.

"Yes, I think so." Lani brushed her fingers over Chime, as if checking to make sure they hadn't slipped into the depths of her bag. "We're just looking for a gate key to the twentieth floor. Can you find that, Sage?"

"I don't know if I can be exactly that specific, but any room connected to a mana fountain should have a high probability of leading to a spire guardian fight," Sage confirmed, adjusting his glasses. "I might be able to tell if the reward for winning is a gate key or not. Is that good enough for you, Nieve?"

"As long as there's a fight involved." Nieve grinned as she cracked her knuckles. "A real fight this time, not against something stupid, like those little urchin monsters."

While Hane didn't entirely share Nieve's lust of violence, they agreed with the sentiment: better to fight one or two big things than hundreds of little things. It had been more challenging than they cared to admit fighting back all the tiny shiuni intent on draining Sage's shroud while he'd been meditating on a solution to the previous room. An agility challenge would be best, though.

While Lani, Nieve, and Emiko filled canteens and waterskins at the mana fountain, Hane followed behind Aldis and Sage to the room's second doorway. They probably could have left through the same door they'd entered through, using Aldis's little portal trick, but it made sense to choose the exit: it was more likely to take them to a gate-key-worthy challenge than the doorway that led them here.

Sage held the door open, and Aldis began flicking through the possibilities. Occasionally Sage would speak aloud, muttering about the things he Saw, his attunement-marked hand resting against the frame of his glasses. Sometimes he'd pause for long moments before shaking his head and saying "Not this one." Other times, his refusal was faster. Each time he declined a room, Aldis worked his magic on the portal's runes, invisible to Hane's eyes, and the view through the door changed.

This wasn't the first team that attempted to manipulate their path through the spire; every team had a different method, ranging from the superstitious to calculated odds, but Hane had to admit: so far, this was the most effective method they had seen. It was simple, too, if a Sunstone-ranked Wayfarer would pull it off. Which only made them wonder: Why had no one tried it before?

If it wasn't a matter of level, perhaps it was a matter of having the right attunements and specializations for the task. It wasn't just Aldis's ingenuity in changing the portal's destination or his travel specialization for portals: it was equally due to Sage's enchanted glasses that allowed them to pick challenges the team knew they could overcome. Not that Seers and Wayfarers were hard to come by when climbing the Tortoise Spire, but perhaps this simple trick hadn't occurred to anyone else just yet. And maybe it wouldn't last, either. Hane had noticed that the spire tended to change whenever a vulnerability was discovered. Possibly by the time they returned here—if they ever returned here—this little trick would no longer work.

Before long, Lani, Nieve, and Emiko were also crowded around the doorway, checking bags and weapons, armor and shrouds in preparation of what Hane expected to be their final challenge of the climb. Aldis was holding the portal steady on a room tiered like an amphitheater in the shape of a hexagon, with long stone tiers descending into a central pit that Hane couldn't see into because of the angle.

"I think . . . this is the one." Sage looked hesitant. "There's something fuzzy about it, but the reward should appear in the middle of the pit in the center of the room, and I See the possibility of a gate key. There's going to be six different combat challenges, but I think the fights will be slightly staggered with opponents appearing from different sides of the room. They're all going to be variations of spire guardians, so it isn't going to be easy."

"Are they going to appear one after another as we defeat them?" Nieve asked. "Or will they appear on timed intervals?"

Sage appeared to concentrate for a moment, then shook his head. "It's too hazy. Way hazier than the last challenge. All I can really see is a lot of fire."

"Well, that makes it easy," Emiko cackled. She glanced back at Hane, smiling widely. "I want to try casting that wave spell you and Nieve did in the maze room."

Hane nodded. Waves from different sides of the room would push any and all combatants into the pit in the center of the room. Once the water filled the amphitheater high enough, Nieve could simply freeze it, bringing about an immediate end to the fight. Doubtless, it wouldn't be quite that easy, but then it wouldn't be a very worthy challenge, would it?

"Okay, so this is it, then," Lani said in a commanding tone. "Is everyone recovered from the last fight? Nieve? Emi? Your shrouds fully functional?"

Nieve and Emiko confirmed that they were in fighting shape again. Sage begged a moment to take a long pull from his canteen, then squared his shoulders. Aldis looked a little tired but pleased that his spell had finally landed on what they were looking for. He shifted to the side, clearing the doorway so that others could precede him into the room.

"Everyone ready?" Lani glanced around for confirmation. "Nieve and Hane go through first. Sage, call out any changes as they come."

Hane sidled up to the doorway, assessing the room. The team would be entering on the highest tier of the six-sided amphitheater, this highest tier being the longest and the widest of four descending tiers to the central pit, which looked to have about ten-foot-long sides making up the final hexagon. Nieve leaned forward, giving the room an evaluating look as well before lifting a brow at Hane. At Hane's nod, Nieve stepped through the doorway. Hane stayed one step behind as Nieve strode forward, standing at the edge of the top tier of stone steps, allowing the others to file in behind them. The stone tiers were wide but not ideal for fighting multiple opponents at once. Hane's plan, in its entirety, would be to knock their opponents down into the hexagonal pit, where a height advantage might be enough for victory, and if it wasn't, at least it would gather up all enemy combatants neatly enough to be drowned or frozen.

Hane heard Emiko begin a chant, but before she could finish, an ominous sound filled the chamber: the rumble of stone tumbling against stone. Hane pivoted, putting their back to Nieve's as they searched for the source of the sound.

"Wait, wait." Sage touched his hand to his forehead, cringing as if pained. "This isn't right. This isn't what I Saw." He doubled over, eyes squeezed shut against whatever he was Seeing. "No, no, no! We have to go! We have to go no—"

Sage spun around, reaching for the door as if to dive back through it. Before he could reach it, the roar of falling stone grew louder, drowning out the sound of Lani shouting out orders. Hane saw it just before the first stone landed: a trap set over the doorway. They were about to be hit by an avalanche.

Transference mana surged through Hane's body, activating almost on instinct in an effort to escape the crush. Rather than leaping clear immediately, Hane dove, sweeping up Emiko into their arms before darting away, twisting in midair to hit one of the angled walls feet-first before dropping to the floor in a crouch. The resounding crashes echoed from all corners of the room as stones the size of boulders rained down. Hane saw Nieve raise a wall of ice, curving it up over her head to protect herself while using the flat of her sword to sweep Lani out of the way, sending the Acolyte tumbling off the top tier of the amphitheater but out of the way of the falling rocks. Hane couldn't make out Aldis or Sage in the tumult of the avalanche, but a breathless second later, Aldis stood by Hane's side, his face coated in rock dust. Emiko struggled free of Hane's arms, eyes wide as she stared at the now-blocked entrance.

"Sage?" Emiko asked in a small voice as the final echo of the last fallen stone reverberated through the room. She trembled violently before calling out again. "Sage!"

Rock dust billowed out from the mound, obscuring Nieve's ice dome as well as the pile of boulders itself. Lani coughed and dragged herself upright, a soft green aura around the hand she held to her chest as she backed up in order to see what had happened on the tier above her.

"Call out, who's injured?" Lani shouted through a cough.

"Sage!" Emiko sounded on the verge of hysterics. Hane could see her shaking. She reached out as if for support, but Hane backed away. They wanted to keep their hands free in case they needed to fight. Aldis took Emiko's trembling hand, looking just as wide-eyed and fearful as she did. Hane moved away from both of them; it was more important to be ready to fight than comfort others over a teammate already lost. "Sage is buried, he's—he's—"

"Emi, focus!" Lani commanded. "Use a wind spell to clear the dust. Nieve, are you okay?"

"I'm here." Nieve's voice came from the cloud of rock dust. Hane could hear the shift and tumble of rocks as Nieve coughed forcefully. "I can't see Sage. Did he get clear? Aldis, did you grab him?"

"He was too far away." Aldis sounded shocked, clinging to Emiko's shoulders seemingly more for his own support than hers. "You were right there, I thought—I thought—"

"Emiko, Aldis, and I are all unharmed," Hane called out, keeping their tone calm and level. Starting a panic now wasn't going to help anyone. "Lani appears to be healing herself. Do you need healing, Nieve?"

"No, I need—I need Sage." The rock dust billowed high and dark, giving Hane only the impression of Nieve stomping around, kicking aside rocks as she searched for him. "Where is he? Did he fall? Did he make it through the doorway? Sage!"

"He's not down here," Lani called, coughing once more before lifting her hand up toward Nieve. "Help me up, I can use Sense Life to search for him. Give me a hand, Nieve." The tiered floor was level with her shoulder, so while it was possible for her to climb up on her own, the tumbled rocks around the ledge didn't leave much space for a solid grip. Nieve reached down and one-handedly hauled Lani up to the highest tier.

"We have to go help." Emiko's eyes were wide; she had a white-knuckled grip on Aldis's hand. "We should—we should go over there. Help them find Sage."

"The most helpful thing right now would be a wind spell to clear the dust," Hane said, looking everywhere but the mound of rubble hiding the entrance from sight. Sage might be okay or he might not be, but either way, the challenge would begin soon and none of them would survive if they were caught off guard again.

"He should have Seen that, shouldn't he?" Aldis muttered, leaning close to Hane's ear. "He's always been good for detecting traps before. How could he miss that?"

Hane refused to answer that. The only way Sage would have missed such an obvious door-trap was if it had been hidden from Sight intentionally. And that didn't bode well for the rest of this challenge at all.

Emiko murmured up a wind spell to carry away the worst of the cloud of dust, revealing Nieve and Lani pulling rocks as large as their torsos off a pile mounded higher than Nieve stood tall. They spared a brief glance at the mound, hoping to see a hand or a boot, but found nothing. Sage was nowhere in sight.

"I think," Hane said carefully, calmly, "that we might have bigger problems than digging out the Seer."

"But he's okay, isn't he?" Emiko asked, voice shrill. "He's just . . . knocked out? Or maybe he got back through the doorway? Sage isn't—he isn't—he's—"

"He's under here," Lani confirmed, face grim as she set her hands on the mound of rocks. "He's still alive, and that's what matters. Nieve, Hane, keep your eyes open for more surprises, Emi, back them up. Aldis, can you do something about these rocks? Or pull Sage out somehow?"

Aldis hurried over to the mound of rubble, stepping carefully around knee-high stones that had spilled outward from the mound. Emiko sniffled, stepping halfway behind Hane.

"His shroud would have protected him, right?" she asked, rubbing her face. "He won't be too hurt and we're almost out of here anyway, right? We could—we could ring out as soon as we get Sage free, can't we?"

Before Hane could tell her they didn't know any of those answers for sure, the light in the room dimmed abruptly, like a midday sky coming over dark with ominous thunderclouds. Emiko gasped and grabbed the back of Hane's tunic. A few of the others cried out, but Hane sank into a sprinter's stance. Sage might not have Seen everything inside this room, but he'd predicted one thing right. This was about to be a fight.

Black smoke billowed from the corners of the room, so thick that at first it looked like a shadow manipulation spell, but Hane's shroud felt the resistance just a touch differently. The smoke didn't carry a scent, nor did it feel acrid or hot, but all the same, Hane didn't want to breathe it in. With one arm swung over Emiko's shoulders, Hane stepped off the stone tier, using transference mana to fall lightly to the next tier down. Nieve jumped down as well, sword held out wide from her side, jaw tight as she looked around the room for the source of the threat.

"Emi, I need you to keep this smoke away from us!" Lani called down. "Everyone, the second we get Sage free, we're all ringing out! Get your bells ready!"

Nieve made a face but didn't argue as she loosened the strings on a belt pouch. Hane understood: it was always hard to walk away from a challenge, but it was worse starting a fight with one team member already down. The priority was getting everyone out with their lives.

"That's not going to be possible." A voice in the smoke boomed at them from all corners of the room, interrupting Emiko's chant for her wind spell by making her gasp and cry out. **"For those who seek to subvert the trials of the goddess, there will be no easy escape. An example must be made of those who cheat."**

"We faced the goddess's trials!" Nieve protested. Hane could hear the rapid shift of rocks and quick, shallow breathing: Lani and Aldis had to be attempting to dig Sage out of the rock pile. Hane swept a hand behind them, reaching back for one of their tonfa. "We thought that choosing challenges that suited our team was a trial of itself. If we were mistaken, we offer an apology. We meant no offense to the goddess!"

A geyser of black smoke erupted from the central pit, its silence no less ominous than the pitiless voice that reverberated through Hane's bones. **"You have already been judged for your repeated offenses and now you must face your punishment. Defeat me or perish, cheating humans."**

Hane removed the tonfa from behind their back, adrenaline flooding their body like a burst of transference mana through their blood. The smoke in the center of the room was weaving itself in a pattern, giving Hane the impression of something impossibly large.

They were about to fight a spire guardian. And if Hane's suspicions were correct, this wasn't just any spire guardian. This was one of the god beast's generals.

Hane wasn't sure if the thrill they felt was more fear or more excitement. How many people got the chance to face off against a general of the god beast?

Or, more accurately, how many faced off against a general of the god beast and survived?

Aldis gave a high-pitched scream, followed by the sounds of rocks dropping to the floor.

"The room is warded against teleportation!" Aldis sounded panicked, breathless. "There's no way out! No way out for us!"

"Did you just try to leave us all behind?" Lani snapped.

"I was trying to take you all with me! Except for maybe . . ."

Sage. While Hane was no expert on teleportation, it probably wasn't possible to move someone buried under all that stone. A high-enough-level Wayfarer might be able to teleport Sage out along with all the rocks on top of him, but along with four other team members, as well as the Wayfarer himself? Especially with Sage buried out of sight and Aldis only Sunstone level, Hane couldn't blame Aldis for attempting to leave Sage behind: sometimes, climbers had to make hard choices, and what were the odds that Sage was even going to survive at this point?

"We can't leave Sage behind!" Emiko cried shrilly. "We have to save him, we have to—"

The black smoke in the center of the room coalesced in a sudden, silent crash, excess sirocco puffing away in a black-smoke halo, revealing a spiked turtle shell, mostly black with the plates illuminated by molten red lines as if lit from within. The shell took up almost the entirety of the central pit of the amphitheater, but from their vantage point, Hane could make out four thick, black-scaled legs, each standing in a pool of flames, and a round, knoblike head crowned with obsidian spikes as long as swords. Hogame. Genbu's general of flame and punishment.

Hane's entire body vibrated with adrenaline mixed with transference mana. This was about to be the fight of their life.

Nieve muttered curses under her breath as she stepped up beside Hane, looking down at Hogame. She cut a quick sideways glance over at Hane. "You good for this?"

Hane never lifted their eyes from their opponent. "Does it matter?"

"I guess not." Nieve flicked her sword, the slim blade growing thicker as ice flowed down over it, turning the narrow sword into a zanbatou. "Lani, call it out! Everyone, watch your—"

Six geysers of lava shot up from the corners of the central pit, and the room shuddered around them. Hane didn't think so much as they reacted, the barest lift of their heels sending them shooting up toward the distant, smoke-shadowed ceiling. They flipped in midair, pushing and pulling through their shroud to land feet-first on the ceiling and run along it to the far side of the room. Just as gravity began to fight against them, Hane kicked off the ceiling, rolled their tonfa out in front of them, and arrowed down at the center of Hogame's spiked shell. It wouldn't be enough to harm the general of the god beast, but Hane needed at least one strike to test how much force would be necessary to break through his shroud.

The moment Hane broke through the black clouds cloaking the ceiling, choosing the seam they wanted to aim their blasts at, one of the spikes from

Hogame's shell launched upward. Hane twisted, rolling in midair to avoid being skewered. They got one foot on the side of the spike and pushed off, holding out both tonfa like the twin barrels of a gun and channeling water mana through both hands, looking for the gaping opening left behind by the projectile spike. The missing plate on Hogame's shell seethed like bubbling magma, a brilliantly glowing bull's-eye in the center of the obsidian shell, but before Hane could get off the shot of water mana, the magma hissed and cooled, turning black just as a spit of magma shot up to form a new spike. Just as Hane reoriented their shot for a molten seam between the plates, a number of spikes fired off in rapid succession. Hane flinched and drew their arms in tight, flooding their shroud with transference mana. Pushing and pulling against the airborne spikes, Hane managed to keep all four from striking, but in the process they got too off course for a shot with their tonfa. Instead, they pushed off the nearest spike and flipped backward, landing on the highest tier of the amphitheater opposite the doorway they had entered through.

Hane wondered why the general of the god beast had only bothered shooting spikes at their aerial assault, but they didn't wonder long. It seemed that Nieve had charged in head-on, taking most of Hogame's attention on herself. Hogame's shroud melted her ice zanbatou when it came too close, but any jets of lava shooting out from the inside of the shell were quickly turned to twisted lumps of smoking stone, thanks to Nieve's ice spells. She stood one tier up from the central pit, putting her just outside Hogame's shroud. For now.

The lava geysers from the corners of the pit had tapered off, leaving sizzling trails of lava and melted stone at each intersection of the tiered stone. The lava on the highest tier was spitting and blackening as it cooled, but each tier lower, the lava ran down, dripping back into the central pit, where it pooled and seethed. Hane made a note to watch out for further geysers: though pushing off water or obsidian spikes for midair changes of direction was easy, using molten lava as a force to push against seemed like a risk Hane would rather not take.

Lani was shouting something that Hane couldn't quite make out across the room and the pitched battle, but then Emiko's voice filled the room, just as Hogame's had before he'd fully manifested.

"Hail, mother of storms/I call upon your fury/Raging waters, rise!"

Rain began to pelt down with enough force to sting. Between the smoke and the sudden deluge, it was getting difficult to see more of Hogame than the cherry-red lines of his shell. Hane saw Nieve back away after creating a thick ice wall between herself and Hogame, putting her back against the next-highest tier. Emiko's conjured rain hissed and fizzled as it struck Hogame's shroud, creating more steam than actual water, but Hane could work with that. Water was the easiest force to work with in terms of pushing and pulling. Weaving a tidal spell to connect the sheeting raindrops, Hane shaped the water into a single, heavy mass—not a cloud, but more like a floating lake. They spun the spell tighter and tighter, creating a dense orb of water, then hurled it at Hogame, hoping both the momentum and the sheer amount of water would get through his heat-haze shroud.

The spell splashed down to fill the lowest pit, a white steam cloud bursting upward and making Hane's eyes sting from the heat. When they could see it again, the view wasn't hopeful. Not an ounce of water remained in the pit with Hogame: it had all been evaporated away.

Water and fire are natural opposites on the mana spectrum, Hane thought, dodging spikes fired off Hogame's shell. *If we can't use water to fight him, how are we supposed to win?*

The stomach-sinking answer seemed to be that they weren't supposed to win. There was no denying that Aldis's trick with the portals had given them an unfair advantage. The spire was coming to collect a past-due debt—one they were meant to pay in blood.

CHAPTER 24

EMIKO

Cloudcaller (lung mark), Citrine

Shards of obsidian showered down almost as constantly as Emiko's rain. Her voice shook as she repeated her chant, the steam and the heat from Hogame having evaporated most of her storm clouds. At least rain was easy; figuring out a spell to help end all this wasn't.

She couldn't stop thinking of Sage, buried beneath the mound of rocks that partially obscured the door—the door that had locked shut at some point after they had all stepped into the room. Her mana reserves were nearly full, her throat and lungs felt healthy and strong, but her will wavered like the heat-haze over Hogame's shell. All she wanted just then was for the rocks to evaporate like her rain and for Sage to stand up, maybe a little battered, but otherwise ready with a strategy and a spell.

But the longer he remained hidden beneath all that crushing weight, the less likely that seemed.

"Emi!" Lani's voice was a whip-crack, drawing her focus back to the real problem. "Keep the rain up. Burn all your mana crystals if you have to. I'm going to go down and give Nieve some backup."

"Wait." The clouds over their heads burst apart and Emiko screamed, thinking it was an obsidian spike, somehow firing down from the ceiling, but it was just Hane, who had somehow traversed the entirety of the room through the smoke and cloud cover hiding the ceiling from sight. They landed in a half crouch, short hair wild and clothes lightly smoking. "There's no way we were ever meant to defeat this monster. Fighting isn't the answer. Finding a way out needs to be the priority if any of us want to survive."

I'm here to make the hard calls. Emiko heard those cold-sounding words again like they were a spell. She hadn't wanted to face that possibility then. She wanted even less to face it now.

"Sage is still alive," she argued, a tremulous warble in her voice. "We need to dig him out. We can't leave—can't leave him behind."

Hane said nothing. A very slight tip to their head and a silent, sidelong glance up at Lani. Lani's lips pinched until they were bloodless, Emiko and Aldis hovering nearby, tense and silent as she came to a decision.

"If we can get Sage out before we find an exit, we'll take him with us. If not . . ." Lani let the words hang in the air, causing Emiko's stomach to plummet like fist-sized hail. "Hane and Emi, keep Hogame distracted. Aldis, see what you can do from here. Test the limits of the anti-teleportation runes and see if you can do anything for Sage."

Lani was touching her fingertips to Chime's pointed tip, jutting up out of her bag; it was an odd thing to notice given the circumstances, but it didn't escape Emiko's eye. Was Lani asking Chime for help? Or was she regretting not ringing out from the mana fountain, as she'd wanted to?

"I have the highest perception mana after Hane," Lani concluded. "I'll go search for an exit." A final glance at Emiko and Aldis, then a look down at Nieve on the lower tier. "Take orders from Hane if you can't get them from me."

"But Lani—" Emiko flinched as Hane launched themself forward off the edge of the stone tier, drawing the fire of more obsidian spikes from Hogame's shell. She marveled for only a moment as they twisted in a tight spiral, then grabbed the edge of a spike, allowing it to pull them up into the purple-black miasma of smoke and storm. By the time Emiko looked around for Lani, she had already rounded the nearest corner, pelting away in search of something that might actually help.

"Well, you heard her," Aldis said, dabbing his face with a cloth. Emiko was sure that the look he gave her was supposed to be reassuring, but the sweat smeared with rock dust only made him look ominously haggard. "I promise to work on freeing Sage. See what you can do to support Nieve and Hane."

Emiko bit her lower lip, feeling tears well up as the mound of boulders caught her eye. She shook her head determinedly, then eased her cloud out over the edge of the tier, looking for something else to focus on.

Hane was barely visible for seconds at a time, diving headlong out of the clouds as if to strike, then using the projectile spikes to ascend once more, lying in wait for the next opportunity to attack. She wasn't sure what they were attempting to accomplish, though she noticed the rising heat in the entire room whenever there were more than five missing plates on Hogame's back. The exposed magma roiled and seethed until it turned black again, forming a new spike that could be fired when Hane next revealed themself.

Maybe they had a plan, or maybe it was just a stall tactic; either way, the most Emiko could do for them was keep the rain falling continuously.

Nieve's fight was closer and more constant: she had the full attention of Hogame's turtle-necked head, the bladelike tines of his obsidian crown parrying strikes from her sword. The ice kept melting off the metal blade, but Nieve determinedly refreshed it, using ice walls as barricades each time Hogame fired off the twin lava jets hidden just inside his carapace. Even with the ice barricades, Nieve's arms, face, and neck were marked with smoking burns, her teeth set in a painful grimace. She seemed prepared to hold on forever, but even Emiko could tell she was steadily losing ground. If her back hit the tier behind her, would she be able to climb to safety before Hogame killed her?

First things first, Emiko thought, popping a mana crystal out of her belt. *If Lani can't be the healer, then I need to be.*

And if she managed to help Sage, too, well, so much the better.

"Gentle Spring come fast/Bring forth new life, heal our woes/Make the flowers grow."

The clouds pressed against the ceiling of the room shimmered and changed, turning silver-gray from their previous purple-black. Instead of pelting, driving drops that stung the skin, the rain turned gentle, falling in a heavy mist. The scents of new growth and petrichor threatened to overcome the smell of sulfur and smoke until they became too diffuse to be distinguished. It was enough to make Emiko feel hopeful, though, especially when Nieve's visible wounds began to wash away, as if they had merely been soot all along. Emiko drew in a cleansing breath to self-soothe, then looked around for other ways to help.

Aldis stood next to the mound of boulders near the door, eyes narrowed in concentration, muttering softly under his breath. Emiko started to ask him what he was doing, but he gave his head a small shake, indicating that he needed a minute. Emiko bit her lip and let him have it: he looked a little like Sage did whenever he was plotting something out. She hoped that whatever it was would work.

Hane was still diving in and out of clouds, dodging obsidian spikes from Hogame's shell to reveal that seething underlayer of bubbling magma. As she watched, Emiko noticed the pattern that Hane was painstakingly drawing out: the more spikes that fired, the slower the scales re-formed on the surface of the magma. Perhaps this was an exposed weakness that Hane was attempting to exploit, or maybe they had another plan in mind. From Emiko's perspective, though, no attack that Hane managed to launch made it through Hogame's shroud without evaporating, so it was hard to guess at what Hane hoped to accomplish.

Lani was nearing the opposite side of the room, her attunement-marked hand trailing along the wall as her eyes roved constantly, even stomping her boots on the floor as if to reveal a secret passage that might allow them to escape. A sudden panicked feeling seized Emiko as she thought: *What if the secret exit is through the ceiling?* But then she rationalized that Hane spent most of the fight near the ceiling, and surely they would have found an exit by now if there were one to be found.

What can I do? Emiko asked herself, hand running over and over the mana crystals holstered in her bandolier. *Water mana should be the natural opposite of fire, but so far, it hasn't been enough. Nieve's ice just melts, an acid would just evaporate, I don't have death magic strong enough to affect a general of the Tortoise Spire . . .*

"Aha!" Aldis's shout nearly made Emiko leap straight off her floating cloud. "I found it! If I place it right . . . there!"

Her heart beating out of her chest, Emiko watched as Aldis pointed down at the tier below the top one, sweat running down his face in streams. His face pinched tight in concentration as slowly, slowly, a section of stone in the lower tier flickered, then began to emit the same heat waves as Hogame's almost-visible shroud.

"What is—" Emiko's heart skipped a beat as she realized what she was seeing. "You opened a portal? But! But! I thought—the return bells!"

"Still won't work," Aldis confirmed, emphatically sweeping his sleeve over his face. "But this room wasn't initially set up with anti-teleportation runes— I think they were added after Sage Saw the room, so the runes were added hastily. There are small gaps I can use to place portals, but only within the confines of this room." Aldis set his foot against a rock balanced on the edge of the upper tier and kicked it forward, sending it careening over the ledge and down into the portal. Emiko followed his gaze, watching the same stone appear over Hogame in the center of the room. It slammed into an obsidian shard and shattered, but Aldis grinned triumphantly anyway. "But it's enough to move at least a few of these boulders."

"It's—you placed the exit inside Hogame's shroud!" Emiko gasped. "They won't melt before they reach him!"

"That's the plan." Aldis shoved a few more stones toward the edge of the stone tier, preparing to drop them through the portal. "I just need Hane to get as many of those shell-plates fired off and maybe we can actually do something instead of just waiting for Lani to save us."

At the mention of Lani, Emiko scanned the room, catching sight of her in a far corner, crouched and examining a wall. That was no good: she couldn't let herself get distracted or else Hogame might realize they were searching

for a way out. The plan wasn't to defeat him: it was to survive long enough
to run away.

I can help, Emiko realized, her hand dancing along her bandolier, searching for a mana type she had very nearly depleted earlier. *I have to help. If we
can just hold him off—if we can just keep Hogame from noticing!*

Emiko drew a breath, filling her lungs with the damp humidity of a sum-
mer storm. She pressed the mana crystal into her diffuser as she let the spell
take shape in her mind.

If I have only one talent, Emiko thought, the words slowly falling into
place, *it's this.*

"Flowing stream of stone/From mountainous cliffs on high." Satisfaction
welled up within her as the spell took shape. Her family had wanted her to
become a poet—had begged her to give up climbing for the safety and beauty
of the words she could weave, the stories she could tell. But here, in this spire
of death and torment, Emiko found her true calling. "Drop by drop, you fall."

A motion spell cast upon the fallen boulders, woven with her last transference mana crystal, shaped by her power and voice. The mound of boulders
shivered, trembled, and then at Emiko's gesture, one by one they began to roll
toward the open portal in the tier below.

Aldis must have gotten through to Hane, because their next death-
defying descent from the film of smoke and vapor was more daring than any
other before. They ricocheted like a bullet off obsidian spike after obsidian
spike, drawing closer to Hogame's shroud than they had dared come before.
Emiko nearly screamed as they missed their grip on a slick-sided spike, the
light from the roiling magma making Hane's clothing glow cherry-red by
its proximity, but then Hane was pointing a single tonfa down at the center
of Hogame's back, and a splash of magma, followed by Hane's rapid ascent,
made her think it could only have been a burst of transference mana, which
allowed Hane to flip themself away again.

Rocks rolled one after another over the edge of the top tier and into the
circular portal Aldis had set below, and one by one Emiko watched them
crash into the exposed magma along Hogame's back. As the giant fire turtle
reeled backward, bellowing a cry of pain, Emiko had one instant to think, to
hope: *We can do this!* before she realized that perhaps making Hogame angry
wasn't the best thing they could have done.

Hogame's head and legs retreated into his shell, the room still shaking
hard enough to make the stones blocking the entrance skitter and slide. Aldis
cursed as he was knocked off his feet, the portal he'd worked so hard to open
snapping shut. Hogame's shell turned black, brittle-looking around the edges,
yet the room never lost its cherry-hot-metal glow. Emiko saw Hane land on

the highest tier of the amphitheater across from the doorway, perched on the edge and looking down. Emiko swallowed tightly and peered over the edge of her cloud.

Red-hot magma was spilling out of the openings of Hogame's shell, spreading into a lake of fire that was rapidly ascending toward the second tier, lifting the shell in a mockery of the principles of buoyancy. Emiko might have simply stared on in horror, but Nieve's shout shook her out of her shock.

Nieve had been fighting Hogame by standing only one tier up from the central pit, where Hogame stood—now floating on the rising tide of magma. She had created an ice pillar beneath her feet, most likely to lift herself to the next-highest tier and escape the lake of magma, but the heat emanating upward and outward had melted the pillar too quickly, sending Nieve skidding backward, flailing desperately on the edge before pitching herself forward onto her hands and knees. Her hair hung in thick, heavy locks around her face as she twisted to look back, watching the steadily surging magma begin to ooze over the ledge on which she stood.

Emiko didn't stop and think—she reacted. She had already seen Sage crushed beneath a door-trap, she was not about to watch Nieve get swallowed up by the lake of molten death.

The heat tore Emiko's vaporous cloud to shreds, but her levitation spell stayed active, carrying her to the corner where Nieve fought to regain her feet, hurling herself against the wall and as far away from the magma as she could. Seeing Emiko, Nieve leapt, hand reaching long. Emiko caught her hand, the additional weight dragging her down, yet she fought to stay elevated as she dragged Nieve up and over to the third tier. Nieve stumbled to the far wall once she crested the lip of the stone tier, looking battered but whole as she scraped soot off her face.

"Thanks, Emi," she gasped, voice ragged from the heat. Emiko started to reach for another life mana crystal to renew her healing rain when a commanding bellow rang out from the distal corner of the hexagonal room.

"Conjure water to cool it off!" Lani shouted, both hands cupped around her mouth to amplify the shout. Before she'd even finished shouting, she held her hand out toward the center of the room, shooting a jet of conjured water down onto the magma, making it hiss and spit and curdle, only to be subsumed by the magma rising around it.

Hane crouched down on the edge of the highest tier, water pouring off their shroud as quickly as they could conjure it. Nieve glanced back down into the pit, where the magma oozed steadily to cover the tier she had been standing on moments before. Rather than cast, she looked up to the next-highest tier.

"Here!" Aldis must have run to get there so fast. He knelt on the edge of the highest tier, reaching down for Nieve's hand. Emiko seized Nieve's other hand, and together they hauled her up to the topmost tier. Nieve steadied herself with a hand on Aldis's shoulder, nodding breathless thanks to each of them before turning around to face the pit. She sheathed her sword and turned her palms out at her sides. After a moment of concentration, water began to spill from her hands, running down into the rising lake of magma.

Emiko sucked in a mouthful of air and added her spell to the mix: "Hail, mother of storms/I call upon your fury/Raging waters, rise!"

Her healing rain spell was all but spent at that point anyway; any lingering life magic would be caught in the fury of the pelting rainstorm. The constant susurrus of falling droplets into the bubbling magma added to the hiss and crackle of Lani's water jet and Hane's spillover. Emiko bit her lip, feeling a tightness in her throat as she watched the magma claim the next tier of the amphitheater. Was the water doing anything at all to slow it down? Or were they only filling the room up faster?

She couldn't help but shoot a look over at the pile of rubble still hiding Sage from sight, though even she couldn't say whether she was still hoping to save him, or if she just wanted the doorway to open and escape this molten domain.

Aldis drew back as the level of magma rose to meet the lip of the final stone tier, the heat warping the sharp-edged stone into something softer, more rounded. Just when Emiko thought, *Here it comes*, it didn't. Instead, the trembling, oozing edge turned brittle and black, growing inward at a leisurely pace, leaving a rugged, steaming crust behind over the top of the magma lake. Emiko felt a hopeful nudge of relief right before Hogame's head and legs burst through the openings of his carapace, a roar of challenge making the room quake and the new crust of dried obsidian crack like glass.

"That's no good," Nieve muttered, drawing her sword again as she squared up. "He's too close to the ceiling now, Hane won't be able to hide as easily anymore."

"Worse," Aldis groaned. "There's no way to open a portal this close to the anti-teleportation runes. I couldn't drop any more rocks on him if I wanted to."

Hogame started to lumber around in a plodding circle, as if curious about what Hane and Lani were doing behind him. Nieve squared up and charged, face set in grim determination as she faced the general of the god beast, drawing enough of his focus to make him forget about the others. Not trusting the newly formed magma-crust, Nieve laid down a sheet of ice beneath her boots, though when she wasn't maintaining it, the residual heat turned it into billowing steam. Emiko had to admire the fearlessness with which Nieve resumed the fight, though she could hardly say she was surprised: Nieve always fought as if she believed it was impossible to lose.

A flicker as silent as a shadow darted at Hogame from behind: Hane bent forward as they ran, tonfa held low and tight to their sides for a sudden strike. Hogame stomped a hind foot, cracking the magma crust and sending up a geyser of fire-colored lava, not only driving Hane back but also sending splatters of lava in all directions. Emiko flinched, knowing she couldn't weave a shield into existence in time to block the droplets of molten stone, but then a violent wind blew past her, sending the lava spray back toward the crusted magma field. Aldis looked as surprised as she did as he swept his hand back through rain-soaked hair to push it off his forehead.

"I don't know what to do," Aldis confessed, anxiously glancing back at the doorway. Or maybe toward Sage. "My mental mana isn't strong enough to touch a monster of this level, never mind a general of the god beast, and my air spells are far too weak to deal any actual damage. I'm not—I'm not heroic, like the others. I don't think anything I can do will help at all."

"We just need to survive," Emiko insisted, eyes drawn by Hane, sliding sideways over the crusted magma, sinking low into the slide to avoid the obsidian spikes that fired off in their passing wake. Hane reversed their direction effortlessly, taking aim at the exposed magma beneath the shell with their tonfa, though Emiko didn't know what type of mana they were shooting. "You can dig out Sage and see if he's—"

A sharp scream cut through the hiss of the rain and the crash of battle. Emiko whirled around in time to see Lani fall through the floor—not the crusted magma, no, but the final tier of stone floor that ringed the walls.

"Lani!" Emiko screamed, her heart compressed so tightly it had to struggle to beat again. She started to dart across the room, heedless of the occasional magma sprays from both Hogame and the crackling obsidian, as well as the spikes that kept firing out in Hane's wake. She just had to get there, no matter what! No matter—

"Wait!" Aldis caught her arm before she crossed from the stone floor to blackened magma. "Wait, I—I don't think it was a trap. It was probably a secret. Right?"

Emiko couldn't speak, couldn't think past her blind terror for her teammate and friend.

"Let me go help," Aldis insisted. "I can't do anything here, but your spells are our best hope right now. If Lani's found a way out, I'm the one who can communicate it to everyone."

Emiko swallowed past the bile in her throat and gave him a tremulous nod. "Okay. Okay, just—save Lani."

CHAPTER 25

ALDIS

Wayfarer—Travel Specialization (hand mark), Sunstone

Aldis only set one foot on the crackling, uneven blackened magma before reeling back and thinking: *Nope, not going to chance that.*

The anti-teleportation runes had him feeling like he was trying to fight with both arms tied behind his back. It didn't help that the smoke and steam, combined with Emiko's rain, made it difficult to see and even harder to keep his footing. Puddles shimmered on the stone pathway that ringed the room, hiding the glittering glasslike shards of obsidian that Hogame's shell-spikes left behind each time he attempted to skewer Hane. It made for quite the obstacle course as Aldis took the long way around the center of the room, slipping and sliding with one hand on the wall to brace himself as he searched for the spot where Lani had disappeared. He felt certain that Lani hadn't tumbled into a pit trap—she was far too cautious for that. And besides, it only made sense for the room to have hidden secrets. However it had been reforged after Sage's initial impression of the room, it was still a spire chamber, complete with secrets and treasures and all the things one could usually expect during a normal challenge.

A peal of thunder made Aldis flinch, lowering himself to the ground only one segment from where Lani had vanished. A twist of his head showed Emiko hovering on a little cloud again, chanting something inaudible over the rain and the crash of battle. A lightning bolt lanced down from the night-dark clouds, striking a patch of exposed magma on Hogame's carapace. There was a roar and then the slam of feet as large as boulders against the cooled magma. Aldis expected another jet of lava to erupt from below, but this time Hogame had put enough force behind his stomp to send a rising, curling wave of magma in Emiko's direction. Aldis held his breath until he confirmed that she'd managed to zip out from underneath it, and then he scrambled back to his feet, skidding dangerously on obsidian fragments until he dropped to his hands and knees at the edge of a perfectly square-shaped pit.

"Lani?" Aldis called down, peering down wincingly before sighing with relief. Lani was at the bottom of a deep pit—one with a floor and no jagged spikes, thankfully—that appeared to be a little more than half as deep as the room had been before Hogame flooded it with magma. Stone ridges were cut into one side like a ladder. It didn't look easy to climb but definitely possible if one was motivated. "Did you get hurt? Need a hand?"

"Not hurt, really, more surprised." Lani's fingertips had been resting on the crystal shard peeking out of her satchel. She pulled her hand away as she moved to stand beneath Aldis, the length of an average-sized person separating them. "Chime sensed the floor was weak here and I thought it was just a false floor. I didn't realize it was this deep when I cracked it open."

"Did you find any—" Another roar followed by the snap of cracking obsidian. Aldis flinched and looked back over his shoulder. Another wave of magma, closer this time, but not quite close enough to be of concern. He turned his palm out, blowing away the splashes that would have caught him.

"I found a key," Lani called up. Aldis checked for more splash hazards before looking down again. Lani held up a simple black iron key, proving her fall hadn't been for nothing. "Help me up. I need a levitation spell or—"

Lani's lips kept moving, but Aldis was deafened by a peal of thunder. It looked like she was reaching for his hand, though even if he lay down flat, Aldis couldn't have reached her, much less have pulled her up. Rubbing his ear, he asked: "Why don't you just climb the—"

The stone ladder, but he didn't get the words out before the ominous crack of brittle obsidian had his gaze whipping sideways. He only barely caught sight of several blackened patches of magma on Hogame's carapace, like scars where new obsidian plates couldn't grow, before the brilliant crimson wave of magma stole his focus. And unlike the others, this one was coming straight for him.

Aldis's first instinct, as always, was to teleport away. He experienced something like a squeezing paralysis that encompassed his heart and lungs, making him gasp from surprise, pain, and panic. He wasn't fast enough to scramble out of the wave's path, and even if he could, would he really leave Lani blind to it in the bottom of the pit?

No.

So in the end, he did the only thing he could think to do:

Aldis jumped.

"Lava lava lava!" Aldis cried, landing painfully on his feet, crowding Lani back into a corner of the pit. "Water air water, now!"

Lani looked stymied, but as the red glow eclipsed the light trickling down into the pit, understanding came over her. Together they raised their hands, palms out, blasting water and air up with enough violence to split the wave as it crested. There were still splashes of lava that rained down, and the upper edges of the pit oozed and melted, but that would all likely cool in a moment; surely Hogame wouldn't bother two harmless climbers this far away from the fight.

Lani made a frustrated noise in the back of her throat. "Now you have to levitate both of us out of here. What good is having a key if we can't get it to the door?"

"Did you find a door?" Aldis asked, carefully using a stream of air to cool the lava dripping over the edges of the pit. The lava on three sides cooled quickly enough, but the side nearest Hogame and the rest of the team kept glowing hot again, no matter how much air Aldis directed over it. "A key on its own isn't enough."

"We think it's the same door we came in through," Lani said. Aldis cocked his head at the word "we." Lani was touching the crystal shard again. "It makes sense, based on the door trap. It wasn't just to catch us coming in, it was meant to block the only exit as well."

"Ah." That did make a certain amount of sense. This wouldn't be the first time a chamber's exit was the same as its entrance, only with a new destination.

Although it could be the last.

Aldis pushed back the negative thought.

"Help me cool the lava on this side," Aldis requested, still channeling his air current over it. "We can climb the stone ladder and test your theory out."

Even though he hadn't been climbing with Lani long, Aldis sensed a sharp tang in Lani's silence, one that made him flinch without even having to look back at her expression.

"The ladder is set against the side closest to Hogame and the lake of magma," Lani said, voice dangerously calm. "Have you tried touching it yet?"

Aldis felt his stomach sink even before he reached out to touch the stone wall, which he now realized was sweating almost as hard as he was. His hand yanked itself back before he was conscious of the gesture, backpedaling until he bumped into the side farthest away from the ladder.

"It's melting," Aldis said, tasting sweat on his upper lip. "That wall is—it's melting into here."

"I know," Lani said grimly. She swept her hand low, conjuring a stream of water that filled the bottom of the pit up to their ankles. Now that Aldis looked properly, he could see a seam of blackened magma along the floor beneath the ladder: Lani had been keeping the lava at bay so far by cooling the wall with water. How much longer would that hold out, though? "That's why I asked you to levitate me out."

"I can—I can do that," Aldis said, gauging the height of the walls. "I can lift us both out of here, we just have to be ready to run the moment Hogame sees us."

"Do you think he knows about the key?" Lani asked, starkly serious. "Because if he does, he'll target us once we get free."

Aldis hedged, uncertain. "I can't say for certain. But making a run for it is the best we can hope for. We can split up and go separate directions around the room—"

"And hope he doesn't melt the one with the key?" Lani asked drily. Steam was rising off the conjured water in the bottom of the pit. Lani held her palm out and added a few more inches to the pool, her face void of expression or emotion. "Our best bet is to wait until Hogame is distracted. Then it's just a roll of the dice as to whether we get the key to the door or not."

Aldis gulped hard, tasting salt at the corners of his mouth. "I'll tell the others to create a suitable distraction. Y-you should hold onto the key when we—"

Aldis nearly fainted as a shadow flickered over the opening of the pit. He lifted a hand to shoot a jet of air at whatever it was, then nearly collapsed in relief when he saw it was only Hane.

"You both have Emiko worried sick," Hane explained, leaning down low to extend their hand. "Hurry, I'll help lift you out. Did you find—"

From his angle, Aldis couldn't see what cut Hane off, but before he could cast a levitation spell on both himself and Lani, Hane's eyes went wide and they vanished almost as abruptly as they'd appeared. Dark shapes flew over the top of the pit, crashing and shattering against the wall to rain obsidian shards down into the pit.

"There will be no escape for those who violated the sacred tenets of the goddess," Hogame intoned, their voice making the room shudder— except for the hot wall inside the pit trap: that one rippled. **"Resign your-selves to your fates, for you will not be leaving this place alive."**

Perhaps Nieve would have had a biting remark for that sentiment, but Aldis felt his knees knock together. A quivering droplet of burning red lava trembled on the ledge closest to Hogame, then trickled down like a tear, the wall growing orange and angry against its slow progress. Aldis felt his joints turning to jelly, his trembling violent enough to send ripples through the ankle-deep water at the bottom of the pit.

Lani swept a hand over her hair, shaking bits of obsidian out of her hair. "Is Hane—"

"They're still alive," Aldis confirmed. He drew a breath of air that burned and firmed his resolve. "Ready for a levitation spell?"

Lani nodded grimly, looking up at the lava-limned opening above their heads. "I'll go left, you go right."

Focusing was the hardest part as the bleeding wall trembled each time Hogame made the room shiver. This wasn't an average levitation spell either. Aldis needed to lift them both higher than a few inches off the ground: he had to get them each high enough to crest the pit, locate a safe place to land, and then cancel the spell so they could each run to the door on the fully opposite side of the room. And as difficult as it was to focus on creating the spell, Aldis suspected that the run to the door might be the worst part of this.

Just as Aldis's feet lifted off the floor, Lani only inches behind him, Hane appeared at the top of the pit again, reaching down to help them up. Their fingertips had just brushed against Lani's when a shout from across the room jerked Hane's head up. Pounding footsteps shook the room, making the melting wall shudder tremulously. Hane seemed frozen with indecision, then withdrew their hand sharply.

"Down!" Hane ordered before leaping away in a shadowlike blur. Lani wobbled, still in the middle of reaching for Hane's hand. Aldis steadied her before she could careen into the lava-spattered wall.

Why would Hane tell them to get down? They were nearly out, why should they stay—

Aldis's head crested the lip of the pit and he immediately saw the problem: Hogame was charging across the room, bulling through ice walls that appeared in the path between him and the pit that Aldis and Lani were desperately attempting to escape. Hogame roared as he spotted Aldis, twin stars of fire-red light appearing inside his carapace to either side of his head. Aldis canceled the levitation spell just as jets of lava shot from Hogame's shell, spattering against the wall just over the pit.

Lani cried out as she fell, landing on her hands and backside in the diminished pool of conjured water. Aldis staggered, careful not to touch the walls as he recovered his balance. Fresh lava was dripping down the side of the pit, faster now as the heat in the small space made Aldis's eyes and throat feel tight and dry despite the steam rising off the water.

"One more time!" Lani demanded, water splashing as she scrambled to her feet. "Quickly this time, so we—"

The shadow that fell over the pit cut off her command as cleanly as a guillotine. Aldis felt Lani crash against his shoulder as they both stared up in horror and awe at Hogame's shiny, obsidian underbelly.

"Can we . . ." Lani swallowed audibly. "Can we hurt him from here?"

"Maybe." Aldis wasn't convinced but didn't want to be the first one to give up, either. "If we can penetrate his shroud with something?"

Lani bit her lower lip, her fingers worrying Chime's crystalline tip as she stared upward, sweat tracking paths through soot and grime on her face. "We need . . . We need Hane and Nieve to distract him. Get him to move."

"I'll tell them." Aldis swiped sweat out of his eyes, reaching out for Hane and Nieve with a communication spell. "They say they're trying but—but it looks like Hogame intends to trap us here. He doesn't want to—"

Aldis was aware of Lani screaming before he could process the cause: Hogame stomped a foot hard enough to make the melting wall tremble, sending both Lani and Aldis reeling away from it. At the highest point of the wall, lava began to bleed through, melting the lip of the pit. It was only after the tremors stopped that Aldis realized he, too, had been screaming.

Still trembling with one arm hugging herself, Lani raised a hand, shooting a jet of water over the blood-colored spill of lava. A moment later, Aldis joined in with an air spell, cooling the lava. Their spells could turn the surface black and brittle, but the molten core kept burning through. They finally thinned the lava to a trickle, then had to stop because the water around their ankles was beginning to burn through their shrouds. Lani conjured more water within the pit, which cooled it a little, but Aldis still found himself hopping from foot to foot, feeling very much like a crab stuck in a pot.

"So." Lani looked up grimly at the underside of Hogame's shell. "What do we do now?"

"I doubt we could move him," Aldis said, mopping the mixture of sweat and condensed steam off his face. "Even if we threw everything we had at him, I doubt we could penetrate his shroud. We'd probably end up cooking ourselves faster if we tried."

"If you levitate me, I could touch him," Lani said doubtfully. "I could try converting his blood to poison or acid."

"Even if you could, you'd never get your hands through his shroud to reach him," Aldis pointed out. "It would be like holding your arms inside a bonfire."

"I could charge my shroud with water—"

"It would turn to steam and burn you." Aldis coughed into his fist, feeling the heat burn through his nostrils into the back of his throat. "I don't think we're going to be able to go through him. Our only hope is for the others to move him."

Lani growled in frustration but broke down coughing. She staggered woozily for a moment before Aldis grabbed her shoulder, steadying her so she didn't crash into a lava-drenched wall. Lani caught her balance but cupped her forehead as if she were suffering a headache, loose braids falling over her face.

"Can you teleport him?" Lani asked in a small, hopeless voice. "Or teleport us?"

He knew he couldn't, but Aldis reached for the magic anyway. The familiar empty squeeze in the depths of his chest had him shaking his head before he could answer.

"I can't—" Aldis stopped, catching a message from Hane. "Hane says that they're doing their best to move Hogame, but he's being stubborn. They want to know if you have any specific orders."

"Tell them . . ." Lani looked up, massaging the palm of her attunement-marked hand. Her fingers twitched like the legs of a dying spider; even if her mana pools weren't exhausted yet, she had likely overused that particular pathway for her spells. "Tell them to keep Hogame distracted. Tell them we'll find our own way out."

"Right." Aldis sent the message before considering the walls of the pit trap once more. The far wall was warped and weeping, the ledges meant to resemble a ladder twisted into frowns, clear bubbles blooming through the stone to drip and weep like glassy tears. Every time Hogame took a step, the wall threatened to buckle inward. Aldis could hear the shatter of obsidian and the crash of metal, yet the shadow above them didn't budge an inch. Without the eerie red glow of the lava, Hogame's shell would have eclipsed almost all light, leaving them trapped in darkness. The pooled lava above was still oozing down all four walls, elongating with the silent malice of a nest of snakes. Despite the heat, he shivered. "We're not . . . we're not going to find our own way out of this, are we?"

Lani's iron resolve didn't waver; her chin didn't tremble, her eyes didn't leak. She considered the thin gap between the top of the trap and Hogame's shell, shimmering with the heat-haze of his shroud that would surely incinerate them if they attempted to crawl through it—if Hogame didn't simply crush them. She grimaced as she shifted her weight onto one foot, then looked to the floor where the weeping wall had begun to buckle into their limited space. She hissed in pain as she turned her palm out, conjuring water to replace the evaporated portion. "No. I don't think so. Unless you have an idea."

Aldis reached into a belt pouch for his return bell, hooking an arm through Lani's before giving it a shake. Then another shake. And a harder shake. He cast a glance upward again, seeking salvation only for another stomp of the god beast's general to make the walls shudder once again.

"It was worth a try," Lani said, making an attempt at a smile. Her stoicism almost broke then, boots sloshing in the ankle-deep water as her gaze darted swiftly away. She thrust her mana-burned hand down and flicked it with an almost violent command, shaping the pool of water to cover the melting wall at an angle, so it no longer pooled about their ankles. She grimaced as she stomped her boots, water squishing out of them. "Can't believe I'm going to die with wet socks."

Aldis nearly laughed then. Not from humor, no, but from near hysteria. "That can't be your biggest regret right now."

Lani's face went tight, jaw clenched fiercely. "No. It's not." Her fingers sought the tip of the crystal shard peeking out of her bag, sliding along it in a gesture like a stroke. She released a slow, shaky breath. "It wouldn't be so bad if—if—" She bit herself off with a rough curse, a squelch sounding from her boot. "I could have tossed Hane the key! Why didn't I think of that?"

"It's not a weakness to think of survival first and strategy second," Aldis reminded her. "And . . . not that it helps, but . . . somehow, I doubt it would have made a difference."

Lani let her breath go all at once. "You're probably right. The fact that Hogame's hovering over us probably means he knows there's a key. He'd just melt down the whole room if he thought there was a chance we might actually escape."

The angled pool of water was steaming endlessly, and the glassy quartz tears were beginning to bleed with red light as the wall glowed an ominous orange. Not ready to give up yet, Aldis turned a circle in the small amount of space allowed to him by Lani. He paused when he noticed her hand still resting on the crystal shard jutting from her satchel.

"Is there any way they can help us?" Aldis asked, pointing. "Any hidden power to save themselves, or any revelations that would get us out of here?"

"I asked already." Lani's grip tightened, her knuckles turning white. "It feels foolish to admit this, but do you know what's worse than dying here?"

Aldis couldn't think of anything worse than dying just then.

"I made a promise." She drew the crystal shard from her satchel, clasping it in both hands. "I felt like . . . like I had a purpose. I was going to reunite Chime with their other pieces and help them reclaim their shrine. And now . . ." Bloodless lips puckered around a sour taste. "If Chime melts here, with us, their consciousness will revert back to the largest piece of themself—which means the sword. Back to serving some cretin who couldn't respect the fact that Chime was fine the way they were."

Aldis swallowed, shifting his eyes away. It felt personal, Lani's confession. He wished—no. He couldn't wish that someone closer to her were here with her just now. Awkwardly, Aldis cleared his throat. "Well, there's still the chance that the dastard who stole Chime from their shrine is dead, so that's . . . that's something," he finished weakly. He cast around once more as the smell of burning something—hair maybe—suffused the pit. "I could try calling Hane back one last time. They might have a trick that would get them close enough so you could toss Chime to them. Seems they've survived more of these disastrous types of climbs than anyone else. If I could, I'd put all my money on them."

Lani looked mildly surprised. "I thought you hated gambling."

The resentment that always felt so present for Aldis seemed such a minor thing now as he watched the far wall warp and droop. It felt like an admission of defeat to speak it out loud. "My parents . . . They weren't gamblers, exactly, they just . . . they were merchants who used a shady information broker to know when to buy and when to trade. It worked out pretty well until . . . Well, they got swindled. Lost everything. More than everything: they'd taken out a few bad loans in expectation of the windfall. I didn't know about any of that, I was still pretty young then. Got used to a certain type of lifestyle and then it was just . . . gone. Even our family name: we had to change it to run from creditors. Ever since then, I just . . . I buried myself in the Teachings of Selys. I think I mostly did it to punish my parents, but . . . that's got nothing to do with you. Sorry, Lani."

"I'm sorry, too, Aldis." Lani didn't smile—Aldis didn't think anyone could smile in a situation like theirs—but the corners of her mouth tightened in an attempt, at least. "I should have warned you about the ladder before you jumped. I should have just tossed Chime and the key up to you and told you to get clear. Maybe you could have found another way—"

"Wait!" Aldis gasped, the heat and sulfur making him hack and cough, eyes tearing as he waved away Lani's offered healing hand. "Another way! I have one! Not for us, I mean, but Chime, at least. And the key, too, for what it's worth."

"What do you mean?" Lani asked, skepticism heavy in her voice. "This isn't the time for false hope, Aldis."

"Not for us," Aldis agreed, crouching down to hold his hand beneath the steaming water. "But maybe for the others . . . Here!" Aldis looked back over his shoulder, grinning. "We're low enough in the room that I can reach a blank space between the anti-teleportation runes. I can create a portal here. Well, a small one."

"A small one?" Lani asked. "How small? I suppose not big enough for one of us to escape."

"No, we're not that lucky," Aldis sighed. "The trouble isn't opening this portal, the trouble is the exit portal. Every other blank space is under lava right now, and I can't create an exit past the anti-teleportation runes. But if I charge it with enough mana—if I go beyond safe mana limits with one spell— I should be able to place the exit within the radius of one of the runes. That would be everything from me, though. I'd have nothing left."

Lani flexed her hand and frowned, likely considering her own safe mana levels, as well as the mana-burn she had to be feeling in her hand. "Enough to get Chime and the key out to the others?"

Aldis nodded. "Hogame wouldn't even know. It's our—their—best bet."

Lani's jaw went taut as she looked up again at the sides of their prison, the orange wall sloughing and bleeding from the top: it wouldn't be long now before it gave way and melted entirely. The sounds of battle had all but faded into background noise, but a roar and a stomp made them both gasp and cringe, waiting to see if this was the moment the wall fell. It held, but only just—it looked little more than the thin rime over a puddle just before dawn. Aldis bit his lip in an effort not to remind Lani how little time they had left to make this decision. Surely she knew they had only seconds left.

"Yes," Lani said, nodding firmly. "Yes, open the portal. And I think I know where you should place the exit portal, if you can."

Aldis crouched again, noting with discomfort that most of the water was gone now; the small bit that remained was bubbling constantly, as if boiling. The portal, unfortunately, could only be placed against the melting wall, as it was the farthest from the effect of the anti-teleportation runes. One of them would have to reach through it in order to place the crystal shard and the key in reach of their teammates. Their friends.

Lani counseled Aldis on the exit portal and he agreed, sweating as he worked the magic—pushed, shoved, and *begged* the magic to take shape on the other side. He drew mana from all parts of his body, drawing from places he rarely used, gathering them all together and forcing them into the shape he needed. At first, it just hurt like an overworked muscle. Before long, it began to burn like a line of fire.

"Ready," Aldis panted, feeling the exit portal snap into place. "Hurry!"

"Good luck to you," Lani whispered to the crystal shard, held close to the black iron key. "May you be whole once more one day."

Without further ceremony, Lani thrust her hand through the open portal, leaving both shard and key in a dark, dry place. She withdrew her hand quickly, and the portal snapped shut. The skin of her hand burned red from the proximity to the wall, but she still had the presence of mind to help Aldis to his feet. Aldis felt watery, wobbly, and weak, and if he had enough minutes left in his life, he would have worried about throwing up. The heat in the air wasn't helping, nor was the distortion effect on the melting wall. Aldis put a hand over his eyes and tried to focus on breathing.

"I think they'll get out," Lani said, more to herself than to him. "They will. They'll find the key and they'll get out."

"They'll find Chime's pieces, too," Aldis said, swallowing down bile. He tried to smile, but his chin felt too weak. "They love you, you know."

For the first time since he'd met her, Aldis saw Lani's eyes tear up. As the far wall turned cherry-red, they backed up as far as they could, casting cautious looks up toward the lava dripping down the wall behind them. When their eyes met, Lani offered Aldis her attunement-marked hand.

"I can heal you through it for a little while," she offered, eyes steady despite the tears. "Just in case of . . . something."

Aldis looked up, then looked to the wall and shook his head. "I'd rather it end quickly."

"Me too."

CHAPTER 26

NIEVE

Champion (mind mark), Citrine

Hogame's twin lava jets, tucked inside the carapace to either side of his head, glowed white-hot, giving Nieve only seconds to erect a barricade of ice. She dropped to a knee in order to duck, watching the water stream off her wall as she judged how long it would take to melt, her free hand sifting through her open satchel to find and grasp a healing potion. She ripped the stopper out with her teeth, refusing to release her grip on her sword for even a second as she gulped half the contents of the potion down. Burns and cuts from shattered obsidian ranging up and down her arms scabbed and healed over. As the lava began to pool around the base of her ice wall, turning brittle and black as it cooled, she pushed herself back up to her feet, holding the open potion bottle slightly behind her as she prepared to defend herself once again.

"What did Lani and Aldis find?" Nieve shouted, her eyes never leaving the god beast's general poised above the opening in the floor. She didn't know exactly where Hane was but guessed they would be close by. "Does Lani have a plan?"

"Only to keep distracting Hogame." Hane dropped lightly down a little behind Nieve. They didn't land in their usual half crouch—in fact, out of the corner of her eye, Nieve thought it looked as if they'd nearly lost their balance. She shot a quick glance behind herself, noting Hane's soaked and steaming clothing, their exposed skin red and chapped from the heat. She couldn't see any obvious injuries, but she held back the half-full bottle of potion in an offering. Hane considered, then accepted, quaffing the bottle as quickly as Nieve had. "If they found something, they didn't tell me, although the pit had the look of a secret, rather than a trap. I imagine they're hoping Hogame forgets about them long enough for the two of them to escape."

That made sense: if Hogame heard that there was a plan to escape—or better yet, to defeat him—no doubt the difficulty of the challenge would spike into ludicrous levels of impossibility. But couldn't Aldis send them a message, so that Hogame couldn't hear it? Or maybe he and Lani were still working out the plan. All Nieve could do was continue to hold out and hope to draw Hogame away from the pit. It wasn't looking good, though: every time she thought she had his attention enough to lure him away, he'd start stomping on the floor, droplets of lava flying off his every footstep. To stop him, she'd had to move in close enough to attack again. Someone had to come up with a better plan soon, because Nieve's magic and resolve were both wearing thin.

A jet of flame through the magma-crusted floor distracted her enough that Hogame scored a hit along her arm with the razor-sharp obsidian tines of his crown. Nieve cursed and parried, gritting her teeth as she refocused on the general of the god beast of the Tortoise Spire.

"Emi!" Nieve shouted, knowing the little Cloudcaller had to be somewhere hidden in the black and gray clouds scudding the ceiling. "More rain! The magma crust is breaking apart!"

Hane sprang away, hurling the empty potion bottle at Hogame as they vanished into the clouds. The glass glowed red-hot as it passed through Hogame's shroud, landing with a splatter against the edge of Hogame's shell. Though that turtle-like face wasn't especially expressive, Nieve thought she saw him eye the molten glass with something akin to a scowl. A moment later, it was impossible to make out the remains of the bottle from Hogame's gleaming, obsidian shell.

Nieve centered herself with a slow exhale, focusing on the strength, speed, and endurance her Frost Form lent her. As much as she loved a good fight, there would be no victory here; she knew her limits and this monster fell outside them. The best she could hope to do was defend and distract and keep Hogame's attacks centered on herself rather than on her teammates. She'd leave the strategy up to everyone else.

Emi's rain drove down hard and stinging once again, sizzling and snapping and creating more steam along the craggy black magma floor. It was a stopgap at best, but at least it helped Nieve's ice barricades last a little longer before the lava beneath the surface melted them. Too often, the crags of the cooled magma breached her layer of ice, creating hazards that could trip her, and she couldn't take that risk—not with those twin lava jets pointed at her.

And the lava jets weren't Hogame's only front-facing weapons, either. Nieve darted to the side as knifelike blades of obsidian fired from the upper curve of the carapace above Hogame's head. He attacked in the wake of the knives, lowering his head and swiping sideways, his black-glass crown swinging like misshapen trident prongs. Nieve shaped the ice along her sword like a spear as she jabbed toward Hogame's bulbous orange eyeball. The ice melted as it penetrated Hogame's shroud, but as most creatures did, Hogame flinched at an attack made toward his eyes. Another round of obsidian knives fired in an arc had Nieve ducking behind a wall of ice once again.

I can't keep this up forever, Nieve thought, her energy flagging, each step and each swing of the sword making her feel heavy, clumsy, and hopeless. *If there's a plan, I need to know it. I need to know that we're going to make it out of this.*

Clouds burst as Hane darted down from the ceiling, obsidian spikes firing off Hogame's shell along their trajectory, though Hane twisted and turned, narrowly avoiding each one in order to draw close enough to fire off several blasts through their tonfa. Nieve could only guess that they were shooting transference mana, by the way it passed through the shroud and sent up splashes of magma in each blast's wake. Hane completed one of their midair direction changes, somersaulted to land on the brittle magma floor, and then seemingly climbed the rain to vanish into the clouds again. A few more obsidian spikes fired after them, glasslike shards raining down from where they impacted the ceiling.

I wish I knew if those hits were actually doing anything, Nieve thought, struggling to draw breath after dodging another swipe from Hogame's tridentlike crown. The blasts of water mana had been all but useless, evaporating before making it through the shroud. The transference mana passed through, but how much of that mana did Hane have to burn? With all the hopping around they were doing, surely they had to be reaching some sort of limit. Nieve could already feel a migraine clouding her vision, making noises seem louder than they were. When sounds became sparks that flared in her vision and assaulted her equilibrium, she would be overextended on her mana, making her all but useless. She wasn't at that point yet, but she soon would be if someone didn't tell her what the reshing plan was.

"Hane!" Nieve shouted, pitching her voice loud, hoping they would hear her wherever they were. "Check on Lani and Aldis! Tell them whatever they're going to do, they need to do it—"

A shift in her footing, then a sharp snapping sound followed by a rushing roar had Nieve dropping to a knee. For a minute, her eyes refused to accept what they saw until understanding caught up to her: one wall of the pit trap had caved in, cracking the magma floor into blackened pieces that floated on the lake of lava. As Hogame lifted his foot and casually flicked a bit of lava off it, Nieve's hand clutched at her heart.

Seething lava filled the pit trap.

"No." Nieve shook her head, hand twisted tight enough in her tunic to clasp the locket hidden beneath it. "No, it—they—Aldis could—" Her gorge rose, bile flooding the back of her tongue. "Lani!"

She missed the moment that Hogame lowered his head and charged. In her shock and grief, she might have let herself be run through by the glass swords atop Hogame's head. But a force slammed into her from the side, tossing her clear of the charge as she and one other person rolled to their feet amid the fragmented and churning plates of obsidian. Nieve rolled to her feet on instinct alone as Hane did the same at her side.

"Stay focused," Hane ordered in a low, calm voice.

"But they—" Nieve choked on an unnamed emotion.

"We don't know anything for certain," Hane said swiftly.

How could they be so calm right now? Nieve felt like screaming, like ripping out her hair, like cutting out her own heart. Her fingers still dug into the center of her chest, reaching beyond the locket for something else.

"They got out, right?" Emiko asked, her eyes as wide saucers as she descended from the smoke and storm clouds that cloaked the ceiling. "Lani and Aldis—they made it out, didn't they? They teleported, or they rang their bells, or they—they—"

"We don't know anything," Hane repeated steadily. "All we know is that if any of us want to survive this, we need to find a way out of here. I know we're all low on mana, but we can't give up right now. If we give up, we're dead.

Like Lani and Aldis, Nieve thought, her eyes seeking the noticeable dip in the floor where the lava had filled in the pit. If Lani and Aldis were still inside when it collapsed—she didn't want to think about it. Couldn't think about it. Not without falling to pieces.

And she couldn't afford to fall to pieces now. Not while Emi still lived. And Sage, maybe.

Stinging pain lanced Nieve's fingers as she forcibly uncurled them from her tunic to grip her elongated hilt. As Hogame trudged a circle to turn and face her, she picked three distant walls around the six-sided room and conjured towering ice pillars, ignoring the lancing pain that stabbed at the backs of her eyes.

"Get a winter wind blowing, Emi," Nieve ordered, steadying her stance. "We need to seal the cracks in the floor, or else we'll all get melted."

"But they're okay, right?" Emi whimpered, her little cloud vibrating so hard that tufts of it tore off and evaporated. "Lani and Aldis. They—they made it out. Didn't they?"

"Hane's going to check." Nieve flicked her eyes sidelong at Hane. They nodded, accepting the order. "Right now, I need wind, Emi. And keep the rain falling. It's too hot in here without it."

"R-right." Emi was still shaking as she carried herself up into the veil of the clouds above. Hane waited a moment longer before darting away. Nieve only hoped they knew better than to crush Emi's hopes; she'd gone to pieces before and they couldn't afford that this time.

The team had barely lived through it last time.

Hogame charged just as a whipping wind circled the room, dragging air away from Nieve's ice pillars to cool the seething floor. The fragment of magma Nieve stood upon was large, but she had no illusions of it holding Hogame's weight. She dove out of the way of the charge, careful to avoid the cracks between the rocking and crashing magma plates. Where she could, she laid down a layer of ice, hoping to cool the lava enough to harden it, but it was getting harder to use her magic with a headache throbbing behind her eyes. Not that Hogame seemed at all sympathetic as he swung his obsidian crown at Nieve like a mace. She parried with her naked sword and backed away, testing her footing before shifting her weight.

Without the pit trap to guard, Hogame followed, alternating attacks from swinging his head, launching a volley of black-glass daggers, and shooting jets of lava from inside his shell. Nieve was careful to cede ground in a circle, so that her back never came up against a wall and she kept to a tight, predictable pattern so Hane could anticipate her moves well enough to dart in and check the steaming lava sloped into a pool near the pit trap. She tried to steel herself as Hane crouched close to the pool as if searching for something. When they stood up and offered a grim-faced shrug, Nieve gritted her teeth and set the thought aside. Either Lani and Aldis had gotten out somehow, or they hadn't. She could grieve later; for now, she had to fight.

No, fighting him isn't going to do us any good, Nieve thought, increasingly aware of the weight of her locket around her neck. *But even if I wanted to, would it work? Could I even use it with my mana as low as it is?*

If I'd tried it sooner . . . could I have saved them?

Hane darted down from the clouds, drawing off a line of obsidian spikes from Hogame's shell. Bursts of transference mana out of the end of their tonfa sent up splashes of roiling magma, spattering on the obsidian floor like blood. Before, those splashes had cooled rapidly, becoming slick patches underfoot, but now they continued to seethe and bubble. As Nieve wiped sweat off her forehead, she realized Emi's wind had failed already. The rain was still falling but in a soft patter rather than the earlier torrents, which signaled the end of the rain spell. Was Emi as drained of mana as Nieve was? Could she keep the wind and the rain going, or was that asking too much of her?

Hogame lumbered forward, the weight of his foot tipping the magma plate on which Nieve stood. Her headache disoriented her, causing her to pitch forward, toward the lowered crown like a ring of spears. Frost Form saved her, reacting on instinct to propel her away, the added strength in her legs aiding her wild leap, the layer of ice beneath her skin protecting her as she rolled across the jagged cracks and spikes of the steaming obsidian. Her head was still spinning as she turned to face Hogame, sinking into a braced stance almost without conscious thought. The god beast's general pulled his foot back, sending the magma plate crashing down. Nieve hissed through gritted teeth as lava spattered the left side of her body, stinging even despite her Frost Form. Taking cautious steps backward, she rooted through her satchel for another healing potion.

A splash of water over her head made her gasp and jump, dropping the potion bottle. Hane caught it, giving her an apologetic look as they handed it back to her.

"Your hair was on fire," Hane explained tersely. "I don't think any of our attacks have hurt him at all. Escape needs to be our priority."

"Did Lani tell you anything?" Nieve asked, trying to ignore the tight squeeze in her chest as she said Lani's name. She quaffed half the potion, then offered it to Hane, who shook their head. "Did they find anything?"

"If they did, they didn't pass it on to me," Hane said simply, backpedaling as Hogame lumbered forward. At least this magma plate was attached to the stone rim around the room—hopefully it would hold. "If your team has a last-chance option, you should—"

"Nieve!" Emiko dropped from the clouds so fast that Nieve moved to catch her. The Cloudcaller's cheeks were streaked with tears, her hands and cloud trembling violently. "I've been trying to call out to Aldis and he isn't responding! We need to get them out and we need to find Sage and we need to get—"

Hogame stomped a foot, and the ground beneath Emiko glowed red-hot in a perfect circle. Nieve threw a hand out on reflex, conjuring a block of ice and hurling it into Emiko's chest hard enough to knock her away just before a pillar of lava burst up from the ground. Before she could see if Emi had landed safely or not, Nieve's headache blinded her, elevating every sound, every light, every tactile sensation against her skin one hundredfold. She pitched forward and vomited, though little more came out than the healing potion she had just swallowed.

That might have been the end but for Hane leaping forward and using Hogame's own trick against him: they stomped on the edge of a piece of floating, brittle magma so that it popped up at an angle just before a force of transference mana burst outward from their body, shattering the hardened magma into thousands of sharp-edged projectiles, all flying at Hogame's face. Hogame retreated a step as they turned their face away from the slivered shards of obsidian.

Great, Nieve thought, swiping at her mouth with the back of her hand. *Now we have a huge hole in the floor.*

"Get to Emi," Nieve spat, using her sword as a crutch to lever herself back to her feet. Her body trembled, but she managed to order it into a defensive stance, her sword gripped tight in both hands. "Say whatever you need to say to get her to make it rain again. We need the floor to stabilize."

Hane lingered just long enough to give the impression of an argument, then leapt into the low-hanging clouds once again. Nieve steeled herself as Hogame turned to face her once again.

She would at least face her death head-on while trying to give Emi even one moment longer to draw breath. One moment longer might be the difference between escape and death. She could hold on for one more moment.

Shards of black glass erupted from Hogame's carapace, making Nieve leap backward. She cursed as she realized she'd been forced toward a wall. She used the distance to gain a wider angle, forcing Hogame to chase after her, rather than continue to be backed into a corner. At least she could use more of the room's space now.

There was no reason to avoid the pit trap any longer.

The center of her chest felt cold, heavy. As if the weight of her locket was making it hard to breathe. Even if there was a chance it could work with her mana as depleted as it was, she would need time to undo the seal. Time that could cost Emi and Hane their lives. It was too big a risk; Nieve put it out of her mind.

But if I'd tried earlier . . . Nieve's eyes flicked to the dip in the floor where the pit trap used to be, then skittered across the room to the mound of rocks that buried Sage. *If I'd thought to try it sooner, then maybe . . . maybe . . .*

She needed it to rain. She needed the magma to cool enough to make the floor solid once more. She needed the distraction Hane offered, she needed the versatility of Emi's magic. She needed Sage's insight, Lani's straightforward planning, and Aldis's ingenuity. She needed her team.

A crimson bubble gasped between two magma plates, drawing Nieve's eye to the collapsed pit, an overwhelming sense of guilt making her stumble over the uneven crust of the floor, allowing one of Hogame's knifelike obsidian shards to open a line of red along her sword arm. As she fought to regain her balance, another cut through a chunk of rain-wet hair. The next time the lava jets burned white-hot, Nieve rolled to the side and sank to a knee, groping inside her bag for another healing potion, wishing it could heal the pang of guilt inside her heart.

No one else, Nieve thought, more plea than promise. *Please . . . no one else.*

CHAPTER 27

HANE

Wavewalker (leg mark), Citrine

What did they find down there? The question plagued Hane even as they kicked off the dying rain to hide among the clouds. *Hogame wouldn't care if it was just treasure: we'd have no way to escape with it. Did they find a door? An exit? But then why was Lani trying to climb out? Why not just have Aldis tell everyone to run for the pit?*

The questions helped keep their mind off the fact that ultimately, they had been the one to leave Lani and Aldis down in the pit. They had thought there would be time for a rescue later, if only they could move Hogame, but that moment had never come. They had reached out to Aldis asking for some guidance, but if they'd known the pit's collapse was imminent, they could have fought harder, tried something trickier, cobbled together a better plan, anything that could have helped move Hogame so Lani and Aldis could escape the pit. If only they had realized before . . .

Hane set their jaw, narrowing their eyes as they pierced the cloud cover to strike at Hogame again, dodging the obsidian spikes that whistled past their ears before they channeled six hard, short bursts of transference mana through their tonfa into Hogame's exposed magma carapace. They weren't exactly certain what effect, if any, the blasts were having, but it was the only attack they could get to penetrate Hogame's shroud.

Berating themself now wasn't going to bring Lani and Aldis back. It wasn't going to save anyone else, either. But figuring out what Lani and Aldis had found—as well as why Hogame had been so particularly interested in preventing them from escaping that pit—might at least save anyone still on their feet.

So what was it?

A doorway makes the most sense, Hane rationalized. *Maybe a locked door? But then, Aldis could have told us to look for a key. Unless it was a door that only opens at the end of a challenge?*

It didn't seem as if this was a challenge designed to be won, so that didn't make much sense. No, the only thing that made sense was if they had found an actual escape route.

Or perhaps . . . a part of an escape route?

No, a key makes no sense, Hane insisted silently. *Lani would have passed off a key. Our hands touched when I tried to pull her out. And even if it was a key, what was it a key to? There's no other door except—*

Wait.

There didn't have to be another door.

The door they had entered through was still visible past the mound of stones that had buried Sage at the beginning. The door was sealed, of course, and when Hane had glanced over it at the beginning of all of this, it hadn't appeared to have a keyhole of any sort.

But just because it doesn't look that way doesn't mean there isn't an illusion over it.

Hane sharpened their vision with a perception spell, flipping upside down within Emiko's rain clouds to peer beyond the filmy veil. The rain made the room look fuzzy, and perception mana wouldn't reveal the same things that mental mana would, like runes or enchantments. But the door was just wet enough for Hane's water perception to detect the hum of a woven spell: it had to be an illusion. It had to be!

But then why wouldn't Lani have passed off a key if she'd found one?

A shout of pain from down below and Hane dropped through the clouds to the hardened-magma floor. Nieve was down, three narrow obsidian blades stuck through her upper arm and shoulder, yet she still kept a grip on her sword as her free hand searched for yet another healing potion in her bag. Hane darted in front of her, taking her place in fighting Hogame head-on so Nieve would have time to heal.

Nieve gasped a word of thanks as she fished out a glass bottle of bright red liquid. Too many more of those and she just might poison herself with them. But that was probably the least of her worries just then.

Hane rolled each tonfa by the handle that stuck out from the side at a right angle, smashing and breaking the black glass projectiles as Hogame launched them. When the lava jets burned hot, Hane dodged and rolled, using the rain to change directions instantly using only small touches of transference mana. The jagged black magma of the floor caught at their quilted clothing, tugged at their bag, jabbed at their shroud. This would be easier with one of Nieve's ice floors, but she had to be running low on mana by now. That, and the lava hidden just under this hard magma layer would probably melt it anyway.

Where was Emiko? What was she doing during all of this? Hane had pressed her earlier to cast another rain spell, but it hadn't fallen with the sharp, stinging force of her earlier storms. This was the problem with climbing with friends: poor judgment, hysteria, an unwillingness to leave behind a lost cause. Hane would have called the climb right after Sage was crushed, but because of the anti-teleportation runes, they were stuck in an unwinnable fight.

At least Nieve was a professional. She'd splashed half the healing potion over her arm, then gripped the neck of the bottle in her teeth as she yanked the obsidian shards out of her arm. She would probably be up on her feet as soon as she finished the potion, ready and willing to take a few more literal stabs at the general of the Tortoise Spire. Her resolve was impressive, under the circumstances. Or maybe she just wanted a little revenge before Hogame got her, too. Either way, she was keeping her head clear and her attention on the fight.

Hane very nearly missed the next volley of obsidian shards. A quick pulse of transference mana through their shroud was the only thing that saved them. How many times had they seen professional, seasoned climbers suddenly lose it and make foolish mistakes when faced with their imminent demise? What if Lani really had found a key but had assumed she would survive long enough to actually use it, rather than passing it off? What if there really was an escape? A real possibility that those of them who were left might walk away from this?

"I'm up!" Nieve shouted, distracting Hane into looking back at her. Emiko's rain tracked thin, red rivulets down Nieve's arm, but she no longer appeared to be actively bleeding. She pulled her arm back, the rounded glass bottle cupped in her palm before she lobbed it at Hogame. "Here, you oversized reptile! Time to get back to the main course!"

Hane doubted that that would have been enough to draw Hogame's focus, but after dodging another jet of lava, they coiled transference mana beneath their feet and leapt for the clouds. Obsidian spikes fired past, one catching their ankle in a jagged line of pain before they concealed themself in the rain clouds once more, leaving Hogame with no other choice than to fight Nieve.

Well, or melt the whole room down.

Hane hoped it wouldn't end quite that quickly.

In the cover of the clouds, Hane flipped open the bag they kept slung over a shoulder and lashed in place with both a latch over their shoulder and a second latch in the middle of their back. The dimensional bag had been a choice bit of loot they'd earned on a previous climb, on a floor higher than this one. It could store far more items than it looked able to hold and could even keep delicate items, like glass-bottled potions, separate from items that might crush or break them. Hane reached into a familiar "pocket" within the bag, confirming that their key collection was still very much intact.

But what key will fit? Hane wondered, thin light glinting over varicolored keys, all collected after completed climbs. A gold key would work in almost any lock, but that was the one color Hane was certain they didn't have. Gold keys were practically a treasure in themselves, while other keys—reds, yellows, blues, blacks, and silvers—were considered little better than trash. A handful of such keys would sell at about the same rate as Carnelian-ranked mana crystals, so most teams didn't mind letting Hane keep a few extras once the climb was complete. And while most keys were able to open more than one lock, Hane was certain they did not have the time required to check each color of key in a keyhole they were only guessing existed.

Likewise, if Hane were to suddenly stop attacking Hogame in order to examine the door, they expected to be melted, much in the same way Lani and Aldis had been.

Checking past the door's illusion for a keyhole was a slim hope, but it was the only hope left to them, so Hane grasped it tight. Sending out Sense Water through the clouds, Hane located Emiko, hidden and silently weeping into her hands. They pushed off the clouds to glide over to her, leaving vaporous trails in their wake. It was a shame that Emiko couldn't keep it together as Nieve could, but then again, her hysteria might just be what kept Hogame from considering her a threat.

"Emi." Hane used the nickname they'd heard the others use, hoping it would soothe her rather than upset her further. They set their hand gently on her shoulder, trying to get her to look up. "I know it's tough for you right now, but Nieve and I need you. There might still be a way out of this if you can keep it together just a little longer."

"B-but Lani." Emiko's eyes were bloodshot, the skin around them raw from rubbing. "S-Sage. Aldis. I can't—I can't—"

"You have to," Hane said, keeping their voice low and level but also firm. "Nieve is still here. You are still here. If you just hide here, Hogame will find you. Perhaps after he's killed me and Nieve. Do you really want to wait for that to happen?"

Emiko sobbed and buried her face in her hands again but shook her head. It was base manipulation, Hane knew that, but they also knew they couldn't leave the fight to Nieve on her own for too much longer.

"Take a moment and pull yourself together," Hane said, taking pains to keep their voice soothing. "But then I need you to do something. Something to help us escape. You can do that, right?"

Emiko nodded, her breathing heavy and blubbery, but at least she was listening.

"I think there's an illusion over the door," Hane explained. "Your perception magic is new, but if you really focus, I think you can see past it. I need you to look for a keyhole. Keep searching until you find it. When you do, shout to me what color key you need and I'll get it to you. Can you do that, Emi?"

"I—I think so," Emiko stammered. "That's not—not so hard."

Hane nodded. They imagined that casting a large breath-activated spell right now might be too much for the little Cloudcaller, but something smaller, designed to save the rest of her team, might just be within Emiko's abilities.

They hoped.

As soon as Emiko confirmed her intentions to follow through, Hane dropped through the clouds, drawing obsidian spikes away from Hogame's shell but holding back from actually firing any mana through their enchanted tonfa. Instead, they replaced Nieve at the helm of the general's center of attention, letting Nieve back away and take a brief respite. She was breathing rapidly, her hand clasped to the center of her chest. Her eyes were still hard, still focused, but her face looked tight and pale. Rather than drink yet another healing potion, Nieve reached for her canteen, drinking greedily before stopping to suck down more air. Hane shattered black-glass projectiles, giving her as much time to recuperate as possible.

For an instant, ancient fear welled up, rising from the pit of Hane's stomach to grip their mind with icy tendrils of panic and grief. The red-orange glow of the room slowly went dark; the floor itself seemed to tip and careen beneath their feet. They felt transported back to that time when the only thing more chilling than the crumpled bodies on the floor were the grim-faced adults holding their notebooks and shaking their heads. Another failure. The next batch will do better. Perhaps they should end the experiment here.

And with only two choices left before them—death by the trial of the goddess or returning with those coldhearted researchers—Hane had forged a third path: they ran. Into the depths of the spire, away from those they counted family, leaving them to die, or, if any survived, to suffer further pain at the hands of the researchers. And in their shameful flight, Hane had never once looked back.

Something slammed into Hane's shoulder, hard enough to knock them to the ground. A white-hot jet of lava seared itself across Hane's vision, making them blink it away fiercely. When they could see again, Nieve stood over them, sword clenched in a white-knuckled grip.

"Get it together," Nieve snapped, her eyes on the general of the Tortoise Spire. "We're still here. Emi's still here. We need to hold."

Hane nodded and climbed back to their feet, a tonfa in each hand as they took a defensive stance.

Finding a keyhole in the door was a slim hope at best, but it was the only hope they had left to them. They had to hold.

For now.

CHAPTER 28

EMIKO

Cloudcaller (lung mark), Citrine

Aldis. Lani. Sage.

Emiko couldn't stop the endless refrain, like a litany of grief inside her head. Portions of poetry, fragmented and staccato, ricocheted and reassembled themselves like echoes of words never spoken, written in the smoke left behind after a firework's explosion. As if three people could be reduced to mere words, common stanzas, their lives nothing more than pretty words in the wind. Emiko felt like she was choking. Drowning.

Like she would be next.

She was aware that her rain spell had ended, but only vaguely, as the clouds lingered still. Soon, they would break up from the heat emanating from the crusted-over lake of lava. From the exposed inner magma of Hogame's shell. Soon, she would have no place left to hide. And then the spire would claim her life, too.

Without the patter and hiss of the rain, Emiko couldn't help but hear the battle below. Hogame's lumbering steps, the crack of the magma crust, the shattering of obsidian projectiles, and the metallic clang of Nieve's sword.

That's right. Nieve is still fighting. And Hane, too. The air felt thick, like trying to breathe through wet wool. Her chest hurt, her eyes hurt, her very soul hurt. *Hane told me to do something. What was it? What can I do? Please, Goddess, we're sorry, so so sorry!*

As if being sorry could bring her friends back.

She saw Aldis's face behind her eyelids, red-cheeked and laughing, sharing food inside the mana fountain room. The inquisitive way he'd asked about her mana diffuser, his interest in trade and enchantments. He was rough around the edges, sure, but his jovial nature had been endearing: Emiko had already accepted him as a new member of the team.

Clever pride all gone . . .

This wasn't his fault. This trial, this punishment, this goddess-forsaken room, Emiko couldn't lay any of it on Aldis's shoulders. They had all agreed, they had all accepted the risk. She had worshiped the goddess her whole life but never thought herself capable of committing a blasphemy that would earn this level of retribution. It didn't seem in line with the teachings at all. Didn't the goddess value lateral thinking? Unique problem solving? If they were wrong, why not allow them to leave, so that they could warn others not to do what they had done? It should be added to the teachings, decreed as an ultimate taboo to protect future climbers . . .

What if this had happened before? And no one knew because none who had tried it had survived?

Then . . . it would happen again.

Emiko scrubbed her cheeks with her hands, sniffling as she peered through the wispy remains of her rain clouds. Hogame was a large, round shape beneath her, with two small, hazy shadows out ahead of him. Nieve and Hane, still fighting. Why? Hadn't they lost already? It wasn't the goddess's will that they survive this.

Unless . . . the challenge was to survive? To make it back and warn other climbers against changing their course through the spire? But how was anyone supposed to survive a fight with Genbu's general of flame and punishment? Where did she even start?

Fearless heart, lead on . . .

Lani had been looking for an exit. An escape. Searching had led to her death, but at least looking for a way out wasn't just giving up. It wasn't waiting to be found so the battle could be over. Emiko was still alive, still mobile with mana to burn, if only she could get the words out. Didn't she owe it to Lani to at least try?

What had Hane wanted her to do? Emiko had barely been able to process their words, so remembering them was difficult. Something about the door? And maybe . . . her perception magic?

That was a place to start, at least.

For three heartbeats, Emiko made an attempt to whisper a spell. A simple one, just a veil of fog to cover herself before descending low enough that Hogame would notice her. It was a spell she knew by heart, yet she stuttered and stammered the words, unable to make it through a single line before the feeling of breathlessness overwhelmed her. Giving up on her fog spell, Emiko skirted the edges of the room, descending only when she was poised just over the room's entrance.

It wasn't often that the entryway was also the point of egress, but it did happen on occasion. Sometimes doorways faded out of existence entirely; other times they were simply covered over by a portion of wall or blocked by bars. This one was covered over by a slab of stone, dense and immovable by all but the will of the goddess. It seemed a hopeless cause, but Emiko placed her hand against it, trying to reach out with her perception mana, though without use of a spell, there was little more that she could tell beyond the fact that there was a doorway there.

"Oh light, show—show the—the—" Emiko choked and shivered, the spell trapped inside her aching chest. "Oh light, make the— Please light, lead the—"

She couldn't make the words come, couldn't find the rhythm that matched magic to melody, couldn't work the spell that might save her remaining team-mates. And hadn't she always known it would come to this? Her team relying on her, and at the critical moment, she failed them. She wasn't strong enough to be a climber, she never had been. She was always the one being carried, never the one to carry the team.

Overcome, she fell against the door, leaning back against it as her levitation spell finally failed. She sank to the floor, her back and shoulders against that stone slab that kept her team from escape and freedom. It seemed a fitting place to end it: trying to be helpful, yet failing all the same.

The room looked blurry, hazy, as if by giving up, Emiko had given up her right to see the end coming. It might have been the tears, or it might have been the heat-haze over the crusted magma floor. It might even have been a mercy of the goddess, who was Emiko to question the point of anything right now? She let her eyes blur, let herself feel the weakness seated in her chest that kept her from breathing, from speaking her spells, from doing anything worthwhile, here at the bitter end. The clearest thing she could see was the low, misshapen mound of boulders, so close to the door that she could kick a stone if she had but the energy.

First friend, wise and true . . .

Sage and all his brilliant plans and foresight, buried at the beginning of all of this. Was that why everyone had seemed so lost from the beginning? Without their compass, how were they to know which path to follow? This wasn't Sage's fault either, though. He'd done his best to peer into this room before they'd walked through the doorway. Surely that meant this was the will of the goddess.

It won't be so bad, Emiko thought, hunkering down to wait. *Sage will wait for me, I know it. We'll wait for Nieve together . . .*

Except—

Was that . . . movement?

Emiko blinked. Scrubbed at her eyes. It was probably just the vibrations caused by Hogame's footsteps causing smaller stones to tumble off the mound. That had to be it. She couldn't have seen . . .

No. No! It really was! A dust-covered hand peeked out from between two stones that stood as high as Emiko's knees. The fingers twitched, tensed, nails digging into the floor as tendons flexed along the back of the hand.

Sage!

Emiko crawled forward, almost blind with fresh tears. She covered Sage's hand with her own. His wrist tried to turn but couldn't. Still, he managed to curl his fingers around Emiko's, his grip too loose to be worthy of the word, but still! Sage was alive!

And most likely hurt.

"Sage, Sage, I'm so sorry I thought you were dead!" Emiko patted his hand once, then grasped the closest stone and pulled it away, using her shoulder and elbow to direct the ones that rolled down after, ignoring bruises and scrapes. "We've never needed you like we need you now. Sage, it's— We might have lost—" Emiko couldn't make herself say it. If Sage was alive, then couldn't Lani and Aldis be alive, too? "Why am I telling you? I'm sure you already know. You probably know more than I do. Sage?"

Rocks shifted and rolled, some pinching her fingers, some slamming into her legs and ankles as she pushed, pulled, and shoved them out of the way. There weren't as many as there had been at the beginning, thanks to her stone spell and Aldis's portal through Hogame's shroud. But there were still more than enough to crush a person, and even though they were long settled by now, rock dust coated the arm Emiko slowly revealed.

Panting, her fingers torn and bleeding, Emiko rolled a heavy stone away and curled her body over it, peering into the opening beyond. "Sage?"

No response.

She could see a partially open space, where two taller stones had formed a sort of roof over Sage's head and the upper part of his back. But if he was breathing, it was too thin to see. Emiko craned forward, reaching out to lift the hair that covered his face. Blood, thick, dark, and clotted with dust, trailed down the side of his face that Emiko could see. His skin was cool, ashen even beneath the coating of dust. And yet a pulse ticked weakly at his throat.

"Sage," Emiko whimpered. She pulled back, looking around frantically. It took her a moment to realize she was looking for Lani.

"That's okay," she said, mostly to herself. "It's okay, Sage. It's going to be okay. Just hold on for me. I can do this. I can do this."

She couldn't make the perception spell work, but she could do this. If it killed her, she would do this. Sage was alive, and at that moment, everything else ceased to matter.

Sage was alive and she could save him.

As her fingers fit the green life crystal into her mana diffuser, Emiko drew a breath. It wasn't deep enough, so she released it and tried again. She had to stand up: her lungs felt too compressed while seated on the ground.

Was someone calling her name? Didn't they realize she couldn't be distracted right now?

"Gentle Spring, come fast." Her breath felt strong, stronger than it had even before Lani and Aldis vanished into that cursed pit. Her wind had left her the moment Sage was buried in stone. It returned to her now, full and deep and powerful. "Bring forth new life—"

Hane was shouting something, probably telling her to focus on the door. She could do that in a minute. She would have strength left over after this.

"—Heal our woes."

Now Nieve was shouting. Didn't she understand? Emiko's concentration couldn't waver. Sage's life was in the balance and Lani wasn't here right now.

"Make the flowers—"

"Emi, get down!" Nieve's frantic tone finally caught Emiko's ear, drawing her eyes up even as she held the spell bound within her chest. Nieve was running, Hane was making a sweeping gesture with a tonfa. All of that registered only an instant before something impacted Emiko's chest hard enough to slam her back into the wall behind her. Even in her stunned state, she refused to let her breath go, instead looking down to see what had hit her.

Oh.

She saw only a sheen of black obsidian, wide and blunt at the end. An obsidian spike. Transfixed through her chest.

She didn't even feel it. Not really. Not as pain, but more as pressure, urging her to release that last breath, to let go of her final spell. She forced herself to hold it, closing her eyes so she didn't have to see Nieve's look of anguish.

Instead, she thought of Sage, lying cold and breathless under a mound of stone.

"Grow," she finished, releasing all her power in her final breath.

CHAPTER 29

NIEVE

Champion (mind mark), Citrine

??? (heart mark), Sealed

"Emi, no! No!"

Nieve hardly recognized the heartrending scream as her own. She wasn't aware of when, exactly, she had turned her back on Hogame, but she had. She couldn't hope to beat the obsidian spike, but she could catch it, couldn't she? Put up an ice wall, wrap Emi up in a dome, something, anything! But as she reached for her magic, Nieve's world spun on an axis, pain erupting in starbursts inside her head. If she used more mana now, she'd risk permanent mental scarring, but for Emi, it would be worth it.

Besides, that wasn't the only power Nieve could draw on.

But even as she reached for the seal on her secret heart mark, she knew it was too late. Emiko was pinned to the far wall, her eyes wide, her mouth an O of surprise. For a moment, as their eyes locked over the distance, Nieve thought it might be okay. If that spike missed hitting something vital, then maybe—just maybe—she could still save her. The cost didn't matter, giving up the secret didn't matter, the only thing that mattered was saving Emi. But between her physical and mental exhaustion—with the pounding in her head and the burn wounds that peppered her body twice over—Nieve stumbled over the words she was supposed to use. She saw Emi close her eyes, then the exhalation of a word she couldn't hear.

As a misty rain began to fall, Emi's head slumped sideways, her tiny body crumpling around the obsidian spike. The open, glassy-eyed stare made it all too clear that once again, Nieve had been too late.

"No no no, Emi! Mi-mi!" Nieve tried to run. To race. To get there in time, because maybe if she did, it would make a difference. Before she took two steps, her Frost Form spell fractured and faded, her strength and endurance vanishing as sharply as if her legs had been cut out from under her. She dropped to her knees, her sword skittering from her grasp across the obsidian. It felt like there wasn't enough good air left to breathe in the entire room.

The blackened magma crust covering the center of the room cracked, obscene lava veins licking at the seams, making fragments rock and bob like broken ice on a lake. Nieve felt the ground beneath her tilt and buckle, droplets of lava hissing as they spurted up between the cracks.

"No!" Nieve snarled, snatching up her sword again and staggering to her feet. "Not now! You don't get to do this to me now."

The words to a spell she'd never used before might have eluded her, but her sheet-of-ice spell came as naturally as breathing, even if she had to rip the magic from her arms, legs, lungs, and heart to cast it. And Emiko's last rain spell helped just enough that Nieve was able to lay ice not only over the top of the magma layer, making it solid once more, but it also helped her encase each of Hogame's legs in a shackle of ice, making him roar and thrash in order to free his legs.

The spell cost her, though: Nieve's vision went dark, her knees buckled, and her gorge rose. She could see each indignant roar of the spire's general in crimson waves that broke against her eyeballs. Her ice was already melting, the cracks and pings like white-blue sparks that diverted and distracted her. If she weren't so certain that she was about to die, she'd be worried about the damage this all would cause her.

"Nieve." Hane was by her side, gripping her elbow to help her to her feet.

"Get away from me," Nieve snarled, yanking her arm free of Hane's grip. With her sword, she pointed, unable to look back lest she lose her ability to fight. "What was she doing there? You told her to try something, didn't you? She could have hid! She could have lasted until the end!"

"I'm sorry," Hane said simply, though the sorrow didn't touch their face. "Should we survive, I'll accept any punishment you wish, but for now, I'm your last ally standing."

Nieve hated that they were right. All she wanted was to grab them by the shoulders and shake them until their neck snapped, but that wouldn't be meaningful. Not now. It wouldn't help her, and it certainly wouldn't help Emi or any of the others.

"Do you have a plan?" Nieve asked, stabbing her sword into the ice around her to lever herself up to her feet. Most of the ice was already gone; Hogame had three legs free already and was violently straining against the sole remaining ice shackle.

Hane said nothing but reached into their bag, their hand emerging with an escape bell cradled in their palm. Nieve grimaced and reached into a belt pouch for her own. She held the bell up to confirm with Hane. They each shook vigorously, then paused, daring to hope, straining to feel the effects of the teleportation magic . . . But of course it failed. Nieve dropped her bell back into her bag, though she might as well have dropped it in a pool of lava for all the good it would do her. She gripped the hilt of her sword in both hands, squaring her shoulders against Hogame as he tore free of the final shackle.

"It was worth a try," Hane said, squaring up beside her. They dipped their hand into the bag again, this time holding up a bottle of bright red potion. Nieve considered it, then shook her head.

"I'd just throw it up." The last few potions already had her feeling ill. "Besides." She turned her face up to the gently falling rain. "I think this is a healing rain."

Hane looked up at the falling rain, nodded, and then put their healing potion away. Nieve found herself grateful that Hane didn't try to spin it as Emi's final hope for them to survive or anything trite like that. The facts were the facts, and nothing more. Nieve could appreciate that, even if she didn't appreciate Hane very much at that moment.

They stood shoulder to shoulder, Nieve's sword braced defensively, Hane poised with a tonfa in each hand, as Hogame lumbered toward them. She wasn't sure how much mana Hane had left, but she had noticed that they were no longer blasting mana through their tonfa, and for some time now, they had been fighting on the ground with her, rather than flipping through the clouds and running on the rain. Perhaps they were saving up for a final attack, or maybe they were running just as dry as Nieve was. It made little difference in the end: a difference of about five to ten more minutes, by Nieve's estimate.

"This has been more fun than I have had in a long time." Hogame's voice boomed off the walls and ceiling, the obsidian crust glowing under each of his feet every time he took a step. **"It is always amusing to watch the antics of humans. But as you two are the last and I can see you are weary, I will make this end quick for you."**

Nieve braced herself, fully prepared to jump away if the floor should turn to lava again. It seemed Hogame knew as well as she did that she didn't have enough power left for another sheet of ice. She could still use the power hidden near her heart if she could undo the seal, but without Emiko or Sage, without Lani, continuing to fight just seemed pointless. She didn't have the strength to break the seal, nor did she remember the correct words to call upon the mystery that was her heart mark. Even if she had the strength and the knowledge, she didn't have the time. No, even if she revealed it now, it wouldn't be enough to save her.

Surviving alone wasn't really surviving, anyway.

The ground beneath Nieve's boots began to burn. Before she could determine whether it was a lava plume or yet another breaking of the floor, a light so brilliant that it made the lava seem shadowed burst across the room in a narrow ray. The ray of light slammed into Hogame's face bright and hard enough that he roared and reeled backward, shaking his head from side to side, yet the light tracked with him.

Nieve whipped around so fast that she lost her balance. Hane grabbed her arm to keep her on her feet and for once, she didn't pull away immediately.

Sage had risen from his cairn of stone, rivulets of rain and blood tracking through the ashen dust that coated him from head to toe. His face looked strangely naked without his glasses and he must have lost his dueling cane, for he held the beam of light in his outstretched palm. He looked like half a corpse, but he was *alive* and, in that moment, Nieve could have kissed him.

"Stand aside, guys, I've got this," Sage commanded, voice loud, determined, as he held his beam of light centered over Hogame's face. "My mana reserves are full and I can See every move he's about to make. I'll protect you!"

That was what he said, but Sage's actions were in complete opposition with his words. He shook his head and made an abrupt gesture with a closed fist that clearly said "Get over here, now!" Hogame reared up, slamming his front feet down hard enough to send thick, red cracks spiderwebbing across the surface of the magma crust, which was all the motivation Nieve needed to comply. She scrambled off the smoking magma and onto the much cooler stone that rimmed the edges of the room, Hane clearing the distance in a single leap. Sage held his beam of light over Hogame's face the entire time, tracking every movement.

"Hane, take the key." Sage held out a hand, his attention never wavering from Hogame. "Nieve." He choked. Swallowed hard. "Get Emi."

Nieve only caught the briefest glimpse of a black key and something thin and shining in Sage's palm before the weight of Sage's request hit her like a punch to the gut. She reached for hope that maybe Emi's last healing spell had somehow saved her too, but hope vanished like rain on lava at the sight of Emi's glassy, unblinking eyes, at the unnatural tilt of her head. There was no saving her. But at the very least, they could bring her back home.

"Hurry," Sage urged, his voice fevered but low. "I can't hold him for long. Get the door open, Hane."

"There's an illusion over it, but I can sense that it is a way out." Hane pressed both palms against the layer of stone blocking the door. "We'll only have a moment once I get it open. Everyone be ready."

Sage shot Nieve a pleading look over his shoulder. She nodded grimly, reversed her grip on her sword, and then slammed the hilt into the wide end of the obsidian spike pinning Emi to the wall. It shattered just enough for her to hold Emi by the shoulders, bitter bile flooding her mouth as she pulled her friend off the part of the spike. For someone who had been so light in life, she was almost too heavy for Nieve to carry in death. But maybe that was just the exhaustion. Nieve shifted Emi's weight up over her shoulder, feeling the seconds tick by as Hane ran their hands over the door, searching for the keyhole beneath the illusion.

"Got it." It was barely noticeable, but as Hane spoke, a black-rimmed keyhole appeared to the right of the door. They jammed the key in the lock, glanced back once, and then turned it.

Hogame screamed as if pained, obsidian spikes erupting from his shell all at once in a mad assault. Nieve dove through the door before it was fully opened, Hane only paused long enough to grab Sage's collar and yank him through as well. They weren't back inside the mana fountain room, which meant they weren't safe by any means, but that was all Nieve had time to notice.

"Lani and Aldis—" she started, looking to Sage.

"I know." Sage's eyes were bright, but somehow they looked older than they had at the beginning of the climb. Weary. Aged. "Sorry, Nieve. I—I Saw it all."

"No time," Hane snapped, ripping their return bell out of their bag and holding it up. The room shook around them: walls and doors were no barrier against Hogame's overwhelming power. "Do you have yours, Sage?"

"No." Sage's bag was gone, along with his cloak, his cane, and his glasses. He still had two belt pouches on his right hip, but the rest had been torn away. His tunic seemed mostly intact, with only a few tears on his sleeves and leggings, so his shroud must have taken most of the impact from the doortrap. The hair over his ear was glued to the side of his head with congealed blood, which was most likely the blow that had knocked him out.

"I have you." Hane looped an arm over Sage's shoulder, tugging him tight to their chest. "Nieve?"

"Ready." She grasped her bell, holding Emi tight against her shoulder as she gave it a hard shake.

In the breathless seconds before the teleportation magic could take hold, the room they had spilled into began to glow with an ominous red light. Nieve heard Hogame's roar of protest growing louder, closer, imminent—

—And then cool, fresh air hit her face so hard that she staggered backward, collapsing under Emiko's weight into thick, deep grass. A coughing fit hit her so hard that her eyes teared up, the sharp, convulsive movements tugging mercilessly on every battle-weary muscle in her body. When she could breathe again, the air was so cold it felt like breathing knives into her lungs. She had almost forgotten what it was like to breathe crisp air, unladen with sulfur and regret. A second deep breath set her to coughing again, her chest compressed by Emi's weight. Shadows fell over her, and Emi was carefully lifted away.

Sage grasped her wrists gently and pulled her up to sitting. She clasped Sage's tunic tightly in a fist, terrified that if she let go, she'd lose her team all over again. She held on until it no longer hurt to breathe, allowing her to blink the tears from her eyes so she could finally take stock of her surroundings.

Sage sat in front of her, watching her through tearful eyes. Hane sat nearby, cradling Emi in their arms. Someone had closed her eyes, and with her head tipped in toward Hane's shoulder, she could almost be sleeping. They were all outside, on the grass beside the Guiding Star Legacy flag, the place where the anchors to their return bells were monitored by the Soaring Wings administration. The Tortoise Spire loomed just beyond the canvas awning, distant yet menacing in a way Nieve had never associated it with until today. The black stone tower harkened an image of a grave marker, stark against the too-blue sky.

Her gaze dropping to Emi's limp body once more, Nieve felt a bubble of grief and pain well up inside her chest, catching in her throat to make her choke. Sage's arms were around her then, pulling her against him in a hug that was more desperate than affectionate. She clung to him with the urgency of an unnamable emotion, uncertain whether the raw-sounding sobs were hers or Sage's as they rolled through her chest.

Hane held their silence, staying close but coming no closer. That made sense, in a way. They were a part of this, of course, but it wasn't the same. If they grieved, they kept it close. Guarded. If they no longer grieved those left behind in the spire, well, they didn't speak to that, either. By the time Nieve's gasping breath was finally beginning to return to normal, Hane said lightly: "The officials are on their way over. They'll be here in a moment."

Nieve nodded, sitting back on her knees to clean her face. There would be paperwork to fill out, affidavits to sign that no team member had maliciously caused the death of another during the climb. There were families to talk to, portions of treasure to be paid out. So much to do that it all suddenly felt more overwhelming than facing down the Tortoise Spire's general of flame and punishment.

"Wait. Before they get here." Sage sniffed hard, making an effort to set his face before holding out his clenched-tight fist. His fingers opened slowly, shakily, as if he had been clutching at something far tighter than he'd needed to.

There it was. The slivered crystal shard Lani had held on to since the beginning of the climb.

Chime.

"How did you get that?" Nieve asked. She'd been sure Lani had it on her, had seen it in Lani's belt pouch when they left the mana fountain. There hadn't been time to ask about the black key Sage had had when he'd pulled his miraculous resurrection, but they had time now. If only minutes before the spire officials descended upon them.

"Aldis and La—" Sage choked. "Lani. They managed to open a portal before—before—" Nieve waved a hand, letting him know he didn't have to finish. "They sent the key. And Chime."

Hane leaned forward delicately, peering at the crystal without letting go of Emiko. "Can you still hear them?"

"No," Sage admitted, closing his hand on the shard. He met Nieve's eyes defiantly. "I know we were against it before, Nieve, but she—she risked everything to get this to me. To us." Sage clutched the shard close to his chest, hand shaking as he lowered his head. "I'm going to do it. I'm going to find Chime's missing pieces and see them restored to their shrine. Because that's what—that's what—"

Nieve's heart ached. She'd thought him only infatuated, which made playing his rival in love a fun game. If he'd really been in love with Lani, then . . . Well, it could only be described as cruel now.

"I'm going," Sage said when he finished choking on his words. "And it's fine if you two don't want to come, but—"

"I'm coming," Hane said, soft but fierce. "I want to. If you'll let me."

"I'm coming, too," Nieve replied wearily, the headache that had been threatening to overtake her imminent. "I can't let you carry out her final wish on your own. I need to make it to the top of a spire anyway, and somehow, I don't think I'm welcome in this one anymore."

Sage's next breath was almost a chuckle, though it was tinged in bitterness. He tucked Chime away in an inside pocket of his dueling tunic. The Soaring Wings officials were close enough now that Nieve could hear them shouting. "Thank you. Both of you. Let's . . . let's talk about it again after."

Nieve nodded, as did Hane.

There was more than enough to deal with just now.

The Soaring Wings officials flocked around them, asking where the rest of their team was and offering healing spells. As an Acolyte pressed cool fingers against Nieve's forehead, she finally gave in to the mana sickness that consumed her from the inside and let herself pass out. The numbing darkness felt like relief.

EPILOGUE

Sage

Seer (hand mark), Citrine

Oppressive silence lay heavily on Sage's shoulders, bowing his head and squeezing his heart. Noise would have been a welcome distraction: conversation, music, or even the soft tinkle of a fountain. Now and then someone shuffled, reminding Sage he wasn't alone, but it wasn't enough to break through his grief, his heartache.

His regret.

Every time he closed his eyes, he saw them die again. Aldis. Emiko. Lani . . .

He'd watched it all, helpless to influence the outcome, silenced by an unforeseen tumble of stone that rendered him helpless during his team's greatest need. He'd seen the general of the god beast Genbu appear, watched the valiant yet hopeless battle, screamed as Lani and Aldis met their end . . . sobbed when Emi met hers.

He'd tried to save Emi. He had. His consciousness had been so close to his body, he struggled to make it move, to speak, to do *anything* to prevent the coming fate. He'd tried to hold her hand, tried to keep her from standing up and making herself a target. He would have traded his life for Emi's. But in the end, he'd been unable to do anything.

Useless. Worthless. Pitiful.

Yet somehow alive.

It was only through his sense of duty that Sage kept himself moving forward. First, to save the ones that could be saved: Nieve. And Hane. Second, delivering Emiko to her family and apologizing fervently, deeply, with his forehead pressed to the ground as they wept for their daughter. He would have told Lani's family but didn't know how to find them; Lani had cut ties with them years before Sage had ever met her. She said it was to protect them from her debts, and Sage hadn't thought to question past that. Nieve, as the team leader, had informed Aldis's family of his death. There was no set date for the funeral yet, but Sage planned on attending if he was able.

The paperwork required for fatalities sustained within the spire was exhaustive enough to serve almost as a respite for Sage. He was able to lose himself in the heartlessness of it. Name of the deceased. Attunement(s) of the deceased. Next of kin of the deceased. Treasure allocation for the deceased. The word "deceased" was repeated so often that it lost all meaning, allowing Sage to fill in answers sans emotional response.

It was only after the paperwork was finished that the grief set back in. Every time he was alone with his thoughts, he saw their faces, heard their voices . . .

Watched them die.

"Sage. Sage?"

His body rocked beneath a hand on his shoulder. He would have startled if he'd had the energy, but as it was, he only looked up slowly, morosely, halfway hoping that whoever it was that roused him would put him out of his misery.

So of course it was only Nieve.

"Hey," she said, expression twisted into one of worry. "They called us. Did you hear?"

Sage blinked and looked around, reminding himself of where he was. The silence was so absolute, he'd almost thought he was at a funeral, but no. This was the waiting room inside the official Dalenos division of the Soaring Wings administration. He rubbed his forehead as he remembered why they were there.

"I didn't hear," Sage admitted. "Sorry."

Nieve tried a smile, but it fell from her face too soon, her eyes darting away from his. As if she found him too painful to look at. "We don't have to take this on, you know. We can just explain the situation and hand over the—"

"No." Sage reached up to touch his glasses, hesitated when they weren't there, then ran a shaking hand back through his hair instead. "No, I want to do this. I have to."

Nieve nodded solemnly. "I understand."

Sage got to his feet, noting the other petitioners seated in the waiting room of the administration hall. The faces were all new since he'd sat down. Strange: he hadn't heard any names being called, nor the quiet murmur from the registration desk as climbers and applicants signed in to await their appointment. Maybe it hadn't been as silent as he'd thought.

Having no idea where to go, Sage followed Nieve, who greeted a woman wearing the badge of a Soaring Wings administrator pinned to her shirt. She smiled and greeted Nieve with a professional's courtesy, motioning for them to follow her. Sage followed on instinct more than by intent. He'd been told the fog of grief would fade over time, but he no longer recalled who had said that to him.

"Welcome, Team Guiding Star Legacy," the administrator said with a painted-on smile as she welcomed them into a warmly furnished office. "I've been reviewing your climber file, as well as your request, and I just have a few—"

The sudden pause didn't alert Sage so much as Nieve spinning on her heel to face the doorway, her hand dropping to the hilt of a sword she didn't wear. Sage dropped his hand to his belt, too, acutely noting the loss of his dueling cane. He'd need to commission a new one, soon, too, if he was going to get one with all the extra features of his old one. That was good: one more thing to keep his mind distracted from its grief.

The administrator had been closing the door to the office when a hooded youth ducked inside with a sinuous twist of their shoulders, a hood pulled low over their face, posture hunched, hands buried deeply in their jacket pockets. Seemingly their appearance had startled the administrator.

"It's okay," Nieve assured her, hand falling away from her nonexistent sword. "That's Hane. They're with us."

Had Hane been waiting with them out in the lobby? Sage didn't remember seeing them. But then, he'd also forgotten that Nieve was there, as well as why he'd been waiting in the first place. He dropped so steeply into darkness whenever he wasn't keeping himself busy.

Perhaps that was why he needed this so desperately.

"Ah, yes," the administrator said, seemingly hesitant over allowing Hane to enter her office. She recovered her clinical smile a moment later, shutting the door before rounding the corner of her desk to sit behind an open file. "Welcome. I'm Administrator Kagomi and I've been assigned to the request you filed about two weeks ago."

Had it really only been two weeks? Time felt slow lately. Especially all the sleepless nights in between.

"First, I have to say how sorry I am to hear of your losses on this last climb." Kagomi's tone was properly sympathetic, but it failed to carry any weight on the word "losses." It sounded like she was reading from a script, rather than truly sorry. "I must say, for as many climbs as you've completed, Guiding Star Legacy looks to be a very accomplished team." She selected a page from the file, one filled out in Sage's neat penmanship and blotted here and there with tears. "I have to admit, it's a bit of a shock that you want to branch out and begin climbing foreign spires. I understand that your loss is very fresh right now, but we'd like to keep you here, in Dalenos. The administration is willing to extend some bereavement funds to all three of you while you recover if you will consider remaining here."

"We're—" Nieve stopped and coughed, a dry, rattling sound. Sage should probably ask her if she'd suffered any permanent damage from that last fight, but doing so would be facing his own guilt for leaving her to fight on her own while he'd remained safely out of the way, and he wasn't ready for that just yet. "We're not relocating due to grief. We have a mission we need to complete."

"A mission?" Kagomi tilted her head, her brows arched in polite curiosity. "Is it from Katashi? Or another visage, perhaps?"

"No." Nieve shifted as if uncomfortable. She glanced sideways at Sage. He met her gaze uncomprehendingly, then slowly understood what she was asking. He reached into his belt pouch, flinching at the first object he touched, then withdrawing the slivered shard that housed Chime's consciousness. He solemnly unwrapped the handkerchief that encased it, then held it up in his outstretched palms. Kagomi leaned across her desk, frowning as she examined it.

"What is it?" she asked inquisitively. "If you need some enchanted item replaced, I can check and see if the administration has a similar item you could utilize on an extended loan."

"No, it's—" Nieve broke off again, clearing her throat, then sipping from a hip flask. She tried again, then shook her head. "Can you explain it, Sage? I halfway didn't believe it, even when I was listening to their story."

"Do I have to?" Sage asked, morose.

"It would be best coming from you," Hane said gently. "It's okay if you don't remember everything. We can help you remember."

Sage nodded stiffly, letting his hands rest in his lap, Chime still cradled in his palm. "You won't hear anything now, but during our climb we discovered this . . . shard. It possesses the sentience of a gateway crystal from the Unclaimed Lands. They . . . they're broken." *Like me*, Sage thought but didn't say out loud. "Our team leader promised we'd make them whole again and return them to their shrine. I need to—we need to keep that promise."

"I'm not sure I understand," Kagomi admitted, sitting back in her chair. "Why can't the entity speak to me now?"

"They don't have enough power in this form," Sage explained. Questions were easy; they kept his mind off darker themes. "You should be able to question them in areas with high mana concentration, if you need to. They said their pieces were broken off in the other spires. We're requesting funds and letters of support in order to search for the missing pieces in the other spires across Kaldwyn."

"Hm." Kagomi tapped a finger on her desk, lips twisted to the side as she considered. "Assuming that to be true, what would the benefit to Dalenos be?" She blinked and smiled suddenly, as if catching herself acting unsympathetic. "Aside from being a tribute to your fallen comrades, I mean."

Sage hesitated, looking from Nieve to Hane. Surprisingly, it was Hane who answered the question.

"We can't speak on behalf of the entity trapped within this shard." Hane's hood cast a shadow over the features of their face, rendering their expression unreadable. "But they've promised to deliver boons to those that help them. Perhaps they can form some sort of alliance with the government of Dalenos. Whether that be in regard to challenges, or limiting entrants from other nations, we can't say at this time."

"Interesting." Kagomi tapped her finger again, eyes calculating variables that Sage couldn't begin to imagine. "Do you think this entity would be open to making such an alliance?"

"Possibly." Hane shrugged. "You would have to talk to them yourself."

"Hm. And what shrine is it the gateway crystal of?"

"*They*," Hane said with surprising firmness, "are the gateway crystal of the Shrine of Singing Waters."

"My apologies." Kagomi addressed the crystal in Sage's hand, but her expression seemed preoccupied. She rested her fingers on a glass paperweight shaped like a pyramid, her fingers pinching the top. "It's a fascinating story. I've never heard anything quite like it. If the gateway crystal would agree to allow Dalenos jurisdiction over their shrine, I could see the administration agreeing to fund your quest. To some extent, at least."

"We need a travel budget," Nieve put in, seemingly unsure as she glanced at Sage. "And equipment and letters of introduction. Money for gear and consumables and maybe even a translator would be helpful."

"I would need to talk to the higher-ups before I could confirm any sort of support to your team, but this is an intriguing tale." Kagomi pursed her lips. Her fingers drummed restlessly on the glass pyramid as if it were a familiar fidget. "There is another option. We can mobilize Soaring Wings teams within the other spires to search for the pieces and bring them here. That way, you won't have to travel so far and you could still complete your promise to the crystal."

"Chime," Sage corrected. "We did consider that, but since Chime can sense their pieces within a spire, we thought it would be faster to take Chime to each spire ourselves. They can guide us that way."

Kagomi's eyes glittered with cold calculation. "We could always—"

Hane lifted their chin, though the shadows beneath their hood never moved. They gave the impression of glaring at Kagomi without ever showing their eyes. "We are not breaking them."

"Of course, of course, that would be very rude." Kagomi sat back abruptly, one finger tapping thoughtfully on the peak of the pyramid paperweight. She held her silence for a moment, mouth twisted thoughtfully to the side. "Your team does have an outstanding reputation—or it did up until this most recent climb, I should say. Miss Nieve and Mister Seiji are two of the legacy's re-founding members, but as I understand it, you"—she pointed to Hane—"are not a formal member of this team."

The silence felt as absolute as a shadow. Hane held perfectly still, as if they were scarcely breathing. Just as Sage began to wonder if Hane was going to walk out on them, something in their rigid posture softened.

"If I am invited to, I would be willing to sign on to the Guiding Star Legacy team as an official member." Hane's shadowed hood turned to face Nieve. "But I leave that decision to the team leader."

Nieve looked startled, as if surprised to find herself in charge. "Yeah. I mean, yes, right?" Nieve glanced at Sage, as if he might object. He wouldn't: Hane had been of far more use in that final fight than Sage had been. "We need you, Hane. Sorry, I should have asked before now, but I—we—for sure want you to join the team. As long as you don't mind, I guess. I know you're not one for joining up."

Hane's shoulders rolled in a shrug. "I'm invested in seeing Chime restored. I can't say I'll stay on for longer than that, though."

"I'm fine with that," Nieve said quickly. "Sage?"

"We couldn't do it without you," Sage agreed, though it made his heart feel heavy to admit it. Could they really hope to accomplish such a feat as reassembling a gateway crystal's consciousness without Aldis's portal magic, Emiko's boundless cheer, and Lani's steadfast leadership? Just the thought of climbing with a new team felt traitorous, somehow.

"Even so, your team is definitely down a few members," Kagomi pointed out, her tone more pragmatic than sympathetic. "Your healer was top-rate; one of the best on record for an unsponsored team. And your Cloudcaller was exceptional by climbing standards. Do you really believe you can repli-cate your former successful climbs without those team members?"

Nieve hedged and looked to Sage, her jaw tight with a gleam of pain in her eyes. Sage turned away, unable to face that pain head-on.

"It won't be the same," Sage admitted slowly, his eyes fixed on the crystal shard resting on his palms. "We'll need help, for sure, and I don't think it'll be easy, but I don't think we'll give up, either." His fingers curled around Chime's silent form like a gentle embrace. "It's not just for us, or even for the gateway crystal. It's for . . . it's for them."

Nieve clapped a hand on Sage's shoulder, her grip so tight it was almost painful. Without looking up, Sage covered her hand with his, appreciating the contact as well as the implied approval. On Sage's other side, Hane made a loose fist and rapped their knuckles against Sage's shoulder, a wordless show of solidarity.

Kagomi nodded, lips pursed as she sized each one of them up critically. "All right, then. I can raise this issue with my superiors and start working on a travel budget for your team. Start reaching out to powerful friends in other nations, grease a few wheels, sow a few seeds, you know how it goes."

"So you think they'll sponsor us?" Sage asked, surprised. He'd hoped they would, but when he'd been honest with himself, he'd expected that they'd have to fund this journey themselves.

"Well, I suspect someone will want to talk to the—" Kagomi covered a sudden cough. "Talk to Chime and hash out a favorable deal in exchange for the support. There are a few locations available for such a chat. I don't imagine you would feel comfortable leaving Chime with—"

"No." Sage wasn't the only one who protested, but he was the one to close his hands around the crystal sliver, pulling it close to his chest.

"We're holding on to them," Nieve stated fiercely.

"We'll meet you at a designated place and time, but Chime stays with one of us," Hane added with something like a threat to their tone.

"Understandable." Kagomi waved a hand as if their reticence was to be expected. "Well then, if you'll allow me a few days to consult with my superiors, I can set up a time and place to speak with Chime and work out a mutually beneficial arrangement for all of us."

"We'll need access to all the spires," Hane put in unexpectedly. "All of them."

"If this venture is approved, we'll be able to provide you assistance at the Serpent, Tiger, Hydra, and Phoenix spires," Kagomi assured them. "The Spider Spire is a little more complicated, but we'll see what we can do." She hedged for a moment, then added: "I can't imagine you'll need to visit the Seventh Spire in the Unclaimed Lands, but if you do, neither Dalenos nor the Soaring Wings has any influence we can assert there. You'll have to appeal to the goddess for that one."

The possibility of visiting the mysterious closed spire of the Unclaimed Lands hadn't even occurred to Sage. He'd heard the stories of climbers making the journey to see the spire, but he'd never heard a single one claim to have been inside it. It seemed unlikely that one of Chime's pieces would be found inside. It was almost equally shocking to consider visiting the Spider Spire; he'd never met anyone claiming to have been there, as its location was the best-kept secret in Kaldwyn. Though he had heard a rumor or two that the Spider Spire was under Dalenos's influence, which would be a lucky turn if it was true.

"I think I have about enough to write up a proposal for your quest," Kagomi stated, making a note inside the file on her desk. "Rest assured that we will treat this information with the utmost consideration and secrecy. Expect a communication from my office in the next few days."

"You think they'll really fund us?" Nieve asked, sounding surprised. "For traveling and gear and other climbers, all of that?"

"I think it will depend upon the deal we strike with Chime," Kagomi pointed out. "But I'm hopeful we'll be able to provide at least something to help get you started." Kagomi shuffled the papers on her desk, halfway closing the file before pausing and looking up. "Unless there is anything else you need to disclose before I take this matter to my superiors?"

Sage cast a look over at Nieve, wondering if they should disclose the reason Chime was broken with their consciousness trapped inside crystalline shards among the spires. It was relevant if the person who had captured Chime against their will was still alive, and perhaps searching for the pieces of their missing sword, but by Chime's own admission, they could have been dormant for a hundred years, in which case Sage didn't think it was worth sharing. Nieve gave an imperceptible shrug, likely thinking along similar lines.

"I think that's everything we know for certain," Nieve said, pushing herself up from her chair. "You'll be able to ask Chime directly for anything else at the meeting." She glanced over at Sage as he delicately wrapped the handkerchief around Chime's form again. "We have somewhere we need to be right now, anyway."

Sage froze in the middle of wrapping the handkerchief tight. He choked on a breath, eyes stinging badly enough that he had to close them. He hadn't forgotten; he just hadn't wanted to think of it.

"Emiko's funeral?" Hane asked, also rising. "May I accompany you? I'd like to pay my respects."

Nieve nodded tightly. She turned to leave, then stopped. Sage flinched at the gentle hand on his shoulder. "Come on, Sage. We don't want to be late."

"I know." It came out as a whisper. It came out as pain. He focused on his careful wrapping of Chime, blinking away tears until he could see again. When he stood, he felt unsteady, yet determined. He wasn't going to miss his chance to say goodbye. He just wished he didn't have to say it.

Nieve led the way out of the Soaring Wings administration building and out into the streets of Tenkai. It was just past midday, and the streets were bustling with shoppers, hawkers, tourists, climbers, and every bit of imaginable humanity, but Sage felt removed from it all. He didn't fit in this cheerful, life-filled scene. He wanted to be alone, someplace dark and quiet. Except, that was also the last thing he wanted: to be alone with his thoughts, his guilt, his overwhelming sense of sorrow.

Keeping his eyes stuck to Nieve's back, he tucked Chime away in his belt pouch, a fresh wave of emotional agony washing over him as he touched the curve of the enchanted object inside. How had this, of all things, remained with him after that climb? He'd lost his enchanted glasses, his custom-made dueling cane, his satchel of supplies, and he'd broken half the enchantments on his dueling vest. Yet this had stayed with him. Why?

"There's a Wayfarer's flag on the corner," Nieve said, pointing. "We can pay for a teleport straight to the Ryotsu estate."

"Wait." Sage caught at Nieve's sleeve as she started to move. She turned back with a question on her face. "Can I . . . I'm sorry, Hane, but could you go ahead? We'll catch up in a minute."

Hane's hood dipped in a nod before they turned away, heading for the Wayfarer flag Nieve pointed out. Nieve sighed as she faced Sage.

"I know this is tough, but we have to be there," Nieve said, her voice hard, but in a brittle way. "I failed her, too. All of them."

"It's not . . . It's not that." Sage drew a shaky breath as he drew the circular object from his belt pouch. He hesitated only a moment before thrusting it at Nieve. "Here. You don't have to use it, I just . . . I can't have it anymore."

Nieve frowned as she studied it. It was round and metallic, like a thick bracelet but too small to fit around a wrist. Enchanting runes marked the sides in a patternlike design. Her mouth twisted to the side as she looked to Sage again. "What is this?"

"It's a hair clasp." Sage felt his guts twist and churn as he explained it. Nieve would know it hadn't been meant for her. Maybe this was more cruel than kind, though he hadn't meant it that way. "Like Emi's. It won't . . . won't fall out, or get messed up. I got it for—for—"

"I get it," Nieve said, turning the clasp over in her hand. "You didn't get this for me."

Sage shook his head, unable to meet her eyes. "It's stupid, I know. You can sell it if you want."

Nieve stared at it a moment longer, then abruptly swiped at her face with the back of her hand. Sage was startled to see tears streaking down her cheeks. She drew a breath that trembled, then grabbed Sage's shoulder, pulling him into a tight hug. He clasped her back just as tightly, as if the hug could soothe the jagged wound open between them.

"I'm sorry," Nieve whispered, voice hoarse. "I'm sorry you didn't get your chance."

"You too," Sage said, throat so tight the words came out half-strangled. "I know you— She—"

Nieve shook her head, a deep breath rocking the two of them. "I think it helps to think neither of us ever had a shot."

Sage chuckled bitterly. "I'll try to remember that when it hurts a little less."

"Yeah. Me too." Nieve patted Sage's back, then broke the hug, scrubbing at her cheeks as she pulled away. Sage pulled a handkerchief from his pocket and dabbed at his eyes. When he could see again, the hair clasp was nowhere in sight; Nieve must have pocketed it.

"Come on." Nieve slung an arm around Sage's shoulders. "We'll drink to their memory tonight. I'll get the first round."

Sage nodded, the pang in his chest eased ever so slightly by the contact of a close friend. "We should invite Hane, too."

"Of course," Nieve said, a false cheer in her tone. "We need to get to know them better if we're going to be traveling as a team for a while."

"Ren and Wyle will probably be there, too," Sage pointed out, unable to utter the word "funeral." "I'll ask if they want to come with us. That would make it a better farewell."

Nieve tipped her head against Sage's for just a moment. "It'll be a better beginning, too. A fresh start."

"Yeah." That sounded good. Hopeful. "A fresh start."

Soaring Wings Climber Registry

GUIDING STAR LEGACY ROSTER

Name: Nieve Yukihara
Attunement(s): Champion, mind mark
Rank: Citrine
Status: Active Climber
Additional notes: Inherited the team Guiding Star from her parents (both deceased while climbing the Tortoise Spire); re-founded the team as a legacy team. Officially the team's leader.

Name: Seiji "Sage" Hayden
Attunement(s): Seer, hand mark
Rank: Citrine
Status: Active Climber
Additional notes: Founding member of the re-established Guiding Star climber team. Despite foreign appearance, is a Dalenos native.

Name: Emiko Ryotsu
Attunement(s): Cloudcaller, lung mark
Rank: Sunstone
Status: Active Climber
Additional notes: Founding member of the re-established Guiding Star climber team. Yes, she is a member of *that* Ryotsu family, so take good care of her.

Name: Lani Nanashi
Attunement(s): Acolyte, hand mark
Rank: Citrine
Status: Active Climber
Additional notes: De facto team leader and a known gambler.

Name: Ren Ikaika
Attunement(s): Soulblade, leg mark
Rank: Citrine
Status: Retired
Additional notes: Recently retired, approved to resume climbing upon application.

Name: Wyle Anora
Attunement(s): Wayfarer, heart mark
Rank: Sunstone
Status: Retired
Additional notes: Recently retired, approved to resume climbing upon application.

Name: Aldis Somers
Attunement(s): Wayfarer, hand mark
Rank: Sunstone
Status: Contract Climber
Additional notes: Contracted to climb with Team Guiding Star Legacy for one expedition, provisional on joining team on a permanent basis.

Name: Hane
Attunement(s): Wavewalker, leg mark
Rank: Citrine
Status: Contract Climber
Additional notes: Contracted to climb with Team Guiding Star Legacy for one expedition only.

ATTUNEMENTS OF DALENOS

Copied from Sage's Pre-Judgment class notes

A list of typical attunements earned from Judgments within the Tortoise Spire, added to climber notebook because some people (Nieve) have trouble remembering the basics. This is by no means an exhaustive list of all attunements that *may* be granted from a Tortoise Spire Judgment, but instead a basic list of the eight attunements normally associated with Visage Katashi.

A note for those who may forget (*ahem*, Nieve): tertiary mana types typically develop once an attuned reaches the level of Citrine. The one notable exception to this rule are Wayfarer attuned, who have access to all three of their mana types at the time they receive their attunement.

- **Acolyte:** Acolytes are flexible healers, treating injuries, poisons, and diseases with equal ease.
  - **Mana Types:** life, water, perception (Citrine level)

- **Champion:** Champions have a combination of powerful defensive abilities and crowd control, using enhancement spells to bolster their own combat abilities and ice magic to freeze their foes in place.
  - **Mana Types:** enhancement, water, mental (Citrine level)

- **Cloudcaller:** Cloudcallers manipulate weather, calling rain and storms, and then alter these storms to cause specific magical effects.
  - **Mana Types:** water air, perception (Citrine level)

- **Illusionist:** While other attunements can make illusions, Illusionists are by far the most potent in terms of scale, capable of making large-scale illusions that create their own sounds and even influence the minds of potential victims.
  - **Mana Types:** perception, light, stone (Citrine level)

- **Seer:** Seers are capable of divining potential futures, making them one of the most powerful sources of information gathering in existence—aka the best attunement of all.
  - **Mana Types:** mental, light, death (Citrine level)

- **Soulblade:** Soulblades bind monsters to their equipment with contracts, creating powerful magical items with unique abilities.
  - **Mana Types:** light, life, transference (Citrine level)

- **Wavewalker:** Wavewalkers can shape the forces of motion to push and pull opponents, walk on water, or even float in the air.
  - **Mana Types:** water, transference, perception (Citrine level)

- **Wayfarer:** Wayfarers are best known for their ability to send messages at nearly any distance, which they can do without parallel. Wayfarers gain access to their tertiary mana type immediately, making them one of two known attunements that can learn teleportation magic.
  - **Mana Types:** air, mental, transference

Acknowledgments

If there is one person ultimately responsible for this collaboration between Andrew Rowe and me, that would be my college friend Jess. We met almost twenty years ago at an anime club (can you believe it's been that long, Jess?!) and we've stayed in touch over the years and across the miles as I moved out of California. At the start of the pandemic, Jess and I, along with a few other friends, maintained our sanity in isolation by watching TV shows and movies via Discord, creating our own head canons and trading wild story ideas. It was during that time that Jess asked me if I'd be interested in collaborating with their partner, Andrew, and the rest, I suppose, is history. Without Jess, the Shattered Legacy series wouldn't exist at all, so the first and greatest thanks has to go to them.

The other person absolutely necessary to making this series a reality is my husband, Andy. I was excited but nervous about stepping into another author's universe and writing in an established hard magic system; I had read all of Andrew Rowe's books prior to being invited to write in the Arcane Ascension universe and was a bit intimidated by the daunting task of meeting both Andrew's standards and those of his enthusiastic readers. Andy worked tirelessly to help me understand the magic system, not just by reading and rereading Andrew's books but by joining the Climber's Court Discord group and diving deeper into discussions on attunements and lore. A love of video games and tabletop RPGs made it easier for Andy to understand the magic system and explain it to me in ways that helped me understand. During character creation, he even helped me roll up D&D character sheets for each of my characters to help flesh them out! Andy's endless support and love has made it possible for me to write full time, and I'll never be grateful enough for that. Thank you, honey! I love you! <3

The idea of an expanded universe with multiple authors would not have been able to gain any traction without the support of Podium and the amazing people who decided to take a chance on a self-published author such as myself. I didn't know what to expect from working with a publisher, but Victoria met with me via Zoom and helped me feel very welcome and comfortable with the publishing process. Podium has been amazingly supportive, and I honestly can't wait to hear the audio version of this book once it's ready!

I have to make a special mention of each of my brothers for their support of both my writing and this novel specifically. As my little brother, Eamon has been an unwitting fan of mine since before he could read, and now he's always ready to take a late-night, hours-long phone call with me to help talk through any creative snarls I happen to get myself into. His creativity and problem-solving have always been an immense help to me, as well as the ability to hold a conversation made up almost entirely of quotes from *The Simpsons*. I also have to add in some congratulations for a major life milestone he reached recently: Congratulations on your wedding, baby brother! Don't forget how lucky you are to have Lisa in your life!

I relied heavily on my brother Alex at the beginning of this collaboration, as his insight and enthusiasm for contract law helped me understand exactly what it meant to participate in another author's intellectual property. His advice helped guide negotiations when accepting this proposal, and his discretion has been absolutely invaluable. And one more thing: Congratulations on your engagement! Welcome to the family, Carly!

One of the most intimidating things about writing in another author's world—particularly Andrew Rowe's world—are the fans. And wow, does Andrew have some dedicated fans! I can't thank everyone on the Climber's Court Discord and subreddit for how supportive and welcoming they've been to a new author writing in the world they love. I am both excited and terrified to find out what you all think of Shattered Legacy, because I know you will hold nothing back! While there are dozens of people who helped shape this first book, there are two community members I feel I must recognize formally for their contributions. First, special thanks to Kester, who really dug deep into the magic system of this book to call out mistakes and advised how to fix them. I'm sure I'll continue to run into this problem in the future, so this type of support is greatly appreciated! And second, I must thank Krista K. for all their wonderful artwork on the attunement marks as well as Chime's spell mark that helped give this story a true fantasy feel. This book would not be complete without either of these two amazing people!

For me, one of the most critical parts of publishing a book is getting feedback from beta readers, and that was especially important here. Andrew and I had to consider both his current audience and new readers who might discover the world of Arcane Ascension for the first time through Shattered Legacy. Our beta reader pool had to include both longtime fans of Andrew's works and people who had never read a book from the LitRPG genre before in order to make the book appealing to a wider audience. I can't thank our wonderful and hardworking beta readers enough for taking the time to not only read the unpolished manuscript but offer their insights and advice, helping us shape this novel into its present state. Thank you to all of our beta readers, including Andy, Eamon, Alex, Matt, Amy Reader-Lalor, Brandon Yee, James Wolter, Jonah L., Krista K., Ryodin, Tyler L. Kowalchuk, Yvonne Etzkorn, John Bierce, Liam Wales, Justin Green, and Michael Kelly.

Finally, the greatest thanks I can give for this novel goes to Andrew Rowe. I feel so honored and grateful for having been invited to participate in this incredibly vivid and complex world, and I can only hope I have done justice in representing his work. Even before asking me to participate in his expanded universe, Andrew has been incredibly supportive of my career as an independent author, offering advice on self-publishing and marketing and even sharing my published works through his blog. Throughout this collaboration, he's been an absolute joy to work with: quick to respond to queries and incredibly detailed in his explanations. He wore so many hats during this process that I don't think I can remember them all, but he served as a copy editor, line editor, sounding board, weird-question answerer, and even an artist for the early renditions of the attunement marks in the chapter headers. A generous spirit even outside of writing, Andrew extended an offer of assistance to me and my family during the Texas winter storm of 2021. Andrew, I couldn't have asked for a better guide, partner, and friend. From the bottom of my heart, thank you for everything.

KAYLEIGH NICOL

After earning her Bachelor of Science in Animal Science at Cal Poly Pomona, followed by years of exhausting (but rewarding!) work with many amazing animals, Kayleigh made the unexpected decision to begin writing fantasy books full time. She stays true to her animal background by loving her real pets, digital pets, and strays, and correcting people on their animal facts. After living in various regions around the United States (the Northeast, the Midwest, California, and Texas) Kayleigh has come to believe that a home is where and what you make it.

You can follow Kayleigh's blog on www.KayleighNicol.com, or follow Kayleigh on Facebook or Twitter.

Other Novels by Kayleigh Nicol

Sorcerous Rivalry

Mistress Mage

Mage Prince

Cursed Realm (coming soon!)

The Mage-Born Anthology

ANDREW ROWE

Andrew Rowe was once a professional game designer for awesome companies like Blizzard Entertainment, Cryptic Studios, and Obsidian Entertainment. Nowadays, he's writing full time.

When he's not crunching numbers for game balance, he runs live-action role-playing games set in the same universe as his books. In addition, he writes for pen-and-paper role-playing games.

Aside from game design and writing, Andrew watches a lot of anime, reads a metric ton of fantasy books, and plays every role-playing game he can get his hands on.

Interested in following Andrew's books releases, or discussing them with other people? You can find more info, updates, and discussions in a few places online:

Andrew's Blog: https://andrewkrowe.wordpress.com/

Mailing List: https://andrewkrowe.wordpress.com/mailing-list/

Facebook: https://www.facebook.com/
Arcane-Ascension-378362729189084/

Reddit: https://www.reddit.com/r/ClimbersCourt/

Podium
DISCOVER
STORIES UNBOUND
PodiumAudio.com